The Italian Garden

By the same author

Reynardine
Till the Day Goes Down

JUDITH LENNOX

The Italian Garden

St. Martin's Press
New York

 For information, address St. Martin's Press, 175 Fifth Avenue, New York, N.Y. 10010.

Library of Congress Cataloging-in-Publication Data

Lennox, Judith.
The Italian garden / Judith Lennox.
p. cm.
ISBN 0-312-09810-3 (hardcover)
1. Women gardeners—Italy—Fiction. 2. Women artists—Italy—Fiction.
3. Renaissance—Italy—Fiction. I. Title.
PR6062.E63I83 1993
823'.914—dc20 93-8998 CIP

First published in Great Britain by Penguin Books Ltd.
First U.S. Edition: September 1993
10 9 8 7 6 5 4 3 2 1

PART ONE

1500–1509

The Garden of Jealous Love

The rose of gardens is planted and sette and tylthed as a vyne. And if it is forgendred and not shred and pared and not clensed of superfluyte: thene it gooth out of kynde and chaungeth in to a wylde rose.

Bartholomaeus Anglicus, *De herbis*

CHAPTER ONE

In Castile, they sold powders of antimony and salts of mercury at a mystery play that lasted for twenty-five days. An epidemic of sweating-sickness broke out among the audience: Donato mumbled Latin verses, Sanchia made tisanes of feverfew. The child Joanna, pulling her tattered velvet cloak around herself, watched as Death and Beauty, Five Wits and the Angel, strutted on the ochre dust.

The end of the century approached. The clouds rained blood, and in France a triple moon cursed the night sky. A thunderbolt seared through the Vatican, hurling the Pope from his throne. There were plagues and epidemics, but they were necessary to Donato Zulian's trade.

In Navarre, Sanchia taught Joanna her letters and the names and properties of plants. Donato stood on a dais in the marketplace, roaring at the crowds, one fist thumping his other open palm, his pointing fingers and wild eyes drawing the sick like lodestones. A musician played the fiddle, and another the tambourine and Joanna danced, chestnut hair whirling in the dusty heat, her bright skirts fanned around her. When the dance was done, people clapped and threw her coins.

In the summer of 1502 they carried vipers coiled in woven baskets to cure snake-bites. Donato sold all his oils and unguents, and a gentleman paid gold for a remedy for the French pox. They dined in the kitchens of the gentleman's castle, and Joanna breathed in the scent of the sweet rushes on the floor, and heard in the distance the sound of a lute. The gentleman, in his gratitude, gave Sanchia a pair of black velvet sleeves and Joanna a fur-trimmed cloak. Later that night Donato drank bottle after bottle of good red wine, and Sanchia bought her daughter a pen and a horn of ink. They had no paper, so they drew letters and faces on the back of Donato Zulian's banner, and Donato, returning from the tavern, laughed, and called Joanna his pet, his kitten.

In Lisbon, they bought ginger and rhubarb from Cathay and, from the Malabar coast, zedoary to warm the stomach. The spices and drugs had been carried by sea from the Indies: Donato, opening another bottle of wine, said that the journeys of the Portuguese sailors would mean disaster for Venice. Sanchia, watching the ships with grey-green, troubled eyes, held her daughter's hand and said nothing.

That autumn, the crops failed, cursed with a dark purple blight that made people mad. Sometimes hungry crowds threw stones at the Jews, sometimes at the gypsies, at other times they hurled them after the travelling physician with his useless remedies and his hollow promises of everlasting life. Donato carefully bound the cut on Sanchia's forehead, and his hands hardly shook at all. Joanna, who was almost eleven now, built up the fire, and cooked the meal, and set heavy stones on the edges of the tent, so that her mother, sleeping inside, should not feel the cold wind. Joanna ate alone, because Donato was not hungry, only thirsty, and Sanchia, lulled by one of her husband's philtres, did not wake. She ate alone, and remembered the expressions on the faces of those who had thrown the stones. *Mountebank*, they had shouted. *Zany*, a boy had spat at her, and she had picked up a stone herself. It had struck him on the forehead and he had fallen to the cobbles, and lain there, quite still.

In the spring, when Sanchia's cough had eased, they travelled north into France. At the fair in Lyons Donato set up his stand and his booth and sold cures for toothache. To kill the worms that wriggled from the head and gnawed into the teeth, Donato burned wax candles studded with henbane seeds. Sanchia had gathered the henbane by the sea. Joanna took the money from the patients as they staggered from the booth. One of them, hazy with henbane, pinched her chin and asked her for a kiss: Sanchia, crouched in a corner, cursed him in Spanish and sent him on his way.

In the gentle valleys of the Loire the grapes ripened in the misty sunlight, and lizards darted among the stones, finding shelter from the heat. At night, they watched the St John's Eve bonfires flare up into the sky and paint the darkness. The light changed the fields and the meadows to gold, gilding the endless flowers, limning the cornfields and the vineyards with bronze. Half closing her eyes, Joanna saw sparks and flames mingle with the stars in the sky. Soon, Donato said, Saturn and Jupiter would be no longer in conjunction. Then the evil times would be past.

The following day they were invited to the castle of a great nobleman, whose daughter was sick of the bloody flux. Donato fortified himself with wine, and talked of the university of Bologna and watching the dissection of corpses in the theatres of Padua. Sanchia, shaking out and sponging crushed and grimy garments, smiled and kissed her husband.

Waiting alone in a cold ante-room in the castle, Joanna studied the single great tapestry on the wall. There was a lion, and a unicorn, and rabbits, and ermines and monkeys and dogs. And there were flowers everywhere – in the grass, in the sky, studding the graceful, spindly trees. If she looked through the one narrow window, she could see the thousand flowers of the valleys outside: poppy and corncockle, larkspur and buttercup and wild rose.

The nobleman's daughter died, and Donato Zulian and his wife and child left town quietly one night. To cheer up her father, Joanna made a new banner out of an old petticoat. The banner bore the name of Zulian, and was decorated with a glorious garden painted in the dyes Sanchia had extracted from the roadside flowers. It pleased Joanna to make flowers from flowers, and Donato looked, and hugged her, smiling.

Winter came early. On All Souls' Day they stood on the grey rocky coast of Brittany looking out to a jagged sea. There were holes in the tent, and none of them knew the language of the Bretons. We'll sail to England, said Donato, narrowing his eyes as though he could pick out England's island coastline from the horizon. A new country – a new beginning . . .

Sanchia had red marks on her cheeks the colour of bruised poppy petals. Joanna watched as her mother took Donato's sleeve and walked with him across the white sand to where the foam whisked patterns of lace on the shore. The gulls circled overhead, their cries as meaningless as the gaunt jabber of the Bretons, and Sanchia spoke, her head resting against Donato's shoulder. Her words were torn to shreds by the wind, but when they returned, Joanna saw that Donato's eyes were wet, as though the sea spray had washed over him. We'll go back to Spain, he said.

Sanchia died when they were within sight of Aragon. Joanna, who had fallen asleep crouched by her mother's pallet, heard Donato's terrible roar of anger and grief.

The next day they walked to the nearest church. Donato carried Sanchia wrapped in Joanna's best fur-lined cloak; Joanna led the mule, which was laden with the tent, the banner, their pots and pans, jars and unguents. The bitter wind tore at the girl's uncovered hair, and tugged at the tattered garments covering Sanchia Zulian's corpse. Donato told the priest that his wife had been shriven: the priest, had he known the truth, would have said that Donato Zulian lied. Donato had no shame, though, he knew that Sanchia would have had nothing to confess.

Donato drank through the spring. Joanna sold simples and salves, wrote letters for the anxious and illiterate, refused offers of easier money with a curse or a flick of a sharp, narrow-bladed knife. In the summer, rousing his shaking, abused body, Donato said that they would go back to Venice, to stay for a while with his brother Taddeo.

They bought another mule, and Joanna patched the holes in the tent. To Joanna, Venice was as unknown a country as England or the Americas. Donato's old reluctance to return to his family, his homeland, increased as they travelled from Toulouse to Avignon, from Savoy to Genoa. Donato rode the mule, Joanna walked beside him. She dosed him with feverfew when his head ached, with ivy and centaurean when his stomach heaved. When he was feeling better, he spoke of his brother Taddeo, and his sister-in-law Isotta. When he tried to speak of Sanchia, he cried.

In Genoa, Donato drew his daughter to his side. He must go back to Spain, he said, to the town where he had met his beloved Sanchia. There was a monastery near by, where his skills had been respected: the brothers would look after him until he was better.

But Joanna could not accompany him. Joanna was a young woman now – Donato's voice trembled, tears started again from his eyes – and a young woman needed a mother's protection. Isotta Zulian would be Joanna's mother, Taddeo her father. Perhaps, God willing, there would be sisters, brothers, too. Donato's most precious treasure must travel to Venice alone. When he was recovered, Donato would join her.

He had written a note to his brother. The tails of the letters formed spider trails, crawling into the margins, blurring into the words below. He would not, Donato added proudly, send her to his brother undowried. Breathing heavily, rummaging through a battered saddlebag, Donato took out a book, a purse and a necklace. The book was Dioscorides' herbal, the purse contained two Genoese ducats, a French écu d'or and a Venetian zecchino. The necklace, which was of jade and black pearls, had belonged to Sanchia. Donato began to weep again.

When he had wiped away the tears, he told Joanna that she would set off the following day. He had engaged a reliable escort for her. He himself would join her in Venice by the end of the following summer.

*

The painter Taddeo Zulian, his workshops and his family, occupied a house in the same square as the church of San Giovanni e San Paolo. The great brick body of the church, its façade as yet unfinished, towered over the piazza with a benevolent, orderly authority.

It was late autumn, and a thin grey mist had begun to settle over the city of Venice, blurring the outline of the church and the nearby Scuola di San Marco, hazing the features of the people hurrying through the streets. At the window of his workshop, Taddeo paused and looked out to the brick-paved campo beyond. He could hear fragments of conversation, the cries of street-sellers, tail-ends of bargains and beginnings of quarrels. Greek and Spanish and Turkish and Slav wafted through the damp air to dissolve in the busy, quiet industry of Taddeo Zulian's workshop. Merchants and sailors, mercenaries and courtesans crossed the campo, hailed friends, carried baskets of shopping. Taddeo's mouth curled at the pretensions of the courtesans, who wore low-fronted, over-ornate gowns, and the white silk headband of the bride. Five crowns for a kiss, one hundred crowns for rather more, Taddeo's brother-in-law Gaetano had told him. Taddeo sniffed.

But as he glanced back round the workshop, his smile returned. The workshop was the largest room in the house, spacious and organized, all the rolls of canvases and fabrics, the jars of paints and sizes and dyes, in their proper places. Taddeo Zulian ran a successful business and an orderly house with the help of only two apprentices and a journeyman. And Isotta, of course, and Lena in the kitchen and Matteo to run errands. He did not squander his earnings on fancy clothes, or on black slaves to row his gondola. He did not envy his betters these things – his livelihood depended on the need of the Contarini, the Querini, the Malipieri, for frescos, portraits and wedding-chests.

He did not envy, and neither did he desire, the responsibilities that were the lot of the families of the Great Council, those families whose names were listed in the Libro d'Oro. Politics – the machinations of the della Rovere Pope, Julius II, the lust for all things Italian of the French king, Louis XII – were simply not his concern. Taddeo's concerns were his family, his house, his guild.

Taddeo Zulian was of medium height, grey-haired, his loosening stomach hidden by black robes. He had selected a wife who neither nagged nor flirted, and he took only hard-working, sensible boys as his apprentices. He resisted innovation, both in his work and in his private life, believing that to stray from existing rules invariably proved foolish. His one regret was that his wife had proved to be barren, providing him with no healthy sons to guarantee the continuance of his name. He prided himself that, years ago, when Isotta's barrenness had become apparent, he had been forgiving and generous. Her dowry had been substantial, and besides, Isotta was a good, dutiful wife in every other respect – hard-working, undemanding and acquiescent, and of good family. On Taddeo's death, the house and workshop would be left to Isotta's brother Gaetano, an arrangement with which Taddeo was perfectly content. Gaetano Cavazza was a strong, capable man, good company, lacking his sister's feminine weaknesses of extravagance and inconsistency.

Taddeo turned his back to the window, checking the industry of his apprentices, Marin and Alessandro. Cursing his deteriorating sight, he inspected the progress of the altarpiece, the wedding-chest, the trays. From below, he heard the knock at the door, but, taking up his paints and brushes, he did not go downstairs to receive the visitor. He was busy: Isotta would tell him if the caller was worthy of his attention.

She had Italian from her father, and Spanish and French from her mother, as well as a smattering of Flemish, English and Portuguese from their travels. But Venice, with its exotic, distorted idiom, almost defeated her. Her father's accent had softened over the years, adapting to other tongues. Joanna sat with her head held high, her lips clamped together, her heart beating unusually fast, as the gondola slid past palaces and warehouses, waterways and bridges.

She had separated from the reliable escort in Cremona after he had tried to climb into her bed one night. Since then, she had journeyed alone along the valley of the Po, attaching herself to groups of pilgrims, merchants or journeymen. She covered her red-brown hair with a black shawl, and she kept her knife hidden in her sleeve. She saw wolves prowling the high plains of Mantua, and mist hazing the marshes of Ferrara. She sold her horse in Chioggia, travelling by barge through the marshes and lagoons up the coast to Venice.

Venice had come to her out of the sea, unreal, floating, suspended somewhere between grey water and grey sky. On the Grand Canal, Joanna alighted from the barge and hired a gondola. The gondolier had laughed at her accent, but had accepted her coin and set off through the darkening afternoon towards the house of Taddeo Zulian. The tall, cramped buildings of Venice crowded over the water, jostling for space. There was no road in front of her now, only the slick black water, the towering houses.

She found her uncle's house in the corner of a small square. Inside, as the servant scuttled away to find his mistress, Joanna waited.

It annoyed Taddeo Zulian to be interrupted in his work, something which he made quite clear to his wife. Isotta was mumbling something about a *girl*, and *Donato*. It took Taddeo a good five minutes to realize that she was jabbering about Donato Zulian, his brother, but when he understood, he frowned and hissed, so that the apprentices might not hear, 'Donato? You've had word? A letter?'

Isotta shook her head. For a moment her faded features looked triumphant. 'Not a letter. Donato's daughter is here.'

The apprentices were staring open-mouthed, but for once Taddeo Zulian did not call them back to work. He put aside his brush and paint.

'Donato has a daughter?'

Isotta nodded, her pale blue eyes wide. 'She is here, husband. Downstairs. Her name is Joanna.'

Unusually, Taddeo found that he wanted to shake his wife, to destroy her pathetic pleasure in being the bringer of such unexpected news. Generally, Isotta induced in him no emotion stronger than mild irritation. Taddeo acknowledged that he was upset.

He said, unkindly, 'You must calm down, Isotta. You're making a spectacle of yourself.'

For once she did not redden and weep; instead, she tugged at his sleeve and said, 'You must come, Taddeo. She's downstairs.'

Taddeo found himself rising to his feet, his curiosity overcoming his irritation. He was half convinced that the foolish woman had got it all wrong, that Donato and the Spaniard were still childless and on their travels, but he followed Isotta to the door and out of the workshop to the small chamber his wife used for mending and embroidery.

The light was poor, the single window faced on to the back wall of the house beyond. The room stank of the canal, of the herbs Isotta scattered to counteract its smell, of the wax candles and pomanders and scented handkerchiefs she collected.

He did not comment on her extravagance this time. Isotta had brushed past him to lead a figure from the shadows. A woman – no, a girl: Taddeo quickly estimated that she could be no more than twelve or thirteen years old. Donato had left Venice in 1490, had sent word of his marriage to the Spanish woman in 1491.

'This is Joanna,' said Isotta, proudly. 'Donato and Sanchia's daughter.'

The girl curtsied. Her clothes were ridiculous: she looked, thought Taddeo, like a gypsy. Her face – when she rose from her curtsy, looking up at him, he realized that she was beautiful. It was the artist that told him, not the man. Taddeo preferred the sort of prettiness that Isotta had once possessed: fair curls, round pink cheeks. Joanna Zulian's long hair was a light chestnut, her eyes grey in a pale oval face. She was tall for a woman, only a few inches shorter than Taddeo himself.

The girl said, quite composedly, 'I'm sorry to appear so unexpectedly, Uncle Taddeo, but if I'd sent a letter it would like as not have reached you after I arrived.'

She wore a red skirt striped with braid, a green bodice and black sleeves. All three were travel-stained and patched beyond what even Taddeo would have considered reasonable economy. Her bare feet were grey with dust.

'Is he dead?' Taddeo said suddenly. 'Is Donato dead?'

He experienced no grief at the thought: he barely remembered his younger brother, had not seen him in fifteen years. And Donato had been such a fool.

But Joanna shook her head. 'My father is still alive, Uncle Taddeo. He has gone to Castile, to the hospital of the brothers in Valladolid. My mother is dead. She died last winter.'

'Ah.' In a stab of the fraternal resentment he had thought long buried, Taddeo saw it all. He laughed humourlessly. 'So my brother found himself saddled with an undowried daughter.' He considered Joanna Zulian's slight body, her heavy-lidded eyes, her small curved mouth. 'And no wife to chaperone her. A liability indeed! Enough to make any man unwell.'

'Taddeo!' exclaimed Isotta, but Joanna Zulian, crouching on the floor to scrabble in a bag, merely said, 'I am not undowried, uncle. I'll not be a burden to you.'

Standing, she showed them her pathetic dowry with such pride that even Taddeo, drawn to the limits of civility by his brother's habitual lack of consideration, found himself silenced. A rubbishy necklace, an equally rubbishy book, and a few odd coins in an old silk purse.

Isotta said hesitantly, 'Joanna can sew and cook, Taddeo. And write. Her mother taught her.'

Isotta could write no more than her name. Isotta already called this ragamuffin, decorative flotsam, *Joanna*. Yet he listened to what his wife was saying. There was always a need for another cook, another seamstress, another clerk. And you did not have to pay a niece. And besides, he knew that he had no choice. The girl bore his own name, the name of Zulian, and he could not leave Taddeo Zulian's niece to earn her bread on the streets, or shout her wares in the marketplace like that mountebank, her father.

Joanna knew within a week that to Isotta Zulian she was the daughter fate had denied her, and to Taddeo Zulian she was another pair of hands to help in the smooth running of the artist's household. She had no objection to either role, she had always expected to work in return for her bed and board. Work took her mind off things. And besides, she would not remain in Venice for long. Her father would come for her within a year.

In the back of Dioscorides' herbal, Joanna noted down the day on which she had parted from Donato. She had ridden from Genoa on the last day of July, 1504. Which meant that her father would come to Venice by the end of the following summer.

Meanwhile, she struggled to accustom herself to life in Taddeo Zulian's house. To eat sitting at a table, to sleep in a bed. The bed seemed cramped and unsafe, horribly high and narrow. During her first week in Venice, she wrapped a blanket round herself and slept on the floor next to the window. But Lena, the cook, found her there one morning and laughed until the tears ran from her eyes. After that, Joanna slept in the bed, her fears of falling exceeded by her fear of ridicule.

Mealtimes, too, were an ordeal. How to hold her cutlery, what to use her napkin for. She was afraid to touch the delicate Murano glass that held her wine, convinced that it would fracture as soon as she gripped it. She went thirsty for two days until she was forced, trembling, to lift the fine-stemmed goblet. Then it seemed a miracle: that this beautiful thing, which appeared to be made of ice or crystal, was strong enough to touch, to hold, to lift to her mouth.

Most difficult of all was to know when to speak and when to be silent. Isotta, showing off her new niece to acquaintances visiting the

Zulian house, went pink when Joanna greeted the adult strangers with a kiss, an inquiry as to their health and a comment on the splendour of their clothing. Later, recovered from her embarrassment, Isotta kindly explained the importance of silence, of not speaking until spoken to, of curtsying and answering only questions addressed to her, briefly, like a respectable Venetian girl.

At night, Joanna's face had grown hot remembering Isotta's gentle admonishments, but it had grown hotter on the day that she had danced in the square. They had been walking home from church, she and Isotta and Taddeo, and there had been a blind fiddler playing in one corner of the campo. Joanna had always liked music: she knew a hundred songs, she thought, in a dozen different languages. She knew also that she danced well: Sanchia had told her so, and the few coins she had earned had always been a useful supplement to Donato's income. So while Isotta and Taddeo had been bowing and talking to one of Taddeo's patrons, Joanna had danced for the fiddler. Not to earn money for herself, she had explained hastily to Taddeo, as he had dragged her away from the square. For the fiddler, whose hat had been empty until she had begun to dance. Taddeo had been rendered almost speechless then, but his face had said everything.

After that, she became more careful. Listening to Taddeo and Isotta, watching the dull daughters of acquaintances, Joanna copied them, keeping her behaviour within the rigid bounds imposed by Venetian society. She felt as though she were acting in a dumb-show, sometimes: she wanted to laugh at herself, or cry, as she played the part that Sanchia's death, Donato's absence, had cast her in. She was not used to houses, to walls and floors and ceilings. She was used to a tent, patched multicolour with odds and ends of material, and the night and the stars glimpsed through the holes in the roof. She was used to the open road in front of her, not the slow dark waterways and congested campi of Venice. Sometimes, in her bedchamber, when the walls seemed to close in on her, and the window grew smaller and smaller, Joanna had to clench her fists and pin them beneath her elbows to stop her beating them against the plaster, to stop her seizing and shaking the bars of the window-frame.

As well as learning to behave like a respectable Venetian girl, Joanna learned the names of the servants of the Zulian household and their functions. There was fat Lena in the kitchen, who had a brother who worked at the Arsenal and a fund of sailors' stories in consequence. Joanna, who had seen more of the world than Lena, had stories in return. Lena's round dark eyes grew rounder at some of Joanna's tales, and she crossed herself several times.

There was old Matteo, the messenger, who pinched her chin and called her his peach. Looking at Joanna, Matteo's eyes would water and he would mumble about the little sister who had died more than thirty years ago. And Joanna would smile and offer to take the messages for him, because Matteo had grown old and slow. And besides, it was hard to spend even one whole day encased in Taddeo Zulian's crowded house.

In Taddeo's workshop there were the apprentices Alessandro and Marin, and the journeyman, Benedetto. Alessandro and Marin were much the same age as Joanna, but spotty; they quarrelled constantly, jostling for position. Benedetto, the journeyman, wore scarlet doublets and part-coloured hose and tried to pinch Joanna's bottom when Taddeo wasn't looking. Benedetto was helping Taddeo with an altarpiece for the Scuola di San Giovanni Evangelista. Scenes of the Evangelist's life blossomed under Taddeo's cold, accurate sketching, Benedetto's flamboyant colouring.

The workshop was high-ceilinged, to accommodate the larger commissions, its walls lined with shelves crammed with jars and bottles and brushes and palettes. It smelt of oil and spirits and canvas, and the floor was littered with wood-shavings and paint-stained cloths. Joanna had never seen a room like it before; inside the workshop, she would stand breathless, silenced, her dazzled gaze darting from the sketches, to the easels, to the gloriously coloured paints.

Her mornings were spent with Isotta, in the dark, poky back room, patching and hemming linen, spinning and weaving thread. Isotta would feed the fire in the grate, and talk of the Paduan family she had left to marry Taddeo, of the sisters she had rarely seen since her wedding-day. She spoke of Gaetano, her younger brother, who was, like Taddeo, an artist. Gaetano was becoming a great man, said Isotta proudly.

Isotta made Joanna a respectable Venetian gown: black velvet with a wide neck and black oversleeves. Joanna thanked Isotta with a kiss, and secretly longed for her colours and her braid. Her feet were blistered with the rubbing of her fine new shoes. Isotta spoke of gowns and jewels and wedding-gifts, of the carnivals and banquets of her youth. Isotta herself rarely left the house now, preferring the hot, safe darkness of the sewing-room.

In the afternoons, as soon as Isotta had fallen asleep open-mouthed by the fire, Joanna would leave the house. In the Rialto, the canal was packed with ships and barges from every country in the world. Sailors called to each other, merchants jostled at the quayside, unloading goods into the warehouses. The barges were crammed with grain and silk, fruit and spices. The scents of the fruits and spices conjured as many memories as the languages. The dry, sharp smell of cinnamon, from a barrel on the dockside at Lisbon . . . the sweet scent of melons that they had once eaten in a garden in Madrid . . . Donato had licked melon juice from Sanchia's mouth, Joanna's fingers had stuck to the dusty skirts of her dress.

Every day she expected one of the figures who stepped from a barge or caravel to be that of Donato Zulian, the tall and handsome physician, wearing his best quilted doublet and fur-lined cloak. Every day, when Donato did not come, Joanna turned from the waterside back towards the city, walking until the pain had gone from her heart.

Inside the Basilica di San Marco, she would stand and gaze up at the exquisite mosaicked prophets, at the golden-winged, inscrutable angels. Once she heard the choir sing, rehearsing for some great ceremony, their voices soaring and echoing off the five golden domes. When she closed her eyes, she could believe she heard the voices of the angels themselves.

As autumn turned into winter, the air grew damper and colder, and the mist never lifted. Joanna was glad; the changing of the seasons reassured her that time had not frozen, trapped for ever in the stillness of the lagoon. She wandered through the Campo di Rialto, with its fish-market and meat-market and money-changers, and she gazed at the treasures of the silversmiths and ivory-carvers. She learned how to repel the attentions of the young men with their black and red hose, their shoulder-length hair and velvet caps and slashed silk doublets. She watched the negro slaves, dressed in the colours of their owners, steering their black-painted gondolas under wooden bridges, gliding past the palazzi of the great families. The slaves had travelled even further than she, and were now trapped here, in Venice, for ever. That thought made her shiver. Through the doorways of the palazzi she could see to the courtyard beyond, to the paved faded gardens with their trees and fountains and frescoed walls. Sometimes she would glimpse ladies stepping down from the gardens into their gondolas, their cloth-of-gold gowns mirrored in the water, their round breasts covered only by the finest of veils.

Sometimes she walked in a different direction, towards the church of San Cassiano. Beggars crouched in the shelter of doorways, tattered garments pulled about them to keep away the cold and mist. There were quarters like these in every city, the quarters of the sickly, the weak, the unlucky. Whores paraded the squares, some of them with the marks of syphilis already on their faces. She had nothing to give the beggars, no remedy to offer the whores.

In the evenings, Joanna wrote in the margin of Dioscorides' herbal the vernacular names of the flowers and their purposes, adding tiny drawings so that she would not forget all that she had learned. She must not forget, because with Sanchia gone she would be Donato's only help. By New Year, there were over a hundred tiny flowers drawn in the margin of the book.

In February, in the last few days of carnival, Isotta's brother Gaetano visited the Zulian household.

He was a big man, dark-haired and muscular, the opposite of his fair, worn-out sister. Gaetano greeted Isotta with a peck on the cheek and an inquiry concerning her health; he flung open the workshop door and, calling Taddeo's name, clapped his brother-in-law on the back. He ran a critical eye over the contents of the studio and realized that though Taddeo had work aplenty, he had long lost what little flair he had ever possessed. He was still churning out the coats of arms and trays and trousseau-chests that were his stock in trade: competent and conscientious every one of them, but so conservative compared with the sort of work Gaetano had begun to do. Gaetano, still only in his early thirties, intended to be remembered. You were not remembered for coats of arms and trousseau-chests.

But Taddeo had a larger commission now: a fresco covering the entire courtyard wall of one of the palazzi by the Grand Canal. He was asking Gaetano's help, Gaetano's advice. Gaetano, seizing a brush, began to sketch on the corner of a blank canvas. Trees, caves, flowers and nymphs grew out of nothing. Taddeo looked dubious at Gaetano's suggested subject-matter, but Taddeo would come round, he always did. Gaetano thought to himself that he would show Taddeo how to paint a fresco that would make him the talk of Venice. He offered to help Taddeo with the commission: he would take note of the measurements so that he could work on the sketches for the fresco on his return to his own studio in Padua. After all, because of the lack of fire in poor Taddeo's loins, the Venetian workshop would one day be his.

He knew by the expression of relief on his brother-in-law's face that he had made just the suggestion Taddeo had been hoping for. The journeyman, Benedetto, would have his nose put out of joint, a thought that did not distress Gaetano one jot. He put the brush aside at last and, smiling, showed the youngest apprentice how to mix exactly the right shade of blue for the Virgin's cloak. Then, his eye caught by something in the campo beyond, he glanced out of the window.

He could see a girl crossing the snow-stained cobbles. She was tall and slender, and her long, reddish hair was pearled with flakes of falling snow. She had, thought Gaetano, the sort of face he had always tried to paint. That thought, unaccountably, hurt him. When she walked to the door of the Zulian house, Gaetano said, curiously, 'You have a visitor, Taddeo.'

Taddeo, whose sap, had it ever risen, had desiccated long since, merely glanced through the window and said, 'She's not a visitor. She is my niece, Joanna.'

Gaetano said, 'Niece? What niece, brother?'

'Donato's daughter. You remember Donato, Gaetano.'

He did, but only after an effort. Donato Zulian was Taddeo's younger brother, the one who had left Venice to go and do something unsuitable. A mercenary . . . a mariner . . .

'A physician,' said Gaetano, remembering.

'A mountebank,' said Taddeo Zulian scornfully.

The door of the workshop opened as he spoke. Gaetano had been aware of the front door opening below, the sound of light footsteps on wooden stairs, long skirts brushing against the boards. He knew again, looking at Joanna Zulian's perfect face, that she was what he had always tried to paint, and he knew also that she had heard her uncle's words, and resented them.

He saw how hard she tried not to betray her anger. She said nothing, but her eyes were very bright and her pale cheeks had flushed. He wondered idly why she dissembled, and distrusted her for her dissembling. Gaetano knew that women were creatures of guile, to whom deceit came almost as naturally as breathing.

He realized, watching Taddeo's niece, that Joanna Zulian was much younger than he had at first thought, little more than a child. He realized also that tonight he would have to leave Taddeo Zulian's small, overheated house and find solace amongst the eleven thousand or so ladies of the night who haunted Venice like lovely, impecunious ghosts.

Carnival, of course, had its own special trail of memories. Donato had often done rather well at carnivals: people made themselves sick with too much food and drink, needed remedies to ward off the consequence of a careless night. Carnivals in Spain, France, Portugal, Navarre and Savoy. There had been different flavours to each of them: the scent of the sea in Lisbon; the wide black arc of the sky flecked with stars in Castile; a procession of ships, decked with flags and flares, gliding down the Loire.

And now, there was Venice. Joanna wore the black gown Isotta had made for her, and a matching black mask. Not that long ago, Sanchia had plaited ribbons into her hair and decked her with beads and baubles. The mask made her feel odd, as though she were someone else. When the Zulian gondola glided past other gondolas, the young men bowed to her and blew her kisses and threw paper roses. *'Bella, bella,'* they called, as though she were a lady, not a child.

Even Isotta had come tonight, finding the courage to quit the safety of the house. Joanna sat next to her, her arm linked through her aunt's. Isotta also wore a mask, which she fiddled with nervously as it threatened to slip from the tip of her small, upturned nose. Opposite them in the gondola sat the two apprentices, Alessandro and Marin, and behind them were Taddeo Zulian and his journeyman, Benedetto. Isotta's brother, Gaetano, stood at the stern of the boat, oar in hand, steering them through the tangle of brightly lit, heavily laden craft. All the men wore masks, long-nosed, animal-eared, frilled with lace. If she half closed her eyes, the figures opposite Joanna blurred and became unrecognizable: creatures from a bestiary.

Disembarking, they tied the gondola to the mooring-post, and Isotta clutched Joanna's arm as they walked through the crowds. The flames of the bonfire in the middle of the square soared as high as the roofs of the surrounding buildings. If she looked up to the sky, Joanna could not distinguish the sparks from the flakes of falling snow, made glittering gold by the reflected light. The flames gilded the paving-stones and the glorious mosaics on the Basilica. Venice was no longer grey, blanketed in mist, but a magical place.

Joanna began to feel alive again, to recollect some of the certainty, some of the joy, that had crumbled steadily away since Sanchia's death, Donato's desertion. Soon, she thought, she would be free again. Donato would be with her by the end of the summer and then they would travel the world. The names of Donato Zulian, physician, and his daughter, Joanna, would be known in the courts of every land. No one would call them *mountebank* or *zany*, no one would throw stones at them.

A band of musicians – trumpeters and flute-players and viol-players – stood on the steps of the Basilica. People had begun to dance, encircling the fire, their bodies quartered like the young men's motley, scarlet by the fire, black by the night. Isotta was complaining of the heat, of the cold. The music worked its old magic, and Joanna began to sway, to laugh. Taking her aunt's fidgeting hands in hers, Joanna started to dance, slowly at first as Isotta squeaked and protested, and then faster, guiding her round the bonfire, leaving the apprentices and the journeyman and Taddeo open-mouthed in the distance.

He still drank the flagon of hot wine, still supplied niceties of conversation to the neighbours Taddeo had introduced him to, but Gaetano's eyes and mind were solely preoccupied with that distant, whirling figure dancing round the bonfire.

He had talked at length, earlier in the evening, to Isotta, his pale, faded sister. Isotta, full of sisterly affection for him, had at least been interesting and informative on the subject of Joanna Zulian. Her father was Donato Zulian (drunkard, physician, mountebank, what you will), her mother had been a Spaniard, from Valladolid. The mother, Sanchia, was dead, the father – according to Joanna – still lived.

Taddeo's talkative neighbour had four plain daughters: Gaetano, subtracting himself effortlessly from the prospect of a tedious duty, waited until Isotta and Joanna had encircled the fire once more, and caught Isotta, breathless and laughing, in his arms. Then it was just a simple matter of passing her to Taddeo, and taking Joanna Zulian's long slender fingers in his.

Her foot was still tapping, her grey eyes, beneath the mask, were as luminous as the bonfire. The square was crowded now, it was easier to dance than remain still, they were sucked into the maelstrom. Beside the musicians, Gluttony, a fat, feather-capped man, his splendid garments hung with lengths of sausages and sides of ham, danced with Lent, a thin old woman dressed in rags. Overhead, the sparks from the fire, the snowflakes, and a few pale, shimmering stars whirled.

Gaetano looked down at her at last. Joanna was tall for her age, and well-developed. He did not feel as though he was dancing with a child. The black velvet mask hid the soft curves of her cheeks, refining them, hollowing her face. Snowflakes clung to her long unbound hair, multi-faceted like jewels. Gold, pink, purple and emerald, colours drawn from the fire. He was glad that she had spared him the boredom of dancing with a plain woman, but he pitied, suddenly, the man that would marry Joanna Zulian. A child, in an ugly, old-fashioned dress, but every man in the square glanced at her as she passed.

He considered idly, as with a flourish of grace-notes the dance drew to an end, the sort of life Taddeo's niece might have led. A drunken, irresponsible father, an exotic tramp of a mother. Gaetano was hot; as he bowed, sweat trickled down the back of his neck and lined the inside of his mask. He could see the apprentices and Benedetto, each of them with a girl resting on his arm, but he could no longer see Taddeo and Isotta. 'We were to dine with Messer Capponi,' said the child suddenly, rising from her curtsy and Gaetano smiled and nodded, following her as she walked away from the piazza in the direction of the Capponi house.

The street closed in, the tall houses on either side abruptly cut off the sound of laughter and music. Gaetano could no longer feel the heat of the bonfire; it had become winter again, an icy Venetian night speckled with snowflakes. The alleyway was unlit, but he could see the girl walking ahead of him by the hazy light of the moon.

They had almost reached the canal when she held one hand out to stop him, a single upraised finger touching her lips. He drew level with her, his shoes silent on the cobbles, his palm curled around the handle of his knife.

He could see four youths silhouetted by the light of the moon and the flares on the bank of the canal. They were dragging something towards the water's edge: some shapeless bundle of dirty rags. The bundle was alive, it moved and moaned. A dog, thought Gaetano, until he saw that the tattered, dirty robes were marked with a yellow square.

Even if he had wanted to, he could have done nothing. There were four of them, each one viciously drunk, each one with a knife in his hand. Gaetano heard the girl gasp as the body was toppled into the canal and the head held under the water. He saw her small flurry of movement, and his hand grabbed her shoulder firmly. '*No*,' he whispered.

She was still then. She would have run forward, called out, Gaetano thought wonderingly, as the man in the canal stopped struggling and the bubbles ceased. Gaetano realized that Joanna Zulian both fascinated and disturbed him.

When the youths had gone, running laughing along the canal bank to the safety of an alleyway. Gaetano glanced down at her. She was still at his side, staring out to the canal as his restraining hand gripped her shoulder. Her grey eyes focused on the last of the ripples that travelled slowly to the water's edge. She had slid off her mask; it lay crumpled on the ground beside her.

'He was a money-lender,' said Gaetano, roughly. 'A Jew.'

He took her hand and dragged her off in the direction of the Ca' Capponi.

The snow failed to settle, Lent passed, and it was spring. Each afternoon Joanna went to the Grand Canal and watched the passengers step from the barges. But still, Donato did not come. It was a long way from Spain, she reminded herself. Joanna thought of the places Donato must travel through, of the rivers he must cross, the mountains he must climb. And all alone, without either his daughter or his wife to help him.

In the mornings, Isotta taught her to embroider. Tiny silk flowers on a woven background, edgings for table-linen, bed-linen, collars and bodices and cuffs. Joanna remembered the flowers she had painted on Donato's banner, and the flowers in the valley of the Loire. Running errands for the workshops, she glimpsed the sketches that Gaetano Cavazza had sent from Padua for the fresco. They were unlike any pictures Joanna had seen before: she thought if she touched those hills, those streams, she would feel grass or pure spring water.

In the early summer, Isotta caught a fever. Joanna made tisanes and poultices; outside, the sky was violet-blue, but Isotta insisted the shutters must be drawn and the fire built up. Isotta coughed and cried, Joanna mopped her forehead, fed her soup from a spoon, brushed away the flies that somehow found a way through the shutters. Joanna held Isotta's hand until she slept, worn out by fits of coughing. Isotta coughed blood sometimes, and Joanna knew no remedy for that.

When she began to recover, Isotta told Joanna about the babies she had lost at birth. Twins, a boy and a girl. She had never conceived again. She wept as she spoke. Joanna must marry young, Isotta sobbed, and have lots of children, and never have to look at an empty cradle as Isotta had done.

Exhausted, Isotta slept. She would not marry, Joanna thought, she would never have children. There would be Donato to look after, and new places to see, and money to earn. Soon Donato would be here, and she would leave Venice for ever. She worried about Isotta being left alone again, and planned the remedies that she would leave for her aunt. She still remembered it all: the treatments for the ague, the plague and sweating-sickness; how to prevent a wound from festering; the principal organs of the body and their purposes, which veins to use for blood-letting; the names of the four humours and their characteristics, the astrological signs and their influences; love-philtres, charms against witchcraft; wallflowers to ease the pain of childbirth, the fruit of the peach tree to cure impotence; nightshade, hemlock, thorn-apple, and cowbane – the darker secrets of the poison phial.

In May, the Fair of the Ascension lasted for fifteen days. As Isotta was confined to her bed, Joanna walked alone down the crowded Merceria to buy ribbons and pins, thread and linen.

Lengths of cloth-of-gold, of brocade and embroidered damask hung, gently swaying in the heat, from the first-floor windows of the shops. The stalls were decorated with flowers, both fresh and of silk. It was as though, thought Joanna, she walked through a golden, gleaming forest, where the birdsong came from the nightingales imprisoned in their cages, and the flowers were scented with the rosewater and sandalwood of the perfumiers. Venice was transformed once more, an enchanter's country.

She saw him as she paused beside the glass-blowers' stall. Spread out on the cloth in front of her were bulbous, translucent jars and wine-goblets, fragile globes of gold and pink and turquoise. And there, when she looked up, was Donato.

He was fifteen yards or so ahead of her, walking away down the Merceria towards the Rialto. His back was to her, but she recognized immediately the set of his shoulders, the threadbare cloak, the shoulder-length greying fair hair topped by a flamboyantly feathered hat. As she began to run away from the stall, the glass-blower called out to her that she had left her purse, but Joanna did not turn back.

The street was swarming with people enjoying the fair; mothers with their children, sailors and their sweethearts, slow old people shuffling along with the help of a stick. Desperately Joanna struggled not to lose Donato in the crowds, to keep her gaze fixed on that familiar bouncing gait, and on the old velvet cap set at its customarily jaunty angle. Her heart felt as though it would burst, her breath was tight in her throat.

She caught up with him as he rounded the last corner and the Rialto came in sight. As the street opened out and the sun poured in, Joanna touched her father's shoulder.

'Donato. Papa.'

The man turned slowly. She realized as he turned, before he spoke, that she had been wrong. She had not followed Donato Zulian, returned to Venice at last to reclaim his daughter; she had followed a stranger.

'Signorina. Good day to you.'

The Italian was poor, the accent German, she thought shakily, or perhaps Flemish. She felt the smile wither on her lips, the pounding of her heart begin to slow.

'I'm sorry – I thought –'

Her voice was feeble, little more than a whisper. Her eyes stung, tears brimming at her lids. The stranger had seized her hand in his, was raising it to his lips, and was asking her something.

At first Joanna did not understand the clumsy, ugly Italian. Then, suddenly, she did understand. He had asked her her price. She began to tremble in spite of the oppressive heat of the crowded, enclosed street.

The stranger's face was crudely made, his eyes pale, his lips thick. So unlike Donato.

Something inside her, fragile since Sanchia's death, broke then. Joanna cursed him in German, in Flemish, and in English just in case. She caught the hand that imprisoned her fingers, and bit it, hard, drawing small pinpoints of blood. Then she ran back through the Merceria, past the armourers and the goldsmiths and the shoemakers, leaving the man howling in the street.

She began to doubt then. For the first time in her short life, Joanna began to doubt Donato Zulian, her father.

Her father – a man of great passions and great generosity. A fine physician, a skilful surgeon. Sanchia's brave and handsome lover, Joanna's guide and mentor: her childhood idol.

Or, a drunkard and a braggart. A wastrel. A man who had made his ailing wife and small daughter walk the length of Europe, with no pity for their limited health and strength. A man who had squandered the education that he had received, who had abandoned the city that would have nurtured his gifts. A man whose wealth and status had declined, quickly and inexorably, throughout Joanna's childhood.

A quack, a hawker of useless potions. A gypsy, a rogue. A trickster who exploited gullibility and pain.

A mountebank. A man who had killed his wife, and deserted his daughter. In Venice, the mountebank's daughter – the mountebank's zany – still waited.

The summer drew to a close. The sunlight that had sparkled the entire width of the Grand Canal diminished a little, so that the water no longer seemed spiked with sapphires and diamonds. The gondolas, whose graceful crescent shapes had been transformed by the sun into crafts of gold, darkened, and were no longer magical gilded chariots, but black-painted boats again, ferrying people about their daily business.

At the end of September, Joanna knew that she need wait no longer. Rising at dawn, silently leaving Taddeo's house, she walked not to the Rialto to watch the disembarking ships, but along the length of the Riva degli Schiavoni.

Bundling up her skirts, Joanna sat at the edge of the quayside, her knees bunched up to her chin. In the distance, beyond the Bacino di San Marco, the vast expanse of the Adriatic Sea glimmered, hazed with mist, reflecting the weak early-morning sun. Venice was silent: the sounds of the city had faded into the distance, and the sun hung heavily on the horizon, painting the sea gold, lilac, crimson and scarlet. A cold breeze fluttered on the water, rippling its smooth surface into a thousand tiny waves.

The summer was over, and Donato had not come for her. Over the past year, Joanna had repeated a litany of faith to herself. That Donato would be here, today, tomorrow, next week. That he had set off already on his long journey from Spain, that he was standing perhaps that very evening in some far-off marketplace, selling cures for snake-bites, offering to set broken bones.

But now her faith had died. It was a terrible thing, to lose faith. A voice in her head said, *Mountebank*, and in her mind's eye she saw a child pick up a stone and hurl it into the screaming crowd. She wondered, as she had wondered so many times before, whether the boy she had struck had died. Once, that thought had haunted her; now, she found that she had almost ceased to care.

Sitting at the quayside, Joanna understood that Taddeo Zulian's home was now her home, that Taddeo Zulian's family was now her family. That she would sleep in a bed, eat at a table, wear shoes, for the rest of her days. That she would never again dance alone in a dusty market-place, or watch the midsummer bonfires burn in a field in France.

Below her, the waters of the canal seemed bottomless, dark and opaque. In the gently shifting water she could see her own reflection: the pale oval face, the long unbound hair. The features were blurred and faded by the movement of the waves. No longer a child, not yet a woman. Something between – something forgotten, something forsaken.

She rose at last, stiff and awkward with cold, her black skirts falling crumpled around her. Alone, she began the long walk back to the Zulian house.

Later that day, Isotta's brother, Gaetano, returned to Venice from Padua, bringing with him the last of the sketches for the fresco.

The five of them – Taddeo, Isotta, Gaetano, Joanna and the journeyman Benedetto – dined that night with greater ceremony than usual to celebrate Gaetano's visit. Dinner was long and over-rich: lamb and venison, crabs and oysters, partridges and guinea-fowl. After dinner, Isotta embroidered. The journeyman, sitting on the floor by the hearth, made eyes at Joanna, and Gaetano and Taddeo discussed the ambitions of the kings of France and Spain, the Emperor, and the Pope.

'Bologna first,' said Gaetano, cutting an orange into quarters. 'And Perugia. Pope Julius II will evict the Bentivogli and the Baglioni from the Papal States. And then he will turn his attention to Venice.'

They were seated by the open window. Outside, the fading autumn light gleamed on the paved square.

'The Pope is Venice's ally,' said Taddeo confidently. 'He will not threaten us. Besides, Venice is impregnable.'

His complacency did not yet annoy Gaetano, who was heavy with good food and wine. 'The Pope is a soldier.' Gaetano refilled his glass. 'And although Venice may be impregnable, what of the cities of the terra firma, Taddeo? What of Verona? What of Padua?'

He knew that the fate of the mainland cities had not crossed Taddeo's self-centred Venetian mind. Gaetano's own house and workshop were in Padua, without any convenient sea-barrier to protect it from those rulers hungry for land or power, or simply impatient for revenge on arrogant, greedy Venice.

Taddeo shrugged, uninterested. Across the room, the journeyman stooped to pick up Isotta's fallen skein of thread, his hand brushing against Joanna Zulian's ankle as he did so. Suddenly Gaetano found that he wanted to shake Taddeo, to rouse him from his self-satisfaction. Controlling himself, he said, shortly, 'Venice is dependent on the terra firma for food, for taxes. She will not be able to survive in isolation.'

'She will not have to survive in isolation,' said Taddeo stubbornly. 'The French have always been our allies.'

Gaetano had ridden from Padua that day, and although he had washed and changed his clothes, he still felt as though he were covered in a layer of dust. Rising, he loosened the ties of his sleeveless doublet, and stared out of the open window. The square below was still crowded: children squabbled over a plaything, mariners, wine-bottles in hand, called to the passing courtesans.

He turned back to Taddeo. 'You say, my brother, that the French have always been Venice's allies, that they only want Milan. But two years ago the French signed a treaty of alliance with Pope Julius and the Emperor Maximilian. A formidable combination, don't you think?'

Taddeo said, disdainfully, 'As you know, the Treaty of Blois did not stand. The signatories fell out on the queen of Spain's death. No, Gaetano, the French are Venice's friends, and they will remain Venice's friends. Because of the spice trade, you see. They need Venice for the spice trade.'

'And we need the French for the fair at Lyons. They are not our dependents – we are interdependent.'

Isotta was coughing, she held a handkerchief to her mouth. A wasp whined, feeding off Gaetano's discarded orange-peel.

Taddeo said, 'Such matters are for the Great Council. They are not our concern.'

The journeyman, Benedetto, was sketching Taddeo's niece, Joanna.

Gaetano felt a surge of anger: Benedetto had not the skill. One day he, Gaetano Cavazza, would draw Joanna Zulian. When she was older, when he had found the right setting for her. Benedetto wore tight-fitting orange and black hose. One leg was striped, the other quartered. His soft boots had ridiculously long pointed toes. The girl Joanna was paying no attention to him; was paying no attention, Gaetano realized, to anyone. When Isotta coughed, Joanna would hold her aunt's embroidery for her, handing it back when the spasm had finished. But her movements were mechanical, her expression detached. Gaetano wondered whether Joanna was unwell: it had been her animation, her obvious life and vitality, that had made him notice her, as much as her good looks.

Quelling his irritation, Gaetano turned back to Taddeo. 'Consider, my dear friend,' he said patiently, 'this possibility. That the Pope, having driven the Bentivogli and the Baglioni out of the Papal States, will decide to march upon the cities of the Romagna, so recently acquired by Venice herself. Consider also that both the French king and the Emperor regard Italy as a box of comfits, to be squabbled over like greedy children, to be shared out for her cities, her treasures, her arts. Consider how many other Italian states – Florence, Milan, Genoa, Naples, for instance – regard Venice as an object of envy, rather than an ally.'

There was a short silence. Then Gaetano added softly, 'It will happen, Taddeo. Bologna and Perugia will fall within one year – two at the most.'

Taddeo frowned. 'Bologna and Perugia may not fall. The Bentivogli, too, are soldiers. Giovanni Bentivoglio will not part with Bologna without a struggle.'

It was dark outside now, and the noise from the square had lessened. 'Giovanni Bentivoglio,' said Gaetano, slowly, 'hasn't a fraction of Julius II's wealth, Taddeo. Bologna will need a great deal of money if she is to pay mercenary soldiers.'

'Venice has money,' said Taddeo stubbornly. 'Venice is the greatest city in Christendom.'

Gaetano knew that his brother-in-law spoke the truth. Outside, beyond the campo, were the canals and harbours, the great warehouses that stored the wealth of nations, and the Arsenal, the largest shipyard in the world. Venice's wealth was founded on the profits of trade: on the silks and spices and wines carried up the Adriatic in her barges and caravels. If any city could defend herself, then Venice could. She was protected by nature, protected by history. It was the jealousy which this sort of wealth inspired that troubled Gaetano; that, and a suspicion that Venice's military success and strength of purpose might neither be willing nor able to extend itself into the terra firma.

But perhaps Taddeo was right. Perhaps the French were their allies, and Julius would be content with Bologna, and Padua would not be left undefended. And besides, he knew that it was futile to argue with Taddeo, who had drunk more than he was used to, and had not the imagination to conceive of the sort of future Gaetano feared.

Gaetano leaned over and refilled Taddeo's glass. 'Let's talk of our fresco instead, Taddeo. Will it make the names of Zulian and Cavazza famous the length of Italy?'

He saw Taddeo's eyes gleam, Benedetto scowl. When he was owner of the Venetian workshops, thought Gaetano, there would no longer be a place for Benedetto. The journeyman specialized in complicated perspective, mathematical renditions of churches and bridges. Benedetto had laughed when he had seen Gaetano's initial sketches for the fresco. He would not laugh when Gaetano Cavazza was master of the workshop.

'We've begun to mark out the pictures on the walls,' said Taddeo. 'We'd best finish the work before winter comes.'

'Aye.' Gaetano laughed. 'You'll not enjoy painting while the snow falls, Taddeo. Your fingers will freeze to the brush.'

Taddeo, too, laughed. Then, frowning suddenly, he added, 'I'll have to look for another apprentice, Gaetano. It'll take two of us to finish the fresco by winter, and that'll only leave two in the workshop. Two is not enough to keep up with the rest of the work.'

'The rest of the work' was, Gaetano knew, Taddeo's wretched wedding-chests and coats of arms. Gaetano smiled. 'You have money enough for another apprentice, brother,' he said. 'The fresco will bring you two hundred and fifty ducats, perhaps three hundred.'

Taddeo nodded. 'We'll be paid by the yard – if we complete the commission in time. But my expenses have risen, brother. Gold leaf is a terrible price – and you can pay a fortune for some of the rarer dyes. And besides, there's the girl, Donato's daughter. We'll not see Donato again, I'm sure, so I'll have to find her a dowry if she's not to go to a nunnery. And if she's her father's daughter, she'll not be satisfied with a nunnery . . .'

The old fool had forgotten the girl was present. Gaetano's skin tingled, he glanced across the room.

Isotta looked up from her embroidery. '*Taddeo*. You should not speak of such things in front of Joanna. She is too young.'

Gaetano did not know whether the shock on Taddeo's face was caused by Isotta's unprecedented reproof, or by his recollection that his niece was in the room. But Joanna Zulian had risen from her seat and had crossed the room to stand opposite her uncle. Her hands clenched the folds of her gown and her knuckles were white.

'I have a dowry, uncle. I showed it to you.'

Taddeo, who had drunk too much, said, 'What man will marry you for an old book and a half-empty purse?'

Gaetano saw something at last in Joanna Zulian's lovely eyes. He had seen that haunted expression once before, at the carnival, when they had watched the boys drown the old Jew. She had disturbed him then: he had understood suddenly that such sights were not new to her, that the life she had led had accustomed her to that sort of random violence. He heard Joanna whisper, 'Aunt Isotta, Messer Cavazza,' and he saw her turn on her heel and leave the room.

'*Taddeo*,' said Isotta again. There were tears in her eyes. 'She is only a child . . .'

She was wrong, of course. Gaetano had realized that Joanna Zulian was not a child, had never been a child, had been a small, knowing adult since birth. He, too, rose, making his apologies, aware that the room was too crowded, too hot, that his need for the night and a different sort of company had suddenly become irresistible.

Joanna did not go to her bedchamber, which was small and dark and cramped. She went instead to the workshop, the largest room in the house. From the window of the workshop you could see the square, the church, the sky. You could believe that beyond the confining sea were other cities, other countries.

But she could not, as she had done so many times before, simply stand at the window and look. She found herself unable to be still, unable to do anything but circle the room, staring at the paintings and sketches on the easels, her fists clenched, her sight blurred. The long, seemingly endless day was drawing at last to a close. And she had not cried, she had not wept for the life she had once had, or for the family she had lost, until Taddeo had spoken those few, careless words.

Now she struggled not to bury her head in her hands and weep. Dignitaries, capped and robed, stared indifferently back at her from the canvases, the perfect brushstrokes blurred by the tears that gathered in her eyes. Townspeople paraded disinterestedly by, dwarfed by towers and bridges. Endless archways of immaculate perspective drew her towards them, triumphal in their dazzling mathematical bravura. Pompous men posed outside pompous houses that mirrored the palazzi lining the Grand Canal. All of Venice's grandeur and pageantry was here, in Taddeo Zulian's studio.

Joanna took a deep, shuddering breath, and wiped her eyes dry with her sleeve. Now the pictures were clear, the lines and colours no longer blurred. She saw that the canvas in front of her was incomplete, sketched in black, the colours indicated with only a few bold washes. Forests and plains, lakes and waterfalls, formed out of the candle-lit void. Her breath caught in her throat, her heart hammered painfully. She knew that this painting was different from the others in the workshop: that when she looked at it she was somewhere other than Venice, somewhere, perhaps, where she might see the stars in the sky through the holes in her tent. The walls and the sea ebbed away: she was in another country.

Beside the painting was a jar of brushes, and a shell still daubed with the remains of today's ultramarine. Dipping the brush into the shell, Joanna Zulian began to paint.

CHAPTER TWO

There were three of them: the first a huge fellow with a stringy pigtail scratching the shoulders of his leather jerkin, the second wearing an assortment of grubby silks and satins, and the third dark-haired, good-looking. An ill-assorted trio. But they were all young, they were all soldiers, and they were all stinkingly drunk.

Martin Gefroy rode after the three inebriated mercenaries, because Martin Gefroy was lost. Travelling from Rome to Padua, he had attached himself, as was his usual practice, to a group of merchants. But he had become side-tracked by a fascinating disease encountered near Pistóia, and the merchants had continued on their way without him, leaving Martin with pustules and boils and excrescences to investigate, and an appallingly poor sense of direction. He had attempted to continue his journey alone, telling himself that geography, like anything else, could be acquired by diligence. He had found himself, eventually, on a wooded river bank, alone in the rain and the grey November twilight. He had known the name of neither the wood nor the river, and he had heard, not far away, the howling of wolves.

Then, when he was debating the possibilities of sleeping in a tree (Could wolves climb? Would he fall from the branches when he dozed off?), the three soldiers had ridden along the track. He had heard them a quarter of a mile away, their songs and raucous laughter drowning the night sounds of the forest, the rushing of the river. He had watched and he had waited, hidden by the trees, and then, when the three were a decent distance ahead of him, Martin had mounted his horse and ridden cautiously after them.

He knew they were mercenaries by the swords they carried at their sides, the breastplates and sallets strapped to their saddlebags. Had it not been for one thing, Martin would have hid from them as he hid from the wolves, knowing them to be just as dangerous. He might have little money, but he had a reasonable cloak, and a good horse, and a bag of medical equipment that would fetch more than a few soldi in any marketplace. Unemployed soldiers had been known to kill for considerably less.

It had been the languages they had spoken that had stopped Martin Gefroy scrambling hastily up the tree, his horse already hidden in the undergrowth. The three men spoke a muddle of dialects, but the man with the pigtail was an Englishman, like Martin himself. The other two were French perhaps, or Italian. Martin trailed hopefully after them, trusting that their superior sense of direction would lead him to a clean bed and a hot meal by nightfall.

Snatches of songs – Italian, French, English, all of them bawdy, the words of none of them complete – filtered through the rain and shadows as Martin eased his way through the forest. The Englishman's voice bawled a riddle over the whispering of the trees and the rain.

> '"I have a hole above my knee
> And pricked it is and pricked shall be . . ."'

His friends responded with a mixture of howls and catcalls. The man in the dirty silks slumped over his horse's mane and pretended to be sick, and the dark-haired soldier groaned, 'Something new, Penniless, *please*.'

'I haven't finished, Toby,' said Penniless, aggrieved. He repeated, enunciating with care:

> '"And pricked it is and pricked shall be
> And yet it is not sore . . ."'

There was a howl of rage from Penniless as the fair-headed man hurled himself at him, and both slipped from their saddles in a tangle of stirrups and reins and leaf-mould. 'Bastard!' yelled Penniless. 'You bastard, Gilles!'

Martin, hidden in the shadows, sighed. His hopes of a clean bed and a hot meal began to recede as the scuffle threw up handfuls of earth and torn fragments of silk from the forest floor. He watched as Toby reined in his horse a short distance away from his squabbling companions. It was too dark for Martin to see the expression on his face.

Then Martin heard, unmistakably, the sound of steel against steel, the rasp of a sword being drawn from its scabbard. Sickened, but unsurprised, Martin struggled to turn away, entrapping himself and his horse in a thicket of thorns and willow branches. He was aware again of the rain and the cold and the isolation. He wondered which of the three soldiers intended to slit his companions' throats.

But immediately following the hiss of the sword, he heard a voice cry out, 'Penniless! Gilles! For Christ's sake . . .', and then Martin turned, and saw that things weren't quite as he'd imagined.

He, Penniless, Gilles and Toby were surrounded by wolves. But the wolves that circled them were not grey-coated and yellow-eyed, but of human form, raggedly dressed, hunger shadowing their gaunt faces. And carrying a daunting assortment of staves and cudgels, knives and clubs.

Dry-mouthed, Martin couldn't count them. Then he realized that the brigands had not yet seen him hidden in the thicket, but had noticed only the mercenaries, with their tempting, saleable clothes and armourer-made weapons.

A cudgel thumped Penniless, still brawling amidst the leaves, on the back of the head: Penniless, stunned for a moment, released Gilles, then shook himself and roared furiously.

The darkness, the drizzle, the noise and confusion, made it impossible for Martin to follow all that then took place. His hand reached for his dagger twice and then retreated, and several times he made ready to clutch his reins and turn about, struggling through the thorns to ride for the hills. But he was held still by a mixture of admiration and horror: a horror of this butchery, which nevertheless was one of the mainstays of his trade; and an admiration for the sheer physical prowess of the three soldiers. Martin, untidy and hopelessly clumsy away from his phials and his philtres, respected coordination, speed, agility.

Soon, most of the brigands had fled, or lay sprawled like split sacks of corn among the mud and bracken. Penniless and Gilles were crouched on the forest floor, rifling the pockets of the dead. Only Toby still fought, the dull steel of his sword whirling in the darkness, his ragged black hair soaked by the rain. Only Martin, watching, saw him pay the price for one too many tankards of ale, and slip on a tree root, staggering backwards so that the back of his uncovered head slammed against the trunk of a beech tree. Only Martin saw the gleam of steel in the darkness, the triumphal grimace on the face of the brigand. He heard himself cry out.

The brigand's knife didn't strike at the man's heart, though, as Martin had expected. Instead, it scored deeply along the forearm, the right forearm. There was a clatter of a sword to the stony ground, as the mercenary's fingers, suddenly losing all strength, let go of the hilt.

Then Penniless was there, wrapping brawny arms around a thin throat in an unloving embrace. And Martin was suddenly aware of the silence, of the gentle sounds of the river and the trees, and of Gilles, who stood in front of him, blue eyes glaring, sword pointing.

Very, very carefully, Martin raised his hands, fingers outspread, palms open. 'I'm a scholar,' he said placatingly. 'On my way to Padua. To study medicine and natural sciences.' He said it first in French, and then in English, and then in Italian for good measure. He was about to try Latin when the sword wavered a bit, and was withdrawn and returned to the scabbard.

'Medicine?' asked Gilles.

Martin slithered off his horse, and began to walk across the copse on rather unsteady legs. Penniless was already lost in the darkness, hacking his way through the trees, howling for vengeance. Kneeling down beside the wounded man, Martin saw the small shake of Gilles's head. Gilles's eyes were fixed on the steady stream of blood that flowed from Toby's sword-arm.

'There's a tavern half a league up the river,' said Gilles softly to Martin. 'Could you . . .?'

Could you take him back to civilization, slung over your saddlebow? Could you attempt to repair the irreparable? Could you find a priest to mutter the last rites?

And yet the wounded man was still conscious. Martin saw Toby's eyes, the dark blue-grey of twilight, stare first at him and then look downwards, almost with disbelief, to the knife-cut that gaped the length of his forearm, showing grey bone beneath the layers of skin and muscle.

Martin Gefroy nodded his assent. Then, with Gilles to help him, he put the wounded man across his horse, and started to ride to the tavern.

Following the path very, very carefully.

Toby dreamed.

The dreams were from far back: before his four years of soldiering, before the schoolmaster and his wife. His father was holding him by the hair and beating him, and though he struggled and spat he could not shake that hold. A vice was tightening around his arm; the pain was unbearable. Through the pain he could smell new leather and beeswax, and see the hammers and nails and lasts of the shoemaker's shop.

Everything hurt: his head, his arm, his back. He was fighting for breath, trying to scream.

Something cool touched his forehead, an unfamiliar voice murmured soothing words, and he opened his eyes. Shaking, gasping, Toby saw at first the square of the window, and then the fire with its flickering flames. At last he focused on the figure standing at his bedside. He blinked, but he still did not know the face.

The stranger said gently, 'You've rejoined us, then?' and a hand held a cup to his lips. He could not swallow the wine, it burnt his throat, making him cough.

The cup was taken away. Toby closed his eyes, exhausted, but he did not let himself sleep. He did not want to sleep: if he slept, he would be a child again, pumping the bellows to keep the fire going, drawing water from the well with icy, bruised hands.

'You were riding through the forest, monsieur. You were attacked by brigands. Do you remember?'

The voice was pleasant, the French slightly accented. Still, opening his eyes again, Toby did not recognize the face.

'My name is Martin Gefroy. I am an Englishman. Your friend Gilles asked me to bring you to this tavern and look after you.'

Martin Gefroy lied, though: it had not been quite like that. Gilles had expected him to die. Suddenly Toby wanted to prove Gilles wrong. Gilles was a conceited bastard.

But the memory of Gilles brought with it another recollection. Of lying in the mud somewhere between Pistóia and Bologna, and looking down at his arm. Toby summoned up the tattered remains of his courage and looked down once again. His arm was swathed in bandages. His right arm, his sword-arm. He felt waves of panic washing over him.

He heard Martin Gefroy say, 'It's a bit of a mess, I'm afraid. I found a competent barber-surgeon, and I did what I could myself as well. It's bleeding a great deal less.'

A priest, a schoolmaster, a notary's clerk . . . A trail of similarly unsuitable professions rattled relentlessly through Toby's aching head. He tried to move his fingers, and could not.

He was too tired to think. His eyes closed again and shut away the present.

Dreaming too much, he slept fitfully until the following morning, when

Gilles woke him with sops of bread in wine and a plateful of boiled chicken.

Gilles was looking pleased with himself; Penniless, awkward and shuffling in the small room, stood behind him. The rain had stopped overnight and the sun glared through the window. Gilles was silhouetted by its rays. Painfully, Toby hauled himself upright.

'We thought we'd have to bury you,' said Gilles conversationally, adjusting the lace at his cuffs. He wore a particularly florid doublet, filched, Toby recalled, from one of his countrymen at the battle of Gaeta. 'There's a nice little churchyard near by. Penniless insisted we buy you flowers. Does it hurt?'

Penniless clutched a ragged bunch of daisies. 'Yes,' said Toby briefly. Gilles, sitting down beside the bed, began to eat Toby's boiled chicken. Penniless jammed the battered flowers into a cup and said mournfully, 'Poor Crow.'

It hurt like hell. So did his head. He wasn't sure whether it was a hangover or a fever. He tried to move his fingers again, and a band of sweat broke out on his forehead.

Gilles was dissecting the chicken with long, elegant fingers. 'One of those bastards had some money,' he said. 'If we don't have to pay the sexton . . .'

A purse was placed on the table beside the bed. The remains of Gilles's sentence lingered in the air, unfinished. Toby knew the gist of it, though: we've money enough so that you'll have food in your belly, a roof over your head. Something to keep you going until you're well enough to become a priest, a schoolmaster, a notary's clerk . . . Poor Crow indeed.

He forced himself to smile, though. Gilles, finishing the chicken, rose, clamping his hat, an extravagant affair of feathers and ribbons, on top of his fair curls.

'We'll look out for you.' Gilles smiled. 'And behave yourself, Toby. The innkeeper has a very pretty daughter.'

The door shut behind them. The smile on Toby's face slipped, faded utterly. Wiping the sweat from his forehead with his good arm, he stared out of the window.

A flock of crows squabbled in the treetops outside. *Poor Crow*: Penniless's nickname for him, a tribute to his black hair the colour of a crow's wing, echoed forlornly round the room, an epitaph to a life that was over with. A void yawned before him, memories he had spent years trying to escape crowded round him, clawing at his heels. He didn't hear the door open or see Martin Gefroy come into the room.

'They've gone,' said the Englishman. 'Your friends. I didn't catch your name, by the way, monsieur?'

'Dubreton,' said Toby absently. 'Toby Dubreton.' Then he added, 'Will it mend?'

Martin sat on the stool beside the bed. 'I don't know,' he said apologetically. 'I'm sorry. I wish I could say one way or the other, but I can't. If you look after yourself and the wound heals well, then yes, you might be able to use your arm again. I've seen worse. But not often.'

Toby stared out of the window again. The crows had flown away, their cawing replaced by silence.

Martin Gefroy added, 'I'll stay here a while. There's some grain merchants travelling to Padua soon, apparently. I'm a scholar,' he explained to Toby. 'I've studied at the university of Paris, and in Rome. I was travelling from Rome to Padua, but I got lost. So I followed you.'

Toby had to force himself to speak. 'Why Padua?'

Martin pushed back his untidy hair from his face, and flicked a torn, trailing shirtsleeve from his plate. His light blue-grey eyes gleamed. 'For the natural sciences, my friend. For medicine. The university of Padua teaches Aristotelian science from the original Greek.'

'You're a physician, then, Master Gefroy?'

'I will be a physician. When I've finished my studies.' The Englishman added, his voice level, 'And I don't think a physician of twenty-five years' standing could tell you whether your arm will fully recover or not. It's just a matter of time. And of trying to prevent the dangerous symptoms that may follow such a wound.'

Toby leaned back on the pillows. Four years ago he had thought his future resolved. Soldiering had answered all his needs, had kept both mind and body occupied. Now, assuming he avoided the infections and gangrene that the scholar had hinted at, the future gaped before him again, another open wound. A priest, a schoolmaster, a notary's clerk . . . All three would give him far too much time to think. He did not want to think: he wanted to sleep, to avoid facing up to the reality of the brigand's knife-cut. But sleep, damn it, had yesterday brought with it dreams of the past. He knew then that he was afraid to close his eyes, afraid to reawaken the old nightmares that waited for him, calling him with cracked, insistent voices, allowing him no rest.

★

It was early spring before Toby was able to ride back to France.

He had parted with the Englishman a couple of months before, saying his farewells as Martin Gefroy set off down the road to Padua with a group of well-armed merchants bound for Treviso. Although he could not yet wield a sword, at least his hands could hold the horse's reins. His cuirass and sallet were inside his saddlebag, and he travelled the more populous routes. Just another civilian in search of a decent tavern and the least dangerous road home.

His journey was slowed by his reduced stamina, and by a gallingly limited ability to defend himself. He did not reach the village until late May. Then, long golden clouds streaked the hills and valleys, gilding the ridged lines of vines. Toby was tired; it took him a while to calculate how long it had been since he had last seen his home. Almost five years, he thought. He did not know why he had stayed away so long.

His adoptive mother saw him as he dismounted from his horse at the corner of the narrow cobbled street. She was pulling weeds from the small garden in front of the schoolmaster's house. She had always liked flowers. Toby held in his bad arm a sheaf of spring blossom he had gathered from the fields: bluebells and primroses and daffodils.

He saw her glance at him, and then glance a second time and freeze. She rose to her feet with tremulous slowness, resting one hand against the plastered wall. And then he was running the length of the street, the horse on its leading-rein behind him struggling to keep up.

His adoptive mother's name was Agnès Dubreton, his adoptive father was called Paul. There had never been any secret made of their relationship to him; there could not have been, because he remembered what had gone before. He remembered, but did not speak of it, and the Dubretons had always respected his silence.

Agnès tutted when she saw his arm, shaking her head over the jagged red scar. Paul brought out the best cognac and poured him a double measure. The flowers were put in a vase on the dresser, and the table was set. Toby was crammed full of chicken and bread and soft runny cheese until he thought he would burst. He slept that night in the small bed of his childhood, in the room where he had played with the toy soldiers Paul had made, charting fortifications with rushes on the stone floor.

He had thought that here, where he had discovered a temporary sort of happiness, he would have been able to sleep. But he could not: each night he dreamed the same dreams, those dreams awakened the previous autumn by fever and fear and pain. The shoemaker's shop, with its fire and bellows and lasts and knives. Bruises on his back, hunger in his belly.

Exhaustion made him touchy, incommunicative. As the days passed, conversation became strained and full of effort. He had been away too long; he knew himself to be haunted, ghost-ridden. How could he speak of what war did to men, to women, to children? How could he speak of what arquebus-shot, cannon-shot, did to limbs, to bodies? Worst of all, how could he escape his own childhood, which snarled like a black dog at his bedside every time he closed his eyes?

In the end, it was Paul who, for the second time in his life, coaxed him back to civility. One morning he gave Toby a hammer and some nails, and ordered him to the schoolroom next to the church.

There were no children in the classroom now; they were all out in the fields helping their parents to shoo the birds from the currant bushes or to hoe weeds from between the rows of vines. The room was dark and cool, the windows high and mullioned.

Paul pointed to the benches stacked in a corner of the room. 'They've hardly lasted out the year. Every leg wobbles.'

Toby raised the hammer while Paul held the bench steady. Toby's arm was infuriatingly weak, the first nail went in crooked. As he battered at the second nail, his chief emotion was suddenly one of anger, anger that some cursed rabble looking for trouble should have disrupted a life that had suited him so nicely. An unlucky wound to the arm, and there he was, unemployable, and nightly plunging back into a hell he had never wanted to see again.

His forehead was beaded with sweat, his arm ached. He would use a sword again only if he made his muscles work hard, bloody hard. And besides –

'Stop,' said Paul. He covered Toby's hand with his own until the muscles in Toby's fingers relaxed, and the hammer slipped to the floor. Toby glared at him. Paul said gently, 'If you spoke about it, it might help, you know. It sometimes does.'

Toby stood up, wiping the sweat from his face with the back of his shirtsleeve.

'You don't sleep,' persisted Paul, 'and you can't sit still. You never were the reflective sort, Toby, but . . .'

The words trailed away, lost in the buzz of a bee and the scuffing of Toby's boots as he restlessly paced the schoolroom.

'Tell me,' said Paul, 'about what you have seen, about what has happened to you.'

Toby paused at the doorway. He heard Paul add quietly, 'I know that I am only a country schoolmaster. I know that I have not travelled, that what adventures I have experienced have taken place, on the whole, between the pages of a book. But I am not without imagination.'

Toby made himself turn and smile. The smile, he knew, was as crooked as the nail he had driven into the bench. 'I know, papa,' he said softly. 'I know.'

Paul had crossed the room towards him. He waited, Toby knew, for some sort of an explanation. He couldn't speak, though. He had lived through the happy part of his childhood – the part with the Dubretons – by refusing to allow himself to think of the past, by creating, almost, another person. Toby Dubreton, the schoolmaster's son, instead of Toby Lescot, the shoemaker's apprentice. At sixteen, finding the village too small for him, and knowing himself well enough to see the possible consequences of that narrowness, he had ridden away before his restlessness could turn into mischief, his boredom into something he might regret. As a soldier, the noise of battle, the varied company, had created yet another man: one who lived for the present, one whose only thought was to stay alive, in one piece, experiencing to the full all the pleasures and terrors of his new life.

But now, the distant past seemed to have flooded into the vacuum of the present. When he heard Paul say, 'War is a terrible thing, Toby. And you haven't told us how you hurt your arm,' he almost laughed out loud.

He managed to say, 'That was nothing glorious, I'm afraid, papa. We were attacked by brigands, and I was too drunk to defend myself properly. It's not *that* . . .'

He shook his head, his sudden amusement utterly gone. He could see, glancing desperately out of the open doorway, the intense blueness of the sky, the wild roses that clung to the walls of the schoolroom. His memories seemed jarring, almost indecent, here.

'It's my father,' he said suddenly. 'I keep thinking of my father. I dream of him.'

Paul was silent.

Toby added, glimpsing his face, 'I mean the shoemaker. He was my true father, after all.' He hadn't meant to be so curt, so brutal.

But Paul only said, 'Of course. Perhaps.'

In the silence that followed, Toby became very aware of the small sounds of the village: the women's clogs as they clacked across the cobbles to the stream in which they washed the clothes, the dogs squabbling over a bone in the gutter.

Toby said, very carefully, 'I meant, papa, that I am of the shoemaker's blood. I did not mean that you are not . . .'

He stopped. Still so hard to find the right words; some of what had been beaten out of him in childhood he had never reclaimed. But there was no hurt on Paul's face; his eyes, as they met Toby's own, were steady.

'And *I* meant, Toby, that Monsieur Lescot was perhaps your father. But I was never sure.'

Staring at Paul, Toby did not move. Incurably restless by nature, he found his feet were sealed to the ground, his limbs as still as a statue's.

'Does it help?' said Paul, looking at him. 'I didn't speak to you about it when you were a child because you seemed to prefer to forget. Does it help?'

Toby shook his head, bewildered. 'I don't know, papa.'

'I found you in Chinon,' said Paul. 'In a cobbler's workshop. You remember that, I expect?'

He did. Fingers always torn from cutting the leather, his back always bruised from the cobbler's hand.

'You were the shoemaker's errand-boy. And apprentice. And whipping-boy. You were about seven or eight years old when I found you. Maybe older – you were a half-starved little thing.' Briefly, he rested his hand on Toby's shoulder. 'As I've said, I've never been sure how much you could remember. Some things are best forgotten, don't you think?'

Toby said, 'Some things are never forgotten. I remember the shop, the yard. I remember being cold and hungry.' His fists were clenched in anger. He saw the pity in Paul Dubreton's grey eyes, and he pulled away from him. He watched Paul cross the room and sit down on a rickety bench.

Paul's eyes were screwed up, his forehead creased, remembering. 'I'd gone to Chinon to buy some books. I was walking past a cobbler's yard when I heard a child screaming. I went in, and saw the shoemaker – your father. He was holding you in one hand, a hammer in the other. I believe that he would have killed you if I hadn't come in then. He was a big brute, built like a bull.'

Toby almost wanted to smile then, at the thought of gentle Paul Dubreton, book in hand, confronting a man who was built like a bull. 'Go on,' he said, evenly.

'I got myself measured for a pair of boots I didn't need, which put him in a better frame of mind. I managed to slip you a coin when he wasn't looking. I went back to my hotel, but I couldn't get you out of my mind. We had no children, as you know, Agnès and I, and it seemed such a *waste*. I went back the following day and bought you.' Paul smiled. 'I had some reservations about what Agnès might say, presented with an undersized infant whose every other word was a curse. But she rose to the occasion, of course. Bathed you in the horse-trough, and had you eating with a knife and a spoon within a fortnight.'

He said to his adopted father, who had bought a pair of boots he didn't need, along with a foul-mouthed son, 'Why me? You've seen a hundred half-starved children, a dozen of them on the streets of Chinon, I expect. You'd have liked to rescue them all, no doubt, but you knew that you couldn't. So why me?'

Paul shook his head. 'Nothing logical. There was just something about you – a brightness, a stubbornness. It struck me, in one so young, in such a place. You should have cowered, Toby, you should have grovelled. But you didn't. But I knew that if you stayed there, he'd beat the last sparks out of you. So I bought you.'

It didn't help, thought Toby. Much of it he could remember: the stranger's coin in his palm, the ride from Chinon to Bourges. Kicking and struggling most of the way, because he hadn't believed a word Paul had said to him, of course. He had known only bad things: he had not been able to conceive of the possibility that a stranger might intend him good.

Paul persisted. 'I'd made inquiries, you see, Toby. In case you had family in the town who might protest at me taking you away. But there was no one. I talked to Monsieur Lescot's neighbours. Lescot had never married, and they thought you'd been in your father's . . . *care*, if that is the word, for only three or four years or so. It seemed odd – why would a man like that take on such a young child? You can have been of little use to him, and I found it hard to believe that he did it out of the goodness of his heart. And if a mistress, for instance, had abandoned her unwanted child – well, there are foundling hospitals, after all.'

The sun was still casting pools of diamonded light on the floor, and the bee buzzed frantically, trapped in a cobweb slung between the rafters. Disjointed thoughts fluttered through Toby's mind, failing to make sense.

'And my father – the cobbler? Did you ask him?'

'I did. He told me you were his son. But –'

Toby looked up, eyes wide. 'But . . . you didn't believe him?'

'I wasn't sure. Would he have sold me his son? Perhaps.' Paul shrugged. 'I guessed that he had no capacity for telling the truth, that he would say whatever he believed would suit him best in the circumstances. He told me that you were his illegitimate son by a girl from Bourgueil.' The schoolmaster added, his voice level, 'There is the possibility, Toby, that though he lied over the details, the gist of what he said was the truth. You must consider that.'

There was a silence. Even the bee, choked by the spider's web, had ceased buzzing. Toby stepped through the doorway into the sunlight, and took in great lungfuls of warm summer air.

He stayed another few weeks with Paul and Agnès Dubreton, making himself useful. He drew water from the well for Agnès, he fed her hens, and held wriggling sheep while she inspected them for tics. In the schoolroom, he repaired tables and benches, and painted walls scabbed by chalk and small grubby fingers with a wash of lime. He worked from dawn to dusk, exhausting himself so that he could sleep soundly at night. By the end of a fortnight, he could have wielded a sword or loaded a pistol, if very slowly.

One evening he waited until Agnès had gone to bed, and then spoke to Paul, who had been alone in his study with his books and quills and papers.

'The cobbler's surname was Lescot, but I can't remember his forename. Nor the street where I lived.'

Paul looked up from his desk. 'You're going to him?' he said quietly. 'Toby, he may be long dead. He drank too much, fought too much . . .'

'I know.' He had had time to consider all that, time also to consider that he might simply be the brutal shoemaker's son, putting his father's belligerence to slightly better use as a soldier of fortune. 'His forename . . . please.'

Paul's nod of assent was scarcely noticeable. 'His name was Pernet Lescot. The shop was in an alleyway off the Rue Haute Saint-Maurice in the centre of Chinon. There was a small courtyard with a baker and a laundry as well. It shouldn't be difficult to find.'

He rose from the desk, stopping Toby before he reached the door. 'Have you thought, *mon fils*?' There was pain in his voice. 'Have you thought what you intend to do?'

'I intend to satisfy my curiosity, that's all.'

Toby knew that he lied. Unlike Paul Dubreton, he could lie very well, having learned that particular skill long ago. It was no tame, biddable emotion like curiosity that sent him to Chinon, but something altogether blacker. Exorcism, he thought. The need to obliterate a very persistent ghost.

Toby saw the fear on Paul's face. He said, in an attempt at reassurance, 'I won't kill him, father. I just need to know.'

The schoolmaster smiled, but his eyes were sad. 'I know you wouldn't kill him, Toby – at least, not in cold blood. But I know also that you won't ride to Chinon, ask your question and accept Monsieur Lescot's answer, and then ride contentedly away. I know you well, my son, and you're not capable of that.'

He had never been anything other than transparent to Paul Dubreton. Fourteen years ago Paul had, presumably, seen through the layers of dirt and sores and lice to something better, something worth preserving.

If Toby had been a different person, then he might have changed his mind, have spent a few months more regaining his skill with sword and pistol, and eventually ridden back to Italy to take part in whatever war his betters next intended to fight. But he was what his past had made of him. And the same itching restlessness that had sent him from this village years before would not allow him to do anything other than ride the following day to Chinon.

Chinon was baked in sun; sunlight glinted on the towers of the castle and caught the pennants flying from the square-rigged boats that slid down the Vienne. The river was green and opaque, trimmed with sandbanks. The castle's vast ramparts dwarfed the town. Less than ten years previously Cesare Borgia, son of Pope Julius's predecessor

Alexander VI, had ridden to Chinon to present King Louis XII with the annulment of his marriage to the crippled Jeanne de France. Louis had then married Anne of Brittany, Charles VIII's widow, thus securing her vast inheritance. Louis XII's gaze had since turned a little further afield, to Italy. Everyone wanted Italy, for its wealth, its treasures, its culture, its availability.

Toby remembered the bridge, and he remembered the boats. He also remembered the castle: Pernet Lescot, in one of his more imaginative moods, had threatened him with its dungeon. Riding through the town walls, he found the Rue Haute Saint-Maurice easily enough. The Grand Carroi branched off to his right, winding steeply up to the castle, climbing past wine-cellars cut into the rockface. The street was busy; it was market day. Stalls were set up at the side of the road, housewives clustered round them, the hems of their gowns trailing in the dusty straw. A pretty girl offered him a bunch of rosebuds for his sweetheart, but Toby smiled and shook his head.

He found the cobbler's workshop hidden in a courtyard at the back of a tavern. He remembered the tavern, too, he had been sent there often enough to fetch ale or wine. There was no longer a baker to one side of the shop, but there were still baskets of dirty washing piled up outside the laundry. Toby was glad that the baker had gone: the smell of new bread had once tormented him.

Looping the reins round the hitching-post, he left his horse outside the cobbler's shop. He pushed open the door and called the shoemaker's name. At first the room was empty, giving his eyes time to adjust to the poor light, and to see the lasts, the knives, the hides, just as before. Nothing had changed: it was merely a little older, a little dirtier. Then he heard a shuffling and a grumbling, and the tattered curtain at the rear of the shop swung aside.

Toby could smell the wine on Pernet Lescot's breath, see the dark stains that spilled down the front of his leather apron. Toby felt instant and almost overwhelming fear. He wanted to run and hide behind the barrels in front of the tavern, to bury himself in the piles of washing by the laundry. He still bore the scars of this man's temper on his back.

But he recollected himself immediately. He was no longer eight years old and in the shoemaker's possession; he was a grown man with a sword at his side and five years' experience of war. And besides, Pernet Lescot had produced a sickening, ingratiating smile, and was already ushering him towards the nearby stool and assessing the condition of his boots.

He did not sit down. He said, 'Monsieur Lescot, I'm not here for shoe leather. You don't recognize me, do you? I'm your former apprentice, the one you sold to the schoolmaster, Paul Dubreton.'

He saw confusion, then shock, then fear, flicker in the cobbler's bloodshot eyes. Then Pernet Lescot began to laugh, a hoarse, obscene cackle that made the skin on the back of Toby's neck turn cold.

'He paid ten écus d'or for you,' the shoemaker gasped. 'The old fool!' The laughter subsided; the shoemaker, wheezing, rested his palms on the table and leaned forward. 'And what do you want with me, boy?'

Anger had begun to replace the fear. 'A little information, that's all. I want to know where I came from.'

His answer was more laughter, and an obscenity. There was a half-full wine-bottle on the shelf next to the row of finished shoes. Lescot took a mouthful from it. 'I needed help in the shop.' His eyes measured Toby, their mockery blatant. 'You're mine, boy. The result of a little misunderstanding between myself and a girl in Bourgueil. She thought I'd marry her – I was damned if I would. She'd have drowned you at birth. Aren't you grateful that I'd the decency to take you in and care for you?'

Sitting inside the peaceful schoolroom, Paul Dubreton had said, *'He told me that you were his illegitimate son by a girl from Bourgueil. There is the possibility that though he lied about the details, the gist of what he said was the truth.'*

Toby had had time to work out the implications of that one. That he was the shoemaker's son by a married woman, or by his first cousin, or by his sister . . . That thought sickened him.

Lescot had lowered the bottle, was wiping the wine from his chin with the back of his hand. He grinned. 'What a fine fellow you are now, though. What did the old fool make of you? A priest . . . a farmer . . . or his catamite? That's what I thought he wanted, a little –'

He did not finish his sentence. Toby's knife was in his hand, his other arm round the shoemaker's neck, squeezing. His right arm, his sword-arm, did not hurt at all just now. He hissed, his voice thick, 'He made of me a soldier, Lescot. A mercenary. *Someone who kills for money.*'

He felt Pernet Lescot writhe, trying to free himself. But the once-hard muscles had turned to fat, the powerful movements had been made clumsy by age and drink. Toby knew that he had only to slice the knife across Lescot's throat, cutting through skin, tendon and windpipe, to avenge himself for all the countless cruelties and humiliations of his childhood.

But there was a movement of the torn curtain at the back of the shop and a voice whispered, 'Master?'

Blue eyes, round with fear, stared at him, then at the knife. The child was not, Toby told himself as his hand started to shake, his former self come back to haunt him, but only the shoemaker's latest apprentice.

The knife slipped, Toby's hold relaxed, and the shoemaker fell forward, hands on the table, coughing and retching. From out of the darkness, his own voice echoed as he promised Paul Dubreton, *'I won't kill him.'*

He moved away from the shoemaker, disgusted suddenly by the stale breath and greasy hair. Pernet Lescot, recovering himself, shouted at the child to be gone. There was another flurry of movement, the sound of bare feet running across the cobbles in the courtyard.

Toby still held the knife in his hand. The shoemaker's eyes were fixed, warily, on the long, thin blade. His breath wheezed like the bellows the child Toby had once used to light the fire in this room.

Toby sat on the edge of the table. 'Let's try again, shoemaker. I want to know how old I was when I came to live with you, where I came from, why you agreed to keep me. The last one's easily answered, I suppose – there must have been money involved. A reasonable sum of money, I'd guess. Which suggests, does it not, that you had me from one of your betters?'

He saw Pernet Lescot nod slowly, as his hand reached for the wine-bottle.

'*Who*, then, shoemaker? And why?'

Toby's hand folded round the bottle; the shoemaker's outstretched fingers paused, twitching.

A shake of the head. 'Don't know. Never knew.'

'I have the knife,' Toby said softly. 'And there's the shop, of course. There's plenty of straw in here that would burn rather nicely.'

Still there was silence. Cradling the bottle against his chest, Toby said dreamily, 'You cannot doubt me, shoemaker. I have a long memory.'

His words hung in the warm afternoon air, echoing around the familiar room. Pernet Lescot mumbled something, and Toby, up-ending the bottle, let the wine trickle to the dirty floor.

'Speak clearly, shoemaker.'

Lescot said desperately, 'You were three or four years old – I can't remember. Too young to be of any use. And wilful. My last boy had died, but I wanted an older lad –'

'But you were offered money to take me?'

The shoemaker nodded, his reddened eyes fixed on the slowly dripping wine.

'A lot of money, presumably, to persuade you to take a child who would be of little use for several years.'

Lescot said bitterly, 'They told me you'd be dead within the year. You'd have been the best bargain I'd ever made if you'd kept to that. But you survived, damn you.'

Toby felt curiously detached, as though Pernet Lescot spoke of some other person. 'And my name? What was my name?'

Lescot's face was agonized. 'Toby. That's all. They never told me your surname.'

The bottle tilted a little further. The tangle of straw and leather trimmings on the floor was stained with purple.

'And who were *they*, shoemaker? Who were *they*?'

'They were . . . they were servants of the Seigneur de Marigny. I saw the colours of their livery under their cloaks. I said nothing, of course. But I thought, that's it, the brat is a du Chantonnay bastard. That's all I know. *For the love of God, give me the wine!*'

Toby handed Pernet Lescot the bottle. His own movements were suddenly clumsy. Calculation and confusion battled for place within him. His lungs seemed to be scrabbling for air, as though it were he, and not the shoemaker, who had had the life almost choked out of him.

He found the boy outside, curled up in a basket of linen, sleeping like some small exhausted animal in the sun. He could see, under the torn shirt, the weals and bruises on the child's back. Crouching, he placed a coin in the child's hand, and the wide blue eyes, so much lighter than his own, stared at him disbelievingly.

'Tell your master,' Toby said, 'when he is sober, that I will be back. Tell him that if you are not warm and well-fed and unmarked, that I will take what he owes me. Can you remember that?'

The boy nodded. Toby straightened, untied the reins of his horse and led it away from the cobbler's yard through the Rue Haute Saint-Maurice.

He did not look back.

It took him no time to discover that the du Chantonnay estate of Marigny lay between Chinon and Tours. By late morning of the following day he had reached the outskirts of the Marigny estate and was standing outside the wall and forest that hid the château.

It was hot, he rode hatless, in shirtsleeves and breeches, his cloak and doublet stuffed into his saddlebags. Beside the path, the river, emerald-green with pondweed, was fringed with reeds and teasels. Reining in his horse, Toby stood for a moment, watching the midday heat shimmer on the river, the distant fields and the enclosing woodland. There was no one about, so he swung off his horse and looped the reins around a branch, leaving the animal standing in the shade contentedly chewing the sparse grass. Then he was over the wall, with only the clouds of dust rising into the air to show the path he had taken.

Inside the boundary wall the forest was like a cave, cool and green and lightless. Branches threaded together overhead to make a roof; underfoot the ground was littered with dead leaves and newly sprouting ferns and pale fungi. There was no breeze; the leaves did not stir, and Toby's feet made no sound on the soft earth. He wanted to see the château de Marigny without being seen. He wanted to measure Marigny's strength.

Eventually the trees just stopped, and there in front of him, across a vast, flower-filled meadow, lay the château de Marigny. Toby gazed with awe at the turrets that soared into the sky, at the majestic walls that shimmered and sparkled in the glassy water of the moat that reflected them. Swans glided to and fro. From the tops of the turrets pennants trailed in the windless air. Although he had hitherto reserved words like *beauty* for pretty girls, or expensive horses, Toby knew at once that this was beautiful.

His throat ached. He thought briefly, painfully, of the shoemaker's shop in which he had spent his infancy. He knew that he could never cross the flower-filled meadow that lay between him and the high doorway of Marigny. Just as the drawbridge and moat excluded him, so did his ignorance of his origins, his years spent crouched in a filthy shop, feeding wood into a smoky fire. Birth and privilege gave you something like Marigny, and he had neither of those. The blood of the du Chantonnays might flow in his veins, but it was tainted, muddied. He was shut out for ever, unfit for the sort of company that dwelled in those high turrets.

He spent that night in a tavern in a nearby village. He did not sleep, because he could not sleep; and when he had sickened of lying awake, he went in search of the serving-woman who had offered herself earlier. She was called Sophie, and she was plump and stupid and generous. With her, he managed to forget for a while that taunting, beautiful house. But only for a while.

When, eventually, she lay still in his arms, her fair hair tumbled against his shoulder, he asked her about Marigny.

Sophie yawned. 'They say' – her eyes were half closed and her voice was dreamy – 'that there's a thousand rooms and a thousand servants. And that her ladyship has a new gown for every day of the year.'

He said automatically, 'The Seigneur de Marigny's married, then?'

Sophie nodded. 'Yes, *petit*. Madame de Marigny's name is Eleanor. My sister-in-law worked in the kitchens of Marigny. Kiss me?'

He kissed her, and thought of Eleanor du Chantonnay who had a different gown every day of the year. Sophie's frayed skirts lay bundled on the floor; her grubby bodice had fallen open to reveal her full breasts. His hand absently stroked her soft skin, and he said, 'Have they children? The du Chantonnays, I mean.'

'Yes. One. A boy called François. A sickly lad, my sister-in-law says.' Turning on to her stomach, Sophie looked up at Toby, smiling. Her hand touched his thigh, then kneaded the hard muscles of his stomach. 'Why, *chéri*? Will you work for the Seigneur?'

The moonlight traced the beginnings of her double chin, her tangled, dirty hair. Toby made himself produce an answering smile. 'Perhaps. Yes, I might.'

He realized, as he rolled her on to her back and began to kiss her again, that Sophie had merely voiced the idea that had hovered in the back of his mind since the afternoon. Perhaps he would work for the Seigneur de Marigny. Perhaps the du Chantonnays, whom the shoemaker had thought to be his progenitors, had need of a mercenary soldier with a sword, a cuirass and a damnably long memory.

★

The image of the château was still imprinted on Toby's pupils when he returned to Marigny the following day. Hidden beneath the sheltering trees, he walked around the perimeter of the meadow. Whenever he looked up, there was the château, pale and perfect, flaunting itself to him from every angle.

The previous day the château had seemed empty and enchanted. It had occurred to him that if he ventured beyond the dark ring of trees that imprisoned the flowery meadow, he too would become motionless, stilled by a fairytale magic. But that was nonsense, of course. It had been early afternoon, and anyone in their right minds would be dozing indoors out of the heat. Only beggars and bastards pounded the land at midday, sweat between their shoulder-blades, damp hair glued to their foreheads. Even his namesake, the crow, had retired to the high treetops, temporarily abandoning the search for carrion.

The sudden sound of horse's hooves made Toby's heart thump, and his hand reach for the hilt of his sword. But, peering out through the branches, he saw that it was only a boy riding full tilt across the meadow. Horse and rider disappeared into the trees ahead of him, and Toby heard the crack of hooves breaking twigs, branches thwacking against the horse's flanks. The rider was a youth of thirteen or fourteen, and he rode awkwardly, stiffly, without instinct.

Hidden in the shadow of a tree, Toby heard shouting coming from another rider still in the meadow. Ahead of him the youth was laughing, a high-pitched nervous laugh, and wiping his long, pale hair back from his face with a flick of a wide silk sleeve. The lad was well dressed, the horse was superb, although the boy used it like a drayman's nag. He was spurring it through the forest, regardless of the tangled undergrowth and protruding tree roots beneath him.

Out in the meadow the other rider paused, wheeling his horse round and calling. Now Toby could distinguish the name that he called. *François*. The boy was called François.

The pounding of hooves suddenly ceased, and there was a tearing of leaves and branches, and a shriek closely followed by a splash. Then silence. Toby began to run through the wood, following the trail the horse had made. He saw the horse, riderless, chewing at the flurries of dog's mercury that edged the ditches, and then he turned and saw the boy.

He was floating face downwards in a pool that was black and still.

Dead, jagged logs lay in the mud at the water's edge. One side of the boy's pale hair was stained pink. The boy circled slowly in the dark water, his arms and legs spreadeagled.

The Seigneur of Marigny had one son, Sophie had said the previous night, who was almost grown. *'François,'* called the distant voice from the meadow. *'François.'* The boy floating in the pool was the Seigneur de Marigny's only son. No, thought Toby. His only *legitimate* son.

Toby came up to the pond and paused for a moment, as though on the edge of a precipice. Then he found himself wading through the mud, seizing the soaking shirt, and hauling François du Chantonnay out of the water. Too easy, thought Toby, too easy. The lad was pale and weak. Letting him drown would offer Toby no satisfactory recompense. He knew, suddenly, that he wanted something more than that. Restitution, perhaps. Redemption. A share in what, in different circumstances, might have been his.

He placed the boy on his front among the leaf-mould and wood-ants, and squeezed the water out of his lungs. François du Chantonnay's eyes opened, and he coughed and choked and finally vomited. And then he cried, wiping his eyes on a muddy silk sleeve.

Toby heard the sound of horse's hooves, much more skilfully controlled this time, coming towards them. *'François,'* called the du Chantonnay's bodyguard again and, jumping from his horse, glancing at the boy's quivering body, he raised a sword to Toby's throat.

Toby's own sword was still in its scabbard, clogged with mud. The bodyguard was six feet tall, three feet wide. The sword scratched Toby's windpipe.

The boy snivelled and said, 'That cursed horse threw me, Meraud. I nearly drowned. You should cut *its* throat.'

Meraud's glance took in the horse still peacefully grazing, and the pond with its trail of muddy footprints. His eyes met Toby's.

Toby said, careful not to move an inch, 'The horse threw the lad – he was riding too fast. His head must have struck one of the logs. I found him floating face down in the water.'

Some of the suspicion ebbed from Meraud's eyes, and the tip of the sword slipped a little. Toby saw the look of contempt that flickered across the bodyguard's face as he glanced again at the shivering youth. François struggled to his feet, using Meraud's outstretched arm as a support.

Toby smiled expansively. 'I'll lead the lad's horse back for you, if you want, Monsieur Meraud.'

François du Chantonnay's bodyguard gave Toby one last measuring glance and then said, 'Aye. You can do that. And then you can have the pleasure of explaining to my lord what the hell you were doing on his lands.'

Toby led young François du Chantonnay's grey out of the forest and across the meadow. Flowers of every colour surrounded him. He crushed their leaves underfoot, and their scents, rich and hypnotic, filled the air. The bodyguard Meraud led his own large chestnut; the youth, pale and damp, was slumped in its saddle. The château de Marigny seemed to have become possible, suddenly: no longer an unreachable mirage. Toby's shirt and breeches began to dry in the hot sun as the house and its shifting twin image in the moat enlarged as he neared them.

They crossed the drawbridge and were permitted to pass through the keep. The du Chantonnay coat of arms, a leopard under three crescent moons, was everywhere: carved above the doorways and windows, embroidered on the banners and pennants that drooped from the pinnacles. And the motto, *Garde ta foy*, repeated itself over and over again as Toby stared dizzily up at the walls and towers surrounding the courtyard.

The horses were handed to a stable-boy, the youth François dispatched to an agitated housekeeper. Toby was led up winding stone steps, past doorways and high, narrow windows, and finally instructed to wait in a small ante-room.

'Stay here. I'll have two dozen armed men looking for you if you're not here when I come back.'

Toby nodded. He had seen a dozen Merauds on the battlefields of Italy. Meraud limped slightly, which had, Toby guessed, curtailed a successful military career. The bodyguard knocked and entered the adjoining room, closing the door behind him.

The walls of the ante-room were bare blocks of stone, the floor was strewn with rushes. Toby scraped some of the mud off his boots against the top step of the stairway and attempted to rearrange his damp, dirty clothes. Outside, glimpsed through the narrow window, he could see the meadow and distant forest. He felt dazed, unconvinced that this was reality, half certain that when he touched the stone window-sill everything would dissolve: château, courtyard and moat would become insubstantial and leave him standing alone again, shut out from all this splendour.

The door opened. 'The Seigneur will see you now, lad,' Meraud said. 'Remember your manners.'

Toby stepped into the adjacent gallery. Again, that sense of shock at yet another overwhelming display of what money and breeding and good fortune could buy. Inside, as the door closed behind him, Toby found himself drenched with colour and light. The ceiling was banded with huge wooden beams, the stone floor covered with Turkey carpets. And the walls . . .

The walls were almost invisible. They were hidden behind tapestries twelve feet in height, vast and multicoloured. He could have been outside in the meadow that surrounded Marigny, for every tapestry was a profusion of flowers, each flower a complex, colourful, perfect shape. He could almost smell them. Animals peered at him from between the flowers: hunting-hounds, lionesses, rabbits and genets. And unicorns. Toby's eyes were seized and fixed by the final tapestry, where a unicorn, encircled by a small fenced enclosure, raised its proud head.

He had forgotten that he was not, of course, alone. A voice said, 'They are exquisite, are they not? Shall I tell you their story?'

Toby realized that he was behaving like an ignorant country bumpkin, gawking open-mouthed at a rich man's treasures. He managed an adequate bow.

The Seigneur de Marigny was taller than average, about Toby's own height, and powerfully built. His rich dark crimson overtunic was lined with cloth-of-gold, and a gold chain rested on broad padded shoulders. A grey beard traced the jutting contours of his chin and echoed the colour of his short hair. Age had begun to dig furrows from nose to chin, but the flesh was firm, well-filled. The Seigneur was, Toby guessed, well into his fifties, the product of money and good food and security. His eyes were narrow and sharp and colourless. Fish's eyes, glazed and greedy. Toby wanted to shiver as those eyes rested on him, assessing him. Du Chantonnay would, Toby thought, see everything.

But he did not yet find himself cast out of Paradise, marked as a pretender, a bastard, an outcast. As the Seigneur moved towards him, Toby noticed that his gait was clumsy, lacking the power and virility of that first impression.

Level with him, du Chantonnay pointed up to the first tapestry. 'Look. The hunters gather. They are armed with bows and spears, their dogs strain at the leash. To hunt the unicorn, you see.'

He shuffled forward a few paces, Toby following him. 'And here, in the second tapestry, the unicorn bends its head to dip its horn in the stream. To purify the water, so that the other beasts may drink.'

The horn pierced the pale, glassy water. A stag, a lion, a panther and a hyena waited on the bank of the stream.

'And here' – the Seigneur pointed to the third tapestry – 'the chase. The hunters surround the unicorn with their spears. They believe that he cannot escape them.'

A few more limping steps. 'But the unicorn fights back. He kicks and strikes with his horn. The hunters recall that he cannot be taken in this way. There's only one way to catch a unicorn.'

Toby found his voice. 'He must be tamed by a maiden, *votre seigneurie*.'

Du Chantonnay smiled, inclined his head. 'Of course! The unicorn must be betrayed by a maiden. Like so.'

Toby looked up. The unicorn's forelegs rested on a lady's lap. One of her hands stroked his white throat, her other hand held up a mirror in which the unicorn was reflected.

'Now,' said the Seigneur calmly, 'the hunters can kill him.'

Spears pierced the white hide, sullying it with blood. A hound gnawed at the creature's living flesh, and the unicorn's eyes were distended in agony. Looking upwards, Toby had to remind himself that he had seen sights far worse than this; that this death was merely an image, woven in silk across warps of wool.

Yet he was glad to turn to the final tapestry, where the unicorn, miraculously brought back to life, caracoled in a meadow. A flowery meadow, the twin of the one that surrounded the château de Marigny.

'A fascinating and instructive story.' The Seigneur turned away from the tapestries and eased himself into a chair. 'Don't you think, monsieur . . . ?'

Toby glanced out of the window. On the perfect flowery meadow of Marigny a crow strutted, a smear of black on the acres of green. He smiled. If it was perhaps unwise to be a Dubreton, then he would use for himself the name that Penniless had given him, far away on the battlefields of Italy.

'Crow. Toby Crow. I'm French, though the surname is English. I come from near Bourges.'

'Well, Monsieur Crow' – the Seigneur stretched out a leg in front of him: Toby could see the heavy bandaging from ankle to thigh – 'I believe I am in your debt. Meraud tells me that you saved my son from drowning.'

Toby said easily, 'Sire, it was fortuitous, that's all. I was in the right place at the right time.'

'Yes. Most fortuitous, as you say. François is my only son, monsieur, and therefore we must strive to keep him alive. It is unfortunate that he is headstrong as well as incompetent – an unpromising combination that makes our task so much more difficult.' Turning his head to glance out of the window, du Chantonnay added, 'Your occupation, sir?'

That was easy. 'A soldier, *votre seigneurie*. I have spent the last five years as a soldier.'

'Fighting for your country?'

'For whichever country would pay me. In Italy, mostly.'

Du Chantonnay's smile failed to reach his small, bleak eyes. 'If you know Italy, sir, then tell me, what will the Pope do next?'

Toby let his mind drift back to Italy. 'Venice,' he said. 'Pope Julius would like to humiliate Venice.'

Du Chantonnay nodded. 'That is my opinion also.' He glanced again at the wall. 'These beautiful tapestries were part of my second wife's dowry. They are what I married her for.' The folds of du Chantonnay's face creased, his shoulders heaved momentarily with laughter. 'I possess paintings as well as tapestries, Monsieur Crow, many of which come from Venice. And I have money invested in Venetian banks. So much more convenient, you understand.'

Toby managed to mumble some suitable reply. He could feel the weight of power, of influence: it bore down on him, crushing him, just as it had crushed him the previous day when he had seen the château de Marigny for the first time. Beside this, he was nothing. He did not even exist.

'It would not suit me,' added the Seigneur, 'if Venice were to be destroyed. Do you see, monsieur?'

He did. He understood suddenly that the Seigneur de Marigny shared with his liege lord King Louis of France a passion for all things Italian. Both of them wanted a piece of that opulent, sunlit country – the country in which Toby himself had spent four years of his life.

'Circumstances have not permitted me to travel to Italy for some time,' continued du Chantonnay. 'My health, you see.' He glanced down at his leg. 'All the physicians in France cannot find me a cure. It's ulcerated – a vile complaint. So it would interest me, Monsieur Crow, if you were to tell me what you have seen.'

He was back for a moment in Italy, where the greatest armies in the world battled for possession and power. Toby said slowly, 'Some of the city-states – Bologna, Perugia – are nervous. But Venice is convinced that she will be able to keep the cities of the Romagna, *votre seigneurie*. She believes Pope Julius has neither the money nor the troops to take them from her – she also considers France to be her friend. Venice doesn't doubt that she has both the men and the resources to keep the Emperor Maximilian, if he marches alone, at bay.'

'And you, sir' – du Chantonnay smiled again, but his eyes, with their unsettling lack of colour, were cold – 'what do you, a common soldier, think?'

The tapestries moved gently in the warm air from the open window: the wounded unicorn, with its tormented eyes, stared down at him. 'I think,' Toby said, 'that all the world envies Venice. For her wealth, for her security.'

'Would you fight for her?'

He shrugged. 'If she paid me well enough. But not for a while. I was wounded last autumn.' He held up his arm, showing the scar that snaked from forearm to knuckle. 'That's why I was here, in your wood, seigneur.' Toby's eyes were disarming, wide open. 'I thought I'd see if Marigny had need of a mercenary soldier who didn't want to go back to war just yet.'

He made his face as honest as possible, and did not flinch from the Seigneur de Marigny's unsettling gaze.

Du Chantonnay said slowly, 'A child could understand the story of my tapestries. The chase, the luring by the maiden, the killing. But there's so much more to it than that, Monsieur Crow, so much that a child would never see. So much that requires an altogether more subtle mind. Did you know, for instance, that the thistle beside the stream from which the unicorn drinks represents the crown of thorns? Did you know that the red rose tells of sensual pleasure, that the medlars and marigolds are antidotes to poison? Nothing is quite what it seems.' He smiled. 'And you, sir, are you, too, subtle? Do you see – or do you *construct* . . . what is not . . . quite . . . there?'

Toby did not move. His heart pounded, and his mind voiced over and over again the thought he had tried to suppress since the interview had begun: *This man could be my father.*

Du Chantonnay added, 'My son's . . . *accident* . . . was, as you said, fortuitous, monsieur. I might almost think, did I not know how appallingly François rides, that you manoeuvred the entire incident. Entrapped the foolish boy, tapped him on the head, dipped him in the pond and waited for Monsieur Meraud to arrive. A subtle course, whose reward would be, you might have hoped, recognition. And money, of course – a mercenary soldier with a damaged sword-arm might be short of a few sous.'

Toby said nothing. He felt, though, a small, cold trickle of sweat run down the back of his neck.

'Had you done that, sir, I might have respected you – even admired you – for your initiative, your imagination. But I would have you put to death, nevertheless. Don't doubt me, don't think that because I despise François's temperament and lack of talent, I would applaud anything that might bring him the slightest harm. He is my only son. Marigny must be his one day. I would dismantle it stone by stone before I let a stranger – or an enemy – take it.'

The sweat chilled, turned to ice. Toby was aware, suddenly, that the sun, dipping below the forested horizon, no longer gilded the stone floor. He was aware also, for the first time, that a different odour was smothering the sweet scent of the rushes, the smell of cut grass and flowers. It was an odour he associated with the battleground and its aftermath. He shivered.

The door opened and a voice from behind him said, 'The child has taken no harm, Reynaud, and Clemente has given him something to make him sleep. Oh . . .' Toby turned. There was a rustling of skirts as a woman walked forward. 'I thought you were alone, Reynaud.' She was tall, elegant, expensively dressed in high-waisted brocade. And she was young.

The Seigneur de Marigny said irritably, 'Eleanor, you interrupt us.' He wiped the perspiration from his forehead with his handkerchief and added, hardly bothering to glance at the young woman, 'This is the gentleman who saved my son's life. His name is Toby Crow, and he's a soldier from Bourges. I'm considering a suitable reward for Monsieur Crow. Monsieur, this is my wife, Eleanor.'

Toby made his bow to Eleanor du Chantonnay. He had expected grey hair and lined skin: it took him a moment to accustom himself to such a different picture. Eleanor du Chantonnay was almost her husband's height, her eyes were dark and well-shaped, her hair visible as two narrow bands of black beneath a russet-coloured velvet head-dress. And she was not many years older than he, Toby realized, jarringly. Too young, he guessed, to be the mother of the boy he had dragged from the pool.

Madame de Marigny turned to Toby and said, 'François has always been a delicate child, monsieur. We've almost lost him so many times. We could not bear such a loss.'

Yet Reynaud du Chantonnay had showed for his son nothing but contempt. Reynaud du Chantonnay's need for his heir was, of course, to do only with possession and power.

Some of his thoughts must have shown on his face, because Eleanor du Chantonnay said, 'He is all we have, monsieur.' She shook her head; Toby was surprised to see that there were tears glistening on her lashes. Madame de Marigny's vivid dark eyes were intense, her skin was pale.

He said, gently, 'Madame, I did you little service. I lifted a dazed boy out of the water and set him on dry ground. That's all. If I could do more for you, I would, and account it the greatest honour.'

Those dark eyes were fixed on him now, and her strong, square white hands were trembling. *My* son, the Seigneur had said. Not *our* son. Young François must, then, be the child of the Seigneur's first wife. And Eleanor du Chantonnay, despite all her youth and strength and beauty, had so far failed to provide her husband with more sons.

And if François had died, Toby realized, then this proud, elegant woman would have found herself in a nunnery. Because Reynaud du Chantonnay was not the sort of man who would let sentiment get in the way of ridding himself of a barren wife. There was no affection in this marriage, only power and fear. Madame de Marigny's belongings and status were dependent on the survival of her predecessor's feeble child.

She said softly, 'I've three dozen men to protect me, monsieur, but I'll remember your offer with gratitude.'

For a fraction of a second her hand touched his. Then she turned back to her husband and said, 'Let me find the poor man some dry clothes, Reynaud.'

'Later.' Reynaud du Chantonnay's tone was dismissive. 'I am glad to hear that my son is well. Now go, Eleanor, I have business to conclude. No, wait outside. You must bandage this accursed leg.'

As she turned to go, Toby recognized suddenly the source of the graveyard odour. The Seigneur had risen and was walking towards him. Toby could see the stains of the ulcers pressing through the bandages, fouling the white linen.

Reynaud du Chantonnay made his offer as soon as the door closed behind his wife. A position in the household of Marigny: an inferior position to begin with, but with the possibility, if Toby proved both apt and trustworthy, of something more interesting, more suited to his talents. The small, colourless eyes glared at him, waiting for a reply.

He accepted, of course. Leaving the room, Toby paused at the top of the flight of stairs and looked out to the meadow and the forest.

He felt reborn. He had a new name, a new profession.

He was Toby Crow, and he had gained admittance to Eden.

CHAPTER THREE

In the workshops of Taddeo Zulian in Venice, they celebrated. Taddeo had a new patron and a new commission. To toast the glittering future Taddeo offered wine (not too much, mind – there was still work to be done) in fine Murano glasses to each of his employees. Six glasses: one each for Benedetto and Alessandro, newly qualified as a journeyman; two more for Marin and the new apprentice, Vittore. One for Taddeo himself, of course.

And one for his niece, Joanna.

She had worked in the painter's studio for two years now, since the night Gaetano Cavazza had found her attempting to complete his own unfinished sketch. Gaetano had laughed at her efforts at first, but then he had shown her how to work with the fine brushes, how to take advantage of the high-quality paints and oils that Taddeo's workshop possessed.

And then he had called Taddeo and Taddeo had agreed that he needed another pair of hands, and eventually, overcoming his natural conservatism, had also agreed that Joanna could come and help in the workshop over the next few busy months. Somehow, the months had grown into years, and she was still in the Zulian workshop, painting a border of flowers around the lid of a Malipieri trousseau-chest.

The fresco that Taddeo and Benedetto had created from Gaetano's sketches had been a great success. The commission had been completed on time, the result admired and copied throughout Venice. Orders had poured in and they had worked, sometimes, for twelve hours a day. Through feast-days as well, for Taddeo never turned down a commission. He had had to take on another apprentice, Vittore, as well as continuing to train Joanna.

She found that when she painted, she could think without pain of Donato and Sanchia, and recall with pleasure the endless dusty roads that had marked the passing of her childhood. Painting dispelled the sense of confinement and despair that Donato's abandonment had left her with. Accepting her loss, Joanna had become – outwardly at least – a respectable young Venetian woman. She kept her memories for her paintings, drawing flowers that Taddeo had never seen, landscapes of countries many miles from Venice. The solace that Joanna had found on that first night inaccurately colouring Gaetano Cavazza's sketches had never deserted her. She had only to choose her colours, to prepare her brushes and sit down at the easel, and there was a certain consolation. If she could paint, she need not be unhappy.

Joanna was a credit to Isotta and Taddeo. In church she sat with her hair covered in a scarf and her eyes hidden by a veil, and gazed upon the glorious mosaics and soaring stone angels. She no longer danced for the blind fiddler in the square, though when Taddeo was not looking she would sometimes slip a few scudi into his hat. When she went with her uncle to visit his patrons, she remembered to keep silent with downcast eyes, only allowing herself to look hungrily round the rich palaces if she was sure that no one was looking.

To begin with, Taddeo had given her only the most menial jobs: cleaning and preparing palettes; binding hogs' hair to quills to make brushes; preparing size for the canvases; grinding pigments for the paints. Joanna took great pleasure in these tasks, proud that she was able to contribute to the Zulian household. She had always worked: for her father she had mixed salves and dried herbs, painted banners and danced.

Gradually, though, as the pressure on the workshop increased, Taddeo began to teach her to draw and to mix colours. To imitate the richness of velvet, the sheen of satin. Joanna painted trees, landscapes and flowers. She did not paint buildings: Taddeo had not yet shown her the complex science of perspective, and so the churches and the squares were left to Benedetto and Alessandro, the newly qualified journeyman. You don't need to know, Taddeo said dismissively. Plenty of people are happy with flowers or fruit. Joanna was content with her apricots or her daisies, but sometimes, unnoticed, she watched Benedetto use the squared drawing-frame that helped him make accurate perspective drawings.

Neither did she paint figures. For that she must study the dissection of corpses and learn to draw from life. Benedetto, Alessandro and Marin sketched from the models who sat, clothed and unclothed, in the studio. It would be her turn next, Joanna told herself, she was fifteen now. While the others drew the model, Taddeo set her to work in the little side-room, grinding pigments in a mortar and pestle, mixing them with oils and spooning them into a stoppered bladder.

In the afternoons she sat with Isotta for an hour or so, but she no longer ran messages for Matteo, who was left to take up his old duties again, grumbling about his gout and the weather, while Joanna returned to the studio and her paints. Aunt Isotta slept more and more: even Taddeo no longer scolded her for idleness, realizing at last that her feebleness was due to ill health. Joanna gave Isotta poppy tea to ease her cough, and made her breathe vapours of betony.

In the evenings she sat in the withdrawing-room with Isotta and Taddeo. She still added to her herbal, drawing new plants and noting their medicinal purposes in the margin of the book. Taddeo no longer sneered at her; she was paying for her keep. Joanna was confident that soon Taddeo would allow her to begin to help with the altarpieces and frescoes that were his more valuable commissions.

Toby Crow, the courier of the Seigneur de Marigny, arrived in Venice in the November of 1507.

He had learned, at Marigny, what Reynaud du Chantonnay wanted of him. Reynaud employed couriers to run errands in France and Italy. Couriers who could collect purchases, make orders, keep him informed about an increasingly slippery political situation. Who could speak Italian, who knew Italy, and who could keep their mouths shut. Who could, if necessary, fight their way out of trouble.

So, within the space of eighteen months, Toby had progressed from stable-hand to errand-boy, from errand-boy to courier. Throughout that time he had, carefully, tried to prise his past from its forgotten shell. But his cautious attempts at questioning servants or neighbours had met with both ignorance and indifference. He had, he thought, acquired only a little more knowledge than he had already possessed on the day he had first seen Marigny. He had learned that the du Chantonnays were of Breton origin, and that Reynaud had a cousin still living in Brittany, and a younger sister, long dead. The sister had been called Izabel; the cousin's name was Guillaume, and he was in his thirties.

He had learned that Reynaud du Chantonnay had married twice. That his first wife, Blanche, had brought him the château de Marigny, and his second wife, Eleanor, had given him the unicorn tapestries. That neither wife had presented him with the healthy son he longed for. But if Reynaud du Chantonnay had ever kept a mistress by whom he had sired an unwanted bastard son, a son whom Reynaud had later apprenticed to the shoemaker in Chinon, then Toby had heard not the smallest whisper to hint at her existence.

It was evening, and the dying sun painted bands of violet and rose on the waterways. Toby saw Venice for the first time hazed with the colours of twilight, rising out of the sea like a rediscovered Atlantis. He had travelled to Florence, to Rome and to Siena, but nothing – nothing – had prepared him for Venice.

Hiring a gondola, he inquired after the lodgings of the painter Arlotto Attavanti. The house was tall and dark, leaning precariously over a narrow canal as though it were about to topple into the black water. Inside, the building was damp, its lower floors stained with the watermarks of last winter's flooding. The stairs twisted drunkenly upwards, curlings of dust in every corner.

'He's a painter,' Reynaud du Chantonnay had said, the evening before Toby had left France for Italy. 'An incompetent painter of trinkets and gewgaws. He counterfeits other men's work, I suspect. But he has a good eye for quality, for antiquity. That's why I use him. Tell Arlotto Attavanti the Seigneur de Marigny has work for him. But be careful what you buy. Check its provenance.'

Toby thought wryly, as he began to climb the stairs to the topmost floor of the house, that his time at Marigny had told him nothing of his own provenance. He might now know a Florentine painting from one of the Venetian school, he might know a triptych from a diptych, a misericord from a pietà, but he knew nothing more of Toby Crow – or Toby Dubreton, or Toby Lescot – than he had on the first day he had crossed the drawbridge of the château.

But he had found something at Marigny. His initial sense of wonder, his fear of exclusion, had never left him. If his place at Marigny was one of servility, if the Seigneur de Marigny was at his best difficult, and at his worst obnoxious, then still, every time he crossed the meadow and rode into the courtyard, Toby was conscious of a sense of homecoming, of an absence of the restlessness that had characterized him all the years of his life. He was not fool enough to translate that sense of homecoming into memory or some half-forgotten knowledge that lingered in his blood – he knew, simply, that Marigny was beautiful, Marigny was an island of peace in a troubled world.

But his continued existence there was dependent on the success of this journey. Rapping on the door of the apartment in the canal-side house, Toby heard, eventually, a shuffling and a cursing, and then the door inched open.

A face peered out, brown eyes scowling beneath tangled brown hair.

'Messer Attavanti?' said Toby. 'I'm a servant of the Seigneur de Marigny. My name's Crow. I've a letter to you from the Seigneur.'

The scowl intensified, then relaxed and was replaced by a broad grin. 'I thought you were a creditor. Or some damned tax-collector. Come in, my friend.'

The door opened. Arlotto Attavanti wore a linen shirt, untied, over his wrinkled hose. The studio was cramped, untidy, littered with papers and materials. On a couch to one side of the room sat a girl, wearing a length of brocade. Arlotto coughed.

'Maria . . .?'

The girl rose, her lower lip pouting sulkily. Dropping the brocade to the floor, she dressed herself unhurriedly in chemise, stockings and gown. 'Maria is my model,' explained Arlotto Attavanti without embarrassment, as he finished reading Reynaud du Chantonnay's letter. 'For Bathsheba.'

Bathsheba, complete with turbaned attendants and black-skinned maids, reclined unfinished on a nearby canvas. Arlotto pressed a coin into Maria's hand, closed the front door behind her, and pulled on his doublet and breeches.

'A dear girl, but not too bright. She wanted to wear *feathers*. In her hair. Can you imagine?' Arlotto beamed, retired behind a curtain, and reappeared carrying a bottle and two glasses. 'To drink your health, Messer Crow. And the Seigneur's health. I thought he'd forgotten me.'

Arlotto Attavanti was short, stout, in his mid-forties. Toby accepted the wine-glass and raised it in salute.

'Reynaud du Chantonnay recommended you to me, Messer Attavanti.'

'Did he now?' Arlotto emptied his glass and made an unconvincing attempt at tidying the litter of knives, bottles, palettes and rags on the table. 'The old bastard. He's never bought anything of mine. Although . . .' He shrugged, then sighed. 'He's no shortage of money. And why buy sacking when you can pay for silk?'

He poured himself a second glass of wine. Arlotto's bright brown eyes inspected Toby. 'The Seigneur generally sends his scavengers in pairs,' he said thoughtfully. 'One to observe the honesty of the other, I'd always assumed.'

Toby's mouth twitched in the smallest of smiles. 'My companion sickened in Florence and died in Ferrara,' he said. 'Sadly, I felt obliged to continue without him. To spare the Seigneur any disappointment.'

He had thought, at first, when his fellow-servant finally succumbed to a fever picked up from the fouled waters of Florence, of returning to Marigny. But he had recognized in the untimely death of his companion an opportunity for himself. Marigny had a great deal to offer to somebody with ambition. If he brought back to Reynaud du Chantonnay something beautiful, something exceptional to add to the perfection of Marigny, then he, too, might be rewarded – by becoming, perhaps, an indispensable part of Marigny. Sometimes he felt that that was his birthright. And it pleased him to acquire, surreptitiously and anonymously, a little of what Reynaud du Chantonnay had excluded him from.

So in Florence Toby had bought a triptych of the Virgin Mary, and in Ferrara a small, exquisite wooden sculpture of Daphne, her fingers fluttering into laurel leaves. He had also acquired letters, noted whispered reports. This was his second journey as courier of the Seigneur de Marigny. If he was successful, he would have velvet on his back and he would ride a fine horse. He would have his own small niche in the exclusive world of the du Chantonnays.

Arlotto swept brushes and scallop shells from a stool and sat down. 'Has he changed? Eyes like a fish and the sense of humour of a snake?'

Toby shook his head and grinned. Although he had found work to replace the employment that the brigand's knife-cut had taken from him, still he knew that he had not found the trust of his master. The Seigneur watched his servants constantly, checking invoices and bills with the obsessive thoroughness of the extremely wealthy. Any carelessness with the Seigneur's money or property and he would, Toby knew, be cast beyond the walls of Marigny.

'How long have you known the Seigneur?'

Arlotto leaned back, rubbing at his bristly chin. 'I first met Reynaud – oh, a long time ago. I was not yet twenty. He was in Venice with his wife.'

Toby realized almost immediately that the painter was not, of course, referring to Eleanor du Chantonnay. He was speaking of her predecessor, Reynaud's first wife, the mother of his son.

'Blanche,' said Toby. 'What was Blanche du Chantonnay like, Messer Attavanti?'

Arlotto screwed up his eyes with the effort of memory. 'Thin, blonde, pale-skinned. She was an heiress, you know. Brought Reynaud the château and the land. Her forebears had all married first cousins, you see, to keep the property in the family. Consequently, lunatics and geldings every one of them. The offspring, I mean, my dear.'

Arlotto raised the bottle to his mouth and swallowed the dregs. 'Blanche herself was rather sickly. Always ailing with one thing or another. She gave Reynaud an heir, though – eventually, after many years of marriage.' He chuckled. 'Reynaud must have been tearing his hair out, waiting for his wife to do her duty.'

Blanche, thought Toby, must have resembled young François: pale and nervous and sickly. Eleanor du Chantonnay was her dark and vigorous opposite, and yet the Seigneur de Marigny had failed to sire a healthy son with either of his wives.

The painter added, 'The Seigneur had come to Venice to choose a wedding-gift for his sister. What was her name? Izabel – yes. She was to marry an Englishman. Called Mandeville, I believe. Reynaud bought her a wedding-chest, a few trinkets. A length of silk for a wedding-gown. Nothing good. Anything good, he said, would be wasted on the English. The old devil.' He shook his head, recalling the Seigneur's meanness. 'He's married again, I hear. I haven't seen the second wife.'

Toby said, 'She's called Eleanor. Dark-haired, dark-eyed, much younger than her husband.'

'Ah-ha.' Arlotto's eyes gleamed, he wagged a dirty finger in Toby's direction. 'Be careful. The Seigneur will have you flayed alive, my dear, and suspended from his highest flagpole if you should lay a finger on his property. Don't think of it. Venice has just as much to offer, at much less cost.'

He did not need Arlotto's warning. Toby knew that for Reynaud du Chantonnay his lands, his wife and his son must remain inviolable. Not because he bore them any affection, but because they were his, paid for, due and necessary adjuncts to his power.

'I'm not here for women, Messer Attavanti. I've come to Venice for different sorts of treasures. Paintings, sculptures, tapestries. Oh – and I need information, too. Who is allying with whom, who is planning to invade whom, that sort of thing. The Seigneur de Marigny keeps money in Venetian banks.' His smile broadened. 'It's safer that way. Think of the gold he'd have to entrust me with otherwise . . . But the Seigneur won't want to keep his money in Venice if his countrymen are planning to sack the city.'

Arlotto Attavanti rubbed at his chin meditatively. Then he rose, tossing the wine-bottle aside so that it rolled amid the tangle of discarded clothing from the chest. He seized his cloak.

'Give me a day or two, and I'll arrange a meeting for you. I've some useful acquaintances. As for the other items – we'll see what's coming in on the ships. And we'll visit the workshops of Messer Bellini and – let me see – dear Gianbattista Cima. I'm sure you'll find something to suit you there. Oh' – Arlotto turned back to Toby, laughter in his eyes – 'We'll go to Messer Zulian's studio, too. Taddeo Zulian's an old fool, and his work is dull, but his studios contain the most *delightful* treasure.'

At Messer Zulian's workshop, they rose at dawn and laboured until the sun disappeared into the sea in a blaze of copper and carmine light. Taddeo, Benedetto and Alessandro worked on the altarpieces; Joanna, Marin and Vittore on the smaller commissions.

Joanna was hurrying to finish the garland of poppies that adorned the lid of the Malipieri trousseau-chest. That morning Taddeo, flustered, had agreed to let her work on the competition-piece for the Scuola di Santa Ursula. Gaetano Cavazza, Taddeo's brother-in-law, had sketched out the subject, the Flight into Egypt, several weeks ago, and Alessandro had squared up the drawings into a full-size cartoon. Small details of the figures had been completed: hands and feet, the sweep of the Virgin's cloak as the Holy Family battled against the wind. Then the picture had been put aside, lost in the urgency of commissions for frescoes, trays, portraits. Taddeo had rediscovered the painting that morning, almost hidden behind a pile of canvases.

Standing beside him, Joanna had looked down to where Joseph, Mary and the infant Christ struggled through a fragmentary landscape of trees and lakes, mountains and clouds. Taddeo had tutted, Joanna had soothed, and made her suggestion. Taddeo had shaken his head, stared anxiously round the crowded workshop, and then, reluctantly, given his assent. Joanna could begin work on the background to the picture. Alessandro would complete the figures when there was time.

Joanna finished the last poppy petal on the wreath and moved the trousseau-chest carefully aside to dry. Cleaning her brushes with a rag, she lifted the *Flight into Egypt* on to an easel. If the workshop remained busy, she thought, then perhaps she might be allowed to complete the picture. She wanted to paint all those swaying trees, every one of those thick, billowing clouds, the pale, glassy lake that would reflect the Virgin's fluttering cloak, and the great barricade of the mountains. Images from her childhood darted through her memory: rivers and lakes and hills.

Soon Taddeo must begin to teach her perspective, must allow her to draw from life. Then, if she worked hard, she could progress from apprentice to journeyman, and eventually from journeyman to master. Then she would no longer be the daughter of Taddeo's hopeless brother, the mountebank; instead, she would have a position, a place, status. She would be able to spend the rest of her life doing something she enjoyed, something that made her happy. She would be able, one day, to leave Venice, to return to the endless roads and hills of the mainland. Painters travelled the world, visiting courts and palaces.

Joanna began to grind the pigments that she would use to paint the sky. Taddeo, looking harassed, was greeting two visitors. One of the visitors was the painter Arlotto Attavanti, an old acquaintance of Taddeo's.

The second visitor, though, she did not recognize. He was younger than Messer Attavanti, black-haired and well-dressed. He looked . . . dangerous, Joanna thought, and immediately wanted to laugh at herself. But he did. She simply could not think of another word for it. She glanced again at the tall, well-made figure, the black hair skimming the shoulders of a velvet doublet, the dark eyes. She could not yet distinguish their colour, but she did not think they would be a warm, friendly brown.

Joanna chose from the range of colours and oils on the table beside her. Carefully, she mixed the first shade that she would use for the sky: a wash of dark slate-grey with scarcely the smallest hint of blue. The white canvas, with its bold black lines, its chance of success or failure, alarmed her momentarily. But only momentarily. With a mixture of fear and excitement, she raised her brush.

'Signorina?'

Her hands shook and marked the canvas with a single stroke of colour. She looked up.

'Signorina Zulian, my apologies. I merely wanted to pay my respects.'

Arlotto Attavanti stood beside her. Joanna put aside the brush, and he bowed and kissed her hand, and, head to one side, studied the painting.

'Mmm . . . not Uncle Taddeo's work, I think . . .' Arlotto squinted. 'No, Messer Cavazza, I would guess.'

Joanna smiled. 'Gaetano Cavazza drew the picture, but I am to paint it, Messer Attavanti. It's for the competition for the Scuola di Santa Ursula.'

Arlotto beamed. 'Then I'm sure it will win the competition, my dear Signorina Joanna.'

Turning, he waved to the man who still stood in the centre of the workshop talking to Taddeo.

'Signorina, let me introduce you to Messer Crow, who has travelled from France to Venice to purchase paintings. Toby, this is Signorina Joanna Zulian, Messer Zulian's niece.'

The second man had wound his way through the easels and stools to stand in front of Joanna. He bowed, sweeping a feathered black cap from his dark hair.

Joanna saw that Toby Crow's eyes were the same colour as the single paintmark her brush had made on the *Flight into Egypt*. A dark slate-grey, lacking, in this light, any trace of blue.

Three days later Toby was introduced to Arlotto's useful acquaintance. His name was Pasquale Gennari, and he was waiting in Arlotto's studio when they returned from the workshops of Gianbattista Cima. Messer Gennari's sword was out of its scabbard as Arlotto opened the door, but Arlotto calmed him, and kicked papers and brushes and skulls and chalks aside to seat both Messer Gennari and Toby Crow at the cluttered table. Messer Gennari was, Arlotto explained as he searched the studio for a bottle of wine, a secretary to the Venier family. Messer Venier was a member of the *Case Grandi* and hence belonged to the exclusive group of Venetian patricians from whom the Doge was selected.

Consequently, Pasquale heard *everything*. Pasquale and he had an arrangement, said Arlotto breezily, as he poured three glasses of wine. Pasquale told Arlotto if the Great Council had any interest in Arlotto's activities; and Arlotto recompensed him with a cut of some of his profits. Toby remembered Reynaud du Chantonnay saying, 'He counterfeits other men's works.'

Arlotto beamed as he handed the secretary a glass. 'Messer Crow is in Venice to buy paintings and information, Pasquale. He comes from France.'

Pasquale Gennari had a thin, pointed face, and short, dark hair. His small dark eyes frequently darted to the door, and the wine was swallowed in one gulp. He nodded a terse greeting. 'I haven't much time. What sort of information do you want, Messer Crow?'

Toby took his wine-glass from Arlotto. 'My employer has money invested in Italian banks and Italian businesses, Messer Gennari. He's concerned about the safety of his investments – about the safety of his Venetian interests in particular. He hears the sound of cannon being hauled across Italian soil. He wonders whether Venice has considered appeasement, rather than confrontation. Whether Venice has considered, for instance, returning to Pope Julius the cities of the Romagna.'

Arlotto yawned, poured himself a second glass of wine. 'The Pope hasn't the money or the troops to attack Venice, my dear Toby. Even I know that.'

Pasquale wound thin fingers round the stem of his empty glass. 'I doubt if Messer Crow's employer's concern is for the ambitions of the Papal States. The Papal States *alone*, that is.'

Briefly, Toby wondered why an intelligent, educated man like Pasquale Gennari should involve himself with a rascal like Arlotto Attavanti. Then he said, 'Ferdinand of Spain, the Emperor Maximilian, Louis de France – what if they should betray Venice, Messer Gennari?'

Pasquale Gennari smiled, but the smile failed to touch his narrow, dark eyes. 'If you are French, Messer Crow, then you will know that Venice considers France to be her friend. If that friendship remains constant, then Venice has nothing to fear.' There was silence for a moment. The door was locked and the windows were closed, excluding the sounds of the city. The secretary continued softly, 'And in answer to your earlier question, Messer Crow, Venice has already offered the Pope some of the cities of the Romagna. But not the ones that he wants.'

Pope Julius, Gennari explained, wanted Rimini, Faenza and Cervia, acquired by Venice from the Papacy only a few years ago. Venice, aware of the dangers of losing her mainland base, wanted to hold on to the cities of the Romagna for as long as possible. 'Venice is playing a dangerous game. While she waits for the Pope to lose interest – or to die of the pox – Julius has time to organize his troops and to make alliances with any other powers that might enjoy seeing Venice put to the sword. It's not a situation that can remain stable for long.'

Pasquale put aside his glass. His nails, Toby noticed, were bitten to the quick. 'The Emperor Maximilian goes to Rome for his coronation next year. We've told him he can't march through Venetian land. Politely, of course. But he won't like it.'

Arlotto refilled the secretary's glass. He raised his eyebrows. 'You don't believe Maximilian will make the journey alone, then, Pasquale, escorted by a few nicely dressed servants?'

Pasquale's dark, thin face was expressionless. 'I suspect that the Emperor will march through the terra firma at the head of a very large army. Having exhumed beforehand any odd claims he has to Venetian lands, of course.'

So Venice had offended not only the Papacy, but the Holy Roman Empire as well. Powerful enemies, thought Toby. No wonder the Serenissima needed to be confident of the continuing friendship of France.

There was just one more question he had to ask. 'And having foreseen this large army, Messer Gennari, how will Venice defend herself?'

He saw Pasquale glance quickly first at him and then at Arlotto.

Arlotto said lazily, 'He's all right, honestly, old friend. I know his employer. Only in it for the money. *Honestly.*'

Pasquale ran his hands through his short hair. He took a deep breath. 'Venice has been talking to the Orsini.'

There was a sound from the stairway outside. Toby's hand went to the hilt of his sword; he saw sweat gather suddenly on Pasquale Gennari's brow. Arlotto opened the door an inch and peered out.

'The old dear next door and her luscious granddaughter,' he whispered. 'Only thirteen years old and the most enormous . . .' His hands gestured wistfully to his chest. Arlotto let the door swing shut. 'Who are the Orsini?'

'Nicolò di Pitigliano and Bartolomeo d'Alviano,' said Toby. '*Condottieri* – mercenary leaders. I fought for Nicolò once.'

'Ah.' Arlotto sat down again and smiled. 'I thought so. Didn't quite see you as Reynaud's lap-dog. I wondered, though. I mean – why exchange a pleasant existence of rapine and pillage to work for that old sod?'

Curiosity, Toby might have answered to Arlotto's question. Or a chance to regain something that had been denied to him.

Arlotto was still grinning. 'Unless you're still hankering after the lovely Eleanor, of course. Lecherous bastard.' He turned to Pasquale. 'I took Messer Crow to the workshops of Taddeo Zulian. He was most impressed with Messer Zulian's property.'

And in his mind's eye Toby saw Joanna Zulian again, hidden in a corner of the studio in a paint-stained apron. As though she were something shameful, he had thought on first seeing her, something that needed to be kept out of sight.

He frowned. 'How long has she worked there? It's uncommon, isn't it? I mean, a woman . . .'

'Precisely,' said Pasquale, drily. 'Joanna Zulian has helped in her uncle's studio for a year or two, I believe.' He rose, throwing his cloak over his shoulders. 'They won't let her join the guild, of course. Taddeo Zulian's making a fool of himself. Everyone knows he's only trying to save money.'

'He'll marry her off soon.' Arlotto went to the door and opened it a fraction. 'Uncle Taddeo doesn't trust her – thinks she's too much her father's daughter. Will bring shame on the house of Zulian. Poor little thing. She's only fifteen, you know. Looks older. She'd make quite a competent artist, if she was allowed to. She's company for the wife just now, but as soon as Isotta Zulian dies, Taddeo will find a husband for Joanna. Lucky devil,' he added with a sigh. 'I'd almost offer myself, but I don't believe there's much of a dowry.' He peered down the corridor. 'It's all right, Pasquale. No one about.'

They watched the secretary walk away down the stairs, swathed in a cloak and with a hat pulled down over his eyes. Arlotto shook his curly head.

'Poor dear. He's got two wives. One in Venice, the other in Verona. You wouldn't credit it, would you? Doesn't look as though he's got the stamina. But he needs the money, you see.'

Joanna put all her energies into the *Flight into Egypt*. The Zulian workshop was still busy, and she worked almost forgotten in her corner, painting storm clouds and windswept fields with painstaking care, drawing tiny flowers – lilies and narcissi and roses – along the path that the Holy Family travelled. Soon the painted sky was blistered purple with the onset of winter and ice had begun to form on the furthermost shore of the lake.

The figures she left blank. She knew whose faces she would have given them, had she the skill and knowledge to paint them. Their heads were bent against the bitter weather, but Donato would have worn his patched, fur-edged cloak, Sanchia's dark hair would have been folded into the nape of her neck, her eyes serene. Looking at those figures, white and featureless against the stormy background, the sense of unease that had haunted Joanna since the beginning of the week increased.

Two days ago, Taddeo had instructed the apprentice Vittore to attend the life-drawing class with Marin and Alessandro. Joanna had waited, delighted, for her uncle to tell her to do likewise. But he had not: he had not spoken to her, he had hardly seemed aware of her presence.

When Taddeo had gone, Joanna had felt confused and upset. Vittore was fourteen, the youngest apprentice. She was fifteen, would be sixteen in the new year. Vittore had been apprenticed to Taddeo for only eighteen months; she had quitted the kitchen and the sewing-room more than two years ago. And Joanna knew, glancing at the heraldic crest that Vittore laboured over, and then looking back at the *Flight to Egypt*, that she painted well. She could almost have plucked petals from the flowers that sprang up around the Holy Family. Vittore's griffin was cross-eyed.

She knew also that she worked hard, sometimes from dawn to dusk. Often her arms and head ached by the end of the day, and her eyes were red-rimmed. And even Taddeo had occasionally grunted approval at her work on the *Flight to Egypt*.

Joanna told herself that her uncle was growing old, that he had forgotten her age, her increasing competence. She would speak to him soon, when he was not so busy. And then she, too, could join the rest of the studio when the model paid her weekly visits, instead of hiding in the paint-room, alone and excluded.

Meanwhile, she sketched the rough outlines of the Holy Family's clothing with the aid of the manikins that Taddeo used in the absence of a live model. The manikins were featureless wooden puppets, their limbs stiff and lifeless. But sometimes, when it was late and dark, and the apprentices had left the studio, and she had grown tired, Joanna thought that beneath the heavy white draperies, she could almost see a flicker of movement in the carefully posed limbs.

★

Gaetano Cavazza made regular visits to Venice now. Partly because his sister Isotta was dying; but more importantly because he had found himself a wealthy Venetian patron. Also, he liked to keep on good terms with Taddeo. The girl Joanna was almost grown now; there was always the risk, however slight, that Taddeo might choose to will his house and workshops to her future husband.

But Joanna, Gaetano acknowledged to himself, had herself become one of the pleasures of visiting Venice. The beauty that he had long ago noticed had not diminished as the girl had grown older. The fining-down of her face had merely emphasized Joanna's high cheekbones, her straight nose and sculptured mouth, her great grey eyes. It amused Gaetano to watch her, perched at her easel in a shadowy corner of the studio, brow furrowed as she bent over her painting. It amused him to consider how he would paint her, when she was older, when she no longer laboured in Taddeo's workshops. When she was married, perhaps, to whichever Venetian lordling would be prepared to overlook her lack of dowry for the sake of her beauty. That same lordling would, Gaetano was sure, wish to commission a portrait of his lovely wife from the painter Gaetano Cavazza.

He was not sure, though, how, when the time came, he would paint her. It mystified Gaetano that he still did not know. Now, Joanna frowned over the picture he had sketched for the competition of the Scuola di Santa Ursula. Her full draped white apron gave her a classical appearance, her hair was plaited tightly to her head. As Diana, spied on by Actaeon, thought Gaetano. As Io, pursued by Zeus in the shape of a bull. Both ideas interested him, but neither seemed quite right. They were too sexless, too passive. Joanna Zulian might look serene, innocent, with her perfect oval face and calm grey eyes, but Gaetano had seen beyond that cleverly assumed mask years ago. If he had been Taddeo he would have found her a husband by now.

Meanwhile, it amused him, when visiting Taddeo, to watch her. She was making a reasonable job of the work for the Scuola: Joanna had talent, Gaetano acknowledged, but not, of course, genius. Women were not capable of genius. She drew pretty flowers and competent landscapes, but she would never paint portraits, or the great heroic scenes that adorned churches and castles. Her paintings were attractive, yes, charming even, but they would never be anything more than that. A woman had not the energy nor the power of concentration of a man: women were fickle, easily distracted.

Today, Gaetano sought help from Taddeo's studio with his latest commission for Messer Venier, his Venetian patron. Taddeo's workshops were, as always, busy, but Taddeo had agreed that Gaetano could take an apprentice to help him measure the Venier courtyard for a fresco. Gaetano's gaze drifted from Alessandro, to Marin, to Vittore.

And then, almost inevitably, back to Joanna.

The autumn sky was blue, the air clear and crisp. The gondola was decorated with the Venier colours and insignia, and rowed by a Venier manservant. Gaetano, notebook, measure and pencils beside him, still watched Joanna seated opposite him. Sitting on the cushioned seat, she had let her hand trail in the cold, black waters, so that a small V-shaped wake echoed the longer wake of the gondola. She wore neither hat nor veil, and Gaetano saw how men stared at her as they glided past. Joanna's eyes were dreamy, absent, but Gaetano enjoyed the other men's stares, enjoyed their envy.

At the Venier palazzo, Gaetano handed her out of the boat and up the shallow steps that were licked with water. He did not release her as they entered the gateway; his hand enclosed her elbow firmly, guiding her into the courtyard. Her arm was warm and firm beneath his fingers; the breeze twisted her auburn hair around her face, sculpting it into curls and tendrils.

Messer Venier himself came out to greet him. Gaetano appreciated the courtesy: some men of Messer Venier's standing would have sent only a servant. Through the open doorway that led off the courtyard and into the house, Gaetano could see three other figures, candlelight multiplying their shadows on the tiled floor.

He listened carefully as Messer Venier explained his wishes. Casually, he introduced Joanna. 'My brother-in-law Taddeo's niece,' he said, noting with pride the interest in Messer Venier's eyes, the straightening of his stance.

A seascape, suggested Gaetano, his experienced eyes wandering over the bare walls that enclosed the Venier courtyard. Neptune, sirens, naiads, that sort of thing. A border of scallop shells, and perhaps, in the centre of the garden, a fountain encrusted with conchs and coral. Gaetano would leave the fountain to an artisan, but he himself would paint the fresco. He would not, like Taddeo, farm out his work to apprentices, journeymen, nieces.

Messer Venier nodded enthusiastically. He would haggle over the price later, Gaetano knew, but he also knew that Marcantonio Venier would eventually pay whatever price was demanded. Both Gaetano and Messer Venier knew Gaetano's worth. Messer Venier's financial troubles, common knowledge throughout Venice, were only paralleled by Messer Venier's acquisitiveness.

Gaetano saw Joanna wander off to stare out through the portico at the canal. Officiously, enjoying the power that he had over her, he called her back to work.

'*Pompous* man,' said Arlotto Attavanti, rather loudly, staring out of the Venier doorway. 'Can't stand him.'

'Gaetano Cavazza?' Pasquale Gennari's dark face twitched in a sour grin. 'He'll have two workshops, soon, Arlotto. His own in Padua and the Zulian workshops in Venice.'

Arlotto snorted and spat on the tiled floor. Toby, standing beside him, looked out to where Joanna Zulian stood, pen and notebook in hand.

He had been in Venice for six weeks now, and had left commissions at the studios of Giorgio da Castelfranco and Gianbattista Cima. He had visited countless workshops, warehouses and apartments. He had acquired a Greek amphora decorated with silhouetted figures and a marble head of a child. Arlotto judged the artistic merit of each piece and estimated its value. Toby just measured the honesty or otherwise of the vendor.

At the house of Marcantonio Venier, the item for sale was a carved boxwood Virgin and Child. French, about two hundred years old, Arlotto said, cradling the piece in careful hands. The serene wooden faces of mother and baby were darkened and smoothed with age, the graceful drapery was frozen for ever in time. Studying the piece, Arlotto's voice had been gentle, awed, his eyes robbed of their customary cynicism.

The Virgin and Child stood on the table cushioned in velvet, waiting to be packed, waiting for Messer Venier to drag himself away from his fresco painter and agree to a price.

'Cavazza's good, though,' said Arlotto grudgingly, looking back out to where Messer Venier and the painter Gaetano Cavazza talked. 'Expensive – knows his own worth.' Arlotto's lip curled. He added,

'Talking of money, my dear Toby, you're to let me settle this one. I'm hoping that dear old Marcantonio hasn't a clue what this is worth.'

Arlotto's eyes focused again on the boxwood Virgin. Messer Venier was coming back into the house. Pasquale poured wine and passed the glasses around; he took one out to the artist in the courtyard. Toby, yawning, left the financial arrangements to Arlotto and Messer Venier, and through the doorway watched the painter and the young Zulian girl.

The weak afternoon sun had disappeared, and Joanna's long, unbound hair blew loose in the chill November breeze. Her expression was serious, absorbed in her work. She wore a stiff square-necked black gown and a fringed shawl around her shoulders. She had a face, thought Toby idly, like that of the carved wooden Madonna they haggled over. 'Two hundred ducats,' said Arlotto. 'Three hundred,' replied Messer Venier, glowering. Toby watched as Joanna Zulian noted figures in a book and held measures for Cavazza. He was a big man, tall and well-built. Whenever he drew near to Joanna, he would touch her. A hand to an elbow, large fingers resting proprietorially on her shoulder. Toby began to dislike him.

Gaetano Cavazza gave the girl's arm an extra squeeze and then walked towards the house, notebook in hand. The girl, staying outside, wandered back towards the canal. Arlotto was toasting the conclusion of a successful transaction with some more of Messer Venier's superb wine; Gaetano Cavazza, his face consumed by a self-satisfied smile, was spreading out papers and sketches on the table for Messer Venier. Toby, bored with money, art and greed, left the house and walked out into the fresh air of the courtyard.

It all happened so quickly then, that he wondered for a moment if he had imagined it. The girl was framed in the doorway that led to the canal, and beyond her he could see gliding down the water a gondola crammed with half a dozen youths. The youths were laughing and shouting and tossing a bundle high into the air. The bundle was hurled upwards one last time and splashed into the cold, dark water. Then the gondola was gone and the noise of the young men disappeared into the distance.

And the painter's niece was walking forward, kicking off her shoes, letting the shawl slip from her shoulders. She walked out of the doorway and down the steps that led to the canal. She did not stop when she reached the water, instead she kept on walking as the black water lapped at, and then submerged, her equally black skirts.

Toby began to run.

She wrote down the figures in the notebook, proud of the clear hand that Sanchia had taught her. She held the measure for Gaetano and noted for him the proportions of Messer Venier's wall. The afternoon was chilling rapidly: she was glad she had taken her shawl. When they had finished, Gaetano patted her arm and strode into the house, leaving Joanna standing in the courtyard.

She could picture the fresco that Gaetano would paint for Messer Venier. Sea horses and sea beasts, whirlpools and cascades. The actual water of the canal, glimpsed through the doorway, would be framed on either side by the painted water on the walls. Joanna wandered over to the doorway, her shawl pulled over her shoulders.

She heard the gondola before she saw it. Half a dozen young men – far too many – cavorted in it. They were making a lot of noise and the gondola was swaying dangerously. Joanna watched, amused for a while, wondering if the boat would capsize.

Then her amusement abruptly vanished. They were tossing something up into the air, shouting as they did so. She recognized what they were throwing: she could hear its cries. Waves of anger and pity swept over her. She dug her nails into her palms. And then they caught it and threw it one last time, and the bundle plunged into the water and the gondola passed out of sight.

Joanna kicked off her shoes, dropped her shawl to the paving-stones. She did not even think as she walked quickly out of the doorway and down the steps and into the water. She could see the scrap of black and orange and white in the centre of the canal, drifting towards the steps of the Venier house. The coldness of the water as it flooded over her ankles took her by surprise, but she kept on walking.

Then the steps stopped, and there was nothing beneath her feet. She knew how to swim, though: Donato had taught her. As an infant she had swam, naked and unashamed, in pools and rivers in France and Spain. Donato had laughed at her, and called her his sea maid.

Her heavy skirts pulled her down, though, and the icy water robbed her muscles of strength. There was water in her eyes and on her lips, salty and foul-tasting. But she reached out a hand and grasped the creature that floated towards her, feeling its warm body in her frozen fingers.

She was only a couple of yards from the steps, but the cold was paralysing her. She gasped and fought off panic as the water filled her nostrils and mouth, covering her head. She heard a voice say, 'Give me your hand, Joanna.' She reached out her free arm and someone dragged her up and out of the water on to the safety of the steps.

She couldn't stand at first. Water poured from her skirts, from her hair. Her legs juddered with cold and exhaustion, so she sat down suddenly, surrounded by the lapping canal.

She looked down at the creature she had rescued from the water. It was a kitten, a tortoiseshell kitten, its tiny body marked perfectly in bands of black and orange and white. It was warm, she could feel its warmth against her skin, but it did not move. She had been quick, it had only been in the water a minute or two, and yet it did not move. Joanna ran her fingers over the small body, conscious that someone had crouched down beside her, the same someone who had helped her from the water. She did not look at his face yet, though: instead, she lifted the kitten into her palms, murmuring to it, trying to coax it into life.

It would not be coaxed, though. The eyes, round and blue, stared at her sightlessly, the head lolled to one side, the neck broken. She remembered the last time the youth had caught it, the small twist of his hands. A voice said, 'Here. Let me,' and the dead kitten was scooped up from her lap and wrapped in a cloak.

Joanna covered her face with her hands. She was shivering violently, cold with the icy water of the canal. She felt a warm arm around her shoulders, helping her to her feet. She felt foolish, bereft. Standing, glancing up, she found that she was looking into the dark, slate-grey eyes of Arlotto's friend, Toby Crow.

She half expected him to laugh at her. She had not behaved like a respectable Venetian woman. But Toby Crow's arms were still around her, supporting her, warming her. She did not want him to let her go. 'They broke its neck,' she said. Her voice shook.

He nodded. 'I know. You did what you could. You should come into the house now, Joanna. I'm sure Madonna Venier can find you a dry gown.'

She let him lead her up the steps towards the house. She had realized that there was no laughter in those dark, duplicitous eyes, but something akin to respect.

*

Gaetano, settling with Messer Venier the last details of the commission, looked out to the courtyard and saw Joanna in the arms of the young Frenchman who had bought Marcantonio's boxwood Madonna. They were framed by the doorway that led to the canal. Although the light was dying, the air chilling, he could see them clearly. He felt breathless suddenly, unable to concentrate on what he was saying.

As Joanna's lovely eyes looked up into those of the Frenchman, they might have been the only two people in the world: their mutual gaze absorbed each other, excluding everyone else. Suddenly, Gaetano found the sight of another man looking at Joanna Zulian offensive, outrageous even. He could not speak, but some sort of noise must have issued from his throat, because everyone in the room suddenly turned and looked to where he was looking. Arlotto Attavanti, Pasquale Gennari and Messer Venier himself stared out to the courtyard. They were all looking at Joanna, and he found that now he hated them to look. Gaetano felt his skin redden, his muscles tremble. He heard Arlotto Attavanti drawl, 'I see that young Toby's found something to occupy himself with,' and Gaetano was out of the door, pushing past Messer Venier, walking fast through the courtyard.

If he had been accustomed to wearing a sword, his hand would have already been on its hilt. He saw, as he reached Joanna, that her clothes and hair were soaking. Water dripped from her gown, trailing over the paving-stones. The damp material clung to her body, outlining the contours of breast and hip. Her feet were bare. The Frenchman's hand was still curled round her shoulder. He did not let go of her as Gaetano approached.

'I fell in the canal, Gaetano.'

It was Joanna who spoke first, breaking the taut silence. She had brushed back her wet hair from her face and straightened herself.

'I went to look at the canal and slipped on the wet stones. Messer Crow helped me out.'

Her voice was clipped, tense, her eyes bright and red-rimmed. Gaetano's gaze moved quickly from Joanna's face to that of the Frenchman.

Toby Crow's eyes met Gaetano's, and Gaetano saw no fear, no shame, but only a sort of mockery.

'She's cold, Messer Cavazza.' The Frenchman's Italian was good, his voice was level. He wore a sword, Gaetano noticed. 'You should take Signorina Zulian into the house, get her a dry gown.'

He did not need to be told what to do by this insolent young puppy. Gaetano took Joanna's hand and pulled her roughly towards him. Then he dragged her into Messer Venier's house.

Returning from the Venier house, Joanna knew why Gaetano was cross with her. She had not behaved, as Isotta would say, like a respectable young Venetian woman. Respectable Venetian women did not swim, and neither did they plunge into canals to rescue animals. She thought of the kitten, with its wet, soft fur, and her eyes filled again and she had to close them tightly.

Rowed home in the Venier gondola, clad in one of Madonna Venier's opulent and over-large gowns, Joanna did not speak to or look at Gaetano. She did not enjoy his disapproval, but she knew that she could not counter it. In the eyes of Venice she had behaved badly – shockingly, even. In her own eyes she had been foolish, naïve.

The sun had gone and, despite the dry gown, Joanna felt desperately cold. Her damp hair stuck clammily to her face, her limbs were covered in goose-pimples. She began to shiver uncontrollably as she sat there and remembered the kitten, the small twist of the young man's hands as he had wrung the creature's neck and the awful, suffocating sense of panic she had felt out there in the canal.

A few days later, Gaetano found Taddeo in the workshop. The room was busy: paintings in various stages of completion were propped against the walls or balanced on shelves. Benedetto and Alessandro were perched on scaffolding on the far side of the room sketching the background to a large narrative scene with the aid of a drawing-frame and squared canvas. Marin and Vittore prepared wooden panels and sized canvases, selecting lengths of charcoal and chalk. In a corner of the room, behind a gauze screen, a fat, squat woman unpinned her hair and began to loosen the fastenings of her jacket.

'We paint from life today,' said Taddeo, after greeting Gaetano. 'I thought it time that Vittore joined the class. He shows no great promise, though.'

Gaetano did not bother to glance at Marin or Vittore, Benedetto or Alessandro. He looked, as he always did, for Joanna, half expecting to see her in the corner of the room, her head bent over an easel. But she was not in her corner, of course. He thought at first that Taddeo had very properly sent her away to Isotta for the duration of the life class. Then suddenly he saw her, shut away in the small room where they made up the pigments. The door was half open, and Gaetano watched her unnoticed.

The simple pleasure he had once found in watching her had, he realized, utterly dissipated. His eyes flickered round the workshop, checking that Benedetto, Marin, Alessandro, even young Vittore, did not watch her also. Taddeo should have sent her away, he thought angrily. Taddeo should never have let her work in his studio. It was not right. It was not suitable. His own part in that arrangement he now regretted bitterly.

The model had removed all her clothes and was arranging herself on a couch behind the gauze screen. She was an ugly woman, coarse-skinned and shapeless. Gaetano glanced at her for only a moment. He looked back and saw that Joanna had left the paint-room and was walking towards Taddeo, paper and charcoal in hand. The model was only a few feet away: Gaetano was aware that his face was reddening, that his clothing felt tight and uncomfortably hot.

Taddeo did not notice Joanna at first. He was scolding Vittore for playing with the bladders of paint, for spraying crimson all over the floor.

Gaetano saw Joanna go to her uncle, touch his arm and ask something. He could not hear what she said. But he saw Taddeo's look of horror and outrage, his vigorous shake of the head. He continued to watch Joanna as Taddeo, taking her arm, almost dragged her out of the studio. Gaetano followed. He heard Taddeo say, as he closed the workshop door behind him, 'Don't be ridiculous, girl, the woman is naked!'

Gaetano almost wanted to laugh: the word *naked* came from Taddeo's mouth as though it burned him. Then, looking at Joanna, he no longer wanted to laugh. As he watched, he saw her face change, saw the mask slip. He could not understand why at first. Then, suddenly, he understood everything. The girl was asking to join the life class and the old fool was refusing her. Surely, Gaetano thought, surely Joanna could not have expected to sit there with the apprentices and the journeymen, drawing Taddeo Zulian's ugly model? Damn it, as Taddeo had said, the woman was *naked*. Surely Joanna must be aware that the length of time she could remain in Taddeo's studio, the sort of work she would be permitted to do, the position to which she could aspire, would be naturally curtailed by her sex? Surely she could not have been so naïve as to believe that she could follow the same path as the male apprentices?

And yet she had, damn it, she had. Or was it naïvety? Suddenly Gaetano remembered the Venier house, glancing out of the doorway and seeing the girl in that damned Frenchman's arms. Her damp gown clinging to her exquisite body, her eyes unashamed, full of guile. It occurred to him that even after three years in Venice, Joanna Zulian might not know how a woman should behave, might still retain her own peculiar, questionable standards.

Gaetano's nails dug deep into his palms, the air was tight in his throat. Watching her, he half thought that Joanna would shout out, cry, make a fuss. But she did not, of course. Instead the mask slowly resumed, and Gaetano realized that there was only he to know that it had ever slipped.

After her interview with Taddeo, Joanna went to her room. It was late afternoon: the sky was already half dark, long shadows painted themselves across the floor, down the walls. Alone, she sat on her bed, her head cradled in her hands.

She realized, as if for the first time, how other women lived. Hidden behind shuttered windows, leaving their houses only for a heavily veiled expedition to church. Isotta's life was not exceptional, it was commonplace. Isotta's deadening, suffocating existence was the lot of most Venetian wives.

The future that she had painted for herself Joanna now knew to be a brittle edifice of glass, unsustainable and impermanent. It was not by oversight that Taddeo had forbidden her to join the life class, it was by intention. He would not allow her to draw from life, because to do so would mean that she looked on a naked body. And he would not teach her perspective, because to do so would involve learning mathematics, and there was no sense in teaching a woman mathematics. However competent she might be, however hard-working she might be, Taddeo would allow her no future as an artist. Vittore, clumsy, talentless Vittore, had a better future than she.

The misery, the sense of futility that had possessed her since the episode by the canal, threatened to overwhelm her. She had been foolish then, walking into the water to rescue a dead creature, and she had been foolish again now. A thousand times more foolish not to recognize what her own eyes should have taught her. Sitting there, she despised herself for labouring so long under the delusion that she could become an artist.

What stupidity, what ignorance! She had only to think of all the other artists' studios in Venice to know that not a single woman worked in them except as drudge or model. Joanna hated herself for having been blind for so long.

She told Lena, when the cook knocked hesitantly on her door, that she had a headache and would go to bed. It was true that she had a headache – it pounded and squeezed at her skull – but she did not go to bed: she knew she could not sleep.

When she had heard Taddeo and Isotta go to their rooms and the house was quiet, Joanna opened her door and went downstairs. She went, as she had gone once before, to the workshop. It was midwinter now, not midsummer, and only the thin light of her single candle illuminated the wicker bottles and glass alembics, the brushes and palettes, the manikins with their blank, featureless faces.

But it was all different now. It no longer fascinated her. She knew that she had ceased to be a part of this entrancing, absorbing world: she was excluded for ever by the mere fact of her sex. What she had once loved, what had made Venice bearable, enjoyable even, had rejected her, refusing to permit her even the smallest part of its magic. Through the window she could see, outlined by rushlights and lanterns, the city of Venice: the houses, the squares, the canals; the lagoons that enclosed the city, barring her for ever from lands she had once known. She did not belong to Venice, she never would belong to Venice. She knew that with utter certainty now.

Joanna paused in front of her picture, placing the candle carefully on the shelf of the easel. The pale light picked out the wintry sky, the twisting, leafless trees, the narrow avenue of meticulously painted flowers. Yet it was not her picture, of course. The *Flight to Egypt* had never been her picture, never would be her picture. A man's name would sign it, a man's name would be announced when it won the competition of the Scuola. And that was unbearable. Joanna knew that something was being taken away from her, something irreplaceable. She knew suddenly that she could not live with that.

Her eyes were blurred, her breathing short and painful. On the table beside the easel were brushes, paints and knives. Joanna did not think as she took a knife from the table and grasped it in her palm. But when she raised her hand, ready to strike, her aim was quite deliberate.

*

In the early evening Gaetano had slipped out of the house. He needed company and had searched the Rialto, the Piazzetta, even the Campo di San Cassiano. But he had failed to find quite what he wanted, and what he had taken, although it had relieved his immediate physical needs, had ultimately proved unsatisfying. As he had undressed, Gaetano had imagined Joanna Zulian naked behind the gauze curtain in Taddeo's studio. As he made love in the small, squalid room, he imagined the whore's fair hair to be that light reddish-brown, the whore's commonplace blue eyes to be a clear, translucent grey. When he opened his eyes, her face disappointed him. He was angry with the girl when he had finished, deriding her for the slut she undoubtedly was. He left her only half of the money she demanded. She had been lucky, Gaetano thought as he reached the Campo di Santi Giovanni e Paolo, that he had not struck her.

As he crossed the square to the house, he noticed the light in the studio, thin and flickering in the darkness. Gaetano went silently up the stairs and saw that the studio door was open.

He saw Joanna standing in front of the picture, her fisted hand raised above her shoulder. He had just time to seize her wrist so that the tip of the knife only scraped the canvas, gouging a single thin line through the paint.

He heard her sudden sobbing intake of breath, felt her try to pull away from him. She was strong for a woman, but Gaetano was stronger. He did not let go of her, not even when her fingers relaxed and the dagger clattered to the floor.

'It's a good picture,' he whispered in her ear. 'You shouldn't destroy it.'

She seemed unable to speak or to look away from the picture. Her breathing was taut and fast. He saw the misery in her distended eyes, and he said, quite gently: 'Taddeo was right, Joanna. You wouldn't be able to join the guild. It's better that you leave the workshop now.'

Gaetano's free arm curved round her waist, his palm was flat against her belly. He could feel the rise and fall of her breath, the fast, steady beat of her heart. She was still staring at the painting, and then her eyes closed suddenly and he saw the tears that beaded her lashes.

Taddeo and Isotta had been hopeless with her, he thought. She was like some high-strung pony that needed breaking and taming. She needed to be shown what to do, how to behave. She needed someone older, stronger, who knew what she was. She was still young enough. Only fifteen.

His thoughts compelled him, and frightened him. His fingers began to stroke her smooth velvet bodice. The movement was rhythmic, soothing: she no longer tried to pull away from him. Gaetano heard Joanna gasp, saw her mouth open slightly. Then, sweeping aside the heavy fall of her hair, he began to kiss her neck. His mouth followed the curve of her shoulder, her slender hollowed throat. She was pliant in his arms. He realized that he wanted to be the first man to know Joanna Zulian, the first man to possess her. She did not stop him, not even when he loosened the ties of her bodice so that he could touch her round white breasts. He wanted her, and yet her compliance offended him. The thought came to Gaetano that she might let other men take similar liberties. His desire dissolved suddenly in fear, and he saw again the Frenchman, his arm around Joanna's shoulders.

There was only one way to answer his hunger, his fear. Gaetano asked his question before he had time to consider the consequences. She did not refuse him. Her acquiescence was in the small nod of her head, the dimming of her eyes as, moving away from him, she retied the ribbons of her bodice.

He did not allow himself to regret his impulse. He realized that he knew now how he would paint her. As he led her out of the studio and watched her walk alone up the stairs to her bedchamber, Gaetano saw the painting in his mind's eye, complete in every detail.

CHAPTER FOUR

As soon as the arrangements could be made, they were married. Gaetano had stayed in Venice; when the ceremonies were done he and his new bride would return to Padua. It would, he thought, give his gossiping old sisters something to talk about.

When the feasting was over, Gaetano took Joanna to the bedchamber that Isotta and Taddeo had set aside for them. The door was closed, the shutters were pulled tight. Isotta had decked the bed with new hangings, and strewn sweet-smelling herbs over the linen. The house was cold and silent, the candles shivering, guttering in the draught.

Joanna's gown was of red velvet lined with yellow silk. White gauze trimmed with gold embroidery showed through the slashings in the wide oversleeves. The velvet echoed the colour of her hair, which flowed long and loose down her back. She still wore the marriage-gifts that Gaetano had given her. Through her hair he had threaded pearls, and around her neck he had strung a chain of silver and lapis lazuli. On each blue stone was etched his own initials. The same initials were engraved on the gold clasp she wore at her shoulder.

Gaetano began to remove the jewellery. The clasp, the beads, the chains. He laid them carefully on the chest, where the letters carved on the stones were drawn deeper by the candlelight. It was right that he should remove the jewels he had adorned her with only a few hours earlier: they were, after all, his. Joanna had brought to the marriage only the few trinkets from her father, and a rather more substantial sum from Taddeo. Taddeo had, as Gaetano had expected, been delighted with the match. Isotta had moped a little at the loss of her niece, but anyone could see that Isotta would not live out the year.

Gaetano left the pearls in Joanna's hair. The picture he would paint as soon as they returned to Padua was vivid in his mind. He thought for a moment that he saw fear in her eyes as he unlaced the ties of her bodice, but he knew that he must be mistaken. Joanna Zulian was afraid of nothing – that lack of fear both fascinated and frightened him. In a woman, fearlessness was dangerous. Women were in thrall to their desires, their appetites. Fear was both natural and necessary to women. It kept them in their proper place.

Joanna had not spoken a word since they had entered the bedchamber. Her eyes were fixed not on Gaetano but on the panelled walls beyond. Gaetano appreciated her demonstration of modesty, but his eyes, observant artist's eyes, noted that her hands trembled, and noted also, beneath the white swelling of her breast, the fast beating of her heart. He thought that she was finding it difficult to wait.

He unlaced her sleeves, untied her bodice, stooped to pull the thin silk stockings from her feet. When he laid the red velvet skirts beside the sleeves, Gaetano felt his own heart begin to flutter and thud. She was naked now. Her skin was white and unblemished, the curves and contours of her body were as perfect as any artist might have drawn. She was clothed only in her long russet hair, shadowed only by the flickering candlelight, the dull glow of the fire. He stood for a moment, staring at her. Her perfection startled him; he did not yet touch her. Momentarily, *he* was afraid – of her inconstancy, her youth, of the power that her beauty gave her.

Almost immediately, though, his fear was replaced by a kind of outrage – that this girl, this fifteen-year-old child, should daunt him! It was ludicrous. It was not to be borne. He took her in his arms, his fingers bruising her smooth pale skin, his mouth searching, kissing, sucking, biting. Pushing her on to the bed, he took what he wanted immediately, without any preliminaries. He was her husband, her body belonged to him.

Afterwards, he rolled on to his back, recovering his breath. Through the glorious release of tension, Gaetano was aware of triumph. Donato Zulian's daughter had been, to his relief, a virgin. He had been the first man to own her, to possess her.

They travelled to the city of Padua two days later. As she stepped from the boat on to the mainland for the first time in more than three years, Joanna felt a rush of excitement. She did not look back as Venice faded into the distance, lost in the grey misty sea that encompassed it. Her only regret was for Isotta, who would be left once more to Taddeo, and to isolation and loneliness. She had left medicinal preparations with the cook for Isotta's continued care, and Joanna knew that her instructions would be followed faithfully. But she also knew that Isotta's condition would deteriorate when spring brought its usual ration of fevers to Venice's marshes and shallow lagoons.

She was happier riding from Venice to Padua than she had been for weeks, but not because of her new status. She had to block all memory of that dreadful wedding-night from her mind. She had known what to expect, of course. For although Isotta's mumbling, red-faced explanations of a bride's duty would not have enlightened anyone, Joanna's own mother had explained everything to her when she had become a woman. But some things in Sanchia's patient explanation did not match Joanna's experience of marriage – love, for instance. Sanchia had undoubtedly loved Donato, and he had loved her. The warmest emotion – perhaps the only emotion – that Joanna felt so far for Gaetano was gratitude that he had taken her away from Venice. She knew that something was wrong: a wife should love her husband.

They rode into the walled city of Padua in the early evening: Joanna, Gaetano and a trail of servants laden with baggage, artists' materials, rolled-up sketches and canvases. For many months afterwards Joanna retained this memory of the day's journey: the sky stretching out over land, not sea; the low, rolling hills; the gentle sway of the green earth; most of all, the road that had seemed to lead forever into the distance. She had felt free again.

She did not realize, until Gaetano led her into his house and upstairs to the withdrawing-room, that her husband had given only the briefest word of his marriage to the elder sisters who shared his home. He had ridden back to Padua for a few days to collect money and belongings, but he had explained little to either Caterina or Nannina. There was no need to explain. He was their brother, their superior.

Now, both sisters gaped wordlessly at Joanna, eyes wide, mouths open. Gaetano, Joanna noticed, seemed to find it all rather amusing. Joanna smiled, curtsied, and kissed each dry, pale cheek in turn.

'Madonna Caterina. Madonna Nannina.'

She wore her red velvet wedding-gown. She had ornamented the hem with green- and cream-coloured braid: it reminded her of a skirt Sanchia had once made for her. She had pleaded with Isotta for the coloured gown, and Isotta had eventually smiled and given way. It had given Joanna great pleasure to abandon the black that Isotta had thought proper for a young Venetian woman.

The withdrawing-room of Gaetano's house was more spacious than Taddeo's, the windows larger and more plentiful. The room was comfortably furnished, trimmed with cushions and hangings and cloths sewn, presumably, by Caterina and Nannina. They were both widows, Gaetano had earlier explained, whose husbands had died too late in life for either woman to have any hopes of remarriage. He had, therefore, received his sisters back into the family home. They were of his blood, after all, and it was not suitable that women should live alone. Both were a few years older than Isotta, many years older than himself.

'Gaetano . . .' Madonna Caterina, after inspecting Joanna, turned to her brother. 'She's very young.' Caterina was dark, like Gaetano, tall and large-boned.

Gaetano smiled, and lowered himself into a chair. 'She's old enough. Joanna has travelled, seen the world, haven't you, my dear?'

Joanna nodded. Caterina stared at her again and sniffed. 'That gown is rather low-cut. And the colour! They may wear such fashions in Venice, but it won't do for Padua. And you should put up your hair, child, now that you are married.'

Nannina, fluttering nervously, poured wine into four glasses. Gaetano yawned. 'Sister,' he said to Caterina, 'I leave it to you to make of Joanna a respectable Paduan matron. But do not make her fat or dull. I have married her because she is beautiful to look at. Like one of my paintings.'

Caterina's straight, dark brows clamped tightly together. Nannina, who had Isotta's snub, pretty features, offered Gaetano the wine, and then, putting the tray aside, knelt in front of him to help him remove his heavy riding-boots. Nannina's stiff black skirts scratched against the wooden floor, her small, plump body wobbled as she found her balance.

'No,' said Gaetano suddenly, as Nannina's short fingers struggled with the buckles. 'I am married now, remember.'

His voice, reproving, was addressed to his sister, but his eyes rested on Joanna. As she took Nannina's place, the joy that she had found earlier in the day began to ebb slowly but steadily away. She felt tears prick at the corners of her eyelids as she unbuckled the boots and pulled them from her husband's feet.

She wanted to cry because she was tired, she told herself. Because the ride had been long, and she was once again among strangers.

*

Gaetano took her to his studio the following evening. The workshop was smaller than Taddeo's and on the ground floor. Unlike Taddeo, he had only a single apprentice and an errand-boy to help him.

She watched him light the candelabra on the table. An easel was set up to one side of the room, and the table was piled with lengths of cloth. It felt odd to be in an artist's workshop again: to smell the rich, heavy oils, spirits and pigments, to see the brushstrokes on the canvases, robbed of colour by the night. It brought her abruptly back to when she had stood in Taddeo's studio, brush in hand, painting lilies and roses and narcissi. Only six weeks had passed since then. A long six weeks.

Gaetano had begun to pin paper to the easel, to break off lengths of charcoal. 'I won't always work on the picture at night' – he gestured to the candles, to the inky blackness between the slats of the shutters – 'I'll need to see you in the daylight, sometimes, to get the details right.'

Joanna stared at Gaetano. 'You are going to paint *me*?'

'Of course.' She saw the charcoal move as he sketched a few broad strokes on the paper. His eyes studied her coldly. He said impatiently, 'Take off your gown behind the screen, Joanna.'

At first, she could not speak or move. If she had spoken, he would not, she thought, have heard her. Her fingers knotted together, her heart was pounding. She was aware of a compulsion to run from the studio, to leave the house, the street, Padua.

Sternly, Joanna told herself she was being ridiculous. She was a married woman, now, no longer the child that had roamed the dusty tracks of Europe. It had been thoughtless, inconsiderate of Gaetano not to have explained his wishes to her, but he was an artist, and it was only natural that an artist should wish to paint his wife. And besides, it was her duty to obey him. Even Isotta had managed to explain that part of marriage.

At last she managed to walk behind the screen. The small table and stool behind it were bare. She realized that she was to take off her clothes for him. Just as Taddeo's models had: those women of the street who had posed naked for a few easy scudi an hour. Her fingers were clumsy as she unlaced her gown. She reminded herself that she had, after all, few other wifely duties: Caterina organized the kitchen, Nannina sewed and visited the market. She should be glad of the opportunity to help her husband.

When Joanna looked up, Gaetano was beside her, a length of bronze silk slung over one arm. Winding the heavy material around her, he made a skirt out of the silk, so that the heavy material fell in twists and folds from her waist, leaving the upper half of her body uncovered. Pearls were threaded through her hair, bracelets pushed on to her arms, a silver chain fastened round her neck. Every now and then Gaetano paused and walked back a few paces, inspecting her, adjusting the folds of silk, the jewellery. Distantly, Joanna could hear the evening sounds of the house: the rattle of pots and pans in the kitchen, Caterina's slow, heavy footsteps as she went to fetch more thread for her embroidery. The sounds seemed unreal, from another person's life. Gaetano's fingers teased coils of russet-coloured hair around the pearls over Joanna's shoulder, behind her ears. He seized her limbs and began to position them: both arms out to her sides, hands fisted as though she held something.

'You must smile,' he said.

She could not smile. She tried to, but her mouth would not obey her, it twitched and twisted. Gaetano did not look at her, Joanna thought, as he had looked at her on their wedding-night, with that strange mixture of resentment and hunger and triumph that she had found so disturbing. He looked at her measuringly, almost coldly, as though she were someone – something – utterly distinct from the woman he had married only a few days previously. She began to fear, for the first time, that he was dissatisfied with her.

'Will I do, husband?' she whispered. Her voice shook.

He nodded, but Joanna realized that Gaetano's mind was already on the paper, those pieces of charcoal. He had returned to the easel and had begun to draw. She could see the charcoal making broad sweeps, see Gaetano's narrowed eyes first studying her and then returning to the easel. The studio was silent except for the scrape of the charcoal, the rustle as Gaetano occasionally rubbed at the paper with a piece of cloth. The room seemed vast. She felt as though there were watching eyes behind every easel, behind every shuttered window. She felt cold, exposed, betrayed. Her arms ached. There were, again, those wretched tears at the corners of her eyes. She would not let them fall, though.

Eventually she said, 'Will I do for *what*, husband?' and her voice cracked. 'What am I?'

Gaetano's head jerked up, his hand paused momentarily. 'Why, you are Judith, of course, my dear. After she has slain Holofernes.'

★

Joanna tried so hard to be a good wife. In December, when she had accepted Gaetano's unexpected proposal of marriage, she had seen no choice, no alternative. She had no place in Venice, she had lost the life she had once had, and had found nothing permanent to replace it. If she had doubted her decision over the weeks that passed between her betrothal and her wedding, then she had hidden those doubts. She had accepted Gaetano, and she would honour the promises that she had made. She would be a good wife: her pride demanded nothing less of her.

Joanna had first regretted her decision on her wedding-night. She had lain awake into the early hours of the morning, dry-eyed, careful not to make any movement which might disturb her sleeping husband. She had felt bruised, she had felt dirty. Worst of all, she had experienced fear. She had believed that in marrying Gaetano she would avoid fear. Fear of desertion, of exclusion, she was already familiar with. She could not name the fear she experienced during the first night of marriage: it had been featureless, black, suffocating. But by dawn she had gathered her courage, and resolved to be of use to Gaetano, who had released her from Venice. She had allowed herself to be blinded by illusion too often before – by Donato, by her own skill with a paintbrush – but at last she had become wise. She was a grown woman now, a wife.

And yet, after only two months of marriage, her resolution was beginning to crumble. Joanna knew that she did not love Gaetano, she did not even think she liked him. He had awakened some sort of feeling in her that night in Taddeo's studio, but it had been fleeting, never since repeated. He had never again kissed her like that, caressed her like that. Gaetano's nightly love-making seemed to Joanna to be something cold and loveless.

She found her lack of privacy hard to bear. Even in Taddeo Zulian's cramped house in Venice she had had her own bedchamber, where she could be alone if she wished. Although Taddeo's studio had been busy, she had worked in it largely unnoticed. She had been allowed to go alone to the marketplace; she had attended church with only the disinterested Taddeo to accompany her. Now, of course, she shared her bedchamber with Gaetano. Sometimes she thought that Gaetano would have liked to take possession of her mind as well as her body. The city of Padua might have ceased at the boundaries of the Cavazza house for all that Joanna had seen of it.

The restrictions on her life were trivial, petty and, Joanna knew, common to most young brides. Yet she resented them with a bitterness she sometimes found hard to control. She could not stand on the balcony of the Paduan house, she could not walk to church unveiled. The servants or Nannina went to the market for her; her only fresh air was taken from the tiny enclosed square of earth at the back of the house. At night she would dream of the sea-shore fringed with black rocks, or of gentle valleys and wooded hills fading endlessly into the distance. In the mornings she would wake and see the shuttered windows and hear, only faintly, the sounds of men at work and children running in the piazza.

Caterina connived at her confinement, because, like Gaetano, she enjoyed power, enjoyed any sort of power, since as an ageing widow she existed on her brother's charity. If it had not been for Caterina, then Nannina might have proved a friend, but she was like Isotta; kind, gentle, utterly subservient, and afraid of both Gaetano and Caterina.

Many evenings were spent in the studio. Gaetano had spent the first few weeks making sketches in charcoal, then transferring the squared-up design to the canvas. He had now begun to paint with oils. Standing there, draped with silk and pearls, Joanna would empty her mind of all thoughts. She knew her thoughts would terrify her if she allowed herself to think. For marriage was permanent, binding, and the prison she had willingly entered would never unlock its doors.

Sometimes Gaetano and Caterina spoke of her as though she were not present or could not hear. 'She was standing at the window a long time,' Caterina would say, 'so I drew the shutters.' And Gaetano, staring at Joanna, would reply, 'You did well, sister.' They made her feel invisible, almost as though she no longer existed. She knew that she was no longer the child she had once been, the child that had danced alone in a Spanish square, her chestnut hair fanning round her like a veil. She knew that she was no longer Joanna Zulian, the physician's daughter, the mountebank's zany. She had become Joanna Cavazza, a silenced, imprisoned creature who was never alone, and never among friends. The confinement, the lack of privacy, made her feel edgy and afraid. She, who had rarely known fear, found herself increasingly consumed by it.

Her right hand would hold the bloodstained knife, Gaetano had explained to Joanna, the left would grip Holofernes' severed head by the hair. He had not yet found a suitable knife, and he would probably have to make do with a model of a severed head, but those were details he could attend to later.

When he painted, he hated her to speak to him. You didn't expect an artist's model to speak. Some were sulky, complaining that he made their poses too demanding; others coyly flirtatious, offering with a flutter of the eyelashes and a dimpled smile much, much more than just a glance. He was thankful that Joanna was not a chatterer; her occasional questions he answered curtly, if at all.

He worked in the studio most nights. He watched as the figure of Judith was brought to life on the canvas by his own clever, patient fingers. Even when he was not working on it, he thought about the painting constantly. It obsessed him, frightened him, its incongruous images of violence and beauty haunting his dreams. More than once he had woken during the night glazed in sweat, expecting to see Joanna herself poised over him, knife in hand. Only when his eyes had accustomed themselves to the darkness, only when his heart had stopped its frantic pounding, would he turn and see her, eyes lidded, curled like an infant on the far side of the bed.

One night he drew Joanna to his side to show her the half-finished painting. The pale, vengeful figure growing out of the darkness, the distant landscape of hills and sky glimpsed behind a half-shut curtain. The woman's proud, triumphant face; the severed head of the man, his silenced mouth parted in agony. In the poor light Joanna's eyes, as she studied the painting, were not grey, but dark and pinpointed by the flame of the candle. Her white, full breasts rose and fell. She should have covered herself, thought Gaetano, suddenly, angrily. Another woman would have covered herself with a shawl.

He felt again that familiar sudden fear for the future. He might be using Joanna as a model, but she was not, after all, one of those whores he hired to come into his studio. She was his wife, and she should behave like a wife. He remembered how other men had always looked at her, desire naked in their eyes. He remembered riding with her in the gondola in Venice, dancing with her at the carnival. She lured men quite deliberately, sapping them of will. Her lack of shame, lack of conformity, encouraged their glances. A man could not be held responsible for the consequences of his desire; it was a woman's duty to cover her body, to veil her face, to keep out of the public eye.

Gaetano's imagination conjured up for him Joanna in some other artist's studio, her beautiful breasts exposed, her lovely face full of guile. Other men looked at her, other men touched her, and she welcomed them. She no longer belonged only to him. He felt anger and fear mixed with a terrible desire. The strength of his desire frightened him, increasing his anger.

All women were instinctively faithless, though, and Joanna, headstrong and temptingly beautiful, might be more faithless than most. He could only enjoy Joanna without fear if he was confident of her fidelity. He needed her both as an exquisite artist's model and as a wife.

Gaetano knew suddenly that he had both the inclination and the ability to remind her then and there of her duties as a wife. There would still be time to work again afterwards. His charcoal-stained fingers began to caress those exposed white breasts, to untie the bronze silk that bound Joanna's waist.

In April, the Cavazza household was crammed with the more prosperous citizens of Padua paying their respects to Gaetano's new bride. It was an occasion that Gaetano had postponed for as long as he was able, trapped between his fear of Joanna's faithlessness and his enjoyment of other men's envy. Once he had caught Octavio, his apprentice, lifting the dust-sheets that covered the picture of *Judith* in the daytime. Gaetano's blow had sent the lad running from the studio, blubbering for his mother.

Now, though, looking at the dining-chamber, at his sisters and his wife, all arrayed in their finery, Gaetano felt nothing but pride. Spotless white damask napkins were folded at every place, and candelabras glowed on the table, their flames doubled in the polished wood. Caterina and Nannina were resplendent in stiff black taffeta and buckram boned like body-armour. Heavy jet ornaments were pinned to Caterina's stout breast, a frilled cap was perched precariously on Nannina's small round head. Tucked into an insignificant corner of the room as Gaetano greeted his guests, Caterina inspected the ladies' dress with disapproving eyes, and Nannina fiddled nervously with her fan.

Joanna was dressed in the red velvet she had worn for her wedding, and Gaetano had again threaded strands of pearls through her hair. It had amused him to insist that she wore the pearls: they reminded him that only he saw her as she was in the studio. These fools could only look and envy. They would never know Joanna as Gaetano knew her, would never own her as he owned her. The covetousness – and the lust – in their eyes was naked, but Gaetano did not yet find himself growing angry with the girl. He knew that only he had the right to see her as Judith, her unusual colouring echoed by the bronze silk, long coils of auburn hair curling over her smooth pale skin. Gaetano worked on the painting almost every night; it was, he knew, the best thing he had ever done. It was a labour of love to him, a labour of joy: an obsession. He worked on his other commissions by day, but he was always impatient to return to the *Judith and Holofernes*. He would ask a high price for the picture when it was completed: Messer Venier had already expressed interest in it.

They dined on pigeon and pasta, dried fruit and jellies. The meal was excellent, Caterina had taken responsibility for its planning. Gaetano knew that though Caterina might be as plain as a nanny-goat, she could be trusted not to put him to shame in company. Caterina saw to the kitchen and the servants; Nannina went to the market and, when she was not shopping, sewed endlessly. Gaetano thought her a silly, ineffectual thing, but acknowledged her usefulness in the house. His sisters' continued presence had meant that the smooth running of the Cavazza household had not altered a jot in consequence of Gaetano's marriage. That suited him admirably: he expected to be able to work uninterrupted, to have his meals served on time, his clothing laundered and kept in good repair.

Every so often Gaetano turned away from his guests to glance at Joanna seated at the far end of the table. To check that her behaviour was what it should be, to reassure himself that he was, after all, married to the most beautiful woman in the room. The most beautiful woman in Padua – Gaetano saw how the men sitting beside Joanna gazed at her, hypnotized, and he experienced again that fleeting stab of fear. But he collected himself, drank more wine and reminded himself that his ring was on her finger, his pearls were wound through her lovely hair. He had, he told himself, nothing to fear.

As the last of the dishes were cleared away, Gaetano rose and led the company into the withdrawing-room. A lutenist had been engaged: songs and dances flowered in the far corner of the room. A ridiculous expense, Gaetano had thought, but Nannina, nervously, had assured her brother that a musician would be essential to ensure the success of the evening. And the music was pleasant, soothing, Gaetano admitted to himself, as he discussed with a fellow-artist the shocking price of azurite blue.

He found himself describing to his colleague the portrait of *Judith*. The technique he had used for shading the dark background into the light foreground; the soft, rounded forms that gave the picture depth and luminosity. Eventually he felt compelled to take the man down to his workshop and unveil the picture, and watch as admiration and a particular sort of resentment – the acknowledgement of a superior skill – blossomed on the other painter's face.

Yet his triumph was more temporary than Gaetano had expected. In revealing the artistry he had also to reveal Joanna as only he should see her: half naked in bronze silk, violence and desire marking her exquisite face. The other man made a coarse remark, and Gaetano wanted to strike him. But he managed to unbunch his clenched fists and return to the withdrawing-room, his guest following behind him.

Upstairs, he could not at first see Joanna. The withdrawing-room was not large and guests lined every wall, were clustered in every corner. The candles in the wall-sconces threw pools of light into the darkness; the notes of the lute, like pale pearls strung on golden thread, filtered through the chatter and laughter. Gaetano's forehead was damp with sweat, his heart pounded out his anxiety.

And then he saw her. She was at the far end of the room, just in front of the lutenist, and she was dancing. Her body was erect and proud; her head, with its weight of coiled hair and jewels, caught the fire's uncertain, flickering light. The same golden light sparkled on the embroidered front of her bodice, on the heavy hem of her gown, with its trim of braid and ribbon. Joanna danced like a dancer in a dream, as though she alone heard the notes of the lute, as though twenty pairs of eyes did not watch her, entranced.

Suddenly Gaetano returned through the years to Venice at carnival-time. His sister Isotta was whirling round the bonfire, as though she were a girl again. Her hands were clasped in Joanna's, and she was laughing. And Gaetano remembered that he had thought, *'Pity the man that marries Joanna Zulian.'*

And he, like a fool, had married her. He knew then, with terrible certainty, that he had made a mistake, that he would lose her, that she would rob him of everything: self-respect, reputation, even his manhood.

As he pushed his way through the crowds to her side, he felt again despair magnified a hundred times.

He pulled her away from her partner, and she looked at him for a moment as though she did not recognize him. As though he was anyone, any stranger. He found, though, that to hurt her eased his pain. Dragging her across the room, he dug his fingers into her arms, pressing through the layers of muslin and velvet, until he saw tears in her eyes.

She did not cry out, though. And he had wanted her to cry out.

Caterina caught a cold which went to her chest. Nannina nursed her, fluttering around the bedside, trying to coax her cantankerous elder sister to take a few mouthfuls of broth or an infusion of heart's ease.

Alone in the withdrawing-room, Joanna looked out of the window. There was, for the first time since her marriage, no one to scold her, or to pull her away, or to slam the shutters. Gaetano was in his studio, Caterina and Nannina in their bedchamber. Carefully she opened the window and went out on to the balcony. There, she took in great lungfuls of cold, fresh air. The air tasted like wine.

She looked down at the piazza. A few ragged children squabbled over a plaything, while their mothers talked to one another by the well, wooden buckets in hand. A cleric threw a coin into a fiddler's upturned hat. Some scholars hailed each other, their arms burdened with books and feathered quills. The scratching of the fiddler's jig reached Joanna watching from the balcony, and her foot began to tap. Hungry for company, she found that she was smiling as her gaze moved from the fiddler to a dog attempting to bury its bone in a flower-pot, and then to a chapman selling dubious cures for the plague.

She heard a voice call, '*Buon giorno, madonna!*', and she looked down to where a man, smiling up at her, swept a rather battered velvet cap from his head. He wore a long robe, one sleeve of which trailed in a puddle as he made his bow. His Italian was slightly accented, his face pleasant and kind, his hair and eyes light in colour. A scholar, thought Joanna. From the Netherlands. Or England, perhaps. She could not help smiling back as he wrung out his muddy, soaking sleeve, shaking his head in mock despair. A wave of a hand and he was gone, lost in the market-day crowds, his robes dragging in the dirt. Joanna rested her elbows on the balustrade again, her hands cupping her chin. She was aware of a feeling of peace, of contentment.

Then she heard a voice call, 'Hey, madonna, catch!' And there was the scholar again, standing below her balcony, tossing something up towards her. A bundle of green and white whirled into the air. Joanna reached out a hand and caught what he had thrown to her.

It was a bunch of lily of the valley tied with a length of ribbon. The flowers were small and perfect, their leaves and petals still beaded with dew, the delicate white and pale green buds half open. She felt as though she held the beginnings of summer in her hands. She held the flowers against her face, her eyes closed, intoxicated by their soft fragility.

'They are beautiful, Messer . . .?'

'Gefroy. Martin Gefroy.' The scholar bowed a second time.

'Are you Dutch, Messer Gefroy? Or English?'

Martin Gefroy stood below the balcony, his eyes screwed up against the weak spring sunlight. 'English, madonna. It's many years since I was last in England, though.'

Joanna's English was both rusty and limited, but she did her best. 'Then good day to you, Messer Gefroy. And I thank you for –'

She did not finish her sentence. A hand gripped her shoulder and pulled her roughly round, a voice shouted curses to the man in the street below.

Gaetano's eyes were dark with fury; his fingernails dug into her skin. 'Whore! Bitch! Do you put yourself on public display when there is no one to watch over you?'

He dragged her away from the balcony and into the withdrawing-room, snatched the flowers from her fingers and hurled them to the floor.

She tried to calm him. 'Gaetano . . . I was not –'

The flat of Gaetano's palm struck her hard across the face, sending her reeling against the wall.

When she opened her eyes and looked up, he was staring at her. She did not move, could not move: she remained crouched down on the floor, huddled next to the wall. She did not understand the expression on his face. She shivered violently, waiting for him to strike her again.

He stepped forward, and she flinched. But he had moved only to pull tight the shutters. Kneeling beside her, so that his breath was hot against her face, he said hoarsely: 'You will keep the shutters closed. You will not stand near the window. You will never again speak to another man without my permission. Do you understand?'

His skin was drained of colour. Joanna nodded slowly. There was blood in her mouth and her right eye had begun to close.

After he had gone, she tried to pick up the scattered lilies. But they were broken, every one of them, and her shaking fingers bruised the fragile remains.

In the piazza below it was now overcast, as the weak spring sunshine yielded to thunderclouds. Martin Gefroy had heard the curses, the shouts, the slamming of the shutters. He had thought he had heard – and had prayed that he was mistaken – the sound of a blow. As he stood there with a chill in his heart, he had considered running to fetch the sword he never carried, beating on the door, forcing his way into the house. But he knew the futility of such action, his own incompetence with a sword, his powerlessness when faced with that woman's angry husband, and, no doubt, several burly servants as well.

Realistically, he knew that anything he might attempt to do would only find him thrown into some lousy Paduan gaol. More importantly, he would make things worse for the lovely girl he had glimpsed leaning over the balcony. For her husband had, in the eyes of the rest of Padua, done nothing wrong. He had merely stopped his wife behaving like a whore.

There was a foul taste in Martin's mouth when finally he walked away from the square. He attended the lecture theatre and watched the anatomical dissection, but for once he did not reap his usual pleasure from all the fascinating array of bone, sinew, vein and muscle that was laid out before him.

Gaetano made her model for him that evening. He was not, after all, painting her face.

He selected his pigments as Joanna robed herself behind the screen, clumsily knotting the bronze silk round her waist, weaving the pearls into her hair with trembling hands. The house was silent, the studio dark, lit only by the candles on the table.

She began to hate him then. Standing there, one hand holding the knife, the other gripping the papier-mâché head, Joanna could no longer shut out her thoughts. That morning Gaetano had taught her to fear him. Gaetano – big, muscular Gaetano – had hit her, and she had cowered on the floor, terrified of his strength, his authority. He had marked her face, he had marked her soul. And slowly the fear was transmuting into hatred, hatred that made her want to curse him as he had cursed her, to use the dagger she gripped in her hand. But she would wait, she would bide her time. She would not court other bruises, other humiliations. Her thoughts jangled through her aching head, as compelling and as inescapable as the fiddler's tune.

Once, she had stood on the other side of a canvas, revelling in her power to create flowers and trees, birds and butterflies. Now she was powerless, feeble. When Gaetano came to her, adjusting the folds of her drapery, positioning her naked limbs, she wanted to spit on him. She understood then that she was not even a person to him. She was no more than an artist's wooden manikin, a lifeless, thoughtless, speechless thing, to be moved and used at someone else's will.

News of the Emperor Maximilian's abortive incursion into Venetian territories reached the château de Marigny in the early summer.

Events in faraway Venice affected Eleanor du Chantonnay only when they worsened her husband's temper. In the course of the last year Reynaud du Chantonnay's temper had grown steadily more uncertain as his physical condition had rapidly deteriorated. Eleanor heard his voice bellowing her name from three rooms away, echoing against vast stone walls, making tapestries and hangings sway in the still, late-spring air.

She went to him as soon as she had sent a servant to the linen-room for bandages and ointments and water. Reynaud was in his bedchamber, sitting on his bed half dressed, his bandaged leg splayed out in front of him. The curtains were drawn, the air was thick and foetid. A manservant cowered in the corner, the mark of his master's fury still glowing scarlet on his cheek. Cousin Guillaume, his handsome face expressionless, lounged by the fireplace.

Eleanor sent the manservant out of the room and pulled back the curtains so that sunlight poured through the windows, gilding the rich furnishings and ornaments. Reaching up, she opened one of the windows, enjoying the scents of the fresh spring air. The flowers were already blooming, sprinkling the grass with gold and white and pink. New green leaves unfurled on the distant trees, and the sky was a clear cobalt-blue. Eleanor knew that she lived in the most beautiful place on God's earth and she was thankful for it. Her fingers slowly unknotted, her clenched jaw began to relax. She looked across to the tennis game on the meadow.

She noticed that her stepson was not playing with his bodyguard, Meraud, as she had assumed, but with Reynaud's courier, the dark-haired young man, Toby Crow. Eleanor's eyes rested on François for a moment, on the lolloping stride, the flailing arms, the small outbursts of petulance whenever he missed the ball. François had inherited nothing from his father except his temper, she thought. Blanche's final act of revenge for the years of misery that Reynaud must have inflicted on her.

Her eyes drifted to the other player. Toby Crow had been at Marigny for more than a month now after having successfully carried out his latest commission in Italy. She had seen him frequently during the past few weeks: he had swept off his hat to bow to her when she had passed him on the stairs, he had waved to her, riding back over the drawbridge with François and his bodyguard. He had always been unassumingly polite, quietly courteous. Now she watched him for a moment: the sweep of slightly ragged black hair, the slanting dark eyes. His movements were strong and graceful, his body well-formed and coordinated. So different from poor François.

To Reynaud's cursing at the sunlight she said, mildly, 'I cannot help you if I cannot see, husband. I must have light.'

Eleanor sat down on the edge of the bed and began to tear linen into strips. She noticed the letters on the bed beside Reynaud, letters that Cousin Guillaume had brought to Marigny that morning. Their seals were roughly torn, the paper screwed into little balls. In anger, she thought. Reynaud had never liked to receive bad news.

'Get me food. My belly is empty,' said Reynaud. His face was crimson with temper. 'And bring me my courier. Bring Toby Crow.'

Eleanor murmured to her waiting-woman nervously hovering in the doorway. The strips of linen were carefully rolled; soothing herbs had been infused in the hot water. From beyond the window, Eleanor could still hear the thwack of the tennis ball and François's squeals of delight and pique and laughter. Then, sounds of voices calling, echoing off the smooth dark water of the moat and the distant trees.

A manservant arrived with a tray of cold game and wine and sweetmeats. Reynaud's fat, dimpled fingers burrowed immediately into the quince jellies and marmalades, the candied fruits and custards. Eleanor noticed the look of distaste on Cousin Guillaume's face, the swift shake of the head at Reynaud's offer of food. Guillaume was such a fastidious man.

There was a knock on the door. Reynaud looked up. Runnels of custard trailed between his fingers; his cheeks and chin were dusted white with sugar from the jellies. His small pale eyes were bright with intelligence and malice.

'Ah. My dear Crow, you should be fluttering close at hand when I have need of you, not playing children's games with my son. I pay Meraud to fulfil that tedious obligation.'

Eleanor's head ached with tension, with the expectation of another outburst. Toby Crow, however, merely sketched a bow and said: '*Votre seigneurie*. Have you work for me?'

The balls of paper on the bed were seized in two sugary fists and hurled to the floor. 'Read *those*, Crow. They come from Italy. From your friend, the painter Arlotto Attavanti.'

Cautiously, Eleanor began to unpeel the fouled bandages from Reynaud's leg. Out of the corner of her eye, she saw Toby Crow stoop and retrieve one piece of paper from the fireplace, another from under the table. She noticed, yet again, the physical grace of his movements, the sweep of unruly black hair as it fell over his face and was tossed impatiently back. She watched him as he straightened out the crumpled paper and began to read.

Eventually, looking up, he said, 'It is as we had foreseen, *votre seigneurie*. That Maximilian would use the opportunity of his imperial coronation to attempt to expel the Venetians from Verona and Vicenza. He failed, as we had also foreseen.'

Eleanor was unwinding the last of the soiled bandages. Guillaume du Chantonnay, from the far side of the room, said: 'The Orsini cousins have recovered all Venetian territories, Reynaud. The Emperor Maximilian has been forced to agree to a truce. It is good news, surely.'

Reynaud's clenched fist struck the table beside the bed, making the water in the bowl sway and lick at the edges. 'Good news? You, too, Guillaume? You and that *fool*' – Raynaud's sticky fingers gestured wildly to the letters that Toby still held – 'you and that fool think that we should rejoice!'

Toby said mildly, 'Arlotto is an artist, *votre seigneurie*. Not a soldier.'

Reynaud hissed with fury. Guillaume pressed a small lace handkerchief to his nose to keep away the stench of the open sores. Reynaud's curses were for Arlotto Attavanti, for Pope Julius, and for Eleanor dabbing at the ulcers with quick, careful, hands.

'Pope Julius will no doubt take the truce as a personal insult. He will consider, madame, that the Emperor's adventures have succeeded only in bolstering Venetian arrogance.'

Eleanor du Chantonnay realized, to her surprise, that Reynaud's courier was addressing her. She was accustomed, on such occasions, to exclusion. Women were incapable of understanding politics, therefore it was not worth the trouble of attempting to explain anything to them. Amused, she acknowledged Toby Crow's explanation with a flicker of a smile and a nod of her head, and then she returned to her work. Her strong hands were gentle, instinctively knowing which were the most painful areas of Reynaud's ulcerated leg. She had always been good at treating the pain of other people. She was good with sick or wounded animals, too. If one of the hunting-dogs caught its paw in a trap, if one of François's pet squirrels was ailing, then the sick creature would always be brought to Eleanor.

She dropped the last of the swabs into the bucket, and began to smooth ointment over the open, weeping sores. The ointment contained self-heal, which cleansed external wounds. She knew that there was no cure for her husband's condition, but she could at least make him a little more comfortable. Reynaud's comfort made life easier for everyone at Marigny. An active man, used to having his own way in everything, his resentment with the bounds that his ailing body placed upon him was immense. He vented his anger on the servants, on his horses, on his son and, of course, on Eleanor. She had grown used to that, though; most of the time she hardly noticed.

But Reynaud knew how, if he chose, to hurt her. When Eleanor's fingers, smoothing the ointment on to the open wounds, touched the reddened lip of an ulcer, Reynaud howled; his outstretched arm flung the bowl, the linen, the ointment to the four corners of the room. Regaining his breath, he hissed, 'Do you wish to be free of me *now*, woman? Do you intend that I should die today?' He gripped her arms through the wide sleeves of her gown. His fingernails dug into her flesh.

Eleanor said, her voice unsteady, 'My lord . . . I'm sorry. But the ointment will ease the pain and help the wounds to heal.'

Beads of sweat trailed down Reynaud's forehead, mingling with the sugar that still powdered his cheeks. There was spite – and calculation – in his eyes as he whispered to Eleanor, 'If you had done what any other woman could have done, and provided me with something more than that feeble dolt out there, then I could die today. Happily. As it is . . .'

He left the rest of the sentence unsaid. His eyes glittered as he released his grip on her arms. Eleanor bit her lip, and her skin flushed scarlet with shame. She hated that Reynaud should say such a thing in front of Cousin Guillaume, in front of the servants. Eleanor's hands shook, her eyes stung. From beyond the window she could hear the sound of François playing tennis again. With Meraud, presumably, this time.

She knew, though, that her husband's cruelty was fully justified. He had married her because she had been young and strong, and yet she had failed to give him the son he so desperately needed. She had never even conceived. She was a barren, useless thing, only half a woman. She still, when Reynaud's health permitted it, shared her husband's bed, but after ten years of marriage there was little hope of a child now. She had brought the Seigneur de Marigny money and treasures, but had failed to give him the treasure that he most needed. That she needed also: her arms ached with emptiness sometimes. She knew that her understanding and affectionate care of her stepson, her unstinting patience with broken-winged birds and ailing beasts, her hugs and kisses for servants' babies and infants, were all futile attempts to fill the void of her childlessness.

A voice said gently, 'Madame?' She looked up and saw Toby Crow. He had gathered the rolls of bandages, the lint, the jar of ointment. 'I've sent your woman for more water, madame,' he said. 'And for someone to mop the floor.'

His words were practical, offering no obvious consolation, and yet she recognized the pity in his eyes. At Marigny, kindness was a precious commodity. She wanted to cry; a solitary tear trickled down her cheek. As a servant arrived with a fresh bowl of water, Eleanor bent her head and quickly finished bandaging Reynaud's damaged leg. As soon as the Seigneur gave her his dismissal, she escaped for the silent sanctuary of her own chambers.

Unlike most of the inhabitants of the château de Marigny, Toby was not afraid of the Seigneur's temper. Domestic tyrants of Reynaud du

Chantonnay's ilk attacked only those weaker than themselves. Reynaud might frighten his wife, his son, his servants, but he could not frighten Toby. And besides, Reynaud du Chantonnay could do no worse to him than he had done almost twenty years before, when he had apprenticed the infant Toby to the shoemaker Pernet Lescot. He knew his employer well enough now to believe him capable of such an action. He still could not, however, quite fathom the motives behind Reynaud's cruelty. Pique, perhaps, at his failure to father a son who was both legitimate and healthy.

The Seigneur's treatment of his wife sickened him, however. In front of his servants, in front of Guillaume du Chantonnay, Reynaud had deliberately humiliated her. Tormenting Eleanor was, Toby thought, like tormenting some small, defenceless animal. Or like tormenting a child. Effortlessly, casually done. Eleanor had only the thin protective covering of her elegance and dignity, a covering that Reynaud could easily pierce.

He hid his revulsion, but just for a moment the beauty of Marigny seemed a façade, a false and flimsy covering that hid something altogether darker. Toby found himself wanting to be away from Marigny, riding back through hills and forests towards Italy.

Aloud, he said, after Eleanor had left the room, 'We have a breathing-space, *votre seigneurie*. I can return to Venice now and collect the paintings. Arlotto says that they are ready.'

Guillaume du Chantonnay had sat down in a chair, his long, booted legs flung out before him. 'The Pope cannot make his move yet. He still has treaties to make, alliances to form. Both Julius and Venice are still courting France. You have time, Reynaud. Just.'

The chessboard was set out, but the pieces were not quite in place. Venice could congratulate itself on its wealth, its independence, for a few months yet. Maybe even a year.

Reynaud du Chantonnay's eyes were no longer angry, but half closed, calculating. 'You should take some men with you, perhaps, Crow . . . It might be advisable this time.'

The Seigneur paused, his thick fingers dissecting the cold roast snipe on the tray. 'I visited Italy first when I was fifteen. My son's age. I would offer him as company, so that he might see what I have seen . . .' His voice trailed off into silence. Through the open window they could still hear the sounds of the tennis game, Meraud calling the score, François providing a continuous whining chorus.

Guillaume said lazily, 'It might be the making of him, Reynaud. A nice long journey – the mountains, the open sea, perhaps.' He glanced up at Toby, his face open, innocent. 'You would enjoy the boy's company, would you not, Monsieur Crow?'

He would almost have taken François du Chantonnay, Toby thought, to release him for a few months from the tyranny of his father, to spare him the teasing of his cousin, to see whether anything worthwhile flourished under the petulance and bravado. Sometimes François reminded Toby of the child he had seen at the shoemaker's in Chinon; of the child he had once been himself. But that was ridiculous: François du Chantonnay lacked for nothing. Toby could detect amusement, mockery, on Guillaume's handsome face.

'It would be too risky, *votre seigneurie*. Too dangerous. There are too many different factions in Italy, too many unemployed mercenaries looking for a fight. And besides, I'd rather go alone, if you will permit it. It would attract less attention. It would be safer.'

Reynaud du Chantonnay's eyes were on him, studying him. Toby, suppressing a grin, knew the calculations that flickered through the Seigneur's suspicious mind: that he might abscond with money or treasures; that he might salt away gold or valuables, claiming to have paid inflated prices for pictures or artefacts. Toby did not resent Reynaud's calculations; he neither expected nor desired complete trust. He himself thought trust to be a commodity of dubious worth.

'Oh.' Guillaume had risen out of the chair, was lolling against the window-sill. 'Something I thought you might be interested in, Reynaud. I heard – rumours only, one can't be sure – but I heard that a friend of yours had returned to Brittany.'

Reynaud looked up from the dismembered snipe. 'A friend?'

'Well,' Guillaume's mouth curled in a small smile, 'perhaps not a *friend*, cousin. Perhaps an acquaintance, an old acquaintance.'

Reynaud, scowling, wiped his mouth with the back of his hand.

'Hamon de Bohun,' continued Guillaume happily. 'You remember the Sieur de Bohun, don't you, Reynaud? He was a kinsman of your first wife, wasn't he? Anyway, I believe he has returned from England. He's been seen in Roscoff. Or someone thought they'd seen him in Roscoff. So hard to be sure when a man's been out of the country for – let me see – twenty years or so.'

The tray of sweetmeats, the plates and cutlery, slithered to the floor.

Red wine trickled over the coverlet and on to the rushes. Reynaud still clutched the half-eaten carcass of the snipe in one hand. 'Hamon de Bohun?' he said, softly.

Guillaume nodded. 'The old Tudor king, they say, is dying. De Bohun was Henry Tudor's friend. Perhaps he does not wish to remain at his son's court.'

'Hamon de Bohun was my first wife's guardian.' Reynaud glanced at Toby. Malice glittered in the small, colourless eyes. 'I married her without de Bohun's permission.'

Ponderously, slowly, in a scattering of bedlinen and tableware, Reynaud du Chantonnay was rising to his feet. Smiling, he said, 'But there's nothing for him here, cousin, is there? Nothing at all.' He began to shake then – not with rage or apoplexy, but with laughter.

'Rumours,' said Guillaume, gently. 'Only rumours.'

Each midday Gaetano, Caterina, Nannina and Joanna dined together. It was August, and the weather was hot and sultry. The heat and the sight of the food sickened Joanna. She had disguised her lack of appetite for more than a week, but now, faced with neat's tongue and boiled pork, her stomach heaved and her heart pounded. She pushed her plate aside, the food untouched.

Caterina said irritably, 'What ails you, girl? You shouldn't waste good food.'

Joanna had suspected her condition for some time, but now she was certain. It might at least, she thought through nausea and lassitude, keep her from Gaetano's bed. She disregarded Caterina and spoke to Gaetano, who was gnawing a lamb-bone. 'I'm not unwell, Gaetano. I'm pregnant. I'm carrying your child.'

She saw Caterina's look of outrage, heard Nannina's splutter of pleasure. 'A baby! A *baby*, sister! How wonderful!'

Gaetano put down the lamb-bone. '*My* child? Is it true, Joanna? Are you sure?'

Joanna said evenly, 'The child is yours, Gaetano. Or perhaps it is the child of your apprentice, or of the blackbird that takes crumbs from my window-sill. Do you think so?'

He looked doubtful for a moment, as though twelve-year-old Octavio might indeed have fathered a child.

Nannina sighed again. 'A baby! How wonderful, Gaetano!'

'If it lives,' Caterina sniffed. 'She's too young to produce a healthy child, brother. She'll produce a feeble brat that dies within a week.'

Gaetano shook his head slowly. 'Joanna will give me a son,' he said, softly. 'I shall have many sons. I am not weak or impotent like brother Taddeo.'

The exhaustion of early pregnancy made Joanna too tired even to hate him. Instead, she rose from the table. She did not offer her excuses for leaving the room, and nor did she answer Gaetano when he called after her. He would not hit her again and put his son – that living proof of his virility – at risk. She heard Nannina say nervously, 'She's going to the garden, Gaetano. It will be good for her to sit in the garden – she often goes there,' and then Joanna was down the stairs and out through the kitchen to the small square of land behind the house.

She had laid claim to her sanctuary in the early spring and it had, she sometimes thought, enabled her to remain sane. Then the garden had been deserted, neglected, the bushes unshaped and overgrown, ivy winding round the flower-beds and terracotta pots. But there had been flowers there, almost choked by the undergrowth: sweet violet, the Virgin Mary's flower, and primroses. And later in the year, roses and honeysuckle and lavender. Gradually she had cleared away the weeds and creepers, and coaxed life from seeds, shoots and bulbs. She had planted a herb garden in the centre of the terrace; a small, intricate knot of thyme and rosemary, chervil and rue.

Joanna sat on the stone bench enjoying the shade that the heavily leaved trees gave from the sun. She did not resent the restrictions and indignities that this new life would impose on her, as she resented those imposed on her by Gaetano. A baby – even Gaetano's baby – represented new life, new hope, a new optimism for the future. A baby might allow her to dredge something worthwhile from the travesty that her marriage had become.

The aroma of pinks and jasmine scented the hot air, settling her stomach. She was not, Joanna thought thankfully, going to be sick again. She would plant wallflowers in the autumn: wallflowers to ease the pain of childbirth.

It was several weeks before Eleanor du Chantonnay realized that she was in love with her husband's courier, Toby Crow. She was in the parlour that she used as a sewing-room, removing a splinter from the paw of one of François's squirrels. François was supposed to be holding the creature still while she performed the operation; but it writhed and squawked, and then the boy howled in pain.

François stood up, bawling; the animal bounded across the room and huddled on top of a curtain-rail. 'It bit me, *maman*! The horrible thing bit me!'

'I told you to hold its head still.' Eleanor, struggling to keep her patience, began to dab at François's hand with the water and lint meant for the squirrel.

'Beastly thing. I should have it throttled.'

There were tears in François's eyes. Eleanor sighed. There would be visitors arriving at the château later, important visitors. François must make no ill-timed display of petulance today, nor develop one of his fevers. There were already patches of scarlet on his pale cheeks, and his breathing was becoming short and strangled. Eleanor acted quickly to avert disaster.

'Sit down, my dear, and take some wine. The squirrel was frightened, that's all. Look.'

She took a handful of hazelnuts from the bowl on the table and went over to the curtain. A few moments' clucking and wheedling, and then the squirrel was in her arms again, cradled against her crimson silk bodice. She stroked it while she spoke to François, gently reminding him of the importance of the evening's banquet.

'The Estates General will call at Marigny on their way to Tours. It is important to Reynaud – important to all of us – that the visit goes well.'

François was still holding the piece of lint over his grazed hand. 'The king is so dull,' he said peevishly. 'He only eats boiled beef. Imagine!'

Eleanor eased out the splinter, and the squirrel did not so much as whimper. 'Then we shall tell the kitchen to prepare plenty of boiled beef,' she said calmly. 'Besides, Louis de France will not be our only visitor. There'll be many other lords. And Cousin Guillaume will be here, too.'

François sniffed. 'I can't bear Guillaume. He laughs at me. He makes me look foolish.'

Eleanor's irritation began to simmer again. 'Then do not give Guillaume cause to laugh at you,' she said as patiently as she was able. 'If you can think of nothing wise to say, then be silent. If you cannot win at quintain or at chess, then you can at least be courteous and civil.'

François rose and went to the window, slouching against the sill. 'I wish Toby was back,' he said miserably. Outside, the sky was cloudy and dull. 'He was teaching me tennis. He said that I was getting quite good at it.'

Eleanor felt for a moment a terrible pity for François. If he had been someone else's son, then he might have been quite content in his mediocrity. As it was, he was Reynaud du Chantonnay's son, and he carried all the burden of that name, and of this great house and lands, on his unsuitable shoulders.

'Monsieur Crow will be gone for a few months,' said Eleanor, attempting to provide some comfort. 'But I'm sure that when he returns he'll play tennis with you again, François.'

She remembered standing at Reynaud's bedchamber window looking out into the garden where François and Toby Crow had played tennis. She realized that she had felt happy then, a wild, fragile sort of joy that had carried her through the remainder of the summer, making the season somehow more precious to her than all the ten dreary summers before. Now, looking out of the window of the sewing-room, she could see only the kitchen garden at the back of the house, fading and gone to seed with the change of season.

'You like him, *maman*, don't you?' said François suddenly.

It was then that Eleanor felt her skin start to redden, the hand caressing the sleeping squirrel in her lap start to shake. But when she looked up at her stepson's face, there was no guile there, only a naked hero-worship that brought her almost to the point of tears. She heard herself say, 'Yes, François, I like him very much.' She knew at once that she spoke the truth, and she knew also the terrible danger and terrible beauty of such an admission. As if Reynaud himself were in the room, and not just her besotted stepson and a sleeping squirrel, Eleanor added hastily: 'He's an honest servant. Monsieur Crow is intelligent, reliable – we should value such servants, François.'

'He showed me how to load an arquebus.' François's voice was excited, his pale eyes gleamed. 'Meraud wouldn't let me.'

She wanted him to go, so that she could have a few moments to herself before rushing to the kitchen and supervising the final preparations for the night's banquet. She wanted to be alone and to recall every time she had seen Toby Crow, from the afternoon that she had thanked him for saving her stepson's life to the morning, just a few weeks ago, when he had ridden out of Marigny and back to Italy. But she saw love in François's eyes, too. A love that, though it might be different in quality from her own, was every bit as painful, every bit as burdened with possibilities of desertion and disillusion.

'Monsieur Crow will return to Marigny in the winter,' she said, rising, the squirrel still cradled in her arms. 'And now let's put this poor creature back in his cage and then decide what you are to wear tonight, François. We'll make you look so grand that even Cousin Guillaume will feel plain in comparison.'

In the early autumn, Isotta died. Taddeo wrote to Gaetano; a few days later a letter arrived for Joanna from Lena, Taddeo's cook, who had paid a scribe to write for her. Gaetano opened the letter first and then tossed it into Joanna's lap after scanning the contents.

'I don't know why this servant writes to you. After all, Taddeo's letter told us everything of interest.'

She went out to the garden to read the letter alone. The air was cold and damp; red and gold leaves fluttered to the ground, covering the flowers. When she felt well enough, which was not often, Joanna would collect and burn the dry leaves, warming her hands over the small bonfire. Now, she sat down on the bench, her shawl wrapped around her.

The letter, a single half-page, told Joanna that Lena had followed Joanna's medical instructions carefully and that Isotta had suffered very little pain at the end. Isotta herself had told Lena that all her jewels – those she had brought to her marriage in her dowry – were to go to Joanna. Lena looked forward to seeing Joanna when she came to Venice for the funeral. The letter was signed with a single, wobbling cross.

Joanna folded the letter carefully and replaced it in her pocket. Threading her hands together in her lap, she let her gaze wander over the chill, dying garden.

She had cried for Isotta already, when Taddeo's letter had arrived. Not for the manner of Isotta's death, but for the waste of her life. Isotta had possessed the ability to love, and yet that ability had been denied a focus, until she, Joanna, who was not even Isotta's blood-relative, had turned up on her doorstep.

Joanna's threaded hands rested on the small swelling of her belly. Would she love this child, Gaetano's child? Even though it had begun to move inside her, it did not yet seem like a living creature, a baby that she would hold in her arms in only a few months' time. Now, it was only something that made her sick, that made her constantly tired, that took away from her even the desire to go outdoors and walk or ride.

She would not go to Venice for Isotta Zulian's funeral, because both Gaetano and Caterina had said that it was not proper for a woman in her condition to be seen in public. She had not argued with them, she had not pointed out that the baby was still so small that no one but herself and Gaetano need know of its existence. She had neither the strength to argue nor the inclination. Her feet and hands swelled whenever she climbed the stairs; she slept late into the morning, and most of the afternoon as well. She knew, when she had the strength to think about it, that this pregnancy was not going well for her. Perhaps Caterina was right: perhaps she was too young to bear a healthy child. Gaetano himself laughed at her now, saying she had become a proper Paduan matron, with her thickening waist and pallid face.

Joanna's eyes began to close, sitting there on the bench. Nannina found her later, huddled in her shawl, hands white with cold. Clucking, she led her into the house.

•

CHAPTER FIVE

Black African slaves, two to an equally black gondola, rowed the guests of Messer Marcantonio Venier through a fog as dark as hell. By the Grand Canal the brothers of the Scuola di San Giovanni Evangelista paraded through the city carrying a cross and lighted candles. Each candle was circled with a corona of amber-coloured light.

'They used to whip themselves,' whispered the painter Arlotto Attavanti. 'You know, knotted scourges and naked shoulders. That sort of thing.'

Arlotto's curly hair was beaded with fog, his eyes gleamed. In the dark autumn night the flares on the walls of the houses sketched the features of his companion: the hooded eyes, the damp black hair slightly curled by the swirling fog, the trace of a smile hovering at the corners of the long mouth.

Toby Crow said, 'Not really to my taste. Sorry, Arlotto.' He had been in Venice for more than a month now. He had ridden across Touraine, through Burgundy, and over the Alps into Italy. He had been accompanied by a handful of armed men and by a new and disturbing ambivalence towards Marigny. He had seen at first hand the sort of cruelty, the sort of greed necessary to the acquisition of an estate like Marigny. He had glimpsed the skull beneath the skin.

In Venice, working off his renewed restlessness, Toby had collected glassware, paintings and sculpture. The larger items had already begun their journey back to Marigny, carefully packed in straw and sackcloth, and accompanied by Reynaud du Chantonnay's armed retainers. Toby himself had intended to leave Venice a week ago, escorting the treasure-filled barge on its journey down the Po. But then Pasquale Gennari, Marcantonio Venier's uxorious secretary, had given him his invitation to this evening's banquet. 'There's something you might like, Messer Crow,' he had said. 'Something special.'

Nothing more. His curiosity aroused, Toby had stayed, although he would risk bad weather crossing the Alps and Reynaud du Chantonnay's wrath. He had bills and invoices, signed and sealed, in duplicate, detailing every one of his Venetian purchases. He had spent what the Seigneur de Marigny had permitted him to spend, and not a zecchino more. Yet.

The gondola had reached the entrance of the Ca' Venier. In the courtyard the bay trees and rose bushes were covered with a fine filigree of mist, and the tiny transparent pearls of water were painted gold, turquoise and rose by the flares. The dampness had soaked through Toby's shirt to his skin. On the walls of the courtyard Poseidon and his sea nymphs cavorted in painted seas beneath painted skies bordered by shells and corals. It was as though they swam in some strange, dark undersea world, their movements slowed and indistinct.

But inside the palazzo, the brightness, noise and colour hit Toby with almost physical force. His gaze was dragged to the windows glazed with coats of arms and mythological scenes, then to the doors of intarsia and the walls hung with crimson damask. To the statues clustered coyly in their alcoves, to the tapestries swaying on the walls, their gold thread shimmering in the flickering torchlight. Columns of jade-green jasper, rising from the tiled floor like great frozen trees, supported ceilings of painted panels. In the panels Toby read the story of Zeus and Danaë: the cloud in which Zeus hid himself was, Toby knew, real gold.

Dining in the vast banqueting-chamber, they ate truffles from Friuli, quails from Lombardy and tiny thrushes from the Romagna. Crabs curled their terracotta claws on silver platters; oysters gleamed grey and blue and opalescent in the candlelight. Between courses, the guests of Messer Marcantonio Venier washed their hands in scented water and dried them on napkins of embroidered damask. The napkins were folded into pyramids, turbans, galleons. The plates were of majolica, the toothpicks gold, and the glittering glassware rivalled the jewellery of the guests for brilliance. Along the sides of the dining-chamber, coloured fish – blue and green and crimson – swam in ornamental tanks. In the centre of the table the branches of an orange tree were hung with gilded baskets crammed with sweetmeats and ornamental fruits. Tied by ribbons to the orange tree were a starling, a thrush and a trembling leveret.

'It's all show, you know,' whispered Arlotto loudly, through a mouthful of vanilla tart. 'Messer Venier is embarrassingly short of cash. Hasn't a ducat.' Arlotto emptied the contents of a bowl of plum jelly on top of the tart. 'As soon as Messer Venier buys something new, he has to sell something. I should think this banquet will cost him a tapestry or two.'

One of the birds attached to the orange tree had entangled a foot in its tether. The gentleman to the other side of Toby said: 'Messer Venier should consider, perhaps, whether such show' – he gestured disdainfully at the sparkling tableware, the equally sparkling dinner guests – 'is entirely appropriate at such a time.'

Arlotto scooped up the last spoonful of jelly. 'Times are no better – and no worse – than they've always been, Messer Giustinian.'

Giustinian had severely cut shoulder-length black hair and a small black beard and moustache. 'Venice's downfall will be her extravagance, her immorality. Have you seen the paintings in the mezzanine of this house?' His sallow face creased in an expression of distaste. '*The Rape of Europa*, complete in every detail.'

Arlotto, leaning back in his chair, flicked some jelly from the front of his doublet. 'I thought them rather fine, Messer Giustinian. Though Europa was distinctly plump.'

'You mock me, Arlotto Attavanti.'

A gentleman seated opposite said soothingly, 'I'm sure that no insult was intended, Antonio. Messer Attavanti speaks as an artist, that's all.'

Arlotto beamed. 'You are correct, Messer Gritti. No insult intended at all. And, after all, female beauty is a matter of taste, don't you agree?'

Gritti smiled. His was a name that Toby recognized: Andrea Gritti, a tall, handsome man in his early fifties, was a diplomat and a soldier. A servant of Venice since his youth, he was now Proveditor of the town of Treviso. In the course of a dazzling career, he was reputed to have fathered three bastards while on a diplomatic mission in Turkey.

Antonio Giustinian had turned to Toby. 'You are a Frenchman, I believe, Messer Crow. Tell me – can you be confident of your country's continuing friendship with Venice?'

In France, Louis XII waited, hungry for Italian treasures. Slowly Toby shook his head.

Giustinian's contemptuous gaze momentarily focused on Toby, and then swept the length of the table. 'Look at them all,' he hissed. 'Look at the patrician ladies who display their bodies like street-women, at the young men who wear jewels in their hair and perfume on their skin. Shall Venice be made safe by such as these? I don't believe so. God himself will punish us.'

On the far side of the table Andrea Gritti smiled briefly. 'We need not wait for God, Antonio. The Pope will do His work. With the assistance of the Emperor Maximilian, doubtless. And' – Gritti nodded his head in Toby's direction – 'the king of France, I suspect.'

Arlotto took a handful of crystallized fruit from a silver bowl. 'Venice is impregnable, Messer Gritti,' he said lazily. 'Always has been. Even Pope Julius cannot walk on water.'

Several people laughed.

Antonio Giustinian said angrily, 'You blaspheme, Arlotto Attavanti! You should consider your own part in our city's shame – you, too, paint jewelled whores, powdered youths.'

'I paint,' said Arlotto, calmly stoning a crystallized damson, 'what I see.'

There was a silence. In the centre of the table the tethered starling lay exhausted on the polished wood, its small breast fluttering rapidly in and out, its foot still entangled in the length of pink ribbon.

People had begun to rise from the table, to drift away towards the sounds of music and dancing. Toby watched them go. He saw that only Andrea Gritti remained seated at the table. He said softly: 'And the terra firma, Messer Gritti? Is the terra firma also impregnable? I have heard that Venice has fortified only the outermost mainland cities. That Verona, Vicenza, Padua, will fall at the first cannon-shot.'

At first, the Venetian did not answer. His eyes met Toby's, and finally he said: 'Messer Giustinian – and many other members of the Council of Ten – would say to you that there may be sacrifices. Necessary sacrifices, of course. To save Venice.'

Toby saw suddenly how it would happen. The cities of the terra firma would fall like a poorly balanced house of cards one after the other. It would need just one resounding defeat, and then the armies of the French king and the Pope from the west, and the Emperor from the east, would overrun the Veneto. The waste of it, the folly of it, made him angry.

'A short-sighted policy, surely, Messer Gritti? How long can Venice survive without the mainland cities? How long can she feed herself?'

The Venetian rose from the table. Andrea Gritti's gesture took in the soiled dining-table, the scattered plates and wine-stained goblets. 'Whilst I would not agree with all of Antonio's sentiments, there is sense in much of what he says. We should be readying our armies for the inevitable. We should be laying up stocks of grain. But we are not, Messer Crow, we are not. And why?' He shook his head sadly. 'Because my countrymen believe that Venice is invincible.'

'Nowhere – no one – is invincible.' The chatter of the guests, the music and the rhythms of the dancing, were no longer audible, but were shut away behind closed, distant doors. The splendid palazzo of Messer Venier had become silent, waiting for a changed, uncertain future.

Gritti looked up at Toby. 'I tell you this despite your nationality, Messer Crow. Venice's unpreparedness, Venice's arrogance, is common knowledge amongst our enemies. Pope Julius will punish us for our arrogance.'

Toby stood up. He saw the inevitability of war; he was aware, suddenly, of an urge to take part in it again. War was simple. You chose your side, you lived or died. Its squalor was blatant, unhidden. The lovely château de Marigny hid a different sort of squalor: one composed of secrets, of hypocrisy and lies.

He took a deep breath. 'Before I was a rich man's servant, Messer Gritti, I was a soldier of fortune. As a soldier, I see now that Venice is unprepared – complacent. You should be arming your mainland cities. Venetian patricians and their sons should be preparing for war. Instead . . . instead, they are dancing.'

Again, that sad, attractive smile, a smile of complicity and understanding and hopelessness. The Venetian said simply, 'I know. A tragedy, don't you think?'

Gritti opened the wide double-doors of the banqueting-chamber. 'You should consider returning to your former trade, perhaps, Messer Crow. Mercenary soldiers will soon be in great demand.'

The doors closed behind him. Gritti's last words echoed among the scattered debris of the banquet. Eventually, Toby leaned across the table and cut with his knife the ribbon that bound the starling's foot to the orange tree. But the creature was dead, it lay limp in his hand, its fragile body already cold.

Toby did not immediately return to the other guests and Venetian complacency, Venetian guilt. Instead he walked alone through the mezzanine storey of the house, looking for air. Finding a balcony, he paused for a moment, gazing out at the night. Venice, that great, unconquerable city, suddenly seemed so small, so fragile. She was nothing more than a feeble harbour perched at the head of a mighty sea, waiting for the waves that would soon sweep over her. And those waves would come, Toby knew that now.

He heard a footfall behind him, and turned. Pasquale Gennari, secretary to Messer Venier, stood beside him. Pasquale's sardonic face was twisted into a grin. 'Are you admiring the scenery, Messer Crow? Come, I'll show you something far more pleasing to look at.'

More stairs, more rooms glittering with gilt and jewels, crammed with chairs, prie-dieus, majolica tables. Toby found himself in the anteroom to Messer Venier's bedchamber.

'Look,' whispered Pasquale Gennari. 'I'm sure Messer Venier will sell. If the price is high enough.'

Toby was looking up at the painting on the wall. 'Judith,' said Pasquale, beside him, but he had known that already, of course. Judith, who had slain Holofernes. But Judith's face was already known to Toby. The woman that gripped the knife in one hand and the severed head in the other was not some ancient biblical heroine. Joanna Zulian, niece of the painter Taddeo Zulian, looked proudly down from the canvas.

'She's superb,' he said at last.

He did not know whether he referred to the woman he saw in the painting or to the girl he had a year ago helped from the canal outside this house. Joanna Zulian's black gown had streamed with water, her hair had stuck to her face and shoulders. The woman in the painting was clad in only a length of bronze silk. Suddenly he felt desire: for the half-naked woman in the painting, for the damp naiad of his memories. He saw the swell of her breasts, her narrow waist, her smooth skin. Her long red-brown hair was threaded with pearls; he had stroked that hair, he had felt it soft and wet and fine beneath his palm. Her face was exquisite, its sculptured, delicate features supported by the narrow column of her neck. But her eyes, those great grey eyes were not as Toby remembered them. Helping her from the canal, he had seen a sort of despair and longing in those eyes blurred first by water, then by tears. But there was nothing in the painted woman's eyes, nothing at all. Her eyes were empty and numbed. He thought it was a failure of the painter at first, and then he knew, instinctively, that it was not.

'Eight hundred ducats,' murmured Pasquale. 'Popular opinion is that it's Gaetano Cavazza's best work. Cavazza is Taddeo Zulian's brother-in-law – he married the niece a year ago. She's pregnant, living in Padua. Did Arlotto tell you?'

Toby shook his head. He remembered Gaetano Cavazza, of course: pompous, possessive, talented Gaetano. And he thought again of Joanna

Zulian shivering with cold and distress, the dead kitten cradled in her lap. An ill-assorted pair, surely.

Pasquale added, 'If you have money – a great deal of money, that is, Messer Crow – you may purchase something else, too. Information.' The secretary's eyes gleamed. 'The Council of Ten are such gossips.'

Of course he had money. Reynaud du Chantonnay's money, safely hoarded in Venetian banks. He also had a promissory note bearing the Seigneur de Marigny's signature. He contemplated withdrawing more than eight hundred ducats tomorrow on Reynaud's behalf for a painting Reynaud had not commissioned, and he felt not the slightest qualm.

Toby's eyes had not yet left the picture. He heard Pasquale say, 'Venice has refused to surrender Messer Bentivoglio and his followers to the Papacy. Julius, it seems, is not pleased. I should make your purchase and return to France quickly, Messer Crow. The terra firma – Italy – will not be a safe place to travel through soon.' The secretary's face was blank. He added: 'The Pope has sent emissaries, Messer Crow, to France, to Spain, to the Empire, the Netherlands, Hungary and Milan. Julius proposes that Christendom shall ally itself against the Venetian Republic, and having done so, it shall dismember her piece by piece.'

The pain woke Joanna one morning in January – a dull, rhythmical ache in the small of her back that stopped her sleeping. She did not realize what it was at first. But she was aware, lying there in the darkness, that something had changed, something was different. Gaetano, however, lying beside her, still snored, and the house was silent.

Careful not to wake her husband, Joanna rose from the bed. It was cold, she was glad of the shawl that she had draped across her shoulders. Her movements had grown clumsy now, her body distorted, but she managed to walk silently over to the window and open the shutter an inch. The garden below was covered in a thin blanket of white. The snow that had fallen in the night hid all the small struggling plants that she had nurtured so carefully and weighed down the leaves of the evergreens. Tiny snowflakes still whirled from the heavy white sky.

Joanna's hands rested on her swollen belly. She noticed that as the pain in her back came and went, so her stomach clenched and became hard. She understood then what was happening to her. She knew that it was too soon, far too soon. Two whole months too soon.

She went back to bed, hoping that if she just lay still the pain would cease. Instead it grew relentlessly more intense. It hurt to move, it hurt to lie still. The light that issued through the shutters was yellow and baleful; fixing her eyes on those slats of orange light, Joanna tried not to panic. She wanted this baby. She wanted to hold it, small and warm and soft, she wanted it to look at her, only her, and smile. She wanted someone to love. Too soon, she thought, digging her nails into her palms, too soon.

Eventually she moaned aloud and woke Gaetano. When he realized that Joanna was in labour, he roared for his sisters. Caterina and Nannina came running, still clad in beribboned nightgowns, hair in long stringy plaits down their backs. Nannina fussed. Caterina pointed out, loudly, that the baby was coming far too early. Eventually Gaetano, losing his temper with both his sisters, sent a servant for the midwife and escaped to his workshop.

Joanna lost track of time and place. As the pain increased in intensity, so her fears for the future, even her longing for her child, diminished. The only thing of any importance was to survive the moment. To remain herself, Joanna Zulian; to remain in one piece and not be torn in two by the terrible, crushing waves of pain. In her mind's eye the bedchamber was transformed into the narrow confines of a tent, so that only the darting snowflakes were visible through the parted canvas. The snowflakes became stars, dancing their endless dance in a featureless sky. She thought that her baby had been born and had died, and she had not even tears left to mourn him. She heard voices in the darkness: Nannina's voice, the midwife's voice, Sanchia's voice. Sometimes they whispered, sometimes they boomed like voices in a cave.

Paolo was born in the evening, as the bell of the church of the Carmine chimed the seventh hour. The midwife dragged the infant from his mother, his body still covered in the slippery caul. Joanna could not speak, could not move her arms to take her baby.

The midwife's voice, unnaturally loud, cried to Nannina, 'Poor thing! She's not much more than a child herself.'

They propped her up on pillows, and placed the infant in the crook of her arm. Her thoughts were slow, confused, in some half-world between sleeping and waking.

Nannina's voice echoed with the midwife's. 'A boy! Gaetano will be so pleased!'

She could feel the weight of the baby, warm against her arm. Focusing momentarily on the shutters, Joanna knew from the heavy silence that surrounded the house that the snow still fell. She managed to turn her head at last, to look at her baby's face. She began to cry then, slow tears that trickled down her tired cheeks. She had not cried throughout her long, painful labour. And yet she could not help but weep now, looking at her tiny seven-month son. She had simply never seen anything so beautiful. His head was crowned with small whorls of black hair, his eyes were dark and almond-shaped. One open hand, star-shaped, waved aimlessly.

As Gaetano and Caterina came into the room, Nannina said, 'There, there, my dear, he's breathing well enough. And Gaetano will find a good wet-nurse for him.'

But the last words she heard before she drifted into sleep came from Caterina. 'A seven-month child! It won't last the week, Gaetano.'

Toby's journey from Venice to France was particularly tiresome: because of the foul weather, because of the awkwardness and value of the cargo he carried, because of the soldiers of fortune that were gradually but inexorably finding their way into the Italian mainland, swords in hand.

He had travelled by water as far as possible, taking passage in a barge sailing along the River Po to Alessandria. He did not catch up with the barge he had earlier sent under the guard of Reynaud du Chantonnay's soldiers. It was mid-winter by the time he reached Alessandria, the weather far too bad to risk crossing the Alps. So he rode to Genoa and sailed on a caravel through choppy grey seas, clinging to the coast as far as the Gulf of Lyons. From Marseilles he rode north, and into the worst winter he had ever known.

The snow had reduced France to monochrome, rubbing out all colour of field and village, altering a landscape that he knew well into an unfamiliar sketch of black and white. His journey became a matter of survival, no longer a race to reach the valley of the Loire in the shortest possible time. Brigands, unemployed mercenary soldiers, were no longer his greatest threat. He struggled against something much greater, much stronger than feeble humanity. The cold that ate into his reserves, that froze the animals in the fields, that made the earth like iron.

On Twelfth Night he took shelter in a great lord's house, and watched mummers and jesters and lutenists, and ate boar's head and roast goose. Later, he was forced by the strength of the blizzards to remain shut up in a village for a week. Once he found himself curled in a corner of someone's barn, kept from death by only the warmth of his horse's flanks and a swarm of seething, foul-smelling hogs.

He saw the casualties of winter as he made his slow, careful way north: the beggars, the children, the old; the birds that froze to their branches like stuffed creatures in a taxidermist's workshop. He gave some of Reynaud du Chantonnay's gold to a farmer whose granary was empty; he buried a mother and her newborn baby, frozen like the birds, beneath flat stones on the banks of the Rhône.

He hid the Seigneur de Marigny's treasures beneath straw on a cart, or in a barge full of manure. Lost, he walked with a herdsman and his gaggle of squawking geese until they found the wintry river again. He changed guises several times, to conform with the allegiances of the villages he travelled through. He was soldier, farmer or scholar as it suited him, but never a rich man's courier carrying a king's ransom in Venetian glass and one superb oil-painting.

He had to fight his way out of a scuffle in a tavern in Avignon; he was obliged to slit the throat of the gentleman he discovered one night, his pockets crammed with gold, standing over him, a dagger in hand. He caught a bellyache from some shellfish he ate in Lyons; vomited for three days and three nights, and then slept for as long. But not before he had hidden the glass in a blanket and the canvas beneath his mattress.

Cutting across country, he attached himself to a group of silk-weavers bound for Chinon. The snow thickened as he rode into the town, smearing the turrets and the ramparts of the castle with a yellow haze. On the bridge that spanned the Vienne, the flags were frozen to their poles; ice crusted the small inlets at the edge of the river. The canvas was hidden in the roll of blankets and matting tied to the back of Toby's saddle, the glassware wrapped in linen and buried in wadding in his saddlebags. Between the layers of material in his doublet were letters: letters from the knowledgeable gentlemen of the Ca' d'Oro, letters detailing the deliberations of the Great Council of Venice.

He ate in a tavern on the Grand Carroi. His saddlebags were at his side. He watched the dice-players in the corner of the tavern cast their lots, and he knew that for him Gaetano Cavazza's painting was his greatest gamble. If Reynaud resented his courier's presumption in buying an uncommissioned picture, then Toby would find himself thrown out of Marigny, once again without work or position. But if Reynaud could see what Toby himself had seen in that lovely, violent figure, then his every ambition might eventually be satisfied. Only it was ironic, he thought with a small smile, that he had recently begun to question that ambition, to wonder whether a small part of Marigny was all that he truly wanted.

What he did need, he thought, as the snow on his shoulders began to melt and drip into small puddles on the floor, was to satisfy his curiosity. What he needed was to *know*. To know whether Reynaud du Chantonnay was his father and why, if so, he had apprenticed his bastard son to the shoemaker of Chinon. To know whether Pernet Lescot had, two and a half years ago, lied to him.

Toby recalled the shoemaker only a hundred yards or so up the street, and he thought, One last time. He would see the shoemaker and question him just once more. There might be something, some small detail, that the shoemaker had neglected to tell him. He rose, gathered up his saddlebags and shook the runnels of water from his cloak. His body ached with weariness from the long journey; he did not think he would ever feel warm again. He wondered, as he walked out of the tavern door, whether this time Pernet Lescot would tell him different lies.

And of course, there was another reason to return to his former employer: his own voice, echoing through the years, saying to Pernet Lescot's latest apprentice, *Tell your master, when he is sober, that I will be back*. And yet he had not since returned to Chinon. Marigny, ambition, curiosity, had all prevented him.

His unease began when he reached the courtyard off the Rue Haute Saint-Maurice. Steam issued from the laundry, clouding the air, making hollows in the snow. But there was no candlelight to be glimpsed behind the unglazed window of the cobbler's workshop; only the light from the laundry jewelled the ice crystals so that they glowed pink and amber and jade-green.

Toby swung off his horse and looped the reins round the hitching-post. Trying the shoemaker's door, he found that it was locked. When he peered through the window, he could see a thin layer of dust over the cut pieces of leather, the tools and lasts. In the fireplace was a mess of blackened ashes; the bellows hung unused on a hook on the wall. He called the shoemaker's name, and his own voice echoed back, mocking him.

Toby became aware once more of the cold, of the snow that found its way beneath his collar and round the cuffs of his gloves. Leaving the shoemaker's, he rapped on the door of the laundry.

A man he did not recognize opened the door, and Toby said, his throat dry, 'The shoemaker, Pernet Lescot, is he ill? Or drunk?'

The man stared at him for a moment, then spat on the ground. 'Not unless they grow grapes in hell.' He laughed at his own joke.

It seemed to take Toby an age to ask his next question. 'He's dead, then?'

The laundryman nodded. Steam billowed out of the open doorway of the laundry, burning Toby's face. 'Hanged a fortnight past. Good riddance I'd say – except the soles are coming off my boots.'

The man turned to go. Toby's hand enclosed his elbow, halting him. 'Why? Why did they hang him?'

He guessed the answer before the other man spoke. The laundryman's words rebounded in the courtyard and were robbed of resonance by the snow. There must have been murder in Toby's face then, because the laundryman started to pull away, to hold out his hands, palms upwards, in a gesture of placation. Toby did not let him go, though. Not until he had the whole story. And then his clenched fists slipped from the man's filthy jerkin and he walked back to his mare and led her through the snow-filled streets of Chinon.

Lescot locked his apprentice in the wood-shed at the back of the workshop. They found him there a frozen corpse. They said the lad had been eating wood, drinking snow.

Toby was not conscious of riding out through the gates of Chinon, of crossing the bridge, of taking the road that led in the direction of Marigny. He saw only a small boy, whose eyes were sometimes a bright, clear blue, and sometimes his own dark slate-grey. He heard only his own voice saying, *Tell your master that I will be back.*

And yet he had not gone back soon enough. He had not gone back because he had spent the last few years like the carrion crow his namesake, picking at a rich man's well-fed bones. He had tried to erase the memory of his earliest years, to lose the odour of poverty and brutality in the château de Marigny's scented halls. But you never could shake off that stench: it clung to you, it seeped through your skin for the rest of your days.

Toby's hands were knotted to his reins in anger; his horse flicked its head and whinnied in protest. The path ahead of him had closed in, palisaded by the trees, the dark, the snow. The sky was a thick amber-grey, the horizon lost in tumbling, clotted flakes. He should have stayed in Chinon, he should have looked for a tavern, but Toby knew himself to be incapable of even the limited civility that asking for a room would entail. The silence of the snowy landscape was complete; he did not think his temper could bear the aimless chatter of his fellow-men.

He realized that he had been careless when he heard the horses' hooves muffled by the snow, and the jangle of harness and bridle. He had been watchful throughout all the long weeks since he had set out from Venice, but tonight, distracted by anger, he had let slip his guard. Automatically, Toby checked the security of the painting and the glass. Then he swung the mare round, his sword in his hand, his eyes narrowed in the gathering darkness.

Three riders barred the path behind him. The metal of swords and knives gleamed dully in the twilight. The riders' faces were darkened by the peaks of their helmets and the heavy shadows of the snow-laden trees. Three fine Spanish swords were pointed at Toby, three equally fine horses circled round him, dislodging the snow from the branches so that it tumbled, a haze of white powder, to the ground.

A rational man would have thrown his remaining gold to the ground, put his spurs to his horse's flanks and ridden for his life. But Toby had left rationality in Chinon, and besides, he wanted to kill.

He heard his voice break the silence as he rode for the first of them. The clash of steel on steel, clouds of snow rising around the horses' hooves. He had forgotten nothing from his years as a soldier, he had not lost an ounce of strength from his right arm. He felt a rush of the old, familiar joy as his sword glanced off his adversary's shoulder and drops of dark red blood pitted the snow. He was smiling.

He fought well, better perhaps than he had ever fought before, but there were three of them, and they were good. Eventually they knocked him from his horse. But he struggled still, though he had lost his sword. He used his fists and feet, but he knew that fists and feet would be useless against the sword-blade that would soon sweep towards his heart. He did not want to die, but he was aware, through a red haze of anger and pain, that there was a sort of justice in it.

The sword-thrust never came, though. Instead, they sheathed their weapons and, like him, used their fists. They hit him until he stopped fighting and lay curled on the snow, choking for air. Then they hauled him to his feet and threw him over someone's horse, and rode away through the night.

There was a fire, the flames dancing scarlet and orange, violet and pink, near the heart where the logs crackled and glowed and spat. The floor of the room was tiled, the wood of the furniture dark, cushioned with rich velvet.

Toby drifted in and out of consciousness. There had been the forest, a pathway, a door, the falling snow. Then, later, the inside of a house. He thought, confused for a moment, that he was at Marigny. He glimpsed tapestries, a carved wooden staircase, and candles bright yellow against the pitted stone walls. He was dragged through a succession of rooms, all warm, all richly furnished. And then he was standing, still shackled to two of his attackers, dripping snow on to someone's fine Turkey rug.

At first, Toby thought he was alone but for the two men beside him. But then a voice said, 'You enjoyed yourselves, then, gentlemen?'

The man still gripping Toby's arm muttered, 'He wanted a fight, my lord. So we gave him one.'

'So I see.' The speaker moved forward. Squinting, Toby could see, silhouetted in the firelight, a man who gave an impression of height, of wealth, of power. Like Reynaud, Toby thought, dazed. A hand reached out and tilted Toby's face to the firelight. 'I hope he can still speak, gentlemen.' The voice was soft and dry, the eyes that examined Toby's battered face were dark, blank and inhuman. Toby's clothes were soaked and clammy, still encrusted with dirty snow. He shivered.

The hand slipped from Toby's face, and the voice whispered, 'Can you speak, my pet? Can you take a message for me?'

Toby's lips were split and one of his teeth wobbled. He whispered, 'A message to whom?'

A wave of the hand, and the two guards were gone, leaving Toby in the room with the fire, and the tiles, and the velvet cushions. The gentleman said, 'To your employer, of course. To the Seigneur de Marigny.'

Toby's head jerked up; he forced his muscles not to judder. The other man's mouth had twisted into the smallest of smiles, but the eyes were still cold and reptilian.

'You are the Seigneur's messenger, are you not?' The cold gaze flickered once more over Toby, lingering on his torn, soaking clothes, his bruised face and hands. Again, that gentle, arid voice. 'There was no need to struggle, my pet – it was not necessary that I should return dear Reynaud damaged goods.'

Every bone in Toby's body ached, and it hurt to breathe. He knew that his mind was sluggish, numbed by the blows of several gauntleted fists. Yet there was still fear, and still an almost animal awareness of some threat worse than physical abuse. He felt as though he was seven years old again, the plaything of someone far greater, far more powerful than he.

The gentleman smiled once more. 'I have been waiting for your return, monsieur. I wished to speak to you because I have heard that your employer is ailing. And that he has but one doltish son.'

Those dark, empty eyes still held him. Toby thought of François: clumsy, foolish François, whom he had coaxed into a half-decent game of tennis last summer. He was tired, and he hurt, and he had no words to express the sudden loathing he felt for his nameless interviewer. Instead he spat, the ball of spittle landing neatly on the man's fur-edged robe.

The dark eyes did not even blink. But a hand reached up and grasped the bunched material of Toby's doublet, just below his throat. And the blade of a dagger suddenly lay cold against his cheek. 'Dear, dear. Such temper. It is fortunate that I am not hot-blooded also, or you would find yourself in a ditch, my pet, minus some of your body's more useful little appendages.'

Toby managed to whisper, while the tip of the dagger dug into his face, *'Who are you?'*

The dagger was drawn slowly downwards, searing Toby's skin. The gentleman said: 'My name is Hamon de Bohun.'

Toby's thoughts were slow, lumbering in their struggle to delve back into memory and find that name. But at last, echoing over the months, Guillaume du Chantonnay's voice whispered, *'You remember the Sieur de Bohun, don't you, Reynaud? He was a kinsman of your first wife.'*

De Bohun was about Reynaud's age. The dagger still caressed the curve of Toby's jaw, and he could see carved into this man's face every one of the Seigneur de Marigny's less endearing characteristics. Ruthlessness, cruelty, rapacity. And yet de Bohun possessed something that even Reynaud lacked. Something that made Toby's flesh crawl.

The dagger slid slowly back into its sheath, and Hamon de Bohun left Toby and walked over to the table. 'Your manners are poor, sir. One day I shall teach you better. But still, I can be patient. Now – the message.'

Toby looked up and saw that in front of de Bohun, rolled on the table but freed from its coverings, lay the painting he had brought back from Venice.

'Tell your master,' said Hamon de Bohun softly, 'that I have come to take what I am owed. Tell him that I will have this' – carefully he unrolled the picture – 'as a deposit. Yes. A deposit.'

Toby moved a few paces forward and stared down at the table. Two months earlier, he had seen that painting on the wall of a glittering Venetian palazzo. Judith, displaying Holofernes' severed head, stared up at Toby with Joanna Zulian's serene grey eyes. And for the first time, Toby, glancing across, saw something in Hamon de Bohun's dark eyes. But he was not sure what.

Refusing Gaetano's offer of a wet-nurse, Joanna tended Paolo herself, dragging her aching body out of bed at all hours of the day and night. Her love for her baby altered everything. The anger, the terrible sense of confinement that her marriage had increasingly brought with it, retreated and became unimportant. Gaetano, Caterina and Nannina were nothing more than shadow-people: there was, for Joanna, only one person of any importance, and that was the small struggling scrap in the cradle.

Paolo transformed her life, giving her existence meaning and direction. The sort of tenderness that had enabled her to coax green shoots from the raw earth, or flowers from tints and canvas, was magnified tenfold and devoted to the care of the baby. When she held him, when he fed from her breast, then she was perfectly happy. Nothing else mattered.

Her happiness was tempered by anxiety, though. Caterina's words echoed always in her ears. *'A seven-month child. It won't last the week, Gaetano.'* Joanna stayed awake throughout Paolo's seventh night, her infant son curled in the crook of her arm, his tiny face warm against her breast. Throughout the hours of darkness, she watched the small flickerings of movement across his face and felt the quick rise and fall of his chest. She thought that if she slept, then he might die. He was still a part of her; her belief that her watchfulness could guarantee his existence was absolute.

Paolo survived his first week, and his second. He did not regain the weight he had lost after birth, though: his limbs seemed to Joanna's anxious eyes to grow slowly thinner. When she laid him in his cradle, he slept for hours at a time. He cried little and his requests for food became increasingly hesitant. A good baby, said the visiting neighbours, as they cooed at the peaceful child, and Joanna nodded and tried to believe them. Babies were supposed to sleep, she told herself, and Paolo slept more now because he had recovered from the ordeal of birth.

Still, she watched him at night. But often, increasingly exhausted herself, Joanna's heavy eyes would close, and she would wake later with a jolt at Paolo's feeble crowings, trembling with guilt and fear as she lifted him to her breast.

Sometimes, she would look at him as she bathed or fed him and his round blue eyes would open wide and meet hers. His gaze seemed to Joanna to contain infinite wisdom, infinite patience.

Afterwards, they threw Toby, none too gently, out of the door in the direction of his horse. He could not get in the saddle quick enough, his hands pulled at the mare's mouth in his anxiety to get away from that house, from that man. He rode through what remained of the night, through heavily falling snow, only stopping to swallow several mouthfuls of wine when he had put a few miles between himself and Hamon de Bohun.

The château de Marigny, frosted with snow, shimmered in the dying sunlight when Toby reached it the following afternoon. The snowstorm had abated: only a few puffy flakes drifted lazily through the cold air. The slender, darting turrets and pinnacles were dyed gold, indigo, ruby-red, in the setting sun: every reed that lined the moat was edged with a fringe of silvery ice. The frozen water reflected Toby's foreshortened figure as he rode across the drawbridge: it blurred, however, the cuts and bruises on his face. There was still that sense of peace, of sanctuary, in entering the safe, enclosing circle of those pale walls, in seeing those triumphant pennants, each one marked with the leopard and three crescent moons.

The marks inflicted by Hamon de Bohun's henchmen made the guard look twice before he called a greeting and opened the portcullis. Inside, reaching the stables, Toby slid from his saddle and stood for a moment, his forehead against the mare's flank, his eyes closed, trying to regain his breath. Only then was he able to unbuckle his saddle and pass it to the stable-lad, only then was he able to take the saddlebags, with their precious load of Venetian glass, from the horse's back.

In the Great Hall flames leaped up high into the mouth of the huge, carved fireplace. Toby stood there, his hands outstretched, steam rising from his soaking clothes. Incised into the stone over the fireplace were the leopard and the moons, and the motto of the du Chantonnays, *Garde ta foy*. Through a haze of anger and pain and exhaustion Toby said his farewells to Marigny. He had gambled and he had lost.

Reynaud du Chantonnay received him in the gallery with the unicorn tapestries. The bleak, noble eyes of the unicorn stared down at him, uncritical, unpitying. Reynaud was not alone: Guillaume du Chantonnay, exquisitely dressed in a pale blue satin doublet and lace-trimmed shirt, lounged against the window-sill. Reynaud was seated in a cross-legged chair. A box of sweetmeats lay on the table beside him: sugar dusted his hands and robes.

Guillaume du Chantonnay's gaze trailed slowly over Toby's dirty, ragged clothing and bruised face. Nodding an inadequate bow, it took Toby only one glance to see how rapidly the Seigneur de Marigny's condition had deteriorated in the six months of his absence. Reynaud's face was puffy, his eyes were two colourless pits in a pale mass of flesh, his hands dimpled at the knuckles. Reynaud's fat fingers scrabbled in the box for a piece of rose-coloured cotignac as he said, 'You are late, sir.'

Toby felt the embers of his temper, ignited so thoroughly the previous day, flicker. He kept his voice and features impassive, though, as he replied, 'The weather was poor.' It hurt to breathe, it hurt to speak. He still felt the imprint of boots on his ribs. Worse, he recalled that dry, caressing voice. *'There was no need to struggle, my pet.'*

Reynaud mumbled through a mouthful of cotignac, 'I had begun to think, Crow, that you had deserted me.'

Guillaume watched silently. A single ruby glittered in his ear, his long fingers waved his refusal of Reynaud's offer of sweetmeats.

'So what do you have for me, Crow?' Reynaud leaned forward in his chair. His eyes were buried deep in his flesh, and Toby could see anger in them, naked and scarcely restrained. 'I am expecting something wonderful, something marvelous, to compensate for your unreasonable absence.'

Toby opened his saddlebags. 'Some glass. Some letters.'

His lack of courtesy was deliberate. His mouth could not frame the words *votre seigneurie*. He would not spit at Reynaud du Chantonnay as he had spat at the Sieur de Bohun, but neither could he mouth the expected pleasantries or fawn to regain this man's approval. He placed the letters and the glassware on the large table by the window. Not a chip, not a scratch, marred the smooth coloured surfaces. Pink and amber and jade-green they glowed, like moonlight on snow.

Reynaud heaved himself out of the chair and caressed the goblets with his large, swollen hands. Toby could see the pleasure, the joy of possession on his face. He himself could take no pride in the artefacts arranged on the table. The price he had paid for them had been, in the end, too high. He wanted only his dismissal, so that he could sleep until his head and ribs stopped hurting, so that he could no longer see a child frozen to death amidst a pile of logs, or hear the voice of Hamon de Bohun whispering in his ear. But he could not leave yet. He had, after all, a message to give.

Reynaud du Chantonnay had broken the seals and was reading the letters. He looked up. 'You are, as I said, late, sir.' His voice was taut with anger, a plump white finger stabbed repeatedly at the papers before him. 'I have this information already, you see. My cousin Guillaume rode to Marigny this morning to tell me that the fate of Venice is already decided. To tell me that the death-warrant of Venice has been signed in Cambrai by Margaret of Austria, for her father, the Emperor Maximilian. And by Cardinal Georges d'Amboise, for Louis XII, Crow, the king of France.' Reynaud's clenched fist thumped the table.

Guillaume du Chantonnay still leaned against the sill, enjoying the scene. Now he said, carelessly, 'I quote from the Preamble to the Treaty of Cambrai, messieurs.' His light drawl echoed round the room. '"Thus we have found it not only well-advised and honourable, but even necessary, to summon all people to take their just revenge and so to extinguish, like a great fire, the insatiable rapacity of the Venetians and their thirst for power."' Guillaume smiled, his blue eyes bright. 'War, don't you think?'

Reynaud du Chantonnay hissed, 'Both Louis de France and the Emperor Maximilian have already ranged themselves with the Papacy against the Republic. Venice cannot stand against such a coalition. You have been too long travelling, Crow. You have dawdled. I shall lose money from the Venetian banks.' Reynaud swept the letters to the floor. 'These are useless – all useless. You have not earned what I pay you.'

Toby thought fleetingly of the ride from Venice to France, of the cold, of the misery that he had seen, of his own appalling overdue visit to Chinon. Again, he felt his grip on his temper begin to slip. He said softly, 'Then pay me no longer. Find another errand-boy. Find another fool to do what you cannot do.' He heard Reynaud's hiss of fury and, from behind him, Guillaume du Chantonnay's half-stifled chuckle of amusement.

'You are insolent, sir!' Reynaud, his face creased with fury, had stepped a few paces forwards, but he did not yet, like Hamon de Bohun, draw his dagger. 'You forget who you are.'

Toby wanted to say, *But I don't know who I am. You haven't told me.* He found that he was laughing, that he was unable to stop laughing. The flat of Reynaud's hand, hard against his face, brought him back to his senses. Through pain and anger and a longing for retribution Toby became aware that his own hand had reached for the hilt of his sword.

'Reynaud,' said Guillaume du Chantonnay lazily. 'The man has travelled far in foul conditions. He is exhausted – ill, perhaps. Let him go. Speak to him tomorrow, when he will be more civil.'

To draw his sword in this room would be fatal. Somehow Toby managed to drag his hand away from the steel. Reynaud had returned to his seat, and there was still that damned, damnable message.

Toby began to pull from the inside of his doublet the receipts, bills and notes of sale he had gathered in Venice. 'You've better reason for dismissing me than my poor manners and lack of speed. I'm afraid that I . . . mislaid . . . a painting.' He found the bill of sale from the Ca' Venier and placed it in Reynaud du Chantonnay's outstretched, sugary hands. 'It refers to a painting by the Paduan Gaetano Cavazza. A portrait of Judith and Holofernes. It was superb, magnificent. I paid eight hundred ducats for it. And I lost it somewhere between Chinon and Marigny.'

Reynaud's fingers clutched the paper. His fleshy skin had darkened with anger.

Guillaume said sharply, '*Lost* it? What do you mean, man?'

'Well . . .' Toby smiled with difficulty. 'It was taken from me. Forcibly. By an *acquaintance* of yours, my lord.'

Reynaud du Chantonnay was still staring at him. His fingers held a piece of cotignac suspended in mid-air.

Toby's voice was bland, careless. He found that he was, for the first time in weeks, enjoying himself. 'His name was Hamon de Bohun. He gave me a message for you, Seigneur. He said that he had heard that you were ailing, and that he had come to take what he was owed. And he took the painting, he said, as a deposit.'

It was never wise to be a bearer of bad news, particularly to someone like Reynaud du Chantonnay. Toby was spared the consequences of Reynaud's wrath by Guillaume, who shoved him out of the room and, kicking aside the scattered sweetmeat box and its colourful contents, reseated the purple-faced Reynaud in his chair. Reynaud yelled after Toby as he closed the door behind him, 'You'll go back to Venice tomorrow, Crow! You'll repay that money, every last sou of it. Or I'll see you hanged!'

Outside, with the sound of his employer's fury reduced to a whisper, Toby sat on the topmost stair and buried his head in his hands. His anger had dissipated; he recognized the utter futility of his display of temper and insolence. He did not know how long he sat there, hands threaded through his hair, his forehead on his knees, before he heard the sound of a footfall, the whisper of silk on stone steps. He raised his head and saw, half-hidden in the shadowed twist of the spiral staircase, Eleanor du Chantonnay. Her face was obscure in the poor light, black hollows emphasized her cheekbones and circled her deep brown eyes. He started to shuffle to his feet, but she stopped him with a gesture. Climbing a few steps, she touched his bruised face with her fingertips.

'Who did this to you?' Her voice trembled slightly. 'Did Reynaud?'

He was surprised at her disquiet. He had not thought her a squeamish woman. He tried to smile. 'Not Reynaud. It was a hard journey, madame, that's all.'

He watched her face. It was odd, he thought, how the embers of curiosity still flickered, even though he knew that he had gambled and lost everything. But he had begun to understand a little of Marigny's past: Blanche, fatherless and unmarried, in possession of the château and lands. Hamon de Bohun and Reynaud du Chantonnay, circling around her like vultures.

He added, 'It's not as bad as it looks, madame. I apologize for alarming you.'

'Alarming?' Instantly, Eleanor du Chantonnay's features became haughty and aloof. 'I've seen far worse, Monsieur Crow. I do not faint at the sight of blood.'

Toby managed to rise to his feet and nod his head in a bow. 'Then I apologize for a second time, madame. For misjudging you.'

Eleanor's attitude relaxed a little. 'It's of no consequence. I only meant, monsieur, to ask whether you would allow me to attempt some sort of treatment. No, you mustn't quibble. I'm an excellent physician. I take thorns from squirrels' paws. I treat Reynaud's hunting-dogs for the mange. I'm sure I can do something for a black eye and a cut lip.'

She gave him bread and soup and a bottle of good claret, then went to fetch water and ointment and clean rags. She dismissed the maidservant from the linen-room, and herself threw logs on the fire. Some of the tension of the past months slid away and Toby began to feel, for what seemed like the first time in ages, truly warm.

The wine warmed him too, taking the edge off his misery. He found that he enjoyed watching Eleanor du Chantonnay's long white hands crush the herbs into their infusion of water and rip the linen into suitably sized pieces. Toby began to relax at last, the echoes of his long journey and its aftermath started to fade into the distance.

She was, as she had said, a good physician. She dabbed with the cloth at his black eye, at his split lip, at the scratch that Hamon de Bohun's dagger had made along his jaw. The scented water soothed, the touch of her gentle fingers soothed even more.

When she had finished, he opened his eyes, but she had already turned away. Her voice was business-like, but still held that slight edge he had previously mistaken for distaste. 'I've done what I can for your poor face, monsieur. Is there more?'

His clothes had begun to dry at last; she helped him remove his doublet, now only slightly damp. She laid it across the back of a chair. 'This is fit only for the fire.' Her fingers smoothed out the tears across the back of the doublet and her dark eyes inspected the ripped sleeve. 'I'll find you something better.'

He was struggling to pull his shirt over his head. It hurt to raise his arms: when he took a deep breath, his lungs seemed to batter against his ribs. There was sweat on his forehead and on the back of his neck. He saw that Eleanor du Chantonnay was staring at him, at the great purple bruises that strung themselves across his chest. Her eyes were intense, narrowed: for a moment Toby almost thought he saw tears in them, but he knew that he must be mistaken.

'I'll mend,' he said cheerfully. 'Like you, I've seen worse.'

Eleanor said nothing. She took her rags and ointments again, and began to dab at his scarred ribs. Her skin, he noticed, as she bent her head, was smooth and pale. Her hair, hidden except for the two semi-circles visible beneath her head-dress, was the same dark colour as her eyes. The flames of the fire leaped up the chimney; the small room had become very warm.

Eleanor paused, straightening. Her hand did not leave him yet, however. Instead, her tapered fingers traced the scar that wound from his wrist to his elbow, the scar that the brigand's knife had made more than three years before.

'*That* was worse,' he said, looking up at her. 'I had a good physician for that one as well. Not so beautiful, though.' He hadn't meant to say that. It was the wine, it was his exhaustion, and the close, dreamy heat of the room.

But Eleanor du Chantonnay's long fingers did not leave him: instead, they followed the path of his arm, shoulder and neck upwards to his face. Then she bent her head, and kissed his forehead. And then, because he looked up at her again, she kissed his mouth. Very carefully, so as not to hurt. There was no other sound in the room than the crackling of the flames and her soft, quick breathing. Toby could see desperation in her eyes now, and fear. He stood up and his two thumbs wiped away the tears at the corners of her eyes.

She was tall for a woman, her head reaching above his shoulder. Her palms cupped his face, tilting his mouth towards hers. The tears were flowing steadily now, so he kissed them as they coursed down her smooth cheeks. And because her mouth trembled, he kissed that also. He no longer remembered Venice, his journey, Chinon. He knew only that there was an ache in him, a hunger: something that this sort of physical contact had always helped to dispel. The scent of her skin and the touch of those strong, confident fingers against his naked back were intoxicating. He forgot who she was, where they were. She was pliant, desperate, helping him to tear aside her heavy layers of winter clothing.

Voices called from the kitchen outside, footsteps pattered beyond the door. He felt her body stiffen, heard her gasp of fear as she pulled away from him. He felt then as though someone had doused him in ice-cold water or thumped him in the stomach. Here he was, a nameless bastard servant of the Seigneur de Marigny, making love to the Seigneur's beautiful wife in the château de Marigny's linen-room. It was unreal. It was preposterous.

Outside, the rattle of pots and pans could be heard as the kitchen staff began to prepare the night's meal. Eleanor hurriedly tucked her hair back under her head-dress and straightened her dishevelled clothing.

And at last he could see clearly what he must do. The brief, intoxicating desire, the anger, the need for revenge, all left him. He saw Marigny for what it was: a prize for greed, for brutality, for strength. He saw his future for what it must become.

Pulling on his shirt, forcing his bruised arm into his tattered doublet, Toby said, 'I'm going back to Italy. Early tomorrow morning, I hope.'

Eleanor turned round. Two scarlet marks burned on her cheeks. She whispered, 'For Reynaud?'

Toby shook his head. 'No. Not to get his damned money from his damned banks. For myself. To fight.'

He saw the bleakness in her eyes, her quivering lips. He glimpsed, briefly, the terrible isolation in which she lived. He knew that he owed her some sort of explanation. He said, haltingly, 'I think . . . I think that whatever relationship I have had with the Seigneur de Marigny is finished now.'His ambiguity was intentional. He knew that Marigny was a dream, an illusion, that he had wasted years of his life searching for something unattainable. More gently he said, 'How could I stay here now, madame? How could I stay?'

She was past tears. She began to shake her head violently, to press her palms against the side of her white face. Her sudden lack of control disturbed him.

'But you'll come back?' Her hoarse voice cracked. 'You will come back?' Her eyes were black, distended, her fingers clawed clumsily at his sleeve.

He heard himself muttering uselessly, 'I don't know . . . if I can . . .' And then he picked up his saddlebags and left the room, closing the door behind him.

He had lied to her, though. He knew, as he walked fast through the kitchens, that he had lied to her. He had made his decision before he had so much as touched the Seigneur de Marigny's lonely wife, perhaps before he had even ridden back through the gates of the château. He had drifted for a short while into the glorious dream that was Marigny, but that dream was someone else's: he had no true part in it.

Joanna slept deeply and dreamlessly. When she woke, she noticed first the rim of sunlight around the shutters, and then the absence of sound, the stillness of the cradle. She realized that she had slept through the night, that Paolo's cries had not woken her. Her guilt was immense and complete. Leaning over the cradle, she whispered her son's name. He did not open his eyes. She touched his cheek. His flesh was already cold, tinged with blue: no longer a child, but something carved out of stone, like the marble amoretti that clustered round tombs in Venetian churchyards.

Someone was screaming. A thin, high wail that drowned all the other sounds of morning. Paolo was in her lap, she was kissing him, chafing his chill hands. Her head was bent over him, her eyes distended, willing his eyes to open. She became aware that there were other people in the room. A hand struck her face, and the screaming stopped. The silence was worse, though. Someone was trying to take her baby from her, but she held him to her breasts, rocking him, trying to warm his tiny body. Her aching breasts wept milk.

They had to prise her arms open to drag him from her. She tried to stop them taking him away, hitting Caterina with her fists, pulling Gaetano's hair, cursing the weeping Nannina. Caterina was wrapping her baby in one of his own small damask sheets, covering his face.

Eventually, they locked her into the bedchamber with the empty cradle. Her clenched fists beat the door until they bled. When no one came, she rocked herself, because there was no baby to rock, and crossed her arms over her swollen breasts.

Much later, Nannina came to the door with a tray. Joanna did not strike her, and had no tears left to cry. She let Nannina help her back into bed, because all will, all resolve, had left her. She could not eat, could not sleep. She closed her eyes and saw Paolo again wrapped in the white sheet.

The hours drifted into days, the days into weeks. They were all muddled, all meaningless. Soon, when she closed her eyes, there was nothing. Trying to picture her son, she found that she could no longer recall the shape of his eyes or the small, soft lines of his mouth.

CHAPTER SIX

At Marigny, they hunted the hare, the lecherous, bright-eyed hare. With hounds and dogs and fleet-footed horses they followed the direction that the signaller chose for them. The chime of the bells on the jesses of the hawks, the call of the hunting-horns and the greedy yelping of the dogs rang through the forest. Through the bright green leaves of spring that clothed the trees, their garments were a flicker of brave colour: crimson and azure and scarlet and emerald. The caparisons of the horses and the livery of the servants were embroidered with the insignia of the du Chantonnays, the motto, *Garde ta foy*, glittering in gold thread. A grey pony was glimpsed in the distance through the trees, for a tantalizing fraction of a second resembling the unicorn from Marigny's great tapestries.

The hare was not the only casualty of the hunt. That evening, six servants carried the Seigneur de Marigny back through wood and field, his great, still living, body borne on a stout wooden door. Reynaud was unconscious, his breathing thick and laboured, blood trailing from the wound at the back of his head. He had tried to jump the boundary wall, and his horse, overburdened by his weight, had stumbled.

They led Reynaud's black warhorse back to the château, following the inert body of its rider. A horse was supposed to weep on the death of its master, a demonstration of fidelity. Eleanor, looking down at her dying husband, could not find a single tear.

Rumours of war, rumours of Venice's last, desperate negotiations with the della Rovere Pope reached Padua, but were of no interest to the young wife of the painter Gaetano Cavazza.

After the birth and death of Paolo, it was two months before Joanna left her bedchamber. At first she had just sat in the withdrawing-room, a shawl wrapped by Nannina around her thin shoulders, eyes focusing on nothing. She had become what both Gaetano and Caterina had always desired her to be: a docile, passive, silent creature. When Caterina, irritated by her stillness, told her to sew, then she sewed – ragged, uneven stitches that Nannina later tactfully unpicked and remade herself. When Nannina begged her to eat, then Joanna ate. When they told her to comb her hair, then, with trembling, clumsy hands, she dragged a comb through the thick, tangled strands. And if they had requested that she hurl herself from the highest balcony to the square below, she would have done so.

Yet with the progression of the seasons from winter to spring to early summer, Joanna began, slowly, to recover. First, the recovery of the body, unwished for but inexorable. She was hungry at mealtimes now, she was no longer exhausted by the climb from the withdrawing-room to her bedchamber.

The recovery of the mind was slower. At first, she had wanted only blankness. To begin to think again, to understand, to remember, was unbearable. But eventually she found herself thinking not only about her baby and her marriage, but about her years in Venice. And about her life before Venice, travelling with Donato and Sanchia – the sights she had seen, the child she had once been. She knew then that something precious had been taken away from her. She had let herself consent to that loss, and in doing so had almost ceased to exist. Sometimes, waking alone in the early hours of the morning, she understood that she could not live like this, that something essential, something that was Joanna Zulian, was in danger of being destroyed for ever.

She had been unwell for months and, although the company of whores had satisfied his immediate physical needs, Gaetano had grown uncomfortably aware that his desire for Joanna, and only Joanna, had not lessened. He had been patient, a good husband. Many men, Gaetano told himself, would not have been so patient. He had slept apart from Joanna while she recovered from childbirth, and had continued to sleep apart from her after the death of the baby, during those weeks when she had lain in bed staring at the ceiling, scarcely speaking. He had buried his son, mourning him, knowing that there would be others to replace him, knowing that Joanna had been, as Caterina had said, too young.

But there would be no more sons unless they shared a bed again. Joanna was well now: she had begun to put on weight, and there was no longer that touch of unreason in her eyes that had earlier disturbed him. He knew that it was time that she accepted the duties of marriage again and took responsibility for the well-being of her husband.

Opening the door of her bedchamber, Gaetano focused on Joanna as she turned in the chair, hairbrush in hand. She had lost her looks, he thought: although Joanna Zulian would never be ordinary, she had lost that sparkle, the magnetism that had drawn him to her, half unwilling. Part of him hoped that she would never regain that magic, the part that recalled how other men had looked at her, had longed for her.

And yet he remembered so vividly the portrait, the *Judith and Holofernes*. Nothing he had painted since had touched that picture; he knew in his heart that it was Joanna herself who was in some way a catalyst for his art, that only Joanna was capable of transforming his talent and industry into greatness. He must paint her again, soon. As Diana, as Io, as Jael . . . As every classical or biblical beauty, as every heroine, every temptress. Painting her, he would release himself from the chains with which she had fettered him. Painting her, he mastered her.

Gaetano took the hairbrush from Joanna's hand and began to draw it through her long, russet locks. The ends of her hair reached past her waist; loose curls gathered round her forehead and clung to her high cheekbones. Her hair was like heavy silk. In his mind's eye Gaetano mixed the pigments to paint it: umber and lake and perhaps a touch of ochre. His hands were gentle, careful not to hurt her as he disentangled the knots. When he looked up, he could see in the darkened pane of glass opposite that her eyes were closed, the sockets shadowed, showing the bones beneath the skin.

He considered, for a moment, leaving her then, with that glorious curtain of hair spread all down her back, and the memory of the warmth of her skin still imprinted on his hands. He considered bending and kissing the crown of her head and leaving the room and waiting for her.

But he did not. Gaetano thought how his acquaintances would laugh at him if they knew that he had scarcely touched his wife for more than three months. He thought how they would mock him if they knew that he was afraid to touch this fragile, exquisite creature. And they would know if there were no more sons. He needed a son to replace the child that he had buried. He needed a son to train as an artist, to inherit the workshops in both Padua and Venice. If he did not have a son, then people would laugh at him as they laughed at Taddeo Zulian, taking him for a weak, impotent old fool.

He made his caresses more urgent, more particular. She did not move. When he looked up, he saw by Joanna's reflection that her eyes were open, but he could not tell her expression; her face was distorted by the uneven glass. She did not rise, so he lifted her out of the chair and laid her on the bed. She was light in his arms, reminding him of the child he had once danced with at the carnival in Venice. He did not look at her face until he was inside her. Pausing then, bending his head to kiss her, Gaetano saw that her eyes were like stones. Two grey stones. She focused on him at last and he saw not hatred, nor anger, but a terrible contempt. A contempt that was proud, pitiless and devoid of any sort of affection or respect.

He managed to finish. When he rose from the bed, she drew the coverlet over her body and he felt those scornful grey eyes watching him, burning into him, as he left the room. His legs shook and he felt nauseated.

It was always the same after that. He hit her once, trying to get some sort of response out of her, but it made no difference. She never spoke, but she made her derision plain by the small, mocking twist of her lips, the stony gaze of her eyes. Eventually, Gaetano found that he did not want to make love to her.

Eventually, Gaetano found himself unable to make love to her.

A dozen times that year Martin Gefroy stood before the door of the Cavazza house, hand fisted, ready to knock. A dozen times he had let his fingers drop, and had turned away, mouth set, blue-grey eyes as wintry as the cold Paduan sky. A likeable, intelligent man, he had discovered the name of the owner of the house, and had then made friends among the circle of men that were Padua's artists. From them he had heard of the birth and subsequent death of Gaetano Cavazza's son, and of the long illness of his wife. He had discovered that Joanna Cavazza was the niece of a Venetian painter. She was, the Paduan painters had told him, a beauty, but Martin had known that already.

He would have liked to give her flowers again, or to prescribe remedies that would help her regain her strength. He would have liked to thump Gaetano Cavazza, who was a thick-set, pompous idiot. But he did none of these things, because he knew that they would not help Joanna. Sometimes, late at night, when his eyes ached with studying and the dregs of the wine were thick and sour, Martin told himself that he was being foolish: he had mistaken the sounds of marital bullying that had followed his gift of a posy; Madonna Cavazza was, after all, another man's wife. But in the morning, waking with a headache and a tongue that clung to the roof of his mouth, Martin continued to make occasional, tactful inquiries among the artists of Padua.

A new concern possessed Martin Gefroy as the fitful spring shifted slowly into summer: in April the French king had declared war against Venice. There were the first rumblings of battle as French soldiers marched into Venetian territory. Pope Julius II had excommunicated Venice and was threatening to excommunicate the Orsini cousins, Venice's *condottieri*. There was a tangible tension in Padua and tempers were easily ignited: in the streets mothers snapped at their children and the young men of the city wore swords. Martin knew that he should leave the university he had studied at for the past three years. There were other universities, in far safer places. He had never taken pleasure in the loss of life, only in the repairing of it. He was an Englishman, and the struggles of the Italian states, of France, Venice and the Empire, were not his.

But he did not yet leave. He had bought her flowers once, and she had suffered for his impetuosity. He owed her something: some sort of protection, or friendship, should she ever require it. Martin stayed because the joy in her eyes when he had tossed the posy up to her was imprinted on the pages of his soul.

In mid-April the French army marched into northern Italy, a gaudy, noisy cavalcade of armour and plumes and pennants and war horses. At their head was the French king, Louis XII. Weeks of indecisive skirmishing with Venetian mercenaries followed: small, pointless engagements for a wood, a bridge, a farmstead.

It was more than two months since Toby had ridden from Marigny, two months spent travelling, training for battle and attempting to pick up the remnants of an earlier life. Questioning his fellow-soldiers, he had almost found Gilles and Penniless a dozen times, and then he had quite by chance found them in Treviglio when his only thought had been to warn the Orsini army of the progress of the French. He was in Italy again, fighting for Venice because Gilles and Penniless also happened to be fighting for Venice, and because he had, when it came to it, no sense of nationality. The past three years had not changed that.

Riding from Treviglio, they had to slow as they travelled south, their progress impeded by irrigation ditches and ranks of budding grapevines. Although it was not yet midday, the sky was darkening. Thick clouds bubbled on the horizon and the trees shivered in the gathering breeze. Gilles was muttering about the impossibility of French troops having crossed the Adda. Toby ignored him.

With the profits of three years spent in the service of the Seigneur de Marigny, Toby had bought himself an arquebus and a good supply of powder. He still had his sallet and his cuirass, and had worn both since crossing the Alps into Italy. Penniless, too, wore half-armour. Gilles's head was covered with an appalling purple hat, although he had a cuirass over his rather splendid doublet. As they neared the river, Gilles said smugly: 'I told you so. Tactics were never your strong point, Toby. A useful man in a fight, but you have to put yourself in the enemy's position. The French aren't –'

Gilles stopped, his mouth half-open, the first drops of rain splashing on to the brim of his hat. They had crested the final ridge and were looking down upon the valley of the Adda, towards the village of Agnadello. They were looking down to where the army of the Venetian mercenary captain, Bartolomeo d'Alviano, faced the troops of the French Viceroy of Milan across the vines and beanstalks. Toby's gaze swept over the ranks of infantry, cavalry, pikemen, arquebusiers and culverineers, over the flags that flickered in the dampening air, over the colours that were tied to the shoulders and headgear of the soldiers. He was the first to speak.

'Where's Nicolò Orsini?'

Penniless stared downwards and shook his head. Gilles's blue eyes raked the horizon. He swore. 'Riding south, someone said. Alviano will send messengers.'

Toby was knotting his colours to his shoulder as they rode down the hillside. He glanced up briefly. 'They'd better. Send messengers, I mean. Because that's less than half the French army. And Louis of France is near by, I would guess, polishing his sword-blade.'

Messengers were sent to Nicolò Orsini, Count of Pitigliano, who was riding south, already a mile or two away from the battlefield of Agnadello. Meanwhile, Nicolò's cousin, Bartolomeo d'Alviano, deployed his troops on the hillside overlooking the vineyards. A good position, from which they could see below them the first heavy drops of rain falling on the grapes, dampening the soil at the bottom of the irrigation ditches. The lower ground, not far from the River Adda, was marshy, dotted with reeds and yellow kingcups, pitted with mud-pockets. As Alviano's artillerymen fired their first volley, Charles d'Amboise, Seigneur de Chaumont, the French Viceroy of Milan, gathered his cavalry ready for the attack.

It was easy at first. Toby, loading and firing his arquebus from the hillside, found a certain amount of pleasure in it. The crack of the gun, the pounding of the horses' hooves, the rhythm of pipe and drum, removed the need for any thoughts other than the most immediate. The images that had dogged Toby Crow since he had ridden from France – the Seigneur de Marigny and his desirable wife, Hamon de Bohun, the child scrabbling among the logs with frozen fingers – became irrelevant.

Now what mattered was to balance correctly so as to absorb the kickback of the arquebus, with a brief prayer each time that the weapon would fire properly and not shatter at the barrel, blowing his face to smithereens. He needed quick fingers and an equally quick eye, and the powder had to be protected from the thickening rain, for otherwise the arquebus would be made useless.

To begin with, the battle went well for the Venetians. Better positioned than the French, Bartolomeo's troops repelled first the French cavalry attack and then the regiment of Swiss pikemen, their weapons bristling like a hedgehog's quills. The irrigation ditches and the short, closely interwoven vines acted like a series of palisades and earthworks. The marshy ground, stirred into a swamp by the heavy rain, made the pikemen slip, weapons jutting uselessly skywards. The sky was a dark steel-grey, the first rumbles of thunder even greater than the noises of battle.

Had Alviano's messengers ever reached the Count of Pitigliano, had the army of King Louis XII of France not been positioned near by waiting for the best moment, then all might have continued to go well for Venice, and the signatories of the League of Cambrai, the pact by which an Italian Pope had invited foreign armies into Italy to subdue an Italian state, might have lost the first pitched battle of war, thought better of the whole venture and gone home.

As Toby put aside his arquebus and mounted his horse, he saw the great army of the French king, pennants flying, drums beating, approaching from the west, riding to the assistance of the Seigneur de Chaumont. And at the same moment, from behind Bartolomeo d'Alviano's army, riding to the brow of the hill, the French rearguard appeared. The Venetians were hemmed in on three sides.

For Guillaume du Chantonnay, riding in the vanguard of the French king, war was a duty imposed on him in consequence of his birth. A not unenjoyable duty – Guillaume found a certain pleasure in hurling himself down a hillside towards twenty thousand disorganized Venetian infantrymen – but a duty none the less. Guillaume, who was at heart a renegade, had always resented authority and the duties authority imposed on him. But subtly. He was never, like his cousin's foolish courier, Toby Crow, reduced to insolence, although he recognized that a servant's means of resisting authority were limited. Guillaume had laughed (though not within Reynaud's hearing) when he heard that the courier had left Marigny the night after his exchange with Reynaud. With the family silver and half a dozen of the best horses from the stables, Guillaume had presumed, and was surprised later to learn otherwise. In Toby Crow's position, Guillaume would have put a candle to Reynaud's precious bloody tapestries.

So at first, when he saw Toby on the battlefield of Agnadello only a few yards away from him, he thought he had conjured the man himself from the shades and placed him there. His features were marked with mud and black smoke, but Guillaume knew him instantly. Toby Crow's sallet, unlike Guillaume's helm, was visorless. Suddenly Guillaume wanted to laugh, there in the middle of a battlefield, as he gripped his sword in one hand, his reins in the other. Guillaume noticed that Toby wore the colours of the Venetian *condottiere* Bartolomeo d'Alviano. He thought, momentarily, of engaging Reynaud's servant in battle, but then he thought how it would please Reynaud if he killed him. It would be better to leave Toby Crow to his own devices, a living thorn in Reynaud du Chantonnay's corpulent flesh. Reynaud, after all, possessed what Guillaume lusted after.

The messengers had never got through to Nicolò Orsini, concluded Toby when he had a moment to think: some clever Frenchman had slit their throats, and the Count of Pitigliano and all his great army had continued to march blithely south.

Toby saw, briefly, Bartolomeo d'Alviano, Nicolò's cousin, although it took a second glance at Bartolomeo's exquisite body-armour and superbly caparisoned horse to recognize him. Even Bartolomeo's own mother would not have known her son: the skin of his face hung in terrible, bloody strips, and he had lost an eye. Yet he fought like a madman, his sword curving through the rain; blood and water streamed from his etched epaulettes and cuirass.

Toby saw an entire regiment of pikemen from the Romagna surrounded and butchered, and was unable to do anything to help them. He saw the Venetian infantry – poorly armed peasants, most of them – cut down where they stood, utterly defenceless against the superior numbers of French cavalry. He saw the rain change suddenly to hail, great hard lumps of ice that ricocheted off cuirasses and sallets like bullets. He saw the vines stripped of leaf and fruit, made sterile sticks by warfare, while the purple juice of the flattened grapes mingled with mud and blood.

He heard the retreat sound as he fought for his own life, slashing at the ribs of the Frenchman who confronted him. He managed to catch Gilles's eye, and Gilles nodded and bawled through the confusion and the carnage for Penniless.

As Toby pressed his spurs to his horse's side and wove and ducked his way from the battlefield, he thought of Venice. The battle of Agnadello would destroy Venice: the Venice of the great gilded palaces; the Venice of the slow, dark waterways and glorious Byzantine churches; the Venice of Arlotto Attavanti and Pasquale Gennari; of Vittore Carpaccio and Gentile Bellini; the Venice of Joanna Zulian, who had risen from the black waters of the canal.

Pope Julius had exacted a terrible price for the city's pride, Toby thought, as he galloped through the wind and the rain.

The news of the Venetian defeat at Agnadello reached Venice on the evening of the fifteenth of May. At first, a dreadful silence spread over the city like a pall, and then the people thronged to the Doges' Palace for news of sons, brothers, fathers, husbands. Four thousand Venetian troops had died on the battlefield. The wounded Bartolomeo d'Alviano had been taken prisoner. Many of the Count of Pitigliano's mercenary troops had deserted.

On the twenty-ninth of May, the Emperor Maximilian declared war on Venice. The Serenissima, abandoning Padua, Vicenza, Verona and

Rovereto to their fates, recalled its mainland administrators and prepared for siege, or surrender.

As soon as Gaetano Cavazza learned of the disaster of Agnadello and the Emperor's declaration of war, he decided to abandon his native Padua and stay with Taddeo Zulian in Venice. The lagoons that surrounded Venice might be shallow, but Padua was almost completely undefended. Gaetano was a painter, not a soldier.

Joanna listened silently while Gaetano gave orders to the family and servants. She even helped with the packing. Gold, jewels, clothing, books, art equipment, were loaded on to mules or carts. Throughout the city, many other families did likewise. Finally, Gaetano instructed his household to assemble in the square, dressed in their travelling clothes.

Joanna went to her bedchamber, but did not put on her hat or cloak. She looked through the window at the small garden she had made the previous summer. She had not tended it this year, but she could still glimpse some flowers struggling for space between the weeds and the remains of last autumn's leaves – cyclamens and carnations and lilies of the valley, and, winding its way up the trellis she had pinned to the wall, a wild rose. The small pond at the side of the garden was clogged with leaves and algae. She would have to empty it, scrub it out and refill it with clear water from the well, and perhaps one day she would make a fountain. The narrow rows of box and lavender that bordered the geometrically patterned herb garden were untidy, their unclipped branches straggling into the beds of marjoram, chervil and sweet rocket. She would cut them back, and enlarge the herb garden to fill the barren space beside the wall. There were so many other plants she needed to grow: all the plants she had once listed so meticulously in the back of Dioscorides' herbal.

She heard Gaetano's heavy tread on the stairs, and knew that he had come for her, knew also what she would say to him. She turned as he entered the room. She had opened the window and there was still the scent of the flowers from the garden below.

'Joanna.' Gaetano was dressed for travel, his face was hot and florid. 'You must hurry. I intend to reach Venice by nightfall.'

Slowly she shook her head. 'I'm not coming, Gaetano.'

He ran his hands through his hair, glancing out of a side-window at the small cavalcade gathered in the courtyard below. 'Are you sick again, Joanna? If you are unwell, then we'll empty the cart and you may travel in that. But hurry – there's already talk that the French have crossed the Adige.'

'I'm not ill,' she said calmly. 'I'm not coming with you, Gaetano. I'm staying here, in Padua.'

He stared at her. Slowly his mouth opened, and stayed open. A few short weeks ago she might have wanted to laugh at him, but now she found that she almost pitied him.

'I will not go with you, Gaetano. You would have to tie me to the horse, and even then I would kick and scream all the way. If you managed to get me to Venice, then you would have to chain me to my bed or I'd swim back over the lagoons.' Her voice was quite steady. Although she had to thread her hands together to stop them shaking, she felt as though she had begun to be Joanna Zulian again, a traveller, a painter of banners and maker of potions. She knew that she must not go back to Venice, that Venice would return her to the brink of madness on which she had faltered after the death of Paolo. She would not return to that place again.

'You are my wife,' said Gaetano, hoarsely, desperately. He had lost his certainty over the past weeks, and now he did not even raise his hand to her. 'You are my *wife*.'

'You may apply, when the Pope is well-disposed to Venice, for an annulment on the grounds of desertion. For myself, I will not use your name again.' She took Gaetano's ring from her finger as she spoke, then the pearls from her ears, the agate beads from her throat. 'The rest are in the box on the bed. All your jewels are there, Gaetano – I'll have nothing of yours. I've kept my dowry and the jewels Isotta left me, that's all.'

He attempted to laugh. 'I'm taking all but one of the servants with me, Joanna. How could you, a young woman on your own, live? How will you fetch water from the well, cut firewood? How will you keep yourself?'

She replied levelly, 'I have survived on my own before, Gaetano. Long before I met you. And besides – we would destroy each other.'

She saw that there were tears at the corners of his eyes. He whispered, 'And when the soldiers come?'

She knew what he implied. She knew that for all of them the future was unknown, dangerous. But she knew also that she must risk everything in order to secure her freedom. She said gently, 'Padua will not fight, we both know that. The Emperor's troops will not sack a city that surrenders willingly.' She stood quite still, waiting for him to go. From outside in the square she could hear the voices of the waiting servants, the voices of Caterina and Nannina.

Gaetano's fists were clenched at his sides. 'You are a madwoman,' he whispered at last. 'A witch. I should have listened to them – I should have listened to myself. You have taken everything from me.' And then he turned on his heel, leaving her standing by the window.

Riding east from the killing-grounds of Agnadello, they argued. Toby, who was once easy-going, passably pleasant company, had become as stubborn as hell.

'The French are going to *win*,' bawled Gilles to Toby, who was riding ahead of him. 'We've lost the rest of our company, and most of Pitigliano's troops have deserted, so no one would know . . .' He left the sentence unfinished. Gilles had been pressing for a tactful change of side ever since they had ridden, beaten and somewhat bloody, from the battlefield. Now, he put his spurs to his horse's flanks, forcing the exhausted animal forwards until he was alongside Toby. He yelled again, 'Venice hasn't a hope. You must see that.' Then, when Toby didn't even glance at him, Gilles seized Toby's reins, so that they both shuddered to a halt in a cloud of dust and curses.

Toby said, looking up at last, 'Damn you, Gilles.'

Gilles, losing patience, seized his second-best hat and hurled it to the ground. 'You obstinate bastard, you're not even Venetian! And I like to win!'

'Then go.' Toby's face was grey with dust, his eyes, half hidden by the brim of his helmet, were hard. 'Go, Gilles. I'm not keeping you.'

Once, Gilles thought ruefully, it had been he who had decided their next venture, their next battle. Over the years of Toby's absence, something had changed.

Penniless had reined in behind them. To the west, they could see the plumes of smoke that blemished the blue horizon, as the troops of King Louis of France burned fields and villages.

'Penniless?' asked Gilles uncertainly.

Penniless didn't even hesitate. 'Venice,' he said.

Gilles groaned and buried his head in his hands. Penniless had simply picked up where he had left off: devoted to Toby, he followed him around like some great, clumsy bloodhound.

'Stupid buggers,' muttered Gilles under his breath, and he spurred his horse in the direction of the Veneto.

The rumour, in a city febrile with rumour, reached the Englishman Martin Gefroy within a day. The rumour said that the obnoxious Gaetano Cavazza had taken his sisters, his servants and his baggage and had left the city of Padua. Rumour added that he had not taken his wife, Joanna.

Martin found himself standing at the door of the Cavazza house again. At first, he was paralysed once more, unable to knock. Then, his mouth dry, he tapped on the polished wood.

The servant, an aged, toothless crone, told him that Madonna Cavazza was in the garden. He found his way there himself, leaving the crone muttering about bread-making and the lack of firewood.

He saw her first through the doorway. She was crouched in a corner of the small terrace emptying buckets of water. Martin coughed.

She rose. The sleeves of her gown were pushed up above her elbows. The ends of her long, full skirts were caught up into the belt at her waist, and the layers of petticoats beneath were splashed with green. But even in the dirty gown she was still beautiful, although Martin the physician saw that she had lost both weight and colour. To his immense pleasure, she recognized him. After a first, initial, uncomprehending glance her face broke into the most glorious smile. Martin felt as though there were two suns now: the first high in the midmorning sky, and the second enclosed with him in the garden.

'The scholar,' she said, rising to greet him. 'You gave me flowers.'

'Unwisely, perhaps.' His words were gentle, but he saw the bruised look in her eyes, the slight fading of her smile.

'Kindly,' she said. 'They were a kind thought, Messer Gefroy.'

For a moment neither of them spoke. Then Joanna said, 'I must apologize for my appearance, Messer Gefroy. I'm cleaning the pond.'

To one side of the garden was a small, circular pond, now half empty. Martin's experienced eyes studied the flowers that bordered it. 'Orchis, buttercups, mare's tail . . . You have a pharmacopoeia here, Madonna Cavazza.'

'Madonna Zulian,' she said gently. 'My name is Joanna Zulian.'

He did not ask why she had abandoned her marital name; accepting its implications, he knew that he had no right to question her. Instead, he knelt by the pond and began to scoop the foul green water into a bucket.

'I've sadly neglected the garden this year,' said Joanna, beside him, as she began to sort weeds from plants. 'I've lost the violets, the yellow pansies . . .'

She had lost her child also, but he did not ask her about that. If she wished to talk he would listen, but he would not press her. They worked for a while in silence, Martin emptying the buckets of dirty water, Joanna cleaning out the pond with rags. He would have brought her every plant in the university of Padua's gardens, if she had wished it. When Martin had refilled the pond, they could see the pebbles clearly through the sparkling water.

For a moment he forgot the threatening future that was almost upon them. But if Joanna Zulian was ignorant of Padua's fate, of her own fate, then Martin knew that he must warn her. Rising, he said, 'You should have left Padua, madonna. The Emperor's troops will be here any day. Anybody left in the city will be captives – hostages.'

She, too, rose, wiping her hands on her apron. He saw that her eyes were a clear light grey, as serene as the still water in the pond. 'I was a hostage before, Messer Gefroy,' she said. 'Now I have my own name and I sleep in my own bed. I can grow my flowers, tend my garden. Perhaps eventually I can mourn my son without bitterness. That is freedom.'

Martin said nothing. He turned to go, waving her farewell. He knew that he, too, had arrangements to make, valuables to hide, before the troops of the Emperor Maximilian began their rape of the city of Padua. Outside it was sunny, the sky sapphire-blue, but the empty houses and silent squares told of impending disaster.

At the beginning of June the cities of Padua, Vicenza, Verona, Cittadella, Riva and Rovereto submitted to the representatives of the Empire, and German troops marched into the terra firma. The news was received in silence by a humiliated, frightened Venice. The cities of the Romagna, the cities that Venice had tried to hold on to at so great a price, had already fallen. In less than a month, the greatest seaport in the world had lost all its mainland possessions except Treviso. Venice's enemies gathered at the salt margins of the lagoon, only three short miles of shallow water from the city of Venice itself.

The manservant handed the letter to Eleanor as she stood in the kitchen helping to weigh out sugar for pickling. The letter was addressed to the Seigneur de Marigny. François stood at Eleanor's side, sneezing as he picked at the basket of walnuts. Eleanor considered for a moment handing the letter to François, but, looking at the boy's reddened nose and swollen eyes, decided against it. She would read it aloud to him: despite all his tutor's efforts, François still struggled with anything but the clearest handwriting. She knew from the seal that the letter was from Cousin Guillaume. Guillaume, who had been in Italy with the French army since the spring, did not yet know of Reynaud's illness. She should have written, thought Eleanor.

Since the day of the hunt Reynaud had neither spoken nor risen from his bed. Gruel, spooned patiently into his mouth by Eleanor, dribbled on to the bedclothes. And yet he still breathed, obstinate to the last. The château de Marigny waited for his death, voices hushed, curtains drawn, frozen in time. Eleanor herself dwelt in a nameless limbo, neither a wife nor a widow. François waited, Eleanor knew, for freedom and respect. The boy seemed to believe, she thought pityingly, that with his assumption of the title and inheritance of the lands, he would also acquire looks, intelligence, dignity.

François started to sneeze again. Eleanor patted his shoulder comfortingly and broke open the seal. Her eyes scanned Guillaume's bold, large handwriting.

At the table, the servant strained the syrup of rosewater and sugar until it was a clear pale pink. 'It's ready now, madame.'

Eleanor smiled and looked up. 'I'll help you with the walnuts, Berthe,' she said and glanced back to the letter.

She turned the paper over and her breath caught in her throat as she saw the name. Suddenly her heart was pounding. The letter shook in her hands as if a cold wind were blowing through Marigny's overheated kitchen.

'Are you ill, madame?'

Her head jerked up. The servant was looking at her anxiously.

'Is it bad news, madame?'

She did not know, in truth, whether it was bad news or not. She had seen his name and was unable to read any further. Beside her, François sniffed, wiping his nose on his sleeve. With an effort unnoticeable to anyone but herself, Eleanor managed to fold the letter and smile.

'No. Not bad news, Berthe. I just feel a little faint, that's all. The weather . . . the heat from the stoves . . . I'll go out into the garden for a while.'

Eleanor heard François's moan of irritation but for once disregarded him. She crossed the courtyard, drawbridge and meadow, and continued walking until she had reached the wood. Only there did she let herself sink to the ground amidst poppies and corncockles and the dipping velvety leaves of the beech trees.

She finished the letter and still could not cry, although the pain was greater than any she had ever known. She had endured Reynaud's taunts and the unending ache of childlessness, but this pain she knew she could not live with; it made her want to scream her agony like a banshee, trapped here between meadow and wood. Foolishly she had thought that there could be nothing worse than his absence, his continued failure to return to her. Now she knew that there was something much, much worse. There was the possibility that he had already ceased to exist, the possibility that she and he might no longer even dwell in the same world.

The letter fell from Eleanor's feeble hands and fluttered momentarily in the breeze before coming to rest amidst the grass and flowers of the forest floor.

Guillaume had written: 'Guess, my dear Reynaud, whom I saw at Agnadello. Your former servant, Toby Crow, fighting for the unfortunate Venetians. Amusing, don't you think? Your vengeance may be unnecessary, therefore. It is probable that he has met his death alongside the four thousand or so others who perished in the army of Bartolomeo d'Alviano . . .'

Padua had changed. Occupied by the soldiers of the Emperor, its streets and squares had become places of ill temper and danger. The city had fallen under Imperial rule without a drop of blood spilt. And yet there was a constant tension in the air. Dogs squabbled on the pavements, women smacked their children, their tempers frayed by the heat, the silence, the humiliation. When she left the house, Joanna was careful to cover her head with a veil and to hide her figure in a shawl to avoid the attentions of the soldiers. To avoid the attentions of her fellow-citizens also: a woman had spat at her in the street, a man had seized her arm and cursed her for abandoning her husband.

Most of the time, therefore, she stayed in the house or tended her garden. The Englishman Martin Gefroy visited her frequently, and she was grateful for his company. Yet she liked to be on her own also, to feel the strength and sanity that she had lost earlier in the year slowly returning. She did not let herself think of the future, of Gaetano's eventual, inevitable return to Padua. She must be gone long before then. She thought often of the past, of her childhood travels through Savoy and Navarre, Spain and France. She remembered the St John's Eve bonfires that lit the valley of the Loire. She remembered the wooded slopes and wide meadows of Touraine covered with flowers. She knew that she must leave Italy: she ached to travel again.

The days passed slowly, each one hotter, more oppressive than the last. Food was beginning to run short; she could buy only enough each time to last herself and the maidservant for a day. Soldiers were burning the crops, people whispered, and often Joanna could see in the distance thin plumes of smoke rising against the sapphire sky. The Emperor's soldiers fed themselves well, of course, and drank well also. Rumours buzzed round the city like the clouds of flies and mosquitoes: Imperial troops had put the entire population of Friuli to the sword . . . the Venetians had invited the Turks to come to their defence . . . the Venetian people had risen up and massacred the Doge and the Council of Ten for abandoning the peoples of the terra firma . . .

Martin began to bring her food and warned her not to leave the house. Joanna knew that he loved her, so she made her refusal gentle and honest. She would not be a prisoner again. She would be careful: she would wear her veil and carry her knife, she would keep to the nearby squares and streets. But she would not be a prisoner again. Because he understood her, Martin accepted her refusal and increased his visits to twice a day.

The disaster, when it came, had the relentless inevitability of a breaking thunderstorm. The troops might not be hungry for food, but they were hungry for the women they had left behind them, and for the fighting that Padua's defencelessness, Venice's desertion, had denied them. In the market one day, Joanna saw half a dozen soldiers beating a youth. The lad was about thirteen or fourteen, a gangling, skinny creature, no match for the thickset soldiers with their heavy boots and gauntleted fists. He had looked the wrong way, said the wrong thing.

She could do nothing, of course. No one could do anything. She was as useless as she had been in Venice watching a boatful of youths toss a kitten into the air. The square was full of old men, women and children. The soldiers were armed, although they did not yet use their swords. Uninterrupted, they vented their homesickness and impatience on a beardless boy.

Joanna knew that she should leave quietly, go home, bolt the doors. Yet she found herself unable to move. She stood frozen at a corner of the marketplace, watching by the half-empty vegetable stalls. Soon the boy no longer struggled, soon he no longer cried. Joanna's throat ached and her unblinking eyes were tearless. The lad lay still, sprawled on the earth, his ragged shirt and breeches patched with dust, reddened with blood. The market square was almost empty, the sun high and unpitying in the sky. One of the soldiers, spitting on the inert body of the boy, looked up.

Her veil had slipped from her face, and her eyes, she knew, said everything. She saw the soldier's slow, unpleasant smile, and her fear enabled her to move at last, to gather up her basket and run, stumbling, back to the Cavazza house. Inside, she bolted the heavy front door and stood for a moment leaning against the wall, her heart pounding. She felt unclean with the heat and with running, unclean with what she had seen. Her hair had become unpinned, it fell damp and tangled round her head. She began to scrub at her face and hands with the corner of her veil, trying to rub away the dust, the memory.

There was a sound from the kitchen, and Joanna turned, expecting to see Beatrice, the maidservant. But instead of Beatrice's old, disapproving features she saw a different face, a nightmare face, still wearing that frightening smile. The soldier had followed her from the marketplace and had entered the house by the kitchen door. Joanna whispered, *'Beatrice?'* but received no reply. Just the distant bang of the open door as it swung on its hinges, and the silence of absence, or death.

The soldier, laughing softly, was sheathing his knife in his belt. There was blood on his tunic, but whether it was Beatrice's blood or the blood of that boy in the marketplace, Joanna could not tell. Her mind raced, looking for escape. The front door was shut behind her, and it would take far too long to slip the bolts. And even if she could leave the house, he would follow her. Who would risk the vengeance of this man's comrades to protect a husbandless woman? Worse, a woman who had abandoned the duties of marriage.

The soldier was beckoning to her, speaking a few low, guttural words. He was obese and unshaven, his tunic and breeches tattered and stained. He did not expect refusal: he knew that she had to choose acquiescence or death. Joanna forced herself to smile, to toss back her long, glorious hair, to walk across the room towards the soldier. His expression changed to hunger, to longing – a look that she had seen on Gaetano's face a hundred times. She said something softly in a German dialect and the soldier, even if he did not understand her, watched her, mesmerized. She raised her face to be kissed, and allowed him to encircle her with his arms.

Joanna slipped the knife from her sleeve as his mouth found hers. Then, as his breathing thickened and his tongue pushed between her lips, she plunged the dagger into his back.

His fingers still gripped her arms tightly, but his mouth drew away. She heard him gasp. His face was only a few inches from hers: the skin was livid and distended, bloodshot eyes stared at her, first disbelieving, then vengeful. Hands clutched at her neck, thumbs pressed her windpipe. And then, as her lungs cried out for air, he slipped to the floor, empty fingers trailing down the front of her gown, blood gurgling from his mouth, throat rattling.

Joanna became aware, eventually, that there had been a sound other than the drumming of her heart and the soldier's last, dying breaths: a persistent knocking at the front door, which had stopped as she pulled her skirts away from those lifeless, grasping hands. The dead soldier's fingers, grimy and outstretched, had mesmerized her. Then she heard the sound of the kitchen door closing, and she looked up and saw Martin Gefroy.

He stared first at the soldier, then at her. He was speechless for a moment. Then he said: 'Change your gown, Joanna. Pack a bag.'

His voice was brusque, harsh. She looked down and saw the long streak of blood that trailed from the kitchen. She whispered, 'Beatrice?'

'Is dead.' He spread out his arms, stopping her from going into the kitchen. He added, 'You can't stay here, madonna. Someone will notice his disappearance – someone may know where he went.'

She looked again at the body on the floor, at her knife still protruding from the soldier's back, and she shuddered. Martin crossed the room and took her two shaking hands in his. He spoke more gently.

'You're all right, aren't you?' And when she nodded, he said once more, 'Change your gown. I'll take care of these.' His gesture took in the dead soldier on the floor and the unseen body of Beatrice in the kitchen. 'Pack a few things. I'll find you somewhere safe to stay. I'll take you away from Padua as soon as possible. Hurry, Joanna.'

Upstairs, she unlaced the bloodstained gown and replaced it with the black one Isotta had made for her, long ago, in Venice. She could hear, outside in the garden, the sounds of Martin digging. Her hyacinths, her wallflowers, her roses, would be thrown aside to make an unmarked grave for her husband's maidservant and a nameless German soldier. If she could have found the words, she would have prayed the devout Beatrice's forgiveness for the lack of ceremony, the lack of a Christian burial. She took a bag and placed in it some clothes, Isotta's jewels, her copy of Dioscorides' herbal and her mother's necklace. Then she put a few coins into an old silk purse: a Venetian zecchino, two Genoese ducats and a French écu d'or.

PART TWO

1509–1510

The Garden of Passionate Love

All night by the rose, the rose,
All night by the rose I lay
Dared I not the rose steal
And yet I bore the flower away.

Anonymous. Fourteenth century.

CHAPTER SEVEN

On the sixteenth of July, a fleet of ships set off from Venice for the mainland. Following the fleet's departure, other ships patrolled the lagoons, making sure no further craft left the city.

In the early morning of the following day, before the sun had fully risen, a group of horsemen assembled in the woods outside Padua. The trees were thick with leaves; the men, their horses and their weapons well hidden by the tangled fronds of willow and alder.

Three carts loaded with corn began the journey from the wood to the Codalunga gate of Padua. There were two men with each cart, all six apparently unarmed, all six apparently concerned with nothing but the price of corn and the unbearably hot summer weather.

The first two carts stopped at the gate, their drivers were questioned, their loads examined by the German *Landsknechts.* Then the drawbridge was lowered, and the carts that would feed the hungry garrison of the Emperor Maximilian were waved through. The third cart, however, stopped halfway through the gate, a wheel was jammed. One of the carters, a huge man with the head and shoulders of a bull, climbed slowly down from the cart to try and heave the wheel back into place. His efforts did not seem to help, though: the second carter, fair-haired and smiling, waved an apologetic hand to the guards.

The guards were going down to help the carters when suddenly there was a drumming of hooves and the shouting of a hundred voices. '*Marco! Marco!*' the men cried as they poured through the gate that was held wide open by the stranded cart. Venetian banners streamed in the early-morning heat, swords flashed in the sunlight, and the lion of St Mark's flared red and gold against the pale Paduan sky.

Almost the first person Toby saw once the worst of the fighting had ended was the Englishman, Martin Gefroy.

The engagement had been short and bloody, a series of vicious hand-to-hand combats that took place in the main square of the city. The

Germans fought well, but the Venetians fought better: encouraged, perhaps, by the recent news of support for Venice on the terra firma, thankful, perhaps, to be taking action after weeks of humiliation.

Toby, gathering his breath, had time to check that Gilles and Penniless were safe, and that the lion of St Mark's now fluttered over Padua's towers and gates. And then, wiping the sweat from his forehead with the back of his hand, he saw the Englishman.

He recognized him instantly. He had, of course, once spent almost two months in Martin Gefroy's company. His right arm, which he had used so successfully today, still bore witness to the physician's skill. And the Englishman, he remembered, had been bound for the university of Padua to study medicine.

Martin Gefroy knelt over one of the wounded men lying in the square. An open bag beside him revealed its contents of linen, ointments and salves. Toby, sheathing his sword, crossed the square.

'Will he live?' he said softly.

Martin shook his head. 'No.' Gently he closed the sightless eyes with his hand and rose.

Some of the elation that Toby had felt on the recapture of Padua dissolved in the weariness and despair reflected in the Englishman's eyes. The young man lying on the ground should have been a merchant, a politician, a banker. Not dead at eighteen in a Paduan square.

'Such a waste,' muttered Martin to himself, and then, focusing at last on Toby, he frowned. 'Toby . . .? Toby Dubreton?' The Englishman's voice was tentative at first. Then he said more firmly, *'Toby!'* and his face broke into a wide smile. Martin grasped the sleeves of Toby's doublet, then clapped him resoundingly on the back. 'My repair worked, then? And today . . .?' Martin's blue-grey eyes – physician's eyes – checked Toby for injury and came to rest on the reddened sleeve of his jerkin.

Toby shook his head. 'Someone else's. I've only a few cuts and bruises. I've been lucky this year. So have Penniless and Gilles.'

Toby saw the Englishman glance round the square at the dead and dying, his smile suddenly absent. Toby, too, turned away. There was work for him, also: streets and alleys to be searched for any remaining German soldiers, the inspection and reinforcement of the city's defences to be organized. The army of the Emperor Maximilian could not be far away.

Martin was already kneeling beside the next patient. But as Toby began to walk away, the Englishman turned suddenly and called out: 'I must speak to you later, Toby. I have a favour to ask of you.'

The city of Padua was scoured for carpenters, labourers, masons. Earthworks were dug outside the city gates, bombards and mortars assembled in gunports. They dug through the intense heat of the day and into the night, their half-naked bodies turned mahogany-brown by earth, sweat and sun. Clouds of flies and mosquitoes from the lagoons swarmed in the evenings, tormenting them, blistering their hot skin. Soon the walls of the city bristled with hackbuts and culverins, each one manned by a watchful gunner. The last few German soldiers were flushed out of their hiding-places, and the fortifications of the city were searched twice a day for the Emperor Maximilian's scouts or spies. Patrols were mounted at the armoury, at the grainstore. The city of Padua, finding its feet at last, ridding itself of the shame of occupation, was preparing for siege.

It was three days before Toby saw the physician again. Days of tension, days of waiting, as though they could already hear the fifes and drums of Maximilian's army. At last the curfew was relaxed, and the inhabitants of Padua were belatedly allowed to celebrate its liberation.

The tavern was hot and buzzed with the ever-present flies. Soldiers and their sweethearts crowded into every corner. Gilles had found himself company: a rather pretty Paduan girl played with the ivory buttons on his cloth-of-gold doublet, and ran her fingers through his curls.

Penniless was drunk. 'I've a riddle,' he announced, hiccuping after draining his sixth tankard of ale.

Toby groaned. Gilles, glancing up from the girl seated on his knee, complained, 'The last time you told us a riddle, Penniless, I had to ride halfway to Naples and back *and* buy a damned bunch of flowers for Toby. And he wasn't even dead.'

'It wasn't my fault.' Penniless, his huge torso naked except for a sleeveless leather jerkin, looked hurt. 'Was it, Toby?'

Toby shook his head. Penniless, happy again, creased his brow in concentration. 'Well, then. Listen.

'"I have a hole above my knee
And pricked it is and pricked shall be
And yet it is not sore
And yet it shall be pricked more . . ."'

Penniless's voice was drowned by Gilles's roar of anger and the girl's squeal as she slid off Gilles's lap. There was a scuffle, the sound of overturning furniture and shattering pottery, and Gilles lay on the floor, the glorious purple hat pulled hard over his fair curls, Penniless seated on his shoulders.

Martin Gefroy's voice called through the clamour, 'A scabbard, isn't it, Penniless? Hello, Toby. Gilles.'

The physician, Toby thought, looked exhausted. Martin Gefroy's eyes were red-rimmed, his skin pale and creased with fatigue. He looked as though he had not slept for a week. Not surprisingly, for after all Martin's work started where Toby's finished.

Penniless roared his greetings. Gilles, his lungs still flattened by Penniless's huge buttocks, managed to wave a hand.

Martin refused all offers of a drink. 'I need to talk to you, Toby,' he said. 'Now.' He shook his head as Toby indicated a place on the bench. 'Not here.'

Outside the piazza was silent and bathed in moonlight. Martin, leaning against the low wall that surrounded the square's fountain, said, 'I need your help, Toby. I need you to help me leave Padua, to guide me out of Italy. Tonight, preferably.'

Toby almost wanted to laugh. Martin simply didn't know what he was asking. Then, looking at the physician's strained face, he said, 'I can't. Not possible. I'm needed here.'

Martin ran his hands through his untidy hair and blinked. 'There're other soldiers in Padua. Gilles . . . Penniless . . .'

Toby brushed away a persistent mosquito and asked, 'What have you done, Martin? Seduced the Venetian administrator's wife? Cured a few too many German *Landsknechts*?'

The air was still hot. Martin Gefroy, his face marked with exhaustion, his clothes tattered and dirty, sat on the edge of the fountain, trailing one hand in the cloudy water. 'It's not for me. It's for someone I know. She killed a German soldier.'

He glanced up at Toby. Toby could see the truth in the Englishman's eyes, and fear also.

'The bastard was about to rape her. She put a knife in his back. I buried the body in her garden, cleaned up the house, took her away, hid her at my lodgings. That was four days ago. The next day *Landsknechts* searched her house. They ransacked the place. I tried to persuade her to let me take her to Venice, but she wouldn't. She won't go near the place. She's determined to leave Italy.'

Toby thought, Martin's sweetheart? Martin's lover? He said, 'Venice is sealed off. Besides, the Germans are gone now, Martin.'

'You know yourself that they will be back. You're not digging trenches to grow turnips.' The physician's voice was scornful. His gaze drifted to the distant walls, the gates and turrets of Padua, black against an indigo sky. 'The Emperor will want Padua back, won't he, Toby?'

In the sultry evening air, Toby's brow was damp with sweat, as though he were still out there, beyond the city gates, coaxing fifty civilian labourers to dig the sort of fortifications that would help Padua withstand the enemy's bombards. He said evenly, 'Of course Maximilian will besiege us. Which is why I have to remain in Padua.'

'Which is why she *cannot* remain in Padua. If the Imperial forces retake the city, then she'll be in terrible danger. Padua will be sacked, you know that. And even if Padua holds out and the Emperor retreats' – Martin shook his head hopelessly – 'then her husband will return.'

'Husband?' said Toby. 'Is she married, Martin?'

'Yes.' The Englishman rose, striking the palm of his hand once with his fist. 'Her husband beats her. I've heard him.'

There was anger in Martin's voice. And at the back of Toby's mind, there was the image of a child, red weals on his back, working the bellows in a shoemaker's shop. For the past six months he had shut away all thoughts of Chinon, of Marigny, and he pushed the image angrily aside. He began to walk quickly back to the tavern. 'I'm sorry, Martin, but I can't help you. I wish I could, but I can't. I'm needed here.'

'You owe me,' said the physician, and Toby stopped halfway across the square, boots dug in to the dusty, hard-baked earth. 'I'm calling in my debt, Toby,' Martin said quietly.

'I'm calling in my debt.' It was hot, airless, and Toby's shirtsleeves were rolled up to his elbows. He could see, etched more deeply by the moonlight and by the light from the tavern, the jagged scar that snaked the length of his forearm. He would not be here if it was not for Martin. Martin had given two months of his life to him, a stranger.

From beside the fountain, Martin said, 'I didn't want to have to put it like that. But, as I said, I need you. I'd take her out of the country myself, but I'd be lost before we reached Verona. We'll be safe with you.'

Toby turned round on his heel. He tried one last time. 'They'll forget, Martin. No one's going to worry about one Paduan woman when there's a siege going on. No one will remember her.'

Martin, leaving the fountain, began to walk towards Toby. He stopped in front of him. 'No one could forget her,' he said, simply. 'Come and see.'

He had taken Joanna Zulian to his lodgings behind the university, smuggling her into the tenement house when no one was looking. He had two rooms, and for the past four nights Martin had slept on the floor in one room, Joanna in the bed in the other. He would have sold his soul to have shared the bed with her, but he knew that she did not think of him in that way. He did not dwell on that, or he would have howled his misery like a mad dog. He had her company, and for now that was enough.

Joanna did not speak of the soldier she had killed or of her husband. She repaired some of Martin's clothes and tidied his rooms. When the battle took place in the centre of Padua, she tore linen into strips for bandages, ground herbs and mixed salves. Martin knew that she would have helped him to tend the wounded out there in the square, but he did not dare let her leave his lodgings.

Martin led Toby through the town and up the twisting flights of stairs to his rooms on the top floor. He was not usually given to strange fancies, but a sense of dread had possessed him for several days now. He knew that his fears centred on Joanna, and he told himself that all would be well now, that Toby Dubreton – practical, experienced Toby Dubreton – would spirit them both safely away from Padua. He began to feel an overwhelming relief: he told himself that the nightmare of the past few days would soon be over. He did not regret forcing Toby to help him: he knew that he had had no choice.

Joanna was still awake when they entered the rooms. She was seated at the table, stitching Martin's one tattered old cloak. Martin, looking at her, experienced a brief, husbandly sense of pride. Then he saw that Joanna was staring at Toby.

'Toby,' she said. 'Toby Crow.'

It was Martin's turn to feel confused. He felt shut out suddenly, excluded from some past he knew nothing about. Toby and Joanna were looking at each other, and he saw surprise, yes, in both pairs of eyes, but something else as well. Knowledge. Kinship, perhaps.

'We've met,' said Toby at last. 'In Venice.'

'Toby *Crow*?' said Martin.

He waited silently for an answer. He saw the flicker of calculation in Toby's dark, slate-grey eyes and stared at him, willing him to tell the truth. He could sense somehow that although the truth was important, Toby was not accustomed to it.

Finally Toby spoke. 'I've worked for a Frenchman for the past three years. The name Dubreton was not suitable.'

Martin knew that he had received only half the truth. Joanna rose from the table. 'I met Messer Crow two years ago in Venice, Martin. I'd fallen into a canal. Messer Crow helped me out of it.'

Her face was composed again, her beautiful grey eyes almost calm. But Martin, seeing them side by side, felt again that troubling sense of foreboding. It was as if in protecting Joanna Zulian, as if in forcing Toby to help him against his will, he had unleashed something unpredictable, something destructive.

At last Toby managed to take his eyes from her.

'I could take Madonna Zulian back to England, I thought,' said Martin. 'Or France. I'm not sure.'

Toby hardly heard him. He said to Joanna, 'The baby. The Veniers' secretary told me that you were expecting a baby.'

The face that Toby remembered so clearly flushed. 'My son died, Messer Crow. He was born too early.'

He recalled the Venier palace, how he had looked up and seen this girl – this woman – walk into the water just as though she were walking out into the street. Later, sitting on the steps, she had cradled the dead kitten in her lap. Her expression then had been as it was now: bruised, trying to hide her distress. He remembered putting his arm around her, leading her back into the courtyard. And he remembered Gaetano Cavazza, whom Joanna Zulian had married.

'Well?' said the Englishman impatiently. 'Will you help us?'

Toby knew that he had no choice. As he gave his assent, he saw some of the exhaustion and tension drain from the physician's face. He felt overwhelmed with bitterness suddenly, overwhelmed with the realization that this girl, the Englishman, his own debt, all conspired to take him yet again from his true business, the business of war.

They left Padua two days later. The memory of his interview with Antonio Giustinian was not one Toby cared to dwell on. 'And if I refuse permission, then you will desert, I suppose?' Giustinian had said, contempt in his dark, ascetic eyes. And Toby, forced into honesty by that glare and by his respect for the Venetian's strength of purpose, had nodded.

Andrea Gritti, the sensualist, was more understanding. 'Is she pretty?' the proveditor had asked, and Toby, assenting, had received his permission to leave the city and to quit the forces of Venice. Abandoning Gilles and Penniless had been even less pleasant. Gilles had merely raised his eyes heavenwards and sighed, but Penniless had offered his services as bodyguard – to the end of the world and back, if necessary. Toby had refused, because the north of Italy was littered with soldiers, most of them unfriendly, and he intended to be inconspicuous. With Penniless you could not be inconspicuous. He had been unable to find the right words for Penniless, and had left the explanations to Martin, the cockney's fellow-Englishman.

They left the city at dawn. Toby and Martin and Joanna were ushered through the same gate that Penniless's cart had jammed open only a week earlier. The rising sun pasted the horizon with streaks of pink and gold and violet, the gate swung shut, and they led their horses through the pattern of earthworks that Toby himself had helped to build. Looking round, checking the progress of his fellow-travellers, Toby saw that Joanna Zulian's face was turned towards the sun. She was smiling, and her unbound hair was turned by the sunlight to gold.

Joanna was not the burden Toby had feared she might be. She rode tirelessly and superbly. When the terrain was unsuitable for riding, she swung off her horse and walked for miles and miles, skirts kirtled up to her waist, petticoats trailing in the dust. She never once complained of weariness, never once grumbled at the irregular meals, the dirt, the heat, the flies.

They rode west, in the direction of Milan and the Alps, away from the approaching Imperial troops. The despoiled towns and villages of the Veneto were almost unrecognizable, altering the aspect of the country Toby had travelled through after Agnadello only two months ago. If there had been no more pitched battles like Agnadello, then the north of Italy itself seemed to have become a battleground. Houses – entire villages – had been burned, crops had been laid waste. The troops of the French king and the Emperor, and of Mantua and Ferrara, had ransacked northern Italy like countless scavenging locusts.

They travelled in the early morning and in the evening to avoid the heat of the sun, as well as the skirmishes and troop movements that were taking place daily. Toby assumed every man, unless proved otherwise, to be their enemy. The plains were busy with mercenaries and deserters, with the profiteers and casualties of war, while the woods and hills were a haven for bandits.

Another enemy began to stalk the towns and villages. High summer was always a bad time for agues and distempers, but this year, the year of hunger and violence, it was even worse. Riding into a village, Toby noticed the silence. There were dogs gathering round the village well, a few skinny chickens scrabbling for food in the dust, but no people – only, from one of the houses, a baby's cry. He saw Joanna slide from her horse, saw her stand still for a moment in the square and then walk in the direction of the baby's cry. Suddenly, the physician, running up behind her, took her arm and stopped her. 'Plague,' whispered Martin Gefroy to Toby, and Toby felt a thin trickle of fear run down his spine.

They were even more careful after that. The constant struggle to find enough food became all-absorbing. Toby shot rabbits and hares with a bow and arrow. Occasionally, a pheasant or a partridge, flushed by their horses' hooves from the undergrowth, would find its way into the cooking-pot. Once Toby, who had been dozing beside a stream, woke to see Joanna up to her knees in water, a wriggling trout struggling to free itself from her hands. In the hedgerows there were raspberries and wild strawberries dusty with the dry summer's heat. They would pick the berries and store them in the hood of Joanna's cloak, eating them later in the shelter of an olive grove. The trees had been stripped of fruit long since by marauding troops and hungry peasants.

One day they came upon a band of ragged soldiers in a steep ravine green with ferns. One of the soldiers still wore the tattered insignia of the lion of St Mark's on his arm, but his eyes were hungry, desperate for the travellers' horses and possessions. They were saved by the speed of their horses and the accuracy of Toby's sword, which killed two of his emaciated former allies within minutes. After that, Toby taught the Englishman to use a sword. Martin had no aptitude for it: he was clumsy, as though he used different hands from the ones with which he lanced an abscess or stitched a wound. But he was persistent, he worked hard, patiently forcing himself to learn something that was unnatural to him. The girl Joanna watched them. Toby knew that she hid a stiletto dagger in the wide folds of her sleeve.

If they were lucky, they slept in taverns or stables. If they were less fortunate, they curled themselves up beneath trees or in ditches. Joanna spoke as many languages as Toby, and he grew accustomed to sending her first into a tavern to inquire for rooms in whatever dialect he judged to be most safe. A woman was not a threat. She was a Mantuan madonna or a Florentine lady on her way to the sanctuary of a German nunnery. Once Toby and Joanna were man and wife, and Martin their servant. They slept three to a bed in the crowded tavern that night, too tired to care about either propriety or desire. Their bodies touched under the patched sheets, and someone else's maidservant snored on the floor.

There were good times, though, times that Joanna later treasured, just as she treasured the memories of her childhood.

There were the gypsies, who gazed impressively at a pack of battered tarots and told them about unexpected journeys, mysterious strangers. There was the pedlar who sold Joanna the coloured braid that she sewed to the hem of the black dress. There was the mystery play they watched by the roadside: three actors and a papier-mâché dragon-head, with the hills and hedgerows as a backcloth. There was the pool they all swam in one evening, soaking away the dust and the aches and pains in clear, cold water.

Joanna knew that she had begun to pick up the pieces again. She was Joanna Zulian, a traveller. She was no longer the anonymous manikin that Gaetano had made of her. She had begun to take pleasure in life again, to shake off the dreadful numbness that her marriage and the loss of her baby had caused.

One evening they stopped at a tavern in a village near Asola. It was as though the intervening years had slipped away. Now Padua and Venice were nothing to her – she had never stopped riding the dusty roads of Europe. The tavern was full, the taproom dark and comfortable. Toby went in search of food and wine, while Martin and Joanna squeezed into a space at a table near the open doorway. The village seemed untouched by the wars: through the doorway, Joanna could see fields of ripening corn laced with poppies and a small herb garden, its contents wilting in the late summer heat.

There were lines of weariness round Martin's eyes and mouth. He grimaced and rubbed his foot. 'I've a blister the size of a hen's egg on my heel.'

Toby, elbowing his way through the crowds, dumped a flagon of wine and three cups on to the table. 'Drink this, Martin,' he said, 'and you wouldn't notice if you'd broken your leg.'

Toby filled the three cups. He had not wanted, Joanna knew, to escort a husbandless girl and a travelling scholar out of Italy, but his ill humour had none the less dissolved on the very first day as they had ridden through the valley of the Adige. The initial tension she had noticed between Toby and Martin Gefroy began to ease, if not to disappear completely. Joanna had recognized in Toby something that she had begun to understand in herself: a need for action, for movement. He looked like someone in a cage if he was forced to stay in the same place for too long.

Toby sat down next to Martin. 'This area's quiet,' he said softly. 'But there've been plenty of troop movements, apparently, between here and Milan. And crops burned – people driven from their homes, that sort of thing. So we'll be careful. Keep our heads down.'

He did not mention the rumours that they had all heard: entire villages put to the sword; men, women and children slaughtered because they had spoken for the wrong side, looked the wrong way, said the wrong thing. The jackals were ravaging the plains of northern Italy and squabbling over the spoils.

The wine was good for parched throats and aching limbs. In the centre of the tavern, a trio of musicians had begun to play. The melody of the fife and hurdy-gurdy began cautiously at first, hesitant and half-heard among the shouts and laughter of the crowded tavern. Then the music grew louder, more confident, and the drum added its own compelling rhythm. Thoughts of the war, of destruction and slaughter, dissolved in the beat of the drum, the drone of the hurdy-gurdy. Joanna's foot began to tap, and she seized Martin's hand.

'I'll show you a cure for blisters.'

A circle had begun to form. Martin, delight in his eyes, drained his cup and stood up. Then they were part of the circle, moving to the right, the left, turning and swaying. He was a hopeless dancer, of course. He didn't know his right from his left, and he trod on her toe three times. But he listened to her instructions as attentively, Joanna thought, as he would have listened to his teachers at the university, his brow furrowed with concentration, his light eyes serious.

'Three times to the right, and three to the left. Hold my hand, Martin, and it'll be easy. Don't look at your feet, just listen to the music.'

The hurdy-gurdy and fife played a jig, and half the occupants of the tavern joined in. The musicians stood to one side of the room, ragged hats shadowing their faces, their patched and gaudy clothing bright in the evening sunlight that poured through the open doorway. Martin's feet began to find their way at last, and his eyes were bright as they circled the room. The beat of the drum grew louder and faster, finishing in a flourish. Joanna was lifted into the air and whirled round, a large kiss planted on her forehead.

'You're a magician, Joanna. A witch. I've always fallen on my face before.'

They limped back to the table. There was food and more wine. The thump of feet on the wooden floor, the hiss of women's skirts sweeping the ground, almost drowned the melody of the fife. But the drumbeat was everywhere: pounding through the table, through the taproom, through the fabric of the building itself.

Martin had drunk three cups of wine. His eyes began to close and he slid sideways on the bench, his head resting on Toby's shoulder. Gently, Joanna rearranged his arms, folding them on the table, cradling his head in them.

The musicians had begun to play again. Toby was already on his feet. He took Joanna's hand in his. They found themselves in the inner circle. Four steps to the right, turn, four to the left, turn. Bow and curtsy, take your partner by the hands. Circle twice. Over and over again they broke apart and came together, Joanna seeing herself reflected in his eyes. The room spun round on its axis like the busy world. She was the axis, the taproom all the world she needed. The music grew faster and louder, filling the tavern. They were driven by the drumbeat: lights, faces, half-lit features flickered past, partly glimpsed, as the circles rotated in opposing directions. There was nothing but the music and the dance and Toby, opposite her, his black hair sticking damply to his forehead, his body moving in perfect rhythm with the music. Nothing but his hands, outstretched to take hers, and the smile on his mouth, in his eyes.

Then suddenly he wasn't smiling any more. The dance had ended in a fusillade of drumbeats. The dancers were shouting and laughing and dropping to the floor exhausted. And Toby had taken her in his arms and was kissing her.

He wasn't kissing her like Martin had kissed her. Martin's kiss had been an act of friendship. There had been love there – she was not blind – but a love that had known itself not to be reciprocated. But Toby's kisses were hungry, urgent. And she wanted them. Just as when she had stood by the canal in Venice, her skirts dripping, she had wanted him never to let her go.

But he did let her go, of course. He stood back, his hands still gripping her hands, staring at her. He said nothing, but his eyes were intense, hungry.

Around them in the darkness of the taproom, Joanna could see other couples entwined, cut off from the world, absorbed in each other. Then the musicians began to play once more, a slow, sad song, and they danced for the last time, Toby and Joanna, treading slowly and carefully through the tables and the upturned chairs and the embracing couples.

Martin woke, briefly, as the drummer beat his last roll. Blinking, rubbing his eyes, he raised his head from the table. He couldn't remember where he was: he had drunk too much, he was too tired. He peered round the room, his eyes propped open by his fingers. When he saw them, he didn't quite believe it. Toby and Joanna in the centre of the room, embracing. He thought he was dreaming, at first, that he was enduring some nightmare called up by jealousy and by an awareness of his own inadequacies. But then the music began again, a song that brought tears to his eyes, and Martin watched them as they danced, perfectly in time, perfectly in step, lost in each other's gaze.

They left the village at daybreak the following morning and continued their long ride west. As the village receded into the distance, so the bloody reminders of war increased. They saw the signs of flight, of chase, everywhere: a path made through a cornfield by someone's running feet; a pathetic bundle of pots and pans dumped beneath a hedgerow.

They rode in silence, cradling their thoughts. Toby held the reins with one hand, and balanced the other on the hilt of his sword. The heat was intense, windless. Sweat trickled down his face and made his shirt cling to his body. The horses' hooves sent up clouds of dust. He thought of Joanna Zulian, with whom he had danced the previous night. Whom he had kissed. Martin had been right, of course. No one would forget her. She could not return to Padua, she would not go back to Venice. She wanted, Toby knew, to go to France. Well, then, he'd take her to France. But for the first time he found himself thinking, what then? Where would Joanna Zulian go then?

He spoke to her as they sat in the shadow of a dusty eucalyptus, breathless with the midday heat, gulping mouthfuls of water and wine. 'We'll reach Milan in a few days, and then we'll head for the Alps. We should be in France by late October.'

Joanna nodded and smiled. Martin was sitting beside them, his back against the tree trunk, his eyes closed, his legs flung out in front of him.

Toby persisted. 'Where will you go then, Joanna? Have you family?'

She looked down, her smile fading. He saw the small shake of her head, and he knew suddenly that she was walking to France just as she had once walked into the canal: by instinct, on impulse, without thought of the consequences.

Restlessly, Toby walked to where the horses nibbled at the sparse grass. Flies buzzed around the horses' heads; a heat haze shimmered on the blue horizon.

'No one at all?' he said angrily. 'A nunnery then, do you think, Joanna? Or don't they take married nuns?'

He saw that Martin's eyes were open now and staring at them, but he couldn't read his expression. Joanna had risen; her skin was slightly flushed, but her voice was level.

'I can write,' she said quietly, 'and I can paint. And I can cook and sew, and I can tend the sick. I'll find something. I'll not starve.'

There was a silence. Her gaze held his, and Toby saw pride and a spirit of independence in her eyes.

'I'll take you to Bourges,' he said at last. Miraculously, the solution had occurred to him. He began to check the horses' harnesses and girths.

'My family live near there. They'll be glad to put you up for a while. Then we'll see.' He thought at first that she was going to argue. So, turning away from her, he took her horse's reins, and held out his hand. 'We should go now. It's too open here,' he said, as he helped her into the saddle.

The heat intensified, the occasional bad-tempered crackle of thunder heralding nothing more than a few useless drops of water. Lombardy was silent, brooding. Flames flickered in the burnt fields, carrion crows circled high over the despoiled crops and buildings. Fragments of blackened corn floated in the windless air, griming their faces and clothes. They were running desperately short of water: the streams were dried up with the heat.

The silhouette of a farm loomed against the horizon, thin plumes of smoke rising from its charred roofs. A farm would have a well, but Toby was aware of danger all around them, thick and almost tangible like the heavy, heat-soaked air. He dismounted from his horse, refusing Martin's offer to accompany him. He walked alone through the tense openness of a scorched cornfield, water-bottles in one hand, sword in the other.

The buildings were silent, deserted. The soldiers had killed even the animals: the scrawny carcasses of cows and pigs were scattered among olive trees like abandoned sacks of corn. The stench was appalling. The only sound that could be heard was the buzz of flies, and the lack of life made the hair rise on the back of Toby's neck. Touching one of the stone walls of the farmhouse, he found that it was still hot. Smoke seeped slowly through the unglazed windows, clouding the farmyard.

He did not look into the farmhouse, but walked quickly towards the well, aware of the close presence of death. Then, as he lowered the bucket into the well, he glimpsed something lying on the dirty straw in the pigsty.

He drew his sword as he walked across the cobbled yard, but returned it to its scabbard when he reached the pigsty. A girl was sprawled in the straw, her skirt and bodice ripped open by someone's knife. She was about Joanna's age, he thought, and she was quite, quite dead. Because of the heat, there were already flies trespassing on her round, young face. Retching, he straightened her clothes and kicked straw over her violated body. Then he went to the well, refilled their water-bottles and walked quickly back.

Joanna was watching for him. She waved, smiling, as he approached. She was so lovely, so untouched. As he walked across the burnt cornfield, the image of that other girl was still imprinted on his eyes. Toby thought how much it pleased him just to look at Joanna, and he thought of that dead face disfigured with blood and straw.

He gave them the water, told them to mount their horses. They would ride north, he said. It would be safer in the hills.

Two days from Milan, Joanna's horse shed a shoe as, at dusk one day, they descended a stony hillside. Slipping out of the saddle, refusing both men's offers of help, she began to walk, leading her horse by the reins. Her feet slid on the loose stones and both her shoes were holed. For the first time since she had left Padua she felt exhausted. Her muscles ached with the effort of walking downhill, the palms of her hands were permanently blistered by the reins. She wanted to lean her head against her horse's warm flank and sleep.

She heard a voice beside her say, 'Don't be silly. Let me.' And Toby Crow picked her up like a sack of corn and swung her on to his saddle. From the superior height of his horse, Joanna could see the valley spread out before her like a tapestry: the fields, a few streams, the patchwork of hedgerow and woods.

She fell asleep in the saddle, hands curled around the reins, riding astride like a man, like a gypsy. Every so often she would wake, and there would be Toby beside her, leading both her horse and his own, his dark eyes gazing downwards to the valley, his feet unfailingly choosing the safest route down the slaty hillside. Dozing, she could hear Martin's horse behind them, and when she opened her eyes, she saw the clouds of dust and small rattling stones that accompanied their descent. Every so often she would slip forward until her face touched the horse's mane, and then she would jerk abruptly awake.

Through confused dreams, she heard Martin ask, 'Is it safe?' and Toby reply, 'It's deserted. Look, Martin. It's burnt out.'

She opened her eyes. It was late evening and the shadows were long and indigo-blue. In front of them, at the end of an avenue of ilex trees, was a house. Joanna, rubbing her eyes, could see the empty windows, the black smoke-stains that trailed down the front like teardrops, the door, half-burned away, swinging on its hinges.

'Some unfortunate Venetian will be pining for his summer palace,' said Toby. His words were flippant, but his expression was grim. 'There might be a room or two still intact, though.'

Inside the villa, the kitchen was more or less undamaged. A sack of flour and an entire cheese had somehow miraculously escaped the attentions of the marauding soldiers. They ate better than they had eaten for weeks, feasting on unleavened bread and dry cheese.

Afterwards, Martin slept stretched out on the bench beside the unlit fire, mumbling and scratching in his sleep. Joanna went out into the garden. Weaving carefully through broken doors and the tumbled detritus of a rich man's house, she squeezed herself through the final, charred doorframe and on to the terrace beyond.

The silence, the perfection of what she saw, seemed a miracle. It was night now, but the moon was a white sickle in the sky and a thousand stars speckled the inky blackness. The acrid smell of the burnt house – the smell of death, destruction and hopelessness – seemed to melt away, to be replaced by the rich scents of thyme, lemon balm and rose.

The soldiers had destroyed the house, but they had not desecrated the garden. Only the weeks of neglect had begun to touch it, tangling the climbing plants, allowing the dying petals of the dipping rambling roses to gather in whisps and whorls on the pathways and lawns. The darkness deprived the flowers of colour: melilots, carnations, love-lies-bleeding were all shades of grey and gold; the waxen petals of the lilies seemed sculptured of stone; on the fruit trees the pomegranates, damascene plums and carnelian cherries hung black and heavy, sheened with moonlight. Paths spread out like rays from the terrace, roofed by arched pergolas.

Joanna heard a footstep behind her and turned. She had known that he would follow her. Toby held a lantern in his hand, and the amber light drew the contours of his face, deepening the thumbprints of weariness beneath his eyes.

She touched his face, as if to wipe away the black shadows, and he caught and kissed her hand, so that her fingers only brushed against his cheek. The scent of the roses that wound over the pergola intoxicated them as they walked. On the lawns, fountains still played, ghostly reminders of happier times, their endlessly moving water a shower of silver and gold. Beyond the pergola the hedges of box and bay and lavender twisted into complex patterns, into hearts and diamonds and crescents, enclosing fragile patches of flowers, their petals blurred and folded now in the night. Joanna fancied that the twisting labyrinthine box hedges spelled out words, phrases, and the thought came to her, through weariness and joy, that if she could only decipher them, then everything might make sense. The war, her marriage, the death of her baby, the loss of her family.

In the centre of the garden the pergolas met to form a room. Trellises arched together, smothered with convolvulus, honeysuckle and jasmine. A green room, a secret room. Peering upwards towards the tapestry of leaves, Joanna could no longer see the house, the moon or the stars. She and Toby were shut away, perfectly enclosed, cut off from the busy world.

Toby had put down the lantern. Moths fluttered round the flame, drawn by the light. She raised her face to him, and he kissed her. She could see the desire in his eyes, and she knew the strength of her longing for him. She wanted to erase all memory of the war, of disease and death and destruction. All memory of Gaetano, of her disastrous marriage, of the stifling years in Venice. She wanted to begin to live again. She did not care that she was dirty, that her hair was tangled and unkempt. She did not care that she was married to someone else. She felt the warmth of his body pressing against hers, the urgency of his hands and mouth, and she knew that this was inevitable, that it was like the garden: planned and perfect, and of a pattern she was not yet permitted to know.

'Are you sorry?' he said, much later. She understood him immediately, of course, and she shook her head. 'Not at all.' Her voice was almost lost in the whispering of the leaves, the music of the fountain. But he heard her, and smiled, and kissed her again.

Martin Gefroy never knew what had woken him – the silence of the ruined house, or the first cold fingers of dawn, perhaps, crawling down the hillside. He felt stiff, he felt twenty years older than he was, as he coaxed his aching limbs from the narrow bench. He saw immediately that he was alone. There was no Toby sprawled in a chair, his head drooping in sleep, his sword at his side; there was no Joanna curled in her cloak on the floor. Leaving the kitchen, Martin began to search through the house.

He saw things that he had not noticed in the darkness of the night before: pictures ripped by someone's violating knife; curtains and hangings torn from their hooks; a child's dress pulled apart at the seams, buttons scattered. Martin shivered in the chill early-morning light, as in his imagination he heard the laughter of the intruders, the terror of the house's occupants. His eyes bleak, he walked out of the house and on to the terrace.

He saw them then. They were walking down one of the paths that led through the garden, their figures grey in the dawn mist. Joanna's arm was threaded through Toby's, her head rested on his shoulder. Martin heard her gentle laughter, and the scent of the roses that surrounded her were heavy in the cool air.

At first he could not move. If he'd had more time, he thought. If he'd been different. If he'd not stood in competition with fearless and good-looking Toby Crow. He had known, he realized, he had always known, that this would happen. That knowledge did not lessen his anger. It was as though some frivolous god had made them for each other, not giving a damn about the rest of the world, not giving a damn about the other poor fools they enchained. He went back to the kitchen before they could see him. He went back and folded himself on the bench, his eyes closed, his heart aching.

As they rode into Milan, two days later, the weather broke. The overheated air spiralled upwards into grey and ominous clouds that massed on the horizon. The first creaking rumbles of thunder were heard as they made their way through the gates.

Milan was a French possession, had been for years. Banners of the great French families hung from the windows of the houses and flared from the chimney stacks of the hotels. The city was busy with soldiers. Pikes and lances were balanced against the walls, catching the irritable crackles of lightning that had begun to arc from the sky. In the stables, French warhorses kept the mules and ponies company. The language spoken in the streets, in the squares, was a mixture of French and Italian. Glancing at the marketplace, Toby saw that food was plentiful, but expensive.

They were still almost a hundred miles from the French border. The two-day ride from the deserted villa had been arduous and tense. Most of their money was gone: bribes for quick-tempered soldiers, payment for lodgings, for increasingly scarce food. Martin Gefroy fortified himself with frequent mouthfuls of wine, but Joanna was looking tired and fragile. Toby had offered to slow their pace for her, and she had refused, anger flashing in her grey eyes.

In the Via San Francesco d'Assisi, Toby gazed at the French standards that lined the walls of the best hotels: the fleur-de-lys, the boar's head, the unicorn and lion; crosses and saltires, chevrons and bends; the arms of the Montmorencys, the Rohans, the Bonnivets. The noise of the street – soldiers calling to one another and elbowing their way through the crowds, street-sellers shouting their wares – almost drowned the approaching thunder.

Toby heard voices calling, 'Make way, make way,' and saw soldiers pushing the street-sellers and their carts aside. Cherries rolled into the gutter, lavender was crushed underfoot. A cart surrounded by mounted men-at-arms was being hauled along the cobbles. The men-at-arms wore the fleur-de-lys of France on their tabards. But another insignia was emblazoned on their saddlecloths: a leopard beneath three crescent moons. The insignia of the du Chantonnays.

Sliding off his horse, Toby pushed his way through the crowds to the cart. Great drops of rain had begun to fall, plunging intermittently from a blackened sky. Someone swore at him, someone else tried to throw him aside, but Toby clung to the wooden railing of the cart and looked downwards into the straw.

Not Reynaud du Chantonnay, of course. Nor his foolish son, François. Instead, Guillaume du Chantonnay stared back at him, pain and curiosity in his bright blue eyes.

Guillaume began to laugh, a hoarse, wheezing chuckle. 'Toby Crow! I thought you were dead. You were on the losing side, weren't you?' His face was white, his lips two thin streaks of scarlet. There was blood showing through the blanket that covered him. 'At Agnadello,' he continued. Raindrops struck his face, mingling with the sweat that glistened on his skin. 'I was there.'

The cart had, at a sign from Guillaume, stopped.

'Not a scratch, Monsieur du Chantonnay,' said Toby softly. He was aware that Martin and Joanna had joined him, were standing beside him. 'I thought you were Reynaud. The insignia . . .'

Guillaume began to laugh again, tears gathering at the corners of his eyes. 'Hauled him on to his warhorse, and posted him off to Italy? Almost, my dear Crow, almost.' The laughter ceased, and Guillaume moved his head restlessly in the straw. 'His ghost was haunting me today, I think. Aiming well with an arquebus . . .' The blue eyes closed, then opened again. 'Reynaud is dead, monsieur. He died after a hunting accident in the summer. I had a letter yesterday from Madame de Marigny.'

Toby gripped the side of the cart. His legs nearly failed him, and his knuckles were white with the effort to stop his hands shaking. He heard Martin say to Guillaume: 'An arquebus wound, monsieur? In the leg?' But although Martin spoke to Guillaume du Chantonnay, he looked at Toby. Suddenly the crowd was oppressive, robbing him of breath. The thunder crashed again, like cymbals, like swords on shields. He wanted to be away from here. He wanted to think. He wanted time to recover the bearings he had so utterly lost.

'Will you weep for him?' whispered Guillaume from the cart. The rain was falling more heavily now. 'As much as I, I suspect . . .'

He would never know. That was what hurt, of course. He would never know whether Reynaud du Chantonnay had fathered him, or why he had abandoned him. Whatever truth he had found, Toby knew that none of it shed any light on his origins. It angered him to think that he was condemned to perpetual ignorance.

Joanna said hesitantly, 'Mr Gefroy is a physician, Monsieur du Chantonnay. He's very interested in the treatment of arquebus wounds. Perhaps you would let him look at your leg.'

'He may look at it as much as he wishes,' said Guillaume, from the straw, 'but I'll not let him saw it off. I'll not be a cripple like Reynaud.'

For Guillaume, the war had ended the previous afternoon. Not on the battleground, but in some damned skirmish for someone's damned chicken-farm. The wound hurt like hell, but he could stomach the pain. What he could not tolerate was the thought that he might never completely recover, that he might be crippled. Physical imperfection appalled him, terrified him. Hauled through the streets of Milan, carried clumsily by his servants up the stairs of his hotel, Guillaume pictured himself like Reynaud, trapped by his infirmity, stinking like a charnel-house. He would, he knew, rather die.

As Reynaud himself had died more than six weeks ago. Eleanor's letter had reached Guillaume the previous day. The letter, somehow finding its way into a herald's bundle bound for Louis de France, had taken weeks to reach him. It told, in Eleanor du Chantonnay's bold, straggly handwriting, of Reynaud's accident, Reynaud's illness, Reynaud's death. If Guillaume had never found anything approaching affection for his cousin Reynaud, he had, at least, discovered a grudging admiration for the manner of his death: jumping over the six-foot Marigny boundary wall, riding the black warhorse he had once taken into battle. The old devil.

But Eleanor's letter only exacerbated Guillaume's impatience with his physical condition. Now that Reynaud had died, Guillaume needed to return to Marigny urgently. Having seen his opportunity, he wanted to seize it with both hands. He had intended to make some sort of excuse to his king and to leave for Marigny by the end of the week. Instead, every movement, every jolt, as they carried him up the stairs, gave him agony. If he should recover, he knew that it would be weeks, even months, before he could ride again.

Both the physician and Reynaud's courier had accompanied him back to the hotel room. The physician was young, fair-haired, badly dressed. He had gently moved aside a corner of the blanket and was looking down at the shattered leg. Guillaume closed his eyes momentarily. He thought that if he looked down he would witness himself turning into the monstrosity that Reynaud had become: a foul, stinking wreck, his limbs dead before his heart had ceased to beat.

He said, 'You'll not saw it off, physician. I'd rather die.'

The physician said mildly, 'You're not going to die, monsieur, and I don't intend to amputate. Prop him up on pillows, Toby. And give him some wine.'

Guillaume was hauled into a half-sitting position. The few mouthfuls of wine that he could swallow revived him a little. Hazily, he wondered why Toby Crow should be travelling through Milan with a physician and a young woman.

When he asked, Reynaud's courier said, 'I was escorting Messer Gefroy and Madonna Zulian to France, Monsieur du Chantonnay. We had to leave Padua in a hurry. The Emperor's soldiers were within a few days of the city.'

Guillaume winced as the physician began to cut away his ripped breeches. Beads of sweat gathered on his forehead. 'Padua is under siege, I've heard,' he muttered. 'You were wise to leave.'

He thought of the girl, with her exquisite beauty and her gypsy clothes, and he thought of Toby Crow. He understood Toby's sort. In Toby's face he saw intelligence and opportunism. He was a good-looking young man, with a gloss of education picked up from his travels and a degree of expertise with a sword. Attractive to women, no doubt. A young man on the make, one of the many thousands of nobodies who intended, by wit and by perseverance, to compensate for their low birth. Guillaume had no quarrel with that: ambition was a quality that he admired. Yet he knew the consequences of ambition, and because of that he, like Reynaud, distrusted Toby Crow.

Closing his eyes again, he recalled, briefly, Madonna Zulian's face. A Venetian name, thought Guillaume. A more fanciful man might have believed out there, looking at her, that he had died and gone to heaven. He had seen that face a hundred times before, in Italian churches, in the paintings that Reynaud had collected at Marigny. High forehead, long neck, straight nose, thin brows. And those great grey eyes. He wondered whether she was Toby Crow's friend or lover.

His thoughts drifted to Eleanor, as they had done so many times since he had received her letter. His leg hurt even more now – the physician was picking out fragments of cloth from the open wound – but the pain that accompanied his thoughts of Eleanor was worse. Guillaume knew that he should be there, at Marigny, reminding Reynaud's widow of his existence. The thought that he might, within a year, possess the glorious château de Marigny was both tantalizing and agonizing. Because here he was, confined to his bed, an invalid for God knew how many weeks.

Losing control for the first time, Guillaume groaned his frustration out loud.

He heard Toby say, 'Can I get you something, Monsieur du Chantonnay? Some more wine, perhaps?'

Guillaume saw suddenly what he must do. Toby Crow had been Reynaud's courier. He knew Eleanor du Chantonnay and was familiar with the château de Marigny. He was intelligent, able, efficient. He was riding to France. And he was – Guillaume stared at Reynaud's former courier – short of money.

Guillaume beckoned to his servant. 'A pen and paper. Yes. Fetch me a pen and paper.' He struggled to sit up. 'You'll write a letter for me, Monsieur Crow. And you'll take it to Marigny, won't you? To the lovely widow – to Eleanor?'

It was not a request, it was a demand. Guillaume's hand clutched

Toby's arm, his fingernails dug into his skin. He saw a flicker of surprise, of resentment, and then of acceptance, pass over Toby's face.

'If you wish.'

Guillaume, exhausted, lay back on the pillows. He said, his eyes half closed, 'I'll pay you well, of course.'

When his servant returned with writing materials, Guillaume began to dictate. Then he gave his instructions: that Toby give the letter to the widow of Marigny in person, as soon as possible. Guillaume feared Eleanor might accept the hand of the first rapacious man to ask for her, simply because she was too foolish to say no.

Guillaume noticed that the physician was staring at Toby Crow. Martin Gefroy said, 'I'll have to find an apothecary. You're to come with me, Toby. I'll send Madonna Zulian to sit with you, monsieur.'

Martin found an apothecary's shop in an alleyway off one of the squares. Toby shook off Martin's grip as they walked across the rain-soaked piazza, but he did not, as Martin thought he might, tell him to go to hell. Inside the shop, which was small and dark and crammed with bottles and alembics and flasks and jars, Martin gave his orders. When the apothecary had scuttled away to the back room, he turned to Toby.

Back there in the street, Toby had looked, Martin thought, as though someone had hit him in the stomach. Martin had frequently wanted to hit him, hard, over the past two days, but he realized that he would achieve nothing other than badly bruised knuckles. Now, he thought with some satisfaction, the wounded man had as much as done the job for him. He recalled the startled look on Toby's face when he saw the insignia.

'Who is he?' Martin asked. 'The gentleman with the arquebus wound. Who is he?'

A bolt of lightning lit up the shop with an unreal orange light. Toby had recovered himself a little and, without even glancing at Martin, said, 'His name is Guillaume du Chantonnay. He has lands in Brittany.'

'I mean,' said Martin, struggling for patience, 'what is he to you?'

Toby stared at Martin, with eyes as cold and bleak as the empty sockets of the dusty skull that stood on the apothecary's table. 'He's nothing to me,' he said. 'Nothing to me at all.'

Martin knew that he was lying. He remembered the other name, the name that had made Toby whiten and grip the side of the cart.

'And Reynaud – the man who died in the summer? And Eleanor? They're nothing to you also, I suppose?'

There was another drumroll of thunder, and the apothecary could be heard preparing unguents in the back room. As he waited for a reply, Martin saw anger darkening Toby's eyes.

'My, my. What curiosity. I thought curiosity was my province.' Toby's voice was cold, hard, dangerously taut. 'I worked for Reynaud du Chantonnay for a few years, that's all. When I couldn't use my sword-arm – you remember, surely, Martin? – I was the Seigneur de Marigny's courier.'

'You promised . . . you promised Joanna that you would take her to France.' Martin was struggling for breath. There was not a flicker of guilt on Toby's face.

'So I will.'

'But you said . . . when you wrote the letter . . .' He knew that he was gabbling like an idiot. He simply couldn't stop himself. He had the satisfaction, though, of seeing a reflected anger in Toby's face.

'I'll take Joanna to my parents' house, and then I'll ride on to Marigny. But it's really none of your business, is it, Martin?'

Martin, peaceable, good-natured Martin, clenched his hands into fists. 'It may not be *my* business,' he hissed. 'But it has become Joanna's business, don't you think? To know a little of your past, your occupation, your *name*, damn it? She's *married*, for God's sake. Or had you forgotten that? Had you thought what will happen to her? My God' – and Martin found that he was unable to stop himself – 'couldn't you have left her *alone*?'

Toby took one step towards him. In the greenish light of the stormy sky, the dried herbs and snakeskins and donkeys' tails hanging from the rafters quivered and then stilled. Toby said, very softly: 'I'll take Joanna to Bourges, as I promised. I'll then leave her there with my eminently respectable parents, in their eminently respectable house. I'll then go to the late Reynaud du Chantonnay's château and deliver Guillaume's letter to the Seigneur's widow. And then I'll go back to Italy. But just remember, Martin' – Toby's finger jabbed at Martin's chest – 'you gave me no choice. I've got you as far as Milan. I'm going to get you to France. If you don't like the service, then find someone else. If you can't do that, then shut up. *You're* the physician, *you're* the one who's spent years learning to fuss about people. I'm only a bloody soldier.'

The apothecary reappeared with a rustling of shiny black robes. Bottles and jars were gathered in a small basket. As Martin turned to take the basket, he heard Toby leave the shop, the door slamming shut behind him.

CHAPTER EIGHT

When they left the room, he wanted to close his eyes and sleep, to shut himself off from pain and fear. But he was afraid that if he slept, he would not wake. And besides, there was the girl – the girl who had accompanied Toby Crow and the physician. He heard the sweep of her skirts on the stairs, on the floor of his room. He felt a hand gently brush back the hair from his face, and begin to dab at his brow with something cool and soothing. He knew it was her. None of his damn fool servants were capable of touching him like that. He wanted to see her face again.

Guillaume opened his eyes. Just for a moment, then, looking at her, he had a glimpse of something different, something better. Something other than the forces that had driven him all his life: his need for Marigny, for the strength and security that the château and its lands represented; his long wait for Reynaud's death. He saw beauty, and dimly, as if in the distance, he saw Marigny as it truly was, a thing of loveliness, not just a symbol of power.

Guillaume stilled Joanna's hand, taking it in his own. 'Madonna, I am obliged to you. But I am . . . *embarrassed*, I think, to be tended by a lady to whom I have not been introduced.'

She smiled, looking down at him. Her eyes were grey, fringed with long feathery lashes, and her hair was a light reddish-brown. She wore a black gown and her head was uncovered.

'My name is Joanna Zulian, monsieur. I was living in Padua, but . . . the wars . . .'

Her voice ebbed away. He saw sadness in her eyes, so he said gently, 'Padua is under siege now, I believe. So you shouldn't, perhaps, regret your decision to leave your home. You'll be safer in France.'

'Yes.' Her wide, serene eyes gazed into his. 'I'm sure you're right, monsieur. Now, are you comfortable?'

She moved gracefully, her wide black skirts settling around her in rich folds of material. Her hair was coiled and plaited on top of her head, and her face was pale, shadowed round the eyes, her cheekbones hollowed. She was very young, Guillaume realized – seventeen or eighteen, perhaps.

Now she was removing the cloth with which the physician had covered his leg and replacing it with a fresh one.

'Madonna . . . There's no need. I have servants for that sort of thing . . .'

Guillaume did not usually feel embarrassment, it was just that she was so young, so clean, so lovely. He didn't want to see her hands marked with blood, to witness her eyes gazing at the squalor of the battlefield.

'Your servants will hurt you, monsieur. I won't.' Her voice was still kind, but allowed him no argument. 'My father was a physician, you see. He taught me everything he knew. So you may trust me.' She looked down at Guillaume, full of concern and sympathy.

Guillaume, unused to being the recipient of kindness, was reminded of the nurse who had tended him from birth. Except, he recalled, with an uncontrollable flutter of laughter, she had had warts and a moustache. Whereas Joanna Zulian had the face of an angel.

She laid the clean cloth carefully over the wound. Clenching his teeth, Guillaume whispered, 'Will I recover, Madonna? Will I walk again?'

Joanna Zulian said, 'The bleeding seems to have lessened. Monsieur Gefroy will know what to do, monsieur. He's the best physician in Italy.'

He wanted her to continue speaking, because her voice halted the progress of those other, terrible thoughts. So he said, 'Talk to me, Madonna Zulian. Please.'

So she told him about her childhood. Guillaume closed his eyes, listening as she spoke of Spain and France, Portugal and Navarre. Of the parents she had loved. Of the home she had never had. He envied her, he who had lived in great houses all his life. He who lusted after the château de Marigny. He who had scarcely known his parents and whose few memories of them were bitter.

Opening his eyes again, he watched her as she worked, noting the curves and angles of her profile silhouetted by the window. Outside, the thunder crashed and the lightning flared and rain battered against the window-panes. But Guillaume felt peaceful. Thoughts of Eleanor, of Marigny, even of his wounded leg, began to melt away.

He was almost sorry when the physician appeared, his hands full of jars and unguents.

*

Martin put Guillaume du Chantonnay to sleep by holding a sponge soaked in mandragora under his nose. The blue eyes flickered and closed.

The treatment of arquebus wounds fascinated Martin. Once, it had been thought that the only solution for such new and terrible wounds was amputation. Then cauterization had become popular: searing the wounds with boiling liquids or the red-hot blade of a sword. But cauterization was not only extremely painful, it also produced fever. Martin, looking at his sleeping patient, doubted if he would survive another shock to his system.

He began to pick out the small fragments of bone from the ragged wound. The shot had only chipped at the bone, and he could see gunpowder blackening the raw flesh. He discovered that the solace he generally found in his work was absent. His actions were skilful, but mechanical. His anger, unleashed after days of containment, had not abated. The thoughts and images that had tormented him since he had seen Toby and Joanna together in the Italian garden were relentless.

He had trusted Toby Crow to act as Joanna's protector, and Toby, damn his eyes, had seduced her. Martin glanced up at Joanna standing beside him, and misery swamped him again. Walking alone back from the apothecary's shop to the hotel, he had realized the implications of what had happened.

As he began to smooth an unguent of rose oil and egg yolk on to the clean wound, he said, 'I'll have to stay here, Joanna. It'll be weeks before Monsieur du Chantonnay is on his feet again. And if I go, some quack will be anointing him with frogs' spawn and goats' turds.' He didn't look at her. He felt raw, like the wound he attended. He knew that if there had ever been any possibility of Joanna Zulian loving him, then that possibility had died the day he had brought Toby Crow to her.

'And Toby?' he heard her whisper. Momentarily he hated her. For leaving him dissatisfied and empty. For robbing him of the equilibrium he had always accepted as his right.

'Toby's going to France,' he replied. His voice was careless, as he strove to disguise his pain. 'He'll take you to his family in Bourges, and then he'll ride on to Touraine. To his former employer's house. To Reynaud du Chantonnay's house.'

At first Joanna said nothing, and when finally she spoke, her voice was small, tight. 'His employer's dead, Martin. Reynaud du Chantonnay is dead. So why should Toby go there?'

Martin began to wind the bandage around Guillaume's wounded leg. 'To offer his condolences to his former employer's widow, I believe.' He smiled unpleasantly. 'Well, I always did admire our Toby's ambition.'

When he looked up and saw her face, he regretted his words instantly, hating himself instead. 'I'm sorry, Joanna . . . I didn't mean it.' Martin closed his eyes, shutting out her white face, the hurt in her eyes. 'I'm tired . . . I don't know what I'm saying.'

I'm jealous, he might have said, if he could have recovered the honesty that had always been part of him. I'm jealous of Toby Crow, who can find his way from Padua to Milan, who can use a sword, who can dance. Who made love to you, damn him.

They found themselves together again in one of the many splendid rooms of the du Chantonnay hotel. Only they weren't together any more. They were three separate people, divided by the events of the day and silently nursing their own private troubles. They made poor work of the excellent meal that the du Chantonnay servants had provided, picking at the roast fowl and jellies. Martin drank too much and Toby was monosyllabic. Eventually, Martin rose and left the room, muttering something about checking his patient. Joanna sat on the window-seat, her knees hunched up to her chin, looking out to where yellow rivers of rain coursed down the soaking streets.

Toby came and stood beside her. 'Your shoes, Joanna,' he said. 'Give me your shoes.' She didn't understand him at first. So he sat opposite her on the window-seat and slid her shoes from her bare brown feet.

'I bought some leather,' he said. 'To mend them.' He held her tattered slippers up to her, so that she could see the holes in the sole.

From walking, she thought. Or dancing. She felt tears prickle at the corners of her eyes as she watched him shape the scraps of leather with his knife. She understood that he, too, was making a sort of farewell.

'Martin said you were going to Touraine,' she whispered.

He nodded, his eyes following the careful path of his knife. 'After I've taken you to Bourges, I'm going back to Marigny,' he said. 'I hadn't thought I'd ever go back.'

'Then why must you go?'

The words came out before she could stop them. The knife was poised motionless in his hand.

'I have to. Guillaume du Chantonnay has asked me to give his condolences to the Seigneur's widow. He dictated a letter to me this morning. He's paying me to take it to Marigny.'

She didn't believe him. Oh, he had a letter, no doubt, but that was only part of the reason he wished to return to Marigny. Martin's words that afternoon still stung.

Toby slid the new sole into Joanna's shoe and squinted at it. Outside, the rain was falling more softly, trailing down the window-panes, blurring the roads and buildings.

'Madame du Marigny . . .' said Joanna. She didn't look at Toby, she still stared out of the window. 'Is she very old? Very grey?'

He laughed. He picked up the second scrap of leather. 'Not at all. She was much younger than her late husband. She was the Seigneur's second wife.'

'Well, I always did admire our Toby's ambition.' A beautiful, wealthy young widow; a good-looking, talented but penniless young man in need of something more than insecurity and uncertainty. It all fitted. Martin had been right. Joanna felt a tear slide down her cheek. She cried because the three of them would part, she thought. She cried for the end of summer.

The door opened. Martin said, 'I gave Monsieur du Chantonnay a draught. There's a slight fever, but no sign of gangrene, thank God.'

Joanna looked at him, but could not speak. The Englishman glanced at her, curled up pale and barefooted on the window-seat. And then at Toby, beside her. Eventually, Martin's cold gaze came to rest on the slippers, the scraps of leather, in Toby's hands.

'Well, well,' he said. 'Aren't you clever? A great man in a fight, and good company for the ladies. A terrific sense of direction – you never lose your way, do you, Toby? And you can mend shoes, too. What an education you must have had.'

The shoes, the leather and Toby's knife slipped to the floor. Martin's blow glanced off Toby's jaw before Joanna was able to call out. Then Toby struck the Englishman on the face, and Martin staggered backwards into the table, knocking plates, cutlery, jellies and fruit to the floor.

She had to throw herself between them before they would stop. Martin, choking, had hurled himself on top of Toby. Joanna felt food and fragments of crockery beneath her bare feet, as she grabbed at the folds of Martin's robes and seized a handful of Toby's hair. 'Look at you – just look at you!' she cried. Her voice cracked and broke. 'Stupid, *stupid* men.'

Blood was flowing from Martin's nose. Toby's shirt was ripped from shoulder to wrist. The superb dining-chamber of the superb du Chantonnay hotel was littered with broken glass and scraps of food.

Wiping his bloody face on his robe, Martin staggered to a chair and sat down, his head in his hands. Joanna heard the door slam as Toby left the room. Then, kneeling on the floor, she began to pick up the pieces of crockery, to attempt to clear up the mess they had made.

Toby and Joanna left for France two days after the fight. Martin's voice was cold, his eyes unforgiving. Joanna made her farewells, kissing Martin carefully on his bruised face, wishing Guillaume du Chantonnay a speedy recovery.

They rode towards the foothills of the Alps. Guillaume had lent an escort to take them to the Italian border: six armed retainers, each clad in Guillaume's colours of blue and silver, each bearing the du Chantonnay arms, rode with them through the highlands of Lombardy towards Piedmont.

They rested that evening in a tavern in Novara. Joanna reflected upon how the fragile relationship between herself and Toby had begun to crack. Since Martin had spoken, since Toby himself had confirmed what Martin had told her, she knew that she had, in the Italian garden, made yet another error of judgement. She could paint, she could tend the sick, she could make gardens, but she could not judge men. She had recognized neither Donato nor Gaetano for what they had been until it was too late, until they had almost destroyed her.

Toby had risen from his seat and was standing behind her. 'Three weeks,' he said, 'and then we'll be in the Dauphiné.'

Joanna nodded. The thought of the journey ahead no longer excited her; instead she felt a formless misery as she realized yet again her lack of direction, her lack of any sort of place she could call home.

'You'll like Paul and Agnès, Joanna,' said Toby. 'They're good people.'

He was looking at her with affection, almost with pity, as though he could read her thoughts. She knew his affection to be a mirage, though, because he was unable to offer her loyalty. Affection was nothing without loyalty. That, at least, she had learned.

'I won't stay,' she said. 'Only long enough to sell Isotta's jewels, to think what to do next. That's all.'

She was aware of a gulf between them as wide as the valleys that parted the distant mountains. Toby stood at her side, restless, impatient to be on the road again. He had never wanted to make this journey. He owed her nothing.

'I'll find work,' Joanna continued proudly. 'A gentleman that needs a housekeeper. A lady looking for a seamstress. Something like that.'

She heard his hiss of exasperation. He took her arm and, almost dragging her, led her out of the taproom, across the courtyard, past Guillaume's lounging servants, to the small dew-pond that gathered in the curve of the valley.

'Look at yourself, Joanna. Go on, look. A seamstress? A housekeeper? Don't be bloody ridiculous.' Toby's hand, pressing at the back of her neck, forced her to look down into the still water.

She wore the red dress in which she had married Gaetano; her hair was combed back into plaits, clipped with two pearl clasps of Isotta's. Her face, perfectly reflected in the dark water, reminded her suddenly of the face in the portrait that Gaetano had painted. Serene, enigmatic, with no trace yet etched upon it of loss or loneliness.

'People don't engage housekeepers who look like that, Joanna. Housekeepers have thick waists and plain faces, and they can't dance.'

Tears hovered at the corners of her eyes. His hand had slid down her back and now lingered at her waist. If she turned to him, he would hold her again as he had held her in the secret room walled with flowers.

But she did not turn to him. She knew that he was wrong, that there was a place for her somewhere. She said angrily, moving away from him, 'What shall I be, Toby? Shall I be a painter, like Gaetano? Or a physician, like my father? Or a soldier, like you?'

When he said nothing, she added in a harsh voice, 'And I cannot marry again, of course.'

His eyes suddenly avoided hers, looking out instead to the heat-soaked valley, to the hills that rose, cool and distant, beyond. 'Do you regret that?' he said.

Joanna shook her head. 'Not at all. I have married once and that was enough to last me a lifetime.'

Her voice was bitter, but she spoke the truth. Her experience of marriage – her own, Isotta's, even her parents' – was hardly inspiring, and yet what else was there for a penniless young woman? A lifetime of drudgery, she suspected, scouring someone else's pots and pans, caring for someone else's children.

'And what happened between us? Do you regret *that*?'

He had asked her that once before. His tone made her cringe and she could not look at him. She did not understand the alchemy that existed between them, but she had grown to recognize his ambitions. She could not hate him for those ambitions – she knew that she possessed some of the same impulses herself. But neither would she be tied to him in any way. She could not trust him. She had understood that the first time she had set eyes on Toby Crow, long ago in Taddeo's studio. Nothing had happened since to alter that first impression. And because of that lack of trust, she knew that she must deliberately destroy the remnants of the affection that had existed between them.

'I needed to erase the memory of what happened to me in Padua,' she said. 'The memory of my marriage.'

He turned to her, his eyes bright with anger. 'And did you?' he asked. 'Did you erase it?'

She nodded. 'A little. It helped.'

She moved away from him and began to walk around the dew-pond. The setting sun sent gold and scarlet streaming over the hills. Guillaume's men had abandoned the courtyard for the taproom.

'It shouldn't have happened.' Her voice was clear and cold. 'You have nothing to offer me, and I have nothing to offer you. When we reach Bourges, I shall thank you from the bottom of my heart for escorting me from Italy, and then we shall part.'

She saw Toby turn on his heel. When he was out of sight, she stooped and picked up a few small pebbles. Then, one by one, she tossed them into the water. Their widening ripples touched and then drifted apart.

Agnès was picking bunches of elderberries from the trees that edged the stream at the bottom of the garden. Her apron was spattered with purple, and some of the juice had run through to the faded grey of her bodice.

Gathering elderberries always made Agnès think of Toby, her son. She had always thought of him as her son, ever since that first day when Paul had brought him home and she had dunked him, spitting and cursing, in the horse-trough, washing off what had seemed like years of accumulated filth and grime. Later that night, when she had managed to persuade the child to sleep in a clean bed with clean sheets, she had wept for the weals she had seen on his back. She had not hated the shoemaker

Paul had bought the child from: she found that sort of cruelty too incomprehensible for hatred.

Now, dropping plump berries into the basket, Agnès recalled the day that had followed the bath in the horse-trough. The child Toby had stared at the garden, at the basket of elderberries. And then he had run to the basket, convinced that such plenty would be taken away from him. He had crammed the fruit into his mouth, juice running down his chin, until his small mistreated stomach had rebelled.

These days she thought of her son constantly, and now found herself listening for the sound of his voice as she washed the dishes or fed the pigs.

She needed Toby now because of Paul. Paul never complained and bore few obvious signs of sickness, but Agnès knew that something was wrong. He had lost weight: clothes that had once fitted well now hung loose on his gaunt shoulders and thin arms. Men of Paul's age, if they were well-fed, generally put on weight. Sometimes he was too tired to go back to the school in the afternoon. If Agnès questioned him, he laughed away her inquiries. But her worries were unceasing and she longed to share them with someone.

Now, looking up from the basket, Agnès heard the sound of horses' hooves. It was a sound that always made her hope. Footsteps crunched on the narrow cinder path beside the house. Two pairs of footsteps. Then the gate opened.

She almost dropped the basket, She had never doubted that Toby would return: she knew his restlessness, but understood also the need that he himself had not yet recognized for an anchor, a safe haven. What made the basket slip and juggle against her breast was the woman who followed Toby through the gate. Walking forward, the basket still clutched ridiculously in her arms, Agnès's gaze darted from Toby to the auburn-haired girl, and then back to Toby. She knew that she could not disguise the question that formed in her eyes, any more than she could disguise the smile that almost split her face in two.

He took the basket out of her arms and placed it carefully on the ground. Then he hugged her, a great bear hug that lifted her off her feet and squeezed the breath out of her body. There were tears trailing from the corners of her eyes as she clutched at his jacket and spoke his name. She touched his brown, sun-stained face: he looked older, harder, as though he had travelled a long way, as though he had seen many things. Then, recalling herself, she turned to the girl in the black dress.

'*Maman*, this is Madame Zulian. She needed an escort to take her to France. I thought perhaps she could stay here for a few days.'

Agnès rapidly rearranged the thoughts that tumbled through her head. Not Toby's wife, then, collected from some foreign country over the past three years. Smiling, she took the girl's hand in hers and raised her from her curtsy. 'You're welcome to stay with us as long as you wish, madame.'

'Joanna,' said the girl. 'My name is Joanna.'

She was younger than Toby. Very young, realized Agnès. Eighteen or so. And quite strikingly beautiful. She had light chestnut hair and grey eyes, an unusual combination that was emphasized by the almost transparent pallor of her skin. Seeing the girl's becoming black gown, Agnès was suddenly conscious of her own purple-stained apron, of her wiry grey curls that persistently escaped her cap.

'Joanna's a widow,' said Toby. 'She's Venetian. She had to leave Italy – the wars, you see, *maman*.'

She led them to the house, chattering inanities to put Joanna Zulian at her ease and to absorb her own outpouring of happiness and shock. Inside, she found them seats and drinks. And then, her hand shaking only a little, she scribbled a note and sent the chimney-sweep's one-eyed son to fetch Paul from the school.

Agnès told Toby her fears the following morning.

She had put on her apron and sent Joanna with Paul into the village. Paul looked better today, happy with his son's return and enjoying the company of Joanna Zulian. If she had not known him so well, Agnès would have been jealous.

She was making elderberry wine. Looking at Toby affectionately, she thought that he had, after all, changed little. He was a man in his mid-twenties now, tall, brown and muscular, but he remained as restless as he was as a child.

Agnès lifted down the sieve from the shelf, and balanced it over a pan. 'Tell me, then,' she said, 'It's three years, this time, not five. An improvement of sorts, I suppose.'

He grinned shamefacedly. 'You were always in my thoughts, *maman*. Always the woman I treasured in my heart.'

'Ha,' said Agnès sceptically. She began to ladle raisin pulp into the

sieve. 'Your Joanna makes me feel like a serving-maid – a scullion.' Her apron was already scattered with blobs of raisin juice and streaked with purple from the elderberries.

'She's not *my* Joanna.' Toby, leaning against the window-sill, spoke mildly, but Agnès noticed how his fingers fiddled constantly with the loose window-latch.

Agnès rinsed the elderberries in the sink. 'You'd do better to repair that latch than to break it altogether, Toby. And if she's not your Joanna, then whose Joanna is she?'

Toby, obediently, began to dig the loose nail out of its slot. 'She needed someone to escort her to France. I was there at the time, that's all. We met briefly a few years before, in Venice.'

Agnès had always been able to tell when he was lying. When he'd stolen biscuits, when he'd painted the pig with limewash, she had always, eventually, been able to coax him into the truth. She had succeeded in teaching him, she had believed, that the habit of lying was a poor one.

Now she knew that he told her only half-truths. Her hurt must have showed, for he put down the hammer and nail and with exasperation said, 'I took Joanna to France as a favour, *maman*. A favour to a mutual acquaintance. I had no choice. It wasn't what I would have chosen to do. I intended to stay in Italy to fight.'

'She's a pretty girl, Toby,' said Agnès steadily. 'Very pretty. Paul is half in love with her already.'

'Your saucepan's full, *maman*. And yes, Joanna is pretty. She's beautiful, in fact. But we're nothing to each other. Joanna's made that perfectly clear.'

Again, she saw deception in his eyes. Self-deception, she realized, as she lifted the sieve off the pan and placed the pot full of elderberries on the stove. But she said nothing more. Toby's affairs were his own, he was no longer a child. He had survived alone, had supported himself for almost ten years, and she had no right to inquire about his private life.

As he began to hammer a new nail into the latch, she said carefully, 'I'm glad you're back, Toby. Particularly glad, this time.'

His anger subsided and he turned to her. He had never borne grudges, she thought, never sulked.

'What is it?' he said. 'Are you worried about something?'

'It's Paul.' Agnès frowned, absently stirring the elderberries with a wooden spoon. 'I don't think he's well, Toby. He has lost weight.'

'He was always thin. Paul works too hard and eats too little.'

She tried to smile. 'Yes. That's it, I expect.'

He crossed the kitchen and put his arm around her shoulder. 'There's more, isn't there? Tell me.'

The elderberries were simmering nicely now. She said, 'He wakes early in the morning. He leaves the bedchamber and wanders around. He tries to work, to read, but I've watched him, and he doesn't turn the pages. He says he's well, but –'

'But you don't believe him.' His voice was flat.

Agnès knew how close Toby had once been to Paul. From behind her, she could smell the rich, sweet scent of the elderberries and raisins.

'No. I don't believe him. It's good to have you home, Toby. Perhaps you can talk to him. Perhaps you could persuade him to see a physician.'

She heard him say, 'I can't stay, *maman*,' and the kitchen seemed grey suddenly, sunless.

He didn't meet her eyes. 'I've a letter to deliver. I worked for the du Chantonnays of Marigny for a while, as a courier. The Seigneur de Marigny is dead now, but I met his cousin in Italy, and he gave me a letter to take to the widow.' He flung out his hands in a gesture of despair. 'I have to go. I can't stay here. You do see that, don't you, *maman*?'

Slowly, she nodded. He was right, of course, there was nothing for him here. He was not a farmer, nor a schoolteacher. If she made him remain here, then the narrowness, the isolation of this place, would crush him. He was not made for contained existence, a life of small events and limited company. What she loved in him – his physical courage, his humour, his quickness of understanding – would be obliterated. He would become ordinary.

Gently, he took her by the waist and lifted her on to the table, so that her face was, for once, level with his. 'I'll come back, I promise,' he said. 'It won't be five years, this time, or even three. And you'll let Joanna stay, won't you? She'll talk to Paul. She'll make him better. Her father was a physician, you see.' He reached inside his doublet. He added, 'And this is to help out until I come back.'

Agnès took the purse that he gave her and peered inside it. Shaking her head, she pushed it back into his hands. 'It's too much, Toby. Much too much. Don't be ridiculous.' There were tears at the corners of her eyes.

'You can buy another pig, *maman*.' She watched as he placed the purse on the topmost corner of the dresser, where he knew she would not be able to reach it down and return it to him. 'Or a sack of corn-seed.'

There was a trail of black smoke and the smell of burning sugar. 'The elderberries!' Agnès cried. She jumped off the table and ran to the stove.

The house of Paul and Agnès Dubreton was a sanctuary, a haven. For the first few days of her stay, Joanna slept and ate and washed months of dust out of her clothes and hair. Standing beside Agnès, scrubbing the mud out of the hems of her gowns in the old wooden tub, or out in the garden, discussing sewing-times and storage methods, and sharing with Agnès the papers full of tiny seeds she had harvested from her garden in Padua, she rediscovered the pleasure of female company.

She helped Paul, too. His eyesight was deteriorating, so she wrote letters for him and took notes from complicated textbooks. They talked for hours: about the towns and cities of Italy, about the painters of Venice and Padua. Guiltily, she kept up the pretence that she was a widow, travelling through France to join her surviving relations. Until recently her need to leave Italy had dominated her thoughts. Now, when she considered her future, she imagined it as both solitary and featureless. She had cherished a childhood memory of France – of St John's Eve bonfires and flower-filled valleys. But her child's France had been peopled with Sanchia, with Donato, with the lords and ladies and villagers who had welcomed a skilled physician into their midst. Now she had no home, no family, no profession.

One windy, grey morning, pegging out sheets in the garden, she told Agnès about Sanchia and Donato. And then, slowly and painfully, about Venice and her long wait for a father who had never returned. Agnès was kind and understanding. She told Joanna in turn a little about her own, less eventful, history.

Two days later, Toby left. Joanna hadn't realized how much it would hurt. Since Milan, everything had altered. Since Martin Gefroy had said, *'I always did admire our Toby's ambition,'* and Joanna had learned that the widow of the Seigneur de Marigny was not old and grey, but young and landed and beautiful. The seeds of mistrust had been sewn, choking what had briefly been beautiful and good. She knew, in her heart, that Martin had been right. Toby was restless, ambitious: she saw her own dissatisfaction with convention and confinement reflected in his dark eyes.

She thanked him, formally and sincerely, for taking her away from Italy. Then she left Toby saying his farewells to Paul and Agnès, to people who had some sort of a claim on him. Slipping out of the door, she walked away from the house, through Agnès's dying garden, past the peach trees and the well, towards the small copse that lay beyond the stream.

The land was low-lying, thick with elder and willow, and carpeted with a smooth, green swathe of moss. Joanna sat on a moss-covered log in a small clearing, her knees hunched to her chin, her arms folded around her knees. She thought of the past, of Donato and Sanchia, of Isotta and Taddeo, of Gaetano and Paolo. Months ago, in the Italian garden, she had thought it had all begun to make sense at last: the abandonment, the partings, the loss. But now there was only another parting.

She heard footsteps behind her, and turned. For one foolish moment she thought that it might be Toby, that they might at last break through the barriers of pride and mistrust they had both built up so determinedly. But instead she saw Paul Dubreton stooping to avoid the overhanging branches, treading through the carpet of moss.

'Agnès thought you might be here. It's one of her favourite places, too. Myself, I prefer the study, with a fire in the grate.'

She looked up at him and tried to smile, patting the log beside her. 'He's gone, hasn't he?'

Paul nodded and sat down. 'Agnès is cleaning the parlour. Lots of noise and dust everywhere. It keeps her mind off things.'

'I thought . . .' Joanna paused. The copse was silent except for the distant rippling of the stream. Overhead, branches threaded, making a black pattern of chequers and crosses on the pale sun. 'I thought things had changed. That I had found a place.' She balled her hands, rubbing them against her eyes. 'Oh – not necessarily even a *place*. Just . . . something. Someone. But I was wrong.'

Paul silently offered her his handkerchief. The trees, the carpet of moss, the stream, had become blurred with her tears.

'Do you love him?' he said. 'An impertinent question, but . . .'

She rubbed her eyes and realized that she did not even know. In the empty months after the death of her baby, she thought that she had lost the capacity for love. And yet, somewhere on the road from Padua to Milan, she had begun to feel alive again.

She shook her head hopelessly. 'I don't know. And even if I did' – she shrugged – 'he doesn't love me. Toby's concerned with other things, isn't he? He is *ambitious*.'

Her voice was bitter. Glancing at Paul's kind, concerned face, she took a deep breath and plunged into the abyss. She had realized over the last few days that she could not live a lie. Not here.

'Besides, even if we did care for each other, it would still be hopeless. I lied to you, you see. I'm not a widow. I'm still married.' She heard Paul's slow exhalation of breath. She glanced up, expecting to see in his eyes disapproval and disgust. Instead she saw disappointment. 'My husband's still alive,' she continued. 'I left him seven months ago. He's living in Venice, I believe.'

Joanna slid off the tree trunk. She was still clutching Paul's handkerchief. She said proudly, 'I'll go tomorrow. Gaetano returned my dowry to me. And my Aunt Isotta left me her jewels. I'll find a room in Bourges.'

She began to walk back through the copse, pushing aside the branches, not caring that they whipped back and struck her. From behind her, Paul's voice floated through the damp autumn air.

'And who will help me write my letters, now that my eyesight has grown so poor? And who will talk about plants to Agnès, and help her plan her flower-garden?'

Joanna stopped, trapped by branches, by hope. Then, slowly, she turned back.

'My dear,' said Paul, 'we collect waifs and strays, Agnès and I. Will you stay with us a while?'

Toby had not properly explained to Joanna why he had to return to Marigny, because he didn't really know himself. To deliver Guillaume du Chantonnay's letter, yes. But for Eleanor? For François? Because ten months ago he had offered at least half a promise to Reynaud du Chantonnay's lovely wife?

Since he had last ridden from Marigny, convinced he would never return, everything had changed. Eleanor had been widowed, and François had inherited both château and lands. Riding across the meadow, Toby half expected the portcullis to slam down, the drawbridge to lift, leaving him stranded and foolish on the furthest bank. A fitting reward for impertinence and ambition. But the drawbridge remained where it was, and the gatekeeper, recognizing him, smiled and waved as he rode into the courtyard.

He had known, leaving Bourges, that in riding away he was hiding from something he did not wish to face. Since he had last seen them, Agnès and Paul had become fragile and mortal. As a child they had seemed gods to him, possessed of limitless patience, wisdom and strength. And there had been Joanna, of course. She still fascinated him: she would, he guessed, always fascinate him. It had been unbearable to live under the same roof and not touch her, not kiss her, not share a bed with her. Joanna had made her lack of interest plain, and Toby still felt a rush of anger at the memory of the conversation that had taken place in Novara. And as both Joanna herself and Martin Gefroy had memorably pointed out to him, she was married. He had nothing to offer her. Irritable with frustration and impatience, Toby had made the easy choice and ridden to Marigny.

Inside the courtyard, Toby slid off his horse and handed the reins to the stable-boy. For a moment he stood surrounded by the banners and emblems of Marigny. He was aware yet again that this place held him, drew him, reminded him every moment of his own small, unknown part in its history.

There was the sound of footsteps, light and fast on the curved stone steps of a turret. Toby turned and saw Eleanor du Chantonnay. It was a meeting he had steeled himself for, anticipating disdain, resentment, contempt – everything Joanna Zulian had reserved for him, and more. A few well-aimed kicks from some of the beefier servants, and he'd find himself lying face-first in the meadow beyond the moat.

But Eleanor did not call for her men or spit in his face. Toby bowed and looked up at her. He saw to his surprise that there were tears brimming over her lids. 'I saw you riding down the path,' she said. Her voice faltered. 'I thought you were dead. Guillaume thought you'd died at Agnadello.'

He saw the pain, the happiness on her face. He experienced a complicated mixture of shock and hope, and a realization that he had once again attached someone to him without thought of the consequences.

He said gently, 'Not a scratch, as you see, Madame. The Sieur du Chantonnay himself has been wounded, unfortunately, but he's recovering. I've brought you a letter from him.'

She made no inquiry about Guillaume, though, and did not take the letter that Toby held out to her. Instead, she walked towards him, lifting one hand to touch his face as if to check that he was real and not a ghost that had ridden from the battlefield.

'Reynaud is dead,' she said at last. Her dark eyes were intense. The black of her gown emphasized the pallor of her face. Toby was reminded of the desperation he had briefly glimpsed that evening in the linen-room.

'You'll stay, won't you?' she whispered.

Her palm, cool and smooth, still touched his face. He thought of Italy, then of Agnès, Paul and Joanna. He felt loyalties and aspirations pulling him in opposing directions; he felt a rush of excitement at the possibility of a different future.

When he did not reply, Eleanor added, 'François needs you, Toby. Marigny is his now. He has dismissed many of the servants for half-imagined slights. He has dismissed Meraud. He isn't ready for . . . for all this.'

There was an urgency in her voice: it wobbled and cracked. The courtyard was darkening, and long shadows threw themselves from the towers and pinnacles, rubbing out the shields and the escutcheons of the du Chantonnays. Eleanor's fingers pressed hard into his skin, and her eyes were dark and brilliant. Gently, Toby enfolded and lowered her hand.

They dined in state that evening, at François's insistence, to celebrate Toby's return. The massive table in the Banqueting Hall was of carved oak, and wooden clusters of grapes adorned its legs. Great oak beams, each one the width of a man's forearm, spanned the ceiling. The fireplace, with its carved frieze and capitals, bore the arms of the du Chantonnays. The same arms were etched into the mullioned windows and displayed on shields hung on either side of the fireplace, the vivid colours of leopard and moons exaggerated by the flames of the fire.

Eleanor had dismissed her women and ordered only one manservant to attend them. It was ridiculous, thought Toby: the three of them perched at one end of the table, lost in this huge room. He was used to dining with the servants, he was used to Reynaud's bellowing voice and towering presence. With Reynaud gone the château had become silent, empty. It was frozen in some sort of limbo and had an air of unsettled, directionless waiting. Conversation was jerky, their voices lowered and hesitant. The echoing vastness multiplied the chink of glassware, the rattle of knives and crockery.

Eleanor was right. François was not yet ready for such a burden. Freedom had intoxicated him like the wine he drank so copiously – freedom from his father's contemptuous eye, freedom to do what he wished with the land and wealth he had inherited.

'I'm going to buy a dozen new horses.' François's eyes gleamed as he turned to Toby. 'The best horses come from the Dauphiné, don't they, Toby?'

Toby smiled. 'The best warhorses. I've seen them in battle – they haven't an ounce of fear. I expect your Cousin Guillaume's horses come from the Dauphiné.'

'Oh . . . Guillaume.' François's nose screwed up in disgust, and he wiped the wine from his chin with the back of his hand. 'I'll have better horses than Guillaume. You'll help me choose them, won't you, Toby?'

He nodded. He'd stay a fortnight or so, he thought. He'd help François choose his warhorses, or François would spend a king's ransom on a dozen florid, spavined, ageing beasts.

'And I'm going to have a new suit of armour made. Papa's is too big.' François signalled to the servant to refill his glass, and began to shovel barley cream into his mouth.

Toby saw the anxiety in Eleanor du Chantonnay's eyes. He said, 'Do you intend to go to war, François?'

François nodded enthusiastically. 'I'm going to go to Italy. Like Cousin Guillaume and papa. Papa wouldn't let me.' His voice had become sulky, his thin hands clenched into fists. Then he said proudly, 'I've been practising with the arquebus, like you showed me. I can hit a target at ten paces.'

Toby had a sudden, vivid picture of François at some other Agnadello, clanking down a muddy hillside at the mercy of Italian swords, Swiss pikes. There was no Reynaud now to forbid the boy such a fate. Only Eleanor to try to instil in him the caution he lacked, and rid him of the nervousness that made him clumsy. Only himself, if he chose, to teach François to make skilful use of the weapons of war.

'That's excellent, François,' he said, forcing enthusiasm. 'But a Seigneur like yourself won't be using an arquebus in battle, of course. You'll have to fight with a lance and a sword.'

'I know.' François, drinking fast, hiccupped. He turned to Eleanor. 'I told you, *maman*. That's why I need the horses.'

The wind roared down the chimney, making the flames of the fire leap and twist. Across the table, Eleanor picked at her food with a spoon, pushing it around her plate.

'We should have music, *maman*,' said François, suddenly. He turned to the servant. 'Fetch Josse.'

The lutenist was called for. François, pleased with himself, refilled their glasses as Josse began to play.

It seemed to Toby that the notes of the lute only emphasized the vast emptiness of the room, the weight of the stones of Marigny. Outside the night had grown dark, and the wind wreathed its way round the chimney-pots and crenellations.

'I used to dance,' said Eleanor suddenly. 'When I was a girl. My sisters and I used to dance together. Do you dance, Toby?'

He recalled Joanna dancing in the tavern in Italy, her black skirts fanning around her, light in her eyes. He shook his head. 'Not much, I'm afraid, madame. I'm a soldier, not a courtier.'

'I'll teach you.' She got up, leaving her neglected plate. Her eyes were bright and dark, her skin white. Circling the table, she took Toby's hands in hers.

They danced in the centre of the room. Her gaze always sought his, her hands waited to grasp his as they parted and then rejoined. A slow stately dance, so different from the rowdy jig he had danced with Joanna. He had no difficulty following the steps that Eleanor called to him. Her voice, the notes of the lute, were the only sounds left in Marigny. Even the wind had died, and not a footfall could be heard from the kitchens and state-rooms. Only in the reflected pattern of the firelight, dappling the stone walls, did Toby sometimes think he could see movement, memory, half-glimpsed forgotten faces.

When the dance ended, she was in his arms. 'Look,' she said softly, and Toby turned and looked back to the table, where François, his head cradled in his arms, slept.

'You have to stay. He worships you. You see that, don't you?'

He did. He did not want that sort of idolization, he had never wanted it. But he saw the sleeping, defenceless boy, and he felt Eleanor's hand clutching his arm. He saw the château and lands of Marigny all around him, Marigny with its grace and safety and beauty. From out of the past came a voice that still inhabited his nightmares: *'Tell your master that I have come to take what I am owed.'* Toby shivered, remembering Hamon de Bohun, with his dark, reptilian eyes, and he glanced again at François, his head on the table, spilt red wine staining his fair hair. He began to see that he could leave behind the mess he had made of his life: his desertion of Gilles and Penniless, his seduction of the young, lonely Joanna, his quarrel with Martin Gefroy, without whom he would not be alive. He saw a place for himself here at Marigny where he belonged.

'You'll stay, won't you?' Eleanor said again.

What could he say? He tried to smile. 'For a while. For as long as you want me.'

Her face brightened so that the lines of anxiety between her eyes disappeared. And then she told the servant and the lutenist to take their master to his bed.

They made love there, in the Banqueting Hall, in front of the fire on the sweet rushes scattered over the stones.

She had waited so long. After the dance had finished, she did not let him go, but stood there, her hands on Toby's shoulders, as Josse and the manservant carried François to his bed. She was no longer aware of Reynaud's bullying ghost that still, for Eleanor, haunted Marigny's rooms and towers. Except for that brief encounter in the linen-room, she had never kissed, never held someone with physical desire. For twelve years she had been starved of love. For twelve years she had endured the physical intimacies of marriage without an awareness that pleasure was even possible.

Now she swooned with the miracle that was Toby Crow's return to Marigny. Her hands clutched at him, her eyes could not leave his face. Every muscle in her body was taut with longing. She thought she would break in two with the strength of her happiness and desire. She saw the concern in his eyes and, speechless, could not explain to him that her tears were of joy, not sorrow.

She let him stroke her until her clenched fingers relaxed and she could breathe more steadily. She removed her head-dress and shook her head so that her long dark hair cascaded down her back. As she rested her head against his chest, she could feel his heartbeat.

When she looked up, he kissed her. For comfort, at first, she thought. And then, as she responded to him, threading her fingers through his black hair, drawing his face to hers, no longer for comfort. For hunger, for having waited so long.

She tore at the laces of her gown, pulled her chemise from her shoulders. She saw the look of desire on his face when she uncovered her round full breasts. Together they sank to the floor and lay side by side in front of the fire, the backlighting of the flames scarlet and gold on their bodies. She knew sexual pleasure for the first time in her life when he touched her stomach, her thighs, the black tuft of hair. When he entered her, she was aware of a deep, warm, joyous feeling of almost unbearable intensity. His arms were around her, his face above hers. For a moment she felt as ignorant and frightened as a bride. Then instinct took over. She began to move in rhythm with him and soon her cries of happiness echoed against Marigny's golden walls.

CHAPTER NINE

For François, life at Marigny had improved immeasurably with Toby Crow's return. Over the next few weeks they bought horses – not the dozen François had originally intended, but still, Toby had assured François, four of the best horses in France. Every day they worked at the quintain Toby had set up on the meadow and practised firing the arquebus. Once, François shot at his pair of squirrels, still imprisoned in their cages. The wretched beasts took fright, though, and he succeeded only in nicking one of them on the tail and scattering stone fragments all over the floor. He took the wounded animal to Eleanor, who scolded him. Toby was angry too, so much so that François had almost reminded him of his place and sent him packing like Meraud. But he had caught himself in time, recalling the dreariness of Marigny without Toby, and managed to mumble an apology. Since then, he had only used the arquebus under Toby's supervision.

The weather had worsened, and on rainy days François played chess with Toby or attempted to write letters and study account-books. Chess bored François until Toby told him it was like a battlefield in which he must plan his army's strategy. The letters and account-books made him yawn endlessly: he could not, he whined to his stepmother, see why secretaries and clerks could not deal with such things. The Seigneur de Marigny should give great feasts or win himself fame in battle. Not struggle with spelling and scrawling columns of numbers.

His attempts to make his mark on the château de Marigny, to remove all trace of his domineering father, were feverish and irrational. Paintings were heaped on bonfires, tapestries – including the unicorn tapestries that had been Eleanor's dowry – were consigned to storerooms and cellars.

At Christmas, François insisted on a great celebration. Servants scuttled to and fro, cleaning, cooking, mending. Fireplaces and doorways were decked with boughs of greenery. Scented logs spat in the grates. Eleanor organized the food, which was wonderful – ten courses of pies and puddings and roasted fowl and glorious sweetmeats. François had a cold and had to wipe his nose constantly, but he still managed to do justice to his favourites, the sweetmeats: the tarts and marchpanes, the fools and creams and custards; the quince pastes and the apple suckets and the plum cakes, all moulded into tiny stars, fishes and flowers.

At François's insistence they hired a consort of musicians and a troop of jugglers. The musicians honked and squawked and scraped, and the jugglers threw coloured balls into the air and coaxed pink-feathered doves from their sleeves. The servants lining the Great Hall of Marigny surreptitiously crossed themselves, thinking that they were witnessing witchcraft, but François, sophisticated François, knew that they had only taken a few birds from the dovecote and stained their wings with plum juice.

Later that evening, they danced. The servants galumphed and cavorted, almost drowning the music of the consort, and François, leading one of the demoiselles that his stepmother had invited to stay, trod with meticulous care the steps of folk-dances and court-dances. Eleanor had taught him the dances, and Toby had explained to him that a gentleman of his years should drink no more than three cups of wine in an evening. François was glad that he had taken Toby's advice: his head was muzzy enough with the food and music and the cold, but he managed to stay awake until the feasting ended in the early hours of the morning.

He was proud of himself, he thought that he had acquitted himself well. He had behaved like a Seigneur of Marigny: he had, he thought tremulously, almost equalled Reynaud. He had neither spilled his drink nor trod on a single toe. He had told one of the demoiselles about his horses and the quintain practice, and she had been impressed, he was certain.

François's only regret, as he fell asleep that night, was that Cousin Guillaume had not been there. He would have like Cousin Guillaume, with his cutting tongue, and his handsome, sardonic face, to have seen him at the head of the table, to have seen him as lord of Marigny.

At the house of the schoolteacher and his wife the Christmas celebrations were a little less elaborate. Agnès and Joanna made rabbit pies and biscuit bread, crystallized fruit and spinach tarts. The hen that had stopped laying was consigned to the pot. Joanna decorated the small stone house with holly and mistletoe and sheaves of crimson-berried yew. Agnès told her that the house had never looked so elegant. Neighbours and cousins called by with gifts of cakes and wine. They greeted Agnès and Paul with affection; Joanna with a mixture of curiosity and suspicion. They tolerated her but did not accept her. Her beauty, her foreignness, her lack of father, brother or husband to protect her, both fascinated and offended them.

The celebrations were marred by Toby's continued absence and by Paul's failing health. On Twelfth Night Joanna found Agnès weeping over the sink. When she had wiped her eyes on her apron and accepted Joanna's hug, Agnès said, 'So silly. It's just that he couldn't even eat the macaroons. Paul always loved macaroons.' She sat down at the kitchen table. 'And he hasn't been out of the house for a month. He's closed the school, and he's found all his paying pupils new masters. There's no money coming in, none at all.' She took a deep, shuddering breath and ran her hands through her untidy hair. 'He's even admitted to me, finally, that he's not well. I'm *frightened*, Joanna. I'm not used to being frightened.'

Joanna could not pretend that it was all right, that Paul would get better when the spring came. She had done all she could. She had made tisanes and poultices, ointments and draughts, but Paul continued to lose weight, continued to suffer the pain that gnawed at his belly. She thought, with no great optimism, that perhaps a physician could do better.

Money worries, though, she could do something about. Running to her room, Joanna found her jewel-box and brought it back to the kitchen. She up-ended it and all Isotta's heavy, ugly jewellery spilled out on to the stained kitchen table. 'There's no need to worry about money, Agnès. I'll sell some of these. My aunt left them to me. We'll engage a physician for Paul.' Briefly, Joanna remembered the previous summer, a summer that now seemed so long distant. She said sadly, 'Oh, I wish Martin was here.'

Agnès had begun to look a little better. 'Who's Martin?'

Joanna smiled. 'Martin's a physician, and a dear friend. He's an Englishman. He travelled with us to Milan.'

She had not heard from Martin Gefroy since they had parted last September. Had the Sieur du Chantonnay recovered from his wound? Had Martin remained with Guillaume, or had he continued on his scholar's travels? To Paris, Oxford, Leiden . . . There were so many unfinished stories, so many loose ends.

'There was a quarrel,' Joanna said, bleakly, remembering. 'Toby and Martin quarrelled. It was all so silly.'

'Men,' said Agnès sympathetically. She gazed at the bracelets, the necklaces, the rings scattered on the table, and took a deep breath. 'You must put these away, my dear. I couldn't take them. You may need them for yourself. And besides, I have some money. If you would stand on the stool, Joanna, and reach up to the top corner of the dresser . . .'

Joanna, standing on tiptoes, found the purse that was hidden there and handed it to Agnès.

'Toby gave it to me,' said Agnès, unknotting the ties. 'I was going to buy another pig. But it will pay for a physician, and it will keep us from begging. And besides, there's the garden. With two of us to tend it, we'll grow enough to feed a family of ten.'

'You should write to him, perhaps. To Toby,' Joanna said hesitantly.

Agnès shook her head. 'No,' she said firmly. 'He has his own life . . . I'll not tie him to me. Toby hates to be tied. And besides, he promised to come back soon. I trust him to keep to that.' She rose, straightening out her crumpled apron, tucking loose ends of hair beneath her cap. Then she helped Joanna pick up the necklaces, the bracelets, the rings, and replace them in the box.

At the end of January, Toby went with François to Tours. François had nagged him incessantly to visit the armourer, and there was a score of other small but essential things that Marigny needed. They travelled with an armed escort, but Eleanor, lying awake for the three nights that they were to be away, thought of icy roads and sudden snowstorms.

So at first she was relieved when on the morning of the fourth day she saw horsemen riding down the path from the wood. Her heart fluttered and the thread slipped from her needle. But when, looking a second time, she could not recognize the riders' banners and saw that their colours were not the red and yellow of the du Chantonnays, her heart slowed and she put aside her sewing.

'The lord Hamon de Bohun,' the manservant said, bowing to her. 'Should we admit him, madame?'

In the intensity of her disappointment she did not at first recognize the name. Then she remembered: the Sieur de Bohun had been

Reynaud's acquaintance, Blanche's cousin, Eleanor thought. She nodded, and the servant left the room.

Her women remained beside her, heads bent over their embroidery frames, hemming sheets, chemises, petticoats. Needles paused and eyes peeked furtively when Hamon de Bohun came into the room. He was a handsome man with dark eyes and pale skin; a few strands of slightly greying dark hair could be seen beneath his velvet cap. Eleanor guessed that he was in his early fifties, but in far better health than Reynaud had been.

'Madame, I must apologize for the unexpected visit, but I was on my way to Orléans, and I heard of the Seigneur de Marigny's death. I knew the Seigneur once, a long time ago. I have come to pay my respects to his widow.'

De Bohun bowed and kissed Eleanor's hand. His silks and velvets proclaimed his status. His voice was deep and measured, slightly accented. His gaze trailed over the Great Chamber as though he were assessing the value of its contents with an expert's eye. He looked at furnishings, hangings and paintings, and finally at Eleanor herself.

Held by those cold eyes, she shivered. Hawk's eyes, she thought, the eyes of Reynaud's beautiful jack-merlin, cold and dark and amoral. They made her aware of Marigny's frozen isolation. She saw herself as some small defenceless animal, the great black hawk hovering hungrily above her. She longed for Toby.

De Bohun and her waiting-women were staring at her. She forced herself into a semblance of composure, and said, her voice slightly tremulous, 'I am glad to receive any friend of Reynaud's, monsieur. You were Blanche's cousin, were you not?'

De Bohun smiled. 'A more distant relationship, madame. I hardly knew her.'

She sent a servant for wine. De Bohun sat down opposite her.

'I have lived in England for many years, madame. But now the old king is dead, and I find myself thinking of returning to Brittany. News travels slowly, I'm afraid. I would have liked to have attended the Seigneur's funeral.'

There was genuine regret in de Bohun's voice. His eyes were no longer cold, but warm and vivid. He was not sinister at all, Eleanor thought. How foolish she had been. He merely mourned the absence of an old friend. Loyalty, the sort of friendship that survived distance and absence, Eleanor had always admired.

'My husband had been ill for some time,' she said as the manservant arrived with the refreshments. 'He died following a hunting accident last summer.'

De Bohun shook his head sympathetically, and accepted a glass of wine. 'Hunting is such a dangerous sport. I have sometimes wondered, madame, if as many men die in the chase as in battle.'

Eleanor thought again of Toby, riding back from Tours that day. His horse's hooves slipping on the icy road . . . an awkward fall . . . his head cracked open on the stones . . . Glancing out of the window, she saw that the path from the woods to the château was still empty. A tight knot formed in her stomach.

The Sieur de Bohun was speaking. Eleanor mentally shook herself, reminding herself of her duties as mistress of Marigny.

'Do you have children, madame? To comfort you in your sad loss?'

'I have a son. Well, a stepson. François is Blanche's child.'

She knew that her voice was jerky, betraying her nervousness. The room oppressed her suddenly: the opulent fireplace, the roof with the heavy beams, the tapestries and paintings that clung to the walls, seemed to bear down, crushing her. She would have preferred to be in the kitchen, pounding dough into shape or beating eggs for a pudding. She took up her sewing again, rethreading the needle. Anything to keep her restless hands occupied.

'Such an exquisite place, madame. Such furnishings . . . such paintings . . .'

She noticed the admiration in his voice and forced a smile. 'My husband was a collector, monsieur. He was a great lover of Italian art. He brought to Marigny treasures from all over the world.'

'We shared the same tastes, once, Reynaud and I.' Hamon de Bohun's gaze trailed once more round the room. 'I have lived too long in a backward, isolated little island, madame. Too much rain and mist and not enough sun. One longs for the sun – for beauty – sometimes.'

Eleanor nodded. She knew what it was to be shut out from the sun. She thought of returning to that half-life again and the needle jabbed into her palm. A ball of crimson blood swelled on her skin, then trickled down on to the cloth.

'Madame.'

Hamon de Bohun had risen, was kneeling beside her. Eleanor looked at him, eyes wide, her hands shaking. She could not move, could not speak. She watched, oddly detached, as he took a scrap of linen from her workbasket and wrapped it round her palm. Then he folded her fingers, so that the makeshift bandage was held in place.

The needle and thread had fallen to the floor. His hand was warm and dry, his voice low and reassuring.

'Does something trouble you, Madame de Marigny? Such a responsibility, a place like this. And your stepson is quite young, I believe. Remember that I was Reynaud's friend. I would consider it a great honour if I could be your friend also.'

His voice was soft, mesmerizing. Eleanor found herself lost in those dark eyes, all thought enveloped in their depth. At last she pulled away from de Bohun and gazed wildly out of the window.

'François is away at present, with his bodyguard. They've gone to Tours. They're late. I expected them back this morning. The state of the roads . . . the weather . . . one is always afraid . . .'

She knew that she was gabbling like a vacuous fourteen-year-old. She felt tears of exhaustion and anxiety sting at the corners of her eyes as she stared out at the snow. But then through the thick flakes of snow she made out a small group of horsemen riding down the path. She could just glimpse the crimson and gold colours of the du Chantonnays. And at the head of the group, her anxious eyes picked out two riders, one fair-haired, one dark. She wanted to cry, to laugh, to dance round the room. She hated herself then for not trusting him, for not trusting God to protect him. Her face suddenly bright with happiness, Eleanor dismissed her women and turned to de Bohun.

'He's here now. François has come home. Stay a while, monsieur, and meet my son.'

François had insisted on wearing the helmet throughout the long ride back to Marigny. He had also insisted on plumes, six of them, bright red and yellow. He ran ahead of Toby through the Great Hall and up the stairs, his boots marking the stone with mud and melted snow, and the feathers bobbing like the crest of an outlandish cockatoo.

Toby followed burdened with packages and parcels. He heard François's voice through the half-open doorway of the Great Chamber.

'The greaves and breastplate will be ready in a week, *maman*, the backplate within the month. The armourer's going to etch pictures in the metal – lion's heads and suchlike. The helmet looks very fine, don't you think?'

Toby heard Eleanor reply, 'Very fine, my dear.' Then another voice drawled, 'King Louis himself would be proud of such a helmet, *votre seigneurie.*'

An ice-cold trickle of fear ran down Toby's neck. A year ago that same dry, gentle voice had whispered to him, *'There was no need to struggle, my pet.'* Still, occasionally, it whispered in his dreams.

Toby paused at the top of the staircase, his back pressed against the wall.

Eleanor's voice echoed through the open door. 'We have a visitor, François. This is the Sieur de Bohun, from Brittany. He was a friend of your father's.'

'Tell your master that I have come to take what I am owed.' Forcing himself to recall his one unpleasant interview with the Sieur de Bohun, Toby knew that whatever motive de Bohun had for visiting Marigny, it had nothing whatsoever to do with friendship.

He did not wait to hear François's muttered greeting, but gathered the ribbons and silk he had collected for Eleanor in Tours and walked into the room.

'Madame de Marigny. Monsieur de Bohun.' He bowed to both of them, and had the satisfaction of seeing the flicker of surprise, quickly suppressed, in Hamon de Bohun's eyes.

Eleanor looked bewildered. 'You know each other?'

Toby's eyes did not leave de Bohun. 'We have met. About a year ago.'

'A memorable occasion,' said de Bohun smoothly. 'Our conversation was most interesting. Though, I have since thought, unfinished.' He smiled. 'Don't you agree, Monsieur Crow?'

'Yes.' Toby dumped the parcels on the table in front of Eleanor. He thought of the portrait of Joanna Zulian that Hamon de Bohun had taken a year earlier and once again felt fear and loathing for this man. Almost casually, as he cut with his knife the knots that bound Eleanor's parcels, he said, 'Are you here to return what you borrowed, monsieur?'

'Borrowed?' Eleanor paused in the act of unfolding the lengths of silk and velvet purchased in a draper's shop in Tours. 'What do you mean, Toby?'

Hamon was still smiling, but Toby had noticed the ripple of anger that had crossed his face.

'Your servant is mistaken, madame. I spoke to him last winter, but merely to send my compliments to the Seigneur de Marigny.'

'Monsieur de Bohun has travelled from Brittany.' Eleanor smoothed out the length of black velvet, and began to open the bag of ribbons. 'Monsieur de Bohun was a –'

'A friend of Reynaud's,' said Toby drily. 'Of course.'

Eleanor had loosened the draw-string of the bag. A rainbow of different colours spilled out, jewelling the black velvet.

'I said *black*,' exclaimed Eleanor. Her voice trembled with happiness. She turned to Toby with a wide smile and shining eyes. Her fingers threaded through the lengths of scarlet, purple, lilac, gold and aquamarine. 'One of every colour you have,' Toby had said to the draper in Tours. Briefly, Eleanor's hand touched his.

'Toby's my bodyguard now,' said François from the window-seat. The gaudy feathers on the helmet quivered as he spoke. 'He's teaching me to ride at the quintain. When I'm seventeen I'm going to Italy to fight for the king of France.'

The helmet was too large for François's pale, thin face, and had slipped drunkenly to one side.

'Really?' Hamon de Bohun's dark gaze moved slowly from Toby to the boy at the window. 'I'm sure that Louis de France will be overjoyed.'

Toby clenched his fists. On the journey to Tours he had, with a patience that surprised himself, persuaded François to stay at Marigny for another year. With any luck, he thought, the wars might be over by then. Failing that, a safe place must be found where François could charge around in his new armour with no danger to himself or anyone else.

Eleanor carefully wound the ribbons round her fingers. 'To Italy? You are too young, François.'

'I'm sixteen, *maman*. I can't stay *here* all my life.' François's sulky voice contemptuously dismissed all Marigny's lands and treasures.

'My stepson wants to travel.' The ribbons were all coiled now, laid neatly on the black velvet. 'Do you have children, Monsieur de Bohun?'

De Bohun shook his head. 'Alas, no. I have never married.' He glanced again at François. 'Your stepson must be a great comfort to you, madame.'

François, his face red with the heat of the fire and the weight of the helmet, was wiping his nose on his sleeve. His mouth still curled with bad temper, and his eyes evaded Eleanor's. Toby wanted to shake the boy, to jolt him out of his self-centredness, so that he would understand the threat that men like de Bohun represented.

A threat that Toby himself did not yet completely understand. Remnants of conversations, with Arlotto Attavanti, with Guillaume du Chantonnay, with de Bohun himself, flickered through his head. Hamon de Bohun had been guardian to Blanche, Reynaud's first wife. And Blanche had brought to Reynaud du Chantonnay the house and lands of Marigny. So Reynaud had acquired the estate of Marigny through his marriage to Blanche. *'I have come to take what I am owed,'* Hamon had said. Was it possible, Toby thought, was it possible that Hamon believed that Reynaud owed him *Marigny*? That Eleanor – François – owed him Marigny? Marigny: something to lie for, something to kill for. Toby gazed first at François half dozing on the window-seat, then at Eleanor standing next to him, her face still vivid with happiness. He was aware suddenly of the cold, the constantly falling snow, and he knew that his fears were not for himself. He was afraid for Eleanor, for François, for their innocence, their defencelessness.

De Bohun was making his farewells. He rose and kissed Eleanor's hand, then bowed to François. *'Votre seigneurie,'* he said, and Toby knew that only he heard the mockery in those two words.

Now de Bohun turned to Toby. The Breton's long fingers grasped his shoulder. 'Good day to you, Monsieur Crow,' he said softly. The tips of his fingers pressed into Toby's skin, and his eyes were dark and brilliant. 'I'm sure we shall meet again.'

A blanket of snow covered the garden, weighing down the bare branches of the trees and forming icy crusts along the banks of the stream. Away from the fireplaces and stove, the house now was always cold.

Agnès was outside feeding the chickens when Joanna found Paul collapsed in his study, a pen still gripped in his shaking hands. Agnès ran inside the house, scattering mud on the flagstones. They carried Paul to his room and put him to bed. He weighs as little as a child, thought Agnès, blinking away her tears. The physician was sent for. Muttering impressively about evil humours, he examined Paul and recommended a surgeon for blood-letting.

The blood-letting seemed to help. Some colour returned to Paul's face, and he managed to speak a few words and sip a little soup. That evening, with Agnès's consent, Joanna wrote to Toby. Sitting beside her husband's bed, Agnès could see through to Paul's study, to the desk where Joanna, head bent, sat writing. The girl was frowning, but her pen covered the page swiftly.

A single candle illuminated Paul's sleeping figure. Outside, the wind rattled the shutters, tossing up snow that squeezed its way through the gaps in the window. Agnès held Paul's hand and thought about the past. She had known Paul all her life. She could not remember a time when there had not been Paul. They had been born in the same village, had attended the same church. Paul's father had been the schoolmaster, Agnès's father a farmer. Her dowry had consisted of a goat, a pig and a sack of grain. An ordinary, some would say dull, life, and yet, looking back, she would not have changed a moment of it.

She remembered the babies that she had borne and lost. She remembered the day that Paul had returned from Chinon and said, '*I have bought you a present, Agnès.*' On his saddlebow a ragged child had sat, cursing at his confinement. Together they had cleaned him and healed him and taught him: together they had grown proud of their son. Now, watching Joanna sprinkle sand on the letter and fold it carefully, Agnès realized how much she longed for Toby's return.

'I'll ride to Bourges tomorrow,' whispered Joanna, coming into the bedchamber and crouching beside Agnès. 'I know a monk called Brother Joachim who is travelling to Touraine soon. I'm sure he'll take the letter to Marigny for us.'

Agnès, managing a watery smile, wasn't in the least surprised that Joanna knew a monk called Brother Joachim. Joanna would as happily pass the time of day with the squire of the village or the legless beggar who held out his cap in the corner of the square. It was partially that openness, that failure to give due importance to status, that made it impossible for many of the inhabitants of the small, isolated village to accept her. That, thought Agnès, and Joanna's face, her nationality, her obvious and unmistakable difference. The thought of Joanna's future worried Agnès sometimes. Another reason for Toby to come back – so that she could explain to him quite bluntly that he could not put a girl like Joanna in a village like this and expect her to become a part of it. Agnès shook her head and tutted, thinking of her absent son.

The two visitors arrived at the same time. Guillaume du Chantonnay, complete with his armed retinue, and Brother Joachim, a fat monk who was forever grumbling about his empty stomach.

Toby was on the meadow, showing François for the hundredth time how to hit the quintain, instead of driving his lance uselessly into the soil while the sand-filled leather bag trembled untouched in the breeze. He recognized Guillaume immediately – by the banners, by the arms, and by the fact that there were, simply, no other du Chantonnays. Toby left François to sort out his lance, put his spurs to his horse's side and rode across the meadow to greet Guillaume.

'An unenviable task.' Guillaume's mocking blue eyes took in the quintain, the lance, and François clambering awkwardly back into his saddle. 'I compliment you on your patience, Monsieur Crow. I would have drowned the lad in the moat by now, I don't doubt.'

Guillaume was immaculately dressed in royal blue doublet and breeches, a fur-lined cloak slung over his shoulders. His gauntlets glittered with jewels, and he wore a single diamond in one ear.

Toby nodded his head in a bow. 'I take it you're recovered from your injuries, Monsieur du Chantonnay?'

'Completely. Your excellent friend, Mr Gefroy, worked valiantly. I have enticed him, by the way, taken him home with me. A strange fellow: he is fascinated by the most repulsive diseases. He insists on attending wretches in hovels – beggars, lepers. But even the remarkable Mr Gefroy has to live, so he has consented to become my physician for a while. Ah . . .' Guillaume glanced again across the meadow. 'François has managed to stay in his saddle. What a relief. Do I take it, Monsieur Crow, that Madame de Marigny has engaged your services as a courier once more?' The cool blue eyes studied Toby. A smile hovered round the long, thin mouth.

'Not quite,' said Toby smoothly. 'François dismissed Meraud, his bodyguard. I'm taking his place for a while.'

Guillaume quietened his restless horse as François, fully armed, clanked noisily towards them. *'François!'* François, red-faced, had drawn level with them. 'You look quite splendid. Such a helmet.

'Oh, Monsieur Crow . . .' Gathering his reins, Guillaume turned back to Toby. 'A monk by the name of Brother Joachim has ridden with us from Tours. He has a letter for you, I believe. Feed him, please, before I throttle him. He has grumbled about his belly for the last five miles.'

With a wave of his hand Guillaume was gone, riding towards the drawbridge with François at his side. And in front of Toby was an oversized Benedictine monk on an undersized mule, a letter in his outstretched hand.

★

He didn't understand the letter at first. He read it, noting the swirl of the *J* in Joanna's signature at the bottom of the page and his own name in clear black ink at the top, but it didn't make sense.

The letter trembled in his hand with the chill February breeze. It was impossible, Toby thought. Joanna had made a mistake. Paul could not be so ill. It had been Paul who had helped him to make sense of his life, Paul who had showed him the possibility of kindness.

He read the letter again. He knew that the monk, straddled on his ridiculous mule, was staring at him. Confused, he thought of bright, vivacious Joanna Zulian, who with holes in her shoes had tramped from Padua to Milan. *You must come home at once,* Joanna had written. *Agnès needs you.*

When he looked up, he could not see clearly. The moat, the meadow, the distant woods were all blurred. He felt anger more than grief. Anger that Paul should threaten to leave him when there was so much that was unresolved. 'Bad news, monsieur?' the monk said hesitantly and Toby turned with Joanna's letter crumpled in his fist. He saw the brief look of fear cross the monk's fat, good-natured face, and then he took hold of himself and remembered his manners. Shoving the letter inside his doublet, he escorted Brother Joachim to the kitchen.

Like Toby, Guillaume du Chantonnay found the absence of Reynaud from Marigny an almost tangible thing. It gave him great pleasure to cross the drawbridge, to ride beneath the gate-tower, to enter the courtyard, knowing that there would be no Reynaud to greet him, taunting him with his ownership of Marigny.

Guillaume had inwardly blessed the boundary wall that had felled Reynaud and thanked the God in which he had long ceased to believe for Eleanor's continued widowhood. The thought that she might have remarried, to protect François, to protect herself, had haunted Guillaume throughout his long months of convalescence. But Eleanor had not remarried, and he was fully recovered, thanks to his excellent physician and his own robust good health.

Guillaume stood for a moment in the courtyard, his need for Marigny washing over him until he felt almost faint with the desire for ownership. Inside the château, he looked at the rooms and treasures with different eyes: eyes that told him that possession of this place was no longer an unobtainable and jeering dream, but a possibility that he could make real.

He greeted Eleanor in the Great Hall, taking her hand in his. 'My dear Eleanor, I have come to offer my condolences. Although I suspect that you, like myself, have been able to contain your excesses of grief.'

He thought her changed for the better since he had last seen her. She had always been a handsome woman, but time, and Reynaud, had added unseasonable lines to her pale skin and given her dark eyes a hunted, bruised look. But now her skin glowed and her face was untroubled.

'Widowhood suits you, Eleanor,' said Guillaume, releasing her hand. 'You should have dropped poison into the old bastard's wine years ago.'

If Eleanor had not, he realized with amusement, been such a transparently honest, transparently conscientious woman, he might in the past have suggested such a course to her. Eleanor laughed, and Guillaume sat in the chair opposite her.

'It's good to see you again, Guillaume.' Eleanor signalled to a servant to give him wine. 'I heard that you were unwell. Are you recovered now?'

Her face was concerned, kind. Guillaume thought of being married to Eleanor, and he knew how the very honesty and generosity that he admired in her would weary him.

'An arquebus-shot in my leg.' He grimaced. 'The repair of such wounds will occupy the physicians for many years, my dear Eleanor. They are not like sword-cuts or lance-wounds. I thought I'd end my days a stinking hulk, like Reynaud. Or following the old devil to the churchyard.'

He shuddered. He had, unlike Eleanor, no faith to protect him against the terror of the grave, no philosophy that might have dulled the fear that had possessed him in his worst moments. The fear that it was over, that he had lost, that the gnawing ache that he had known since he was a boy would never be quelled.

'I found a good physician, fortunately,' he added. 'An Englishman. I've brought him back to Nantes with me.' His eyes narrowed momentarily. 'I met Toby Crow outside. Attempting to teach dear François to use a lance.'

Eleanor's smile blossomed. He thought again how she had improved since he had last seen her – damn it, the woman looked ten years younger.

'Toby is working for me now. I have employed him as François's bodyguard. François dismissed Meraud, you see.'

'Did he now?' Guillaume fingered his cleanly shaven chin as he thought about François. François was a fool, an incompetent: every insult that Reynaud had ever bestowed on him was fully deserved. It had been a great comfort to Guillaume to see how Reynaud's heir had disappointed his father, how the boy's sickliness and lack of talent had galled him. It had made Guillaume more kindly disposed to François, although he was never able to resist teasing the boy. François was so easy to tease.

The blackest time had been when Reynaud had remarried: to Eleanor, middle daughter of a rich and landed family. Guillaume had hated Eleanor to begin with, but found that his hatred could not survive her appalling humility. When it had become obvious that Reynaud's ageing loins would father no child and Guillaume himself witnessed how badly Reynaud treated his barren wife, then Guillaume had almost pitied her. Except that he was not capable of pity.

'François intends to go to Italy,' said Eleanor. For the first time that morning a trace of anxiety darkened her face. 'To fight, Guillaume. It worries me. I don't think he's strong enough. He has attacks of breathlessness. They've become more frequent recently.' She forced a laugh. 'Perhaps I shall have to borrow your excellent physician, Guillaume.'

'Why not? I'll send him to you, Eleanor. Martin takes nothing but pleasure in curing the most disgusting of complaints.'

He was silent for a moment, drinking his wine, watching her. Then he said, making his voice sound tentative, concerned, 'Have you considered your position here, cousin? Have you considered François's position?'

Eleanor looked at Guillaume, puzzled. Impatiently, he thought how blind women could be, how unaware they sometimes were of the world that surrounded them.

'My position, Guillaume? François's position? François is now the Seigneur of Marigny, of course. And I will remain at Marigny for as long as François needs me. Until he finds a wife, I suppose. I'm looking for a suitable girl.'

Guillaume thought, fleetingly, of the unfortunate creature that would find her way into François du Chantonnay's bed. Would the wealth and power of Marigny be sufficient compensation for such a husband? Privately, Guillaume doubted whether François was capable of the duties of a husband.

'François may not marry for years,' he said. 'And he is not healthy, Eleanor – you've just pointed that out. You should consider your position, cousin. It is somewhat precarious.' The stupid woman still didn't seem to understand. He added, patiently, 'You should remarry, Eleanor. That way you'll protect François and yourself. And Marigny.'

It was Marigny he cared about, of course. But he'd make a tolerable husband to Eleanor du Chantonnay. He'd not torment her as Reynaud had – there was simply no need for that sort of barbarity. Guillaume, unlike Reynaud, was subtle. He would keep his mistresses well out of sight, while he and Eleanor lived separate, comfortable lives. As for François – well, the boy might die of a fever tomorrow. And if not, then he'd do whatever Guillaume told him to. Guillaume had never bothered to charm the lad, but knew instinctively that François would eat out of his hand if given so much as a kind word.

'I'm asking you to marry me, Eleanor,' said Guillaume, putting aside his wine. 'It would solve a great many problems.'

Her short peal of laughter did not offend him. It would take her a while to get used to the idea. He had never thought her a bright woman.

Eleanor shook her head. 'I couldn't possibly, Guillaume. It's ridiculous. And unnecessary.'

'It isn't unnecessary. You know that yourself. Both you and François will be prey to any fortune-hunter who happens to set eyes on Marigny.'

She still looked amused.

Suddenly and brutally, he said, 'People kill for land, Eleanor.'

The amusement vanished. She glanced round the room, fearful at last, as though bidding a silent, premature farewell to the glorious château.

'I can't remarry yet,' she said eventually. 'Reynaud died only last summer. Less than a year ago, Guillaume.'

Guillaume frowned. *'Eleanor –'*

'No, Guillaume.' Her voice was quite firm. 'I cannot even consider marriage before the year is out. It wouldn't be right.'

The set of her mouth and the expression in her eyes appeared unusually stubborn. Guillaume, quelling his irritation, stood up and pulled on his gauntlets. He had intended to stay the night, but while he did not have ownership the place tormented him. And he knew that he needed to give Eleanor time to think, time to see the advantages of his proposal. She'd come round to it eventually, he thought: beneath her veneer of bovine conformity, Guillaume was aware that Eleanor possessed a deep well of common sense.

He must be patient for a few more months. At least he could now be secure in the knowledge that she would marry no one else.

He turned to Eleanor. 'Will you think about it, though, cousin? About marriage?'

His forbearance was rewarded by the smile on her lips, the joy in her eyes. 'Yes. I'll think about it, Guillaume,' said Eleanor.

After Guillaume had gone, Eleanor searched the house for Toby. She found him in the kitchen sitting beside a Benedictine monk. The monk had a red face and a shiny head, and was surrounded by empty plates and bowls. Toby didn't seem to see her at first, so she said his name gently. He rose to his feet.

'This is Brother Joachim, madame. He brought me a letter.'

Eleanor felt only guilt when faced with a member of the clergy. She had given an incomplete confession for weeks now, knowing herself unable to confess to the nature of her sins. Fornication and lechery: she felt the heat rise to her face at the dreadful thunder of those syllables. But she managed to greet Brother Joachim with a smile and listen politely to a long speech about the cold weather, the poor roads, the cockroach-infested inns. When the monk paused for breath, Eleanor turned to Toby.

'A letter?'

She saw the flash of anger in Toby's eyes, the inquisitive stare of the monk. She knew that she should not have asked: if she allowed Toby no life of his own, then she would lose him. And yet the mention of a letter, of a contact with the outside world, was a reminder that he had another life, a life he had allowed her to know so little about. She needed to know everything about him. She needed to be safe.

Toby said in a level voice, 'From my family, madame. My father is unwell.'

And then it was as though she could see herself, ageing and plain, inquiring about this young man's private life in front of a stranger and the servants, surrounded by the clatter of pots and pans and the steam and smoke that filled the kitchen. Her head began to ache and tears stung behind her eyelids. She was tired, she thought, exhausted by a night interrupted by one of François's attacks, and by that rather startling conversation with Guillaume. She was tired, stupid and old.

She heard Toby say, his voice taut, 'I'll have to go home for a while.'

It was as though he had struck her. She glanced up at him. The prospect of parting appalled her. She whispered, 'No. I can't spare you. We need you. François needs you. He's not well.'

She knew that the monk and the servants were staring at her. She felt a pain in her chest. In the stifling heat of the kitchen she could not breathe, and she loathed herself for her lack of pride and trust. She heard herself say tremulously, 'You'll stay the night, won't you, Brother Joachim?', and the monk, his mouth full of pastry, thanked her profusely and cut himself another slice of apple pie. Eleanor found that her legs were shaking as she climbed the steps from the kitchen.

Eleanor did not go to her chambers, but crossed the courtyard and drawbridge to the meadow. To one side was the quintain and François's discarded lance. The grass was still crisp with frost and the air was chill and clean.

Toby, catching up with her, said, 'If François is poorly, then perhaps you should send for a physician.'

'I have.' She looked up at him, trying to learn by heart his young, unlined face, his slim, muscular body. 'Cousin Guillaume's new physician, in fact. He should be here in a day or so.'

She saw Toby frown. She said, unable to stop herself, 'You won't go, will you?'

'I must.' His voice, she noticed, had become patient again, tolerant of an old woman's whim. 'Only for a few days, I hope. If François has taken to his bed, he won't have much need of me.'

Eleanor knew that her own need would be constant. She thought of what Guillaume had said, of the glorious idea that Guillaume had unwittingly given her, and she took Toby's hands in hers. Her words tumbled out. 'When you come back . . . when you come back, my love, I thought that we should marry.'

She waited, hardly daring to breathe, knowing that rejection would be unbearable. She could not interpret the flicker of expression in his eyes. But Toby said, as she herself had earlier said to Guillaume, 'Don't be ridiculous, Eleanor. We couldn't possibly marry.'

She was aware then of the bitterness of the wind, the coldness of the earth. She saw herself suddenly as he must see her: a useless, ageing crone. Loathing the years that there were between them, she cried out, 'Because I'm too old?'

But his eyes were shocked suddenly, and he was shaking his head. 'Old? You're not old, Eleanor. You're young, you're beautiful.'

She was glad of his words, even though he lied. She pulled him to her, laying her head against his shoulder, not caring that all Marigny might see them together.

'You can't marry me,' Toby said gently as he stroked her hair, 'because you're the mistress of Marigny, and I'm nothing. It wouldn't do at all. You must see that, Eleanor.'

She saw only his face above her, his black hair blown about by the wind, his dark eyes looking down at her. 'I told you, my darling,' she whispered. 'I don't care. Not one bit. And if you married me, you would be something.'

At first she regretted her words, because he turned away. But then she noticed how with a look of love and longing he gazed at the turrets and crenellations of the château. She did not care: if he wanted Marigny, he could have Marigny. He could have anything she was able to give him.

'You should go back to the house,' Toby said. 'You're cold.'

He was right. Her fingers were tinged with blue and the chill had crept beneath her layers of clothing.

Toby rubbed his hand over his eyes, as though he, too, were tired, and then he said: 'I must go to Bourges, Eleanor. I'll be back in a few days.'

Toby, troubled and confused, knew only that he did not want to be at Marigny when Martin Gefroy called to see François. And so he left early the next morning, bidding farewell to a tearful Eleanor, a coughing François and Brother Joachim was was eating his breakfast. Once over the drawbridge, he spurred on his horse and galloped across the meadow and through the forest, leaving a cloud of hoar-frost in his wake. Only when he had ridden eastwards for an hour or two did he slow his pace and allow himself to think.

Eleanor had offered him marriage. She had offered him Marigny and, if not the name of du Chantonnay, the chance to live as a du Chantonnay. The chance to live bulwarked by money, beauty and land. The chance to ride a warhorse into battle, to wear a visored helmet and carry a lance. The chance to get out of the mud that lay always underfoot at the bottom of the hill, waiting to suck you down. The chance to forget the past and reclaim what might have been his.

And yet, slowing to a trot, ducking to avoid the coppiced branches of the trees, Toby knew, if he was honest, that it was Marigny he loved and not Eleanor. He respected and admired the mistress of Marigny, he would happily have spent every night of the year beside her warm, generous body, but he did not love her. He could not give back to her what she gave to him.

Did it matter? As the path broadened, cutting into the edge of a wide meadow, he thought coldly that to her it did not. What she had now, little though it might be, was so much more than she had had before. And she needed him – for François, as well as for herself. Toby's thoughts drifted, as they so often had over the past few weeks, to Hamon de Bohun. '*I have come to take what I am owed.*'

He told himself, as he coaxed his horse carefully along a path slippery with ice, that he could protect Eleanor by marrying her. As Eleanor's husband, instead of Eleanor's servant, he could re-engage the men that Marigny needed to defend itself; he could safeguard François and free Eleanor from the attentions of those who were hungry only for gold and power.

There was another way of looking at it all, of course. You've had Reynaud's wife, the voice whispered in his head, why not have his house and lands as well? What better vengeance for the past? The prospect fascinated him, tempted him, appalled him.

If it had not been for Paul, he would have been glad then of Joanna's note, glad of the excuse to leave Marigny. He knew that over the last few months it was as though he had been suspended in time; that Marigny had worked its old enchantment, cutting its inhabitants off from the outside world, stilling them in a bewitched existence. He had stayed there too long: conscious of the dangers that threatened both Eleanor and François, he had neglected Paul, Agnès and Joanna. He had neglected people to whom he owed something. Outside Marigny, beyond those favoured walls, Toby was suddenly aware of the progression of events, of the need for crisis and resolution. Nothing stayed still.

The countryside was a monochrome of white and grey and black. The sun gleamed dully behind a covering of cloud, its rays failing to thaw the frost or to soften the iron-hard ground. The mare's breath clouded the clear, cold air, mist swirled from the frozen ponds. Toby thought once more of the distant past and his own muddled beginnings. Sometimes it was as though he almost saw the truth hidden somewhere in the half-glimpsed strands of history. The shoemaker's description of the men-at-arms who had taken the infant Toby to Chinon. *'I thought, that's it, the brat is a du Chantonnay bastard.'* Reynaud's hasty marriage to Blanche, to secure the château de Marigny. De Bohun: *'I have come to take what I am owed.'* But then the strands separated, failing to make a pattern.

He let the horse have its head, and speed cut out the need for thought or decision. For a long while the only sounds were the clink of bit and bridle and the clatter of his horse's hooves on the icy grass. The sky curved wide and white above him, the fields and trees were veiled by frost.

Toby saw the riders as he opened a gate and made his way through a field of sheep. At first he thought that those black silhouettes against the blanched grass and sky were nothing to do with him.

Then he realized that they were everything to do with him. He put his horse into a gallop, but they surrounded him, half a dozen of them, riding towards him from every direction. The cold wind drove against his face, making it hard to breathe. His throat ached, his head pounded. Swiftly he unsheathed his sword.

It all happened just as before. He even recognized one of them. He fought as he had fought a year ago, but with desperation this time rather than anger. Because he saw, too late, and with a terrible clarity, the trap he had constructed for himself.

He did not know at first whether the voice whispered in his dreams or in reality. *'Wake up, my pet. We need to have a little talk.'* Toby groaned and tried to move his aching limbs. He opened his eyes.

Everything was blurred at first: a pattern of black and red. Like Hell, he thought, wearily. He was in Purgatory, beginning a long payment for past sins.

Then Hamon de Bohun said, 'That's better. You may drink if you wish to,' and he knew that he was not in Hell. Not yet, anyway.

Toby gulped some water from a bucket beside him. It was brackish and dirty, but it moistened his parched mouth. His eyes focused at last, and he saw that he was not, as before, in some splendid house, but in a stone hut. There was no glass in the windows, and straw was scattered on the dirt floor. A fire burned in the chimneyless grate, marking the walls with a scarlet light.

He was lying on the floor, curled up like a baby, deprived, of course, of sword and knife. Shuffling himself to a sitting position, he raised his eyes, at last, to Hamon de Bohun.

De Bohun said, 'I thought we should have a little talk before I kill you. You do know why I'm going to kill you, don't you?'

'For Marigny,' Toby croaked. His head was beating like a drum, and his lip was split and swollen.

Hamon de Bohun smiled. His dark eyes glittered with delight. 'Of course, for Marigny. I made inquiries, you see, Crow. The lady's pleasure on receiving your gift was so touching.'

Those damned ribbons. Briefly, Toby remembered the smile on Eleanor's face, her undisguised pleasure in his feeble gift.

'I wouldn't want your little flirtation with the lady of Marigny to go any further, you see. After all, she wouldn't be the first ageing widow to warm her bed with a servant.'

De Bohun had moved a little closer. The fire made his dark shadow loom over Toby. Toby's hatred was pure and cold and useless.

De Bohun, bending his head, whispered, 'You didn't think, did you, my pet, that I would let you have Marigny? After all, I have lost it before.'

Toby's bruised lips stretched into a semblance of a smile. 'To Reynaud.'

Surprise registered briefly on de Bohun's face. 'My, my. You are well informed, Crow. And what else do you know?'

Toby wondered in a detached fashion whether Hamon de Bohun himself would slit his throat or whether his half-dozen henchmen still lingered beyond the cottage door waiting to do the task for him. He said, piecing together the motley clues he had collected in Venice and France, 'You wanted to marry Blanche. Reynaud got to her – and Marigny – first. So you retired to England to lick your wounds.'

Hamon de Bohun shook his head. 'Now there you are mistaken, my pet. I don't believe in licking wounds. I believe in vengeance.'

There was a silence. Toby shuddered. The cold, white light of midday filtered through the single small window, and the unseasoned wood crackled and spat in the fire. Toby leaned his back against the wall. His lungs hurt but, then, he shouldn't have to use them much longer.

Finally he said, 'And did you have your vengeance?'

'Oh yes. Oh yes.'

The expression on Hamon de Bohun's face made Toby shiver again. Nausea churned restlessly in the pit of his stomach.

De Bohun continued, 'And you, Crow? Such looks, such talent. Such *flair.* It is unfortunate for you that you possess an ambition inappropriate to your station. You should have stayed a common soldier, don't you agree? And not meddled in the affairs of your betters.'

De Bohun's face, closer to him now, had become hazy. Toby did not know whether the haziness was due to the smoke from the fire or to his battered vision. Toby said drowsily, 'I thought that the affairs of my betters were my own affair,' and he closed his eyes for a moment.

The voice cut through his dizziness. 'Wake up. I haven't quite finished.'

A hand grasped his shoulder, shook him. De Bohun said, 'You fantasize, Crow. You are deluded. My affairs, Reynaud's affairs, were never your concern. You were foolish enough to interfere in a private quarrel.'

Toby heard himself reply as if he were in a dream, 'I thought Reynaud du Chantonnay was my father, you see.' Then he closed his eyes again and drifted pleasantly to where no one could touch him.

Ice-cold water woke him, as Hamon de Bohun up-ended the bucket over his head.

De Bohun's voice was sharp. 'You thought Reynaud was your father? What do you mean?'

When Toby remained silent, Hamon added, 'You can die quickly or slowly, monsieur. I'm sure you've seen slow deaths often enough not to court *that.*'

Toby realized that it didn't matter now. Reynaud was dead, and he would never again have Eleanor, never have Marigny. So he explained, haltingly and through thickened lips, about the schoolteacher and his wife, about the cobbler. *'I thought, that's it, the brat is a du Chantonnay bastard.'* If he stumbled, then Hamon de Bohun prompted him. If he dozed off again, he was struck.

When he had finished, he thought suddenly how pointless it all had been. Such a fragile web of history, such futile curiosity. Five years of his life that had, in the end, brought him to this.

De Bohun's back was to him; he was facing the fire. The outline of his head and body was sketched in red by the flames. There was a long silence.

When Hamon de Bohun turned, he was smiling. 'You see, my dear, you have it entirely wrong. *I* am your father. You are *my* son.'

Hamon de Bohun didn't kill him, after all. Instead, barely conscious, Toby was aware that they had embarked upon a journey. Sometimes he travelled slung over the saddlebow of someone's horse, at other times dumped in the bottom of a cart among sacks and straw and a few wizened turnips. The sky changed from white to black and then to white again. He was cold or he was frozen, he had forgotten even the possibility of warmth.

The journey became confused in his mind with other journeys: riding back from Italy, his arm still weak from its wound; the winter journey from Venice to Chinon; travelling from Padua to Milan with Martin Gefroy and Joanna Zulian. Once he thought himself to be in the garden again, where the air was scented with honeysuckle and pinks but, opening his eyes, he knew that to be an illusion.

He never slept deeply: sounds echoed on the edges of his dreams. The sounds of town and village: pedlars calling their wares, dogs barking, horses' hooves on cobblestones. Of the countryside: the cawing of crows, the bleating of sheep. Or of those who travelled with him, as they asked directions and called for food outside taverns.

And always, always, Hamon de Bohun's voice. *'I am your father. You are my son.'*

The possibility that de Bohun had spoken the truth was appalling, terrible, unable to be contemplated.

Eventually, Toby heard a new sound. A crashing and roaring, unrecognizable to him at first. Then he smelt salt in the air and he knew himself to be by the sea.

He was hauled out of the cart, and made to stand amid the barrels and nets and lobster-pots that cluttered the harbour of a port he did not recognize. Perhaps Brittany, he thought, seeing steep cliffs and rocky beaches. Perhaps Roscoff. He wondered in a detached sort of way why Hamon de Bohun had decided to kill him in Brittany.

It was either early morning or late evening, he was too tired to work out which. The sun was halfway into the sea: the garish pink and purple and crimson light hurt his eyes. The harbour was almost deserted: boats bobbed in the grey water and only a few dark figures moved in the distance, uninterested in what did not concern them.

At first he couldn't stand. Hands held him roughly upright as he struggled for balance. His legs shook, as weak as a baby's. The cold salt air jolted him, though, whipping his hair around his face, forcing its way into his bruised lungs. Looking up, he saw Hamon de Bohun standing in front of him.

Toby found himself lost in those lightless eyes.

'I've decided that I don't need to kill you,' said de Bohun softly. 'I dare say you'll find that life has lost its savour anyway. I am allowing you to satisfy your rather unattractive curiosity, my pet. I think that you should meet your mother.'

De Bohun moved closer. There was a knife in his hand, its long, thin blade painted gaudy rainbow colours by the nightmarish sun.

'But before we part, a little memento. You were insolent to me once, Crow. I dislike insolence.'

They had torn open his doublet and shirt. He felt the knife pierce his skin just below the collarbone, and then the point was dragged diagonally down across his chest.

'Bend sinister,' whispered Hamon de Bohun. 'For bastardy, my pet.'

CHAPTER TEN

Joanna had allowed Toby a week. Two or three days for Brother Joachim to ride to Marigny, a similar length of time for Toby to make the journey to Bourges. Since his collapse, Paul had not risen from his bed. Joanna saw the resignation, the fear, in Agnès's face every time she looked at her.

It hurt her to see Agnès's distress as the days passed and Toby did not come. Joanna knew that Paul would not work again, and that Agnès's smallholding could scarcely provide even one person with a reasonable living. She would remain there only as long as Agnès needed her: she would not depend on her generosity. She wanted more than mere survival. She wanted independence, and she wanted security. She wanted a home, a place, a future. Those were things that Joanna knew she must find herself, alone. She wanted to be no one's duty, no one's responsibility. Duty and ownership were far too closely linked.

The cold weather eased only grudgingly; when she went out Joanna wrapped herself in cloaks and shawls. In the marketplace and at church the villagers stared and whispered. *He was well enough until she came. Dosed him with herbs and potions, didn't she?* The village women, drab and starved of colour, gazed with envy and hostility at her braid, her low-cut Venetian gowns, her fur-trimmed cloak. The men consumed with hungry eyes the long, loose red-brown hair, the colour of a fox's coat, the slender, ringless hands. Joanna felt as she had eventually felt in Venice working in Taddeo's studio: an oddity, a freak. It saddened her that she should have travelled so many hundreds of miles to find herself still outcast, still so helplessly different.

Toby, she thought, Toby. Taking her turn at the sick man's bedside, Joanna read voraciously books from Paul's library, filling in the gaps in her erratic education. From the distant past, she remembered a favourite quotation of Donato's. *'Love is very fruitful,'* he had said, *'both of honey and of gall.'*

*

The journey seemed endless. Later, or perhaps even at the time, it all seemed mixed together, a hopelessly muddled jumble. Like his origins, Toby thought. Like his tainted, lousy provenance.

The rise and fall of the ship became confused with the pounding of horses' hooves. There was always noise, all of it unnatural-seeming, beyond his usual experience. Darkness was the only constant: it was dark in the ship, where his head lay on the bare boards and he could smell salt, and it was dark in the cart, where straw scratched his face and his body was covered with sacking. Sometimes there was water to drink, and sometimes there was not. His hands were tied, his fingers numb. Once he was sick; strangely detached, he listened to the retching of his stomach.

He did not realize that the journey had ended at first. The ground still swayed, there was still the clatter of hooves. But then he heard a voice say, *'That'll do, Tomaz. Let's be gone before the taverns close.'* He was dropped off the back of a horse, and he rolled into a hollow in the grass and lay motionless.

It was dawn when he was awoken by the cold. Opening his eyes, Toby looked around him. Stones rose like the dolmens of Brittany from out of the grey haze. Mist swirled around the stones, hovering over the grass, blurring the tall building opposite him. Toby hauled himself into a sitting position, his knees hunched up to his chin. He blinked.

He was in a churchyard. The dolmens were gravestones, and the building was a church. His back was to the wall that Hamon de Bohun's men had dumped him over, and to either side of him were yew trees. Shivering, he began to work his wrists free of the knotted rope.

It took a long time to force his fingers back into movement, and his wrists were red and raw. He felt too tired even to try to understand. Since Hamon de Bohun had said, *'I am your father. You are my son,'* he had realized only that he had misunderstood everything. He had been clumsy and foolish, a blunderer.

He managed to stand, though, knowing that if he did not move now, he would soon be unable. Every bone in his body ached, and Hamon de Bohun's knife-cut seared his chest like a brand. Holding the wall for support he looked around him, trying to get his bearings. He did not see one familiar object: the church, the landscape, the bundle of houses and the dirt road behind the wall, were all strange. The silence, the emptiness, frightened him. He was in a country peopled only by ghosts.

He heard voices at last, distant and unintelligible, approaching along the lane. He remained where he was, silent and hidden by the wall. Soon he was able to make out syllables and sentences, but he hardly understood a word that was said. He slid back down the wall, his legs juddering uncontrollably. *English*. They had spoken in *English*.

His sense of shock would not let him think clearly. His fingers clenched, clawing at the frosty grass. His forehead was damp with sweat, and waves of nausea washed over him. He rested his head on his knees until the dizziness passed. Hamon de Bohun's parting words flickered through his exhausted brain. *'I am allowing you to satisfy your rather unattractive curiosity, my pet. I think that you should meet your mother.'* It made no sense to him. None of it made any sense.

Eventually he pulled himself to his feet again with the aid of the wall. There was a lich-gate to one side of the churchyard, still wreathed in mist. He began to walk towards it – slowly, holding the wall, the trees, the gravestones for support. Beyond the gate he could see the straggling cottages, the well, the more substantial house that was framed by the hill in the distance. The village was beginning to come to life. In the dawn light, dogs snuffled for scraps in the gutter; women walked to the well, buckets in hand.

It hurt to move; it hurt, damn it, to do anything. But he made himself stumble across the road, towards the well on the village green. He was breathless by the time he reached it, and had to lean on the stone well-head for support. Voices – English voices – fluttered across the grass. He wondered, briefly, whether he was still dreaming. But he knew that he was not: this nightmare was of Hamon de Bohun's making.

A woman was lowering her bucket into the well. She glanced at him curiously. She was pretty, fair-haired and blue-eyed. She offered him water, and he, cupping his hands, drank deeply. When he had finished, he managed to ask her, stumbling over the unfamiliar words, for the name of the village.

'Why, this is Lydney Mandeville,' she said.

Her accent was strange to him, so different from Penniless's. He knew that she watched him as he began to limp away.

At first the name meant nothing to him. Lydney Mandeville – angular, unpronounceable English syllables. Hobbling back to the churchyard, Toby mumbled them out loud, testing them. So strange . . . But then out of a confusion of memory there was something. He frowned, clutching the wooden supports of the lich-gate. Lydney Mandeville. *Mandeville.*

He stood still for a moment, swaying. Memories, fragments of the last four years, fluttered around him like dead leaves. He was aware of more curious stares, more whispered comments. Then he walked, as fast as he was able, into the churchyard. He blundered about the gravestones like a madman, trampling on flowers and carefully plaited wreaths. He lurched from stone to stone, knocking aside the tall grass, peering furiously through lichen to read the names carved in the limestone. All English names, and every inhabitant of the black, dank ground was unknown to him.

Until he found the Mandevilles. They occupied the best corner of the churchyard, of course, a little apart from the rest. Their stones were cleaner, finer, more artistically carved, trimmed with skulls and scrolls, angels holding out the keys to heaven. Toby forced his eyes to focus: on the older stones he read the names of Hugh de Mandeville, Alan de Mandeville, Cecily de Mandeville, his wife. On the newer stones the Norman prefix had been dropped: John Mandeville, another Hugh. And at last he found what he had been looking for. The gravestone that Hamon de Bohun had sent him to see. Izabel Mandeville, who had lived for only twenty-seven years, the last six of them away from her native Brittany.

Hamon de Bohun's voice echoed round the churchyard. *'I think that you should meet your mother.'*

The church doors were unlocked. Inside, there was a smell of incense. Toby lit some candles to dispel the darkness, then sat in one of the hindmost pews.

Izabel Mandeville had been Reynaud's sister. She had remained in France until after Reynaud had married Blanche. Then, long before François's birth, she had been sent to England to marry a Mandeville. Hugh Mandeville, thought Toby, recalling the gravestone adjacent to Izabel's.

Beginning to understand, he stared bleakly at the altar with its jewelled, golden cross, and then his gaze drifted slowly upwards to the roof of the church. Angels, their wooden wings outspread, supported the roof-beams. If he thought, *Izabel Mandeville was my mother, and Hamon de Bohun my father . . .* the dizziness swamped him. The wooden angels were ready to fly, to swoop down to the clay below them, outstretched wings creaking, vengeance on their perfect faces.

'I think you'll find that life has lost its savour,' Hamon de Bohun had said, and he had been right, of course. The walls, the roof, the floor of the church seemed to heave inexorably together, crushing him like a fly trapped between two palms. Every possibility was sickening, every possibility intolerable.

At last he found the solace of sleep. He lay stretched out on the pew, his arms curled over his head, as the candles guttered and died.

When after a week, Toby had not returned to Marigny, Eleanor told herself not to worry. The weather was still poor, she reminded herself, and the roads were always troublesome at this time of year. She had doubted him before, and she had hated herself for it: she refused to let doubt consume her again. Faith was, after all, a part of love. And besides, she had something else to think about now.

For she was pregnant. She had hardly dared to believe at first that such a miracle was possible. She had endured twelve years of barren marriage to Reynaud, twelve years in which her monthly courses had appeared with relentless regularity. She could have timed the waxing and waning of the moon by the rhythm of her body. Bitterly, she had tried to come to terms with her permanent childlessness, had struggled to accept that she would always be denied the one thing that could have made her marriage worthwhile.

Now, though, she was almost a fortnight late. At first Eleanor thought that the change of life had come early, that the alterations in her body were those of age. The thought frightened her: once again, she feared that she would lose Toby. But then that morning she overheard a whispered conversation in the kitchen. One of the serving-maids – a silly wench of fifteen – was pregnant. The women had discussed the girl's symptoms in disapproving, fascinated detail: sore breasts and sick every morning. Eleanor, who had had to loosen the bodices of her gowns, and whose stomach was still churning at the sights and smells of the kitchen, knew then, with sudden, utter certainty and an unquenchable joy in her heart, that she was pregnant.

Someone was gripping his shoulder, was shaking him so hard that every bone in his body rattled. When he managed to open his eyes and sit up,

Toby saw a priest standing beside him. He was holding a candlestick and gazing at him with fear on his face. Toby couldn't understand his fear at first, but then, as he rubbed his eyes with his fists, he thought how he must appear.

The priest said hesitantly, 'It's almost time for evensong, my son.'

Toby's tongue had stuck to the roof of his mouth. He croaked, 'A drink, father?' and the old man nodded and shuffled off in the direction of the vestry.

Consecrated wine, he thought, gulping down the cupful the priest brought for him. To wash away his sins. For a brief moment he wanted to laugh. The priest was watching him warily. Trying to size me up, thought Toby. If his clothes had been homespun, then it would have been easy: another vagrant throwing himself on the mercy of the parish. But his clothes, though torn and dirty, were of silk and velvet.

He managed to say her name, struggled to ask his next question. But the English words eluded him, his request for directions to the Mandeville estate turning into a hopeless jumble of French and Italian. He saw the priest step back nervously, still staring at him, and he made one last, terrible effort, searching back for the Latin that Paul Dubreton had once patiently taught him. The effort of memory exhausted him so much that he didn't understand a word of the priest's reply. But the priest, seeing perhaps the distress in Toby's eyes, overcame his fear and, taking him by the elbow, guided him out of the church and back to the lich-gate.

His head pounded so much that he recognized only the name, *Mandeville*. But he looked in the direction of the priest's pointing hand and saw the house set back from the village green, amber and violet in the dying sunlight.

At Izabel Mandeville's house there were the first tentative signs of spring: snowdrops huddled next to the walls, and a drift of acid-yellow celandines glimmered beneath the trees. The paved forecourt was lined by a wing of the house on one side, by stables on the other. The grass in front of the house was high and spitted with reeds where a marshy stream trailed. Ivy crawled up the yellow stone walls, and box trees formed mounds of evergreen at the forecourt's sides.

But no candles flickered within, and no horses pawed the cobbles in front of the stables. Stepping forward, Toby saw the air of palpable neglect that permeated the manor house of Lydney Mandeville: the dusty, empty windows; the swirls of dead leaves around the doorstep; the spiders' webs that festooned the furniture half-glimpsed through grimy window-panes. The house looked as though it were in mourning. Toby wanted to walk away, longed to separate himself from this place and whatever miserable story it hid.

But he could not, of course, walk away. Instead he limped to the large wooden door and, standing on the topmost doorstep, seized the wrought-iron knocker. He heard the thud as the knocker struck the door over and over again; he heard the sound echoing through the rooms and corridors, reverberating against plaster and glass and wood. He found himself waiting, his entire body tensed, for approaching footsteps, for an answering voice.

There was nothing, though. The house was deserted and there were no ghosts to answer the questions he no longer wanted to ask. He began to stumble around the building, gazing up at the bay windows, the arched windows, the oriel windows. Chimneys pierced the greying sky. Statues – grotesques – crouched on the roof-arches. Mandeville was a part of him. He was there somewhere in its history. Hamon de Bohun is my father, he thought, and Izabel Mandeville was my mother. He did not for a moment doubt de Bohun: had he been nothing other than Reynaud du Chantonnay's overambitious courier, then de Bohun would have killed him in France. He was an instrument of Hamon de Bohun's vengeance, the precise paths of which he had not yet traced, did not want to trace. But here, he guessed at the violence that had stained his creation, exhaustion providing, as it always did, leaps of imagination, of understanding. He thought that if he closed his eyes he would hear, echoing through the years, the pain that Hamon de Bohun had taken pleasure in inflicting on Izabel Mandeville. That sort of suffering was not forgotten, it lived on in the bleak aspect of the place, the cold walls and shadowy grounds. *'Bend sinister. For bastardy, my pet.'*

Crouching in the long grass behind the house, Toby rested his forehead on his knees. Dizziness washed over him in sickening waves, and the blackness of his vision was not only the blackness of night. Up in the tall beech trees to the side of the house, crows cawed, welcoming the darkness.

When, after a fortnight, Toby did not return, Eleanor struggled to keep calm. She told herself that she was being foolish. Toby's father might have taken a turn for the worse and his son been obliged to stay at Bourges for longer than he had anticipated. A letter would arrive any moment, or she would see Toby himself riding down the long, winding path through forest and meadow.

But no letter arrived, and the path was always empty. In the chapel, unable to confess the true nature of her sins, Eleanor told the priest, 'I'm lonely, I'm frightened.' The priest, well-fed and bored, reminded her that in the presence of God she need never be lonely, never afraid. Afterwards, she knelt on the cold stone floor of the chapel, her eyes fixed on the altar. Surely God would not prevent her legitimizing a union that had been so wrong, so utterly wrong in the eyes of the Church. Parted from Toby, the gravity of her sins appalled her, waking her in the early hours of the morning.

François whined for Toby and Eleanor wanted to hit him. Digging her nails into her palms, she told the boy to be patient, that Toby would soon be back. She had begun to disbelieve her own words, however: they sounded hollow, empty. Watching François deal incompetently with all the duties of a great landowner, she remembered Cousin Guillaume's words, *'People kill for land, Eleanor.'* When she saw, reflected in the dark waters of the moat, her pale, tired face, she told herself that Toby would return because he had wanted Marigny. Guillaume had been right: everyone wanted Marigny.

A fortnight passed, and she was constantly sick. Her breasts hurt to touch, and even walking across the meadow exhausted her. She struggled to hide her condition from her serving-women. She could not retreat to the kitchen, her usual solace, because the smell of food was nauseating. And besides, from the kitchen she could not see the path.

She took to her bed, claiming illness, but found herself unable to rest. She could not concentrate enough to read, and her fingers had become too clumsy to sew. Her women's chatter made her want to scream.

Rising, she despised herself. How could there be love, she thought, when there was not faith? She must have faith in Toby: something must have prevented his return. She sent riders to Bourges, to inquire after a family by the name of Crow. When they returned, having found no such family, having found no trace of Toby, Eleanor began to see how God was punishing her. For lust, for fornication. For having betrayed her birth, her position. For having believed that earthly love was both possible and permissible. In eight months' time all the world would know how she had sinned.

The following day Hamon de Bohun came to Marigny.

Eleanor was in the chapel trying to pray. It was evening, and the dying sun filtered through the stained-glass windows, making pools of purple and azure, viridian and carmine, as though the colours of a painter's palette had been spilt on to the flagstones.

Eleanor heard the chapel door open and she rose to her feet. The door was in the shadow of a stone archway, and the darkness etched shadows on the figure of her visitor, subduing the greyness of his hair, making hollows in his face.

For a moment she thought it was Toby. Then the flicker of false similarity that the darkness had created died, and the thudding of her heart, the dryness of her throat, reminded her of the irrational persistence of hope.

'I apologize for intruding upon you, madame. Your steward told me that you were here.'

Hamon de Bohun's voice echoed in the small chapel. As he stepped forward, the candlelight illuminated his features: the strong, well-cut face, the dark, hypnotic eyes.

'There's no need to apologize, Monsieur de Bohun. I have finished.'

She had not been able to pray. The words had curdled in her mouth. The only thing she wanted, God would not grant. Eleanor walked to the chapel door.

'I am on my way to Tours.' De Bohun smiled. 'I had the temerity to hope that you would permit me to break my journey at Marigny.'

Eleanor managed to find a suitable reply.

He had taken her arm, and was now leading her out of the chapel towards the courtyard. 'Would you walk to the meadow with me, Madame de Marigny? The château looks so beautiful from the meadow.'

It was almost, she thought, as though she were the visitor, not he. But she found herself acquiescing, aware that the power of decision had deserted her during these last, terrible weeks.

On the drawbridge they paused, looking down to the still surface of the moat. Two swans glided past, mirrored in the dark water, drawing a widening wake behind them. For the first time Eleanor thought of toppling over the bridge, of sliding beneath the water. It would be so easy, so restful. Yet she knew that she would not. Suicides could not be buried in consecrated ground. And besides, to kill herself would involve committing the greatest sin of all: the murder of her own child.

'You look tired, madame.'

She had forgotten Hamon de Bohun's presence. She managed to force a smile. 'Such a busy week . . . and my son has been unwell. We have found him a good physician, but he still ails.'

Painfully, she thought how easily untruths came to her now. She who had not known deceit until she had met Toby Crow. Her whole life had become a lie.

They began to walk again. Eleanor saw, framed by the rising moon, Hamon de Bohun's men, positioned on the meadow beyond the drawbridge. Forty or fifty of them, armed, mounted, dressed in their master's colours. Panniers and saddlebags on each horse, and two carts laden with chests. As though he intended to stay for a year, she thought, dazed. So many of them.

'The roads are treacherous,' said de Bohun smoothly, following her gaze. 'One must travel in company. A group of pilgrims were robbed and murdered near Angers not so long ago. Did you hear about that, madame?'

Eleanor shook her head, her eyes wide. The dark, the moonlight, the shadows, seemed to multiply the men waiting on the meadow, until they were no longer a retinue of servants, but an army, swords and lances readied, poised outside the drawbridge of Marigny.

'Murdered?' Her voice faltered.

'A dozen of them.' For a moment Hamon de Bohun's dark, fathomless eyes held hers, and then he turned and waved his men towards the drawbridge. Slowly, the portcullis opened and they passed into the depths of the château.

De Bohun watched until the last of his men had disappeared through the gateway. Then he began to walk again, past the turrets and towers, the walls and gates of Marigny.

'Such an exquisite place, madame. I have travelled widely, and I have, as you know, lived in England for many years. But I have never seen anywhere quite like Marigny. It is enchanted, don't you think? It weaves a spell.' De Bohun's eyes were still fixed lovingly on the château.

Eleanor nodded, unable to speak.

They walked for a while in silence, following the circle of the moat. The spring flowers in the meadow were budding. The château was dark except for an occasional candlelit window. They came to the kitchen garden which straggled untidily behind the house on the far side of the moat, the only blemish on Marigny's perfection.

Throughout the years of her marriage to Reynaud, thought Eleanor, Marigny had been a solace, a comfort. She had known herself privileged to live in such a beautiful place, to be cut off from hunger, from war, from the chaos of the world. And then, when Toby had entered her life, Marigny had become a paradise, a Garden of Eden. Since his departure, though, she had felt herself trapped, mocked by the beauty of the building, the loveliness of the land.

'I saw your courier,' said Hamon.

Her breath caught in her throat, there was a sudden pain in her chest. She stopped and stared at de Bohun.

'Your son's bodyguard, I should say. Monsieur Crow.'

She waited for him to go on, but he said nothing more. His eyes met hers, and she could see nothing in them except, improbably, the smallest touch of amusement. She said, 'Where, Monsieur de Bohun? Toby went away almost three weeks ago. I have had no word from him . . .'

Hamon de Bohun shook his head. A smile touched his lips. 'Young men are so fickle, are they not, madame? You would think that he would be content to stay with a generous employer, such as yourself, my dear Eleanor – I may call you Eleanor, mayn't I? And a boy like François to educate, to coach in the arts of war.' He sighed, spreading his hands in a gesture of resignation. 'But inconstancy is a fault of the young. It is those of us who are older, wiser, who appreciate stability and endurance.'

'*Where?*' she whispered a second time. 'Where did you see Toby Crow?'

De Bohun's shadow was black against the pale moonlit walls of Marigny. He added softly, 'I saw Monsieur Crow in Chinon, madame. A week or so ago. He was with a girl – a fair-haired, pretty little thing. Not yet twenty, I would guess.'

She knew then that her treasured hopes had crumbled. She began to walk again, blindly, stumbling on the paths of the kitchen garden that threaded through clumps of cabbages and onion-heads. She knew herself to be trapped: trapped by her folly, trapped by her pathetic desire for a faithless young man. She began to shiver.

Hamon de Bohun said, 'But you are cold, madame. How thoughtless of me – we must return indoors.'

They walked back round the moat to the front of the house. Hamon de Bohun took her arm once more. His touch was firm, as he guided her towards the drawbridge. He gave her direction. Without him, she would not have known which way to go: she would have wandered for ever like a madwoman round the gardens of Marigny.

Eleanor lay awake throughout the night. The bed seemed wide, empty and cold. The ordered world she had once known had disintegrated, leaving her stranded like a beached fish gasping for air. She saw suddenly how right Guillaume had been, how vulnerable they were, herself and François. Her fear for François was that night as desperate as her fear for herself, and for the bastard child in her womb.

She rose early, as the sun hovered, pink and misted, over the distant trees. For Eleanor, the world had tilted on its axis, had become for ever out of joint, unreliable. It surprised her to see the sun rising at its appointed time. It should have been swallowed by dragons; the day should have remained as black as night.

She went to Reynaud's ante-room. In the emptiness of the gallery beyond, where the tapestries had once hung, she pictured the images of betrayal: Toby, his arm round a pretty young girl, kissing her, caressing her, bedding her. Eleanor closed her eyes very tightly.

When she opened them, Hamon de Bohun was beside her. He said nothing, but she allowed him to take her in his arms and to stroke her long unbound black hair, as Toby had once done.

Paul Dubreton died at the end of March. In the graveyard, a raw wind tugged at the skirts and cloaks of the mourners, and rain drummed intermittently on the slate roof of the church. The church was full, but Agnès's hurt, disbelieving eyes constantly raked the crowded pews for one particular face. Joanna knew who Agnès was looking for.

Afterwards, most of the inhabitants of the village gathered in the schoolteacher's house. Joanna and Agnès had spent much of the day and night that had passed since Paul's death in the kitchen, making bread and cakes and boiled mutton for the funeral dinner. It had been impossible, stirring sauces, pounding dough, for them to absorb the reality of Paul's death. They couldn't stop listening for his voice, couldn't stop expecting him to peer round the kitchen door, sniffing the tantalizing smells.

For the funeral, Joanna had picked the braid from her black gown and had covered her face with a veil. Her eyes were red with tears. Like Agnès, she had listened constantly for the sound of horse's hooves, and glanced round in the church at every creaking of the door. Just as with Paolo, just as with Donato, it was so hard to accept death or desertion. So hard to believe that she would see neither Paul nor Toby again. The mixture of anger and desolation was almost overwhelming.

Agnès and Joanna fed their guests bacon, mutton and boiled chicken; the Dubretons' small cellar was drunk almost dry. Joanna's head ached and her feet hurt. The stone walls of the cottage echoed with the clamour of conversation that accompanied the release of tension after the ordeal of the funeral.

'You should stay for a while with Cousin Philippe. You know you adore the children. And my hens are not laying at all, Agnès. One egg for the whole of March. You must give me your advice . . .'

'Jeanne gave me a length of cloth from the fair at Bourges. I've made breeches for each of the boys, and there's still half an ell left . . .'

'Box leaves and pennyroyal. Boil them for a few minutes, and then strain the liquid . . .'

'I've left the water-meadows fallow. The soil's too clogged to take the plough . . .'

'She should marry. It's not right, is it, a woman like that? Agnès would think the best of anyone . . .'

'A bad year, Vincent. The curé says there's a great deal of sickness in Orléans . . .'

'And if pennyroyal doesn't work, then you might ask Joanna. She cured Hortense of a fever . . .'

'Agnès'll not see him again. Paul Dubreton was a good man, but a fool. Bad blood, you could see it in his eyes . . .'

'A cold winter and a wet spring. God punishes us for our sins, Vincent . . .'

'I told Agnès she should go to Philippe. Without the Italian woman, of course. I'll not have *her* look at my hens. They'd be dead within a week . . .'

Joanna escaped into the kitchen. The sink was piled with dirty plates, the dresser bare except for a single holly branch, forgotten from Christmas, trailing from the uppermost shelf. Angrily, she climbed on to a stool and seized the branch. The spiky leaves pricked her fingers, and tears began to ooze from her eyes. These days they seemed to overflow constantly – a fleeting memory and they would ache and fill and the tears would trickle down her cheeks.

Joanna stepped down from the stool and dabbed at her eyes with a handkerchief. She broke the holly branch in two and tossed it into the fire. The shiny brown leaves crumpled and blackened, the shrivelled berries spat.

She knew that she had stayed here too long. She had not intended to stay so long. It was a home: a warm, loving home. But not *her* home. As she began to heave dirty dishes into the sink and scrub at them with a bundle of twigs, Joanna saw what she must do. She must go to Bourges: both to sell her jewels and to discover whether fat Brother Joachim had ever delivered the letter that she had written to Toby Crow.

Impatiently, Guillaume had marked the weeks he allowed Eleanor. He knew that she needed time: time to accustom herself to the idea of remarriage, time for the fact of François's incompetence and her own defencelessness to sink in. Thwarted by Eleanor's respect for convention, Guillaume still hoped that she might be persuaded to a betrothal before her year of mourning was out, even if she would not consent to an immediate marriage. Guillaume was aware of the many hungry eyes that gazed in the direction of Marigny. He was disturbed by Hamon de Bohun's return to France. But de Bohun was old, he told himself. De Bohun had long ago forfeited whatever claim he had once had to Marigny. Still, he would be more forceful this time, Guillaume thought, he would not allow Eleanor to prevaricate. Martin Gefroy had visited Marigny twice now to attend the wretched François. Both times, on his return, he had reassured Guillaume that Eleanor was still widowed, Marigny still attainable. But Guillaume was nervous, untrusting. He had waited so long and, besides, he had no faith. He knew fate to be capricious.

The weather improved at last, and sunlight filtered through the unfurling leaves as Guillaume rode through the village of Marigny towards the château. He wore blue silk trimmed with lace, and the blue mirrored the colour of his eyes. He had jewels in his ear, on his doublet, on his gloves. Like a bridegroom, thought Guillaume, mocking himself. The unmarried village girls were bareheaded in the sunlight; sly, enticing eyes caught Guillaume's gaze as his retinue wound through the narrow hilly streets.

Guillaume felt quite at ease as he rode towards the château. Birds sang the first songs of spring, golden buds sprouted from the marsh marigolds floating on the river. It was only when he glimpsed the wrought-iron gate in the boundary wall that he had a premonition of disaster.

Two men-at-arms stood beside the gate, their gaudy tabards catching the fragile sunlight, their emblazoned insignia harsh against the subtle colours of field and forest. Guillaume thought at first that they were François's men. Some petty pomposity set up by the sickly youth to substitute for his lack of intellect and manhood. Place a few muscular fellows with coats of arms and quartered devices around your demesne, and the world will cease to notice your beardless face, your backwardness. Only they weren't du Chantonnay arms, Guillaume realized as he drew closer. There were no familiar crescents, no leopard. Only two golden pikes, teeth bared, glittering in gold thread on the breasts and banners of the soldiers.

Halfway up the slope to the gate he had to take a deep breath and pause for a long moment. Thoughts, possibilities, all of them insupportable, stuttered through his head. Guillaume's jewelled leather gauntlets gripped the reins, and he cursed out loud when one of his men tried to speak to him.

Eventually, however, he coaxed his horse forward. Whatever his faults, he had never lacked physical courage. Guillaume gave his name and rank to the men-at-arms. With difficulty he restrained himself from striking them for their insolent smiles.

The gate was opened and he was permitted to ride into Marigny. As he rode through the forest and across the meadow, the image of those snarling golden pikes was imprinted on his mind. The arms were unfamiliar; Guillaume went methodically through the insignia of the great families of Brittany and France, but the *luce d'or* bordered with black was unknown to him.

More men-at-arms, wearing that same damnable insignia, were stationed on the meadow and at the end of the drawbridge. The drawbridge, damn it, was not even lowered. As though Marigny were under siege, thought Guillaume. The moat cut him off, stranded him.

He waited, trying to disguise his anger, as finally they lowered the drawbridge, with a great scraping and screeching of wheels and cogs. He rode slowly across, thinking of the pikes that swam in the moat below, far beneath the surface of the water. Great aged fish, golden and cunning, hatching plots, waiting to bite.

In the courtyard, he saw no Eleanor, no François. No Berthe from the kitchens. Only someone else's unfamiliar servants, and someone else's banners with those voracious embroidered fish grinning triumphantly down at him.

He had managed to take control of himself, to hide his fear and fury beneath the mask he always assumed at Marigny. Guillaume's voice was light as he instructed his men to wait for him in the courtyard. He swung off his saddle, threw the reins to the stable-lad and walked into Marigny's Great Hall.

It was all changed. Even if he had not seen those betraying men-at-arms, Guillaume would have known that Marigny was different. Something alien had transformed the rooms that he had known intimately since he had first come there as a child – when his father, whispering, had shown him what Cousin Reynaud had done. *'He's made us look fools, boy. He's appropriated lands three times the value of ours. He's made us look like hedge-squires.'* Stupidly the child Guillaume had voiced his wonder at the place. To Reynaud, of all people, and within his father's hearing. Halfway home, his father had taken him from his horse and struck him across the face with his gloved hand. Twice, with all the servants watching. Guillaume had never again been stupid after that. He had learned to be clever, cunning, detached.

Now, as he followed the manservant to the Great Chamber, he found his detachment tried to the utmost. Furniture had been moved, old paintings taken down and replaced with new ones. It outraged Guillaume to see a single stone of Marigny altered by another's hand. It was like a violation.

And then, at last, he was face to face with Marigny's violator. He heard Eleanor's voice greeting him.

'Guillaume. How pleasant to see you. This is the Sieur de Bohun, my husband.'

They had married two nights previously. Guillaume took a seat, accepted wine, watched Eleanor speak, watched her mouth jabber like a wooden marionette's. Her voice was nervous but toneless. She had lost the sparkle that widowhood had given her: her eyes were dull, her face pale and puffy.

She was telling him about Hamon de Bohun. His family, like the du Chantonnays, had originated in Brittany, she said, but Guillaume had known that already, of course. Long ago, Reynaud had taken Blanche – and Marigny – from Hamon de Bohun. De Bohun now owned lands in both Brittany and England. After he lost Marigny he retired to England, exploiting Henry VII's favour, which he had acquired during the Tudor King's sojourn in Brittany. Guillaume had not taken sufficient account of the threat that de Bohun represented. He had underestimated both de Bohun's ruthlessness and the length of his memory. He knew now that he had made an unforgivable mistake.

He managed to congratulate Eleanor and to greet de Bohun, although he would have liked to shower them both with curses and run them through with his sword. Long practised in self-control, he did not often wish for physical violence, but now, looking at Eleanor's anxious, stupid face and at de Bohun's clever, knowing features, it was hard to resist.

But anger was for fools, or for servants like Toby Crow. So instead he let his eyes wander around the room, while he drank, quickly, a cup of Marigny's excellent red wine. He allowed a servant to refill his glass as he murmured pleasantries about the weather and the yields of his own paltry estate. Hamon de Bohun was courteous and polite, but Guillaume knew that really de Bohun was laughing at him.

Now his gaze wandered slowly to the new painting that hung above the carved stone mantel of the fireplace.

He recognized the subject of the painting immediately: Judith and Holofernes. For a moment Guillaume allowed himself the pleasure of imagining Hamon de Bohun's features on Holofernes' severed head. He stood up, put aside his cup of wine and walked towards the fireplace, ignoring Eleanor's bleating voice.

He stared at Judith. He could not take his eyes from Judith. Because he had met her the previous autumn in Milan. Joanna Zulian. The woman that Toby Crow had escorted to France.

He stood a few feet back from the fireplace, staring up at her. Her long auburn hair, her pure classical features, her lovely grey eyes, were all familiar to him. Joanna Zulian looked down at Guillaume as she had looked at him in Milan, when she had tended his wounded leg.

In Milan, Joanna Zulian had worn a black dress trimmed with braid, dust around its hem. She had looked, he thought, like a gypsy. A wild and desirable gypsy. In the painting, though, she wore only jewels and a skirt of bronze silk. Her arms, her shoulders, her breasts were bare. Guillaume's mouth was dry suddenly.

Guillaume heard Hamon de Bohun beside him say, 'She is an enchantress, isn't she? Marigny is the only setting for her,' and he turned and looked at the Breton.

He saw, to his surprise, that in Hamon de Bohun's dark eyes as he gazed up at the picture was some reflection of his own longing, his own despair. And then, knowing he could tolerate Marigny no longer, Guillaume du Chantonnay made his bow and walked out of the château.

Martin Gefroy had been drinking. Since Milan, when he had stood and watched Joanna Zulian ride away with Toby Crow to France, he had needed to drink to erase, however temporarily, the echoes of the past. He did not drink when he was working, of course. He knew that if he started to drink by day, if he needed wine before he could dress a wound or tend a fever, then it would be the end: his skill, his future, his solace, would be destroyed. So he confined his weakness to the evenings, despising himself. He drank with Guillaume du Chantonnay or with Guillaume's steward if either of them wanted company, and he drank alone if no one wished to drink with him. Then he could sleep.

Guillaume had gone to Touraine, to pay court to the widowed lady of Marigny. Toby Crow worked at Marigny as bodyguard to Madame de Marigny's son. To his immense relief, Toby had always been absent when Martin had called at Marigny to tend the ailing François. No amount of wine had succeeded in extinguishing the memory of that last day in Milan. The quarrel, the fight, Joanna's white, shocked face. The sound of his own sickening jealousy: *'I always did admire our Toby's ambition.'* Jealousy was such a contemptible emotion.

It was late when Guillaume returned, and the sky was inky black, the house quiet. One bottle lay empty in the grate in Martin Gefroy's room, another had been opened. The steward came to fetch him, and Martin swayed a little as he followed after him.

Guillaume, still cloaked and booted and spurred, was in the parlour. The table was laden with bread and cheese, roast chicken and a leg of mutton. Guillaume poured two glasses of wine and dismissed the servants. Martin hesitated to pick up the glass.

Guillaume, flinging his cloak on to a chair, said lazily, 'I haven't the pox and the ride didn't give me saddlesores. Only a raging thirst. So you may drink as much as you wish, my dear Martin. I'll see that one of the servants puts you to bed at the end of the evening.'

Martin took the glass and swallowed a mouthful of wine. Guillaume, tearing off a piece of bread, sat in a chair beside the fire, his long booted legs flung out in front of him. Martin could see the rage in his bright blue eyes, in the tension of his mouth.

'Now, *I* am drinking because I have just lost the game I have been playing for years. The game I had almost won. The prizes of that game were, my dear Martin, land and power' – Guillaume held his glass up to the light and gazed at the clear crimson liquid – 'which are, of course, the only gods worthy of adoration. I suspect, though, that you drink for a different reason. What have you lost, Martin? A home? A country? A woman?'

Martin winced. He thought, briefly and painfully, of Joanna Zulian, from whom he had parted last September. He said, steadily, 'The lady Eleanor will not have you then, Guillaume?'

Guillaume, draining his glass, shook his head. He was smiling, but his eyes were still incandescent with fury. 'Worse. Much worse. I should have taken the silly woman to my bed a month past. Once the deed was done, she'd not have had the wit to refuse me.' His eyes narrowed, and his long mouth curled at the corners. He looked up at the physician. 'Eleanor has married, Martin. I had to give her my felicitations. Can you imagine it?'

For one heart-freezing moment Martin thought of Toby – that Toby, restless, hungry Toby Dubreton, had married the widowed Eleanor du Chantonnay. Martin sat down and watched his fingers tremble as they clutched the narrow stem of the wine-glass. 'Not really.' His voice was unsteady. 'Your tongue must have struggled, Guillaume, to make its way round the necessary consonants.'

'Gall,' whispered Guillaume, staring into the fire. 'I have tasted gall today, my dear physician. And the worst of it is – the worst of it is that I have lost everything through my own stupidity. *That* is the hardest thing to accept.'

Martin got up, took the bottle and refilled both their glasses. His voice was level. 'Who has Madame de Marigny married, Guillaume?'

'She has married – and she will discover it herself before too long – the last man on earth she should have wed.'

The beating of Martin's heart, the drumming in his head, subsided as he heard Guillaume speak of Hamon de Bohun, of Blanche du Chantonnay, of Reynaud. He only half listened: these people were, he knew, of no importance to him.

At the end of his discourse, Guillaume said carelessly, 'The boy won't last the year, of course. Poor foolish François. He'll have a fatal stomach upset, or he'll fall into the moat, or he'll die suddenly and tragically in his bed one night.'

Martin, shocked out of his own misery, blinked. It took him a few moments to understand fully what Guillaume was saying. 'You believe that de Bohun will kill the boy?'

The glass in Guillaume's gauntleted hand shattered suddenly, crushed between his strong fingers. Guillaume smiled. 'Of course he will. Like *that*.'

The flames roared up the wide mouth of the chimney, and in the centre of the fire the logs glowed pink and blue. Martin shivered. He thought of François du Chantonnay, the young Seigneur de Marigny. With care, with the right sort of attention, the boy should reach maturity.

Martin, cradling his glass in his hands, shook his head. 'Surely not, Guillaume. Surely de Bohun would not –'

He couldn't finish his sentence. The scattered shards of Guillaume's glass glinted in the firelight. There was a long silence.

Eventually Guillaume said, 'The lady you travelled with to Milan, Madonna Zulian. Do you see her, Martin?'

Martin laughed, a harsh, ugly sound. 'I haven't seen Joanna since Milan. You remember, Guillaume – Toby Crow escorted her to France.'

Martin noticed that the anger had died from Guillaume's eyes, which were now cold and thoughtful. 'But Toby Crow,' said Guillaume gently, 'went to Marigny. So where is Madonna Zulian?'

Martin ran his fingers through his untidy hair. He was aware that Guillaume was watching him. He had not forgotten, of course, where Toby had taken Joanna Zulian. But neither had he attempted to go there. He had considered it every day of the past six months and yet had known the futility of making such a journey.

'In Bourges, perhaps,' said Martin at last. 'With Toby's family. If Toby kept his word.'

The warmth of the wine was coursing through his body, dulling the pain. Guillaume's voice flickered through the haze of heat and alcohol.

'If you loved her, why didn't you marry her?'

Martin's head jerked up. 'Damn you, Guillaume,' he said softly.

Guillaume was not offended. 'Why else should a worthy man like you choose to drink himself to death? For love, of course, for love. And she was exquisite, I admit. I ask again, Martin: why didn't you marry her?'

Martin's eyes were bleak. 'I couldn't. Nobody could. Not even bloody Toby. She's married already.'

Guillaume frowned.

'To a Paduan painter called Gaetano Cavazza. The bastard,' Martin added angrily. Then he blinked. 'Shouldn't have told you that. *Her* business. No one else's.'

There was another silence. Martin, huddled in his robes, half closed his eyes. Images of the last year repeated themselves in the flames of the fire: Joanna standing on the balcony in Padua; Joanna beside the fish-pond in the garden that she had made, the hem of her dress stained with green; Joanna laughing as she faced him in the dance; Joanna in the Italian garden . . . Martin shut his eyes very tightly.

He wanted to sleep, but he heard Guillaume say: 'I'd like to speak to Madame Zulian. I believe I should thank her for helping me in Padua. Near Bourges, you said, Martin? Then I'll look for a family by the name of Crow near Bourges.'

Martin mumbled, his face half-hidden by his robes, 'Not Crow. Dubreton. You should look for a family by the name of Dubreton. Our Toby has two names, you see, Guillaume.'

The festivities that followed the marriage of Eleanor du Chantonnay to Hamon de Bohun lasted for weeks. By day, they hunted or played tennis or jousted on Marigny's flowery meadow. By night they feasted, watched dumb-shows and masques, danced to the music of the lute. Marigny was reborn: the château shook off the quiet enclosing chrysalis of Reynaud's illness and Eleanor's widowhood, and became something glorious, something splendid, something that looked forward to a brighter, more confident age.

For François, Marigny's transformation almost compensated for the desertion of Toby Crow, his bodyguard. When Toby failed to return to Marigny, François lost his mentor and hero. He sulked at first and complained that the house had, for him, begun to feel empty again, but eventually he noticed that his freedom had increased rather than declined with Toby's departure. François's dislike of Hamon lessened when

Hamon gave him a new sword, new clothes and a fast horse. Much to François's relief, his bodyguard was not replaced. Hamon had agreed with François that the Seigneur de Marigny did not need a nursemaid.

François found himself freed of the tedium of supervising the château's expenditure and checking Marigny's complicated accounts, for Hamon agreed with him that the Seigneur should not have to attend to such trivia. Hamon supervised the finances of Marigny himself. Eleanor did not quibble, and even François noticed that marriage had quietened her. She no longer attempted to interfere in François's affairs. And Cousin Guillaume no longer turned up at Marigny to mock the cut of François's doublet, to voice with devastating accuracy François's own gnawing lack of confidence in himself.

For Eleanor, the days had become indistinguishable, meaningless. She no longer expected fiery dragons to swallow the sun: she knew that the house, the estates, the country that surrounded them, would remain the same. That she would continue to eat, to drink, to sleep. The pain of Toby's betrayal had diminished, replaced by a numbness that made the colourful banquets, the noisy hunts, seem dull and silent. She continued to do what she had done for the past fifteen years: to fulfil her duties as the chatelaine of Marigny and oversee the organization of food, drink, linen and tableware; to ensure that every one of Marigny's many guests was comfortable, well-fed and content. But she felt, always, as though she walked in a dream where nothing quite touched her, where, when she tried to run, her limbs were trapped and held back by a cloying and invisible force.

Four weeks after her marriage, Eleanor waited in her bedchamber for her husband. She knew that Hamon would come to her; he had done so every night since their wedding. She had been married for a month now and knew that she must tell him of the child tonight. She dared not wait any longer.

She heard his tap at the door and called for him to enter. She wore a nightgown and robe, and her black hair was brushed loose down her back. The sheets of the bed were folded back, the bedcurtains already half drawn. She felt, as she always did, a brief frisson of repugnance for what was to take place, coupled with a flicker of guilt at the deception that was necessary for her survival.

He kissed her hand, led her to the bed. She was aware, once again, of his strength, his certainty. The mixture of fear and respect that he had conjured in her on his first visit to Marigny had never altered. If she no longer looked for happiness, then at least, she thought, her marriage had provided security for both François and Marigny.

She folded her fingers over his hand as he began to untie the ribbons of her gown. 'My lord,' said Eleanor, her voice shaking slightly, 'I have something to tell you. I am pregnant. I am going to bear your child.'

He straightened. She saw the gleam of pleasure, of pride, in his dark eyes. 'Are you sure?'

'Quite sure, Hamon. I have been unwell for some days now. I consulted a physician yesterday.'

She had spoken to Monsieur Gefroy, who attended François. She had described her symptoms and the physician had confirmed what she had known for two months: that she was expecting a child.

Nervously, Eleanor watched Hamon rise and walk to the window, his back to her. She remained seated on the edge of the bed, her gaze fixed on his wide, muscular shoulders and on his dark, greying hair. She thought how little she knew him. She had married a stranger, because he had been there during her moment of desperation, and because he had asked. To protect herself and the cuckoo in her womb, to protect Marigny and François.

The pride and delight she had long ago lost was vivid in Hamon's eyes. 'You have made me very happy, Eleanor. You must take care of yourself. You must take care of my son.'

He left the room then. It surprised her at first that he did not stay and make love to her, but then relief overcame the surprise. Eleanor drew the bedcurtains and pulled the blankets over herself. Then, for the first time since Toby's betrayal, she wept. For herself, for the loss of love, and for the child she no longer wanted.

Bourges was grey and drab. A spiteful wind tugged at Joanna's cloak and skirts as she tramped from jeweller to jeweller, looking for the best price. She kept only her mother's necklace and a ring belonging to Isotta, memories of different lives long done with. The rest she sold, aware that the money she earned would keep her for six months or perhaps a year, no more.

Finding Brother Joachim proved more difficult. She had met him by chance in Bourges the previous December. He had been walking back to his monastery, when a pile of books and half a dozen buns slipped out of his hands. Joanna had shooed away a hungry dog snapping at his ankles, and had helped him pick up the books and buns. They began to talk. Brother Joachim, who had travelled in his youth, reminisced about Lisbon and Madrid, Brittany and Navarre. Joanna recommended camomile for the rash on his hands, and Brother Joachim lent her a book for Paul. After that, it seemed to Joanna that whenever she went to Bourges on an errand, Brother Joachim was there: browsing in the bookshop, waiting to be served in the baker's, or feeding the pigeons in the square.

But it turned out that he had left for Touraine more than two months earlier. The monk at the monastery who slid aside the small wooden lid over the peephole a suspicious inch or two could give no news of him. Small, wary eyes inspected her face and clothes, and noted her lack of an escort. As she walked away from the monastery, the beggars that crouched at the gates clutched at her skirts and whined their pitiful stories. She threw them coins, and thought, Five months now. What then?

Her spirits lifted as she rode alone back over the plain to the village. She was never afraid when she travelled: the muddy paths, the fields with their swathes of young green corn, seemed an enticement, a promise of better days to come. The open road, the emptiness of the landscape, never daunted her. It was only houses, whispering voices and confinement that made her feel afraid. The dour colours of poverty, superstition and irrational hatred oppressed her. Travelling, she felt free.

Sunlight had begun to filter through the thinning clouds. Joanna threw off her cloak and hat and rode bare-headed, enjoying the warmth, celebrating the end of winter. She had crested the top of the hill when she saw the horsemen, their clothing flashes of silver and azure on the green and grey landscape. Joanna checked, instinctively, for the knife that she still carried in her sleeve.

She did not need the knife, though. Eyes narrowed, she studied the emblems on the banners that the small cavalcade carried: a leopard beneath three crescent moons. Suddenly she was back in Milan, dusty and saddlesore, waiting for the thunderstorm to break. Her face bright with pleasure, Joanna waved and called to Guillaume du Chantonnay.

'Monsieur du Chantonnay! I am pleased to see you well.'

Urging his horse into a trot, Guillaume rode to her side. He swept off his hat, and the pale sunshine gleamed on his fair hair.

'Well met, Madame Zulian. What good fortune.'

He wore pale blue and black. Jewels glittered on his gauntlets and around his neck. Joanna gave him her hand and Guillaume raised it to his lips. Behind him, banners fluttered in the breeze.

'I have been searching Bourges for you, Madame Zulian. But there are a great many Dubretons in Bourges.'

His long, narrow eyes studied her, bright with some private amusement. Joanna reclaimed her hand. 'Have you a message from Toby, Monsieur du Chantonnay?'

Guillaume shook his head. 'No, madame. I have been looking for you so that I might thank you for your kindness to me last autumn. My physician suggested that I might find you in Bourges.'

Joanna felt a flush of disappointment, as though the clouds had again covered the face of the sun. She frowned. 'Your physician, Monsieur du Chantonnay? Martin Gefroy?'

The amusement on Guillaume's face blossomed into laughter. 'Monsieur Gefroy is, as you told me in Milan, an excellent physician. I managed to persuade him to come back to France with me. He busies himself on my estates, tending peasant women in childbirth, old crones with dropsy. He finds an hour or two, occasionally, to attend to my needs. As for Toby Crow' – he shrugged – 'I saw him last in February. A Benedictine monk who had travelled with me to Marigny took him a letter.'

Joanna's heart plummeted even further. So Toby had received her letter: he had known of Paul's illness. Poor Agnès. She began to walk her horse slowly in the direction of the village. Still she found it hard to accept Toby's refusal to return to his childhood home. Hard to accept that the man who had once waded into a Venetian canal to help a silly girl out of the water would not spare the time to visit his dying father.

She began to see how Toby had changed. How his enthusiasm had hardened into ambition, how his talents had become a vehicle for self-seeking opportunism. She said, simply, 'Toby's mother has need of him. His father died a few weeks ago.'

Guillaume was riding beside her. His voice was solicitous, his expression sympathetic. 'Toby Crow is no longer working at Marigny, Madame Zulian. He left before my cousin remarried, I believe – I have no idea where he is now.'

Bewilderment mingled with the bitterness. 'Do you think . . .' – remembering Milan, Joanna was hesitant – 'do you think that Martin Gefroy might know where Toby is?'

Guillaume laughed. 'I doubt it, madame. My physician does not speak of Monsieur Crow with any great affection. But I'll make inquiries if you wish.'

They had reached the top of the slope and were within sight of the village. The fields, the trees, the tightly furled vines, shivered in the heat haze. The path lay ahead of Joanna, but she reined in her horse, remembering her manners. 'Will you dine with us, Monsieur du Chantonnay? Agnès – Madame Dubreton – would be honoured to meet you.'

And she herself, she realized, would find it a pleasure to share Guillaume du Chantonnay's company for an hour or two. He was clever, witty and urbane. Recently, Joanna had found life bleak again, confined and narrow.

The dull sunlight gleamed on the diamond in Guillaume's ear, and lightened the blue of his doublet. 'A generous invitation, madame, but I must be on my way. Another time, perhaps. I merely wished to thank you for your kindness in Milan. It was not unappreciated.'

He was silent for a moment. He looked at her. Not as Gaetano had looked while he had painted her, with consuming and covetous eyes, but with an impassive gaze and a thoughtful expression. He added, 'If there is any way in which I could help you, madame, I would consider it a small repayment for your past kindness.'

She stared at him for a moment. She thought of the dreariness of her future, the muddle she had made of her life. She thought of how Guillaume du Chantonnay must live, and she almost said, Have you a position in your house, Monsieur du Chantonnay, for a maidservant, a seamstress, a gardener?

But she remained silent. Instead, she smiled and shook her head. 'I have everything I need, monsieur.'

She started to ride down the hill, when she heard Guillaume call from behind her, 'You should not ride out on your own, madame. Be more careful. Not everyone is to be trusted . . .' But she only turned and smiled again, raising her hand in farewell.

CHAPTER ELEVEN

Toby had been in England for more than three months. On that first day he had slept in the garden of Izabel Mandeville's house, waking before dawn and walking out of the village. He had travelled blindly, with no particular direction in mind. His only thought had been to put as many miles as possible between himself and Lydney Mandeville.

His boots were worn through, he stole, scavenged and begged for food. The cut on his chest had become infected, giving him a fever, and his head ached constantly, making him feel nauseous. Eventually he stopped walking and slept in someone's hayrick. When he woke, his hands and feet were numb with cold, but the fever had gone and he had kept hold of his sanity.

The following day he found work helping a swineherd to tend his pigs. He thought how Agnès would have smiled. At first the swineherd had less to say than his pigs. He seemed incapable of curiosity, Toby's own failing – or one of his failings. But when the swineherd began to greet Toby in the mornings with a smile and pleasantries about the weather, Toby knew that it was time to move on. He was a foreigner without permission to be in England, and with only a very limited command of the language. With his meagre wages he bought homespun to replace his ragged silk and velvet. A few days later he began to walk to the next village.

He worked for a mason, hauling blocks of stone from quarries to carts; he served for a fortnight in a tavern in Winchester; he cut logs for a great house by the Thames – because he was young and strong and fit, he did not find it difficult to obtain employment. He told no one about his past, and he believed that he had no future. When he saw beggars – blind, crippled or pox-ridden – driven out of towns and villages, he shut his eyes, unable to watch, frightened that he witnessed his own destiny. When he rolled in the stables with the innkeeper's wall-eyed kitchen-maid, he laughed, knowing that he had found his true level at last. Dirty straw beneath his elbows, horse-shit in the stalls, and the woman's grunts and groans mingling with those from the pigsties next door.

Eventually, he found himself twenty miles west of London, at Richmond. The palace at Shene, rebuilt by the first Tudor king, glittered in the dying afternoon sun, its turrets and crenellations reminding Toby briefly, distantly, of another house, set in a meadow studded with flowers. Richmond's market square was littered with vegetable peelings and a few squawking hens that had somehow escaped their baskets. Toby began to tramp round the shops and inns, looking for work as the church clock struck five.

Martin Gefroy, since his conversation with Guillaume, had frequently attended the young Seigneur de Marigny. Although he doubted that Hamon de Bohun would kill François du Chantonnay, as the bitter and jealous Guillaume had suggested, nevertheless he rode from Nantes to Marigny at least once a month to keep a careful eye on François's health.

As the weeks passed, Martin became even more convinced that Guillaume was mistaken. François's health had improved slowly but noticeably since Martin's first visit. His lungs, though they would never be strong, had cleared somewhat. François did not suffer, as Martin had originally feared he might, from phthisis, but from asthma. A serious enough condition, but one that, if François was sensible, he could survive. If Martin worried for anyone at Marigny, it was for Eleanor. Glimpsing her one morning walking back through Marigny's complicated rooms and passageways, he observed that her face was white and strained, her eyes darkly circled. Her pregnancy was obvious now, and if she had stopped to speak to him, Martin would have suggested rest and recommended a competent midwife. She did not stop, though. Instead, she fluttered away, a pale, distorted ghost, as Martin, dismissed by François, was greeted by Hamon du Bohun.

'Monsieur Gefroy.' De Bohun smiled. 'You'll take a glass of wine with me?'

Martin, gathering up his bag and medicine chest, shook his head. 'My apologies, monsieur, but I must be on my way.' He had made it an inviolable rule to drink nothing other than ale before the evening. When he sewed up wounds or inspected eyes and throats, Martin's hands were still steady. He intended them to remain that way.

'Then a word with you, Monsieur Gefroy.'

It was an order, of course, not a request. Martin followed de Bohun into a small parlour on the first floor. The sound of the servants sweeping last winter's soiled rushes from the floors melted into the distance. Even this small room was hung with tapestries, and its fireplace was decorated with coloured and gilded paintings of mythological beasts. Sometimes Martin, who rarely considered material things, found himself understanding Guillaume du Chantonnay's obsession with the château de Marigny.

'I thought,' said Hamon de Bohun, beckoning Martin to sit down, 'that we should discuss my stepson's health.'

De Bohun spoke in English, Martin's native tongue. It was pleasant to hear his own language again.

'The Seigneur is in good health at present, Monsieur de Bohun. I'm pleased with his progress.'

De Bohun smiled, but the smile, Martin noticed, did not reach his eyes. A cold bastard, thought Martin, suddenly wanting the interview over with. A man whose pleasures were the exercise of authority, the outward display of wealth. De Bohun stood in front of the narrow mullioned window, almost blocking out the strong July sun. Martin, irritated, wished he would sit. His physical presence filled the room.

'Then we can be confident, Monsieur Gefroy, that François will reach adulthood?'

Martin nodded. 'If he is sensible, if he takes good care of himself. The Seigneur must avoid excessive exertion, of course, and keep warm and well-fed. But I don't think' – he glanced again at the tapestries, the pictures, at de Bohun himself, splendid in silk robes – 'that should be too difficult.'

Again de Bohun smiled. 'Of course not, Monsieur Gefroy. My stepson lacks for nothing.'

De Bohun turned, opened the door. Martin understood that he was dismissed. De Bohun held out a small purse to him. As Martin left the room and made his way out of the château and across the drawbridge, he thought of Eleanor du Chantonnay, who had chosen to marry that ice-cold despot. He found himself almost wanting to talk to Toby again, to fill in the gaps.

Toby had found employment, ironically enough, at a cobbler's. The cobbler needed someone to cut logs and haul them to the fire, as well as to heave the heavy bales of leather from his cart. The cobbler was small, wizened and old and not a bit like Pernet Lescot. There was a boy to work the bellows and to sweep the floor, but Toby saw nothing of himself in Mr Kett's undersized apprentice. All that – Chinon, the Dubretons, Marigny – had, after all, happened to someone else.

The shoemaker watched him carefully for the first few days, suspecting both his honesty and his sobriety. But Toby's fingers never found their way into the chest where Samuel Kett kept his gold, and nor was his weakness the bottle. If Mr Kett ever wondered why an able young man with a foreign accent should work in a cobbler's yard in Richmond, then he never voiced his curiosity. He was merely thankful, perhaps, that he had found someone competent to take over the tasks he was no longer fit for.

For the first time since Toby had left Marigny, the days and weeks had a kind of rhythm. He rose at dawn, when he would light the fire in the workshop and unlock the doors and windows. Then, after breakfast with Samuel Kett and his runny-nosed apprentice, he would take the horse and cart to the tannery to load up with leather. Mr Kett, dubious of Toby's capacity for civility, took care of the customers; the boy Nathaniel swept and dusted and ran errands.

While the shoemaker slept in the house above the shop and the apprentice in the small partitioned area between the workshop and the stables, Toby had to make do with the workshop itself, where he lay wrapped in a horse-blanket on the cobbler's bench. He did not sleep well, he dreamed too much.

It could have gone on like that for months had Samuel Kett's success and parsimony not been quite so well known in Richmond. One night, Toby woke staring into the darkness. The hair stood stiff on the back of his neck and he was drenched in a cold sweat. Before he remembered where he was, he heard footsteps and the boy's cry, suddenly silenced. He took a knife from the cobbler's workbench without pausing to calculate how many thieves in the night climbed Samuel Kett's winding stairs in search of the shoemaker's gold.

He stabbed the first of them as he bent over the chest they had hauled out from under the sleeping cobbler's bed. Samuel Kett woke at the wounded intruder's cry and sat up, blinking and ridiculous in frilled nightshirt and tasselled cap. Toby's bare feet slipped in blood, as he turned to face the next thief. As Toby struck him in the stomach, sending him clattering halfway down the crooked stairs, he realized that he was enjoying himself. Then, with Mr Kett quivering beneath the bedclothes and the apprentice Nathaniel squawking somewhere downstairs, he dealt with the third and last thief. This one had a sword, Toby only a long narrow-bladed knife. He could have despatched the fellow in a moment if he had had a sword too – fighting, after all, was what he was good at. Without one the struggle lasted a little longer. Eventually he disarmed his opponent, stabbing at his sword-arm, slamming the man's hand against the window-ledge so that the fingers opened and the sword clanked uselessly to the floor. And then they swayed for a moment, hands at each other's throats, until the rotting frame of Samuel Kett's bedchamber window gave way, and the thief tumbled backwards through the waxed-paper panes, bouncing on the stable roof before sliding downwards to land, yelping with pain, on the cobbled courtyard.

Toby stood still for a moment catching his breath, waiting for his heart to stop pounding. And then slowly he turned. The shoemaker, unharmed, was still under the bedclothes. The boy Nathaniel was tugging at the bunched sheets. 'Mr Kett! Mr Kett!' he shrieked. The boy's eyes were round with wonder, a thief's blow still reddened his chin. 'Mr Kett! Mr Crow has killed three men!' Toby went off to look for aqua vitae to comfort the shaking shoemaker, and below, alone in the workshop, he found that he had at last recalled who he was.

He was Toby Dubreton, he was Toby Mandeville, he was Toby de Bohun. He was Toby Crow, a scavenger and a fighter for the rest of his days.

Guillaume returned to Joanna Zulian in July. He had used the intervening weeks well: he had spoken at length to Martin Gefroy and had received as much information as Martin was prepared to give him. Plied with a great deal of wine, Martin had told him about Gaetano Cavazza, whom Guillaume guessed to be the painter of Hamon de Bohun's *Judith and Holofernes*, and about the long, troublesome journey from Padua to Milan. He had admitted that he loved Joanna Zulian, would always love her. Guillaume, a perceptive man, filled in the gaps that Martin left. Remembering Joanna with her black skirts and uncovered head riding alone along the road from Bourges, he found that he almost pitied Martin.

At the Dubretons' house Guillaume's arrival was announced by the swarm of small boys and yapping dogs that clamoured around his entourage. The villagers gawped, the toothless crones mumbled behind ragged shawls, the young men, returning home for their midday meal, stared slack-jawed and dull-eyed. The summer heat was blistering and airless, but Guillaume travelled in a style suitable to his station; he had half a dozen servants attending him and was resplendent in his colours of pale blue and silver. He wanted Joanna to understand what he was able to offer.

The door was opened by a small, fine-boned woman.

'Madame Dubreton?' said Guillaume, guessing correctly.

In the depths of the house he glimpsed Joanna Zulian's lovely face, surprised, questioning. Even if it had not been for Hamon de Bohun, Guillaume knew that he might still have wanted Joanna Zulian: for her face, which was perfect; for the intelligence and generosity he recognized in those great grey eyes. The rough edges of her background could be softened. Not too much, though. Guillaume was clever enough to know that much of Joanna's charm resided in her lack of convention.

Guillaume bowed and kissed Agnès Dubreton's hand. The door was closed behind him. His servants remained in the narrow street outside, where, hot beneath complicated silk tabards and plumed caps, they eyed the village girls.

Joanna came forward out of the gloom.

'This is the Sieur du Chantonnay, Agnès. We met in Milan. He is a cousin of the late Seigneur de Marigny, who was Toby's employer.'

Guillaume thought how out of place Joanna looked in the cramped little house. He himself found the low ceilings and small unglazed windows oppressive; the smell of the kitchen and the farmyard that permeated the entire house was distasteful to him. But he recognized also the flicker of anxiety on Agnès Dubreton's pleasant face at the mention of Toby's name. He felt, unexpectedly, a pang of envy. He did not think anyone had ever worried for him.

He ate wild strawberries and drank cool white wine in the small garden behind Agnès Dubreton's house. He admired the pig and the sheep, forcing himself not to press a perfumed handkerchief to his nose to keep out the stench from the sties. He was shown the flower border that Joanna had begun to plant beneath the kitchen window, a complicated pattern of squares and curlicues, winding twists of rosemary and lavender, lilies and carnations. Even Guillaume, who had no interest whatsoever in gardening, recognized that here was something different, something unusual. Like Joanna herself, he thought, as out of place in this hovel as an exotic bird trapped in a tawdry cage.

Agnès Dubreton made her excuses and went back into the house. Guillaume helped Joanna up from the grass and took her arm as they walked through the garden, towards the stream that flowed at the bottom of the garden. Joanna still wore black, but in his mind's eye Guillaume saw her dressed in bronze silk, pearls strung through her hair. Gaetano Cavazza had painted her well, he thought. They paused beside the stream. Small white flowers bordered the edge of the marshy ground, and the air was sharp with the scent of cress. The clear runnel of water, sheltered by trees, had not yet been dried up by the sun.

Guillaume, who hardly ever experienced embarrassment or awkwardness, said, 'I have not come to Bourges only to eat your strawberries, Madame Zulian. I have a suggestion to make to you – a proposal. You will think me impertinent, no doubt. Insulting, even. But I would like you to hear me out. Will you promise me that?'

She assented. Amused, he watched her push her way through the thicket of branches and ferns that separated the wood from the stream. She was such a curious mixture, he thought, of ragamuffin and great lady. He could imagine her in silks and satins at the court of King Louis XII; he could picture her equally well scrambling over hills and dales, barefoot, the wind in her hair.

The copse was small, private, shut off from the smells and snufflings of the farmyard. It seemed odd to make his proposal in such a place. Guillaume preferred splendid halls, opulent bedchambers. Covering a log with his short cloak to make a seat for Joanna, he chose his words carefully.

'Madame, since we last met, I have made inquiries concerning your situation. Yes' – he held out his hand, silencing her – 'I am presumptuous. I warned you. But I have learned that Madame Dubreton is grieving and impoverished. And that her son, her adopted son, is not to be found.'

He saw a frown pleat Joanna's smooth forehead. He watched her carefully, because during the past weeks he had wondered again about her relationship with Toby Crow. Her face told him nothing, however, and besides, it no longer mattered. Toby Crow was unimportant. Toby, had he ever been a player, had abandoned the game.

'Toby Crow – Toby Dubreton – has presumably found more lucrative employment in some other lordling's house. Or he has returned to Italy to fight, perhaps. Or he has gone to meet his maker – who knows? He is not to be found, madame. I have made inquiries, as I promised.'

Guillaume paused, letting his words sink in. Then he added, softly, 'I know also, madame, that you have no family. And that you are married.'

The branches that threaded overhead shadowed her face and darkened her eyes. Joanna stood up and Guillaume's silk cloak slithered to the mossy ground.

'I have made no secret of my position to Madame Dubreton, Monsieur du Chantonnay. I have assumed widowhood because the people of this village would find my true status abhorrent. My husband is in Venice, I believe. I'll not live with him again. If the irregularity of my situation offends you, monsieur, then I regret that. But really, it is no business of yours.'

Joanna's eyes sparkled with anger, her stance was rigid with pride. Any moment now, Guillaume thought with amusement, she would slap his face and stalk back to the house, leaving him stranded in the copse.

He said mildly, 'Madame, I meant no criticism. I simply wanted to convey to you that I understand the nature of your difficulties. And would wish to relieve you of some of them.'

Her anger faded a little. 'I hope that one day Gaetano might petition the Pope to grant him a divorce, but . . .' Joanna shook her head.

'The Pope has other concerns just now,' said Guillaume. 'The humiliation of Venice, the increasing strength of France. That sort of thing. I, too, will have to return to Italy soon, I suspect. The obligations of rank, my dear Joanna.'

There was a silence. Then she said bluntly, 'What do you want of me, Monsieur du Chantonnay?'

'To help you. To offer you a place in my household.'

Joanna blinked. She said, bewildered, 'As a serving-maid? A seamstress?'

He allowed himself to smile. Guillaume shook his head, and said smoothly, 'Certainly not, madame. As my mistress.'

Now she would strike him. He saw her fists clench, her eyes widen. He waited, almost pleasurably, for the stinging blow to his cheek. He had considered everything carefully. Joanna Zulian could not marry, so she must therefore be in need of protection and, he suspected, money. The life she now led, cut off from comfort and civilized company, must be stifling to her. She only needed her options pointed out.

There were scarlet marks on her cheekbones, and she stared wildly round the copse, looking at anything but at him. He thought fleetingly of taking Joanna Zulian to his bed, and found that he anticipated the task with pleasure.

He said gently, 'I offer you no insult, madame. Consider my proposal, if you please, in the spirit in which it is made. As a homage to your beauty, your grace, your wit.'

She managed to speak at last. He saw that she was trembling, though the air was thick and hot. 'Monsieur du Chantonnay . . .'

He took her hand in his. He would have liked to stroke her, to soothe her as he might calm a frightened pony, but he knew how cautious he must be. He guessed how easily she would take offence.

'Madame Zulian – Joanna – I am offering you nothing squalid, nothing shameful. I am offering you a household of your own, servants, all the clothes and jewels you might desire. I am offering you freedom from poverty. I am offering you a place in a world sophisticated enough to appreciate you. I am offering you the setting you need – that you deserve. Something to match your beauty.'

'Why?' she whispered. She had withdrawn her hand, and now her slender fingers pleated the folds of her gown. '*Why?* You could have any woman you want. You could marry any great lady . . .'

'The lady I wished to marry has attached herself to another. I told you, madame, when we last met.'

She said, confused, 'Your cousin's widow? Madame de Marigny?'

'Madame de Marigny has wed a Breton by the name of de Bohun. Who will make her even more miserable, no doubt, than Cousin Reynaud did.'

His voice was flippant, but his words were bitter. Guillaume's mouth had curled into a sour smile, and his eyes were hooded. 'I intended to marry Reynaud's widow. Then I would have had Marigny, you see. It is the only thing I have ever wanted.' It surprised him that she had inspired him to honesty. He had meant to flatter her, to pretend passionate love for her. 'There,' he said softly, 'I have broken the rule of a lifetime and spoken the truth. Does it offend you, madame, that I set a house – lands – above the woman I have asked to be my mistress? That I do not covet you, beg you, *implore* you to come with me?'

Joanna's eyes met his. Her voice was level. 'I have known that sort of love, monsieur, and I would not seek it again. Nor would I be owned again – *imprisoned* again.'

He touched her arm. 'I would not confine you, Joanna. You would have an establishment of your own, a life of your own. You would keep what company you chose, you would travel where you wished. I promise you this.'

She was silent for a moment, looking up at him, studying his face. Then she said again, *'Why?'*

He took a few strands of her hair, running them through his fingers like silk. When he looked up, he said, 'A whim. A caprice. The fancy of a man who has found the ordinary things of life far too easy. Who has always hungered after the exotic, the exceptional. You are exotic, Joanna, you are exceptional. If I cannot have Marigny, then I would have you. Please.'

His hands lightly rested on her shoulders. He thought how fragile her bones felt beneath their covering of black cloth. For a moment, he almost regretted what he intended to do, but then his fear overcame his fleeting regret. He knew that he should have courted her for weeks – months – but he had been unable to permit himself such a luxury. He was afraid of losing her. Afraid of losing Joanna Zulian, who would be his weapon.

'Consider what I say,' he whispered. 'Don't refuse me yet, I beg you, madame. Think. Consider what I can give you. I'll come back to you at Michaelmas.'

She started to speak, but his finger touched her lip, silencing her. Guillaume escorted her back through the copse, over the stream, to the smallholding and garden. The small, intricate flower-beds she had planted were bright in the late-afternoon sunshine, a winding tracery of purples, blues and pinks.

He said, 'I could give you a garden, madame – oh, ten times the size of this.'

She said nothing. She stood there, as tall and lovely as the lilies that grew against the wall of the house. Guillaume, who knew that he had planted choice, opportunity, bowed and took his leave.

After Guillaume du Chantonnay had left, Joanna did not immediately go into the house. She remained in the garden to catch her breath and make sense of what had happened. Eventually Agnès came out and sat on the grass beside her.

'I saw him go. All the village watched, I believe. We don't often see such splendour.'

Joanna managed to smile.

Agnès added, 'He's handsome, noble and rich. I don't mean to pry, Joanna, but I shall burst with curiosity.'

Joanna wrapped her arms around her knees. 'Monsieur du Chantonnay made me an offer, Agnès. Not an honourable one, though. He wants me to become his mistress.'

Agnès's eyes were enormous. 'Goodness! And you said . . .?'

'I said I'd think about it.' Her gaze flickered sideways to Agnès. 'Are you shocked, Agnès?'

Agnès said faintly, 'Shocked at him, or at you?' She shook her head. 'To be honest, I don't know, my dear. I am a little . . . a little *stunned*, I think.'

Joanna smiled wryly. 'So am I. I thought Monsieur du Chantonnay wanted a seamstress.'

Agnès fell silent.

Joanna, similarly speechless, thought of Guillaume du Chantonnay. A man who had blue eyes, had met her three times, and now asked her to be his mistress. It was preposterous.

'He knows about Gaetano,' she said eventually. 'Martin Gefroy, the physician I spoke of, told him.'

'Do you like him?' said Agnès suddenly. 'Do you love him?'

Joanna stared ahead, past the garden, past the stream and the copse, to the horizon where the plain met the sky in a haze of blue and violet. 'No. I don't love him. But I don't dislike him. And I think that love is perhaps . . . overrated.'

Agnès said gently, 'I did not find it so.'

'No.' Joanna's voice was sad. 'But you have always had a home, a family, a place. I've never had anywhere. Those that I love abandon me. Those who love me wish to possess me.'

She thought of Donato and Sanchia, of Gaetano, of Paolo. Of Toby and of Martin. Agnès, reading her thoughts, said, 'Had Monsieur du Chantonnay seen Toby?'

Joanna recognized the hope in Agnès's eyes. She hated to disillusion her, but shook her head and watched the hope fade.

'He'll turn up,' said Agnès, scrambling to her feet, determinedly cheerful. 'Toby is like one of those things that knights hit with their lances, that always bounce back. *You* know, Joanna . . .'

'Quintains,' said Joanna helpfully, rising, shaking out her skirts.

*

At Marigny, François mounted his horse, and rode, as he did each afternoon, across the drawbridge and over the meadow. The horse was splendid, a great black stallion, a present from Hamon. François thought, as he jerked the creature into a canter, of the impressive sight that he must make. He wore a new doublet – quilted, with winged shoulders and a tight waist – and the helmet with the plumes.

On his way towards the woods, he passed the quintain, motionless in the hot August sun. Briefly, he felt lonely. There had been Meraud, whom he had taken for granted, and there had been Toby, whom he had adored. Eleanor, who had irritated him constantly with her fussing, had taken to her bed. As for Hamon – François admitted to himself that he was afraid of Hamon. Hamon reminded him of his father.

François, heading for the wood, almost laughed at himself. No, Hamon wasn't a bit like Reynaud. Hamon had no authority over him, and if François chose to, he could drive both Hamon and Eleanor from Marigny tomorrow. And as for loneliness – how could the Seigneur de Marigny possibly feel lonely? The château was brimming with servants, and recently there had been numerous banquets and hunts. And in a year he would be married. He had chosen a wife – Hamon had helped him. She was thirteen years old, plump and tongue-tied.

Slowing only a little, François rode into the wood. Beneath the trees it was dark and green, the sunlight only occasionally piercing the roof of leaves with narrow shafts of gold. François chose his path carefully, avoiding the route that took him past the pond in which he had almost drowned four years ago. The heavy foliage cut off all sound from the château and the meadow: there was only the thud of his horse's hooves as it cantered through the ferns and dead leaves.

He rode deeper into the forest. The air was cool and fresh, a relief after the oppressive heat of the open ground. A rustle of leaves and the crack of a twig broke the silence. A deer had broken from its covert, a young beast, its back still speckled with white markings. François, whooping, dug his spurs into his horse's flanks.

His heart pounded and his breath came fast as he chased the fawn through the forest. He had only vague ideas of how he would make his kill: he carried neither bow nor arrow, only his sword. He would corner the creature by the boundary wall, leap from his horse and slit its throat. Then he would sling the dead animal across his saddlebow and take it back to Marigny. He thought how they would all admire him for hunting a deer single-handed.

He crouched over his horse's neck as he raced through the forest, taking care to jam his feet firmly in his stirrups. *He* was not, like Reynaud, going to fall. Spurring his horse through a thicket of bramble, François saw the wall, and the deer. The deer quivered, trapped, exhausted.

It was then that he heard the noise from behind him. Twigs snapping beneath heavy feet, branches pushed aside by strong arms. François turned round and saw the men that surrounded him.

There were three of them. Big, rough-set brutes, eyeing him in a way that made François shiver. They said nothing. He tried to speak, to tell them to be on their way, but he could not find the words. They were trespassing, intruding on his land. They were thieves perhaps. They were looking at François as he had looked at the deer.

He was frightened, his face and back suddenly glazed with sweat. He wanted Meraud, he wanted Toby. He even, briefly, wanted his father. He waited, mesmerized like the deer. Then he thought, I am François du Chantonnay, the Seigneur de Marigny, and he saw himself as he had earlier, with the fine sword that he wore at his side, the plumed helmet on his head. Clapping his heels to his horse's sides, he swung the stallion round, intending to jump the boundary wall. But the horse, its mouth hurt by the roughly jerked bit, reared, and François, losing the reins, slipped in the saddle. His foot caught in one of the stirrups, and a strong hand seized his reins. He fell sideways out of the saddle, dangling ridiculously and painfully upside-down, trapped by the stirrup. The helmet tumbled from his head, and his fair hair swept the dirt. François felt hands pulling at him, and the last thing he saw was the deer still standing motionless by the wall, shivering with fear.

Martin Gefroy, riding late that afternoon down the wide path that wound through Marigny's forest, saw the small group of du Chantonnay servants emerge from the trees and begin to walk across the meadow. Squinting, his hand sheltering his eyes from the sunshine, he saw that they were carrying something. When he realized what they were carrying, when he saw the riderless horse that they led, Martin cantered across the meadow towards them. He made them stop and lay the stretcher on the grass. They did not want to stop but, finding an authority in himself that he had not known he possessed, Martin overcame their objections. Kneeling on the grass, he lifted the cloak that covered François's face.

He took a deep breath to steady himself. Then he undid the torn doublet and opened the silk shirt that covered the boy's fragile body. He noted every one of the bruises, the position of every one of the marks on François du Chantonnay's white skin. A shadow fell over the sunlit ground and, looking up, Martin saw Hamon de Bohun's steward.

'He had a fall,' said the steward. 'His horse must have thrown him. He was always a poor horseman.' There was not a trace of pity in the steward's eyes. He turned to the other servants. 'Take it to the château. Madame de Marigny is not to see it. It would be unwise for her in her condition.' The impassive gaze moved slowly back to Martin. 'Don't you agree, physician?'

Martin, unable to speak, nodded. Rising, he began to feel afraid. He watched the servants bear the body of François du Chantonnay towards the drawbridge, and his gaze drifted towards the château, to the blank, black windows that faced out to the meadow. He thought that he saw the pale oval of a face behind one of the windows, but he could not be sure.

Glad of the escort that Guillaume had provided, Martin mounted his horse and rode away from Marigny. Travelling back to Nantes, he realized what he had done. He saw, in his mind's eye, that bruised, defenceless body, and he heard his own voice say, *'The Seigneur is in good health at present, Monsieur de Bohun. I'm pleased with his progress.'*

When he reached Nantes, Martin took two bottles of wine from the cellar and, alone, drank himself into unconsciousness.

The shoemaker rewarded Toby with a handful of gold coins from his chest; Toby rewarded the shoemaker a few weeks later by taking his leave of him one morning. He had drawn attention to himself, Richmond was no longer safe. Nathaniel, the hero-worship in his eyes reminding Toby uncomfortably of François du Chantonnay, followed him through torrential rain to the outskirts of the town, bidding his farewells.

With the shoemaker's gold Toby bought himself a sword and a horse to take him to Dover. At Dover, he took passage on a ship bound for Normandy.

Summer returned when he set foot in France. At first, standing on the quayside at Calais, an English possession, the cobbled streets still swayed beneath his feet with the motion of the ship. But the sky was blue and cloudless, the air warm. He changed his gold to French coinage, and looked for another horse to replace the one he had sold at Dover. Walking from one stable to the next in search of a healthy beast, he knew that he had a decision to make. Bourges or Marigny. He dreaded what he would find at either. He decided, as he checked the teeth and hooves of a sprightly chestnut mare, that he would go first to Bourges. He was weary of loose ends: he would finish the journey he had begun five months before.

He reached the village on a Sunday morning. He waited by the poplar trees in the churchyard until the church had emptied and the curé and congregation had gone home. Then he began to search among the newest gravestones.

He found what he had feared, and was overwhelmed by a drowning sense of anger and despair. PAUL DUBRETON, BELOVED HUSBAND OF AGNÈS. He saw clearly how he had abandoned everyone, and he knew there was no remedy for it. Hamon de Bohun had robbed him of that, too: the chance to say his farewells.

He walked away from the churchyard, back to the trees where he had hidden his horse.

Joanna, who had returned to the church to collect the shawl that Agnès had dropped beneath the pew, saw him leave. At first she was not sure. He looked unfamiliar, somehow, and besides, it seemed impossible that Toby Crow, having been absent for so long, should suddenly be here. She didn't want to make the same sort of mistake she had made a long time ago in Venice when she waited for her father. Staring, her heart hammering, she walked quickly after him.

When she caught up with him, he had reached his horse and taken hold of the bridle and reins. Joanna caught a glimpse of his profile, and she was sure.

'Toby.'

He turned. He looked dazed and confused rather than pleased. 'Joanna . . .' He did not let go of the reins. He did not take her hand, kiss her or even smile.

Joanna said, unbelieving, 'You're not going, are you? You haven't seen Agnès.' It was inconceivable that he should try and leave without speaking to Agnès, but Joanna understood suddenly that that had been his intention.

Toby's dark eyes had flicked back to the churchyard. 'I seem to have left things a little late.'

Her heart began to pound again, but with fear now, not happiness. Watching him as he stood beneath the elms that backed the churchyard, Joanna saw how Toby had altered. He was poorly dressed in broadcloth and linen, his eyes had a bruised, deadened look about them.

'What *happened* to you?' she whispered. 'Where have you been? Have you been ill?'

'A little. Nothing much.' He tried to smile, but his face was bleak. 'I fell among thieves, that's all. Or had fallen among them a long time ago, but didn't have the wit to recognize them for what they were.'

She didn't understand him. For a moment his gaze met hers. He did not move, though. She realized that if she touched him he would draw away from her.

Toby said, 'I was . . . delayed.'

That was all. *Delayed.* She waited for him to go on, to add some sort of adequate explanation for his absence, for his desertion of the Dubretons, but he said nothing. Joanna thought of all they had endured over the past months, of Agnès's unhappiness, of Paul's illness and death, of the emptiness of her own life, and for a moment she felt hot with anger. Her voice was taut as she said, 'Guillaume du Chantonnay told me that Brother Joachim had given you my letter.'

The emotionless eyes blinked, startled at last. 'Guillaume – you've seen Guillaume?'

Joanna nodded. 'Monsieur du Chantonnay rode here to thank me for helping him in Milan.' Guillaume's other, extraordinary, motive for calling on her was none of Toby Crow's business. She added, 'Martin Gefroy is Monsieur du Chantonnay's physician. He told Monsieur du Chantonnay where to find me.'

Toby closed his eyes momentarily, rubbing his hand across them. 'I need to find out what has happened at Marigny.'

Her anger deepened. He would not see Agnès who had cared for him as a child, but he would go to the du Chantonnays. As though they and not the Dubretons were his family.

Joanna said, coldly and deliberately, 'Eleanor du Chantonnay has married. Did you know that?'

She could not guess from his expression whether he had known or not. Then he whispered, 'Hamon de Bohun,' and she saw the revulsion in his eyes. Toby Crow, who had looks, intelligence and luck, who had a man's freedom of movement and choice of vocation, had lost the biggest gamble he had ever made.

She had been right, then. She had meant nothing to him. What had happened in the Italian garden had been nothing more than a dalliance. She said softly, 'You loved her, didn't you?'

He did not reply. He just stood staring at her, as if mesmerized, his face shadowed by the long leaves of the elm trees. No, she thought bitterly, she was wrong again. Toby did not even love Madame de Marigny. After all, Martin had explained matters to her last year in Milan. Martin had said, *'I always did admire our Toby's ambition.'* Toby loved no one.

'No. You wanted her for Marigny, didn't you?'

She saw him wince, his face bleached of colour. He looked sick. He was shivering, as though the sky were not a clear, burning blue, as though the midday heat did not shimmer on the plain.

He turned slowly and climbed into the saddle. Gathering the reins, he looked out to the road ahead.

'I don't think there's much point in me seeing Agnès, is there? "Sorry, Agnès, I got sidetracked and couldn't make it to the funeral." It's better for me to go, don't you agree, Joanna?'

She couldn't speak at first. Then she reached out and grabbed the reins, pulling the mare's head round so that Toby was forced to look at her. 'Agnès may have to leave the house, Toby. She hasn't much money.'

She had meant to hurt him, and she knew that she had succeeded.

He smiled humourlessly and shook his head. 'Neither have I, Joanna, neither have I. I've a horse and a sword, and a handful of sous in my pocket. That's all.'

A dry wind rustled the leaves. He said, 'I ask you not to tell Agnès that I was here.'

For a long moment she hated him. 'You ask too much.'

He turned away. 'Yes,' he said. 'But then I always did, didn't I?'

She let go of the reins then. She watched him put his heels to the mare's sides, easing her into a trot, and then ride along the road and up the hill. She wasted no tears on him. He was not worth tears.

Over the last three days, Martin Gefroy's resolution had faltered. He drank now not to hide pain, but to dull the edge of his fear. With a bottle of wine tucked into his saddlebag, Martin could still ride to the villages on Guillaume's estates, could still call at the houses of Guillaume's neighbours. Without the wine, he knew that he would not have dared leave his bedchamber, but would have skulked indoors, the blankets pulled over his head, listening for the footstep on the stairs, the swish of a sword as it was drawn from its scabbard.

Three days earlier he had ridden out to attend a woman on one of the nearby farms. On the journey back Martin's horse, a placid, amiable beast, began to buck and cavort like an unbroken stallion. Had one of Guillaume's tenants not managed to catch the bridle, Martin would certainly have been thrown. Removing the saddle, Martin found a shard of glass an inch long hidden beneath the saddlecloth. He stared at it for a moment in bewilderment, concocting complicated explanations for its presence. Then, feeling suddenly cold, he understood. A couple of small incidents which he thought unimportant at the time suddenly seemed more sinister: a street-fight in Nantes, in which Martin had unwittingly found himself involved; a band of vagabonds who had attacked travellers along the road he had originally intended to take home. Common enough events, he had thought at the time, congratulating himself on his good fortune in escaping injury. But, glancing down at the shard of glass in his palm, Martin realized that these incidents had taken place during the fortnight since François du Chantonnay's death. Since he had seen François du Chantonnay's body.

That was when he began to tuck the wine-bottle into his saddlebag. To glance frequently over his shoulder. To wear the sword he had never bothered with. To try to recall some of what Toby Crow had taught him on the road from Padua to Milan. He had considered leaving Guillaume's service and heading for Paris or Leiden, or even back to England. But he trusted no one to accompany him and knew himself incapable of undertaking such a journey alone. Despising himself for both his fear and his incompetence, Martin knew that he would see assassins round every corner, hidden behind every tree.

Now he was riding home from a visit to one of his patients. The fascinating symptoms the patient had been suffering from – the lesions, the cysts, the putrid discharge – had distracted Martin temporarily from his fears. He made the old man more comfortable, and spent the first half of his solitary journey homewards considering possible courses of treatment. Then, riding through a wooded incline, he heard the rustle of leaves, the faint jangle of harness and bridle.

His heart began to beat at twice its usual speed, his stomach squeezed and churned. Even now, a part of him still noted with scientific detachment the physical symptoms of fear. He glanced wildly round for an escape route and, finding none, drew his sword from its scabbard, conscious that his sweating palm slipped against the chill steel.

The sky had clouded over, the leaves of the trees met thickly overhead. Martin cursed himself for choosing this path at this time of day. He should have travelled back through the fields at midday when Guillaume's tenants would have been lying among the newly shorn corn, resting from the rigours of the harvest. Martin strained to focus in the dim light. The dark shape of a horse and rider moved towards him. Raising his sword, he tried to force his features into lines of determination and aggression. A voice filtered to him from out of the trees.

'If you wave your sword around like that, Martin, you'll fall off your horse. I told you before. Close to the body.'

The sword, pointing towards the treetops, wavered and then relaxed. Martin's entire frame was shaking as he urged his horse forward.

'Toby,' he whispered. 'Toby Crow.'

He was, he realized, very glad to see him.

Toby dismounted from his horse as Martin reached inside his saddlebag and took out a bottle.

'Guillaume thought you were dead,' said Martin, staring at him. 'I have to say that for a while I hoped he was right.'

Toby took the bridle of Martin's horse. He watched Martin rub his forehead with the sleeve of his robe and then unstopper the bottle.

'Someone sent me on an errand,' said Toby. 'It took me rather a long time to find my way back.' He noticed that the physician's hand shook as he raised the bottle to his lips. 'And you, Martin? I had to force you to carry a sword before, I seem to remember. And you don't look well.'

Martin swallowed several mouthfuls of wine. 'I'm not ill. You frightened me. Well . . . terrified me. I thought you were . . .'

His voice trailed away. Toby looked up at him again. Since Milan, Martin's physical condition had deteriorated: his skin was pale and slack, his eyelids were red. Reaching up, Toby eased the bottle out of Martin's trembling fingers.

'I need you conscious, Martin. For a half-hour at least.'

With a quick intake of breath, Martin said softly, 'Damn you, Toby. Can't you manage a few more run-of-the-mill vices?'

Toby ignored him. 'I need to know about Marigny. About Eleanor. About François. And not from a du Chantonnay or a de Bohun. I couldn't stomach either just now.'

There was just the faintest glimmer of curiosity in Martin's red-rimmed eyes.

'Madame de Marigny has married. A Breton called de Bohun – but you knew that, surely? She's expecting her first child. I don't know . . .' – and Martin paused, looking down at Toby – 'I don't know if she will survive the birth. She's old to be giving birth for the first time. And she looks unwell.'

Toby did not allow himself to think of Eleanor dying in childbirth. 'Do you attend her, Martin?'

Martin shook his head, ran his hands through his dishevelled hair. 'No. I attend – I *attended* – the Seigneur. François.'

Martin's expression was unreadable, and Toby swiftly considered the possible implications of his change of tense.

Then the physician said, 'François du Chantonnay died a few weeks ago. He fell from his horse. Well' – and he laughed humourlessly – 'his stepfather says that he fell from his horse.'

For a moment Toby was unable to speak. A wind had picked up, rustling the leaves on the trees. Finally, he said, 'But you don't believe that, do you, Martin?'

Martin shook his head and slid from the saddle. Pushing past Toby, he sat on the bole of an old beech tree, the long skirts of his robe trailing in the soil and dead leaves. 'I saw the body. Nobody meant me to, I was just in the right place at the right time. I believe that François du Chantonnay was dragged from his horse and deliberately put to death. Throttled, in fact. There were bruises on his neck.' His voice was matter-of-fact, clinical. 'The boy was buried the following day. Because of the heat, they said. Eleanor du Chantonnay never saw her stepson's body. She wasn't allowed to, Toby. For fear it would harm the unborn child.'

Toby bowed his head. He thought of François du Chantonnay, whom he had dragged from a pool four years ago after considering, if only briefly, leaving him there to drown. Incompetent, unconfident François, with his runny nose and his ridiculous helmet and his failure ever to strike the quintain properly with the lance. He looked up at Martin Gefroy.

'Hamon de Bohun.'

It wasn't even a question. Martin grimaced. 'Since François's death . . . well, de Bohun has assumed the title, of course. To go with the land . . . and the château . . . and the lady of Marigny.'

Toby saw to his surprise that there was something of his own shame, his own awareness of failure, mirrored in the physician's eyes.

Martin said bleakly, 'Guillaume warned me. I didn't believe him. I signed the boy's death-warrant, Toby. I told de Bohun that with proper care and attention François should reach maturity. A month later he was dead.'

Poor François, thought Toby. Poor bloody François.

He listened as Martin continued, 'Since then – since I saw the body – I have feared for my life. He is watching me, he is waiting. I know he is.'

Rising, Martin took the wine-bottle out of Toby's hands. When he had swallowed, he told Toby about the fight in Nantes, the footpads on the road home, the fragment of glass hidden under his saddlecloth. He whispered, 'Tell me that I am foolish, Toby. Tell me that François du Chantonnay, an incompetent rider, tumbled from his horse and broke his neck. Tell me that the wine has affected my reason at last, that I am seeing spectres and phantoms where none exist. Tell me that Monsieur de Bohun is a pleasant, well-meaning man who grieves for his stepson.'

Toby could tell him none of that, of course. Instead he said, 'Hamon de Bohun is everything you imagine him to be, and worse. I should know, Martin. He's my father.'

He had not intended to say that. He understood, though, that he had offered the truth in return for something – trust, friendship or forgiveness, he was not sure.

'Christ,' said Martin, dazed, staring at him. 'I wish I was sober. I can't think . . .'

'You can think of it tomorrow, Martin, when you've opened the next bottle of wine. When you're looking to see whether de Bohun's behind you with a knife in his hand. Or alternatively you can think about it when you're halfway to Italy with me, having chucked the remainder of that bottle into the bracken. It's up to you.'

Martin said nothing.

Toby added softly, 'He let me live, Martin. He let me live not because we are of the same blood, but because he didn't think me worth the trouble of killing. I intend to show him that he made a mistake.'

'What?' Martin's voice was unsteady. 'Kill him?'

Toby had turned to face him. 'Patricide, you mean, Martin? Hardly a run-of-the-mill vice.' He shook his head. 'No.'

In England, he had seen only one possible route for himself.

'I'm going back to Italy to fight. I'm going to find Gilles and Penniless, if they'll have me, and anyone else who'll join us. I'm not going to work for anyone, though. I'll be my own master. I'll hire us out to whoever will pay for us. It'll take time, but we'll have kings and emperors begging us to fight for them. I promise you that, Martin. We'll need a physician, though.'

He saw the uncertainty in Martin's eyes, the confusion. And then he saw Martin turn and up-end the bottle so that the dark dregs trickled over the curling fronds of bracken.

In September, seven weeks after the death of François du Chantonnay, Eleanor de Bohun's baby was born.

The hot summer had lingered. The meadow that surrounded Marigny was parched yellow, its flowers long dead. Dust gathered in the courtyard, on the stairs and passageways of the château. The rope that lowered the bucket into the well had to be lengthened.

No one saw Eleanor du Chantonnay fall down the small flight of steps that led from the chapel to the courtyard. It was midday: some of the servants were out on the estate helping the peasants to bring in the last of the harvest, the rest were indoors, dozing, hiding away from the heat and the dust.

One of the maidservants finally heard Eleanor's cries, and found her, prone and in pain, at the foot of the chapel steps. Helping her up, they sent for the midwife. Muttering behind their hands that the fall had made the baby come too early, they prophesied that Marigny was soon to experience another tragedy. A double tragedy, perhaps. The Seigneur Hamon de Bohun, having been told that his wife was in labour, nodded and stood by the window of the first-floor hall in silence, his dark eyes surveying the towers and pinnacles of Marigny, its meadow and its forest.

To Eleanor, the long and difficult labour seemed an appropriate punishment. She thanked God that the child was three weeks late. At first she almost welcomed the pain as the first true sensation she had experienced in months. When Toby had lived at Marigny, she had felt with sharp awareness the beauty of the countryside, the warmth of the sun, the comfort of his caresses. With him gone, she felt numb with self-loathing: for her own folly, for her ageing and increasingly grotesque body. Even the death of her stepson had not touched her as it should have. It seemed as though her head were stuffed with straw, so that she was unable to feel or think coherently. She had not cried for François: when at the funeral the tears began to gather, she had blacked out. She thought afterwards that it was God who refused her the natural release of grief.

Now, though, she endured, now she suffered. As night slowly turned to day, everything that had passed before – her marriage to Reynaud, Toby's desertion, François's death – became insignificant. The only thing of any importance was the pain, which possessed her in great, terrible waves. She heard herself scream aloud: she whose humility had made her hide her unhappiness all her adult life. She wanted to die, but she guessed that God would not allow her to die. She believed that she deserved every degradation, every loss of dignity.

The baby was born a full day after Eleanor's tumble down the steps. The rain had begun at last: dimly, as Eleanor's son was dragged from her body, she became aware of the drops falling heavily against the window. With a twist and a slither, her child was parted from her.

She felt nothing then, not even relief that her ordeal was over. When they showed her her son, she saw only that he was not two-headed or hunch-backed as she had expected him to be. There was no visible mark of the sin that had conceived him.

Eleanor, unable yet either to move or to sleep, watched as her husband was brought into the room to greet his first-born son. Lying in bed, still damp with sweat and blood, Eleanor noticed that he did not even look at her. But she saw clearly his face as he bent to see the child in the cradle: there was nothing of love, only triumph and the joy of possession.

When she walked out of the village, and took the road west – the road to Tours, Nantes, Brittany and the sea – Joanna half expected to see those flickering banners of blue and silver glinting on the plains below.

She had made her plans with care. She had mentioned Agnès's poor health and lack of spirits to Cousin Philippe, and Cousin Philippe had duly responded with an invitation. She had refused to accompany Agnès, promising instead to look after the pig and the sheep and the garden. As soon as Agnès had departed, small and tearful, riding pillion on Cousin Philippe's pony, Joanna consigned Hortense and the sheep to the care of a next-door neighbour. Then, in Paul Dubreton's small study, surrounded by books and rabbit skulls and strange glittering stones, she wrote her letter.

She left the letter on the table, weighted down by a jar of bottled plums. The letter thanked Agnès for her kindness, care and affection. She knew that words were not enough, but they were for now all she possessed. Then she bundled her clothes up in a shawl, hiding her money between the layers of material in her bodice. She took one last look around the small stone house and then walked out of the village.

It was Michaelmas. Joanna had decided to commit Guillaume du Chantonnay to chance. If she met him, then she would go with him; if he did not return, then she would not wait for him. She would never again wait for a man. She walked alone, her long overskirt kilted up to her waist, her bundle of belongings clutched in her arms.

She saw him when she reached the top of the hill and looked down into the valley. He came from another world. A world she had so far glimpsed only fleetingly. A world of silks and jewels and music. A world of beautiful castles, of exquisite gardens. She waited at the top of the hill while his small entourage drew near. She thought, waiting, that her life until now had been a series of illusions, each one temporarily convincing, each one crumbling as soon as she had tried to reach out and grasp it. There had been Donato, for whom she had waited faithfully for a year and who had never returned to her. There had been the years she had worked in Taddeo's studio, deluding herself as to the limitations her sex imposed on her. There had been her marriage to Gaetano, a doomed attempt to live the life of a respectable Italian wife. There had been Paolo, whose leaving of her had reduced her almost to insanity.

And there had been Toby. She knew now that, however briefly, she had loved Toby. She knew also that Martin Gefroy had loved her. Both of them had loved the wrong people. And Toby, whose ambitions had pushed him too high and too far, had loved no one at all.

They had drawn level with her. Banners flickered in the breeze, the plumes on Guillaume du Chantonnay's cap shivered. Dismounting, he held out his hand to her. She was selling herself to a stranger, she was bartering her beauty because that was the only exchange permitted her. She let Guillaume help her on to his saddlebow, and she passed to his servant the bundle in which she had hidden her dowry. A jade necklace, a copy of Dioscorides' herbal and a few coins in an old silk purse.

At Marigny, Hamon de Bohun held his infant son in his arms. The child had dark eyes and dark hair, like both his parents. He was a lusty child, strong for a premature infant. His arms waved aimlessly, his mouth pursed into an *o* as he made ready to howl. Guy de Bohun was quite unlike Reynaud's pale, feeble offspring. Hamon knew, studying his son, that he would be healthy, capable, intelligent.

He smiled, looking from the child to the window that framed the demesne of Marigny, and then back to the child again. It was all complete now, he thought. There was nothing more for him to do. The past, the future, he had remade.

PART THREE

1512–1514

The Garden of Obsessive Love

And in your castinge . . . the hyer and the further that ye cast your corne, the better shall it sprede, except it be a great wynde.

Fitzherbert's *Boke of Husbandry*

CHAPTER TWELVE

On the battlefields of northern Italy the alliances and enmities shifted like dice in a cup, like a well-shuffled pack of cards.

In the February of 1510, the five envoys of the proud Republic of Venice knelt for an hour on the steps of St Peter's, their heads bowed in submission, while the Bishop of Ancona read the confession documenting Venice's sins and her capitulation to Rome. As her representatives kissed the feet of Pope Julius II, the Serenissima was granted absolution.

Enjoying his revenge, Julius turned upon a new enemy. The French, whom he had invited into Italy, now possessed vast swathes of Lombardy. Riding through the snow to evict a French army from the garrison of Mirandola, the Pope, sword in hand, cried, 'Let's see who has the bigger balls, the King of France or I!' The relief expedition of the French general, the Seigneur de Chaumont, delayed because a stone-filled snowball had broken the Seigneur's nose, arrived too late to stop Papal troops scaling the walls of Mirandola.

Scheming like an ageing, aggressive spider, Julius devised a new League to replace the abandoned alliances of Cambrai. A Holy League, to include the Papacy, Venice, Spain and the England of the bellicose young Henry VIII. And the Emperor Maximilian too, if Maximilian, always dilatory, could be stirred to action. Venice, meanwhile, fought off French incursions into the Veneto and Friuli. The dashing young nephew of King Louis XII, Gaston de Foix, the Duc de Nemours, took command of the French army. The Papal army attempted to retake the city of Bologna; Brescia and Bergamo, rebelling against French rule, tried to return to their old Venetian allegiance. Marching night and day through foul weather, the army of the Duc de Nemours, fighting barefoot to give themselves better purchase in the slippery ground, retook Brescia. The rebel city was sacked for five days, and it was another three days before the fifteen thousand corpses could be cleared from Brescia's streets.

*

Guillaume du Chantonnay, riding with the Duc de Nemours, witnessed both the triumph and the carnage.

He saw the leader of the revolt beheaded publicly in Brescia's main square, he saw French and German troops stream through the city's streets like a huge, destructive tidal wave. He saw the French commanders lose all control of their men, so that the chivalrous Seigneur de Bayard and the handsome twenty-two-year-old Duc de Nemours were impotent witnesses to the worst horrors of war. Guillaume neither raped nor slaughtered, he merely watched, silently, as the French army and its mercenary troops fell upon men, women and children. He knew that what happened at Brescia merely confirmed his opinion of the human race; what he did not know was how it would gnaw at him, how, every time he closed his eyes, he would see the images of violence and degradation imprinted on his inner eyelids.

After Brescia, they returned to Milan to gather fresh troops. Civilized, elegant Milan welcomed them with banners and poorly rhymed poetry. Then, with an army of twenty-five thousand men, they marched into the Romagna. At the beginning of April, the vast army of the Duc de Nemours laid siege to the city of Ravenna.

On Easter Sunday, the battle lines having been drawn up on the swampy plain below the city, the fighting began. Because they were fighting on level ground, there was no opportunity for clever tactics, no use for their magnificent cannon. Spanish gunfire drove the securely entrenched French troops out of the ditches. Then they slogged it out with sword and lance, pike and culverin. There was no pattern to it, no great design, no opportunity to display the knightly arts of war. Eventually Guillaume, like so many of the rest, had to dismount from his horse, which had sunk up to its hocks in black mud, and fight hand to hand like an infantryman.

His splendid blue and silver colours became caked in mud and blood; his fine Milanese armour was a hindrance, weighing him down in the mire. He abandoned the greaves and the gauntlets and fought in his cuirass and bascinet, the visor raised, sweat pouring down his face like tears. The plain of Ravenna began to resemble a butcher's shop, a slaughterhouse. The fighting was relentless, exhausting, futile – like battling with a river or thick fog. Guillaume tripped over the bodies of his own soldiers, and his boots trampled the emblems of France into the mud.

The French won, though. It didn't feel like a victory to Guillaume, as he gathered together the ragged remains of his men. There were ten thousand dead out there, both French and Italian, scattered on the marshy plain. Food for carrion, thought Guillaume. Images flitted through his head, disjointed and vivid, like nightmares. The flower of French chivalry had died on the marshes of Ravenna, their silks and their plumes ground into the mud. Worse, the Duc de Nemours himself had fallen, hacked to death while attempting to cut off the Spanish retreat.

The Seigneur de La Palice, Nemours's replacement, failed to prevent the rape of Ravenna by its occupying army. Guillaume didn't even attempt to control his soldiers. It was worse than Brescia. He found himself wanting to join in, to lose himself in the orgy of death that the triumphant French army inflicted on Ravenna's citizens. Then he wouldn't have to watch. Stumbling through the chaos, sword still in hand, Guillaume came across a girl. She was hiding behind some empty barrels, but he glimpsed the hem of her dark green dress soaked by rain. He didn't really see her face as he dragged her out from behind the barrels, he noticed only that she was very young and very afraid. Afterwards, he recalled nothing of the act; only the ripped green cloth between his fingers, the smell of fear. Walking away from her, Guillaume began to vomit, disgorging the contents of his stomach over the fouled streets.

He was never really well after that. He was a fastidious man, and his inability to control the functions of his own body disgusted him. The privy, with its flies and its stench, disgusted him. His fouled linen, his damp bedsheets, disgusted him. He thought that the stench of decay and death had begun to cling to him, as it had clung to Reynaud.

Sometimes, when he woke early in the morning before his guts had begun to torment him, he thought of Joanna back in Brittany. But he could not picture her; the details of her face, her body, mingled with his fleeting memory of the girl he had raped in Ravenna. He thought that perhaps Joanna was dead now, that she had not survived pregnancy, would not survive childbirth. Guillaume was almost glad: he was unable to imagine himself ever touching her again. He did not want to infect her with his ailment. She existed, like the Arthurian ghosts of the forest in which she dwelt, in a dream, in a fleeting vision of something better.

It had started in a very small way – an extension, almost, of the days when Toby, Gilles and Penniless had tramped the battlefields of Europe, attaching themselves to whichever war offered the better prospect of money and entertainment. There were more than three of them now, though. Toby had gathered fifty men, each one wearing colours of black and scarlet, and marching behind a standard bearing the device of a carrion crow. Those fifty men were well-trained and paid regularly. Even Gilles grudgingly admitted that, in little over a year, it was an impressive achievement.

They were encamped outside Verona with the Venetian army of the Bolognese *condottiere* Lucio Malvezzo. News of the Papal defeat at the battle of Ravenna had begun to filter through the marshes and plains of Ferrara and Emilia to Verona.

'The Swiss didn't arrive in time,' Martin Gefroy explained. 'The Spanish army was cut to pieces. Cardona escaped, but most of the rest are dead. Toby's trying to find out what Malvezzo intends to do.'

Gilles Ruvelli, picking the last fragment of meat from a rabbit-bone, looked up at Martin Gefroy and said, 'Stay here if he's got any sense.' He threw the bone into the fire. 'Or change sides again.'

They had commandeered a barn south of the city. Some men played cards or dice, others slept. Martin Gefroy eyed Gilles critically.

'I was *hungry*, Gilles, you bastard.'

Gilles said, with not a flicker of remorse, 'It was superb. Penniless cooked it. Not a brain in his head, but he can stew a rabbit.'

Penniless, chipping dried mud off his boots with his knife, grunted. Martin searched among the cooking-pots and swords and armour, and found half a loaf of stale bread. He sat down on a bale of straw. 'Will we retreat, do you think?'

Gilles shrugged. 'Perhaps.' Running his hands through his blond curls, he grimaced. 'Probably not. If dear Toby has anything to do with it, we'll be marching again, I suspect. Day and night. Through blizzards, preferably.'

Martin grinned. 'Tired, Gilles?'

'Exhausted.' Gilles's hat, a splendid affair of green felt and gold braid, topped a sunburnt, unlined face. 'Twenty times – *twenty bloody times* – I was required to load and unload my arquebus today, Martin.'

Penniless snorted.

'Toby's with Malvezzo and Andrea Gritti just now.' Martin tore the loaf of bread in half. 'So you'll know soon enough, Gilles, whether you've to put your boots back on or not.'

Gilles scowled. 'He's a slave-driver, a damned slave-driver. He always was an irritating little bastard, but now . . .' Gilles raised his eyebrows in despair. 'Once, he could at least be amusing company on occasion. Now he's rapidly turning into a sour-faced old tyrant. Like Malvezzo. Like Gritti. Drinks no more than you do, dear Martin. Has taken vows of chastity, I believe . . .'

Martin said gently, 'A *successful* sour-faced old tyrant, Gilles. Toby's done damned well for himself.'

'But what's the point?' Unstoppering a bottle of wine, Gilles took a mouthful. 'If there's no pleasure in life any more, what is the point?'

He passed the bottle to Martin, and leaned back, closing his eyes. Martin swallowed. Enough to wet his palate so that he could eat the bread, no more. He was careful now, had been careful ever since he had ridden out of France at Toby's side. He had seen himself then, quite clearly, for what he would become. The steady but inexorable decline from physician, to barber-surgeon, to quack, to mountebank. He had known that he would, quite simply, rather be dead. It was better to ride with Toby, better to take upon himself some of the risks that Toby's profession demanded, to seek distraction in the sort of endless, exhausting work demanded by war. If he worked hard, bloody hard, if he gave himself no time to think of anything but the ailments that dogged soldiers in camp and the wounds caused by battle, then he could survive. He might have earned far more, achieved far higher status, by attaching himself to some great lord's house. But he had tried that, and it had almost destroyed him.

Gilles was asleep now, snoring gently. Chewing the tasteless bread, Martin considered the events of the past two years. The journey from France to Italy. He had expected assassins around every corner, Hamon de Bohun's assassins. He had been glad of Toby's protection, Toby's sense of direction. Then, as they rode further into France, a new torment. The self-imposed, but necessary torment of abandoning the wine-bottle. If he lapsed, Toby's scornful eyes were on him as he retched and shook. He had hated Toby again then, when he had been forced into the saddle, sweating and cold, after a sleepless night. *'Hamon de Bohun is my father,'* Toby had said and, barely able to keep upright as he rode, Martin had begun to believe him. Cold bastards the pair of them, utterly lacking in the better human qualities of sympathy, warmth, understanding.

By the time they had crossed the Alps, though, the worst had passed.

Martin found that he could drink a cup of wine without needing to empty the bottle; that he could sleep at night, physical exhaustion at last taking its natural toll. He was forced to become fit again simply to keep up with Toby, who was single-minded and utterly relentless in the pursuit of his goal. Martin, if not Gilles, knew why Toby coaxed and bullied and threatened them into shape, and found himself reluctantly beginning to admire Toby's ruthlessness, as he witnessed him turn a sword and a horse into something to be proud of, and then into something to be feared.

They had found Gilles and Penniless the following spring, aimless and poverty-stricken in Venice. Extracting the best possible terms, Toby had eventually hired his small company out to the Bolognese *condottiere* who had replaced the Count of Pitigliano, who had died two years previously. The fighting had, on the whole, been successful for Venice. The Serenissima had resisted much of the French offensive, keeping hold of the cities of the Veneto and Friuli – those cities that Venice had so painfully learned were necessary to her survival. Venice paid her *condottieri* with money and respect, promises of land and houses.

They had been successful, as Martin had said, but still Toby never let up. Bundling his robes over his head to cut out the sound of someone's tuneless singing, Martin wondered whether Toby had merely replaced one unsuitable ambition with another. A different mainspring this time, perhaps.

There was one subject they had never discussed, though. For a moment Martin allowed himself to think of Joanna Zulian, whom he had once loved. But all that – Padua, the ride across Italy, the parting in Milan – seemed a very long time ago.

The victorious French army marched west to Bologna to await the submission of the cities of the Romagna. Guillaume, marching with them, understood the fatal dangers of delay, but was too ill to care.

He entered Bologna on horseback, however, his armour shining and clean again. *He* did not feel clean, though. His guts were still cramped and tangled in waves of sickening, debilitating pain; he still vomited – black bile, sometimes, which increased his self-loathing. He could not eat solid foods, and had become like some gross, fouled baby, he thought, to be fed on paps and gruel.

He knew that the failure of the French to follow up the victory of

Ravenna might prove disastrous. There was Maximilian, still dithering in Germany, and in England there was the aggressive young Henry Tudor, who never dithered. The Seigneur de La Palice, however worthy, however experienced, could not fill the vacuum that Nemours's death had left. And the French army was, like Guillaume himself, exhausted. They had fought too long and too hard.

Sitting in his room in a hotel in Bologna, Guillaume tried to write to Joanna. But the tip of his pen only touched the paper, making a single black mark, saying nothing. There was nothing he could say. The images of Brescia, of Ravenna, filled the blankness, sickening him, so that he retched over and over again, his head clutched in his hands.

In Guillaume du Chantonnay's house in Brittany, Joanna bent over the cradle of her sleeping baby. Sanchia was three months old now. A perfect baby, pink-cheeked and blue-eyed, a few pale-gold curls clustered round the back of her head and on her crown. Her eyes were open, her mouth gaped in a wide smile. Joanna lifted her daughter out of the crib.

'We shall walk round the garden, my darling. I shall show you the flowers.'

They left the nursery, walking down the stairs and out into the sunshine. The house was small – less than a dozen rooms – but Joanna had loved it on sight. Surrounded by the forest, the sunlight filtered through the beeches and oaks, sparkling and rippling on the lichen-covered stone walls. The house seemed not an intrusion into the forest but a part of it, as though Guillaume's forefathers had grown a dwelling-place from the still pools and secret caverns of Finistère.

Joanna knew the forest as she knew the house, intimately, lovingly. She knew each tree, the route of every stream, the beginning and end of every path. She knew the great boulders that scattered the river-valleys as though giants had tossed them like fivestones into the dark, peaty water. She knew the woodland flowers as well as she knew the flowers of the garden she had made around the house: the clusters of windflowers that blanketed the valleys like snow in the early spring; the great swathes of bluebells that later turned the forest floor to azure; the wild roses and old man's beard that tangled the hedgerows in the open glades; the orchids that hid among the grass and heather of the heath.

There was no moat around the house, no obvious indication of a defensive purpose. Just a single turret topped with a cone of tiles and a few crenellations over the front doorway. That was all. Either Guillaume's forebears had not suffered from Guillaume's lack of faith, or they had trusted the forest to defend them. The nearest village was half a day's walk away, the nearest town of any size the market town of Morlaix, many miles distant.

She was never hungry and had no need to work. The prospect of poverty had disappeared the day she had climbed on the saddlebow of Guillaume du Chantonnay's horse. She had a chest full of beautiful gowns, the finest linen, two dozen pairs of shoes. She had ropes of pearls, golden earrings, jewelled head-dresses. She had books, she had servants. Her child slept in a crib trimmed with silk and lace, and sucked from the plump breasts of a healthy wet-nurse.

Sanchia's birth had been easy. If in pregnancy Joanna had recalled Paolo and dreaded that sort of loss again, her fears left her as soon as she held her newborn baby in her arms. She had not needed to count fingers and toes: she had known as soon as she looked at her daughter that she was perfect. Sanchia had remained healthy, growing steadily, resisting colds and coughs despite the apparent delicacy of her frame.

And there had been Guillaume himself, of course. She had ridden to Brittany with a stranger, she had shared her bed with a stranger. A stranger who had been courteous, patient, undemanding. A stranger who had made love to her expertly, if not with passion; who had received the news of her pregnancy with equanimity, if not with joy. And when, eventually, Guillaume had ridden away to Italy, he had still been a stranger. She did not know him at all.

Joanna had begun to make her garden the day she had arrived at the house. First she sketched the paths, parterres, archways and pools, and then, with the help of some of the manservants, cut her design into the scrubby turf that surrounded the house. The following spring she had begun to plant seeds, cuttings, small shrubs and trees stolen from the forest. The garden had grown well, watered by the Atlantic squalls that broke over Brittany's high lands and fed by the soft, dark soil.

Now, as Joanna sat in the garden, Sanchia lay in her lap clutching at petals, following with a wide-eyed gaze the path of a bumble-bee.

Joanna murmured in her baby's ear. 'See – there's the pergola, my darling. The roses and honeysuckle are only half grown, but in a year or two they'll meet at the top. And there's the herb bed. I found the violets in the forest, and the rosemary and thyme are from the heath. We shall buy chervil and rue next time we ride to Morlaix.' She rose from the camomile seat. Cradling the baby against her shoulder, she walked through the pergola, past the pond and the herb garden, to the orchard. 'And here are apple and cherry trees. Look, Sanchia, see the blossom.'

The baby's plump hand reached out, enclosing the white petals. The scent of the box hedges that surrounded the orchard was sweet in the warm summer air. A light breeze rustled the leaves and the grass.

In the Venetian army encampment near Verona they still waited, restless, nervous.

Penniless tossed dice endlessly. Martin treated the cases of dysentery that had begun to break out in the camp. Gilles slept and ate and complained about the weather. The commanders of the Venetian army discussed tactics, siege plans, contingencies.

In the tent of Lucio Malvezzo, Andrea Gritti, the Proveditor of Treviso, and Toby Crow gazed at the sketch of Italy spread out on the table. Malvezzo's thick thumb stabbed at the paper.

'We're *here* – in the east. The French are to the west and the south. De La Palice is still in Bologna, but he could be outside the gates of Verona in less than a week, if he chose.'

Toby recognized the concern in Malvezzo's faded blue eyes. All three of them knew that the Venetian army was not capable of beating the French in a pitched battle. They simply had not sufficient men. The threat to the French must come from further afield than Venice: from the Emperor Maximilian in Germany, or from the young Henry VIII in England.

Toby said, 'It's a question of who makes the first move, isn't it? If the French still had the Duc de Nemours, then they wouldn't be sitting in Bologna now. They'd have marched north from Ravenna.'

'Vicenza, Padua and Verona.' Eyes narrowed, Gritti studied the map. 'The French must lay siege to each of them in turn. Then they'll be able to threaten Venice herself.'

And if the French chose to march north, then there'd be damn all, Toby silently acknowledged, that either he, Gritti or Malvezzo could do to stop them. However well he had chosen his men, however well he had trained them, there just weren't enough of them.

'But they haven't got Nemours, of course,' said Toby thoughtfully. 'They've got de La Palice. Who is cautious and competent, but . . .' He shrugged.

A smile spread slowly over Lucio Malvezzo's weathered face. The *condottiere* said drily: 'Which is why, of course, de La Palice is still alive, and why Nemours is dead at twenty-two. But caution, my dear boy, doesn't necessarily win wars.'

Malvezzo's eyes, weary and experienced and cunning, met Toby's. Rising to his feet, he poured out three cups of wine.

Andrea Gritti, accepting a cup, said, 'Ravenna, it appears, Toby, was less of a victory for the French than we had assumed. The casualties on both sides were enormous.'

Toby had heard rumours of that already. That the army of France was exhausted, ill and demoralized by the loss of their hero, Nemours.

'It's all getting rather interesting,' said Toby slowly. 'If Maximilian doesn't turn up, if Henry Tudor remains safely in England, then the French will, I suppose, eventually march north. But perhaps even Maximilian will stir himself. And if he does – and if de La Palice's troops are really in a bad way after Ravenna – then I can't see the French taking on Maximilian. And neither can I see Henry Tudor missing the opportunity to invade France. With most of France's army in Italy, Henry can just cross the English Channel and walk in.'

Andrea Gritti was smiling. 'You should have been a diplomat, not a soldier, Messer Crow. You have the mind of a diplomat.'

'Low and cunning.' Lucio Malvezzo spat on to the grass. 'But you're right, of course. And if Henry of England invades, then Louis's army will be obliged to return to France. Victory or no victory.'

It was like a chess-game, Toby thought, as they second-guessed their opponent's moves. Outside, through the parted flaps of the tent, he could see the encampment of the Venetian army. The weapons piled outside the tents glittered in the morning sunshine, the horses nuzzled at the grass.

'So what do we do?'

Malvezzo folded the map and replaced it inside a chest. 'You go and remind the sentries to keep an eye open for Maximilian and de La Palice. And otherwise – otherwise, we wait.'

Waiting, Toby thought as he left the tent and mounted his horse, was something he had become good at. Somewhere between Izabel Mandeville's desolate house and the war-ravaged plains of Italy, the restlessness that had been his since birth had hardened into something colder, something more destructive. He waited for justice, for recognition, for the day that Hamon de Bohun would recognize that he, who had planned and schemed and achieved everything he had ever wanted, had made just one error. *'I've decided that I don't need to kill you,'* Hamon de Bohun had said to his creation. The thought that de Bohun might have made a mistake was the only thing that had kept Toby alive and sane.

He had told no one except Martin of his connection with de Bohun. There was no need to tell anyone else – Gilles would not be interested, Penniless would not understand. And for the moment, even Hamon de Bohun must wait. An impoverished soldier-of-fortune could be no threat to the new Seigneur de Marigny. Toby had made the mistake of arrogance before. Riding round the battlefields of Italy, living by his sword and on his wits, he had been the insignificant puppet that de Bohun had intended him to be. He knew that he must become more than that. With each day that had passed since leaving Richmond he had devoted everything to making himself more than that. *'We'll have kings and emperors begging us to fight for them. I promise you that, Martin,'* he had said, and he had worked day and night, summer and winter, through drought and storm, to fulfil that promise.

Eventually and with great difficulty, he had written to Agnès. The letter had been short, uninformative, laying out some of his regrets for the past, sketching a carefully edited version of his intentions for the future. He had sent money, too. He had not visited Agnès because he knew himself unable to lie to her. He could have lied to anyone else, but not to her. Nor could he have told her the truth: people like Agnès couldn't even conceive of the sort of thing that Hamon de Bohun had done. To dent her belief in a benevolent world would be cruel and pointless. If nothing else, he could protect her from that.

Otherwise, he had kept his distance from everyone. From Martin, who understood him too well, from Penniless and Gilles, from Lucio Malvezzo and Andrea Gritti, and all others concerned with the theatre of war. If he wanted the company of women, then he found a girl from among the camp-followers that swarmed after the army – someone who wouldn't comment on the thin scar drawn raggedly across his chest, who would be content with a night or two and a few coins so that neither of them misunderstood the nature of the arrangement.

Two days later, a Venetian scout, watching from the hills that cradled Verona, saw the cloud of dust that blossomed against the summer sky.

A great mist of it, a column that billowed upwards, red-brown against the blue distance, blurring the horizon. A forest fire, the scout thought at first, realizing a moment later that the ground was not yet dry enough.

The scout's heart began to hammer a little faster, his eyes strained to see clearly. Glancing at the dust again, he knew suddenly that the long wait was over. Putting his spurs to his horse's sides, he rode hell-for-leather back to the Venetian encampment.

The column of dust was made not by fire but by the horses and cartwheels of the Emperor Maximilian's army. Only half a day's ride away, perhaps, Maximilian's vast, lumbering army hauled cannon and siege-engines down from the Alps towards the city of Verona.

The Emperor Maximilian had decided to join the party.

Guy was almost two now. He toddled round Marigny's Great Chamber on small, stout legs, pulling at tapestries. He clambered on to the window-seat, hurling cushions to the floor, battering a clenched fist on the mullioned glass that separated him from the lawns and the forest.

'*No,* Master Guy.'

The nursemaid, waddling across the room, lifted the child from the window-seat and carried him to his mother.

'The Seigneur took him to the stables this morning, madame,' said the nurse proudly. She kissed the child, ruffling his thick, dark hair. 'He sat Master Guy on a horse – one of the big hunters. He wasn't a bit afraid.'

Eleanor made herself smile.

The nursemaid said hesitantly, 'Would you like to hold him, madame?'

Reluctantly, Eleanor nodded. She let her son be placed on her lap, she made herself touch him, hold him. She did not, she thought, as she looked at Guy, hate him. It was indifference that she felt, an indifference that had remained with her since his birth.

He was an attractive child, bright and strong, walking and talking early. Her arms loosely around him, Eleanor knew that if she had tried, she would have seen the lineaments of Toby's features in Guy's soft, round face. But she did not try, and the child, catching her uninterested eye, wriggled off her lap and ran back to the window-seat.

'Take him away, Thérèse,' said Eleanor, rising. 'I have a headache.'

After the nursemaid and the infant had gone, Eleanor rose and went to the oriel window. Absently, she straightened out the cushions that Guy had disrupted and checked that the small panes of glass were still firm in the lead.

It was, she thought, her greatest punishment that she could not love her first-born child. The difficult birth, her own guilt, misery and exhaustion, had initially robbed her of any interest in her baby. And when at last, weeks later, she had risen from her bed and begun to pick up the threads of her former life, she found that Guy reserved his first smiles for his wet-nurse, Thérèse. Eleanor herself had forgotten how to smile, how to laugh. When she had held him, Guy looked up at her with dark, knowing eyes, not a flicker of recognition on his small face.

Her first-born child, her only child. There would be no others, because her marriage had ceased with Guy's birth. No – before that, when she had told Hamon of her pregnancy. He had not touched her since. He did not taunt her, or curse her, as Reynaud had done – Hamon was, Eleanor thought, as indifferent to her as she was to Guy. She had realized many months ago that to Hamon she had been nothing more than a means of acquiring Marigny. Toby had tried to warn her, long ago, and she had not heeded him. She did not care: in a way she was glad. Hamon had used her, and she had used Hamon. His indifference evened up the debt between them.

Her headache was growing worse; her temples throbbed. Ever since Guy's birth her health had been poor: she tired easily, fell ill frequently.

Her gaze lingered on the meadow, then drifted to the forest beyond. It was odd, she thought, how persistent was her memory of François, who had been so ineffectual, so hopeless, alive. In the window-seat Eleanor pictured not her own son, laughing as he beat his fist on the panes, but François, Blanche's son, sprawled clumsily, a plumed helmet lopsided on his head. If she looked out to the meadow, she could still see the quintain, unmoving in the windless air. If she closed her eyes, she could picture François as he rode, lance poised, grimacing with effort.

The Emperor Maximilian, having joined forces with the Venetian army near Verona, ordered all Imperial subjects fighting with Louis de France to quit the French army on pain of death. De La Palice's German *Landsknechts* slunk unwillingly home; more French troops were recalled to France to protect their country against the threat of English invasion.

Guillaume du Chantonnay found himself crossing back over the Alps in August. The great victory of Ravenna had gone sour, curdled into a mess of shifting alliances, demoralized troops, threats from every quarter. France had quit Italy, losing everything she had gained, including Milan. Guillaume did not care: another month in Italy would, he believed, have killed him.

His progress home was slow, exhausting. The worst symptoms of dysentery had passed, but the marks of his illness showed in the gauntness of his face and body, his loss of spirit. He felt tainted: what he had seen, what he had done, had become a part of him.

He reached Brittany at the end of September. He stayed for a few weeks at his house in Nantes: there, he dismissed the most incompetent servants, rewarded the best, and harangued the mediocre so that his lands would once more yield a satisfactory crop and support the appropriate number of skinny cattle. Then, having done his duty, he rode on to the house of his mistress.

Inland, Finistère was thickly wooded; Guillaume rode alone through the forest. He was not afraid of the wolves that howled their hunger in the evening, or of the maze of paths and streams and thickets. It was cool in the forest, the ponds and lakes were bottomless, dark and mysterious. Once, the forest had been Guillaume's favourite place. As a boy he had played there for days at a time, catching minnows in pools, building hideouts in trees.

But then his father had taken him to Marigny and, on their return from the château, had hit him in front of the servants. He had realized then that his father, who had never showed him affection, loved only Marigny. Like some fatal, hereditary disease, Guillaume too had begun to want Marigny.

For Marigny he had taken Joanna to Brittany. For Marigny he had sent her servants, musicians, tutors, dressmakers. He had sown the seeds that he believed must flower at last into envy; the roots were already there, established years ago in the rivalry that flourished between the families of de Bohun and du Chantonnay. Guillaume intended to plant the doubt and covetousness that he himself endured in Hamon de Bohun's mind. The object would be different, of course: a woman, not a house. Tired and sick, Guillaume thought of Hamon de Bohun, and of what de Bohun had done to him.

He reached the house the following afternoon. Dismounting from his horse, he stood for a few moments in the shadow of the trees. He stared with wonder at the winding paths of box and lavender and rosemary, the archways, the pools, the parterres. The garden was, he thought hazily, like a painting or a tapestry: green shapes filled with drifts of colour; emblems drawn in flowers. The garden had bloomed since Guillaume had left for Italy in the early spring. He smelled a heady scent and saw the arches of the pergola entwined with pink and yellow and red roses that drooped and scattered petals on the grass. And on the seat at the far end of the garden he saw Joanna.

She wore a grey gown with wide sleeves and a tight bodice, and her hair was loose. She had not yet seen him, and Guillaume studied her for a moment in silence. She cradled something on her lap, something wrapped in loose folds of material. Just for a moment, watching her, Guillaume forgot all that had happened to him, all that he had always longed for. He felt the hunger and the despair slide from his shoulders, leaving him weary, incapable of wanting anything other than solace and acceptance. His head bowed suddenly, as he stood there in silence.

But the habit of desire was too deeply ingrained in him, and he began eventually to walk forward, leaving his horse tethered to a branch. He heard Joanna's voice – she was singing a song that threaded through the sounds of the forest, mingled with the rustling of the leaves, the tinkle of running water. She looked up, and the singing stopped.

'Guillaume.'

Joanna smiled. Her hair gleamed gold in the sun, fine strands curling round her face. Her skin was pale and unblemished, her eyes that familiar calm light grey.

And on her lap lay a baby. Guillaume was startled. He could not at first understand why she held a baby. Then he remembered. Joanna had been pregnant before he had left for Italy. Before Brescia, before Ravenna. Before he had seen children slaughtered in the streets for revenge, for pleasure. Before he, too, had joined in the carnage, because watching and listening had become unbearable.

Joanna stood up, cradling the baby against her shoulder. Guillaume could not kiss her; he bowed stiffly, gracelessly. His eyes were fixed on the child, his child.

'I called her Sanchia,' said Joanna very gently. 'If you sat down, you could hold her, Guillaume.'

He found himself sitting on the camomile seat. He wanted to explain to Joanna that he could not touch his daughter, that she was too innocent, too perfect. She was so fragile, he knew that he must hurt her. But he could not find the words, and besides, Joanna, kneeling beside him, had sat the baby on his knee. He could feel the warmth of her small body against him, smell her clean, unblemished skin.

He did not move at first, but then, slowly, hesitantly, his fingers brushed her smooth round cheek. His daughter looked up at him, and Guillaume saw that her eyes were a deep blue, the mirror of his own. He felt tears burning at the corners of his eyes. He could not remember when last he had cried.

Since Hamon de Bohun had acquired the estate of Marigny, the château had altered. He had engaged painters, sculptors, carpenters, faience-workers; he had sent not one over-ambitious courier to Italy to purchase works of art, but half a dozen. He had engaged whole workshops of artists to labour over Marigny's ceilings, Marigny's walls. Consorts of musicians played for the de Bohuns in the evenings, troupes of actors entertained their guests with improbable and complicated masques. For Eleanor the château had become unfamiliar, as though some strange and exotic butterfly had sprung from its chrysalis.

Marigny entertained the great lords and ladies of France and Brittany – and King Louis himself sometimes. It was Eleanor's responsibility to oversee the dinner and sleeping arrangements. The kitchen bubbled and steamed, seething with overheated and anxious cooks, while Eleanor tasted and inspected, running an experienced eye over the plates of fruits, pies, pickled and salted meat, puddings and cakes that were piled on every available surface. In the linen-room she folded sheets and blankets, counted tablecloths and napkins. She selected the best glassware and tableware from the pantry, instructing the servants to polish the goblets and wash the plates and finger-bowls. When the pastry-cook had hysterics, Eleanor rolled up her sleeves like the kitchen-maids and plunged her arms up to her elbows in dough. When the boy burned his hand on the spit, it was Eleanor who anointed the blister with goose-fat.

Leaving the kitchen for the courtyard, Eleanor sat in the warmth of the late summer afternoon, regaining her breath. Her head ached again and the veins in her temples throbbed, as she watched her husband lead a horse out of the stables.

Eleanor herself had scarcely ridden since she had given birth to Guy. At first she had been too unwell; later, she had found that she no longer took pleasure in riding. She seemed to have lost the capacity for pleasure. Besides, there was little need to travel: Marigny grew and made its own food, wove its own cloth. If she wanted silks or velvets, then tradesmen from Tours or Blois would be only too delighted to call on her. She had no need to ride to church, because Marigny had its own chapel. She rarely hunted now: Hamon, unlike Reynaud, took little pleasure in the hunt. Deliberately she had confined herself to Marigny. She had no wish for contact with the outside world; the outside world, in the form of Toby Crow, had brought her only pain.

But now, looking up at the horse that Hamon led from the stable, and at the rider perched upon it, Eleanor's heart lurched. The rider was Eleanor's own son, Guy. He wore a small black velvet cloak, and his head was topped with a black cap, its single plume clasped with a jewelled pin. His eyes were serious, his teeth pressed into his lip with the effort of concentration. He sat upright in the saddle, gripping the pommel, his legs too small to curve round the horse's flanks.

The horse was a large stallion, its coat gleaming black. Once again, the image of François, lance in hand, scowling as he rode for the quintain, fluttered through Eleanor's mind. She heard Hamon say to Guy, 'The horse will know if you are afraid. If you do not fear him, then he will respect you.'

The sight of the child, small, dark and motionless on top of the huge beast, made a cold shiver run down Eleanor's spine. She crossed the courtyard.

'Hamon, do you think this is wise? He is too young . . .'

Hamon's gaze did not leave the child. 'A boy can never be too young. He must overcome fear now, or he shall be a slave to it later. No son of mine shall be a coward.'

'A coward!' said Eleanor faintly. 'Hamon, Guy is barely two years old.'

He did not answer her. Instead, he detached Guy's small hands from the pommel and threaded the reins through his fingers. Then he unclipped the leading-rein, and stood aside.

Eleanor could not bear to watch. She did not love Guy, but neither did she wish to see him fall to his death on the cobbled courtyard. She looked at Hamon instead, but found no solace in the naked pride in his eyes.

Eventually she could bear it no longer. 'Take him down, please,

Hamon,' she whispered. 'His nurse will be waiting for him – it's time for his supper. That horse is far too big for him.'

For a moment Eleanor thought that he was not going to answer her. But then Hamon turned, his dark gaze running slowly the length of her, taking in her stained gown, her untidy hair.

He said, slowly, 'Would I put my own son on an unsuitable horse? You are foolish, Eleanor. You would make a milksop of my son. Guy will greet our guests riding this horse. He will bow to them, he will welcome them to Marigny. I have taught him to do so. And as for you, Eleanor, I would recommend that you change your gown, or you will be mistaken for one of the serving-maids.'

Hamon led the black stallion away. For a moment, Eleanor couldn't think why she felt so upset. But the image of François came again to her: François riding a black stallion that had been too large, too temperamental for him. A black stallion that had been Hamon's gift to him.

The French had quit Italy, but the Emperor remained. Maximilian, having stirred himself into action, was unwilling to renounce the lands that he had occupied. The Emperor, the Pope and the king of Spain discussed at length the correct apportioning of the disputed territories of northern Italy. Venice, much of whose wealth had found its way into Holy League coffers, fumed disregarded on the sidelines.

Toby Crow found himself back in Venice in the autumn. Venice was chill and angry. Its canals and squares brought back memories of Arlotto Attavanti, Gaetano Cavazza, Joanna Zulian.

He dined with the Proveditor of Treviso, Andrea Gritti, and the Venetian ambassador to the Papacy, Antonio Giustinian. Giustinian's splendid apartments faced on to the Grand Canal: through the half-open window Toby could hear the lapping of the water, the jostling of the gondolas.

Gritti, finishing his meal, wiped his mouth on his napkin. He looked tired, thought Toby: dark shadows circled his eyes, his skin was slack and yellow.

'I asked you here, Messer Crow, because I have just returned from Rome. The outcome of Venice's discussions with Pope Julius was unsatisfactory, I regret.'

'If not unexpected,' added Antonio Giustinian, drily.

'If not unexpected,' repeated Gritti. His crumpled napkin lay discarded on the polished wood of the table, his fisted hand rested beside it. He looked up at Toby.

'Venice, therefore, finds herself in the position of falling out with her former allies. The Emperor Maximilian requires that Venice return to him the cities of the terra firma. The Pope backs the Emperor.'

Toby rose and walked to the window. Outside, the sun had begun to lose itself in the Adriatic Sea, washing the city of Venice, its lagoons and its islands, with a coral light.

Giustinian said bitterly, 'Agnadello, the siege of Padua, Ravenna – we are no better off than we were four years ago. Worse, we have lost money and men. A fruitless war, gentlemen.'

'It has kept people like me in business.' Toby, leaning against the window-sill, saw the flicker of disapproval on Giustinian's face.

'Quite.' The ghost of a smile touched Andrea Gritti's lips. 'Maximilian's greed, the Papacy's lack of faith, will, no doubt, keep the carrion crows busy for years to come.'

Toby's head bowed briefly in acknowledgement. Momentarily, he almost pitied wealthy, arrogant Venice, forced once more to weave and twist to avoid the envy of her neighbours. He said, watching Andrea Gritti, 'I suspect, though, my lords, that Venice is already considering ways out of her difficulties.'

'I told you, Antonio.' Gritti, leaning back in his chair, glanced along the table to the other Venetian. 'Messer Crow has the mind of a soldier, and the soul of a diplomat. If diplomats have souls, which' – a trace of humour sparkled in his blue eyes – 'I sometimes doubt.'

The humour vanished. Andrea Gritti's gaze rested on Toby. 'I have work for you,' he said. 'Venice needs messengers.'

Outside, the sky was dimming. The boats, the canal, the people, were no more than brief brushstrokes on a fading canvas. Toby closed the window. 'Messengers,' he said happily, 'who speak fluent French?'

Giustinian glared at him. 'You are of French birth, I believe, Messer Crow?'

Toby recalled briefly Izabel Mandeville's house: the locked doors, the cobwebbed windows. 'I am a mongrel, Messer Giustinian. A base-born concoction of doubtful pedigree. If you wish to question my loyalties, then I would remind you, as I have previously reminded others, that my loyalty can be bought. If you are prepared to pay enough.'

Giustinian cursed, striking the table with his fist.

Gritti said mildly, 'My young friend taunts you, Antonio. Remember that he has fought for Venice for many years now. Remember Padua.'

'Messer Crow left Italy for France before the siege of Padua began, I seem to recall.' Giustinian's hand hovered at his sword-hilt, his mouth curled in a sneer.

'I found myself forced to repay a debt, Messer Giustinian. To an Englishman and a Venetian woman. Loyalty, you see.'

There was a short silence. When he spoke, Andrea Gritti's voice was weary. 'Gentlemen, this really is no time for bickering.' He turned back to Toby. 'I brought you here, Toby, to ask you to travel to France. To Blois, to the court of King Louis.'

It was two years since he had left France. Two years since he had urged an ailing, foul-tempered Martin Gefroy across France and over the Alps into Italy. He had always known that he must some day go back. Not as a bastard foundling, not as a shoemaker's apprentice, though, not as a rich man's courier.

'As what, my lord?'

'As the representative of the Signoria. As the trusted messenger of the city of Venice.'

Gritti's gaze held Toby's. Giustinian was silent. Gritti said, 'I need, as you pointed out, someone who is fluent in both French and Italian. Someone who will be both unobtrusive and unrecognized. Someone who, if intercepted by the agents of the Papacy, will keep his mouth shut.'

It had gone full circle. Once, the king of France and the Pope had combined against the city of Venice. Then Julius, resenting France's success in Italy, had enlisted Venice to help him expel the French. Now the Venetians, abandoned by their former allies, courted France.

'It will not be uninteresting, I think,' added Gritti. 'And Venice will, of course, reward you suitably. You have fifty men fighting for you at present? If the negotiations are successful, if you play your part well, then you could have double that number when you return. Maybe more.'

Guillaume had hoped that in Brittany the past would become less significant. He had sometimes thought of Brittany as a fairy world, where time ceased to follow its relentless course. When he left the forest, he had imagined that he would find all his old servants and companions long dead, his house at Nantes crumbled to dust.

Now, though, the magic seemed to have failed. Guillaume's temples throbbed continuously and nightmares interrupted his sleep. When Joanna dosed him with the balm of Gilead and hound's tongue, the pain in his stomach eased, but the mental wounds stubbornly refused to heal.

If Joanna handed Sanchia to him, then Guillaume would hold his daughter fearfully, his arm cradled round her as though she was made of glass. He would watch the baby for hours – as she slept, as she sat and laughed in the garden, as she grabbed clumsily at a rose-petal, or a piece of thistledown, or a wriggling worm. If she cried, then he would call for Joanna or the nurse, terror on his face. 'Is she ill?' he would say. 'Is she hurt?'

He wouldn't touch Joanna, though. He was afraid to touch her, afraid to be alone with her. To begin with, he had no desire for her, but then, as his physical health began to improve, desire returned. But he had lost his attitude of amused detachment; he no longer trusted himself. He thought of the future so that he would not have to think of the past. He thought of Marigny, which Hamon de Bohun had taken from him. He began to plan, weaving schemes in the chill morning light, orchestrating elaborate plots for revenge. Anything to avoid thinking of Brescia, of Ravenna.

Letters arrived from Nantes, from Blois, letters that made Guillaume tremble with apprehension. His schemes shifted to something more solid: together he and Joanna rode to Morlaix, to visit jewellers and to engage dressmakers. In her bedchamber Joanna opened chests, unlocked jewellery boxes. Guillaume held Sanchia in his arms, studying with intense care every detail of her tiny face, her fragile limbs.

'She is very thin. Is she ailing?'

His thumb and his forefinger could encircle the widest part of the baby's arm: anxiety, familiar and exhausting, began to flutter in Guillaume's chest.

'She's the right size for her age, Guillaume,' said Joanna firmly. 'She's only six months old. Would you want a seven-foot giant for a daughter, with arms like tree trunks?'

He managed to smile. He sat down on the window-seat with the baby on his knee. Sanchia's eyes met his and her lips parted in a wide, gummy smile. Each time she smiled it seemed to Guillaume to be a miracle.

'She shall be beautiful, charming and rich. She shall dance at the king's court. Won't you, my darling?'

Sanchia, laughing, tugged at a lock of Guillaume's hair. Closing his eyes, holding her to him, he pictured her fully grown. With her golden hair and blue eyes, she walked on a wide meadow studded with flowers. He realized that, without meaning to, he had pictured her at Marigny.

When he opened his eyes, Joanna was lifting her gowns out of the chest, laying them on the bed. The colours, vivid in the greying evening, startled Guillaume. He noticed that Sanchia lay still, and her eyes were closed. His heart pounding, he checked carefully, painfully, for her breathing. She was only sleeping, and Guillaume was suddenly aware of his exhaustion.

'She's tired, Guillaume, that's all. I'll call her nurse.'

Sanchia, curled against his side, whimpered in her sleep. Guillaume thought again how fragile she was, how defenceless. He knew that only he could guard her against the terrible cruelties of life, only he could build walls around her so strong that no one, however clever, however powerful, could touch her.

He let Joanna scoop up the baby and carry her, still sleeping, to the nursery.

When she returned, she said, 'These are all I have, Guillaume.' She had laid out on the bed every one of her gowns, gowns that he had ordered and paid for. The bed was splashed with their colours: green, white, scarlet, gold and crimson. Rising, Guillaume's free hand touched the silk, the velvet, the cloth-of-gold. The bodices of the gowns gleamed with pearls and silver lace, the sleeves were puffed with interlinings of gauze, trimmed with ribbons and braid and fur.

He went to the window and placed his aching head against the cool glass. He stared out at the darkening forest.

'I'll put one of them on, Guillaume. I'll dress myself in my favourite for you.'

He didn't turn, he just nodded. His eyes were still focused on the distant pattern of leaf and branch, but he thought constantly of Blois, of the king's court, of Hamon de Bohun. He thought of showing de Bohun the treasure that he had bought, of seeing the envy, the rage, on de Bohun's face. He smiled, but then Sanchia's small face came before him, shimmering on the uneven glass, and his chest tightened, his eyes began to twitch.

'Look, Guillaume.'

He turned. He heard Joanna say, 'This is my favourite. Do you like it?' but he saw only the colour of the gown, a dark emerald-green.

She offered her back to him so that he could lace up the bodice. Standing behind her, he smelt the sweet warm scent of her skin, the sharpness of the rosemary in which she rinsed her hair. His hands shook as he picked up the laces of the bodice and she lifted her long bright hair out of the way. He saw the arch of her neck, the way her breasts rose, full and round, as she raised her arms. He saw a hem of green cloth soaked by the rain, peeping out from behind a barrel in Ravenna.

He began to kiss her shoulders, the narrow indent of her spine. He groaned as he pushed aside the buckram bodice and cupped her breasts in his palms. Her skirts fell to the floor, a crumpled circle of emerald. The bed was strewn with silks and velvets of every colour. Pearls dug into his elbows, gold lace scratched his face. His climax was a temporary bliss.

Afterwards, she tried to embrace him, to speak to him. But desire had died, and Guillaume knew that he dared not allow affection to replace desire. It was almost dark, and the leading of the windows formed bars and chequers on the stone floor. As he rose from the bed, Guillaume was aware of his aching head, of his fears for the future. He feared for Joanna, he feared for his daughter. He saw suddenly the dangers that attended his every move, but he lacked the will to alter the path that he had made.

And besides, he knew in his heart that it was too late. It had been too late the day he had recognized the woman in Hamon de Bohun's portrait; too late, perhaps, the day he had met Joanna Zulian in Milan. Too late now, because he had realized that he needed Marigny more than ever. Needed it for Sanchia, so that she could hide behind that wall, that forest, that meadow and drawbridge. So that she would always be safe.

Marigny seethed with activity again: seamstresses checked gowns for fallen hems and loose buttons, arrangements were made to cover the Seigneur's absence from his estates. Hamon and Eleanor de Bohun were travelling to Blois, to attend the court of King Louis XII.

Hamon had engaged a tutor for Guy. *He is too young*, Eleanor had wanted to cry again, but she had kept silent, knowing the futility of speech. The tutor was a middle-aged scholar called Clement Flore, who was superbly qualified for his post, having degrees from the universities of Montpellier, Bologna and Louvain. Degrees from Montpellier, Bologna and Louvain did not, however, enable him to deal with a lively two-year-old boy.

The horses in the stable were far more enticing to Guy than Master Flore's attempts to teach him Latin. The meadow, which seemed to Guy unimaginably vast, was far more exciting than making meaningless chalk marks on a slate. Master Flore's complaints were frequent, muttered irritably to nursemaids and the priest; when Guy bit his tutor, however, leaving two neat semicircles of teeth marks on the bony wrist, Master Flore took his outrage to both the Seigneur and his wife.

Hamon was sorting through papers, Eleanor wrapping jewellery in folds of silk.

'*Look*, madame.' The tutor hauled up the elaborate sleeves of his gown, his face crimson with vexation. 'The boy is quite undisciplined. He is like a wild beast.'

Eleanor said soothingly, 'Guy is very naughty, Monsieur Flore. If you go to the kitchen, Berthe will find you a salve and linen.'

The tutor sniffed.

'And you should take a glass of wine, monsieur. I shall speak to Guy.'

Master Flore, slightly mollified, turned to go.

Hamon, seated at the table, put aside his papers and said slowly, 'One moment, monsieur.' He rose and crossed the room. 'My son bit you, you say?'

The tutor nodded. His voice was shrill with indignation. 'I was showing Master Guy his numbers, *votre seigneurie*. He knows most of them, but he confuses his sixes and nines. If I've shown him once, I've shown him a hundred times,' he added peevishly. 'He lost his temper and went quite wild. Kicking and screaming. I told him to be silent, and he bit me.'

'He shall be sent to his room,' said Eleanor. She was weary suddenly of trying to pacify the teacher of a child who should still be in a nursery: there was the servants' clothing to be organized, still her own gowns to be folded and packed ready for the journey.

'Sent to his room?' Hamon's voice was cold. 'I think that disobedience – temper tantrums – demand a little more than that, don't you, Eleanor?'

'Many children of Guy's age have temper tantrums,' she said patiently. 'You wouldn't want the boy to be lacking in spirit.'

The tutor, glancing at his master and mistress, mumbled something, made a hasty bow and fled the room.

'You are a fool, Eleanor, a fool. But Guy will not be a fool. He is my son – he is the heir to Marigny. He will not behave like *other children*. He will not be lacking in spirit, but neither will he behave like a wild beast.'

He left the room. After a moment Eleanor, picking up her skirts, followed him down the stairs, across the Great Hall and outside into the courtyard. She watched as he disappeared into the stables. She could not at first think why he was going there. Then Hamon emerged with a whip in his hand.

'If Guy behaves like a wild beast,' he said, 'he shall be treated like a wild beast.' Then he walked off and left her standing in the courtyard surrounded by gawping stable-lads.

Eleanor felt so little for Guy, and yet she could not stop herself from crying out as she ran after her husband to the upstairs parlour where the boy took his lessons.

She seized his wrist as he took hold of the door-latch. 'My lord, he is a child – little more than a baby! He must be taught his manners, yes, but not like *this*!'

Hamon let go of neither the door-latch nor the whip. 'If you cannot stomach what is necessary for the good of your child, Eleanor, then perhaps you should return to your needlework.'

There was still no anger in his voice. That was what frightened her most, the lack of anger. Eleanor's fingers slipped from his wrist, and Hamon walked into the parlour. The door slid shut. She heard the tone of his voice as he spoke to Guy, but could not make out the words.

There was a silence, and then she heard the child cry out. Once, twice, three times. She wanted to run away, but would not let herself. Guy was her son, not Hamon's. He was her responsibility: her sin, her folly, had brought him into the world. Whatever happened to Guy, she had brought upon him. Eventually, though, sickened by the child's screams, Eleanor covered her ears with her hands.

When the door opened, she was still there, hunched on the top stair. She couldn't bear to look into the parlour and see her son. Lowering her hands, she looked up at Hamon.

He didn't even mention Guy. He was smiling slightly, and he looked content, satisfied. He still held the whip: its tip rested against the calf of his leg. He was talking, of all things, about the château, the garden. Through the terrible sobbing from the parlour, she heard Hamon say: 'I meant to tell you, Eleanor. I intend to start work on the garden when we have returned from Blois. The meadow – the kitchen garden – does not do Marigny justice.'

She rose from the step. She saw from his expression how he despised her, how little he counted her for. He had begun to walk down the stairs. In the parlour, the child's sobs had distilled into a desolate high-pitched wail.

'I *love* the meadow,' said Eleanor softly. 'You will not change the meadow, Hamon.' Her face was level with his, and she did not flinch from his dark, opaque gaze.

CHAPTER THIRTEEN

The court of King Louis XII, wearying temporarily of both war and the endless circuits of the valley of the Loire, paused at the château de Blois.

At his birthplace of Blois, Louis gathered his nobles around him, entertaining them with jousts and hunts and tennis by day, feasting and dancing and music by night. In return they would fight for him when he marched to Italy, would follow him back across the Alps to regain the lands that his treacherous former allies had stolen from him.

His vassals arrived at Blois in bright flurries of colour, gaudy processions against a fading autumn landscape. Their mules and packhorses were laden with finery, with jewels, with gifts suitable for a king. The servants who attended them laboured up the road from the town, their pennants unfurled and limp in the cold autumn air, their tabards stitched in the colours and emblems of their masters. The Montmorencys, the de Foix, the de Rohans, were there. Present also was the Duc d'Alençon, Prince of the Blood, married three years ago to Marguerite d'Angoulême, sister of the heir to the throne, François de Valois.

And of course there were the du Chantonnays. Guillaume du Chantonnay, head bowed and kneeling before his sovereign, told Louis about the woman he had brought with him to Blois. She was gentle, gifted and beautiful, he had said, attempting to counter Louis's disapproval. She was married to a Paduan painter, but the coward had fled to Venice when Maximilian took the city, leaving his wife penniless and unprotected at the mercy of the German *Landsknechts*. Louis, who had no great liking for Maximilian just now, relented a little. Later, his queen told him what of course he had already guessed; that Joanna Zulian was Guillaume du Chantonnay's mistress. Tired, Louis did not alter his decision to receive Joanna Zulian at Blois. Guillaume du Chantonnay, he explained to Anne of Brittany, had fought valiantly at Agnadello, at Brescia, at Ravenna. And besides, by that time Louis de France had seen Joanna Zulian.

The weather worsened. The Seigneur de Marigny arrived three days later with his wife and a great column of attendants, their banners stitched with snarling golden pikes bordered with black. Louis sniffed disapprovingly as the de Bohun entourage curled into the rainswept courtyard of Blois, a vast, glittering black and yellow serpent. Louis disliked show, was suspicious of the outward display of wealth. He himself lived frugally, wore carefully mended clothes, ate little. Drumming his fingers on the stone sill, Louis de France watched as the Seigneur de Marigny and his wife Eleanor were admitted to Blois. He recalled the château de Marigny, with its mighty walls, its wide moat, its glorious Italian treasures. Coveting all things Italian, Louis struggled to recall the details of Hamon de Bohun's inheritance of Marigny. He could not remember clearly; he forgot so much nowadays. But he thought, vaguely, that the inheritance had been dubious, stained with death.

The Sieur du Chantonnay and his mistress Joanna Zulian travelled to Blois, a three-day journey from the house in the forest, leaving Sanchia in the care of her nurse. Riding at Guillaume's side, Joanna knew that the distance between herself and her lover, never quite closed, had enlarged. They might be equally adoring parents of their tiny daughter, they might share a bed, but they shared, Joanna knew, nothing else.

The château de Blois, perched over the town, was made of brick and stone. Inside, the rooms were hung with paintings and tapestries, the fireplaces and doorways decorated with Louis's emblem, the porcupine. Logs scented with juniper and pear smouldered in the great hearths, and the floors were scattered with sweet herbs. On the tables were displayed silver plate, Venetian glass, books and reliquaries. Carefully, almost surreptitiously, Joanna touched them, her fingertips brushing the cool, costly surfaces. Through the windows, she could glimpse the gardens, and beyond, hazed in the late-autumn sunshine, the forests.

The rain began two days after their arrival. Great sheets of it, scything down from a dark grey sky, battering against the roofs and windowpanes. Mud was trodden into the clean rushes and the expensive Turkey carpets, and yellow puddles gathered in the courtyard. Guillaume's anxiety returned: he stood at the window, tense and silent, staring out at the rain.

A day of waiting, and then his good humour snapped back into place.

He took Joanna's arm, steering her out of the banqueting-chamber and up the stairs. 'Dress yourself in the bronze silk.' Guillaume's eyes were hard, glittering. 'Relations of mine have arrived. I'd like to introduce you to them, Joanna.'

The journey had been foul. The heavens opened up as they rode through the gates of Marigny, and it continued to rain all the way to Blois. One of the carts had been swallowed by the mud, and it had taken six serving-men, digging in the quagmire with their bare hands, to free it. A chest fell from the cart and burst open, the finery it contained ruined by the downpour within minutes. The Seigneur de Marigny had had the servants responsible flogged by the roadside.

Reaching Blois, they were made to wait for an hour in a draughty ante-room, and then obliged to listen to their sovereign ramble interminably and pointlessly about the duties of the *seigneurial*. They had not even been permitted to change their clothes: the king received Hamon and Eleanor de Bohun, cold and weary, in the soaking riding-clothes they had worn for their journey, mud embroidering their hems, their furs rank and curled by rain. Hamon disliked travelling, disliked the discomfort it enforced upon him. It was necessary, though, that he should attend King Louis's court at Blois: necessary that his ownership of Marigny, his adoption of the title, should be publicly accepted.

They were dismissed at last. The king's servants closed the double doors behind him, as Hamon and Eleanor backed out into the ante-room. It was late afternoon and the light was poor – only the fire was lit, Louis's parsimony objecting to the use of rushlights before evening.

'*Votre seigneurie* – Eleanor . . .'

A voice, vaguely familiar to Hamon, drawled from out of the darkness. Eleanor, beside him, cried, 'Guillaume!'

Hamon had encountered Guillaume du Chantonnay only once before, at the time of his marriage to Eleanor. A meeting that he still recalled with pleasure.

'Eleanor.' Reynaud's cousin moved forward out of the darkness and kissed Eleanor's hand. 'Seigneur.' He swept a plumed hat off his fair head and bowed to Hamon. To Eleanor he said, 'You look a trifle bedraggled, cousin.' But his gaze took in Hamon's soaking, muddy clothes. Guillaume made no attempt to hide his amusement.

'The weather was poor . . . it rained constantly . . . my horse threw a shoe . . .' Eleanor, stammering, was scarlet with delight. 'It is so *good* to see you, Guillaume. It has been so *long* . . .'

Hamon wanted to hit her. But he realized for the first time that Guillaume du Chantonnay was not alone. He was beckoning to someone: a woman walked forward from the shadows and Guillaume took her hand.

'This is Madame Zulian, who has accompanied me to Blois. Joanna, this is my cousin, Madame de Marigny.'

Again, the words were to Eleanor. And again, Guillaume's eyes, an intense blue in the firelight, met Hamon's.

Joanna Zulian rose from her curtsy. She wore a gown of bronze silk, and pearls were threaded through her hair. Her face was quite, quite perfect, and it was a face that Hamon recognized immediately. He had seen her before, of course: her portrait, which he had stolen from Reynaud's courier – his own misbegotten son – hung in Marigny's Great Chamber. He himself had shown Guillaume du Chantonnay that portrait: Judith holding the severed head of Holofernes. The sense of shock almost overwhelmed him. It was as though the living woman had stepped from the painted image, shimmering with silk and pearls.

Guillaume said blandly, 'Joanna, let me present you to the Seigneur de Marigny.'

Hamon was chill with anger. He knew what Guillaume du Chantonnay was really saying, of course.

You have Marigny, but I have Joanna Zulian.

The messenger from the Signoria of Venice arrived at Blois one crisp autumn morning, having ridden day and night from the distant lagoons of the Adriatic.

Toby Crow paused in the town of Blois long enough only to make himself fit to be received by a king. The letters from Andrea Gritti and Antonio Giustinian were safely stitched into his saddlecloth. In a tavern room Toby changed out of his muddy riding-clothes and plunged his face and hands into icy water. He emerged clean and ready to play his part in the complex negotiations between the city of Venice and the kingdom of France.

First, of course, he had to wait for hours in one of the château's cold and draughty ante-rooms, kicking his heels, looking out to the copper-leaved forest that smudged the horizon. But eventually he was escorted by a poker-faced attendant to the state-rooms of Louis de France.

As Louis had led his troops into battle at Agnadello, he had shouted that not even gunfire could harm a king of France. Now, kneeling before him, head bare and bowed, Toby noticed with a single glance how the Valois king had aged.

The Venetian letters were handed over. On one side of the wide, sparsely furnished room sat Anne of Brittany, surrounded by her ladies. Glancing momentarily at her serene, fragile face, Toby was reminded of the boxwood Madonna he had bought for Reynaud du Chantonnay from Marcantonio Venier. The same carved, sad features, the same resignation in her light, oval eyes. Both Louis de France and his queen looked as though time had suddenly touched them, marking their faces, their gestures.

Louis inspected the seals and signatures of the letters. 'I will study these later, Monsieur Crow.' His faded eyes drifted to Toby, still on one knee in front of him. 'Messer Gritti says that you are a soldier, Monsieur Crow. And that you are of French origin.'

Toby said easily, 'I was brought up in France, your majesty. My parents have never acknowledged me. And, yes, I am a soldier.'

Louis de France shifted in his chair. The letters in his hand shook slightly as he studied them. 'You are not a common soldier, though, monsieur, but the leader of a company of fifty men.' Louis's voice was dry and wavered a little. 'A company that you have hired out to the Signoria of Venice. Perhaps, Monsieur Crow, as a Frenchman, you should consider fighting for the country which raised you, fed you, educated you?'

The floor was cold and hard beneath Toby's knee; he was aware suddenly of how fast he had ridden, how far he had travelled. 'Majesty, it is my hope that in fighting for Venice, I will soon be fighting for France also.'

Louis gave a terse chuckle of amusement. 'Mine also, Monsieur Crow, mine also,' the Valois king said softly. 'You may rise.'

Toby rose, and immediately the atmosphere of the room, tense and expectant until then, lightened a little. One of the ladies began to whisper, Louis's attendants dared to move their limbs.

Louis de France said, 'You will stay with us, monsieur, until I have time to study these letters. I will give you my reply as soon as possible. France is as anxious as Venice for the settlement of suitable terms of alliance.'

★

Toby slept most of the rest of the day, in a room not far from the Tour de Foix. From his window he could see the town of Blois and the wide lazy curl of the River Loire, grey and shimmering in the thin autumn light.

He was woken by a rapping on his door, the summons of a servant to attend the banquet that Louis would give for the lords and ladies of France that night. Dressing himself in black silk, suitable for dining in the presence of a king, Toby followed the servant down dark, twisting passageways to the banqueting-hall.

The room was splendid, lit by great banks of candles and the fire that roared and spat in the wide hearth. There were frescoes on the walls: hunting scenes, tournaments, dancing demoiselles, the brushstrokes bold, the colours garish in the yellow candlelight.

Toby found himself seated at one of the two long tables that ran the length of the hall. Faces swam before him, elegant and beautiful, plain and old. In the background a consort of lutes played, their plangent sounds almost drowned by the chatter of the guests. Beside the dais on which Louis de France, his queen and the Princes of the Blood dined, a dwarf pranced, bells jangling, small feet tapping the floor to the rhythm of a jig. Looking up from his plate of salted mutton and barberry jelly, Toby saw, seated at the table opposite him, Hamon de Bohun and his wife, Eleanor.

Eleanor ate nothing and answered questions in monosyllables. She found the endless, complicated meals, the ritual and etiquette of court, exhausting. She tolerated it because she had no option but to tolerate it. She had attended court with Reynaud before his health had become too poor, and she had, long ago, as one of five well-dowried and beautiful sisters, stayed at Blois in the company of her father. The tedium, the long days that stretched into the night, were an inescapable part of the life of a well-born woman. Though she might have gained far more pleasure from making pastries in the kitchen at Marigny, Eleanor would not have dreamed of quibbling at the duties that her rank imposed on her.

Now though, quite suddenly, her exile at Blois had become intolerable. The meeting with Guillaume had jarred her, a peculiar mixture of pleasure and pain, forcibly reminding her of a life she had once lived, people she had once known.

She had half expected to see Guillaume, knowing that he had spent the last few years fighting for his king, knowing that he was ambitious.

But nothing had prepared her for a meeting with Toby Crow, nothing at all. She had thought she would never see him again.

She was in the middle of an interminable conversation about hawking, when she looked up and there he was. Her polite replies died on her lips, her stomach lurched. She glanced again, sure that she had been mistaken, sure that it was just the wishful thinking that had once made Toby appear in every marketplace, every village square, an inconvenient and incongruous remnant of a folly that she regretted bitterly.

But she was not mistaken. The man across the table was her former lover who had betrayed her. The gentleman to Eleanor's side droned on endlessly about harriers and tiercels, jesses and lures. Eleanor, no longer even pretending to listen, stared at the familiar face, the dark eyes, the unruly black hair, the straight nose, the mouth that she had kissed so many times. She saw that he had changed, that he had grown older, that he smiled less. She saw that he did not speak, but let his gaze wander slowly over the banqueting-hall of Blois, the king and his guests. And then, suddenly, his eyes met hers, and she bowed her head, looking away, her heart thudding like a hunted deer's.

The gentleman beside her, offended, had turned away, was talking to his neighbour. Eleanor's hands shook visibly, the sight of her food nauseated her. When she had recovered her composure enough to walk, she gathered her skirts and began to rise from her chair.

A hand enfolded her wrist, halting her. Hamon de Bohun said softly, 'You're not going, are you, Eleanor?'

She managed to say, 'I feel a little unwell, Hamon.'

'You were well enough, my dear, until you caught sight of your former husband's messenger-boy. Does his presence trouble you? Or are you thinking, perhaps, of running to his side, to discuss old times?'

His fingernails dug into her wrist. Unable to look away from him, she saw the malice in his eyes. Slowly, shaking her head, she almost fell back into her chair.

'I thought he was dead.' Hamon spoke very softly, but Eleanor heard him, and his words were drops of acid, etching themselves into her mind.

He let go of her wrist. 'You must learn, my dear Eleanor,' he said, lightly, 'not to be so impulsive. Would you not agree that courtesy to your king is more important than an exchange of pleasantries with an untrustworthy former servant?'

She nodded dumbly. Staring downwards, Eleanor crumbled a piece of bread between finger and thumb, until her plate was covered with a fine white dust, like snow.

Toby had known that the de Bohuns might be at Blois, of course. It had been a possibility that he had attempted to consider quite calmly. But the reality was different. The reality was Eleanor's strained, ageing face, his own almost physical revulsion for the man that she had married. His father. He noticed the brief interchange between man and wife, saw the whiteness of Hamon de Bohun's knuckles as he gripped Eleanor's wrist. He knew, had known for a long time, that de Bohun gained pleasure from inflicting pain on other people. Toby had never been fool enough to think that the marriage could be a happy one, but still he felt anger rise in him as he witnessed de Bohun's small, almost casual, mistreatment of Eleanor. He fought against the anger, knowing it futile, self-defeating. The scar he bore was a memento of the consequences of untimely loss of temper. *'Bend sinister. For bastardy, my pet.'*

He made himself turn away from the de Bohuns and study the other guests of the king of France. He knew some of them by sight, some by reputation. The corrupt, cynical Duc d'Alençon, the avaricious Jacques de Beaune, receiver-general of Languedoc. There were faces that were familiar to him from the Italian wars. He recognized Guillaume du Chantonnay, and then his eyes lingered for a moment on the lady seated beside Guillaume.

She was dressed in red, a deep, warm red that echoed the shades of her bright hair. Her head-dress was studded with pearls, her wide red velvet sleeves were slashed and braided, cloth-of-gold puffed through the slashes. Her neck was long, white and slender, her profile, turned away now from Toby, appeared perfect. He watched her for a moment, appreciating her beauty.

Then she turned and looked across the room at him. *'Joanna!'* Toby exclaimed loudly, dropping his knife.

The woman opposite, the gentleman beside him, smiled.

The gentleman whispered, 'I have been trying to make myself known to the lady for the past three days, but Guillaume du Chantonnay guards her like a eunuch in a harem.'

Toby frowned. 'Guillaume du Chantonnay?'

'Madame Zulian is Guillaume du Chantonnay's mistress,' said Toby's neighbour.

*

After they had dined, they danced, their shadows flickering against the stone walls, mingling with the frozen figures painted there. The long hems of their gowns whispered on the bare floor, their slippered feet gently echoed the rhythm of the tabor.

When Joanna Zulian danced, all the room watched. Eleanor watched her because she had noticed the striking similarity between Guillaume's beautiful mistress and the portrait on the wall at Marigny. Guillaume watched her because he needed all France to see what he had bought. Hamon de Bohun also watched her, his eyes just once turning away to meet Guillaume's. The message in Guillaume du Chantonnay's bright blue eyes was perfectly clear. Hamon knew that Guillaume was taunting him.

Toby, too, watched Joanna dance. He had seen her dance before, of course, in an inn on the road to Milan. Dusty skirts whirling in the darkness of the tavern, her hair loose, tangled, trailing down her back. Afterwards, he had kissed her. Later, he had made love to her. And now Joanna Zulian was Guillaume du Chantonnay's mistress. He, Toby Crow, had brought them together. That they should have stayed together was not a possibility that Toby had ever considered. He walked away. He didn't want to watch her any more. Instead, he found himself facing Hamon de Bohun.

'Did you enjoy your journey to England, Mr Crow?' said de Bohun softly. 'Did you give my compliments to your mother?'

They stood a little apart from the rest of the guests in a corner of the vast banqueting-chamber. Toby said nothing at first, because he could not speak. The notes of the lute, the tapping of the dancers' feet, suddenly lacked resonance.

'My poor pet, you have been struck dumb. Or has the discovery of your origins taught you your proper place at last?'

Toby had last seen Hamon de Bohun on a quayside in Brittany, when de Bohun had drawn the tip of his dagger across his chest, marking him for life.

'There are still . . . gaps, Monsieur de Bohun.'

Toby had forgotten the power of de Bohun's physical presence. Hamon de Bohun was as tall as Toby and strongly built – not running to fat as Reynaud had been, nor yet touched by the frailties of old age.

'I am glad to see, my pet, that you do not sully the relationship that exists between us by addressing me as *father*. But I would remind you that I have another title now.'

Toby thought he saw a flicker of amusement in de Bohun's dark eyes. 'I had heard, *votre seigneurie*,' he replied. The courtesy almost choked him.

'As for you . . . Reynaud needed to be taught a lesson. I had claimed guardianship of Blanche, you see. She was only fifteen. I'd have married her, of course, to be sure.'

Toby thought how this sort of rivalry always damaged the innocent. Blanche – little more than a child – had been as defenceless as François against greed and the desire for power. He said hoarsely, 'And Izabel Mandeville?'

De Bohun smiled. 'Ah, Izabel. I had gone to England, you see, Crow – I had found favour with the Tudor king. I discovered that Reynaud had married his sister to an English gentleman. So I went to Lydney Mandeville.' De Bohun leaned forward, his voice low and confidential. 'It was not premeditated, you understand. I usually plan, but on that occasion . . .' He shook his head. 'I was inspired, I think. To violate Reynaud du Chantonnay's beloved sister seemed a sort of justice.'

Toby whispered, 'You raped her?'

De Bohun nodded. 'To punish Reynaud for taking Marigny. Marigny was mine, you see, it was my due. And the gods were good to me.'

The consort had stopped playing. Toby's voice sounded unnaturally loud in the sudden silence. 'What do you mean?'

'Hush, my pet. You wouldn't want anyone else to overhear our little tête-à-tête, would you?'

De Bohun's long fingers brushed against Toby's face. The touch appalled Toby.

'I mean – well, it was a stroke of luck that the bitch was so easily impregnated, and yet another stroke of luck that she did not see fit to dispose of you at birth. She tried to hide the pregnancy, of course, sent away most of her servants, but I found out. I was watching her. Hardly daring to trust my luck. And people are so venial, don't you find? A few coins to the right man, and he'll tell you anything you want to know.'

Toby took a deep breath. There was sweat on the back of his neck, on his upper lip. '*You* sent me to France. *You* sent me to Reynaud du Chantonnay.'

De Bohun smiled. 'Yes. It was a fitting punishment, don't you think, for greed, for importunity? Imaginative, even. I left you long enough in England to be sure you survived. Long enough for the bitch to become attached to you. She hadn't told Reynaud, of course. How she howled when I took you,' he added, meditatively. 'How she wailed. I thought she'd be glad to part with her little changeling. I thought I was doing her a service. Yes, I sent you to France, my pet, clutching an explanatory letter.'

De Bohun narrowed his eyes, furrowed his forehead. The lutes had begun to play again, but their jaunty melody seemed incongruous. De Bohun lowered his voice, so that only Toby could hear. 'I gave Reynaud a choice, you see, Crow. He could consign you to the gutter, or he could bring you up at Marigny as his own pampered nephew.'

De Bohun's eyes, wide open now, focused on Toby. 'I think that he took the former option, don't you? I think that he apprenticed you to the most vile employer he could find. I expect he hoped that the shoemaker, your master, would kill you.'

Suddenly all trace of amusement left Hamon de Bohun's face. He whispered, 'I would advise you to maintain your silence about our relationship, Crow. I cannot evict you from this house as I would like to do. But may I suggest that when your liege lord gives you leave to return to whatever sty you generally wallow in, that you do so as soon as possible? If you should falter, if you should hesitate to obey me in this, then remember that I can do to Eleanor what I did to Izabel Mandeville every night of the week, should I so choose. Quite legally, of course. The task would be distasteful to me, no doubt.' Hamon de Bohun's small mouth pursed consideringly. 'Eleanor has become such a plain, matronly creature. But I could stomach it. For your sake, my pet.'

Toby wore no sword, but his hands had fisted. 'You –'

'Bastard?' There was a glitter of amusement in the dark eyes. 'I thought I had explained everything. That particular epithet, Crow, belongs only to you.'

If he lost his temper now, if he struck Hamon de Bohun in the presence of his king, then he would only find himself in whatever unpleasant dungeon the château de Blois had to offer. The last two years, the struggle to become something instead of the nothing that de Bohun had intended him to be, would have been pointless.

He pushed past de Bohun, loathing even that brief physical contact. The warmth of the room, engendered by the heat of the fire and the quantity of people, had become unbearable. Forcing his way through the crowds, bowing sketchily in the direction of his king, and muttering some acceptable excuse to the servants that hovered by the door, Toby found himself in the ante-room beyond the banqueting-hall.

The room was cool, dark, silent. Echoes of the conversation he had just endured jangled through his head. He was not alone, though, and he needed to be alone. He had seen Joanna follow him, a flicker of red velvet through the crowds. But he didn't want to see her just now. He didn't want to see Joanna, or Guillaume, or Eleanor, or any of the others he had entangled himself with. He was not fit company for anyone. Especially not for du Chantonnays or de Bohuns. Or their mistresses.

He heard her say, hesitantly, 'Toby?'

He looked up at her. The flickering candlelight fitfully outlined her features. He leaned against the wall, regaining his breath. He could not stop looking at her.

She was no longer Taddeo Zulian's talented niece, she was no longer the mermaid he had dragged out of the canal. She was no longer the gypsy he had travelled with across the plains of Lombardy. She was no longer the woman that he and Martin Gefroy had once fought over, to the sound of breaking crockery in a Milanese hotel. She had become a great lady, exquisite in red velvet and cloth-of-gold, elegant and composed and graceful. She wore jewels threaded through her hair, round her slender white neck, on her fingers. He could not now imagine touching her, kissing her, making love to her. Guillaume du Chantonnay had taken Joanna Zulian, had changed her, and made her into something that he, a bastard and a soldier-of-fortune, could never touch again.

'I saw you talking to the Seigneur de Marigny,' said Joanna. She stepped forward and now stood only a few paces away from him.

He saw in her face bewilderment, and sympathy. He bitterly resented the sympathy. He said lazily: 'The nunnery wouldn't take you, then, Joanna? You couldn't find a suitable old gentleman in need of a housekeeper?'

She understood him. She flushed, and her eyes sparkled with anger. 'You yourself pointed out, Toby, how few choices there were for me.'

'So you chose instead to become Guillaume du Chantonnay's whore?'

The flat of her hand struck his face before he could duck. He must be tired, he thought, stifling a perverse wish to laugh. He had spent his entire adult life ducking arrows, bullets, cannon-balls, but Joanna Zulian's hand, ringed and manicured, had successfully found its target.

One of her rings caught his lip. Toby wiped the blood from his mouth with the back of his hand as he watched her turn on her heel and stalk quickly back into the banqueting-hall.

Toby Crow had left the room, thank God, and she could begin to think clearly again. When the dance ended, Eleanor found Guillaume beside her.

She had realized, since she had arrived at Blois, how much she had missed Guillaume. Often, she didn't understand him, but she had always been convinced that something good lay beneath the veneer of cynicism. Tonight, his was a face from another life, a life that she had almost forgotten.

'Are you well, cousin?' she asked, recovering her breath. 'Do you prosper?'

He took her hand and escorted her to a seat. 'Very well. And my estates prosper as much as they ever did. Not quite like Marigny, you understand – sheep in the courtyard, hay drying in the hall. Not the sort of thing you are accustomed to, cousin.'

Eleanor flushed, and sat down, her skirts spread out around her. She said, tremulously and proudly, 'I did not *choose* Marigny, Guillaume. Indeed, it was not what I would have chosen.'

He stared at her for a moment, and then he laughed. 'No,' he said. 'You'd have chosen a nunnery, or a farm, wouldn't you, Eleanor?' He shook his head. 'God mocks us both, don't you think?'

She did not, as she once would have done, protest at the blasphemy. Instead, her thoughts turned again to the past, to François. A memory, fleeting and dim, hovered at the edges of her consciousness. She struggled to seize it.

'And your physician, Guillaume? You had a physician, didn't you? He attended François. He was a Netherlander, a Scotsman, I can't remember his name . . .'

'An Englishman,' said Guillaume blandly. 'Martin Gefroy. Haven't seen him for years, Eleanor. He left my service – oh, a couple of weeks after François died. Didn't bother to inform me of his intentions, I'm afraid. Just upped and went.'

Once more, that fleeting memory, the sense of something slipping away from her, almost seen. 'He was a good man,' she said, struggling to recall the English physician's face, his manner. 'François improved so much.'

Again, that short, humourless bark of laughter. 'Even Martin couldn't cure poor François of his real ailment, could he, Eleanor?' Guillaume's tone was bitter. 'His inheritance, I mean.'

The king had risen and the evening was ending. Guillaume moved away and Eleanor saw her husband come towards her from out of the crowds. Toby Crow, thank God, was still nowhere to be seen.

Eleanor frowned, not understanding Guillaume's last remark. What connection could François's inheritance, which had been everything a man could desire, possibly have with his untimely death?

The rain stopped that night, and at dawn the sun gleamed purple and pink on the horizon. A frost had touched the damp leaves and the dying flowers, edging them with a rim of silver. To the mournful call of the hunting-horn the lords and ladies of Blois gathered to hunt with the king of France.

Along the woodland rides ran the twenty-five pairs of hounds, the scores of servants and grooms and footmen that followed the hunt. The taffeta and damask, the velvet and satin of the great families of France, were bright against the sombre colours of the autumn woodland. Cloth-of-gold and cloth-of-silver flickered between the huge tree trunks; the sheen of the swords, the gleam of velvet scabbards and plumed and braided caps, caught the dull white light of the sun. They rode slowly, heads high, waiting for signals from the great brass horns to guide them to their quarry.

Around the dark pools that glimmered beneath the trees the ground was marshy and threaded with reeds. They were hunting boar today: once Joanna caught a glimpse of a small piglet, its back striped and bristled, careening through the undergrowth. Then another half-dozen piglets and a great sow, her belly already swollen with next spring's litter, hurtled past, rushing for safety. The hounds picked up the scent and, howling, altered their direction. Directed by the Captain of the Nets, the huntsmen and dogs spread out through the forest, circling wide.

They paused at midday, gathering to refresh themselves in a clearing. Manservants had arranged trestle tables on the thin grass, wine-bottles cooled in a nearby stream. A few rays of sunlight found their way past the treetops, illuminating the pewter tableware, the trenchers of bread and meat and game. Louis, seated at the head of the table, crumbled black bread and picked at boiled beef.

Joanna, dismounting from her mare, knew that neither her temper nor the echo of Toby Crow's words had faded. *'So you chose instead to become Guillaume du Chantonnay's whore.'* Her hand had stung after she had slapped his face; for an hour afterwards her palm had been mottled pink and white. He had insulted her, and she had hit him. Because the insult had been quite deliberate, and because he had spoken the truth.

She was Guillaume's whore, and Sanchia was Guillaume's bastard. Safe in the forests of Brittany, it had not seemed to matter. But here at brittle, orderly Blois, the rules were different. The rules were those of society, which dictated both the precariousness of her position and the insecure status of her child. In a single well-aimed sentence Toby had destroyed whatever pleasure she had taken from Blois, from its glitter and finery, from the splendid people who inhabited it.

She had slept poorly, the remnants of her anger still with her when she had risen at dawn. She had dressed in her best, though: black velvet to emphasize the pallor of her skin, to contrast with the bright sheen of her hair. She had not, like the other ladies of the court, contained her hair with head-dresses and nets. Her head was covered only with a tasselled velvet cap worn to one side; beneath it, her hair flowed long and loose down her back. She wore Guillaume du Chantonnay's diamonds at her throat and on her gloved hands. She did not intend to give Toby Crow the pleasure of believing that he had hurt her.

'We might as well,' drawled Guillaume, as he handed her down from her horse, 'be peasants, eating black bread in hedgerows and ditches.' His eyes surveyed the trestle tables disdainfully. 'I do appreciate a little comfort.'

Joanna laughed slightly too loudly. Other huntsmen and women were arriving: on the far side of the glade she glimpsed Toby Crow dismounting from a chestnut stallion.

'Hardly a hedgerow, Guillaume. There are musicians, servants . . .'

Guillaume sniffed. 'I prefer my food hot, my table on solid ground. A fire in the hearth, that sort of thing. I am out of place here.' He smiled at her. 'Whereas you, my dear, are in your element. You have misled me, Joanna. You are not Venetian at all, you are a gypsy.'

She let him take her hand and raise it to his lips. She could not see, taking one swift glance across the clearing, whether she had marked Toby's face last night. Her palm still itched with the memory of the blow.

Guillaume escorted her to the tables, introducing her to the other guests of Louis XII. She could see admiration in their eyes as they bowed, kissing her hand. The sackbuts and rebecks scraped and hooted, their melody lost in the open air. Joanna smiled and laughed and accepted elegant compliments. Flocks of crows beat their wings, flying from the treetops; in the forest the lymerers and signallers still prowled, seeking their quarry.

Joanna found herself seated next to the Seigneur de Marigny and his wife. Madame de Marigny, Guillaume's cousin, hardly spoke. The Seigneur complimented Joanna on her dress, inquired about Guillaume's estates. The tic returned to Guillaume's face and his long, ringed fingers drummed at the table.

'And you, son, Eleanor?' asked Guillaume, addressing his cousin at last. 'Is he well?'

Toby Crow, Joanna noticed, was within earshot. Swallowing the remainder of her wine, she made her smile brighter.

Eleanor de Bohun said, 'Very well, Guillaume.' Her voice trembled slightly. Her face was haunted, shadowed. Once, Joanna recalled, she had thought that Toby Crow had loved the lady of Marigny. Once, she had cared.

Hamon de Bohun said, 'Guy thrives, Monsieur du Chantonnay. He is of excellent health – a strong, capable child. He rides excellently for his age, and I have engaged a tutor for him. Guy can already recite some Latin verse.'

Guillaume said nothing for a moment. Then, his expressionless blue eyes turned to de Bohun: 'So different from poor François, don't you agree, monsieur?'

In the distance, the hunting-horn sounded a low, mournful call. The king had risen. His courtiers and ladies stood, heads bowed. A light rain had begun: droplets gathered like beads on the velvet of Joanna's gown.

Joanna enjoyed the speed of the canter and the cold air on her cheeks, as she followed the distant call of the horn. Branches flicked against her mare's flanks, hooves trod bracken underfoot. Her longing for Sanchia, for Brittany, which had been quite unbearable that morning, faded until it was no more than a dull ache. The hunting-horn sounded again, more urgently this time. She heard horse's hooves behind her as she pursued the call. She had separated from Guillaume, from the de Bohuns; she enjoyed the solitude of the forest. There was no one in front of her, she was heading the field. The old, inevitable excitement of the chase seized her.

Her long skirts, her loose hair, streamed out behind her. The pounding of hooves grew louder until it was like thunder in her ears. A horse and rider had drawn level, black satin and silver accoutrements gleamed in the gloom of the forest. Glancing across, Joanna saw Toby Crow.

She put her spurs to the mare's flanks and tried to outride him. Bushes and trees streamed past her, blurred by speed as she pushed ahead of him. Her horse exhaled white clouds of vapour in the cold air; the only sound was the clatter of hooves, the jangle of bridle and bit. Crouching down over the mane, Joanna urged her mare to go faster. Pheasants, startled by the noise of the hooves, blundered into the air; a rabbit darted from the undergrowth. She wanted to win. She wanted to leave Toby far behind, open-mouthed, feeling foolish.

He was level with her again. Out of the corner of her eye she could glimpse his head bent like hers over his horse's neck. Joanna's cloak streamed out behind her, and her tasselled cap was slipping from her hair. Hooves pounded through puddles, through mud, breaking twigs, pulping leaves. Joanna's heart was battering against her ribcage, her mare was lathered with sweat.

Joanna wanted to scream with fury when Toby's horse, stronger and bigger than hers, forged ahead. Her mare fell back, exhausted. Toby reined in his horse, straddling the narrow path; access to the forest was blocked by thickets on either side. Joanna's cap slipped from her head to the muddy ground; angrily, she pushed her damp hair out of her face.

'Let me through,' she said breathlessly.

They were alone, far away from the main body of the hunt; no one travelled along the path behind them.

'I need to talk to you,' Toby said. He, too, sounded breathless.

Joanna stared at him angrily. He was hatless, and his short cloak fluttered in the breeze. She noticed the fine cut of his clothes, the remains of the summer sun on his skin, the confidence with which he guided the horse, with which he handled himself. She remembered the last occasion she had seen him, at the churchyard where they had buried Paul Dubreton. He had looked so different then: sick, pale, beaten.

'I don't believe we have anything to talk about, Messer Crow. Let me pass.'

He didn't move, though. 'We must talk,' he said, 'about Guillaume du Chantonnay.'

'Guillaume!' Her anger simmered, threatening to boil over. 'You intend to insult me again, then?'

He shook his head and swung out of his saddle. Crossing the short distance between them, Toby stooped and picked her cap out of the mud. Brushing it clean, he stood at her side, touching her hand as it lay upon the reins. For the first time she noticed the small bruise to the side of his mouth, where her ring had caught his lip.

'No,' he said. 'I apologize for last night, Joanna. I'd drunk too much.'

But he did not sound apologetic, and besides, she did not believe that he had drunk too much. Toby Crow never drank too much. His hand still covered hers. She did not know whether to snatch up the reins and ride away or to grip his fingers hard. Her indecision and weakness reignited her anger.

'You look well,' she said, glancing scornfully down at him. 'Successful. Have you prospered, Toby? Have you achieved your ambitions at last?' She was pleased to see the answering anger on his face.

His free hand played with her cap, winding the tassel around his fingers. 'Some of them,' he said. 'Not quite all.' He took his hand away from her reins. His eyes were cold and hard. 'I have prospered. I've fought in Italy since we last met, Joanna. Fifty men fight for me. I hire us out to whoever will pay for us. We have been – yes, as you say – successful.'

'You are content, then?' she said. 'You have enough?' She saw the quick shake of his head.

'No. Not enough.'

She knew then that he had not changed one bit. The trappings might have altered: Toby Crow might wear silks and jewels instead of broadcloth and linen, might dance with the great families of France instead of in roadside taverns, but really, he had not changed at all.

She lifted her heels, made ready to ride away, but he seized her reins again, stopping her. 'Don't go, Joanna,' he said. 'Not yet.'

She said tightly, 'Let me go, Toby. You have *no right . . .*'

'No. Of course not. None at all.'

His eyes met hers, and she knew, instinctively, that he, too, was recalling the Italian garden. The rose trees, the pergola, the fountains, seemed to cast such long shadows.

Toby said, 'I wanted to talk to you about Guillaume du Chantonnay. To warn you about him. Don't trust him, Joanna. Leave him. He is using you to avenge himself for the loss of Marigny.'

She hardly heard his last sentence. His arrogance was limitless, she thought. Glaring down at Toby, Joanna hissed, 'Guillaume has given me a roof over my head, clothes to wear on my back, food for my belly. And a *daughter*. Do you think I would leave *that*?'

She pulled the reins through his gloved hands, freeing herself. He said, 'Your hat, Joanna,' and tossed her velvet cap into her lap. Then she swung her horse around and cantered away.

The boar was trapped. Eleanor du Chantonnay, riding inside the circle of nets, saw the great beast turn and turn again, searching for escape.

Like Joanna, Eleanor used the speed and violence of the chase as a distraction. She rode beside Cousin Guillaume, having found herself separated from her husband. She was glad to be spared Hamon's company for a few hours: fragments of conversations, glimpses of dreams and memories, flickered constantly through her aching head. That morning, she was filled with a dreadful unease, a suspicion that if she just sat quietly thinking, everything would fit together, and the past would begin to make terrible sense.

The Captain of the Nets and his men moved slowly inwards, so that the circle shrank. The huge black muscled beast lowered its head to charge, its curved tusks scratching the earth. But it could not gather any speed: with increasing desperation it paced round the enclosure, churning up the forest floor, tossing leaves and earth into the cold air. The boar's snarls and squeals echoed through the trees.

Louis de France accepted the gilded boar-spear from the Captain of the Nets. The Valois king moved forward, the spear raised. In the dim late-afternoon light, he looked for a moment like a young man again. The gilded spear pierced the thick black hide; the animal's high-pitched squeal stabbed the silence. Dark blood trickled from the wound. The illusion of youth was gone, and Louis de France was an old man again, prematurely aged by ambition, by war. Eleanor, watching, shivered.

It began to rain more heavily as they rode back to Blois. The muddy paths speckled elegant boots and skirts with dirt. Eleanor's headache worsened, coloured lights flickered on the perimeters of her vision. She thought longingly of Marigny, of the flowery meadow, of the turrets and chambers, all with their burden of memories. She was sure that when she went back to Marigny the recollection that nagged at her would return. It centred, she thought, on Guillaume, or perhaps on Guillaume's physician. The veins in her temples throbbed with the effort of memory.

She wanted to be back at Marigny. She no longer had the energy or the enthusiasm for social gatherings. And it was unendurable, of course, that she should have to see her former lover, Guy's father. The intensity of her loathing for Toby Crow frightened her; the possibility that she might find herself loving him again frightened her more.

It was dusk by the time they returned to the château. Flares hissed in the dark and the rain, illuminating the courtyard and the high walls of the building. The hunting-horns called again, and the huntsmen drew up in ranks against the stone walls, their long shadows cast by the flambeaux trembling in the rain.

The great carcass of the boar was placed in the centre of the courtyard. Around the dead beast the hunt was re-enacted: the chase, the capture, the slaughter, were all performed once more in dumb ritual. The sound of the horns was magnified by the walls of the château. When they had slain the animal a second time, the boar's head was hacked off and thrown to the hounds. The dogs, brindled and bay and brown, yelped and whooped and squabbled around it.

As the clamour of the dogs died away, another sound filled the rainswept air. A great army of musicians, their song sweet and proud. Eleanor, looking up, discovered that there were tears in her eyes. A long and glittering entourage was riding slowly into the courtyard. She saw the most gloriously caparisoned horses, the most exquisitely dressed gentlemen and gentlewomen. The flower of France gathered before her, untouched by the foul weather, lit by the flickering light of the flambeaux.

'The Duc de Valois,' whispered Guillaume beside her. 'It seems that the heir to the throne has decided to favour us with his presence.'

They feasted that night to celebrate both the success of the hunt and the arrival of François d'Angoulême, Duc de Valois, heir to the throne of France. François, young, dark and sardonic, sat to one side of Louis de France, the Duchess of Brittany to the other. Next to the Duchess sat François d'Angoulême's betrothed, the Princess Claude. Squat and lopsided, her plain face was made beautiful by her obvious adoration of her attractive future husband.

With the arrival of the heir to the throne, the tempo of the day seemed to alter. Blois cast off the last remnants of its frugality, and the energetic, seductive personality of the Duc de Valois dominated the banquet. The château was brighter, noisier, the sound of laughter and conversation almost drowning the music of the consort.

When Toby looked at Joanna, she was laughing. Or dancing. He found himself momentarily hypnotized by the bright swirl of her hair, the sway of her skirts. Her laughter and smiles, which were for everyone, angered him. He thought of her living in Guillaume du Chantonnay's house, wearing clothes that Guillaume had bought, cherishing the daughter that Guillaume had fathered. He had tried to warn her, to make her understand Guillaume's motives, Guillaume's reasons for making her his mistress. But she had not listened, and he knew that he had not found the right words. He himself did not truly understand Guillaume: he remembered only Hamon de Bohun's face as he had studied the stolen picture of Judith and Holofernes.

He did not attempt to speak to her again. Joanna was surrounded by a gaggle of fawning courtiers: the greatest men in France danced with her, laughed with her, bought her cups of hippocras, plates of sweetmeats. He saw how she revelled in their attentions, how her eyes shone, how happily she accepted the hands of her dancing partners. Buffoons pranced in the centre of the room, jugglers hurled coloured balls into the air, but none of them commanded quite the same attention as Guillaume du Chantonnay's mistress did. Toby found his anger waning as the evening progressed. There was, after all, a pleasure just in watching Joanna Zulian. He had always found that, from the day he had first seen her perched behind an easel in a Venetian artist's studio. And, as he had pointed out, as she had reminded him, what else was there for her? She could not have been a painter, a physician, a soldier. Her dowry was her beauty, her grace.

It was just that, he thought grimly as he swallowed his wine and rose from his seat, he had not thought she cared for money, for position. He had not believed Joanna driven by the same sort of lust that had possessed both Hamon de Bohun and Reynaud du Chantonnay. He had thought her free from all that.

He was dragged into the dance, part of one of the concentric circles that filled the Great Chamber. They all danced: François and his beautiful sister, Marguerite, plump little Princess Claude with her poorly disguised limp. The young men of François's entourage, who would follow their ambitious lord into battle in Italy as soon as the opportunity arose. The circles twisted and turned, wheels within wheels. The faces of Joanna Zulian, Guillaume du Chantonnay, Hamon de Bohun, flickered past Toby. He forced himself to face his father's eye, forced himself not to flinch. The nightmares would come later, he knew, when he was alone in the darkness. They always did.

He found himself opposite Eleanor when the dance stopped. He had tried to avoid her, knowing the futility of telling her anything approaching the truth. He hoped to see in her pale, strained face indifference or dislike, but instead he saw despair. Almost three years ago, in England, he had lost the arrogance that once might have led him to think that he could find words of comfort for her. Her dark eyes reflected his emptiness: the emptiness that forced him to work all hours of the day, bullying and beating his men into something worthwhile. So that he would not have to remember his mother's house, with its blank, sad windows. So that he would be something more than Hamon de Bohun's hostage to fortune.

He said, hesitantly, 'You look well, madame.' He knew instantly that she recognized his deceit.

She whispered, 'I look *old*.'

It was true: he could see the tracery of fine lines on her skin, the grey that peppered her tightly bound black hair. But the lineaments of beauty were still there – in the hollow dark eyes, the high brow, the proud tilt of her head.

There was nothing to be said, and yet the silence ached between them. He picked up a thread of a half-heard conversation from the morning's hunt.

'You have a son, I hear, madame.' He saw her gather herself up, a tall, stately woman, as if her reply was a great effort to her.

'His name is Guy,' she said.

He was glad that she had a child. He remembered Eleanor's gentleness, her tenderness with small animals, other people's babies. She should have had half a dozen children. If Hamon de Bohun had taken from her the stepson that she had loved, at least he had fathered the baby she had always longed for.

'You must be proud of your son, madame.'

She stared at him. Then, to his horror, he saw her clamp her fingers over her mouth and begin to shake. He found himself backing away as her laughter, high-pitched and uncontrolled, began to escape from behind her threaded fingers. The music had begun again. Her tall, staggering figure was lost in the bustling crowds.

A voice beside him said softly, 'You have upset my wife, Crow. She is easily unbalanced, I grant you, but I think it better that you do not speak to her again.'

He turned. Hamon de Bohun was beside him. Toby caught a glimpse of Eleanor surrounded by her women at the side of the room.

He said, 'I leave Blois tomorrow.'

It was true: he had been summoned to the presence of the king earlier that evening and given permission to leave Blois the following morning. A bundle of letters bound for Venice was already stitched inside his saddlecloth. He did not know the content of the letters, but he had guessed from the attitude of Louis XII that they would be favourable to Venice. The beginning of lengthy negotiations, no doubt, but it seemed likely that Venice would find herself a new ally.

De Bohun's hand stroked the black satin sleeve of Toby's doublet. 'An appropriate colour, I think, for a carrion crow.'

They were the same height, Toby thought, he and de Bohun. The same height, the same colouring. What never ceased to haunt him was the thought that they might be fired by the same distorted dreams: greed, vengeance and ambition.

He made himself touch de Bohun's cold fingers and remove them from his sleeve. 'I should have died young, shouldn't I?' he said softly. 'But I didn't, did I? Too bloody stubborn, I suppose. Too unwilling to accept what fate doled out to me. Like you, *votre seigneurie*.'

He heard de Bohun's hiss of anger, he heard, more distantly, sobbing, as Eleanor de Bohun's hysterical laughter turned inevitably to tears. Then he turned on his heel and left the room. If he could have left Blois that night, have ridden alone through the darkness and the cold back to the sanity of Venice, he would have.

Joanna saw him go. She was dancing with the Seigneur de Fleurange, the boyhood companion of François d'Angoulême. She had danced all evening – pavanes and galliards and reels – but she had not danced once with Toby Crow, because he had not asked her.

He had not danced with her, he had not even attempted to speak to her. The excitement engendered by the hunt and the banquet and by the wine she had drunk had faded. She made her excuses to the Seigneur, and fled the Great Chamber, looking for silence, for solitude.

The passageways of the château were cold and dark. As the clamour of the banquet faded to nothing, she paused at a window, leaning her hot face against the cold glass. Tonight she had danced and laughed and flirted. She could not remember the names of the men she had danced with. She had behaved, she thought dully, like Guillaume's whore. And Guillaume, like any bawd, had encouraged her.

Outside the rain still fell. Her anger evaporated and a tear slid from her eye. She was weary of Blois, weary of fine clothes and rich food and flowery compliments. She wanted to be back in Brittany with her daughter and her garden. She wanted to walk through the woodland that surrounded the house; she wanted to travel again, all the countries of the world spread out like a vast and glorious tapestry before her. Closing her eyes, she could almost smell the soft scent of Sanchia's skin and the last fading roses in the garden.

That night, Eleanor dreamed.

François was riding through the woodland that surrounded Marigny. His horse was a fine black stallion. The colours of the du Chantonnays, red and yellow, were bright beneath the darkness of the trees.

The stallion caught a hoof in a protruding tree root, and François was thrown. He fell not among the ferns and dead leaves that surrounded him, but into a pond, dark and cold and circular. Eleanor saw how he thrashed about, heard him calling for help. A man stepped out from behind the trees and waded into the pond. Eleanor could see only his silhouette, but she knew that it was Toby. She felt a delicious, drowning warmth, a sense of having come home at last. She watched as Toby took hold of the floundering boy.

Then she saw that instead of helping François from the pond, Toby was pushing him deeper into it. François made no sound, but Eleanor saw the bubbles that rose through the black water, bursting on the surface of the pond. The water was thick and viscous, like honey. François's face was smothered, his frantic movements finally stilled.

She cried out, and slowly Toby turned. Then Eleanor saw how she had been mistaken. The man was not Toby, but Hamon. The dark hair thinned and greyed, the eyes cold and blank, the body heavier, less agile. François floated motionless in the pond. Hamon began to walk towards Eleanor. He was smiling. Eleanor screamed.

Waking, she found herself alone, the first light of dawn filtering through the bedcurtains. At first she could not believe that there was no one else there: she flung aside the curtains, lit with shaking hands a candle on the nearby table, stared wildly around the empty, unfamiliar room. But there was nobody and everything was just as it should have been.

And yet something was different. The fleeting memory that she had struggled for weeks to regain had returned to her, vivid and precise, as if it had never been lost.

She saw herself standing at the window of the gallery in Marigny. The wall, stripped of the unicorn tapestries, was lit by the sun behind her. Her hands were folded over her swollen, pregnant belly. She was worried for François, who had been gone too long. She saw the men coming out of the forest. They were carrying a stretcher. On it lay a motionless bundle which turned Eleanor's apprehension to terror. Then she noticed something else. She saw a figure break off from the small group of horsemen riding down the path. The figure ran over to the stretcher and, kneeling, began to examine the body. She recognized the figure because of the untidy, flailing physician's robes. Guillaume's physician, Martin Gefroy.

Even in her alarm, her grief, it surprised Eleanor that Master Gefroy had not ridden with her stepson's body into the château. But he had not. Instead, Hamon's steward, the one he had engaged to replace bumbling old Stefan, joined the group. And Martin Gefroy rode away.

CHAPTER FOURTEEN

Of all things, Guy de Bohun liked best to ride his pony.

Sometimes his father made him ride the big black stallion. Then the ground seemed a long way away, and his feet could not reach the stirrups. Guy tried very hard not to clutch at the reins, because his father tapped his knuckles with his whip if he clutched the reins. Guy was afraid of the whip.

When his father was away, Guy rode his small dappled pony, Perle. Riding Perle, Guy's small booted feet tucked neatly into the stirrups and his fat little hands reached out confidently to pat the mottled grey mane. He was happiest when his father was away and Master Flore had a stomach-ache. Then one of the stable-lads would lead Perle out of the château to the meadow.

The meadow seemed vast to Guy, the forest that edged it mysterious and sinister. The forest was a magic place, Guy knew, peopled with fairies and wolves. The *loup-garou*, half man, half wolf, with his long, yellow teeth, and his dark, consuming eyes prowled the depths of the forest. Guy's father had eyes like the *loup-garou*: sometimes Guy would stare at him, half expecting to glimpse sharp incisors, pointed ears.

Guy never asked the stable-boy or his nurse to take him into the forest. The meadow was Guy's favourite place. He had once, sliding from Perle's barrel-shaped back, tried to count the flowers. Master Flore had taught him to count, but whenever Guy got beyond twelve the numbers would start muddling themselves up, and he had to start all over again. He decided that there were a thousand flowers in the meadow, because Thérèse had told him about a tapestry belonging to his *maman* which had a thousand flowers sewn on to it. Escaping from his tutor, Guy had clambered around the château one wet March morning, looking for the tapestry that was like the meadow. He had not found it, though, and for his disobedience to his tutor he had received another beating. Afterwards, gulping his misery alone in the nursery, he had understood for the first time in his short life the need to think carefully before acting. He would hide only from Thérèse, he decided, and not from Master Flore. Thérèse would not tell his father. Guy lost the habit of spontaneity before he was three years old.

On the meadow, though, as the warmth of spring began to waken the flowers, he was a small child again. He lay on his back in the grass, staring upwards, wondering at the clouds, the sapphire sky. He imagined himself sitting on a cloud, and could almost feel it, as soft as the softest goose-feather mattress. He thought that if he looked long enough at the vast blue sky he would be able to see beyond, to the heavens.

The return to Marigny was as though someone had woken Eleanor from the trance in which she had lingered since Toby's desertion and her marriage, as though someone had tapped her on the shoulder and said, *Wake. Look around you.*

She woke and, looking round, saw that François was dead, that Marigny had changed, that she was married to a man who rarely acknowledged her existence. She woke and, looking again, saw for the first time the emptiness of the past two and a half years. It was as though she had died and now, unwillingly, was beginning to live again.

In the early hours of the morning thoughts would tumble through Eleanor's head, chaotic at first, then forming into an appalling pattern. Guillaume, warning her that she must marry. To protect herself *and François*. Hamon de Bohun himself, appearing at the gates of Marigny with fifty armed retainers to do his bidding. If she had refused him, would he have forced her? Her own hasty marriage, to protect both her reputation and her unborn child.

François's death. She had not been allowed to pay her last respects to her stepson, had not been permitted to see his body. François had died alone, falling from his horse. Hamon had given François the horse, Hamon had agreed with François that his bodyguard need not be replaced.

What if, she would whisper out loud, what if? What if Hamon de Bohun, acquiring Reynaud's house and lands through his marriage to Reynaud's widow, had decided that Reynaud's son should not inherit? What if, once Eleanor herself had finally proved capable of bearing children, Hamon had decided that the child he believed to be his should be heir to Marigny?

Often, Eleanor thought of what Guillaume had said to her a long time ago at Marigny. '*People kill for land, Eleanor.*'

Back in Venice by the end of January, Toby delivered the king's letters to Andrea Gritti, and then paid a short, irritable visit to the encampment of his soldiers.

Most had returned to their families: the roads were too poor, the weather too foul, to permit much campaigning in winter. A few remained, housed in reasonable comfort on a deserted farm not far from the walls of Padua. Cannon-balls, remnants of the ten thousand or so missiles that the Emperor Maximilian had hurled at Padua during his unsuccessful siege, were still to be found in the hedgerows or sunk in muddy ponds.

'I wouldn't mind,' grumbled Gilles, spitting on the dulled steel of his breastplate, 'if he was civil. Or if there was any point to it all. But it's just bad temper. Too much work, too little to drink, too few women – that's the trouble.' He seized a cloth, and began to rub half-heartedly at the burnished metal. 'Don't you agree, Martin?'

Martin was scribbling something in the flyleaf of a book. The ink-horn was balanced precariously against a stook of hay. 'A malignant humour,' he muttered, blotting the ink with the hem of his robe. 'Black bile, perhaps, leading to moodiness, violent rages and sleeplessness.'

He thought, privately, that Toby's touchiness had a more fundamental cause. Gilles had thrown aside his breastplate, and was shaking straw from a rather splendid cloak. Penniless was disembowelling a hare, ready for the pot.

Martin rose, knocking over the ink. Gilles said optimistically, 'A drink, Martin? The tavern's still open.'

Martin shook his head and, stooping, mopped up the spilt ink with his sleeve. 'The fire-master has a fever,' he said, nodding vaguely in the direction of the tents outside. 'I've made up a cordial for him.'

Outside, it was dark and cold, and bloated flakes of snow floated down from the sky. Martin's feet crunched on the grass and his fingertips were stung by the chilled air. Pulling his robes up to his ears, he walked through the falling snow to the fire-master's quarters. He made the man as comfortable as possible, administering the cordial, soothing with a herbal ointment the rash that covered the unfortunate man's body. Whilst reassuring his patient of his imminent recovery, silently he debated whether fever was transmitted by corrupt air or by contagion. When the fire-master slept, he left the tent.

He was going to return to the barn and Penniless's hare stew, when he saw the candlelight in the window of the farmhouse. Shivering, Martin strode across the icy courtyard, and pushed open the door. Toby was seated at a battered table, his head bent over sheaves of papers and maps, quill pen in hand. The farmhouse and the surrounding fields had been burnt three and a half years ago by the Emperor Maximilian's soldiers during the siege of Padua. Only a few rooms remained intact, their windows hung with sacking in an unsuccessful attempt to keep out the cold, their floor swept clean of burnt straw and litter.

'It's late,' said Martin, when Toby looked up. 'Penniless is cooking – you should join us.'

Toby's head had bent again, his hand began to move across the paper. 'I've eaten.'

Half a loaf of bread lay on the table, a few scraps of cheese beside it. Martin said reasonably, looking at the letter, 'You could leave that until tomorrow. I don't think the Pope will invade Venice just yet.'

The pen paused again.

'The Pope's dying, Martin. They'll be choosing his successor soon. But I doubt' – and Toby pushed his unruly hair out of his face – 'if that'll make much difference to Venice.' He sat back in his chair. The candle on the table underlit the dark rings round his eyes, the set of his mouth.

Martin said again, gently, 'It's late, Toby. Leave it till tomorrow. You're tired.' He saw the crease of irritation gather between Toby's brows.

'Don't fuss, Martin. Keep your sympathy for the ailing babes of Padua – their mamas knock at my door in search of you. I'll finish this letter, and I'll have something to drink. Then I'll go to sleep.'

A dismissive wave of the hand. Martin, looking at him, said, 'No you won't. You'll sit there until dawn. Or you'll walk twenty times round the perimeter of the encampment, annoying the sentries. Or you might even find a pretty girl to take your mind off things for an hour or two. Anything but sleep.'

Toby glared at him.

'I take it you saw Hamon de Bohun at Blois?'

I take it you saw your father at Blois. The unspoken words hovered in the chill air between them.

Toby said softly, 'Damn you, Martin.'

Martin, untroubled, perched on a corner of the table. 'I'm your physician, Toby. You can't go on like this for ever. The candle's been lit in this room every night for the past week.'

Toby still gripped the pen, but he no longer wrote.

'A memorable encounter?' inquired Martin.

The quill pen, flexed beyond endurance, snapped in half. 'Not particularly. A few threats issued, insults exchanged – that sort of thing. The Seigneur de Marigny explained more clearly to me . . . his methods, shall we say, Martin.'

There was a short silence. Then Martin said, 'Such a pity that disease is not more discriminating, I've always thought. The ailment to suit the character, I mean. Monsieur de Bohun would be writhing in agony.'

Toby managed to smile. 'Heresy, my dear physician. Don't let Messer Giustinian hear you.'

A wine-bottle and two cups stood on the mantelpiece. Martin, rising, poured two measures: half a cup for himself, a full one for Toby.

Toby said, 'I saw Joanna, Martin. She was with Guillaume du Chantonnay.'

Martin clutched the pewter cup tightly. He could not even clearly remember Joanna Zulian's face, he thought sadly. But the days – weeks – he had spent with her were still etched vividly in his mind. He could recall entire conversations word for word. And yet he could not feel the warmth of her skin, or picture the precise colour of her eyes. He tried to assimilate the news; he did not want to make a fool of himself again. He remembered that he had told Guillaume du Chantonnay where to find Joanna Zulian.

'She's married to Guillaume?'

Toby shook his head. 'Gaetano Cavazza is still alive, I presume. Joanna is Guillaume's mistress.'

Martin, unable to stop himself, cursed. 'Did you speak to her, Toby?'

Toby grimaced. 'I'm afraid so. I was . . . tactless. Well . . . insulting.'

Martin said painfully, 'Is she happy?'

Toby had gone to the window, was lifting aside the sacking to stare outside at the wind-blown snow.

'Very happy. She is in her element, Martin. Fine clothes, good food, adoring company. What more could she want?'

The undisguised bitterness in his voice took Martin by surprise. Martin almost said, *But you never loved her.* He managed to bite his tongue.

Toby placed the folded letters inside his doublet, and stoppered the ink-horn. Outside, the wind howled, scooping up the snow and hurling it against the ruined walls of the farmhouse.

Martin said, 'I can give you something to make you sleep, if you wish.'

The smile faded. Toby looked very weary, Martin thought.

'I could sleep,' Toby said, rubbing his eyes, 'but I don't want to. I dream, you see, Martin.'

Hamon de Bohun was travelling again. The journey was tiresome, and he particularly loathed riding through the country of his birth. He had travelled through Brittany three years previously, when he had escorted Izabel Mandeville's misbegotten brat to Roscoff, but then he had kept to the coast, avoiding the forest that sprawled inland. Hamon got lost several times, trapped with his entourage in the maze of paths that threaded through the forest. The density of the trees was such that he was unable to distinguish familiar landmarks or keep his bearings. The rain was tumbling from the heavens in drops the size of English pennies and Hamon was beginning to think that the directions he had followed were wrong, when at last he reached Guillaume du Chantonnay's house.

It was tiny compared to Marigny. Even if Guillaume du Chantonnay added it to his larger estates at Nantes, he still could not have competed with Marigny. The thought pleased Hamon and compensated for the discomfort of his soaking furs and velvets, the chill that the forest had settled on him.

He noted the single turret, the lack of a moat, the thatched roof and the unguarded steps running up the side of the house. There were hens pecking in the courtyard, and pigs snuffled in a trough against the wall. Then his gaze wandered to the garden and the fruit trees heavy with pale pink buds. Rain rolled off the furled leaves, made pools in the grass, streamed from the roof and gutters. Hamon de Bohun's eyes lingered on the garden for a moment, and then he walked forward and beat at the door.

He gave his name to the servant, and was led through sparsely furnished rooms to a parlour on the first floor. Then he saw her. She wore a pale gown, and there were jewels in her hair. Staring, trying to focus, he half expected her to hold a dagger in one hand, a severed head in the other.

'Seigneur?'

She had moved forward, away from the oriel window. He realized that her gown was not of bronze silk but of grey velvet, and that the jewels in her hair were amethysts, not pearls. Only at Blois had Guillaume du Chantonnay taunted him with the image of Joanna Zulian as Judith. But Guillaume du Chantonnay was in Nantes: Hamon had made sure of that.

Recovering himself, he bowed. 'Madame Zulian, your servant. I apologize for the unannounced visit, but I was travelling to Roscoff, and became lost in the forest. One of my horses has become lame. The roads are so poor . . .'

She stood only a few feet away from him. He could not take his eyes from her, could not help but compare every feature, every shade of her colouring, with his memory of the picture at Marigny. At Blois, his primary emotion had been one of anger that Guillaume du Chantonnay should have had the temerity to try and provoke him. Now though, alone with her, his emotions were of a different sort.

'You are welcome, *votre seigneurie*. I remember that we met at Blois. Have you travelled far?'

'From Marigny, in Touraine.' Hamon pictured, suddenly, Joanna Zulian at Marigny. Walking in the gallery, riding beside him, sharing his bed . . . Long ago he had replaced physical longing with a different kind of desire: the desire for land, for position, for power. He had believed himself impervious to physical desire.

'The de Bohuns were from Brittany originally,' he said. 'But I married the widow of Marigny a few years ago.'

'Yes,' she said. 'Guillaume told me.'

Jealousy was as unfamiliar to Hamon as desire. It had not been envy he had felt all those years ago, when Reynaud du Chantonnay had usurped Marigny by marrying Blanche, but a cold, intense rage. He would not be bettered. He had known then that his gifts, his talents, outnumbered Reynaud du Chantonnay's by far. And yet Reynaud, by marrying Blanche, had won. Hamon de Bohun's desire for vengeance, his desire for Marigny, had been a simple need to right the balance that Reynaud du Chantonnay's arrogance had upset. In fathering his bastard upon Reynaud's sister, in sending that bastard child to Marigny, to be deposited like some unwanted gift on Reynaud's doorstep, he had tipped the balance resoundingly in his favour. What had happened since – his marriage to Eleanor, the murder of François – had only secured what should have been his years before.

Hamon said smoothly, 'Guillaume du Chantonnay is the cousin of my wife's first husband, as you know. Have you known him long, madame?'

The servant arrived with refreshments. Trays of wine and biscuits were placed on the table.

'I met Monsieur du Chantonnay in Milan, *votre seigneurie* – oh, three and a half years ago. I had been living in Padua, but was obliged to leave before the siege. Monsieur du Chantonnay was wounded. I helped nurse him.'

Hamon was surprised at his sudden surge of anger. He knew that Guillaume, of course, had wanted Marigny. Guillaume, too, had intended to marry the widowed Eleanor. But Guillaume had delayed too long.

Hamon rose, putting aside his wine, and walked to the window. The brilliant pinks and greens and yellows of the garden were blurred by the rain. He recalled Guillaume du Chantonnay's visit to Marigny. Guillaume, ineptly trying to disguise his fury, had walked over to the fireplace and looked up at the picture of Judith and Holofernes. And he, Hamon de Bohun, had said, '*She is an enchantress, isn't she? Marigny is the only setting for her.*'

His anger hardened, as it always did, and turned to ice. He understood that Guillaume du Chantonnay had recognized Joanna Zulian then and had taken her not from love or desire or any other such futile emotion, but as a potentially valuable piece in the game that the du Chantonnays and the de Bohuns played. With Joanna, Guillaume taunted him.

Almost idly, his gaze followed the pattern of the garden: its paths, archways and rose-bushes. He realized, as Guillaume had once realized, that Joanna Zulian had made something new, something different. Something more complex than the gardens of Marigny, its ancient meadow scattered at random with flowers, its straggling kitchen garden hidden out of sight. The garden, irredeemably medieval, was the only aspect of Marigny that Hamon disliked.

'Your garden is exquisite, madame. Did you make it yourself?'

She smiled, and rose to stand beside him. 'Yes, *votre seigneurie*. It is an Italian garden. I copied much of the design from the garden of a villa in Lombardy. It is much smaller, of course. The forest does not permit me to make it any greater.'

He found her physical proximity disturbing. He had believed himself no longer prey to the commoner failings of men: years ago he had realized what fools men made of themselves over women. But now he noticed the fineness of Joanna Zulian's skin, the silkiness of her hair. No shadows or lines marked her face, as they did Eleanor's. Eleanor's looks, never much to Hamon's taste, had deteriorated so much since the birth of the child.

'You are Venetian, I believe, Madame Zulian?'

The leading between the window-panes cast shadows on the pale grey velvet of her gown. 'My father was Venetian, *votre seigneurie*, but my mother was Spanish. I lived in Venice for several years.'

He would have liked to ask her more, but he knew that he must be careful, cautious. He would make inquiries about Joanna Zulian, he needed to understand her. He would possess her, as he possessed Marigny, as he possessed everything that had once belonged to the du Chantonnays. Because he was patient, because he was intelligent, he had always been able to get everything he wanted. And besides, he knew that it was just a question of offering the right price. Three years ago Joanna Zulian had sold herself to Guillaume du Chantonnay. He, Hamon de Bohun, could offer her ten times more than Guillaume. But he would wait, he would be patient. It was not yet time. And besides, the beginnings of an idea, uncertain, half formed, hovered at the back of his mind.

'You should see my garden at Marigny,' he said. He frowned. 'Yes. You will come to Marigny, won't you, Madame Zulian?'

He saw the flicker of surprise in her eyes, and then the small bow of her head.

'I would be honoured, Monsieur de Bohun,' she said.

Eleanor rode to Nantes with only one of her women and a couple of manservants for an escort. She needed time to think, and besides, these days she trusted so few of the servants at Marigny. Hamon had replaced most of those who had served Reynaud with his own men: there was only Berthe in the kitchen and the handful of women she had brought with her to Marigny that Eleanor truly trusted.

She reached Nantes after two days' travelling, arriving at Guillaume's estate in the late afternoon. She thought, as she handed her reins to a groom and let herself be helped out of the saddle, that Guillaume had exaggerated at Blois. A few geese squawked in a corner of the courtyard, but there was not a stook of hay to be seen in the Great Hall. Eleanor sent her serving-woman to the kitchen for refreshment and warmed her hands at the fire.

As she waited for Guillaume's steward to find his master, she considered what she would say. An awkward subject to discuss, she thought, with a rush of slightly hysterical laughter. Murder and usurpation. Hardly parlour talk.

She greeted Guillaume with a smile and a kiss. He was impeccably dressed as usual, but he looked tired and strained. He seated her in a chair and then made a great show of peering out into the courtyard.

'Your respected husband, complete with fifty men-at-arms? They shall have to sleep in the stables, Eleanor. I have not bedchambers for them all . . .'

She shook her head. 'Hamon left Marigny a few days ago, Guillaume. I have only three servants with me – I'm sure you will tuck them in somewhere.'

He glanced at her. She saw the intelligence behind his vivid blue eyes, an intelligence that had, in the early days of her marriage to Reynaud, daunted her. An intelligence, coupled with an icy wit, that had always alarmed poor François.

'Do I understand,' said Guillaume carefully, 'that the Seigneur does not know of your visit?'

Eleanor did not avoid his gaze. 'Someone will tell him, no doubt, after I return. But no, Hamon did not know my intention.'

Guillaume was frowning. She saw him walk slowly to the door to call for his manservant, and she shook her head.

'No, Guillaume. I want neither food nor drink. I need to talk to you. That is why I am here.'

'Without de Bohun's knowledge,' finished Guillaume. 'I had not thought –'

He broke off. Eleanor, looking up at him, said proudly, 'You had not thought that I was capable of disobedience, cousin?' She smiled sadly. 'I have been weak in the past, I know. But I can learn.'

The fire had begun to warm her, and she moved aside some of her layers of furs. She took a deep breath, knowing that she must keep hold of the calmness and rationality that had enabled her to set out on this journey. She must not retreat into the hysteria that had seized her at Blois. She must not behave like the weak woman Guillaume believed her to be.

'What do you wish to talk about, Eleanor?'

'François. I wish to talk to you, Guillaume, about François.'

The shock in his eyes altered quickly to curiosity. Guillaume had sat on a bench by the fire; now he looked up, meeting her gaze. He said nothing to help her, though.

'I have wondered . . .' – Eleanor pressed her nails into her palms – 'I have wondered recently whether François's death was accidental.'

Guillaume's flurry of laughter echoed round the high-ceilinged room. When he had recovered himself, he said, 'As accidental as the beggar who is hanged in the market square for theft, my dear cousin. Or the sheep-stealer who swings from the gibbet at the crossroads.'

She could not speak. She stared at him open-mouthed, wide-eyed, understanding slowly that what to her was a terrible possibility had always been a certainty to Guillaume.

She whispered, '*Hamon* killed François, Guillaume? How do you know?'

He shook his head. There was still a bitter humour in his eyes. 'I have no proof,' he said. 'No one does. The present Seigneur de Marigny is not a foolish man, Eleanor. But I have no doubt, no doubt at all, that François was murdered. It is what Hamon would do.'

The simplicity of his words appalled her. *It is what Hamon would do.* She saw with renewed clarity how directly her own folly and lust had led to François's death.

Eleanor said hoarsely, 'Hamon agreed with François that he did not need another bodyguard. And Hamon bought him the horse. It was not a suitable horse for François, Guillaume. He was always such a poor rider.'

Guillaume shrugged. 'All that proves nothing, Eleanor. Doubtless the lad was dragged from his horse in the forest and put to death. Or perhaps he fell, and de Bohun's henchmen finished off what the boy's incompetence had begun. We shall never know. François is dead and buried; Hamon de Bohun has Marigny. For myself' – and his eyes were hooded, hard – 'I intend to lessen his enjoyment of Marigny as much as possible. There is nothing else I can do.'

She did not understand him. But she said, recalling the day she had watched from the window as François's body had been carried out of the forest, 'I saw your physician, Guillaume. The Englishman, Martin Gefroy.'

Guillaume looked uninterested. Outside, the geese clacked and squawked as someone threw them stale crusts of bread.

'On the day that he died, cousin. You remember that Monsieur Gefroy was treating François's cough. He visited Marigny on the day that François died.'

Now she had Guillaume's attention. Guillaume, frowning, studied her.

'Monsieur Gefroy saw François's body, Guillaume.'

She had to describe everything then. The small procession bearing her stepson's broken body, the arrival of the physician, Martin Gefroy's abrupt departure after he had spoken to Hamon's steward. Eleanor's surprise that the Englishman had not come into the house.

After she had finished, Guillaume was silent for a while. Even the geese had stopped hooting. Eventually, he said: 'Martin Gefroy left my employ soon afterwards, Eleanor. I wasn't at home, unfortunately. I didn't find out about François's death until I returned to Nantes.'

She said tremulously, 'I think that we should speak to him. To Monsieur Gefroy.'

He looked up at her, and to Eleanor's amazement there was a flicker of admiration in his eyes.

'Yes. It would be interesting to know, for instance, why Monsieur Gefroy left my employ quite so precipitately. He was such an appallingly conscientious man.'

She let him rise then, and call for his servants to bring food and drink. While they were waiting, Guillaume said: 'The problem is, cousin, that I haven't the least idea where Martin is. He left no word, you see. He could be anywhere.'

He didn't say it to Eleanor, but it was all too possible, thought Guillaume, that Martin Gefroy was dead. He had been drinking himself into an early grave three years ago when he had been Guillaume's physician. Still, saying his farewells to Eleanor as she headed back to Marigny the following morning, Guillaume promised to search for his missing physician. The prospect interested him, excited him. If Martin had seen François's body, then Martin, a physician, might know how François du Chantonnay had really died. Had Martin Gefroy seen knife-wounds, cudgel marks? Could Martin have left Guillaume's employ so abruptly because he feared the consequences of what he had seen?

Martin's integrity, which Guillaume had always regarded with a sort of amused derision, could become a positive asset. *If*, thought Guillaume, as he watched Eleanor ride out of the courtyard, if Martin Gefroy too had believed François's death to be deliberate, if Martin could be persuaded to make his suspicions public, then he, Guillaume du Chantonnay, could claim Marigny, could take his tiny and fragile baby daughter and hide her behind those strong walls, where she would be safe for ever.

If he could find Martin. The following day Guillaume sent out messengers to the universities of Orléans, Angers and Bourges.

On the twenty-first of February Pope Julius II died, and was succeeded, after lengthy deliberation, by the Cardinal Giovanni de' Medici, who took the name of Leo X. A month later, a treaty was signed at Blois guaranteeing that France and Venice should stand by each other in mutual defence. Venice had secured herself a new and powerful ally; France began to think of regaining the Italian lands that she had lost. Andrea Gritti and Antonio Giustinian, who had carried out the delicate negotiations, heaved large sighs of relief and returned to Venice. Andrea Gritti rewarded Toby Crow with a large sum of money and a house in Venice for his part in the successful conclusion of the treaty. Gritti then escaped from diplomacy for a while and found solace in the arms of his paramour, the nun Celestina.

At Marigny, the workmen had begun to dismantle the old, winding staircase, and to take down, stone by stone, the immense fireplace that had dominated the Great Hall. Hamon intended to build a new staircase, three times the width of the old one, that would rise straight from the centre of the Great Hall to the first-floor gallery. Eleanor hated him for his desecration of Marigny almost as much as she hated him for what he had done to François. It hurt her to see the balustrade and chimneypiece taken down, the lion's head finials abandoned to roar noiselessly in the rain, the leopards and moons carved around the fireplace thrown aside, scarred by workmen's hammers. It hurt her to see the stone-dust tramped through Marigny's passageways, to hear the hammering of mallets and rasping of saws shattering what once had been peace.

Since her conversation with Guillaume, Eleanor had kept to her rooms, increasingly unable to tolerate even the sight of her husband. They lived as two separate people, the brief intimacies of marriage long forsaken.

She refused to accompany her husband to Blois for a second time, and she found herself delighting in the anger her refusal prompted. A small revenge: fear was changing, slowly and inexorably, to anger, as she relived the past three years of her life. The stonemason's hammers beat out the rhythms of her hatred, as she fitted pieces together like a child's puzzle. She understood at last that Hamon de Bohun had always wanted Marigny, that he had intended to marry Reynaud's widow and kill Reynaud's son from the beginning.

She ate alone in her rooms, she walked only in the meadow that Hamon disliked. Once, she encountered her son there riding a squat dappled pony, laughing with his nurse at the sky, the flowers, the birds. She greeted her dark-eyed child as she would have greeted a chance acquaintance, but she remembered what Hamon had said to her at Blois, when she had first sighted Toby Crow. '*I thought he was dead.*'

She began to wonder then whether she had also lost Toby to Hamon. She would never know the truth, she thought. She watched the child ride round the château until he was out of sight, and she felt her fear of Hamon alter inexorably to loathing and spite. She felt herself becoming a hard, brittle creature, someone who wanted the whole world to know what Hamon de Bohun had done. She gloried in her lack of fear. If she was unafraid of Hamon, if she feared neither his tongue nor his arm, then he could not hurt her. Since he had taken away from her everything that she had valued, she had nothing left to lose. She could take her revenge – François's revenge – in whatever way was open to her, because, when it came to it, she placed no value at all upon her own life.

But she knew herself to be as powerless as ever, trapped by her sex and her physical weakness, unable to procure the sort of vengeance she would have chosen. As the coloured lights startled the perimeter of her vision and the pounding began behind her eyes, Eleanor walked back towards her rooms before the headache blinded her.

Guillaume's messengers had returned from the universities of Angers, Orléans and Bourges. They had found no trace, though, of Martin Gefroy, Guillaume du Chantonnay's English physician.

The excitement that Guillaume had felt when Eleanor had suggested searching for Martin Gefroy began to fade. The English physician was dead or wandering in some forgotten byway of the world, never to be seen again. Or had been silenced by Hamon de Bohun years ago, so that his body now lay in a leafy ditch, the flesh eaten away by worms. He was too late: it was his principal weakness, Guillaume thought, his failure to seize the moment.

He sent his servants out again, though. Further afield, this time, to Heidelberg, Louvain and Paris. Doubt gnawed at him, but he struggled against it. While he waited for his messengers' return, Guillaume readied his horses, his armour and his most trusted men-at-arms to ride with him to Italy. The duties of his class weighed heavily on Guillaume: at night his dreams were gaudy with images of violence. Scenes of past wars played out for him over and over again, making nightmares of hideous intensity. Through them flitted a figure of a girl. She wore a green gown, and she cried out when he hurt her. Sometimes her green gown was bloodstained, sometimes her skin was scarred, pocked by disease. Sometimes she had fair hair and blue eyes. Sometimes her face was Sanchia's face.

When she rode out of the forest and saw the château for the first time, she reined in her horse and just looked.

One of her servants said, 'Madame?' but Joanna shook her head, and slid off her horse and stood, still looking.

Mirrored by the moat, swans glided, small and pale and perfect, crossing and recrossing the reflected image of the château. In the water the pale, smooth turrets shimmered and the delicate pinnacles seemed almost ready to float away into the sky. The meadow, to either side of the path, was scattered with flowers: daisies and periwinkle and clover dancing in the breeze. The scent of grass and flowers was heavy in the warm air.

You could have lost, Joanna thought, both Uncle Taddeo's house and Gaetano's house in the château de Marigny. The ruined villa in Italy, which she had thought so splendid, had been but a fraction of this. Even the king's court at Blois seemed dull by comparison.

Swallows pitched and swooped around the high walls of the château. A light breeze ruffled Joanna's hair. There was a silence, a stillness: the distant tiny swans seemed made of ivory, the moat a polished looking-glass. She thought herself out of place: she, who had been born in a shabby tent, who had been homeless for the first twelve years of her life. Sometimes she found it hard to believe what she had become, what Guillaume du Chantonnay had made of her. Now, the silk hem of her gown brushed the soft grass, and three servants paused on the path behind her.

A ripple of laughter broke the silence. A little boy was playing on the meadow not far from where a plump woman, presumably his nursemaid, dozed in the shade of the trees. Wholly absorbed in his games, the child did not notice Joanna. Picking up her skirts, she walked towards him. She understood that the boy was counting. Numbers in random order fluttered through the air as he pulled flowers from the lawn. Every now and then he would stumble over the hem of his long-clothes and fall laughing to the ground.

He had gathered a large bunch of flowers: as he added to it, clovers and daisies slipped from his grasp, scattering the lawn. Laboriously he picked them up again. He was older than Sanchia – about three years old, Joanna guessed. This child was the opposite of her fair, tiny daughter – a dark-haired, dark-eyed, sturdy, pink-cheeked little boy. Joanna thought painfully of her own son, Paolo. He had been dark-haired: had he lived he would now have been four years old.

As she approached, he looked up. Caution replaced the laughter. Joanna smiled at him. 'Good day to you, sir. What pretty flowers.'

Squatting on the grass, he still clutched his bouquet. He had large blue eyes and a mop of black hair. His expression was serious, thoughtful. He stumbled to his feet. 'Good day to you, madame.' His head bobbed, the hand holding the flowers sketched a careful bow.

She sat down on the grass beside him, her skirts spread out around her. 'My name is Joanna. Will you tell me your name?'

'Guy,' he said. 'My name is Guy de Bohun.'

He was, then, the Seigneur de Marigny's only son. This pretty infant was the heir to all that surrounded her: château, meadow, forest. Every acre of it, every tree, every flower, every stream, would one day belong to him. Oddly, Joanna found that she felt sorry for Guy de Bohun.

'Won't you show me your flowers, Guy?' she said gently. 'Shall I tell you their names?'

A pause, and then Guy held out the battered blooms.

'This is clover,' she said. 'And this a forget-me-not. And these are daisies. If you fall over and bruise yourself, a poultice of daisies will take away the bruise within a day.'

The beginnings of a smile flickered again in his solemn eyes, and then he looked beyond Joanna. 'Papa,' he whispered.

The flowers slipped from his grasp, the smile died. Joanna, hearing footsteps behind her, rose to her feet. The Seigneur de Marigny was crossing the meadow to join her.

'Madame Zulian. I cannot tell you what pleasure your visit gives me.'

The Seigneur bowed and kissed her hand. He wore crimson velvet; it was difficult, she thought, to estimate his age. His hair was greyed, his face lined, but there was vigour in his movement, power and strength in his frame.

He turned to his son. 'Should you not be at your lessons, Guy?'

'Master Flore had a stomach-ache, sir.' The child's voice was almost inaudible.

The nurse had woken and was hurriedly brushing grass and leaves from her skirts.

Hamon du Bohun said, 'Speak clearly, Guy, and stand up straight. The heir to Marigny must not cower like a servant.'

The child's eyes darted from side to side. The nurse took his hand.

'A more profitable employment could be found for my son, don't you agree, Thérèse?' said de Bohun.

The nurse reddened, and bobbed another curtsy, mumbling an apology.

De Bohun turned back to Guy. 'Dairymaids and farmer's daughters gather flowers, Guy. Such pastimes are not suitable for gentlemen.'

De Bohun reached out, intending to draw the child towards him. But Guy stepped back, avoiding his touch. Joanna, watching, saw the expression on the child's face. She understood suddenly that Guy de Bohun was very, very afraid of his father.

'Guy.' De Bohun's voice was sharp. 'You are uncivil, sir. You will go to your room.'

The nurse took the child's hand, half dragging him back across the meadow. De Bohun frowned.

'I must apologize, Madame Zulian, for my son's manners. He shall be taught better.'

He took her arm. For a moment, Joanna found herself wanting to pull away, to shrink from his touch as the child had done. But that was ridiculous. She had nothing to fear from Hamon de Bohun.

An untidy kitchen garden was hidden behind the back of the house. A dovecote, a huge circular brick structure, was built on the slope between the kitchen garden and the forest. An orchard of plum, apple and pear trees merged with the encircling forest.

'You like to make gardens, don't you, Madame Zulian?' De Bohun's hand briefly touched Joanna's. 'Tell me, if you were to make a garden for Marigny, where would you start? What would you do?'

Joanna smiled. She imagined making a garden for Marigny, with its limitless acres of land. She looked around her.

'I would start with the kitchen garden. I would set the new garden to the right – the aspect is better, Monsieur de Bohun, and I suspect that the soil is richer too.'

She began to walk through the straggling rows of cabbages and carrots, looking to left and right. 'In monasteries in Spain and France they make kitchen gardens that are divided into squares – like chessboards. Each square is differently planted. And the colours – the colours are glorious. Green and red and gold . . .'

'And then?' he said. 'After the kitchen garden, what would you do, Madame?'

Her gaze drifted upwards, upwards, beyond the moat and the walls of the château, across the towers and the roofs, to the topmost point of the highest pinnacle. She imagined herself looking down from the highest window of that pinnacle to the garden below. She saw then, so vividly, the garden that she would make. Its colours, its plants, its trees and paths. Its meaning. It was as though the scrubby turf was already dug and planted, as though the flowers had rooted and bloomed.

'Then I would make a flower garden. I saw one in Italy – it was like paradise. You would be able to see it from your topmost tower, seigneur. Look.' Joanna pointed to the round, pepperpot-shaped tower. 'It would be like looking down at a tapestry.'

Hamon de Bohun was looking neither at the garden nor the tower, but at her. 'Make your garden for me, madame.'

She thought at first that she had misheard him. Then her hands clenched together, and she turned and looked up at him. She couldn't speak.

He shook his head. 'I apologize for my presumption, madame. You are offended. Forgive me.'

'I am not . . . offended.' She closed her eyes for a moment, dizzy with longing. 'Do you mean it? Would you really let me make a garden for Marigny?'

He took her elbow, turning her so that she no longer saw the château, but only the garden that he would permit her to remake spread out before her. She felt the beginnings of an unquenchable excitement well up in her, and found herself unable to protest her lack of experience. If she wondered why Hamon de Bohun should choose her then she pushed that thought aside.

'All this?' she asked, spreading her hands wide to gesture at the garden in front of her. 'All this, seigneur?'

He nodded. 'All this,' he said, softly. 'And more, if you wish it, madame. Will you help me?'

She had a sudden, vivid memory then of the Seigneur de Marigny as she had first seen him at Blois. His furs were soaked by the rain, his boots spattered with mud, but her impression had been one of power, of a ruthless strength barely contained by the courtesies forced upon him. She had thought then of claws sheathed, voracious eyes gleaming.

She gave her assent, though. Because she wanted to make the finest garden in France. And because she wanted to be something other than Guillaume du Chantonnay's whore.

The woman that her husband had engaged to redesign the garden was Guillaume's mistress, Madame Zulian. Over the long, hot weeks of summer she visited Marigny frequently. Often, Eleanor watched her from the uppermost room of the tower.

She had seen the woman before, of course. At Blois and, long before that, at Marigny. At Blois, Eleanor had recognized Guillaume's mistress as the model for Hamon's picture of Judith and Holofernes. She had always hated that picture: she thought it both cruel and lecherous.

When Joanna Zulian visited Marigny, Eleanor, hidden in the tower, would watch the tiny figures moving in the garden below – the gardeners and labourers that Hamon had engaged to do the heaviest work, Hamon himself, of course, and, increasingly often, Eleanor's own small son, Guy. Eleanor would see Guy peering out from the thickly leaved boughs of the pear trees, or crouched in the feathery darkness of the dovecote. He reminded Eleanor of Toby, then: someone who watched and waited, someone who had learned caution and self-protectiveness. When Guy finally crept out of the undergrowth to speak to Guillaume's whore, Eleanor felt, to her surprise, an unexpected bitterness.

From the tower, she witnessed the progress of the garden. The clearing of the old, scrubby grass; the digging-in of dung and horse manure; the levelling of the ground; the pegging-out with sticks and twine of the new beds; the raking, the hoeing, the planting. Patterns emerged out of nothing: criss-crosses, mazes, whorls. As she watched, Eleanor's hands would fiddle constantly with the pendant she wore round her neck, and her eyes would become dark and angry.

In the turret, Eleanor watched and waited, nurturing her hatred.

In May, the French army marched into Italy. At the beginning of June the French, preparing to lay siege to the town of Novara, found themselves surprised by an unexpected Swiss attack.

For Guillaume, the battle of Novara was a reworking of an old nightmare: Ravenna, with its mud, marsh and carnage. Artillery-shot pierced armour, making holes in visors and breastplates. The ground was churned to a sticky swamp. Faces, colours, plumes, were black with mud. Again Guillaume had to dismount from his horse and fight hand to hand. Again the slaughter was immense.

There was a difference, though. Instead of gaining a victory, the French were routed. Panicking, they fled, abandoning their hopes of regaining Milan. Reaching the Alps, the great army of Louis de France straggled back over the mountains, their invasion ended.

Guillaume du Chantonnay, however, did not return to France. After Novara, he fell ill, as he had at Ravenna. But this time it was worse. A gnawing pain in his belly made him double up in agony and his entire body was soaked in sweat. For a fortnight he was bedridden in a tavern in the foothills of the Alps, eating nothing but paps and gruel. Like Sanchia, he thought, seeing in his mind's eye his baby daughter laughing as her nurse fed her her breakfast.

The tavern was a midden, the bed infested. When his fever rose, Guillaume could see the bugs scurrying across his pillow, but was too weak to crush them. He had his servants change the linen daily, but the straw mattress was crawling. He knew that he could not survive the five or ten miles' journey to a cleaner tavern. He thought, as the last remnants of Louis XII's great army left Italy, that he would not fight for his king again. He would make his excuses, he would seek advancement another way.

Lying in his insect-infested bed, Guillaume's thoughts drifted again to Hamon de Bohun, to Marigny. He needed Marigny for Sanchia, as well as for himself. Many miles from home, Guillaume wondered whether he had been wise to allow Joanna to go to Marigny. To *encourage* Joanna to go to Marigny. To dangle his beautiful mistress in front of Hamon de Bohun like a rare and glittering jewel, something without which even Marigny would be incomplete. Doubt gnawed at him again, worse even than his sickness.

He recalled his first meeting with Joanna, in Milan. His servants had been dragging him through the streets in that damned cart, and then suddenly there was Toby Crow, who had once been Reynaud's courier. Even then, fearing for his life and his limbs, Guillaume had noticed the beautiful girl who stood beside Reynaud's courier. Later, Joanna and the English physician had cared for him.

It was evening. Several hours had passed since Guillaume had last eaten, and the pain had subsided a little. The pain was always worse after a meal. Guillaume managed to haul himself to a sitting position. You could not think clearly stewing in your own sweat, watching the bedbugs crawl across your pillow. He realized suddenly how stupid he had been, and he cursed aloud, waking his dozing page-boy. Martin Gefroy was not attending the universities of Angers, Orléans or Bourges. Nor, Guillaume had discovered before he had left France, did he study at Heidelberg, Louvain or Paris.

He began to issue his orders before his servants had rubbed the sleep from their eyes. They would ride, Guillaume told them, to the universities of Ferrara, Pavia and Bologna. Guillaume knew, with utter certainty, that Martin Gefroy had gone to Italy.

With Toby Crow, of course.

At Marigny, the garden had begun to take shape in the newly cleared earth. In Finistère, Joanna had found pen and paper and had sketched out the garden she would make, just as she had once sketched on the canvases in Taddeo Zulian's studio. She coloured the design with dyes from the flowers and herbs in her garden – the blue of the leeks, the jade-green of the feathered carrot-tops, the red-veined leaves of the beetroot. The herb-garden would be octagonal in outline; inside it, the herbs, with their small, differently shaded leaves, would weave a complicated pattern. As a child, she had once seen a ceiling with a similar design in a Moorish palace in Granada. Over and over again, she had tried to follow the golden, labyrinthine pattern.

She rode to the garden of Marigny every month or so, but she rarely entered the house. Riding through the wooded highlands of Brittany, or watching her own creation take shape in the turned earth, Joanna was happy. She refused Hamon de Bohun's offers to accommodate her in the château: if necessary, she stayed overnight in a tavern in the nearby village. She admitted to herself that she did not trust Hamon de Bohun, that she found the château de Marigny with its countless rooms and limitless treasures daunting – stifling, even. It was the garden she wanted, only the garden. Not to possess, but to create, to see her ideas grow and flower in the sunlight.

She tried to befriend one of the inhabitants of Marigny, but it was as difficult as getting close to one of the wild birds that pecked at the newly turned earth. She would glimpse Guy de Bohun watching her, hidden in the branches of a fruit tree in the orchard or peeping out from behind the curved walls of the dovecote. If she pretended not to notice him, he would edge cautiously closer to her, creeping through the tall grass that lay between the dovecote and the garden. If she waved or called to him, he would scurry away.

One day Joanna brought sweetmeats with her from home. Sitting at the edge of the half-made garden, her skirts gathered around her, she spread them out on the grass. When she heard him approach, she turned and smiled, holding out a gilt gingerbread pig. Guy was half hidden by the long grass. He stared at her, his eyes dark with excitement and fear. If she moved too fast or said the wrong thing, he would be gone, seeking refuge in the apple tree or disappearing behind the brick dome of the dovecote.

But this time he did not run away. Guy crept cautiously towards her, his gaze fixed on the tiny golden pig. Sunlight sparkled on the moat and lit the topmost towers of Marigny. Still staring at the sweetmeat, he reached Joanna's side, his small feet touching the hem of her gown.

'It is for you, Guy,' she said gently, placing the gingerbread pig in his lap. Hesitantly, he touched it, stroking the gold-painted surface.

'Do you like him?'

Guy nodded. He was almost smiling.

'A friend of mine has a great fat pig called Hortense. She eats a bucketful of apples and acorns every day.'

Guy whispered, 'Does Hortense have a little curly tail?'

'She has a little curly tail and a long snout. She snuffles like this . . .' Joanna made a snorting sound. Guy giggled and then clamped his hand over his mouth to silence himself.

'There, I have made you smile, Guy de Bohun. Now, eat your pig, and when I visit you again I shall bring you a gingerbread horse.'

He said, through a mouthful of gingerbread, 'Like Perle?'

'Is Perle the name of your pony? That is a splendid name for a splendid pony.'

Guy began to tell her about his pony. Perle had jumped the little brook that lay between the dovecote and the forest; Perle cantered as fast as the wind. In his excitement, Guy dropped the gingerbread pig. He leaned forward, searching in the long grass for the scattered gilt crumbs.

His silk shirt slipped from his shoulder and Joanna saw the red weals across his back. There were scars underneath. Horrified, she said without thinking: 'Did you fall from your pony, Guy?'

He shook his dark, curly head. He gathered the crumbs of gingerbread; carefully, he picked off the ladybirds and strands of grass that stuck to them. 'I never fall from Perle.'

'But you have hurt your back . . .'

Guy looked up at Joanna, and then his gaze anxiously shifted from the garden to the château. 'I was a bad boy.'

Joanna only just caught the whispered words. Then, hearing and understanding, she could not for a moment speak. Sickened, she watched as Guy's lip trembled and his small plump fingers wound together. She wanted to take him in her arms, to hug and kiss him. But she knew instinctively that the moment she reached out to him, he would run away and hide again.

Joanna said, very gently, 'You are a good boy, Guy. You are the best boy I have ever met. I will visit you again, and I shall bring you a gingerbread horse that looks just like Perle.'

The summer progressed, hazy with heat. Salad rocket and sea kale, Good King Henry and rock samphire, pushed through the earth at Marigny. Sage and plantain, borage and honeysuckle, flowered in the herb beds. Great clouds of bees and butterflies sucked nectar from the blossom.

Joanna made the gingerbread horse herself, adding a small plaited mane and a dusting of finely ground sugar. She made another, smaller, horse for Sanchia, and sat with her in the garden in Brittany, watching while the baby chewed and sucked at the gingerbread. Sanchia was a year old now, a bright, happy, affectionate infant. She could take a few tottering steps; she could, to Joanna's immense pride, lisp, 'Mama.' She was adored, as was her due, by both her parents. She was disciplined, only occasionally, by her doting nurse. Her hair, a curly pale gold, already touched her shoulders. Guillaume would not allow it to be cut.

Joanna wrote letters to Agnès and Guillaume. She sent the letter for Guillaume to Blois, trusting that it would be forwarded to Italy. The day after she had sent the letter, news reached her of the disaster of Novara. She wondered whether Guillaume was alive or dead; whether Sanchia still had a father, whether she and her daughter were still entitled to live in the small house in the forest. The precariousness of her situation alarmed her, but then she thought of Marigny and Guy de Bohun. Sanchia was happy, well-cared for, unafraid. There were no bruises, no weals on her slender back. Joanna knew that she would not for the world have changed her daughter's future with that of Guy's.

At Marigny the spring and summer plantings had been completed: leaves, green and red and jade, began to open out to the sun. Watching her garden come to life, Joanna made small adjustments. A path to be widened here, a bush to be trimmed there. At the corners of each of the squares she made double archways, training vines or damson trees over them. Bay trees, planted in terracotta pots, punctuated the corners of the squares. Joanna dusted the shiny green leaves, breathing in their scent. Sometimes she would kneel in the earth to free a plant from a choking weed, or to clip a tiny apple tree to the exact height she wanted. She fed the thirsty plants with a bucket of water from the moat while Guy made mud pies beside her. His plump hands patted the mud into indistinguishable shapes: a castle, a mountain, a river.

A shadow fell over them, blue-black on the pale dusty ground.

'I shall have the gardeners flogged, Madame Zulian – you should not be doing such work.'

Joanna saw Guy's face whiten and the clods of mud slip through his fingers. She took the child's small dirty hand before he could run away and rose to her feet. 'I like to grub in the earth, *votre seigneurie*. And I apologize for my appearance – and for Guy's. I asked him to help me.'

'To your rooms, sir.'

De Bohun's voice was sharp. Guy scurried away, zigzagging along the paths of the kitchen garden.

Hamon de Bohun said, 'There is no need to apologize, madame. You look exquisite, as always. Please allow my servants to find you water and towels. And then you must take a glass of wine with me.'

He walked at Joanna's side through the half-finished garden. She saw him glance at the neat rows and squares with pride.

'You have done well, madame. I congratulate you. You are making a garden that does justice to Marigny.'

He took her arm, leading her back around the château towards the moat. The old kitchen garden had been harvested now: in the rows of earth a few yellowed leaves wilted in the heat.

'What next, madame?' Hamon de Bohun turned to Joanna. 'The orchard . . . the meadow . . .?'

She would not, thought Joanna, touch the meadow. The meadow was beautiful: the meadow, Guy had confided to her one day, was his favourite place.

She surveyed the remains of the old kitchen garden. 'If you wish it, seigneur, I shall make a flower garden here.'

He looked down at her. 'A garden you can see from the highest tower?' he said. 'A garden that will be a tapestry of flowers?'

She smiled. He led her into the house, calling for his servants. In a splendidly furnished bedchamber, Joanna plunged her hands and face into water perfumed with clove carnations and dried her face on a towel as soft as thistledown. Studying herself in a silver mirror, she rearranged her hair and shook the dust from her gown.

Afterwards, the maidservant escorted her back to Hamon de Bohun. Walking down winding stairways and through splendid chambers, she marvelled at how Marigny glittered – with ornaments of gold, with silken wall-hangings, with coloured glass. The château seemed to catch the sun, to magnify it, to seize the colours of the spectrum and intensify them. The pictures, the tapestries, the gold and silver, dazzled her. She felt dazed, diminished by the wealth that surrounded her.

She was shown into a large chamber that overlooked the meadow. Hamon de Bohun stood at one end of the room, a glass of wine in his hand.

He raised the glass. 'To Judith,' he said.

She did not at first understand him. Then, turning her head, she followed the direction of his gaze and saw the painting on the wall.

Judith and Holofernes. Judith's face was her own.

CHAPTER FIFTEEN

'The painting is very fine, don't you think, madame? I came across it several years ago. One of my better purchases, I think.'

Joanna could not speak. She had last seen the painting in Gaetano's studio in Padua. When she looked at it, she imagined herself back in that studio, pearls in her hair, a length of bronze silk tied round her waist. Hating Gaetano, hating the empty-headed manikin that she had become.

'It has given me such pleasure,' said de Bohun softly, 'to watch you over the past months. When I saw you at Blois, it was as though you had stepped from the frame. Art translated to reality.'

Frightened, confused, her mind darted back to her first meeting with Hamon de Bohun. At Blois, she had worn a bronze silk gown and she had threaded pearls through her hair. It had been Guillaume who had insisted that she wear that gown, those jewels. Sun still streamed through the windows of the Great Chamber, but a chill had touched her. Joanna shivered.

'Drink your wine, my dear Joanna – I may call you Joanna, mayn't I? And sit down – you are tired, you have laboured too long.'

She didn't sit down, nor did she take the glass of wine that he held out to her. She went instead to a window and looked out at the moat, the meadow and the winding path that led from the forest. Anything other than that painting.

'You were the painter's model?'

He was standing behind her. They did not touch, but she was very aware of his nearness. She felt small and powerless.

'I was the painter's wife,' she said. Her voice was hoarse. 'I *am* the painter's wife.'

'Ah.' A soft sound, like a sigh. De Bohun's hand touched Joanna's shoulder: comforting, fatherly. 'But now you are the Sieur du Chantonnay's mistress.'

The chill altered to warmth; she felt colour flood her cheeks.

'I married Gaetano Cavazza when I was very young, seigneur. It was not a happy marriage. I left him and came to France – I was penniless and without friends. The Sieur du Chantonnay was generous enough to offer me both a home and friendship.'

Not true. It was not friendship that Guillaume had offered her. What promises he had made he had kept: she had comfort, independence, some sort of place in society, a measure of security. But not, of course, love. Guillaume loved Sanchia, he did not, Joanna had always known, love her.

De Bohun said, 'I could offer you something better, madame.'

One of his fingers had begun to stroke the soft skin at the back of her neck. She did not move. She did not dare move.

'You must let me reward you for your labours. Think – I can offer you so much more than poor Guillaume. Look at my house, Joanna, look at my lands. Have you ever seen such splendour? And each day, each month, I strive to make Marigny more beautiful. One day it will outshine even the palaces of the king, don't you agree?'

He had bent his head, she felt his lips brush her neck.

'How can I possibly recompense you for what you have done for me – for Marigny? What do you want, Joanna? Money, jewels, a house? I can give you all that. I can give you whatever you desire.'

She was caught between de Bohun and the window. Joanna's heart pounded, his hand and mouth still caressed her neck. She felt nauseated, trapped. What she wanted was to be outside, running up the long winding path that led through the forest, away from Marigny.

She forced herself to turn and face him. 'Guillaume gives me all that, seigneur. Truly, I want nothing other than to make the garden. That is all.'

She saw the flicker of surprise on his face, the momentary bewilderment. His hands slid slowly from her shoulders and rested lightly on her upper arms.

Part of her mind still struggled to work it all out: the portrait, Guillaume's suggestion, years ago, that she become his mistress. A voice said, *'I want to warn you about Guillaume du Chantonnay.'* Toby Crow's voice.

Nothing made sense. She felt a weariness: from her journey, from the work in the garden. And, stronger that that, a sense of aching disquiet. A realization that there were secrets she had not been permitted to know, motives she had not been meant to guess.

'I would much rather,' said de Bohun softly, 'possess the woman than the painting.'

She almost picked up her skirts then, almost pushed past him and ran from the room like a scullery-maid pursued by her lecherous master. But the door opened, and Eleanor de Bohun came into the room.

'Husband,' she said. Eleanor's dark eyes glittered.

'I must congratulate you on the garden you are making, madame. A fine piece of work.'

Eleanor's gaze moved slowly from Joanna to Hamon de Bohun. Hamon's hand still rested on Joanna's sleeve.

Eleanor smiled. 'Was my husband paying you for your services, Madame Zulian?'

Joanna did not stay in the village of Marigny that night, but rode fast towards Nantes, towards Brittany, leaving her servants struggling to keep up with her. She wanted to leave behind the shock and humiliation of her interview with the de Bohuns. She wanted to be alone. She wanted to think. She wanted to try and remember clearly what Toby Crow had said to her at Blois. Most of all, she wanted to work out how Hamon de Bohun had acquired the painting of Judith and Holofernes.

Eventually, listening at last to her servants' pleadings, Joanna agreed to take rooms in a tavern overnight. She could not rest, though, her anger and misery kept her wide awake. She walked out alone, tramping up and down beside the river that lay beyond the tavern's untidy kitchen garden. She couldn't look at the clumps of drought-wizened cabbages and yellowed turnips without thinking of Marigny, and her garden, and Guy de Bohun. She did not think that she would ever go back to Marigny. She could have wept both for her garden and for Guy.

The river was cloudy, foetid, fringed with bullrushes. Dragonflies darted above the water, catching the last rays of the setting sun. When she was tired of walking, Joanna stood on the bridge over the river, her arms resting on the parapet, and stared down at the dark green water. She thought, continually, of Hamon de Bohun, and of Guillaume du Chantonnay.

She had no doubt that Guillaume had seen the painting of Judith and Holofernes at Marigny, no doubt that he had chosen her as his mistress solely because he had recognized her as the model for Gaetano's painting. He had seen her portrait, he had persuaded Martin Gefroy to tell him where to find her, he had searched Bourges for her. And then he had given her a house and servants, clothes and jewels, and a darling baby daughter. Eventually, he had taken her to Blois. Not to show her to the king and the court, but to show her to Hamon de Bohun. He had dressed her in bronze silk and pearls, and he had presented her to the Seigneur de Marigny. Why?

Frowning, running her hands through her tangled hair, Joanna repeated Toby's words to herself once again: *'I want to warn you about Guillaume du Chantonnay.'* To warn her that Guillaume was using her in some private quarrel with Hamon de Bohun.

The sun sank below the horizon: the river was lit only by fireflies and the pale sickle moon. Joanna looked down into the dark water, and part of the puzzle fell into place. Gaetano had sold the picture of Judith and Holofernes to his patron, the Venetian Marcantonio Venier. On the day that she had tried to rescue the kitten from the canal, Toby had been at Messer Venier's house, buying pictures and artefacts to take back to his employer, Reynaud du Chantonnay. Could Toby have bought Gaetano's painting for the former Seigneur de Marigny?

Joanna went back to the tavern. In the morning she rode with two of her servants for Brittany. She sent the other, bearing a letter, to Blois, where she had last seen Toby Crow.

After Joanna Zulian had gone, Hamon de Bohun hit Eleanor once, hard across the face. She staggered backwards, tripping over her skirts, falling sprawled on the floor. He noticed, though, that she did not look frightened. Instead, she dragged herself to her feet and, without even glancing at him, walked unsteadily out of the room. He thought then of going to the stables and fetching the whip, and punishing her as he punished Guy. But he did not. Something stopped him.

Hamon de Bohun found himself possessed by a mixture of emotions. His anger with Eleanor seemed somehow less important than his sense of shock that Joanna had refused him. He had never considered that she might refuse him.

Leaving the château, walking out in the twilight, he criss-crossed the chequerboard pattern of the kitchen garden, and reached the spot where he had discovered her that afternoon. Guy's abandoned mud pies were baked hard by the sun; Joanna's trowel lay beside a clump of plants. Hamon felt, for the first time in his life, a feeble flickering of regret.

It was intolerable, he thought, that he should not have Joanna Zulian.

Intolerable that a du Chantonnay should continue to possess her. He knew that the situation must be salvaged, reparations must be made. He would write to her, would offer profuse apologies both for his own clumsy advances and for Eleanor's insult, and assure her that such a scene would never take place again.

What did she want, though? What did she want? In the dying light of the evening, the question plagued him. He had offered her a house, money, jewels, and still she had refused him. He had shown her Marigny, he had made it plain to Joanna Zulian that he had many times what Guillaume du Chantonnay had to offer. And yet she wanted the garden, only the garden.

Well, then, she would have the garden. Hamon could not bear that Joanna should return to Guillaume du Chantonnay and never visit Marigny again. She would come back to him, he thought, and she would make her flower garden, her garden that would be like a tapestry.

His customary certainty, his self-assurance, returned as he walked through the kitchen garden towards the orchard. The warm evening air was filled with the buzzing of bees and the scents of lavender and honeysuckle. Hamon knew that Joanna Zulian's refusal of him was merely a counter in the game that she, like all her sort, played. He had not yet offered her the right price, that was all.

As he walked, it occurred to him for the first time that what Joanna Zulian wanted from him was, perhaps, marriage. She would not be the first base-born but beautiful young woman to want a name, a position, as well as money. Her temerity both offended and fascinated him.

Yet there was still Joanna's husband, the painter Gaetano Cavazza. Guillaume du Chantonnay taunted Hamon with a woman who wanted the ultimate prize, yet who was not free herself to claim that prize. Hamon de Bohun experienced a flicker of respect for Guillaume du Chantonnay.

Guillaume's servants straggled slowly back to him across the war-torn north of Italy. Guillaume had removed himself to a better tavern; the fever had gone, so that he was able to eat and sleep a little. Martin Gefroy, said his returning servants, was not to be found at the universities of Pavia, Ferrara or Bologna. Guillaume, standing at the window, groaned; his stomach clenched and twisted. But someone, added one of his servants hesitantly, had heard that Martin Gefroy was in Italy. Not attending a university, but working for a band of mercenaries in the pay of Venice. The mercenaries were led by a man nicknamed *Il Cornacchia.* Guillaume blinked, and rubbed the sweat from his forehead. 'The Crow, my lord,' said the servant helpfully, and the breath caught in Guillaume's throat.

They left the next day. After the humiliating rout of the French, the Venetian troops had retreated hastily back to the Veneto, isolated once more and threatened by the armies of the Holy League. Guillaume, enduring dangerous roads and uncomfortable taverns, drank milk and ate soft bread: anything else gave him agony. He thought, with bitter humour, that he had another reason now to seek out Martin Gefroy, his former physician. His illness gnawed at him: he had lost weight, the bones had begun to show through his skin, and his eyes were dulled. To ride was to journey through purgatory. Only his hunger for Marigny, his fear for the future, kept him in the saddle.

He lost track of the days and weeks. Survival became all-important: forcing some food down his throat, staying on horseback. He lost one of his manservants to a fever in Mantua, another to a band of brigands somewhere near Roviga. His progress was erratic, dictated by the poor state of his health and the sporadic fighting. He disguised his nationality as far as he was able, he paid out a fortune in bribes. Money bought information from soldiers-of-fortune who had already spent a summer's wages in the taverns and brothels. When Guillaume forced himself to calculate the cost of his journey, when he added it to what he had already spent on Joanna's wardrobe, jewels and establishment, the fever returned again. His lands could not maintain that sort of expenditure. Land, and the money that land generated, were the only true security. In his dreams, he saw Sanchia barefooted and hungry, begging her living in the marketplace. In the mornings he would wake up cold and sweating, certain of failure.

The fever retreated again, and luck paid Guillaume a fleeting visit. News of the successful defence of Padua spread through the Veneto. The Venetian army was travelling south. Ramón de Cardona, denied Padua, glowered at the edges of the Venetian lagoon, his cannon spitting spitefully and uselessly across the water towards the city of Venice itself. The army of Bartolomeo d'Alviano hovered close by, readying itself, collecting the young Venetian noblemen who had left the city in response to Doge Loredan's call for soldiers. Toby Crow's company, Guillaume discovered, was in the pay of Bartolomeo d'Alviano.

Hope, newly rekindled, enabled Guillaume to remain upright on his horse through the last few miles of his quest. He thought of Marigny again: glorious, exquisite Marigny. He thought of Sanchia as she would be in ten years' time: a beautiful young girl, walking in Marigny's graceful rooms, dancing on Marigny's flowery mead.

The summer of 1513 was tolerable because, with his services so much in demand, Toby didn't have time to think of the past. Venice bore no responsibility for the disaster of Novara, but much credit for the successful defence of Padua. The mainland cities were not left unprotected, as before, but still the summer's campaign had been, Toby knew, a bitty, piecemeal affair. Too many untrained peasants armed with nothing more than billhooks and scythes, too few Venetian noblemen, reluctantly answering the Doge's call to arms.

They were encamped at the farm near Padua again. Toby was billeted in the farmhouse as before. A few more cannon-balls had pitted the charred and crumbling stone walls; some of the roof had fallen away, so that a patch of sky, ink-blue and dotted with stars, could be glimpsed.

Toby was poring over his maps when Gilles kicked open the door and called his name.

'General Cardona asking for a bed for the night?' said Toby mildly, looking up. 'Or the Pope himself, perhaps?'

'A visitor for you. Demands to speak to you in person. He won't give his name. But he's French, I think,' Gilles added, suspiciously.

Gilles, perching on the table, straightened the frills of dirty lace at his cuffs. Toby folded the map, stoppered the ink-well. Then he buckled on his sword and followed Gilles out into the darkness.

'*One* visitor?' asked Toby, as they walked across the grass.

Gilles nodded. The feathers on his hat danced in the evening breeze. 'French, though,' he repeated. 'A spy, do you think? Shall I call Penniless?'

Toby shook his head. Owls hooted somewhere in the twilight, bats darted, fragile scraps of black against an ultramarine sky. Toby pushed open the door of the barn.

His heart thudded when he recognized Guillaume du Chantonnay. His hand slid from his sword-hilt as Gilles closed the door behind them.

'Monsieur du Chantonnay.'

He saw immediately how Guillaume had changed since he had last seen him at Blois. Weight had tumbled from him, his face was strained and grey. He looked, Toby thought, as though he had aged ten years in less than one. He was still fastidiously dressed, though. Reasons for this unexpected visit rushed through Toby's head. He found that he resented deeply the random way in which the du Chantonnays and the de Bohuns appeared and reappeared in his life. As though he was still their pawn, still their hostage to fortune.

Guillaume bowed. 'I must apologize for my unexpected arrival, Monsieur Crow – and for the unseasonable hour. You are not an easy man to find.'

Toby pulled a battered stool from a corner of the barn and sent Gilles to find some wine. The simple, routine movements gave him time to think. To consider why Guillaume du Chantonnay, who was Joanna Zulian's lover, Eleanor de Bohun's kinsman, Marigny's claimant, should trouble to seek him out of the chaos of northern Italy.

Guillaume sat down on the stool, his satin cloak brushing the dusty floor.

'A social call?' said Toby, watching him. 'You've ridden from Brittany, sieur, to make inquiries concerning my health – to give me news of your family?'

A flicker of anger crossed Guillaume du Chantonnay's face, but his voice remained level. 'Not quite. I am glad to see you thriving, though, Monsieur Crow. My own health is, as you may have realized, somewhat uncertain. That is why I have sought you out. I am looking for my physician – the Englishman, Martin Gefroy.'

Gilles had returned with a bottle of wine and three cups. Guillaume du Chantonnay's eyes were a pure, bright cornflower-blue. Innocent eyes, honest eyes. 'Martin left my employ rather suddenly a few years ago,' he added, accepting a cup of wine. 'He was a rare man – his potions actually made you feel better rather than worse. Someone told me that he was with you. I thought I'd see if I could persuade him to attend me.'

Outside, the sky was almost black. Toby stooped and lit, with fairly steady hands, the stub of candle on the window-sill.

'I heard that Master Gefroy was working for you, Monsieur Crow. I was surprised – army doctoring is barber surgeons' work, is it not?

Hardly a suitable trade for a man of Master Gefroy's abilities. I can offer him better employment than that.'

Gilles had collapsed on a pile of straw, his legs stretched out in front of him, his hat over his eyes. 'Martin enjoys all that,' he said lazily. 'He likes getting his hands dirty.'

Guillaume, with bright, feverish eyes, glanced sharply at Gilles. 'Martin Gefroy is here, then?'

'Was,' said Toby. 'Sadly, Master Gefroy left us only a few days ago.'

'He has gone to Venice? To Rome?'

Toby shook his head. His expression was mournful.

'I regret to have to tell you, Monsieur du Chantonnay, that Master Gefroy is dead.'

Gilles was about to speak when Toby, crossing the barn to refill Guillaume's glass, kicked him hard in the shin as he passed. Gilles howled, and Toby muttered insincere apologies.

Guillaume's glass trembled as Toby poured the wine. *'Dead?'* he asked in a voice little more than a whisper. Gilles, rubbing his leg, said nothing.

'As my friend said, Martin liked getting his hands dirty. He wouldn't stay in the camp, you understand, where it was safe. An arrow in the neck, I'm afraid, at Fusina. Just unlucky.' His words were soft with regret. 'A rare man, as you said, Monsieur du Chantonnay. Nothing could be done, of course. He was dead within the hour, I was told. I heard this morning.'

Martin Gefroy, far from being dead of an arrow-wound in Fusina, was asleep in his tent. He slept in a sea of jars and potions, fully dressed, one arm flung over his face, the other hand still loosely clutching a pen. He woke with difficulty when Toby, having trodden carefully through the debris, shook his shoulder.

He sat up, rubbing at his eyes with his sleeve. 'Is it morning?'

'No. About midnight, I think.'

Martin, recognizing Toby's voice, groaned and collapsed back on to his blanket. He mumbled, 'Is someone ill? The fire-master . . .?'

'The fire-master is quite healthy, I believe. It's your own well-being I'm concerned for, Martin.' There were a few shuffling sounds, and Toby added, 'It's damned dark in here. Haven't you a candle?'

Martin rolled over and dug out some tinder and a candle from beneath a pile of books. The light glimmered, underlighting Toby's features and the patched arc of the tent. 'What do you mean, my own well-being?'

'Guillaume du Chantonnay is here, Martin, looking for you.'

Martin's fingers knotted together suddenly, and he felt horribly awake.

'Here?'

'I spoke to him a half-hour ago. He's been searching Italy for you. He said that he was ill – he wants you to go back to France with him, as his physician.'

Martin's mouth was dry. He longed for a drink. 'And you said?'

'I told him you were dead.'

Toby's eyes were black in the candlelight. He sat on one side of the tent, having cleared a space from the chaos.

'Did he believe you?'

Toby grimaced. 'I think so. But it's up to you, Martin. If you'd like to speak to him, if you'd like to go back to France with him, you can always stage a miraculous recovery. After all, I'm only assuming that he's lying.'

Martin shook his head vehemently. He knew that France was the one country on earth in which he would not practise his trade. He still remembered Hamon de Bohun's cold, dark eyes, and the bruises around François du Chantonnay's neck. He still remembered his own shameful, blundering part in François's death. He still experienced physical fear when he thought of Hamon de Bohun, and he despised himself for it.

He muttered incoherently, 'I couldn't . . . I can't . . .'

'Or you could,' said Toby coolly, 'tell the truth.'

He understood immediately what Toby meant. Tell whoever was interested – Guillaume, Guillaume's notary, the officers of the court of France – what he had seen. He imagined himself at Blois describing to the French king the rope-marks on François du Chantonnay's neck, the circumstances of the heir to Marigny's death. If there was no longer unimpeachable evidence, there was, Martin suspected, still sufficient doubt to spark off the train of events that would lead to de Bohun's downfall.

He knew instantly, though, that he could not bear witness against Hamon de Bohun. The thought sickened him, so that the surface of his skin chilled sharply.

'I can't,' he whispered. 'I know I should, but I can't.'

He shook his head and lowered his eyes. He felt shame wash over him, hot and unforgiving, taking away the chill of fear.

'Then you must leave here,' said Toby. There was no judgement in his voice, Martin noticed, no contempt. 'Italy isn't safe for you any more.'

Martin said hesitantly, 'I've been thinking of travelling again. I've never studied at Heidelberg . . . and there's a good man in London . . . Thomas Linacre . . . or I could go home . . .'

Toby rose to his feet. 'I'll find you a competent guide, Martin. Or you'll end up making potions for the Shah of Persia.'

Joanna retired to the house in Brittany to look after her child, to wait for a reply to her letter to Toby, to wonder whether Guillaume was alive or dead.

Sanchia was walking and talking now, but still no word came from Toby. A message, eventually, arrived from Blois. Guillaume du Chantonnay was alive, it was believed, but he had remained in Italy due to poor health.

She felt a measure of relief that she was not yet homeless and penniless. Another letter arrived, from the Seigneur de Marigny. Joanna read it once and consigned it to the fire without replying. Two more letters arrived: she did not even break their seals. When she thought of her garden, the garden that she had intended to make next spring, her fingers itched to reach for her pen. When she thought of Guy, she despised her pride.

On most fine days she walked in the forest, gathering seeds, making cuttings. She only half admitted to herself that these plants were for Marigny, and not for the house in Finistère. At night, when she woke, the garden that she would make was clear in her mind's eye. Only sometimes did she remember Hamon de Bohun's cold lips upon her neck, the expression in his eyes as he had stared at her image in the painting.

In the autumn, the campaigning season over, Toby returned once more to Blois. He took with him letters from the Venetian Proveditors: letters reaffirming the tattered rags of the French alliance, letters attempting to extract some sort of dignity from the disasters of the summer.

At Blois, there were some familiar faces and, thank God, some absences. In the evening, conversation darted over the chink of glasses, flurries of well-bred laughter. The notes of a lute marked out the patterns of the dance: the shadows cast against the painted walls trod out the measure. If he let his sight blur, Toby could see faces on the shadows: Joanna Zulian's, Eleanor's, Hamon de Bohun's.

The following morning, he made tactful inquiries of a small, disaffected card-school. The card-players, skulking in an obscure corner of the château to escape the rigours of the hunt, moaned about the wet weather and the miserable temperament of the king. Anne of Brittany is dying, said the gentleman sitting beside Toby. Louis has no son. Will he marry again, do you think? Cards were fanned on the table, bets made, money scooped into palms.

The de Bohuns, answered the card-player to Toby's inquiry, had not been received at Blois this year. It was rumoured that the lord and lady of Marigny no longer spoke to each other. A delicious rumour, didn't Toby agree? A plump hand squeezed Toby's arm, red lips smiled complicitously. It was rumoured also (a whisper, hand cupped round mouth) that Louis himself was displeased with the Seigneur de Marigny. The château was, people said, becoming grander than any of the king's residences. The ringed hand fondled Toby's sleeve, and rain pelted at the window-panes.

Cards were placed face down on the table. Coins gathered themselves in front of Toby. 'You have a lucky face,' whispered the gentleman at Toby's side. Another card-player relieved himself into the fireplace: steam, spitting and foetid, hissed on the logs.

'A garden, too,' said Toby's neighbour. 'The Seigneur de Marigny is making a splendid garden.'

The dealer giggled. Cards clicked on to the table. Toby picked up his hand.

'Well,' explained the dealer, 'Madame Zulian, Guillaume du Chantonnay's mistress, is making the Seigneur a garden. And goodness knows what else besides.'

Toby's fingers fumbled, the cards flailed from his hands. The coins, in columns on the table, rolled to the ground, tracing wide arcs to all corners of the room.

Toby reached Finistère three days later, having begged leave of absence from a preoccupied Louis de France. The path twisted and meandered through the ghostly forest. Menhirs, great grey rocks that stabbed through the earth, raised themselves brazenly to a watery sky; rain danced on the flat roofs of the stone dolmens. Superstitious villagers left offerings of food beneath the dolmens: palliatives for the fairy-folk. Toby feared neither the supernatural nor the wolves and boars that prowled the forests of Brittany. He feared only for Joanna, for Eleanor. He remembered the blank, black eyes of his enemy, his father.

He arrived at midday. The rain had stopped earlier in the morning and the house was bright in the sunlight. The grass and dying leaves were glistening and pearled with rain.

Madame was not at home, said the housekeeper. Madame was out in the woods, picking blackberries.

Instead of accepting the housekeeper's offer to sit and wait, Toby walked out into the forest that surrounded the house. Small signs dictated his route: the most well-trodden path, the trampled ferns and broken nettle stalks, a footprint in the soft mud. He climbed high, skirting around the huge boulders that protruded from the hillside, stepping over the streams that rushed down to the valley. The tall trees were all shades: golden, amber, russet and yellow. Their fallen leaves gathered in the ditches and were borne away by the streams.

The path skirted high above a river: he stood on the edge of a rock and looked down. Below him there was the sound of water splashing and the wind in the falling leaves, and, through it all, the voice of Joanna singing. She wore a russet wool gown, the hem of the overskirt tucked into her waistband. Her long hair was plaited, the plait trailing carelessly down her back. She wore no jewels, no lace, no ribbons. Toby smiled to himself. This was the Joanna that he knew: the Joanna that he had helped from a canal in Venice, the Joanna with whom he had ridden across the plains of Lombardy. She sat on a smooth rock, and her bare feet splashed the peaty water of a pool. A collection of small baskets were spread out on the rock beside her, and a handful of smooth pebbles glistened in the rays of sunlight that filtered through the trees. As Toby watched, Joanna slid off the rock into the pool, her skirts gathered up with one hand, her other hand trawling through the sandy bed beneath the water.

Toby called, 'It's too cold for swimming, Joanna. Remember Venice?'

She glanced up quickly. He saw by the immediacy of her smile that he was forgiven, that his insolence at Blois was put aside, if not forgotten.

'Of course I remember Venice,' she said. 'I'm not swimming. Look.'

He jumped off the rock, scrambling down the steep path, strewn with ferns and hart's tongue, that led to the pool. Water cascaded from between the boulders, and a small spit of sand jutted from the path into the water. Leaves, orange and green, star-shaped and oval, floated at the edge of the pool. Toby stepped on to the sand.

'Look,' said Joanna again. She held out something on the palm of her hand.

It was a mussel-shell, gleaming and iridescent. 'We used to mix paints in them,' she said, 'in Uncle Taddeo's workshop.'

She placed the mussel-shell carefully on the rock. Toby took her wet hand and kissed it. He glanced at the baskets.

'Blackberries, your servant said.'

'A few. It's a bit late in the year. The devil has spat on them, Agnès would say. But there are crab-apples, and hazelnuts, and walnuts, and puffballs. Eat, Toby.'

He stepped from the sand on to the rock. She still stood below him, up to her knees in water, her skirt tucked around her waist, her petticoats trailing in the pool. He touched the apples, the nuts, and then he picked up another, smaller, basket. A handful of round, shining, black berries glistened in the wicker.

'No. Not those.'

Joanna scrambled out of the water. Her bare wet feet made clear imprints on the dry rock. She took the small basket from Toby's hand and set it aside.

'Belladonna,' she said. 'The fruit of deadly nightshade. They are very poisonous, Toby – you must not touch them.'

He helped her sit down, moving aside the other baskets. She sat on the rock, drying her feet with the hem of her petticoat.

'I distil an infusion of nightshade. Ladies put drops of belladonna in their eyes. It enlarges the pupils, you see, makes their eyes look more beautiful. I sell it in Morlaix.'

Toby grinned. He could imagine Joanna in busy, bustling Morlaix, selling potions and tinctures to the plainer ladies of the town. He took a crab-apple, enjoying its tart taste after his long ride.

'You got my letter, then?' said Joanna.

He blinked, bewildered. He tossed the apple core into the pool, and said, 'What letter?'

It was her turn to look confused. 'I wrote you a letter. Several months ago. I sent it to Blois. I thought someone might know where you were.'

Toby shook his head. 'I've been in Italy throughout the summer. And I doubt if I've been in the same place for more than a few days at a time. Your letter didn't find me, I'm afraid, Joanna.'

She had unplaited her hair and spread out its damp tendrils over her back to dry in the sunlight. 'Then why are you here?'

It was on the tip of his tongue to say, *To see you.* But he remembered Guillaume du Chantonnay, and the silks and jewels that Joanna Zulian had worn at Blois. She didn't always dress in wool and linen and paddle in streams.

'I heard . . . something,' he said carefully. 'I wanted to find out whether it was true.'

She frowned, but she did not turn away. She said coldly, 'You heard something about me?'

Blois was most certainly not forgotten. Toby took a deep breath.

'I heard that you were making a garden for the château de Marigny. For Hamon de Bohun. Did I hear wrong?'

Her eyes, a cool grey, met his. 'You did not hear wrong.'

He rose to his feet. Looking down at her, he said, 'Do you only make the garden, Joanna? Is that the extent of your relationship with the Seigneur?'

He had not, this time, lost his temper. It was simply that he needed to know. But she had stood up and made to strike his face.

'How *dare* you . . .'

Because he had not lost his temper, he was able to catch her wrist. She was breathing fast; two patches of scarlet lit her cheeks. He said, blandly, 'I take that as an assent. You only make the garden.' He let her reclaim her hand. Her back turned to him, she began to pull on her stockings, to buckle her shoes. He saw how her fingers slipped in her haste and anger. 'Joanna. Don't go. Please. I needed to know.'

She was gathering up the baskets. Blackberries tumbled on to the rock, staining it purple; the mussel-shell slipped from her fumbling fingers and splashed into the pool.

Toby jumped in the water and scrabbled in the sand for the missing shell. Water, peat-stained and icy, poured into the tops of his boots and soaked the sleeves of his doublet: he gasped at its coldness.

He heard an unexpected sound. Turning, Toby saw that Joanna was laughing, her fingers clamped over her mouth, her shoulders shaking.

'Look at you!' she cried. 'Look at you, Toby!'

He saw himself suddenly as she saw him, dressed for riding, wading in a pool, scrabbling ridiculously in the sand for a shell. Grinning, he placed the recovered mussel-shell back on the rock and hauled himself out of the water.

'You'll have to empty your boots.' Joanna's voice was still unsteady. 'You may have caught a fish.'

He pulled off his boots and up-ended them, peeled off his stockings and doublet. Water cascaded back into the pool. Then he turned to face Joanna.

'I'm sorry,' he said. 'But I had to know. It was important.'

He saw the small nod of her head. Her eyes were shining suspiciously. Without thought he pulled her to him, so that her head rested against his chest. He did not kiss her, he only hugged her and stroked her wet hair. Something brotherly, something born of affection and a long knowledge of each other.

'You're all wet,' she said eventually. Her voice still shook, but she wasn't laughing.

'So are you.'

He let her go. He had realized how careful they had to be with each other. A fragmented history of strange meetings, sudden passions, equally sudden pain. He was too tired, too brittle, to endure any of that again.

'The letter,' he said. 'Why did you write to me, Joanna?'

She sat down on the rock, her skirts folded round her knees. She said hesitantly, 'Because of the garden. Because of Marigny.' She was turned away from him: he couldn't at first see her face. Then she looked up at him, her eyes narrowed because of the sunlight. 'Hamon de Bohun has a painting of me, Toby. He has a painting of Gaetano's at Marigny.'

She began to tell him about the *Judith and Holofernes*. But he knew all that already, of course. And he should have guessed, shouldn't he, that that painting would adorn Hamon de Bohun's château at Marigny.

He sat down beside her. He saw the distress on her face, and he covered her hand with his.

'I thought . . .' she began. 'I thought that perhaps you had bought the painting from Messer Venier for Reynaud du Chantonnay.'

Toby stared down into the brown, iron-stained water of the pool. 'I did,' he said. 'Messer Venier sold it to me, I took it back to France. But it never reached Reynaud.'

Joanna, frowning, looked up at him sharply. 'But –'

He interrupted, 'Hamon de Bohun stole it from me.'

'Tell your master that I have come to take what I am owed.' And, by God, he thought, Hamon de Bohun had taken his payment, over and over again. He dreaded, though, explaining all that to Joanna Zulian. The stain of his birth, of his creation, still disgusted him. He assumed that it would disgust anyone. He had merely to make sure that Joanna never went back to Marigny. He took a deep breath.

'De Bohun took the painting from me by force on my journey back from Venice the year after I met you. I arrived back at Marigny late, having spent almost a thousand ducats of Reynaud du Chantonnay's money on something I no longer possessed. Reynaud, not surprisingly, made it clear that he didn't require my services any more. So I went back to Italy to fight. And in Padua, I found Martin. And you.'

She had wrapped her hands round her knees; she stared down at her reflection in the water. 'And I made you take me to France.'

He said, lightly, 'It was not an onerous task, Joanna. I've done worse. I once had to help haul a cannon across the Veneto. That was worse.'

She looked at him, and at last the smile returned to her face. She shook her head. 'You are quite impossible, Toby Crow.'

He thought for a moment that he would have liked to stay there for ever: that this was the sort of place they could be happy in, he and Joanna. But mid-morning had shifted to mid-afternoon, a chilly autumnal mid-afternoon, and the shadows of the trees and rocks were falling long and dark.

'You won't go to Marigny any more, will you, Joanna?'

The smile disappeared. Her voice was small, almost lost in the immensity of the forest.

'I want to finish my garden.'

'Christ.' He rose to his feet, pushing his hair angrily out of his eyes. 'You can't. You mustn't, Joanna.'

She, too, scrambled to her feet. 'I can't? I mustn't? Who are you, Toby Crow, to tell me what I cannot and must not do?'

Her eyes were blazing with resentment. He felt tired suddenly: having avoided emotional involvement for so long, such an interview exhausted him.

'No one,' he said flatly. 'Nothing. I simply ask you – *beg* you – not to see Hamon de Bohun any more.'

She crossed her arms in front of her. 'Why?' she said coldly.

It was his turn to evade her eyes. 'Because of what Hamon de Bohun is.'

He pulled his damp boots back on, slung his doublet over one shoulder. He began to walk away from her then, because he knew what he was going to have to say to her. In the last three years he had told only one other person of his relationship with Hamon de Bohun: Martin Gefroy, because he had owed Martin some sort of honesty, and because Martin, the physician, was accustomed to seeing human beings at their worst.

He heard her say, 'And what is he?' and he answered, turning briefly round to face her, 'He is my father.' Then he walked on.

He became aware, eventually, of her running footsteps, of the black crows whirling overhead in the high tops of the trees. He kept walking, though, until she seized his arm and pulled him round.

When he didn't speak, she took his hands and said, gently, 'Tell me, Toby.'

Her gentleness was worse, he thought, than anything else. He forced himself to speak. 'You know that the Dubretons adopted me. Well – I am Hamon de Bohun's bastard son. He has never acknowledged me, of course. I found out a few years ago.'

The colour had gone from her face. There was a short silence. Then she whispered, 'And your mother? Who was your mother, Toby?'

He almost lied to her. He almost said, a maidservant, a dairymaid, a pretty seamstress. But he knew it would be futile, and so he said: 'Reynaud du Chantonnay's sister was my mother. Her name was Izabel Mandeville.' He added, 'I'm quite well connected, you see, Joanna. Reynaud du Chantonnay was my uncle, François my cousin. And Guillaume – I'm not quite sure of the relationship with Guillaume. Second cousin? First cousin once removed . . .'

'Don't.'

Joanna's skin was white, her lips blue. Toby took his doublet from his shoulder and wrapped it round her. 'Only the sleeves are wet, Joanna,' he whispered. 'It'll do, won't it?'

There was, he noticed, no disgust in her eyes. He had at first expected disgust, but then, slowly, he began to realize how her life must have been: a series of accidents and desertions, abandonments and hopeless couplings. He began to understand, at last, why she might have gone to someone like Guillaume du Chantonnay.

'How long have you known?' she said. She was shivering.

'Three years,' he answered bleakly. 'I found out three years ago.'

She was silent for a moment, working it all out. 'The spring Paul Dubreton died. That was when you found out, wasn't it, Toby?'

He had always been aware of her intelligence, as well as her beauty. He nodded.

'So Izabel Mandeville was Monsieur de Bohun's mistress?'

'Not quite.' For a while he couldn't go on. At last he managed to say, 'De Bohun raped her. To avenge himself against Reynaud. Reynaud took Marigny from him, you see.'

The sky had clouded over, and the returning raindrops made dark, circular marks on the rocks around the pool. Joanna was silent for a few moments, and then said, 'You'll help me carry the baskets back to the house, Toby. And then we'll eat. And I shall introduce you to my daughter.'

She took his hand and led him back to the rock pool. He carried three of the baskets for her. He was very tired and very hungry. Joanna slipped the mussel-shell into her pocket, and her hands cradled the basket of shining nightshade berries.

She made him eat and drink, and play with the child. Toby made Sanchia straw dollies, and blew soap bubbles, which, laughing, she chased round the room. Joanna lit the candles and locked the shutters, closing out the night. When they had eaten, Toby claimed weariness and went to bed.

She saw him next at dawn. Unable to sleep, she waited for the first glimmering of sunlight, and peered out at the garden through the slats of the shutters. He was walking, hands dug in his pockets, collar up to keep out the cold air. Joanna threw a cloak over her nightgown and went outside.

His route seemed aimless. He walked, she realized, so that he would not have to think. He, too, had endured a sleepless night. Frost had formed on the grass, and her bare feet were ice-cold. Joining Toby, she touched his arm and saw the shock in his eyes quickly alter to recognition.

'It's cold,' he said. 'You should go inside.'

She shook her head. There had been another dawn once, in a garden bright with blossom, heavy with perfume. Now, the last petals had fallen from the autumn damask roses, and the pond was fringed with ice.

'Tell me,' she said.

He blinked. She put her fingertips up to his face, as though to rub away the crease between his brows. 'Tell me everything.'

So he told her. He did not stop walking, and her hand clutched his arm to keep up with him. She forgot the cold, she heard only his clear, emotionless voice as he listed the origins and pattern of his existence. The shoemaker, Agnès and Paul, Marigny. His mistaken conclusions, his first meeting with Hamon de Bohun. His relationship with Eleanor, his interrupted attempt to visit Paul Dubreton. Crossing the English Channel, the village of Lydney Mandeville, Izabel Mandeville's neglected house. His wanderings in England, his eventual return first to France and then to Italy. The death of François du Chantonnay: Martin Gefroy's suspicions concerning that death.

When he had finished, Joanna could not immediately speak. That someone should create a child solely for the purposes of revenge, that someone should take that child – his own blood – and send him from his home, from the country of his birth, to an unknown, terrible future, she was at first unable to grasp.

But then she remembered Guy. The legitimate child might be well-fed, well-clothed, housed in one of the most beautiful estates in Touraine, but still de Bohun possessed an awful, unforgivable need to force this son into nothing other than a glittering reflection of himself.

'But you came back,' she said at last. 'Why did you come back?'

'I carry messages from Venice to Blois.' He had stopped walking at last, but his hand fiddled constantly with the winding tendrils of honeysuckle that spiralled up the trunk of an apple tree. Fragments of bark flaked to the frosty ground, dry leaves were crushed to powder beneath his fingers. 'And I have a responsibility, don't I?' Toby's eyes were dark, bleak. 'To Agnès. To Eleanor. And to you.'

She couldn't answer. She bowed her head, staring at the hoary grass. Her eyes ached.

She heard him say, 'I can do nothing for Eleanor, of course. I construct absurd schemes in the night, and discard them in the mornings. I once thought I could protect her – what a fool I was! As for Agnès – well, I have now, at least, money. Agnès need never fear poverty. The rent of the house is paid each month, and she has enough to live on.'

Joanna looked up. 'Enough to live *well*.' She smiled. 'She has bought another pig, Toby.'

His eyes flickered briefly in her direction. 'You write to her?'

She nodded. 'I am trying to persuade her to visit me. It's a long journey, though.' She pulled at his sleeve, forcing him to turn back to her. 'You should go and see her, Toby.'

He shook his head.

'Why not?' she said gently. 'It would make her happy.'

He didn't answer. She wasn't sure that he had heard her. He took her hands in his, his palms warming her cold fingertips.

'And you, Joanna? I tell you all this only so that you understand about Hamon de Bohun. So that you do not go back to Marigny.'

Her hands slipped from his, she stood tall, proud. Lying awake at night, she had at last seen clearly what she must do.

'I have to go back, Toby. I will go back.'

Her voice was firm, checking any argument. 'Because of Guy,' she explained. 'Eleanor's son. How could I leave him with someone like that?'

'Eleanor's son is not your responsibility,' he said. But she thought that his voice lacked conviction.

She said fiercely, 'Guy de Bohun wears silks and velvets and never lacks for food. He has a pony of his own, and a tutor who was educated at the Sorbonne. He also has a mother who never speaks to him, and bruises on his back. Rather a lot of bruises, Toby.'

She began to shiver with the memory. She saw the pain and then the acceptance in his eyes. She turned and walked back towards the house. The sun, pale and misted, had touched the top of the trees: Sanchia would soon be waking.

Reaching her as she walked through the doorway, he said, 'Be careful, Joanna. De Bohun is not to be trusted, but neither is Guillaume. He is using you to taunt de Bohun. To show him that though he may have taken Marigny, he hasn't been able to take everything.'

She heard the baby's cry as she began to walk up the stairs. She turned back briefly. 'Ah, but Guillaume has a weakness, you see, Toby.' A smile touched her face, and the first rays of sun, magnified by the window-glass, began to warm her limbs. 'Or a saving grace. It depends how you look at it. Unlike Hamon de Bohun, Guillaume loves his child.'

At Christmas, Eleanor de Bohun received a letter.

The letter was from Cousin Guillaume, who had been in Italy since the spring. Eleanor read it and then tore it into innumerable little pieces, sending them fluttering like snowflakes to the floor of her bedchamber. Her serving-woman, who was helping her dress for the evening, did not speak. Eleanor shoved her arms into bracelets, twisted rings on to her fingers and strung ropes of pearls round her neck as tight as a noose. When she was dressed, she glittered, like the reborn Marigny.

Eleanor had consented to attend the Christmas celebrations for the sake of the few remaining servants who were her friends. A huge apple bough, a foot in diameter, glowed in the fire; holly branches and mistletoe ornamented the fireplace and window-sills. After they had eaten, she sat at Hamon's side, enduring songs, dances and jesting. She could think only of Guillaume's letter. She had not realized how much she had counted on his success. She fiddled constantly with the beads round her neck, and her fingers pulled at the buttons of her gown. When she looked down, she saw that they had gone and strands of thread protruded crazily from the silk.

Her son, Guy, was brought forward to recite a poem. His small voice filled the vast room and spoke the words fluently. But then he caught his father's eye, and, faltering, he gabbled the last lines, the words tumbling over each other. Eleanor understood not a word of the poem, because it was in Latin. Alone, Eleanor could not remember Toby's face; looking at Guy, though, she could recall his features. The dark eyes, the straight nose and mouth, the black unruly hair. She thought of Toby, she knew, because of Guillaume's letter.

Suddenly she was crying. Tears spilled over her eyelids, she had no control over them. Salt water stained her bodice. She had mislaid her handkerchief, so she rubbed at her eyes with her sleeve. As Guy's tutor escorted the boy away, she heard muttering. When she looked up, she saw that people were staring at her. Some looked sympathetic, some horrified. Some were laughing.

She felt Hamon seize her arm, haul her to her feet. He did not, as she expected him to, call for her women. Instead, he dragged her out of the Great Hall.

'I shall send you to a nunnery,' he hissed, when they were alone. 'No one will require me to remain tied to a madwoman.'

Eleanor's head had begun to pound; she wanted to lie down and sleep. But, raising her head, she drew herself to her full height. There was pleasure, after all, to be found in taunting Hamon.

'Ah,' she said, 'but what tales would I tell to the nuns?' He stared at her. She saw, to her delight, that he had actually blenched. 'I would give them good advice,' she continued. 'I would tell them not to ride alone in the forest.'

She started to walk up the stairs, holding the skirts of her gown clear of the steps. She knew that soon her vision would begin to flicker with coloured lights: she must be careful. She heard him run up the stairs after her. The steps were narrow and winding: the shadow of the single rushlight deepened the lines on his face, and emphasized the thinning of his hair. She thought, You will not live for ever, Hamon. Not even you.

'You had a letter from your cousin,' he said.

She inclined her head. 'I had a letter from Cousin Guillaume.'

She started to walk on, but he caught her wrist. His fingers tightened round the bone: her eyes widened as he hurt her.

'You have nothing to fear,' she managed to say. 'Guillaume was looking for his physician, Master Gefroy. He saw François's body, Hamon. Did you know that? But you have nothing to fear. Master Gefroy is dead.'

Her voice fractured, broke. He let go of her then. As she reached the top of the spiral, she heard his footsteps, walking downwards, back to the dining-chamber.

On the top stair she paused. She felt exhausted: coloured lights and circles flickered in the darkness. Hearing a noise Eleanor turned, her hands fisted. But it was only Guy, peering out at her from behind a curtain. She thought him a strange child: forever hiding in corners, looking out with his bright blackbird's eyes from behind furniture and balustrades.

Eleanor's hands gripped one of the pearl necklaces and snapped it in two. She caught the pearls in her palms, and then, with Guy watching, let the small pale beads bounce down the winding staircase, hitting corners, jumping off steps. She laughed, and was touched to hear Guy laugh too.

*

Hamon de Bohun realized that he had been careless. He had been preoccupied with Marigny and, though he hardly admitted it even to himself, with Joanna Zulian. He sent out men to Nantes, to Blois, to trace the whereabouts of Guillaume du Chantonnay. His men took money, wore swords. There was more than one way of finding out what you wanted to know.

He sent someone to Finistère, too. Not too close, though: to watch and to wait. Joanna Zulian still had not replied to his letters.

Guillaume returned to Brittany in midwinter. He knew by then that he was dying. He still fought, though, forcing food down his throat, coaxing himself to survive the long journey back to France.

From Nantes he travelled, slowly and painfully, to visit his mistress and daughter. There, he submitted himself to Joanna's care. He let her put him to bed, dose him with physic, spoonfeed him with tasty morsels. The pain in his guts subsided, and for the first time in months he slept soundly at night. Finistère was magical again: if he stayed in Finistère, he might live.

Lying in bed, he watched his daughter play on the floor beside him. It never bored him to watch the fleeting expressions dart across her small, fragile face. She rarely cried, often smiled. One day, when he was well enough, Guillaume left his bed and went to the window. Snow was falling: great white flakes that danced and floated in the cold air. Carefully, he lifted Sanchia to stand on the window-sill. His hands gripped her tiny waist: even though the panes were firm, the bars solid, he feared that she might fall. Guillaume watched the wonder on her face as she stared at the snow. Her blue eyes were wide, her mouth open. When she spoke, she was at first incoherent. Then she clapped her hands together and laughed.

Guillaume heard Joanna come into the room. He turned round, still clutching the folds of Sanchia's gown.

'You should be in bed. You are not yet strong enough, Guillaume.'

Her words were cross, but her tone was not. She stood beside him, looking out of the window, like Sanchia. He watched her for a moment. He wondered for the first time if she were more important than Marigny.

'You won't ever leave me, will you?' he said hoarsely. 'You won't, will you, Joanna?'

She looked at him, surprise and a sort of pain in her eyes. Sanchia's small fingers scratched at the glass, trying to catch the snowflakes.

Joanna smiled and, standing on her tiptoes, kissed his cheek. 'Of course I won't, Guillaume.'

CHAPTER SIXTEEN

In the spring, Joanna went back to Marigny. Walking through the gardens, looking up at the pinnacles and towers, she began to understand. To Toby, Marigny had meant perpetual exclusion. To Hamon de Bohun it had been the one thing of value that had been denied to him. To Guillaume, Marigny was security, somewhere that would reassure him of his own worth.

On the site of the old kitchen garden, Joanna began to mark out the shape of the flower garden that she would make. Since Toby's visit the meaning of the garden, its pattern and its colours had become quite clear to her. An Italian garden: square in shape, the square divided into four quarters. The four quarters would make four gardens: the Garden of Jealous Love, the Garden of Passionate Love, the Garden of Obsessive Love, the Garden of Tender Love. She would tell, she thought, so many people's stories in those four gardens. The garden was a way of telling the truth.

She gave orders to Marigny's gardeners that the ground be prepared, horse dung dug in to make the soil more fertile. In her garden in Finistère she had collected seeds, grown cuttings and planted tiny seedlings in the most sheltered corners. Lavender, germander and box to outline the patterns; flowering plants and physic plants for their scent, colour and properties.

Working in the garden, Joanna rarely looked up at the château de Marigny, never stepped inside it. Her dislike of the château had hardened into something fixed and unchanging: that great stone edifice, those numberless rooms, frightened her. She recalled how she had felt as a child in Venice: how the walls and ceilings of Uncle Taddeo's house had crushed her, how the complexities of daily life had daunted her. She had longed then for open roads, for fields and the wide sky above her. She was no different now.

She felt him watching her, though. She knew that Hamon de Bohun's courtesy as he had greeted her on her return to Marigny had been a studied, careful display. He had helped her down from her horse, he had kissed her hand, and she had loathed his touch. She had thought of Izabel Mandeville, whom this man had taken by force. She had thought of the infant Toby, taken from his home and shipped to France. If Hamon de Bohun had not been so distant and polite, Joanna knew that despite Guy, despite her garden, she would have climbed on her horse and ridden back to Brittany.

She did not see Guy, though. She could not tell whether he was watching her, whether he had forgiven her for her long absence. She sometimes thought she heard whisperings from the dovecote or the orchard, but that could have been the birds beating their wings or the wind among the apple blossom. She left the sweetmeats that she had brought with her wrapped in a handkerchief, hidden in the grass at the edge of the garden. Just in case.

Hamon de Bohun's heart had pounded when his steward, knocking at his door, announced Joanna Zulian's name. She had never replied to his letters, had given no word of her coming. He ran down Marigny's new staircase, his breath catching in his chest. He was no longer young, and as he came up to her his lungs tightened and his ribs hurt. He hid his discomfort, however. He knew that he must not let Joanna Zulian see him as an old man, a man lacking in vigour.

He helped her down from her horse and greeted her. She wore a gown of green silk and her hair was held in place by a jewelled head-dress. His heart still pounded as he looked at her. Throughout the winter there had been only the painting, and the painting, he had discovered, was no longer enough.

She refused to accompany him into the house, refused his offer of refreshment. He did not press her; instead, he watched as his steward led her back across the drawbridge towards the garden. He watched her long, rippling hair as it spread out behind the veil of her head-dress, he stared hungrily at her small waist, the swell of her bosom. Then he went back into the house and, looking out of the window to the garden, he waited.

He felt desire, which had troubled him so little throughout his life, begin to flicker and then burn. He knew that he must have her, would have her. He had learned from the servant that he had sent to Nantes that Guillaume du Chantonnay was ailing, his estates burdened with debt. He thought, for the first time, of sending messengers to Venice, to inquire after Joanna Zulian's absent husband, the artist Gaetano Cavazza. He realized that in thinking thus, he had considered offering her marriage. Considered disregarding Joanna Zulian's lack of birth and dowry, her dubious status, her bastard daughter. Hamon de Bohun's hands fisted on the window-sill, his gaze did not falter from that small, green-clad figure far below in the garden.

He left the window at last, forcing himself to think of other matters. His lack of a warm reception at court over the winter had disturbed him: he had put it down to the death, in January, of Anne of Brittany. Mourning her deeply, Louis's temper had altered: he had become dour, surly. Rumour said that he was becoming senile. Hamon began to court the heir to the throne, François, Duc d'Angoulême, with gifts and compliments. Just in case, he thought. Just in case Guillaume du Chantonnay had started rumours of his own. Just in case echoes of Eleanor's careless tongue had reached Blois.

Guillaume's servants, parted from their master at Nantes, had proved susceptible to bribery, and one thing that they had revealed disturbed Hamon greatly: it had been Toby Crow who had told Guillaume du Chantonnay that Martin Gefroy, Guillaume's one-time physician, was dead. Hamon, of course, did not trust his bastard son. He was a liar, an upstart. It had offended Hamon to see his son at Blois, it continued to offend him to hear reports of his successes in Italy. Increasingly, Hamon de Bohun regretted not killing Toby Crow four years earlier. He did not believe that Martin Gefroy was dead, and, as Guillaume had once done, sent out messengers to inquire after the English physician in the universities and in the houses of the wealthy.

Hamon returned to the window, and looked out once again at Joanna. It was as though she compelled him, drew him. He had, he realized, never felt like this before.

In the early summer, Eleanor visited Guillaume at his house in Nantes. She found herself shocked both at the alteration in her cousin and at the alteration to his estates. Distracted from her own misery for the first time in years, she noticed the greyness of his skin, the gauntness of his frame. His house, too, had a dishevelled, uncared-for appearance. Eleanor's fingertip, after she ran it along the window-sill, was thick with dust.

'I have let go some of my servants,' said Guillaume, seating her in a chair. 'The harvest was poor last year. Too many mouths to feed.'

He was still immaculately dressed, he still wore a few carefully chosen jewels. Eleanor felt a fleeting admiration for him: for the pride that enabled him to maintain the picture of careless elegance to a critical world. She herself made no attempt to hide her greying hair or replace her unfashionable gowns.

'Yet you keep a mistress,' she said bitterly. 'And a child. Two households must be a considerable expense, Guillaume.'

He pursed his mouth, stared into the depths of his wine. 'Joanna is worth every last sou I spend on her, cousin.'

She looked up at him angrily. 'If you value her so much, then why do you permit her to come to Marigny?'

He said carelessly, '*Permitting* – or denying – anything to Joanna does not enter our relationship, my dear Eleanor. I do not tell her where she may or may not go, whom she may and may not see. That was our original agreement. If I break it, she will leave me.'

She did not believe him. 'And go where?' she said scornfully.

'Who knows? She would tramp the country like a gypsy, perhaps. Dance for her supper. Sell her cordials and potions in the marketplace.' Guillaume was smiling.

Eleanor's fingers clenched the stem of her wine-glass. 'Or, she would find another lover. Someone who can offer more than you, Guillaume.'

His eyes, a pure sapphire-blue, focused on her. 'Hamon, you mean, cousin? Never.'

'He lusts after her. I have seen him . . .'

His eyes were still cool, his voice calm, detached. 'Does he? Good. I hope that he hungers for Joanna as I have hungered for Marigny. I hope his lust for her eats him. I hope it destroys him.'

She stared at him, unable to speak at first. Then she said, her voice slightly unsteady, 'You underestimate Hamon, Guillaume.'

He shook his head. 'I do not. You underestimate Joanna. He shall not have her. She has promised me. And she is an honest woman.'

She found herself wanting to laugh. 'An honest woman . . .!'

'Yes.' His voice was level, his eyes held hers. 'Yes. Joanna is a strange creature, you see, Eleanor. She does not desire power, money, status, all the usual trappings. Hamon shall not have her.'

Eleanor said very softly, 'People are laughing at me, Guillaume. Soon they will laugh at you, too.'

He came towards her, and knelt on the floor in front of her. He took her restless hands in his. 'It was not my intention to humiliate you, Eleanor. Simply to make Hamon suffer. Come. Don't you like to see him suffer?'

She nodded slowly. Then she said, hesitantly: 'If you are in need of money, cousin, I still have the jewels from my dowry . . .'

His bark of laughter echoed against the bare stone walls. 'Has it come to that?' Guillaume shook his head. 'Not yet, Eleanor. But it was a kind thought.'

She took the glass that he held out to her, and had to drink deeply before she could frame her next question. The sunlight made pools of light on the dusty floor: she stared at the flickering shadows, trying to force herself to say the name she had not spoken for years.

'I want you to tell me about Italy, Guillaume,' she said. 'All of it. I want you to tell me about Toby Crow. He was a loyal servant once.'

He was a loyal servant once. She gave a small smile, knowing how she lied, how she had learned to edit everything she said. Her loyal servant had been her lover, the father of her only child.

She listened as he told it all from the beginning. The battle of Novara, the tavern in which he had found himself, sick and without friends. She realized, as she listened, what the years had done to him. Guillaume, like her, was scarred, permanently damaged. She heard him describe his journey across Italy: the sights he had seen, the places he had travelled through. And then his meeting with Toby, his discovery that Martin Gefroy was dead.

When he had finished, she asked, 'How was he? How did he look?'

Guillaume glanced up at her, incomprehension in his eyes. 'Who?'

She said his name again. There was still, she realized, the faintest echo of the pleasure she had once had in simply speaking his name. 'Toby.'

'He did well to leave France. He is no longer at anyone's beck and call, Eleanor. He has more than a hundred and fifty men fighting for him. Oh . . .' Guillaume frowned, remembering something. 'He asked after you.'

Eleanor put down her glass. She said nothing, she just recalled, in the long silence, the months that she had loved Toby. A few months of happiness. How many of her kind, she thought, had that? Women like her married not for love, but to increase the power and wealth of men. Blanche, Izabel and she had been powerless pawns in a game whose prize was the acquisition of land and property. Their consolation in their loneliness was the certainty of food in their bellies, clothes on their backs, roofs over their heads. It was only the outsiders, the nameless and penniless, who risked everything, or gained everything.

She made her excuses soon after that. Hamon's servants had travelled with her; they waited in Guillaume's hay-strewn courtyard, watching the lengthening shadows cast by the sun. They had not even unsaddled their horses.

Eleanor reached Marigny the following afternoon. Dismounting from her horse, she entered the château and climbed the stairs, lifting her skirts out of the mortar and stone fragments that the masons had left.

She had intended to go to her bedchamber, but as she walked past the library, she saw her husband. He was standing at the window, looking out to the garden. Eleanor felt a sudden wave of hatred wash over her. She knew that it had been Hamon who had taken Toby from her, just as it had been Hamon who had killed François. Momentarily, she wished for a knife in her hand and the courage to use it.

She had no knife, though. Her only weapon was her tongue. She said clearly, 'So Guillaume's whore has visited us again?' He turned. She saw how white his face was, how dark his eyes. Eleanor smiled. 'Won't she come to your bed, Hamon? Do you hunger for her, Hamon?'

She had stabbed, she realized then, as deep as she could have with any dagger. Hamon wanted Joanna Zulian, and not just because she belonged to a du Chantonnay. Hamon wanted Joanna Zulian, Eleanor thought, as much as she herself had once wanted Toby.

'Perhaps she craves blue eyes and an unlined skin. Perhaps she wants a young man's arms around her. Perhaps she thinks, husband, that you are too old to do in bed what Cousin Guillaume can do . . .'

Eleanor's voice whispered tauntingly. She crossed the room to stand in front of him. She saw him raise his hand to strike her, and she ducked, running behind the table. 'You are in love with a harlot!' she hissed. 'You are in love with Cousin Guillaume's harlot!'

Moving quickly, he seized her wrist. She thought that the pressure of his grip might turn her bones to powder. 'Love?' he said. 'Love is for fools and servants. You should know, Eleanor.'

She did not understand him. She grinned, baring her teeth. 'Marigny is not enough for you, is it, Hamon? You thought it would be, but it isn't. You want *her* as well. How does it feel, Hamon, to be prey to such a common ailment? To such a tawdry passion?'

She could not evade his blow this time. The flat of his hand struck her hard on the side of her head. She fell to the floor in a shimmer of stars, a billowing of velvet blackness. She held on to consciousness, though, feeling triumphant, happy. She knew how greatly she had wounded him. Her bruised lips had already begun to thicken; her skirts were rucked up to her knees. She mumbled, 'How they will laugh at you at Blois, Hamon. How they will laugh at you . . .'

He stood over her, a small smile on his lips. He said softly, 'As they laughed at you, dear wife, when you lusted after your manservant.' The smile grew, blossomed. The expression in his eyes began to frighten her. 'You were pathetic, Eleanor. I almost pitied you. What did you intend to offer your stepson's bodyguard to make him endure a night in bed with you?'

She gasped. The colour had drained from her face.

He looked down at her, at her sprawled, open legs, at her dishevelled clothing. 'Cover yourself,' he whispered. 'You revolt me.'

She pulled her skirts over her knees, staggered to her feet. The blow had made her head start to ache again.

Hamon had reached the door. His hand gripped the handle, and he turned it, looking back at her. He said pityingly, 'Did you offer him marriage, Eleanor? Did he baulk even at that?'

Her anger redoubled. Her eyes were distended, her skin paper-white. She said fiercely: 'I should have married him. Yes, I should have. I shouldn't have waited, I should have married Toby after Reynaud died, and not cared a jot what the rest of the world thought!'

'Poor Eleanor,' he said as he opened the door. 'Ah, well, take comfort, my dear. The father or the son – is there a great deal of difference?'

She didn't understand him at all. Shadows had begun to gather in the room as the sun lowered itself through the sky. Eleanor stared at Hamon. Her face hurt.

'Didn't you know?' said Hamon de Bohun. 'No. Why should you? I don't suppose Mr Crow would wish to broadcast his parentage.'

She managed to move at last. She shuffled across the room to stand in front of him, her defiance, her brief recovery of confidence, gone. 'What do you mean?' she said hoarsely.

'Well, his birth was rather irregular. I fathered him on Reynaud's sister, you see. Reynaud wasn't too happy about it.'

He had turned to go. Eleanor shook her head slowly. 'I don't believe you,' she whispered.

Hamon, pausing in the doorway, creased his brow in a frown. 'It's hard to prove, I'll admit. But you'll know, perhaps, that Izabel and Reynaud quarrelled. Because of the brat, you see. Izabel Mandeville tried to hid her little changeling, to protect him. God knows why. Rather an extreme instance of maternal feelings, I'd have thought.'

Eleanor felt herself shrinking. Her shoulders bowed, her face crumpled.

'I found the benighted infant, though, and sent him to Reynaud. That was a long time ago, before poor François was born. Some sort of revenge, you see, my dear Eleanor. After all, Reynaud had taken Marigny from me.'

She shook her head. A low moan escaped her bruised lips, a formless, keening sound.

'So you need not regret your hesitation, perhaps, Eleanor,' Hamon continued. 'Toby Crow and I are of the same blood, as I explained. You simply wed into a different generation.'

Her moaning filled the room. He was smiling. She pushed past him then, stumbling through the doorway. She did not at first know where she was going; she no longer recognized the rooms and stairways through which she passed. Eventually, she found herself blundering up the steps of the highest tower. She had to crawl on her hands and knees; the stairs were winding, short-treaded. She could see clearly only what was directly in front of her: everything else was misted by a haze of whirling lights.

When she reached the topmost room, she hauled herself to her feet, and leaned against the window-sill, looking out. The far-distant ground whirled below her. Squinting, she could see the new gardens: the squares of the kitchen garden with their zigzag patterns, their mazes, the squares within squares. The kitchen garden was vast and geometric, like a chess game set out for giants. The designs, spinning in front of her distorted vision, seemed almost to form themselves into words and names.

Eleanor turned away from the window. She saw, rolled up in the corner, the tapestries. *Her* tapestries, the unicorn tapestries. She began to pull apart the ropes that bound them. The twine tore at her fingers, breaking her nails. She unrolled each one until she found the one she was looking for, and then she gathered it in her arms and dragged it down the stairs. Her chest hurt, as she struggled for breath. The tapestry was heavy, and her arms ached. She slipped once or twice on the winding stairway but managed to regain her balance.

Reaching the foot of the tower, she began to heave the tapestry through Marigny's passageways and chambers. The servants stared at her. Some of them spoke to her, but she did not listen. One of them tried to take the tapestry from her, but she hissed at him, and he retreated as though she had struck him. She saw fear in their eyes; she saw serving-women and grooms scuttle back to the kitchen and stables.

At last Eleanor reached the gallery. She pushed a stool over to the wall. Lighter squares of stone showed where the tapestries had once hung. The hooks that had held them in place still protruded from the walls. She stood on the stool, lifting up one corner of the tapestry. Beads of perspiration ran down her face. She was a tall woman, but her fingers could only just reach the hooks. It took her three attempts to slip a loop over a hook. Each successive loop was easier, though.

When she had finished, she climbed down. The tapestry, only slightly askew, hung where it had always hung. She felt a brief sensation of pride, that she had bought this to Marigny, that these beautiful things had been her dowry. She looked up. The borders of the tapestry, with the glorious flowery meadow that she loved so much, were lost to her, hopelessly blurred. She could see only the unicorn, its forelegs resting on the maiden's lap, its great sad eyes half closed.

For the betrayal of innocence, she whispered to herself. For François, whom she had failed to protect. For Guy, whom she had been unable to love.

Eleanor left the gallery then. Marigny was silent and deserted: only her skirts rustled as she walked to the top of the new staircase and looked down to the Great Hall. She saw Hamon standing at the bottom of the wide steps. In the silence his tread on the raw, unweathered new stones seemed unnaturally loud.

The staircase was almost finished. Even then, as he watched Eleanor at the top of the stairs, it occurred to Hamon how their width, their height, improved the appearance of the Great Hall.

Eleanor had lost her head-dress: her hair was tangled loose around her face. Her gown was covered with grey strands – cobwebs, Hamon realized. He noticed how faltering her steps were, as she edged along the balustrade.

Her voice did not falter, though. She said, 'I'm going to Blois, Hamon. I'm going to tell the truth about François. And about Toby and Izabel, too. They will take Marigny from you.'

He knew that he would never let them take Marigny from him. He said, 'No one will believe you. You have no evidence.'

She took her first step down towards him. The stairs were still littered with workmen's tools: hammers and chisels and awls. She didn't seem to see them, though. He would have thought, did he not know better, that she was blind.

Her foot twisted. The chisel on which she had stepped slid and clattered to the stair below. She reached out and failed to grip the banister as her foot slithered off the edge of the stair. Then she fell heavily on her back, tumbling downwards until she lay at the foot of the stairs, only a few feet from Hamon.

Hamon knew before he touched her that she was dead. Her head lolled at an impossible angle; her eyes were still half open.

There was a sound from behind him. He turned. He might, he thought, need witnesses that this death had been accidental. But it was only the child, his son, peering out from behind the table.

Guy's steady gaze rested first on the broken body of his mother, and then he slowly turned to Hamon. Hamon recognized, in those dark, slate-grey eyes, a mixture of emotions. Grief and fear and defiance. Momentarily, the child reminded him of someone, something. He shook his head, struggling to capture the fleeting memory. He saw himself standing at a quayside in Roscoff, a knife in his hand. *'Bend sinister, for bastardy,'* he had said, before he had marked his son's skin. Toby Crow had looked at him then with eyes like that.

He heard the footsteps, the weeping of Eleanor's women, but he still stared at the child. *'I should have married him,'* Eleanor had said, of his first-born son, Toby Crow. Now Hamon wished that he could wake Eleanor from her sleep. He wanted to seize her and to shake her into life again. He wanted to know the truth. What if she had not merely lusted after her serving-man? What if, in spite of her appalling innocence, in spite of the goodness that he had always despised, she had broken the bounds of convention and taken Toby Crow to her bed? Ignoring the tears of the women, the suspicious mutterings of the men, Hamon began to think back, to calculate.

He had married Eleanor in March, and the child had been born in September. A seven-month child, they had said, and yet the infant Guy had not been undersized, had not struggled for life. Indeed, he had been a fit, healthy baby of good size. He remembered Eleanor's fall down the chapel steps, a fall that no one else had witnessed. A fall that had supposedly brought on her premature labour. He remembered, finally, how quickly she had consented to their hasty marriage. How quickly she had become pregnant.

Hamon stepped back, away from the body of his wife, towards his child. The wailing of the women filled the Great Hall. Hamon thought of Eleanor: the hours she had spent on her knees in the draughty chapel, her simplicity, her conformity. She had not, he told himself, been capable of that sort of sin.

The child had covered his face with his hands now, was rocking silently backwards and forwards. Hamon did not speak to Guy, but gave orders for the disposal of the body of his wife.

For the French the summer of 1514 was disastrous. They had lost all their possessions in northern Italy, and the English were rampaging through northern France, capturing towns, laying siege to cities. Venice's prospects, in consequence of their ally's faltering strength, were poor.

Toby was in Venice when he received Joanna's letter. It was August. The city was hot and uncomfortable, teeming with flies. The canals stank, their stagnant waters thick and green.

He was received by Andrea Gritti in his splendid palazzo overlooking the Grand Canal. Even Gritti's house buzzed with mosquitoes, though, and the scented pomanders, the wormwood and rue in bowls on every window-sill, could not disguise the stench of the canal.

'I can offer you wine, grapes, sweetmeats,' said Gritti, greeting Toby. 'I cannot, sadly, offer you anything to take the heat from this infernal weather. Did you know that the Moors haul ice down from the mountains to cool their food and drink in the summer? Such a sensible people, I've always thought.'

Toby, grinning, refused Gritti's offer of refreshments. Letters, some of them with their seals broken, others still folded and tied with ribbon, were spread out on the Proveditor's desk.

'News?' Toby asked, indicating the letters.

Andrea Gritti frowned. 'Rumours,' he said. 'That France and England will soon make peace. That the treaty will be sealed by the marriage of the French king to Henry Tudor's sister.'

Toby looked up. 'Mary Tudor is betrothed to Charles of Castile. And besides, Louis de France is a widower in his fifties, and the Princess Mary is –'

'Eighteen years old and reputedly the loveliest woman in Christendom,' finished Gritti drily. 'There are advantages, don't you agree, Toby, to rank?'

A fly had settled on the dish of sweetmeats. Gritti brushed it irritably away.

'Still . . . rumours,' said Toby.

'I've always put great faith in rumours.' The Venetian looked up at him. 'I asked you here for two reasons, Toby. The first is that you might consider going to France, to investigate the source of these rumours. I am uncertain as yet what effect an alliance between France and England might have on Venice.'

Toby said nothing. He went to the open window and looked at the canal with its litter of bustling ships. He did not want to return to France. He had not returned to France since he had told Joanna Zulian of his relationship with Hamon de Bohun.

He said, 'And the other reason? You said that there were two reasons for inviting me here, Andrea.'

'Ah, yes.' Gritti sifted through the pile of papers on his desk. 'I have a letter for you. It was forwarded from Blois.'

Toby did not recognize the handwriting, and the seal was an undistinguished blob of red wax. He broke the seal and saw the signature.

When he had finished reading, the bright sunlight glittering on the canal seemed inappropriate and obscene. He crumpled the letter in his fist as he stared out at the meaningless jumble of masts and sails. The ceaseless industry of busy, clever Venice seemed futile, worthless, and his own efforts over the past four years equally laughable, yet another symptom of his pathetically limitless arrogance.

Gritti rose from his desk and stood behind him. 'Bad news?' said the Venetian gently.

Toby nodded. He could not yet speak. One of his hands clutched the window-sill, the other crushed Joanna's letter into an illegible ball.

'I'll speak to you later,' he managed to say, 'about France.'

His voice sounded odd even to his own ears. He couldn't meet Gritti's eyes; he could only walk out of the room, the house, as fast as he was able.

He lost track of time as he walked. The sun beat down on his head and neck. His hair was damp with sweat. He walked past canals and palaces and piazzas, but he did not see them. He saw only Joanna's bold black handwriting.

I wanted to tell you, Toby, before you heard from anyone else, that Eleanor de Bohun is dead.

Joanna had been at Marigny on the afternoon of Eleanor's death. Her description of the circumstances of that death was brief, factual, softened, Toby suspected, for his consumption. Eleanor de Bohun had fallen downstairs and broken her neck. The inhabitants of Marigny, Toby thought bitterly, were rather prone to bad falls.

He found himself at the end of an alleyway that opened out on to the Grand Canal. He sat at the water's edge, one knee bunched up to his face, his eyes screwed tightly shut. Mosquitoes attacked his bare forearms, but he did not move.

He found, when he looked up, that he recognized this stretch of canal. Just beyond the curve of the water was the palazzo of Marcantonio Venier. He remembered watching Joanna Zulian walk out of the courtyard of that palazzo and into the water. He remembered how her long hair had floated on the water like bright seaweed, how her skirts had belled around her. How, just for a moment, her head had bobbed under the water, and he had called her name and reached out to grasp her flailing hand.

It was as though, he thought wearily, at every branch in his life he had chosen the wrong fork. There was a temptation to slide into the opaque, green water. Just so that he didn't have to think again. Just so that he didn't have to dream again.

But Toby got to his feet and began once more to walk. Past the quaysides, past where they loaded and unloaded the ships that crammed the lagoon. He thought of taking passage on one of those boats, of setting sail for the far corners of the earth. To Cathay, Africa, the Indies. The sun dipped into the Adriatic, blistering the smooth water with a carmine light. Toby watched the slow perpetual pageant of the ending of day, the beginning of night.

He returned to Andrea Gritti's palazzo, and told Gritti that he would go to France. There was really nowhere else for him to go to.

It took Joanna a considerable gathering of courage to return to Marigny after Eleanor de Bohun's death. She did not go back until the funeral and all its complicated aftermath were over with. She did not belong in a house of mourning: Eleanor de Bohun had, she knew, despised and resented her. She went back to Marigny only because of Guy. And for the garden that would tell the truth.

She found the château and its people altered with Eleanor's death. The drawbridge was raised, the guard at the boundary gates had been doubled. Shutters were closed, windows curtained. Servants whispered behind their hands, women rubbed reddened eyes with the hems of their aprons.

Guy came to her, though. She was kneeling on the ground, planting tiny lavender bushes into great wild curves, when she heard the sound of hooves behind her. He was riding his pony, the fat, dappled Perle. He halted the pony in the shadow of the dovecote, and stared at her with his dark eyes anxious, questioning. Joanna rose to her feet, brushing her hands and skirts free of earth.

'I have a piece of marchpane,' she said, when she reached Guy. 'Do you think that Perle likes marchpane?'

He did not smile, he only nodded his head slowly. 'I save my sweetmeats and give them to Perle for breakfast.'

Joanna held the marchpane out on her open hand. The pony's soft lips nuzzled at her palm. She said gently: 'Shouldn't you be at your lessons, Guy? Shouldn't you be with your tutor?'

The child's eyes were wide and dark. He shook his head. 'Master Flore has gone. He went away when *maman* died. I don't have lessons any more.'

His lips clamped together, his eyes darted back to the great mass of the château. Joanna stroked the pony's mane and studied Guy. He appeared, as always, well-fed and well-dressed. Yet the collar of his silk shirt had begun to fray a little, and there was a hole in one of his stockings. She could not tell whether there were bruises on his back.

She saw him often after that. She took Guy into the forest once, to show him that the woods were peopled only by trees and animals, and not by monsters. She told him the creatures he must respect and avoid –

the wolves, the wild boars – and she told him the names and properties of the plants. Guy listened; he rarely spoke. Joanna walked with him along the winding paths, past the dark, circular ponds. Sitting on a fallen log with Guy on her knee, Joanna showed him the pages of her herbal, fragile and yellowed with age. The script of Donato's signature inscribed on the title page had faded so that she could hardly read it.

In the Garden of Obsessive Love she planted the seeds that she had gathered from the forest and the coast in Brittany. Cowbane, hemlock, thorn apple and nightshade. Destructive plants to show the destructive nature of that sort of love. She taught Guy to respect those plants as he respected the wolf and the wild boar; not to be tempted by their fascinating, gleaming, poisonous fruits.

All four gardens were planted now. Next summer they would be in flower. Summer had changed to autumn, leaves whirled again from the trees. Black berries gleamed on the deadly nightshade; the thorn apple put forth its curious, spiky fruit. Guy de Bohun's tutor was not replaced: the little boy had begun to have an ill-kempt, bedraggled look. No one, as far as Joanna could see, cared particularly for Guy. When she asked him the whereabouts of his nurse, Thérèse, he shook his head and sucked his thumb and rocked himself.

She would have liked to take him home with her, to bathe him and hug him and comb the tangles from his hair. She would have liked to watch him learn to play with Sanchia, to tuck him safely up in a cot in the house in Finistère each night. But she had to be content with seeing Guy de Bohun briefly, every six weeks or so, and with watching him grow more and more silent, more and more lonely.

Toby went to Joanna because he couldn't think whom else to go to.

He hardly slept now: if he closed his eyes, he would wake struggling for breath what seemed like only a few moments later. His dreams were many-coloured and vivid. Too many memories to choose from, he thought wearily.

He had deliberately isolated himself over the past four years: now he paid the price for that isolation. The price was loneliness, the absence of anyone to unburden himself to. In France, Toby delivered messages to the court at Blois and discovered details of the treaty signed between France and England. In August, the proxy wedding of Mary of England and Louis XII of France took place in Greenwich. Princess Mary lay in bed while the Duc de Longueville, standing in for the French king, removed one of his stockings and in the presence of witnesses placed his naked leg across her body. Mary would travel to France, as queen, in the autumn. As in Venice, to Toby it all seemed futile, a complicated and pointless dance of ever-changing partners. Work no longer gave him the respite that he needed. He heard the names of Eleanor and Hamon de Bohun mentioned in banquet-rooms and state-rooms, and he made his excuses and left Touraine for Brittany.

He travelled from dawn to dusk, stopping only when the light had grown too poor to distinguish the path through the forest. He lit himself a fire to keep away the wolves, and roused himself in the morning by dipping his head in the icy water of a pool. He was within a league or two of Guillaume du Chantonnay's house, he thought. The red light of dawn filtered through the trees. He saddled his horse and rode on, deeper into the forest.

He heard horses' hooves as the narrow path opened out into a glade. The hooves were drumming the forest floor: whoever followed him was travelling faster, Toby thought, than he would have cared to ride in such conditions. Grass edged with scarlet-spotted fungi floored the glade. Toby's hand rested on his sword-hilt as he reined in his mare, and waited.

He saw four men and a woman. The men were plainly dressed in broadcloth and linen, leather jerkins covering their backs. The woman wore green silk; her long red-brown hair streamed out behind her like a banner. The woman's horse, brought suddenly to a halt with a twitch of her reins, reared. Toby, sliding from the saddle, ran to catch her bridle.

'Are the hounds of hell chasing you, Joanna? It's dangerous country.' His voice sounded irritable, impatient, even to his own ears. She kept in the saddle, though, as he held the bridle and soothed the frightened animal. Soon the mare settled down and her hooves stopped pawing at the grass.

'I like to ride fast,' Joanna said.

Her eyes were bright, her hair dishevelled. She dismounted from the horse. Toby managed to bite his tongue. How she rode, where she rode, was Joanna's business. Some of the mistakes of the past he would not repeat.

She called out to her servants, who were hovering, bored and cold, at the edge of the glade. 'Ride on, Patrig. I will join you shortly.' And then, when they did not move, 'This gentleman is a friend. Be off with you.'

A final sharp stare at Toby, and the men rode away, their horses' hooves kicking up the dead leaves and mud. Toby looked down at Joanna.

'Are you well? Have you travelled far?'

'I am well. And I have travelled from Nantes. And before that, from Marigny.'

'Ah.' He noted the defensive tone of her voice, the pride in her eyes. He made himself say, 'Monsieur du Chantonnay . . . How is he?'

Joanna's eyes met his. 'Guillaume is dying, Toby. I know it, he knows it, yet we do not speak of it. He intends to travel to Normandy, to attend the marriage of the king. He wishes to keep the king's favour, you see.'

Her face was set, expressionless. He thought how easy it had once been to read Joanna Zulian: how her thoughts and feelings had once been constantly reflected on her beautiful face. Now she, too, had learned deception. He wanted to say, *Will you mourn him?*, but he did not.

Instead, he forced himself to say: 'And the Seigneur de Marigny? Does he suffer from the plague, or the sweating sickness, or leprosy?'

The defiance in her eyes faded a little. She shook her head. 'Sadly, no.' Just for a moment, Joanna folded her gloved hand over his. 'You had my letter, Toby.'

He nodded. He couldn't speak. There was a sound, and he saw her look around, startled. It was only a pheasant, though, wings whirring as it beat against the air.

'On the ride back from Nantes,' Joanna said slowly, 'I thought that someone was following us. That was why we were riding so fast.' She shivered. 'I have felt that before, here in the forest. Eyes . . . footsteps.'

Yet she had never been a fearful woman, Toby thought. The ghosts that had haunted Eleanor du Chantonnay throughout her life had never lingered long with Joanna. She had fought her own battle with loneliness, isolation and envy, and she had won.

She shook herself and smiled at him. 'We'll talk at home, Toby. I need to see my daughter. And I'm cold.'

He helped her back into her saddle. As they rode from the glade the path narrowed again, imprisoning them between tall trees and thickets.

As he neared Guillaume du Chantonnay's house in Finistère, occasionally Toby thought he heard the sound of footsteps. But when he looked round, there was nothing. Wolves, he told himself.

After she had hugged and kissed Sanchia and had warmed her frozen hands before the fire, Joanna repeated at Toby's request all that she had written in her letter. How she had been in the garden, alone, marking out the next part of the pattern with stakes and twine. How one of her shocked servants, who had been waiting in Marigny's stables, ran to her with the terrible news.

'She fell down the stairs,' Joanna said, pouring Toby hot wine flavoured with spices. 'The Seigneur and his son were the only witnesses.'

He just looked at her, but she knew what he was asking.

'I don't know, Toby,' she said flatly. 'I suspect, to be honest, that Madame de Marigny fell. She had been unwell for some time. Bad headaches. Megrims, Guillaume said. And I think that had de Bohun wished himself rid of his wife, he'd have found a different way to do it. After all – his stepson . . .'

Her voice trailed away. Toby did not, Joanna noticed, drink his wine. He rubbed at his eyes with his fingers, as if to rub away bad memories.

She added, 'Guillaume says that there are rumours, though.'

He looked up then. 'At Blois?' He grimaced. 'He's right, Joanna. Someone told me that the Seigneur and Madame de Marigny quarrelled just before her death. Their servants heard them.'

'Which is why,' Joanna said drily, 'Guillaume goes to court. To stir up the rumours. To keep them alive.'

Toby smiled. The smile was hollow, hopeless, and did not touch his eyes. 'For Marigny,' he said. 'Guillaume will hope to bring any scent of scandal to the ears of the king. He will urge Louis to confiscate the estates from de Bohun, and disinherit his son. All of this, of course, in the belief that the estates will eventually be returned to their rightful claimant, Guillaume du Chantonnay.'

Eventually Joanna said, 'Will Guillaume succeed, do you think, Toby?'

Toby shrugged. 'Perhaps. Though de Bohun is very plausible face to face. And at the moment Louis is, of course, rather preoccupied with his marriage to the Princess Mary.'

She watched him as he spoke. He looked, she thought, exhausted. 'And you, Toby,' she said. 'Do you care who wins? Do you care who finally has Marigny?'

He was staring into the fire; his fingers, which had fiddled endlessly with the stem of his goblet or drummed on the table, stilled suddenly. 'No,' he said. 'I thought I did once. But now . . .'

He rose then, and went to the door, mumbling something about seeing to his horse. She did not try to stop him. As he left the room, she thought of the endless cycle of death and destruction that the de Bohuns and the du Chantonnays had set in motion, of the innocence they had trampled underfoot – wantonly, thoughtlessly, as an insignificant by-product of something they had believed to be important. They had been wrong, though. Stones and mortar, fields and vineyards, even the lovely meadow that imprisoned the château de Marigny, were not worth the tears of Eleanor de Bohun, of Izabel Mandeville, of François and Guy.

Joanna persuaded Toby to stay. She was, she told him, nervous. That was not quite true: in Finistère she was never nervous, but still there were the footsteps, the eyes. She could not quite rid herself of the sense that she was being watched.

She realized, after Toby had been in the house a couple of days, that he did not sleep. In the evenings he would prowl round the house and gardens, checking the stables, securing the locks and bolts. At dawn, when Joanna woke, he would still be out there, hands dug deep into his pockets, collar up, walking. The walking was directionless, she realized. Something to stop him thinking.

Sanchia was cutting her back teeth. Joanna, returning from the nursery in the early hours of the morning and passing the room in which Toby slept, saw the thin gleam of light beneath his door. She knocked gently.

'I saw the candlelight,' she said, pushing open the door.

He was dressed in shirt and breeches and was pulling on his boots. He looked up at her, startled. 'I was going to . . .'

His voice trailed away. Joanna put her candlestick down on the table.

'See to the horses? Walk ten times round the garden? Try and lose yourself in the forest?'

Toby, knotting the laces of his doublet, said nothing.

'You are like me, Toby,' said Joanna. 'You know every path in the forest. You couldn't lose yourself if you walked blindfold.'

The lace snapped; Toby closed his eyes very tightly. There was a furrow of pain between his brows.

Joanna sat down on the bed next to him. 'Think of Martin,' she whispered. 'Martin always lost his way. He couldn't cross Padua without having to ask for directions. That's why he had to ask you to take me to France.'

She touched his hand then. She saw him flinch, but she did not let go. 'But you never get lost, Toby. So you have to face what's inside your head. It's the only way.'

'No,' he said. 'You don't know what you're asking.' His refusal was flat, final. He didn't even glance at her.

She said, suddenly: 'Why did you come here, Toby?'

He looked up at her then, eyes wide. 'Because of Eleanor,' he said eventually. 'I needed to know.'

She almost believed him. But she said, trying to force him to see himself clearly, 'I told you everything in my letter. You needed to talk to someone, it's true. But why didn't you go to Agnès . . . or Martin . . .'

'Martin has gone back to England. And Agnès – I haven't spoken to Agnès for some years. I can't . . .' He left the sentence unfinished.

He persistently evaded her, she thought, evaded anyone who might come close to him. She realized that he was almost unable to live with himself, that he teetered on the brink, avoiding disaster only through the violence and constant demands of his profession. He did not know himself; he refused to acknowledge the need he had of other people.

Joanna took a deep breath. 'What troubles you most?' she said. 'Eleanor, or your childhood, or de Bohun?'

He pulled away from her and went to stand at the window. In the dim light she could see only the outline of his shoulders, the shape of his head as he laid his palms on the sill and stared through the glass.

'All of it,' he said softly. And then, correcting himself, 'No. Not true. It's the house that haunts me, Joanna. It's the house that I dream about.'

It was cold in the room; the fire had died hours before. Joanna, crouched in the corner of the bed, pulled the blankets around her. 'Marigny?' she said.

She saw the small shake of his head. 'No, not Marigny. The other house.' She didn't understand him. Then he turned and said, 'Izabel Mandeville's house.'

Joanna frowned. 'The house in England? The house that Hamon de Bohun sent you to?'

Toby said slowly, 'I dream of it every night. The empty windows, the cobwebs, the dust on the sills, on the floor. That's all. Nothing more. Just an empty house.'

He was silent for a while, and then he added, his voice low and angry, 'I have seen wars, sieges, reprisals for sieges. I have seen men, women and children slaughtered. I have almost died myself, more than once. As a child I endured hunger, loneliness, mistreatment. And yet I dream of an empty house. And I am terrified, Joanna. I am *terrified*.'

Rising, the blanket wrapped around her shoulders, she saw in the candlelight the anger in his eyes, the whiteness of his face. She feared for him then. She understood the terror that a single image could conjure. For her, it was the portrait that hung on the wall at Marigny, or the memory of an empty cradle. For Toby, it was a deserted house.

'I hear his voice,' Toby whispered. 'Hamon de Bohun's voice, at Blois. *"How she wept. How she wailed. I thought she'd be glad to part with her little changeling."* He was talking about my mother.'

She rested her hands on his shoulders and laid her head against his chest. Closing her eyes, she could hear the fast beating of his heart.

'I was a small child, Joanna. An infant – Sanchia's age. There was such pleasure in his voice. My *father*!'

She began to shiver. Cold air leaked in around the window-frame and a draught blew through the chimney. In her mind's eye she saw the infant taken by force from his home, the mother howling at her loss. He had recalled, painfully, the desolation she had felt at the death of her son. But she was aware, even as his arms folded momentarily round her, pulling her to him, of a discrepancy, something not quite right. Something to be considered later, when she was alone, when she could think clearly.

She heard him say: 'You're cold. Go back to bed, Joanna.'

In the distance, Joanna heard her daughter's cry. A thin wail pulling her back from the past to the present. Toby's hands slipped from her, as if suddenly he recalled his distrust of human warmth. She was about to speak when he picked up the cloak that lay on the bed, but, seeing his expression, she said nothing. She had pinpointed it now, though, that curious thread, gleaming in the darkness like gold.

Joanna rose early the following morning and told Toby that she was going to talk to a woman in Commana about Sanchia's teeth. She told

Sanchia's nurse the truth: that she would be away for four or five days, and no one was to worry.

To find Guillaume du Chantonnay, she went not to Nantes, but to Rennes. Guillaume was travelling to Abbeville, not far from Boulogne, on the coast of Normandy. Rennes, Joanna thought, was a reasonable guess.

Rain blackened the gates and ramparts of the town, swelled in yellow streams down the cobbled streets. The overhanging half-timbered houses gave partial shelter; Joanna huddled under the plastered storeys while her servant, irritable with the weather and the journey, made inquiries.

Her guess proved a good one; Guillaume was staying in a hotel in the Rue de Chapitre. She was led up a carved wooden staircase that clung precariously to the inner wall of the house. Water dripped from her gown on to the stairs; her gloved hands left damp patches on the bevelled banisters and on the grotesques that leered from every corner. The servant announced her. Guillaume, looking up from his desk, glanced first at Joanna and then at the pools of water that gathered around the hem of her gown.

'I was remaining indoors, my dear Joanna, to avoid the inclement weather. But you seem to have brought it in here with you.' He rose and untied the cloak from her shoulders, and laid it over the back of a stool next to the fire. 'I hope you've brought more clothes with you than that. Or do you intend to witness the marriage of our sovereign lord dressed in a rather muddy travelling-gown?'

Joanna shook her head. 'I'm not coming with you, Guillaume.'

He took her hand and raised it to his lips. 'Then why,' he said, 'are you here?'

'I've a few odds and ends to sell to the apothecary,' she replied, smiling breezily, deceitfully. 'Seeds and berries and suchlike. They'll give me a better price here than in Morlaix.'

She didn't know whether he believed her or not. But he nodded, and let go of her hand.

'Dear Joanna,' said Guillaume. 'Always so busy. Gardens, potions, nostrums. I don't know another woman who would ride out on a day like this for the sake of a few seeds.'

'I thought perhaps we could dine together. And I could dry out a little.'

He led her to the fireplace. Then he unpinned her head-dress and, putting it aside, began to free her damp hair from its plaits. His hands were gentle, careful. Looking into the fire, she thought of what he could have been. She thought, as he combed his fingers through her long wet locks, that she could have loved him.

He said, 'Won't you come with me to Abbeville, Joanna? All the world will be there.'

He meant, she knew, *Hamon de Bohun will be there*. She had never told Guillaume of the conversation she had had with Toby, never told him of the painting she had seen at Marigny.

'Think about it,' he said softly, when she did not reply. 'I shall send for some food.'

Over capon and fish, pears and cheese, she said casually: 'At Marigny, Guillaume, someone mentioned to me that the former Seigneur – your cousin – had a sister.'

Guillaume put down his goblet, looked across the table to Joanna. 'Izabel,' he said. 'Reynaud had a sister called Izabel.'

'Is she alive?'

He shook his head. 'She died – oh, a long time ago. Reynaud married her to an Englishman. I can't remember his name. She died a few years after the marriage. There were no children, thank God.'

Wrong, Joanna thought, looking down at her plate. Her face felt hot suddenly. There had been one child, a son. But that child had been illegitimate, and therefore was no obstacle to Guillaume's claim to Marigny.

She looked up. 'Did he like her?'

'Who?'

'Reynaud. Was he fond of his sister?'

Guillaume had, Joanna noticed, eaten very little.

'To begin with, yes. Izabel was about the only person the old bastard was fond of. Couldn't stand his wife. His first wife, I mean – Blanche. She irritated him. And he loathed my parents. And of course, François was a great disappointment to him. But Izabel . . .' Guillaume shrugged, his blue eyes half-lidded in the effort of memory. 'Everyone liked Izabel. I can remember her only a little. But she was kind, affectionate.' He laughed. 'Hardly a typical du Chantonnay.'

Though it was only midday, the sky, bloated with rainclouds, was a dark greenish-grey. Joanna took a deep breath. 'You said that Reynaud loved Izabel *to begin with*. What happened, Guillaume?'

He pushed aside his plate. 'I've no idea. But he disinherited her. He left her nothing. Not a book, not a bauble. Though in the end, of course, she died long before he did. Even then, he didn't go to her when she was ill. Reynaud left Izabel to die alone in a foreign country.'

Hamon de Bohun had taken the infant Toby from England, and sent him to Reynaud, at Marigny. Had Reynaud disinherited his sister then? The sister he had once loved? Although her gown had dried, although the fire roared in the grate only a few feet away, Joanna shivered.

'They quarrelled, I suppose,' said Guillaume. 'God knows, though, what they quarrelled about. Izabel was never an undutiful sister.'

Joanna swallowed the remainder of her wine. She noticed that Guillaume's hands were clenched over his belly, as though it hurt him.

She said, gently, 'Don't go to Abbeville, Guillaume. Go back to Nantes. Or come to Finistère with me.'

He shook his head. He had relaxed his hands, but his face was still paper-white.

'Sanchia,' she said. 'You could see Sanchia.'

He crossed the room towards her. 'I can do more for Sanchia in Abbeville than I can in Finistère, Joanna. I have to be there. It is important that Louis sees that I am there.'

She rose from her seat. Her hair had dried. He reached out and stroked it. 'Come with me,' he said again.

Joanna shook her head. She saw the future then, quite plainly. If Guillaume managed to oust Hamon de Bohun from Marigny, then Guillaume would marry. He would marry an heiress, a woman with a name, land and a dowry. He would father an heir. He might love Sanchia with all his heart, but for Marigny he would need a son. Joanna knew that there was no place for her in Abbeville or at Marigny. She existed only on the fringes of that sort of society – as Guillaume du Chantonnay's fascinating, beautiful mistress, as the creator of Marigny's Italian garden. She laboured still in a corner of a vast and beautiful room. She could not leave the corner for the centre, the sunlight.

'No, Guillaume,' she said. 'I'll not go with you to Abbeville.'

She felt him lift her hair and separate it into strands. She stood quite still as he wove two long plaits. Her eyes blurred as she stared into the fire. What he gave her was something limited, distorted by the weight of his dreams and desires. It was not enough.

PART FOUR

1514–1517

The Garden of Tender Love

She armeth herself by eating Rue, against the might of the Serpent.

Dioscorides, *De Materia Medica*

CHAPTER SEVENTEEN

A day later, Joanna was back in Finistère. It was evening: the wind picked up the rain and hurled it to the ground. Under his breath Joanna's manservant cursed the weather, the country, his damned difficult mistress.

Reaching the house, she had hardly dismounted from her horse when Toby appeared. Seizing her arms, he shook her, making her bones judder and the hood of her cloak slip off.

'Where have you *been*, Joanna? Christ! It's been *five days!*'

'Let me go,' she said faintly. 'You're hurting me.'

He let her go briefly, but then seized her hand and dragged her inside the house. The stable-boy and servant looked on in fascination.

'I went to see Guillaume,' Joanna said, freeing herself, pushing past him, climbing the narrow stairs. 'To talk to him about Izabel Mandeville.'

He turned swiftly to face her. 'Izabel Mandeville? *Why?*'

She didn't answer him. She heard his fist strike the wall, once, but she ignored him. When she reached the solar, Joanna peeled off her soaking gloves and raised her hands to the fire.

'You went to Nantes – with one servant . . .'

'To Rennes.' She turned round to face him. 'I told you, Toby, Guillaume is going to Abbeville, to see the English princess. And if I'd taken more than one servant, you wouldn't have believed that I was riding to Commana.'

He hissed with exasperation.

Joanna said quickly, 'Listen to what I have to say, Toby. Listen to what Guillaume told me about Izabel. Guillaume told me that Reynaud du Chantonnay was very fond of his sister *at first*. Then, some time after she'd been married, he cut off all communications with her, disinherited her, wouldn't even go to her when she was dying.'

She wasn't even sure that he was listening. His anger had lessened a little, though; the habitual expression of disinterest, detachment, that she knew to be a mask, had returned.

He shrugged. 'Reynaud was an obnoxious bastard with no loyalty to anyone. I could have told you that – I worked for him. That's no excuse for riding round Brittany in a gale.'

The remains of her patience evaporated completely. *'Toby,'* she cried. '*Why* did Izabel protect you? Why did she try and hide you?'

He looked down at her, bewildered.

'Your *mother*,' whispered Joanna.

He blinked. 'Because she was afraid of de Bohun. She thought he might come back, I suppose. And he did.'

'So why did she care? Why did she *want* to protect you? The child of rape . . .'

She saw him wince, but she took no notice. 'The child of her enemy,' she added. 'Don't you see how hard it was for her? Don't you see the price that she paid for hiding you?'

There was a silence. Eventually he said, 'Does it matter? It was all a very long time ago. It's all done with now.'

It wasn't all done with, though. She knew him not to be stupid, and that his obtuseness was entirely deliberate. 'Guillaume,' she said scornfully. 'Does Guillaume believe that it's all done with? Will Guillaume let Hamon de Bohun remain the Seigneur de Marigny?'

'I don't give a damn for Guillaume,' said Toby. His voice was cold and clear. 'He's your lover, after all. He's nothing to me.'

His eyes glittered. You're jealous, she thought suddenly, but you won't admit it. Her fists were clenched, her fingernails dug into her palms. Aloud she said, trying to keep her temper, 'Did you talk to anyone at Lydney Mandeville? Did you speak to anyone about your mother?'

There was a flicker of annoyance behind Toby's supercilious glare. 'Rather difficult even to pass the time of day when you don't speak the bloody language, Joanna.'

'You went away, didn't you? Ran away, because you couldn't face the truth?'

'*Christ!* You obstinate –' He stopped himself just in time.

She said softly, 'Bitch? Marginally better than whore, I suppose.'

He looked suddenly ashamed. The wind howled like the wolves, breaking the taut silence. Branches scratched at the window-panes, as sharp as fingernails. She had almost reached him, but now he had closed himself off again. His face was blank. He said, 'The gutter's blocked, the kitchen will flood. I must go . . .'

She grabbed his arm, halting him. He stared at her for a moment, and then he said, 'Don't meddle, Joanna. It's dangerous to meddle. I've learned that, even if you haven't.'

She heard the sound of small, running feet in the next room, and then the door swung open. Joanna caught up Sanchia in her arms, hugging and kissing her as the nurse hurried after her charge, gasping her apologies. When she looked up from her child, Toby was still there, watching her, and she saw what she had to do.

'Martin,' she said casually. 'I often think of him. He's in England, you said, Toby?'

'In Oxford.' Toby reached out a hand and was about to touch the child's silky golden hair. He opened his mouth to speak again, but then he turned on his heel and left the room.

The English Princess Mary endured an appalling Channel crossing. The wind howled, the rain lashed at the feeble spars and sails of her ship. One of her escort vessels sank, and her own ship ran aground off the port of Boulogne. A gentleman lifted her in his arms and carried her through shallow but seething seas to the safety of the town.

The rain continued, increasing in venom as she rode towards Abbeville. To meet her bridegroom, Mary wore a gown of cloth-of-gold and crimson and a little red cap cocked over one eye. By the time Louis, staging a supposedly accidental encounter with his bride outside the town of Abbeville, met her, the gown was dark with rainwater, the cap no longer jaunty.

Mary's youth and beauty was undiminished, however. Hamon de Bohun, attending the wedding ceremony in Abbeville Cathedral, was reminded of Joanna. Mary's hair was lighter, her eyes more blue than grey, but she had Joanna's height and slenderness. As the princess stood at the far end of the long aisle, indistinct amidst the incense, it could have been Joanna standing there, repeating the vows of the proxy wedding.

Since Eleanor's death, Hamon had been careful, though. He had, as propriety had demanded, mourned his wife; he had not appeared at court until the marriage of his liege lord had demanded it. He had avoided speaking to, or being seen with, Joanna Zulian. His name must not be linked so soon with such a woman. He must wait, must be patient. He was aware that rumour buzzed like flies among his peers. He was aware also of the great irony that suspicion should focus on a death that had, after all, been accidental.

Two days later, Mary was crowned at Saint-Denis. As she rode into Paris, crowds lined the streets waving banners, and flowers perfumed her path. No one expressed out loud their revulsion that such a young, lovely girl had married an ailing old man.

Hamon de Bohun's messengers were waiting for him in Paris. One told him that the physician Martin Gefroy was, as Hamon had suspected, alive and living in England; the other told him the news that he had longed to hear.

The painter Gaetano Cavazza, the husband of Joanna Zulian, had died four years ago in Venice of the plague.

At Roscoff Joanna paused, looking out to sea. The letter to Martin was safely hidden in the bodice of her gown. She thought of the day that she, Donato and Sanchia had stood on the coast of Brittany, looking out across the English Channel. So long ago. All done with, as Toby had said.

Turning, she smiled at Padrig. 'A ship,' she said. 'We need to find a ship bound for England.'

Padrig spat on the cobbles. The sea, grey-green and swollen, heaved against the quayside. The icy wind picked up the folds and layers of Joanna's clothing and flicked them spitefully into the air. They began to walk along the harbour.

Writing the letter had been easy, thought Joanna, as Padrig trawled his inquiries to each vessel they passed. Just like talking to an old friend. She knew Martin well enough to guess that any old antagonisms and jealousies that had once existed had been forgiven long ago, if not forgotten. Hiding her intentions from Toby had at first seemed easy too. Rising in the early hours of the morning to comfort a teething Sanchia, Joanna had seen Toby through the open door of the solar, fast asleep on the window-seat. He was quite still, his head resting against the glass, the furrow still etched between his brows. She had wanted to smooth the deep cleft away with her fingertips, but instead she had bent her head and lightly kissed his forehead and he had not stirred at all. Then she had collected her letter, and thrown a few belongings in a saddlebag, and called Padrig.

Her departure had seemed so simple then, but now in Roscoff she felt quite differently. The rain had already turned to sleet, and heavy, threatening clouds massed themselves on the horizon. Remembering her daughter's hot, pink face, she did not want her journey to take any longer than necessary. Picking up her skirts, she ran after Padrig, coaxing him to act with all speed. They soon found what they were looking for: a small cog bound for the south coast of England. She had only the haziest idea of the whereabouts of Oxford, but Padrig, translating for her the English captain's rudimentary Breton, assured her that from Southampton the letter would reach Oxford within a couple of days. Joanna handed a purse to the captain, and promised more money in the event of a reply. She guessed at the muttered threats that Padrig was issuing. Then she walked back across the quayside to where they had hidden the horses.

Joanna was anxious to get back to the house. She scarcely heard Padrig's grumbles about the weather or his pleas that they postpone their return until the next morning. She recalled too clearly Sanchia's feverish face, and was guiltily aware that she had left no indication of her whereabouts for Toby. She began to regret her haste as they travelled down the promontory to Morlaix, and were crossing the lands of heath and forest that covered the heart of Brittany. The sleet had turned to snow: it stung her face. The daylight had not lasted out the afternoon; the snowcloud turned the remains of the light to a dull greyish-green, so that she could hardly distinguish Padrig riding ahead of her, so that the familiar paths of Finistère became strange and threatening.

And there was that lingering sense that they were not alone, that someone, not too far away, was watching them. Joanna pulled the hood of her cloak lower over her eyes, and brushed away the snowflakes that clung to her eyelashes, easing her horse carefully through the stones and heather.

Left in peace by Joanna's servants, Toby did not wake until after midday. When he opened his eyes, he was without any sense of time or place. He had slept deeply and dreamlessly and, looking out of the solar window at the dripping sleet, he was aware of an unaccustomed sense of contentment.

Then, standing up, stretching his cramped limbs, he remembered who he was and where he was. He heard the distant clatter of pots and pans, a baby's cry. He realized that he was very hungry. He fetched himself something to eat from the kitchen and, working out from the brightness of the sky that it must already be afternoon, he finally noticed Joanna's absence. The house seemed dead and dull; he missed her quick, light footsteps, the sound of her voice.

He went from room to room, flinging open doors, his temporary good humour dissolving with each step. He threw a cloak over his shoulders and walked the bounds of her bedraggled garden. He knew she was not there, though. Standing there as the sleet turned to snow and stung his face, he knew that she had gone away. The absence of her was almost tangible. In the stables, Toby found, as he had known he would find, that two of the horses were missing. The remains of his cheerfulness evaporated in anxiety and anger. Back in the house, he discovered, by bullying and threats, what he needed to know. Sanchia's nurse, snivelling and dabbing her eyes with her apron, told him that madame had gone to Roscoff. When Toby swore, the baby began to cry as well.

He saddled his horse, and packed provisions and a spare cloak in his saddlebag. He took his sword and his knife, too, because he, like Joanna, suspected that some of the wolves that watched the house in Finistère had human eyes. Then, as the snow swirled silently round the lawns and arbours of Joanna's garden, he started through the forest.

He found them on the open heathland, sheltering behind one of the great slabs of rock that rose like broken teeth into the darkening sky. When he rode forward out of the blizzard he saw that her servant, Padrig, had already drawn his sword, and that Joanna herself held in her gloved hand a short, narrow-bladed knife. He had time to see in her eyes, before she recognized him, that she was capable of using the knife.

'Toby!' The single word was a gasp of relief. Then she drew herself up in the saddle and added proudly, 'There was no need to come. We thought we'd stop a while and wait for the snow to die down a bit.'

Dismounting, he reached inside his saddlebag, took out the dry cloak and threw it over her shoulders. He handed her a bottle of wine and watched her hands shake with cold as she opened it. Taking the bridle of Joanna's horse, he led it through the maze of rock and marsh that he had only just crossed.

When at last he felt able to speak, he said, 'Why Roscoff?', and when she didn't answer, he added sarcastically, 'Teething potions for the baby, I suppose, Joanna?'

She went pale. 'Is Sanchia unwell?'

'She's quite well. Missing her mother, that's all. Who were you sending the letter to, Joanna?' His voice was hurled about and robbed of timbre by the wind. He couldn't see her face, but heard her swift intake of breath. He added: 'I am practised at reducing grown men to tears with a few well-chosen words. Sanchia's nurse was easy prey. She told me that you'd taken a letter to Roscoff. To send to England, I assume.'

They had crossed the marshland and reached the forest. Toby climbed back into his saddle. He could see Joanna's profile now, lit by the unreal whiteness of the snow.

'I hoped I'd be back before you woke. I sent a letter to Martin. An English sea-captain agreed to take it for me.'

He said savagely, 'Inquiring after Martin's health, I suppose?'

'No.' She had reined in her horse. 'Asking him to make inquiries at Lydney Mandeville.'

He was silent at first. He was aware of Padrig, a respectful pace behind them, and he was aware, in a detached sort of fashion, that he was about to say something unforgivable.

'Christ,' he said viciously. 'I can see why they found it difficult. The face of a bloody Madonna and the temperament of a harridan. No wonder they found it hard to cope. Gaetano, I mean. Uncle Taddeo. Your father . . .'

Her head bowed suddenly. He heard her gasp. He watched as she walked her horse forward and began to ride along the path that she knew better than anyone. He put his spurs to his horse's sides and rode after her. The slowness of their pace, dictated by the weather and the thick undergrowth of the forest floor, was a torment to him. What he wanted, suddenly, was to shut himself away, to speak to no one. Or to ride as fast as he was able, for hours and hours and hours. Or, best of all, to take part in a nice, violent battle, not caring whether he won or lost. The fleeting peace of mind that he had experienced earlier that afternoon in Joanna's house had gone utterly, lost in the memories she had reawakened.

And in something else as well. He recognized what it was as he rode after her, his mouth set in grim lines, snowflakes battering icily against his face. His irritation at her meddling had been nothing compared to the fear he had felt for her. The thought of Joanna lost on the heathland in a snowstorm had terrified him. He had not trusted Padrig to protect her: he trusted only himself.

The realization shocked him. He looked up, seeing clearly at last, letting the regrets and misunderstandings of years roll away from him. He wondered why she had undertaken such a cold and uncomfortable journey. Why she had left the warmth of her house, the child she loved. The snow had eased a little, and a silver moon peeped out from behind the clouds. He could see misery in every line of Joanna's silhouette. His last words to her echoed in his head in rhythm with the pounding of hooves. He had acquired, he realized, the capacity to hurt her: which meant that she loved him, a little. Until tonight, he had been unable to acknowledge that love. He had never rediscovered the trust that his checkered past had deprived him of. He recognized, though, riding past trees and thickets, trying to regain his sanity, his equilibrium, that there was a limit to how much anyone could hate themselves. He had passed that limit: he had, therefore, to go to Joanna Zulian, who had endured insult, desertion and neglect from him, and beg her forgiveness.

They had reached the house. She slid from her horse, leaving it standing in the garden, and ran inside. Her footsteps pattered fast on the stone steps. He heard the slam of the door to the solar as he ran after her. He took a deep breath and pushed open the door.

She was sitting in the middle of the stone floor, her face buried in the folds of her cloak, her head covered with her hood. The fire was unlit, the room chill. He recognized the small shuddering of her shoulders, and he groaned.

He said her name, and she looked up. Her eyes were red-rimmed, her face blotchy. He felt, just then, terribly sad. The living, after all, were more important than the dead. If he could not repair what he had done to Izabel, to Eleanor, to Paul Dubreton, then he could at least put right what he had done to Joanna.

He took a deep breath. 'What I said was unforgivable and untrue. If you can endure my company any longer, then let me make a fire and find you something to eat.'

She didn't speak. So, kneeling in front of her, he untied the ribbons of her soaking cloak and lifted it from her shoulder. Her hair was wet and darkened to copper, still jewelled with snow crystals. He bent down and kissed the top of her head, and she did not push him away. He had forgotten his own tangled concerns, he had been dragged out of his misery by a need to salvage their fragile relationship.

She didn't send him away, she didn't move at all. She sat there, shivering, as he quickly built and lit a fire. He fetched food and wine from the kitchen, and watched the smooth clear curve of her brow and cheek as she ate, saw her begin to smile again. He thought of the roads they had travelled together, he and Joanna, the places they had seen. He found himself regretting once more the turnings he had taken, the company he had forsaken.

The stone walls of the solar were flecked black and orange by the light from the fires. Their shadows, his and Joanna's, were long and dark. He saw clearly for the first time the thread that had taken them from an artist's workshop in Venice, through the hills and plains of northern Italy, to this room, this night. That thread, sometimes bright and strong, sometimes fragile, almost broken, had drawn their lives together. That he wanted her now was only inevitable.

Her hair had dried: it fell in great silky curtains to her shoulders. She was another man's mistress, another man's wife, he reminded himself. Once they had danced, once he had made love to her in a garden full of flowers. Then something had pulled them apart: his ambition, her need for independence. If the future daunted him, if the past was unreadable, still it had occurred to him at last that only the present counted.

He wanted to caress her hair, to touch again her soft skin, but he did not even reach out his hand. He recalled, so vividly, her feel, her scent, her warmth. But he was hopelessly unsure of what she wanted, of what he meant to her. It crossed his mind, though, that she might, against all reason, give him a second chance.

He saw the marks of tiredness in the shadows around her eyes and the whiteness of her skin. He bent at last to kiss her eyelids. Then he kissed her lips and felt some of the tension drain out of her. When he lifted her in his arms and carried her out of the solar and into her bedchamber, he saw joy in her eyes again.

Joanna stepped into the darkness as she had done before, but this time he was beside her, watching her, holding her.

In the bedchamber she found herself unexpectedly shy. Her fingers fumbled awkwardly with the ties of her gown; a button fell off and rolled to a corner of the room. As Toby took her in his arms, she could hear someone singing in the kitchen below. A bawdy Breton love song, shrill and tuneless, echoed against the stone walls of the house. Joanna smiled, then giggled. Her shoulders shook and tears ran from her eyes. 'They are serenading us,' she managed to say.

Toby's eyes gleamed dark and wicked. She forgot her nervousness, she no longer heard the singing. They were, after all, old acquaintances. With old acquaintances, you could make mistakes, you could be foolish. Lying back on the bed, Joanna let him unlace her bodice, let him drop her velvet sleeves and skirts to the floor. His hands touched her breasts and trailed down to her stomach and thighs. Then his mouth traced the contours of her body. She shivered, but not now with cold. She knew, of course, what to do, how to respond. How to give love, how to return love.

He had pulled the bedcurtains around them, they were enclosed in their own small, exclusive world. The curtains were green, embroidered with flowers. If she half-closed her eyes they were in the green, secret room again. The room where all paths met, in the centre of the Italian garden.

Toby didn't think once that night of his mother's house. His nightmares had fled, banished outside to the darkness of the forest, where they belonged. Here, in Joanna's house, he was safe. He thought, fleetingly, of the letter that Joanna had written to Martin Gefroy, but only to bless that fragile piece of paper for the catalyst it had been in bringing them together at last. He had forgotten past and future, and lost himself in the miracle of her skin, her flesh, her long red-brown hair.

They took their time that night. If the urgency of their passion was no less than it had been four years before, then they had learned to be careful with each other, both eager to give as much pleasure as they received. He could not see her in the darkness, and the blizzard still howled its anger outside. He rediscovered her by the smoothness of her skin, the silkiness of her hair against his face, by the rounded contours of breast and buttock, by the scent of the flowery perfume that she wore, soon to be drowned in the heavy, sweet scent of sex. The pleasure almost annihilated him, so that he fell back on the pillows, gasping for breath, groaning. Her mouth caressed him, her fingertips touched him so that he found himself wanting her again and again. Unseeing, he knew that he had come home at last.

Martin Gefroy had returned to his birthplace by a circuitous route. Leaving Italy in the autumn of 1513, he had travelled north through the lands of the Holy Roman Emperor, attaching himself to whichever reliable group of pilgrims or merchants happened to be journeying in a suitable direction. He had stayed for a few months in Heidelberg, longer in Amsterdam. But eventually, looking across the grey North Sea, he experienced once again a desire to return home. He took passage on a wool-trading ship bound for the East Anglian coast, enduring sea-sickness and cold, inadequate food and unclean water. In England, he headed immediately for London. He found that London had changed in the ten years of his absence: brighter, noisier, more quarrelsome. He got himself lodgings and slept, on and off, for a week.

When he had recovered from his journey, he wrote a letter introducing himself to Thomas Linacre, the physician who had once been tutor to the young Prince Arthur. He spent, eventually, a delightful few weeks with Master Linacre, discussing such niceties as the accurate translation of the anatomist Galen, and the possibility that Henry VIII might found a college of physicians. Martin found himself accepted easily back into England, and totally exorcized of his desire to travel. The years of his absence, of his journeying round Europe, began to recede into the background. They had been, he realized, a necessary preparation for the sort of life he wanted eventually to lead, but not his whole life. He mentally said his farewells to the men and women who had peopled those travels – Joanna, Toby, Guillaume du Chantonnay, Hamon de Bohun – with varying degrees of relief or regret. He believed that part of his life done with, a line drawn with a final flourish.

He began to realize that the flourish was not quite as final as he would have liked it to be when he learned that he was being watched. The apothecary's boy, a bright, impudent youth, told him. Martin himself would never have noticed that the man standing at the corner of the street was anything other than a gentleman visitor to London with too much time on his hands.

'He talks funny,' the lad said. A chill settled on Martin's heart as he delved deep into his pocket to find a coin to give to the apothecary's boy. He decided then to return to Oxford, his birthplace.

At dawn, when Joanna woke, Toby was lying on his side, propped on one elbow, looking at her. A little of the old anxiety, the old defensiveness, had come back into his eyes.

'What now?' he said.

She understood him. A chapter had closed – or opened. 'It's up to you,' she said slowly. 'It always has been. Events just . . . just distract us a bit.'

He traced the contours of her face with his fingertip. 'Such optimism,' he said softly. 'How far have you travelled since you were born, Joanna?'

'A long, long way.'

She thought of the years of her childhood, of Sanchia, who had died, of Donato, who had forsaken her; of the years in Venice, the gaining in the artist's workshop of some sort of contentment; of the disaster of her marriage, a disaster that still clung to her, shutting off paths that she might choose to take.

'And you still believe that you *choose*?'

'Of course.' She slid her hands up to his shoulders, and hugged him. She felt, quite suddenly, perfectly happy. 'Of course I do. I chose to leave Italy. I chose to go to Guillaume. I chose to make the garden at Marigny. And to come here, with you. We make mistakes sometimes, that's all.'

'I seem to have made rather a lot of mistakes.' Toby shook his head, but his eyes didn't leave her face. 'Eleanor . . . Agnès . . . You . . .'

'I'm still here,' she said. 'Aren't I, Toby?'

The beginnings of a smile touched his mouth. 'Yes. God knows why. You're a stubborn woman, Joanna.'

She raised her face so that he would kiss her again. Outside, snow tumbled from the trees and drifted against the walls of the house. She was glad of the snow: it made her feel safe, walled off from the rest of the world. For a little while they could forget both the past and the future.

Once, far away, long ago, rose petals had fallen from the branches, and the air had been perfumed with jasmine. It did not matter; it made no difference.

In Oxford, a few weeks before Christmas, Martin received Joanna's letter.

He had taken two rooms in a lodging-house in Catte Street. The landlady occupied the ground floor. She had a daughter, a plump, bright girl of around twenty. Sometimes, when Martin returned to the house after visiting a patient, Lucy would run after him, picking up the papers that he had dropped, inviting him to the parlour for a cup of spiced ale. She was, like her mother, a good cook, and he knew that she could write with a clear, round hand. Martin had wondered recently whether a methodical, pleasant girl like Lucy might ever look at an untidy, obsessive physician like him. He rather hoped that she might.

He was sorting through the clutter in his room, looking for some missing notes, when Lucy knocked at the door. She held the letter out to him. 'A sailor brought it,' she said. 'From France.'

The inscription, Martin noticed, was vague, and there was no insignia on the blob of sealing-wax. His hands shaking slightly, he broke the seal and opened the letter.

It was not, though, as he had expected, from Toby. Seeing Joanna Zulian's signature at the bottom of the page, Martin's heart paused, waiting to beat. He sat down rather suddenly on the edge of the bed.

'Are you well, Master Gefroy?' asked Lucy anxiously. 'Is it bad news?'

She had to repeat her questions twice before he heard her. Then, having skimmed through the contents of Joanna's letter, he was able to smile and say, 'No, no – not bad news at all, Lucy. And I'm quite well.'

He heard the door close behind her. He read the closely written letter through again carefully.

He was inclined to agree with Toby, he thought, that things were best left alone, that the sort of violence and covetousness that had peppered the past should not be reawakened. Better not to meddle, not to provoke again the vengeance that Hamon de Bohun was capable of. Martin could think of nothing to be gained in visiting, as Joanna had requested, Lydney Mandeville. Remembering Toby bent over his desk in Italy, his face furrowed with exhaustion, he thought that his demons were best left alone in the jar that Toby had succeeded in driving them into, with the lid tightly stoppered. Toby was strong; Toby could live with that sort of knowledge. His demons escaped only briefly at night.

Martin glanced at the letter once more before he rose and began to pack potions and instruments, ready for the day's work. Joanna's signature, a swirl of black ink, looked back at him from the page. He recalled her quite vividly now, with immense affection, with the respect due to someone who had opened his eyes a little. Desire had died, thank God, and with it, jealousy.

He pushed aside the uncomfortable thought that it was his own reluctance to become involved again, his own remembered fear, that made him unwilling to comply with the request that Joanna had made in her letter.

★

That night, after he had written his reply, Martin set to work. He was writing a herbal. He had, during his years on the continent, encountered many plants not native to England. He had investigated their properties by studying the writings of the ancients and by talking to the peasants who used such plants. Some of these plants he had tested on himself, rubbing a little of the sap into his skin or nibbling at a berry, and he had more than once made himself rather ill.

Now he attempted to arrange his findings. By day, he practised as a physician, treating the citizens of Oxford for their various ailments; by night, he worked into the early hours of the morning, seated at his table, delving into memory, into the numerous notes and jottings he had accumulated over the years.

He heard the clock of All Saints' Church chime the midnight bells as he stoppered his ink-well. His candle was burning low, starting to gutter. He yawned and stretched, and knocked some papers to the floor. He was scrabbling beneath the table, trying to pick them up, when he heard the noise.

It was only a very small noise – the squeak of a wooden stair-tread. It was, however, a noise that should not have occurred. Lucy and her mother went to bed soon after dark; the two young gentlemen who occupied the middle floor had returned to their families for Christmas. A shiver traced itself slowly down Martin's spine. The candle flickered and died. For a moment he crouched under the table, heart thudding, unable to move. He heard another creak, then a footstep, soft and unmistakable, on the upstairs landing. *His* landing.

He had not locked his door: he never locked his door. He felt sick; sweat ran like tears down his face. He wore, of course, no sword at his side, and his cries for help would never reach the ground floor. Besides, he had no wish to involve either Lucy or her mother in his own tangled affairs.

He heard the outer door handle turn. He thought of Lucy, who would find him in the morning with his skull caved in or a knife in his breast. He thought of François du Chantonnay, whom he had unwittingly betrayed years ago. He thought of Hamon de Bohun, who assumed that you could buy anything with money or by force.

Martin's hand, of its own volition, reached out and touched something in the darkness. A pewter mug. The remains of the spiced ale had long since gone cold; he had, not unusually, become absorbed in his work and forgotten to eat or drink. Martin's fingers shook slightly as they folded round the handle of the mug. Then he backed carefully out from beneath the table and stood up. For once he did not trip over the trailing hem of his robe.

As the door from the outer room opened, Martin was standing by the door jamb, clutching the pewter mug in his hand. The thin circle of light from the assassin's candle widened, illuminating his desk, his papers, his vast collection of seeds and skulls, his phials and powders. As he raised the tankard ready to strike, he felt a terrible, overwhelming anger. As he brought the cup down on the intruder's unprotected head, he might have shouted aloud – for François, for Mistress Mandeville, for Toby!

The noise, as the mug struck skin and bone, was appalling. The man slid to the floor with a thud. Martin's arm arched with the force of the blow. Gasping for breath, he waited for the intruder to rise, for the fight that must inevitably take place. But the man just lay there quite still, surrounded by a puddle of ale, sticks of cinnamon and pieces of nutmeg. The pewter mug dropped out of Martin's suddenly nerveless fingers, clattering to the floor. He sat down on the edge of the bed, unable to move.

When he looked up, Lucy was framed in the doorway, a candle in her hand. 'I heard a noise,' she whispered. And then, hardly audible, staring at the body on the floor, *'Master Gefroy!'*

Martin slid from the bed and crouched down beside the prone figure. He felt for the pulse at the throat.

'He isn't dead,' he said.

Blood oozed from the wound on the man's scalp.

'A thief?' asked Lucy.

'Something like that.'

Martin rose to his feet. He had no doubt, he thought grimly, that his assassin, when he recovered consciousness, would turn out to speak Breton, not English. No doubt that when he, Martin, mentioned the name of de Bohun, there would be a flicker of recognition in the man's eyes.

He saw on the table the reply that he had earlier written to Joanna. He had been wrong, and Joanna had been right. It was not all over: that sort of thing was never all over. He crumpled his letter into a little ball. His eyes were hard with anger.

'I shall have to go on a journey,' he said. 'Tomorrow morning, after I have taken this fellow to the authorities.'

He was surprised to see a flicker of disappointment in Lucy's eyes. Leaning across, he kissed her lightly on the cheek.

'Not for long,' he said. 'There's some unfinished business, that's all. I'll be back.' He began to bundle clothes into a bag.

'I'll do that,' she said. Her face was slightly pink as she picked up crumpled shirts and doublets from the bed, the floor and beneath the desk.

He watched her for a moment, distracted even from the immediate future as Lucy's clever hands smoothed out broadcloth and linen, and folded his bedraggled garments into small, neat shapes. The man on the floor groaned: his eyes opened briefly and then closed again. Frowning, Martin began to consider the difficulties involved in reaching Lydney Mandeville in one piece before the year was out.

He didn't get lost once. He asked for directions at every cottage, every tavern, and followed those directions meticulously. He gave the quest that Joanna had entrusted to him the same sort of care he gave to the most troublesome infection, the most obscure fever.

The village was small, only a hamlet, the Mandeville house one of the few buildings of any size. The late-afternoon sky was heavy and white. Frost laced the edges of the ivy that clung to the yellow stone walls and turned the evergreen box trees to grey. In the stream, the reeds and bullrushes were frozen in the icy water.

Martin left his horse by the side of the house near the silent stables. When he looked upwards, he saw the weathered chimneys and the grotesques that perched on the roof. The corners of the chimneys, the faces of the stone monkeys and lions, had begun to crumble away.

He walked round the house, pausing now and then to peer through the windows and to try the doors. All the doors were locked, though, and the cobwebbed glass gave only muted glimpses of the interior. Snow began to fall, a few fine, chill flakes. Martin saw what Toby, four years before, had seen: the melancholy, the sense of neglect, as though the ghost of Izabel Mandeville still fluttered here, chained to the earth by her suffering, her loss. Martin shivered and returned to his horse.

He knew that he was being watched. Not by Hamon de Bohun's man, though – he languished sore-headed in Oxford Gaol, doubly incriminated as a house-breaker and an alien. Here the watchers were the villagers who whispered behind their hands, who studied with narrowed eyes his unfamiliar face. He smiled as he led his horse back to the village green. He was, after all, in his own country. Then, with the sort of methodical thoroughness he was supremely capable of, he talked to every one of the inhabitants of Lydney Mandeville.

They both knew that their time together was limited, but Toby did not ask again, as he once had, *What now?* Instead, they concentrated on the present. The three of them – Toby, Joanna and Sanchia – celebrated Christmas alone, glad of the snow that still walled them off from the rest of Brittany. It was as though the world had paused for a while, allowing them time to breathe.

The present had never seemed so precious. Watching her daughter feed crumbs to the robins, watching Toby cut wood for the fire, Joanna knew that she would not have exchanged her life with anyone else's. That this was what happiness was: a deep contentment in the small things of life, an ability to weather all petty difficulties and irritations. She realized that her need of him was only equal to his need of her.

They made a snowman in the garden for Sanchia. A battered hat crowned its head, and Joanna carefully sculptured its features. On the house, the icicles hanging from the eaves grew longer with each passing day. Toby hurled snowballs at the high branches of the trees and powdery snow tumbled like fine sugar to the ground. Snow rimmed the archways of the pergola in the garden so that they were like white lace against the bleached background.

Martin, having found what he wanted in Lydney Mandeville, continued his journey. He had attempted to discover, as Joanna had suggested, the names of the servants who had worked at the manor house in Izabel Mandeville's time.

Knocking on doors, accosting every suspicious villager, he had discovered that the name of Izabel Mandeville's cook was Dorothy Fisher, and that she lived in nearby Stroud.

In Stroud, the roofs were lightly frosted with snow and the cobbles glistened with ice. Martin slept one night in a tavern in the High Street and then, rising early, made inquiries of the landlord. The landlord pointed to the baker's shop halfway down the road. The snow had stopped falling and a weak sun attempted to shine.

The baker's door was half open, the floor and shelves of the shop were white with flour, as though the wintry weather had found its way indoors. The heat from the vast bread ovens hit Martin with an almost physical force.

The baker led him through the shop to the room behind it. It was a wide, deep room, made muggy by the heat from the fire and the ovens. There was a clutter of furniture and a throng of people. A baby, tethered to a table-leg by a length of ribbon round its waist, crawled on the floor; children gathered round the doorway and squabbled over a basket of pegs and a piece of chalk; adults young and old occupied every stool, every bench. Some stood at a wide table rolling pastry or mixing fillings for pies and cakes. The smell of mutton pies, macaroons and batter puddings was overpowering.

The baker led Martin to an old lady seated by the fireplace. Layers of petticoats, skirts, bodices and shawls thickened her bulky frame, and a lappeted cap covered much of her grey hair. Martin stooped to speak in her ear. She waved him cheerfully away.

'I'm not deaf yet, young man. Nor daft. Of course I remember Mistress Mandeville. I was in her service – oh, for two years or so.'

She was in her sixties, he guessed, stout and comfortable.

She smiled. 'She wasn't a difficult woman to cook for, for all she was a foreigner. I thought it'd be all fancy dishes and suchlike, but she was content with what I made for her.'

The baby, tripping over its tether, began to bawl, and Dorothy Fisher called out to one of the children drawing with the chalks on the stone floor: 'Pick him up, Emmie! Give him a hug!'

'Yes, Aunt Doll,' answered the eldest girl obediently, and, dropping her chalk, she stooped to pick up the baby. From the shop, a loud voice called out for a dozen more pies.

'Quiet today,' said Mistress Fisher, adjusting her skirts. 'It's this weather, I shouldn't wonder.'

Martin wanted to laugh. The noise and heat were appalling: he pulled at the collar of his doublet and let his cloak slide from his shoulder.

He framed his question carefully. 'Did you work for Mistress Mandeville before or after her husband died, Mistress Fisher?'

She glanced at him sharply then. 'Both,' she said eventually. 'I was engaged as cook when she married. But she was widowed very young, poor lady. I left her – oh, a year or so after the master died.'

The baby was still crying. 'Give 'im here, Emmie,' said the old lady. The howling infant was placed in Dorothy Fisher's lap. There was a bruise the size of a penny on his forehead.

'There, there, Toby,' said the old lady. 'Hush, now. Nanny's here.'

Martin stiffened. 'A cold poultice,' he said absently. 'A handful of snow, perhaps, wrapped in a cloth.' His fingertips gently touched the bruise on the child's forehead. *'Toby,'* he said, looking up at Izabel Mandeville's former cook. 'Is it a family name?'

Emmie had scuttled away outside; the door banged, letting in cold air.

Mistress Fisher shook her head. 'No. It was given to a child of mine who died. My daughter's baby reminded me of him.'

The baby in Dorothy Fisher's lap was dark-eyed. *It was given to a child of mine who died.* Not, *It was the name of my son.* Emmie came back into the kitchen, a snowball in her hand. Martin wrapped it in his handkerchief and placed it against the infant's bruised forehead.

The baby's howls increased, but Martin managed to say: 'Who died, mistress, or who was taken from you?'

The old woman stared at him but said nothing. Loyalty beyond the grave, he thought, and was touched.

'He died,' said the old woman finally.

The snow had begun to melt. Martin removed the handkerchief from the baby's face. The bruise had gone down a little and the baby's cries had abated.

'I don't think so,' said Martin. 'I think he's still alive. I met him in Italy, you see, mistress. Toby, I mean. Izabel Mandeville's son.'

She whispered, *'Who are you?'*

'I am a physician,' he answered simply, 'and Toby Crow's friend. I mean neither him nor you any harm. Toby found out who he was several years ago. It's just that some of the details didn't seem to quite fit. You looked after Toby, didn't you, Mistress Fisher? You brought him up?'

At last she nodded. She said proudly, 'A lady like Mistress Mandeville couldn't be seen to have a child out of wedlock, could she?'

'So she hid the pregnancy?'

'The mistress dismissed most of her servants, kept only the handful she trusted most. She told everyone that she was ill. I delivered the child when her time came.'

Martin thought rapidly. 'So you took the baby here, and looked after him.'

Dorothy Fisher bent and kissed the child in her lap. 'I'd often take him back to Lydney Mandeville, though. I gave out that he was my own child. We went back every month or so. The mistress doted on him, you see.'

He found that he couldn't ask the sort of questions he needed to. They seemed both obscene and unimportant. That Izabel Mandeville had loved her illegitimate child, thought Martin, in spite of the horror of his creation, was the only thing of any significance.

He heard Dorothy Fisher say, 'We were at Mandeville when *he* came back.' Her voice was a frail whisper. Martin saw fear in the old lady's eyes. He didn't need to ask who *he* was.

'Hamon de Bohun,' he said softly.

'He was a devil. A devil.'

She crossed herself. The baby was sleeping peacefully now. Dorothy Fisher's old eyes stared past Martin to where the flames rose scarlet and orange from the fire.

'I tried to tell him,' she muttered. 'But he wouldn't listen. They hit me. The mistress was crying so – screaming like a madwoman. I thought she'd lost her senses. Just the sight of him –'

She broke off. Martin knew that she had forgotten him, that she saw only her own terrible memories, pictured in the flames. He had to lean forward to hear her soft, mumbling voice.

'He said he'd come to take his son. I thought that if I told him the truth, he'd leave the child alone. But I couldn't make them listen. They didn't speak English – just some outlandish tongue. And they hurt me. I tried to tell them, you see.'

A cold shiver ran up Martin's spine. A forewarning, a flicker of unease. He leaned forward again. 'What did you mean, Mistress Fisher, when you said that if you told de Bohun the truth he'd leave Toby alone?'

A single tear ran down one of the channels that old age had carved into her face. 'I've always thought, you see, that it was my fault. Not that she blamed me – I only blamed myself. She died soon afterwards, poor thing. But I've always thought that if only I'd been able to make them understand . . . But I couldn't find the right words. I just couldn't find the right words.'

When the snowman was no more than a ragged hat lying in a puddle on the grass and the icicles had long since crashed to the ground, the wind picked up, refusing to allow Brittany a glimpse of spring. Tall trees tumbled in the forest like ninepins, and the streams were fast and swollen with the melted snow.

The visitor arrived during a lull in the storm. Joanna, leaning out of the window, knew from the bedraggled cloak and unimposing horse that it was not Guillaume.

'A pedlar, perhaps,' said Toby beside her. 'I'll go and make sure.'

As he turned to go, she reached out and grasped his sleeve, stopping him.

'No, Toby. *Look.*'

Toby looked. Then, *'Martin,'* he said.

He was given hugs and kisses, food and drink, dry clothes. The story that he had to tell bubbled up constantly in him, but he knew that he must wait until they had time and privacy. Just now, there was Joanna's daughter, and Joanna's daughter's nurse, and servants bustling round him, bringing him hot water, rabbit pie, warm ale.

Later, when Sanchia had gone to bed and the three of them were alone in the solar, he looked at Joanna. He knew that he had not looked at her properly yet. What did you say to someone you had not seen for five years? To someone you had once loved so completely, so jealously? He saw that she had changed. That the beauty that had already been hers at eighteen had blossomed into something quite exceptional. That her clothes, her jewellery, her deportment now complemented her natural gifts. He still loved her, he thought. Events, time, absence, never quite killed love.

His gaze shifted to Toby. They sat side by side on the bench, Toby's arm curled round Joanna's shoulders. Martin acknowledged at last what he had always known in his heart. That they were two halves of the same whole. His life had been bound together with theirs for a while, but those bonds were now severed. He found that he feared for them.

He told his story. He chose words that were gentle and honest; he knew how easily the wrong words could hurt them. He told them about Oxford and Lucy and the arrival of Joanna's letter. He told them about his journeys to Lydney Mandeville and to Stroud. About Dorothy Fisher, and the plump dark-haired baby called Toby. He dug deep into the past, and told them about Hamon de Bohun's second visit to Izabel Mandeville.

Lastly, he told them what Dorothy Fisher had said to him, the words that had made him take ship and travel to the France that he feared.

'The mistress's steward was called Toby. Well, she wouldn't be the first lady to warm her bed with a handsome serving-man, would she? She was lonely, poor lady.'

Joanna found Toby in the garden. He had stumbled out of the solar, and, pausing only for a moment to speak to Martin, Joanna had followed him.

He was standing at the edge of the lawn. The wind had died down a little and the sun gleamed through the bands of dark grey clouds, painting the bare branches of the trees with light. She went to his side, and threaded her hand through his arm.

He didn't look at her, he only said, 'I'll never know, will I, Joanna? Not for certain.'

She said gently, 'Does it matter?'

He shook his head. 'Perhaps not.'

'Your mother believed you to be her lover's child,' said Joanna firmly. 'And not Hamon de Bohun's. That was why she named you Toby; that was why she protected you. That was why she loved you.'

She was looking out to the forest; her profile stood out against the background of leaf and sky.

Toby said, 'I'll have to go back to Italy soon. I can't stay here. Come with me, Joanna. Please.'

For a long while she didn't answer. Then she whispered, 'No.'

He had known already what she would reply. It was like a physical pain, though, a deep stab to the chest.

She turned to him. 'I can't,' she said softly. 'There is Guillaume. I could not take Sanchia away from him. And I would not leave her. And I am still married, remember, Toby. I am still Gaetano's wife.'

He felt as though someone had seized his heart from out of his chest, cracking ribs, tearing skin.

Tears spilled over her lids, as she continued to speak. 'It would start again, wouldn't it, Toby? If I left Guillaume, if I came with you. The envy and revenge and destruction. I could not do that. *I could not.*'

He knew that she was right. He rubbed the back of his hand across his eyes, and he held her to him for a long, long time.

★

Later, they dined together. No one spoke much. But halfway through the meal, Martin put down his knife and frowned, as if remembering something. 'There's something else,' he said. 'I thought I'd better warn you. Some bastard broke into my rooms at Oxford. He had a knife in his hand. I hit him with a pewter mug.'

Toby's eyes widened. *'Martin!'* exclaimed Joanna.

'I know,' said Martin, rather sheepishly. 'I lost my temper, I'm afraid. Anyway, he was Breton. One of Hamon de Bohun's. He didn't speak much French, and I know little Breton, so we hadn't much to say to each other. But he recognized his master's name.'

Joanna's fingers tightened around the stem of her goblet. There was a cold flicker in Toby's eyes as he asked, 'Did you kill him, Martin?'

Martin shook his head. 'I disclaimed all knowledge of him, and escorted him to Oxford Gaol as a common thief. They don't take kindly to uninvited foreigners in England.'

Martin took a deep breath. He could see his future quite clearly now, and it pleased him. His work, his home, Lucy. *His* future might be plain, but for Toby and Joanna, he guessed, nothing was quite so clear.

He said, 'I'll stay here for a while, if you like. I'll go to court, tell the truth. About François du Chantonnay, I mean.' He didn't regret his words. 'You can't go on hiding for ever, can you?' he added. 'And it has always *irked* me – my lack of courage.'

Toby said nothing; Joanna leaned forward, holding out her hand.

'Dear Martin,' she said. Her fingertips touched his face. 'You visit plague-ridden villages, you nurse men through the smallpox, and you say that you lack courage?' She smiled, and then she rose and walked to his side and kissed him. On the mouth. For the first time, and the last time.

'Go back to Oxford,' she whispered. 'Marry your little English girl who loves you dearly. Have half a dozen children, and hope they all grow up to be as brave as you.'

Two days later Toby and Martin said their farewells to Joanna. As Toby rode with Martin as far as Roscoff, the memory of Joanna's face, the warmth of her last embrace, was constantly with him. Inside him there was a pain that not even the long, hard ride could obliterate. The impulse to turn the clock back, to right a parting that was so utterly wrong, was almost overwhelming. Yet he did not ride back to the house in Finistère. Instead, after leaving Martin, he rode to Bourges.

It was raining when he reached the village. The pain of separation remained, but he felt calm and clear-headed now. His life had finally adopted some sort of order. He believed that he had only to wait. For years, if necessary, but he had not lost her for ever.

He found himself walking down the cinder path at the side of the schoolteacher's house. He thought how empty this house must now seem to Agnès who had loved Paul just as much as he loved Joanna. He hoped that he could lighten the emptiness, just a little.

She was in the kitchen, making bread. He watched her for a moment. Her hair was now completely grey, and the fine lines at her mouth and eyes had etched deeper into her skin. Then he said her name.

She looked up. Her expression was first one of shock, then fear, and finally hope. He waited in the doorway: for forgiveness, for absolution.

'My dear,' said Agnès shakily. 'Five years this time. Too long. You *promised*.'

Then she held out her arms to him.

CHAPTER EIGHTEEN

When his messenger had told him the name of Joanna Zulian's visitor, Hamon de Bohun had struck him across the face with his horsewhip.

He had been riding back to Marigny, returning from Paris. The courier, his cloak battling against the wind, his horse lathered with sweat, caught up with him at the gate. He gave his message and Hamon de Bohun raised his whip and lashed it down across his face, cutting the man's eye and mouth. Hamon had hoped then that it had blinded him, struck him dumb.

Now, though, three months later, the same messenger cowered in the Great Chamber opposite him. The remnants of the wounds could still be seen on his face. Over the fireplace, Joanna Zulian's calm, beautiful features gazed down on them. The messenger blurted out his information.

'The man – Crow – has gone, Seigneur. I don't know where he went. I thought it best to come here.'

Hamon rose from his seat. The messenger backed away a couple of paces. 'Come,' said Hamon soothingly. 'I'll not hurt you. A token of my appreciation.'

He pressed a gold coin into the man's hand. The messenger was young, fair-featured if you ignored the ragged scars at his mouth and eyelids. Briefly, Hamon touched the damaged face.

'You have done well, my pet,' he whispered. 'Now, return to Brittany. Watch and wait.'

The man shuffled quickly outside, closing the door behind him. Hamon de Bohun looked up at the painting of Joanna Zulian.

Whatever his bastard son had offered her, he thought, it had not been enough. Only he, Hamon de Bohun, the Seigneur de Marigny, could offer her enough. Joanna, like himself, had been made for Marigny. Marigny had been made only for the two of them. Power and beauty: only they were equal to Marigny.

He would ride out to Finistère, he thought, as soon as the weather improved. Just now, squally storms hurled themselves at the peninsula, lifting trees from their roots, making the forest impassable. Looking out through a window, he thought that the wind was already dying.

And Guillaume du Chantonnay was still at Blois, paying court to the new king. Hamon laughed out loud when he thought how fate had aided him. Louis XII had died after barely two months of marriage, worn out, some said, by the demands of his young and beautiful bride. And François d'Angoulême – ambitious, greedy, virile François d'Angoulême – had succeeded him. François wanted Milan, wanted Italy. François did not care a jot about the ownership of Marigny.

Hamon looked up at the picture again. He thought, looking at the knife, the severed head, how inappropriately the dead painter had cast Joanna. The sort of winds that had induced the prophetess Judith to become a murderess blew far away from Joanna Zulian's auburn hair and cool grey eyes.

Because of Sanchia, Joanna was able to endure the parting from Toby. She forced herself back into the normal routines of life: the feeding and clothing of her child, the gathering of whatever treasures the forest had to offer, the business of keeping warm in the middle of a harsh Breton winter. But what had once satisfied her, what had once been enough, was no longer enough. There was something missing, something important.

Sanchia was investigating the contents of her mother's sewing-box. The needles and pins and tiny buttons had all been removed, well out of reach. Joanna watched her daughter arrange the coloured skeins of thread. She knew the cause of her pain. *She* had sent him away. That, of course, was what was so unbearable. Because of Guillaume, because of Sanchia, there had been no alternative. That made it no easier, though.

Balls of wool, hanks of silk thread were strewn all over the floor. Sanchia had unwound a length of ribbon, and was attempting to tie it round her hair.

Joanna rose and went to the window. The winter had not ended yet, she thought. Although the wind, which had broken branches off the trees and hurled them to the forest floor like matchsticks, had died down, it was still cold, the trees still leafless. Only the snowdrops, pale heads pushing through the leaf-mould, danced in the taut remains of the breeze. The rest of the garden was battered, damaged by the gales. The arches of the pergola had been blown to fragments, the camomile seat and the herb garden were littered with twigs and dead leaves.

There was no pattern any more, she thought. The cold wind had destroyed what she had made, blurring the careful lines she had drawn, making an anarchic jumble out of the order stolen from the wilderness. Nothing fitted together. And yet she knew what she must do. Clear up, start again, pick up the fragments. Sweep the broken pieces of wood into a bonfire, rake away the old leaves so that the tiny new flowers could push their way to the sunlight. It was all she could do, for now.

Toby was back in Italy in the spring. With the death of the old French king, history had rearranged itself once more.

'At his coronation, King François took the title of Duke of Milan,' said Andrea Gritti. 'He has a vast appetite, don't you think, Toby?'

Gritti had ridden to the encampment outside Padua, where mercenary soldiers had once more begun to assemble as the campaigning season approached.

Toby grinned. 'For Italy, Andrea?'

'And for women,' said the Proveditor drily. The sexual appetite of François de Valois was common knowledge.

They began to walk round the perimeter of the encampment. Sunlight filtered through the clouds; soldiers squabbled in the barns and outbuildings, or slept off the sour remnants of the night before.

'The world will be ruled by young men soon,' said Gritti thoughtfully. 'The king of England and the king of France already glare at each other like strutting turkeycocks. The Emperor Maximilian is growing old – his grandson Charles waits, no doubt, to assume his mantle. Young men are envious, greedy. They think that there is no limit to what they can do, what they can own. They like to make love. And they like to make war.'

He paused, standing still in the centre of the grass arena between the farmhouse and its outbuildings. Lines had etched Andrea Gritti's handsome face; the blue of his eyes had begun to fade a little. The accoutrements of war were assembled around them: pikes and halberds were balanced against walls, warhorses pawed impatiently at the grass.

'And Venice?' said Toby softly.

'Ah, Venice.' Andrea Gritti's voice was sad. 'Venice grows old. I sometimes think, dear Toby, that her days of glory are almost done.'

They both fell silent. Toby's thoughts drifted, as they often did these days, to those other men who had once squabbled over land, over power, over women. Reynaud du Chantonnay was dead now; and Hamon de Bohun must, surely, grow old at last. Another generation elbowed them out of the way. He hoped they would not make the same mistakes.

He felt Gritti clap him on the back. They began to walk again.

'Still, my friend' – Gritti's gaze trailed over the men and their weapons – 'we will find a little glory this year, I think. The Treaty of Blois has been renewed. France and Venice are allies once more. François will ride for Milan before the year is out. And with a young man to lead us, how can we lose?'

When Hamon de Bohun came to the house in Finistère, Joanna was sitting in the solar. Sanchia was playing at her feet, taking smooth pebbles, shells and fir cones from a basket. By the light from the window, Joanna unpicked tiny stitches to let down the hem of one of her daughter's gowns.

She heard the clatter of horses' hooves on the cobbles before she saw them. For one brief, glorious moment she thought, *Toby*. But almost immediately reality returned. She had sent Toby away, so that he would be safe, so that she would not provoke again the terrible patterns of the past. She rose and looked out of the windows.

Not Guillaume, though, as she had expected. The banners were black and gold; she glimpsed the golden pikes, hungry and snarling, embroidered on the black cloth. Looking down, Joanna saw Hamon de Bohun surrounded by half a dozen of his men-at-arms. She called for the nursemaid and had Sanchia and her basket of cones and pebbles taken away. She could not bear that Hamon should even see her child. Sanchia howled her vexation; her cries subsided as the nurse's steps retreated.

'Seigneur,' said Joanna when de Bohun was shown into the room.

He took her elbow, raising her from her curtsy. His touch disgusted her.

'May we speak alone, madame?'

She dismissed her maidservant. She hated to be alone with Hamon de Bohun. *Guillaume*, she thought. Guillaume was sick, dying . . .

'Have you news for me, Seigneur?' Joanna gestured to a chair, bade him sit down. 'News of Monsieur du Chantonnay?'

She realized from his frown that his motive in coming was not to inform her of Guillaume's death.

'My dear Joanna,' said Hamon de Bohun. 'I must apologize for alarming you. I last saw the Sieur du Chantonnay – oh, two or three months ago. At the funeral of our late king.'

Joanna's heart stopped pounding. 'Then why are you here?'

'To ask you to marry me.'

She gasped with astonishment. De Bohun was smiling slightly and his long white fingers had folded round the carved arm of the chair.

She said faintly, 'You know that is impossible. You know that I am married already, to the painter –'

'Gaetano Cavazza. Who died five years ago, madame, of the plague, in Venice.'

His eyes were dark, amused. He looked at her, Joanna thought, as though he already owned her, as though he had already bought her body and her soul.

She turned away from him, unable to bear the greedy gleam of those eyes, the thought of those long, pale fingers caressing her skin. She rested her hands on the sill and looked out of the window. She did not see her garden, but instead saw Gaetano, and Venice: all the images of her earlier years. Simply to hear his name vividly brought back her sense of confinement, her grief at the loss of her first-born child, her overwhelming need to be herself again, to be owned by no one.

And yet, Gaetano was dead. She could not grieve for him, but she grieved, she found, for the pictures he had not painted, the colour and light he had not had time to imprison for ever on canvas. He too had used her and tried to imprison her, had been unable to give her the sort of love she valued, and yet he at least had left behind something worthwhile, something beautiful. And now he was dead. Dead five years past of a vile, incurable, humiliating disease. And she had not known.

'I apologize again,' said Hamon de Bohun behind her. 'I had not thought that you would mourn him.'

She turned back to him. 'I don't. But it's not an end any of us would choose, it is, *votre seigneurie*? Poor Gaetano.'

'My servant told me that the artist left Padua because of the war, and fled to Venice. He did not return to Padua – he thought, I suppose, that Venice would be safe. Because of the sea, its isolation from the land. But

Venice is a cramped, crowded city. Messer Cavazza could not buy himself safety from the consequences of that.'

His dark eyes never left her. She could almost feel them minutely examining her face, her body.

Hamon de Bohun said gently, 'You have not answered my question, Joanna.'

She wanted to run: out to the forest, to the open fields, the sea. She made herself whisper, 'No. I cannot marry you, Seigneur.'

A brief tremor of shock crossed his face. 'Because of your birth, Joanna? Because you lack a dowry?'

She said proudly, 'I am not ashamed of my birth. My father was a physician from Venice, my mother the daughter of a Castilian merchant. I was born in wedlock, Seigneur. I bear my father's name. And I have a dowry. My father made sure I had a dowry.'

Once, a child of thirteen, she had stood in a house in Venice, and showed her uncle and aunt a necklace, a copy of Dioscorides' herbal, and a purse containing a Venetian zecchino, two Genoese ducats and a French écu d'or. She had kept her dowry: it was upstairs, hidden in the bottom of a chest.

'Not a large dowry, perhaps, Joanna, or you would not have gone to Guillaume du Chantonnay.'

He measured her, she thought. He was watching her, assessing her, calculating her worth. He placed her in one scale, and heaped money, jewels and land in the other.

'I will not wed you, Seigneur,' she said steadily. 'You should leave.'

She saw something in his eyes at last. Pain, closely followed by calculation. He did not rise, though.

'The mercenary, Toby Crow. Is it because of him that you will not share my bed?' His voice was clipped, cold.

At first Joanna could not speak. She shook her head slowly, willing him to believe her, willing him not to see the fear in her eyes. 'You have been watching me,' she whispered.

He inclined his head. 'Merely . . . protecting my property. Protecting what I believe will one day be my property. I would not, my sweet Joanna, wish you to keep the wrong sort of company. That young man is not to be trusted.'

She wanted to say, Toby is not your son, you did not make him. Fate cheated you. But she felt herself balanced on a knife-edge, seeing danger all around her. She thanked God that Toby had returned to Italy.

'I will keep what company I choose,' she said. 'That was my agreement with Guillaume.' Her voice shook a little, but she did not let herself shrink from his glance.

'Then Guillaume is a greater fool than I had believed. What is Toby Crow to you, Joanna? Is he your lover?'

She clasped her hands together, pressing her nails into the palms. 'Toby is my friend,' she said. 'I will not marry you, seigneur, because of Guillaume.'

There was a silence. De Bohun's fingers drummed against the arm of the chair. 'Ah,' he said. 'You are enamoured of him.'

Again, she could not force the lie. 'No. I am *indebted* to him.'

'Debts can be paid,' he said softly. 'What little Guillaume du Chantonnay has, he may lose. He neglects his estates – he has overspent. On you, my dear.'

She whispered, 'People can be bought. That's what you believe, isn't it?'

He had risen from the chair. 'Well, they can, can't they? After all, Guillaume bought you.'

He placed a hand on each of her shoulders, turning her round to face the window. He stood behind her. His fingertips felt cold, his voice was low and soft.

'Look what Guillaume du Chantonnay has – what Guillaume is, what he has given you. What do you see, Joanna? A dilapidated house in a benighted land. Wolves howl at your doors, farmyard animals foul your courtyards and gardens. Each year the forest encroaches on you. The thatch moulders on your roof, the window-panes crack and shatter. You are at the mercy of foul weather, of disease, of any marauding band of brigands who happens to be travelling through the forest. *This* is what Guillaume gives you. You have seen what I can give you.'

Just for a moment, looking out of the window, she saw it with his eyes. The narrow band of garden, the constant struggle to protect it from being swallowed up by the forest. The insecurity of her position, all the overwhelming dangers of the outside world.

Then she heard a cry from the nursery. She spun round, freeing herself from his hands.

She said fiercely, 'We do not live in the same world, seigneur. I do not want to live in your world. I would never, ever marry you. Never. Now go.'

She thought, for one small, heart-stopping moment, that he might force her, as he had forced Izabel Mandeville.

But he did not. Instead, he bowed. He said, 'But you'll come back to Marigny, won't you, Joanna? For the garden. I know how much the garden means to you.'

Then he turned on his heel and left the room.

At Amboise, his favourite residence, King François I asked the Sieur du Chantonnay to ride with the French army to Italy. Guillaume, head bowed and bare, accepted with a gratitude that was only partially feigned.

In Nantes, he made his preparations. He sold off parcels of land to repay his debts, he bought new horses, had his armour repaired and polished, and gathered together what men he could. Then he rode to Finistère, to say his farewells to his mistress and daughter.

Sanchia was three years old now, a fair-haired darling with blue eyes and a dimpled smile. Greeting her father, she curtsied, balancing carefully as she bobbed to the floor.

'I am teaching her to dance,' said Joanna, kissing Guillaume on the cheek. 'She is very light of foot.'

'Like her mother,' said Guillaume, embracing his daughter.

Later that evening, after Sanchia had been put to bed, they dined together. Rumours, fragments of conversation, had reached Guillaume too.

'I heard that Toby Crow was here,' he said.

Joanna looked up. 'He has gone back to Italy, Guillaume,' she said.

His eyes met hers. He thought how their relationship had changed over the years. He had made love to her rarely of late: there would, he knew, be no brother or sister for Sanchia. He wanted no other children: you could not improve on perfection.

Guillaume dismissed the servants. When they were gone, he said, 'The company you keep, the places you visit – they are not my concern, Joanna. You have been everything I wanted you to be, and more. But I will not lose Sanchia. I will not lose my daughter. If you should choose to leave me, then you may do so. But you will not take her.'

He saw her eyes lid, the candlelight make shadows on her face.

'You need not fear Toby, Guillaume.'

'I don't,' he said calmly, studying her.

He knew then that she had loved Toby Crow. Travelling from Padua to France in the company of Reynaud's former courier and the English physician, it had always been a possibility that she would. He had known that since the day he had met her in Milan. He wondered if he minded, and realized that he did, a little. He swallowed a mouthful of wine, and considered her last sentence. *You need not fear Toby, Guillaume.*

With a flicker of intuition and calculation, he said: 'And Hamon de Bohun. Must I fear the Seigneur de Marigny, Joanna?'

'He was here.'

He saw her shudder, and it shocked him. He did not associate Joanna Zulian with fear.

'He asked me to marry him.'

The world spun suddenly on its axis.

'And you said?' inquired Guillaume very carefully.

'I refused him, of course. He disgusts me.'

He could not help but smile. His crow of laughter echoed against the low stone ceiling, the small thick panes of glass. When he saw the expression on her face, though, he stifled his laughter.

'My apologies, Joanna. I do not mock *you*.'

He wiped his eyes with his napkin, struggling to regain control of himself. The thought of Hamon de Bohun, on bended knee, asking Joanna to marry him, would keep jittering into his mind. And she had *refused* him. He would, Guillaume thought, have given almost everything he owned to see the expression on de Bohun's face.

He heard her say, 'I'll not go back to Marigny, Guillaume. Not for you, not for anyone.'

He realized at last how angry she was. Rising, he took her hand in his. 'I shall have Marigny within the year, Joanna. I know it. I have spoken to the king. He knows that it is mine by right. He has favoured me. If I do well in Italy . . .'

She had pulled away from him. She looked at him at last. Her eyes were bitter. 'You are going to Italy, Guillaume?'

He felt himself shrinking from her cold gaze. 'It is my duty. The duty of all my class. You do not know, Joanna, you do not understand.'

'I ask you not to go. I have never asked anything of you before.'

He said patiently, 'I must go. It will be the last time. Once I have Marigny, then I can claim ill health, my increasing years, whatever you wish. I'll never leave Marigny. I'll never *want* to leave Marigny.'

'And Sanchia?'

'When I have Marigny, then Sanchia will be safe. It is a fortress, Joanna – you've seen it.'

'I've seen it.' Her voice was harsh. He did not dare touch her. 'Do you think that Hamon de Bohun will ever give it up? You endanger yourself, Guillaume, by claiming Marigny, You endanger me. You endanger Sanchia.'

It was his turn to feel angry. That this woman, whom he had taken homeless and penniless, and had made into something, should dare to criticize him. He said coldly, 'If you are afraid, Joanna, then I will send extra men. Or you may keep to the house, avoid the forest. Or you may bring Sanchia to my house in Nantes, if you wish.'

He knew, though, that while he lived, Hamon de Bohun would not dare touch Joanna. Too many rumours had already attached themselves to de Bohun's name. Guillaume's own years of striving were at last coming to an end.

Joanna said softly. 'I'll not imprison myself for you, Guillaume. Nor for Hamon de Bohun.'

He stared at her. The pain in his stomach had begun to flutter, but he ignored it. He said, 'You need me, Joanna. You need what I can give you.' The anger had retreated. There was a determination, a pride in her face that almost frightened Guillaume.

'Perhaps,' she said. 'Perhaps I have used you as you used me. But I'll not go back to Marigny, Guillaume. Not for you, not for Hamon de Bohun. Never.'

On the twelfth of August, the French army marched out from Embrun in the Dauphiné towards the Alps. François had chosen his moment well. The armies of Spain and the Papacy were busy fighting Venice; both the Venetians and the city-state of Genoa had asked France to come to their aid. Archduke Charles had agreed not to help his grandfather, Ferdinand of Spain, and even the bellicose young Henry VIII, impatient and jealous in England, could not wage war without allies.

Four armies gathered against the invader, France: the army of the Pope, commanded by Giuliano de' Medici, the army of Spain, under General Cardona, the Milanese troops of Massimiliano Sforza, and the fierce Swiss mercenaries who had annexed part of Massimiliano's Duchy. Armies moved through northern Italy like pieces on a chessboard: the

Swiss and the Milanese to guard the principal passes through the Alps, the Spaniards to Verona to prevent the Venetians from reaching their French allies, the Papal army marching along the Po to protect Piacenza.

But the French Marshal Trivulzio was by birth a Milanese. While the Swiss assembled themselves at Suza to guard the passes of Mont-Cenis and Mont-Genevra, Trivulzio, on the other side of the mountains, talked to Alpine shepherds and deer-hunters. The pass through which the French army chose to haul its cannon, its horses, its field guns, its supplies, was little more than a poorly linked collection of pathways and defiles.

It would, however, give François the sort of surprise attack necessary for victory.

He had, at first, no doubt that she would come. The flower garden, planned and planted the previous year, waited for her. The tiny lavender bushes budded, the box hedges perfumed the warm air. Hamon had the gardeners of Marigny trim them, coaxing them into hearts, squares, circles. An army of men laboured day and night over what Joanna Zulian had made. Water was pumped from the stream to the garden; fountains cascaded into the heat, sparkling like diamonds in the sunlight. Lilies floated on the pools; dragonflies, like flecks of gold, danced. The seeds in the kitchen garden, sown in the spring, rooted and flowered, repeating the strong colours and patterns of the previous year. Great bold squares of leaf and blossom echoed the perfect symmetry of Marigny.

Spring turned inexorably into summer. The honeysuckle and carnation bloomed, their scents intoxicating in the windless air. Grapes ripened on the vine; peaches and apricots, their skins like velvet, swelled in the sun. Roses scrambled up the archways and quince trees fruited in terracotta pots.

When the damask roses flowered, he knew that she would not come. In the Great Chamber the portrait of Judith looked down on him, her smile small and triumphant, as he stared out at the empty pathway, the unpeopled meadow.

She had not come back to him. He knew how much she had loved the garden, how much she had wanted the garden. Standing there, looking up at her portrait, Hamon de Bohun recalled the last conversation he had had with Joanna Zulian. Her eyes, then, had mirrored

Judith's eyes. Hatred and anger, staring out at him, scarcely masked by beauty.

The fear that had begun to haunt him during the winter returned, doubled. That Joanna Zulian loved Toby Crow, his own bastard son. He would have laughed at the irony of it, had he not to struggle against the pain. That his own bastard child, whom he had forced into the world, whom he had uprooted from his home and sent to this very house, should take away the woman who could make Hamon's inheritance complete, was quite intolerable. The pain and anger he now endured reminded Hamon of the weeks that had followed Reynaud du Chantonnay's marriage to Blanche: the sense of being cut off from something unimaginably precious; the sense of being denied what should have been his by right.

And Eleanor's voice, whispering among the exquisite tapestries and flowery mead of Marigny, mocked him. *'You are in love with Cousin Guillaume's harlot . . . Such a tawdry passion . . .'*

Love. He had avoided love all his life, knowing how it weakened men. And yet a half-bred vagabond had ensnared him with her chill grey eyes, making even Marigny valueless, a futile heap of stone and mortar. Love, he thought, was sister to Hate. He hated Joanna Zulian for her casual dismissal of him, for the way in which she had made his life incomplete. She was nothing – a harlot, as Eleanor had said. Yet he had offered her Marigny, and she had refused his incomparable treasure as though it had been a shepherd's hut. Eleanor had been right: love degraded him.

He would have her, though. As, years ago, he had planned to regain Marigny, Hamon began to plan now. Joanna Zulian had looked at him with hatred in her eyes: so she knew, he concluded coolly, of Toby Crow's provenance. She had not hated him before she had spent those weeks in the company of Izabel Mandeville's son.

Which meant, of course, that they had been lovers. You did not impart that sort of information to a casual friend. And Joanna, in Finistère, had not denied that she loved Toby. She had only denied loving Guillaume du Chantonnay, who had ridden to Italy with the king.

There were ways of resolving all that, though. Toby Crow should, after all, never have been born. He had served a purpose, and that purpose was long done with. He could be removed from this world as easily as he had been placed there. Such simple acts: to kill, to make love.

Scrambling through the Alps, the French army blasted rocks with gunpowder and cleared aside rubble and boulders in order that the field-guns and carts could be hauled through the pass.

The remains of Guillaume du Chantonnay's optimism, his precarious belief that events might right themselves, trickled slowly away the higher they climbed into the mountains. Like every member of the French army, including the king himself, he had to walk, dragging his horse by the bridle as they marched single file through the great walls of stone. He watched, shivering, as crevices were bridged with flimsy planks of wood, and guns and supplies were hoisted across ravines with ropes.

The plains of rock, soaked by the thawing snows of summer, frightened Guillaume. He knew, looking up to the heights, or down into the terrible chasms, that he was nothing. His aspirations, his hopes, he now knew to have always been laughable. If a god existed, that god mocked him now, as he dragged himself through immense and terrible passageways of rock, overheated in his armour, sweat pouring down his face.

When the stomach pains began again on the second day, Guillaume knew that he was trapped in a prison of stone and snow for ever. The pain had narrowed itself to one bright, burning circle of fire: something inescapable, something final. The French army climbed higher, towards the Col d'Argentière. Horses slipped on the ice, falling silently to their deaths half a league below. When François's soldiers spoke, their voices echoed against the mountainside, throwing empty words feebly back at them.

Finally Guillaume collapsed, sliding to his knees in the snow and clutching his belly. He was no longer aware of the great army of France marching past him. The pain gathered and soared, and he vomited. When he opened his eyes, he saw that the white snow was stained with gouts of dark crimson blood.

Only his retinue and one of the guides stayed with him. They moved him aside to the shelter of a rock. His page dipped a handkerchief in the snow and laid it on his master's forehead, staring at him with young, anxious eyes. Then they wrapped him in his saddlecloth and cloak.

Guillaume looked up at the mountains. Their summits circled above him, grey against a sapphire-blue sky. He thought he was at Marigny again, lying on his back on the flowery meadow, staring up at the pinnacles and towers. His own banners, blue and silver, flared in the sunlight. He could smell the scents of the carnations and roses. He could feel the soft grass beneath his head, he could hear the gentle whispering of the leaves on the trees, and the trickle of running water as it flowed from the stream into the moat. The sun looked kindly down at him, warming his face.

The pain in his belly flowered to unimaginable intensity and then, just as suddenly, was gone. Guillaume smiled. Close by him, his daughter Sanchia was playing. He called out her name.

Then he closed his eyes and slept.

The Venetian army commanded by Bartolomeo d'Alviano, carefully avoiding the Spanish, reached Lodi, ten miles from Milan.

The summer of 1515 had passed for Venice in a series of skirmishes, which had staved off the constant threat represented by the Papal and Spanish armies. For the soldiers of Venice, the campaign had been the usual mixture of boredom and fatigue, the excitement of battle contrasting with the tedium of inadequate food and shelter, and the long wait for action.

They were waiting now – a short, nervous respite, as they recovered from the forced march across the north of Italy towards Milan. Twelve thousand men lay sprawled in the parched fields outside Lodi, readying their weapons, scrabbling for food and drink. Their edginess expressed itself in short, violent squabbles or in a retreat from conversation and company. Swords were sharpened, prayers muttered, powder horns filled.

Penniless was swallowing the last few crumbs of a loaf of bread; his jaw was swollen and bandaged. Gilles was attaching scarlet plumes to the brim of a hat. Propped up against his saddlebag, with his legs flung out in front of him, he grumbled about the girl he had left behind in Verona.

'A bakery, Toby – she wanted me to marry her and look after her father's damned bakery.' He jabbed a pin through the quill of the plume and looked up, aggrieved. 'Can you imagine? Flour everywhere and a dozen brats running round my heels.'

Toby, kicking his heels on the dusty plain, grinned. 'A steady income, Gilles – much more reliable than soldiering.'

Gilles spat on the ground and tweaked the plumes into place.

Penniless, nursing his jaw, looked up. 'Is there news, Toby?'

It was late afternoon. The sunlight, thick and hot, beat down on the Venetian encampment. Soldiers, nervous and expectant, turned their heads towards Toby.

'Not yet.' Toby shook his head. 'How's the toothache, Penniless?'

Penniless scowled.

'I've offered to pull it for him,' said Gilles virtuously. 'A piece of thread, tied tightly, a little tug . . .'

There was the sound of horses' hooves. All around them men rose to their feet, gathering their weapons and looking out to where a small cloud of dust rolled across the plain towards them. Toby, seizing his horse's bridle, jumped into the saddle.

By choosing an obscure Alpine pass, the French had caught the Swiss by surprise, taking seven hundred men-at-arms as well as their capable commander, Prospero Colonna. After a decent interval of haggling, bribery and treachery, the Swiss had refused the French king's offer of money in return for leaving Milan. And on the thirteenth of September the Swiss army, fifteen-thousand-strong, had marched towards Marignano, vowing to take no prisoners except the king. François, with the vanguard of the French army, had sent the Venetian General Bartolomeo d'Alviano post-haste to Lodi so that he could bring his army to the aid of the beleaguered Constable de Bourbon, with the advance guard. So began the battle of Marignano.

The sun beat down relentlessly on the plain. Noblemen cooked in their heavy plate armour. Swiss pikemen clashed with German *Landsknechts*. Arrayed in square formation the two sides looked like huge spiky porcupines. When François, riding a warhorse caparisoned in sky-blue velvet and gold fleur-de-lys, entered the field, the *Landsknechts* fighting for France took heart, hacking with renewed vigour at the Swiss with pikes and axes. French cannon pounded the Swiss squares, and the cavalry, a glorious spectacle of bright armour and coloured device, charged across the plain.

They were still fighting when night fell and moonlight washed over the field. The line of Swiss soldiers never broke: enduring terrible losses, they marched across the plain, pushing back the French. Dust stung their eyes and clogged the visors of their helmets. Vine stakes tripped them up, and they waded up to their ankles in the swampy rice-fields. Eventually, both armies sank to the ground exhausted, sleeping where they fell, propped up against their shields or pikes.

At dawn, Alpine horns and French trumpets woke them. The fighting increased in intensity, a relentless slogging match, where even the king fought on foot, a pike in his hand. The French cannon and artillery boomed like thunder in the heat, as the Swiss mounted a fresh onslaught. The possibility existed, for a few, dreadful hours, that the disaster of Novara might be repeated. That François and the remains of the French army might find themselves once more straggling ingloriously back over the Alps.

Red dust billowing into the air marked the site of the battle of Marignano. Toby, riding full-tilt from Lodi with the rest of the Venetian light horse, heard first the sonorous pounding of the cannon, then, as they drew still closer, the cries of men and horses, the clatter of steel on steel. He urged his horse on, his hair flowing in the slipstream, and the cry of *Marco! Marco!* echoed around him as the first company of Venetian cavalry flung themselves into the fray.

Three hours later, the rest of d'Alviano's army arrived. Toby found himself in the thick of the battle, Penniless and Gilles beside him, struggling against a detachment of four hundred Zurichers. The heat of the day was such that his body, covered by a light breastplate, felt as though it were being boiled alive.

The Swiss were retreating to a deserted farmhouse, pushed back across the swamp of vine stalks and rice seeds by the Venetian cavalry. Knowing the inevitability of defeat, they fought like madmen. That the Swiss, the most successful mercenary nation in the world, should be defeated at the battle of Marignano, was inconceivable. Toby, sword in one hand, reins in the other, could see the desperation, the disbelief, in their eyes. A Swiss pike sliced at his thigh, and he battered it aside with his sword blade. Blood smeared his leg, but he did not feel any pain. Crossbow bolts hissed in the air around him: arquebuses, their unreliability increased by the dust, spluttered. Around him, he saw his men fall – men he had paid and trained, harangued and drunk with, tumbling from their horses to the dusty, bloody ground.

A few hundred Zurichers reached the farmhouse and scattered into the barns and outbuildings. The plain was littered with men bearing both Swiss and Venetian colours. The bulk of the Swiss army had gathered up their wounded and retreated to Milan. The day was almost over.

Toby withdrew his men as the French wheeled out their heavy cannon. He looked on as the great bronze guns, hauled over the Alps by French artillerymen, hurled their missiles into the farmhouse. Fires flared among the old straw and furniture. Cannon-balls turned the roof to powder, pounding at the terracotta tiles and weathered walls. He turned away when the roof caved in, and what had once been a house became nothing more than a pile of rubble, spiked with a few swords and pikes. Dust settled on the sprawled bodies of the Swiss, and a silence fell at last over the plain of Marignano.

There were three of them, Penniless, Gilles and Toby, riding back from the battlefield. Gilles had taken a bottle from his saddlebag. All were drunk – on aqua vitae, and the joy of being alive.

Toby had wound a makeshift bandage round his thigh. Penniless had been hit hard on the side of his head. He gingerly touched the bloodied purple lump, then poked one dirty finger inside his jaw.

'My toothache's stopped.'

Gilles, riding between Penniless and Toby, said, 'Three daughters. Marietta, Marta and . . . something else. Daughters of a silk-merchant in Milan. Damned pretty girls.'

Toby tilted the bottle and drank long and hard. 'Which one will you have, Gilles?'

'Oh – all three. A wager, Crow – all three within the week.'

'Not at once? And Penniless?'

Gilles hiccupped. 'There's a woman tends pigs outside Padua. Sleeps with 'em, I'm told, so she mightn't notice the difference.'

Penniless with a roar clouted Gilles on the side of the head. Toby reached inside his doublet.

'Five ducats, Gilles. I'll wager five ducats. A respectable merchant's respectable daughters wouldn't look at you.'

'Why?' Gilles was outraged. He looked down at himself: at his slashed and beribboned tunic now smeared with dust and blood, at his puffed part-coloured breeches. 'What's wrong? I had these from a Spaniard at Schio.'

'That hat,' said Toby.

'*Oh*. That.' Gilles, leaning precariously across, seized Toby's sallet and replaced it with the scarlet ostrich-feather hat. 'A sober citizen,' he said, plonking Toby's sallet on top of his fair curls. He grinned and glanced at Toby. 'There. You don't look quite such a gloomy old bastard.'

Toby adjusted the feathered hat so that he could see beneath the wide brim. 'I am a reformed character, Gilles. I shall laugh and dance in the streets. I shall wear striped hose and cloth-of-gold doublets.'

Gilles attempted to seize the bottle from Penniless, who was emptying the last few drops of aqua vitae into his open mouth. Penniless, with one large fist, tried to beat him off. There was a hiss, little more than a whisper, and Gilles slumped suddenly in the saddle. Then he slid drunkenly sideways, the reins slipping from his grasp.

'For God's sake, Gilles,' said Toby impatiently. Penniless licked the rim of the empty bottle and threw it into the undergrowth.

Gilles said nothing. Instead, he slid slowly to the ground, a foot catching in one of the stirrups. Toby seized Gilles's bridle.

Penniless was staring. '*Gilles,*' he bawled. 'He's hurt,' he added, bewildered.

Toby knelt on the ground beside Gilles. If he had not been so fuddled with alcohol and exhaustion, then he might have realized quicker. Gilles's bright, lucid blue eyes were staring up at the sky.

'Gilles?' said Toby uncertainly.

He rolled Gilles on to his front. He saw then why Gilles neither moved nor spoke. A crossbow bolt protruded from a small, crimson hole in his spine.

Toby rose to his feet. Several hundred soldiers were straggling slowly back from the plain of Marignano. Some were drunk, many were wounded. Some carried their fallen comrades on their backs, others carried bundles of booty – weapons, clothes, dead men's boots. Toby's gaze darted wildly from face to face, from hand to hand, but no one now aimed a crossbow.

Toby drew a hand across his face. The scarlet hat still shaded his eyes, the extravagant plumes were unmoving in the windless air. He turned slowly back to Penniless, who was kneeling on the ground beside Gilles.

His oldest friend, Toby thought, dazed. Aged sixteen, Toby had ridden from the Dubretons' house, crossed the Alps and turned up eventually in Milan. He had been raw and ignorant, incapable of defending himself, let alone anyone else. He had met up with Gilles and

Penniless, and they had kept one another alive through countless battles and skirmishes, brawling in a hundred forgotten taverns and encampments.

Penniless was cradling Gilles's head on his lap. Tears trailed unchecked down the Englishman's face, great clumsy hands gently closed Gilles's eyes. Penniless looked up at Toby, as he had looked up at him over and over again throughout the past twelve years. For reassurance, for comfort, for someone of greater intelligence and a more agile mind to say, *It's all right. I'll take care of everything.*

Toby looked down at them. He could say nothing.

When his servant brought her news of Guillaume's death, Joanna began to ready herself to leave Finistère. She packed a bag full of clothes for herself and Sanchia, tucking her dowry carefully underneath. That night, she told the servants of the death of their master, and the following morning several of them left, uncertain of Joanna's ability to pay them. She had wondered what effect Guillaume's death would have on her, and now found that she was not frightened. As she awaited the inevitable repercussions, she was calm: she had gone penniless into the world before, and, if necessary, she would do so again.

She waited, equally calmly, for news of Toby. At the beginning of October, the first rumours of the great battle that had taken place near Milan reached Brittany. Joanna was in Morlaix, selling dried herbs and nostrums wrapped in small silk purses. The French had won a great victory, someone said; the Swiss army is routed, cut to pieces, said another. Not a single voice spoke of the fate of the Venetians.

Back at the house she collected the remaining produce of her garden, tying herbs into bundles and hanging them in the still-room, making jellies and pastes from the fruit. Holding Sanchia in her arms, she found herself quite unable to tell her infant daughter of the death of her father, the changes that must happen in her life. There were no words for that. Instead she sang songs, and kissed and hugged the little girl. Sanchia's small, gentle fingertips dabbed in the tears that ran from Joanna's eyes.

That night, Joanna had a dream. She was a little girl again, not much older than her own daughter. She rode on the mule with her mother, her fingers clutching the coarse grey mane. Her mother's arms were around her, embracing her, her hands holding the reins. Donato held the bridle as they battled against wind and rain, circling a lake. Purple clouds filled the sky, the waters of the lake were jagged in the breeze. Donato's strong voice filled the air, his song drowned the wind and the patter of the rain.

The following morning, she went early to the forest. She felt the change in the air that overnight had turned summer to autumn. The leaves on the trees were beginning to yellow, and in the treetops great clouds of birds were preparing to take wing. As Joanna walked along the paths, past the pools and caverns, she felt her restlessness become almost intolerable. She waited for the event that, like a snap of thunder, would alter for ever the pattern of her days. She waited, she knew, for Toby.

She returned to the house at mid-afternoon. Rain had begun to fall, marking dark circles on the boulders beside the paths, and splashing into the pools in repeated flurries as it had done on the glassy plane of the lake in her dream. She had only a handful of wild mushrooms and a few hazelnuts in her basket. A poor harvest for a day's work.

Back in her garden, she stood for a moment, her eyes trailing slowly over the autumn damask roses and the pear trees. She was, she knew, saying her farewells. To Guillaume, who had died alone so far from home; to this house, this garden, in which she had for a while found sanctuary. She picked a single rose, cradling it between her palms. The delicate petals, beaded with rainwater, were beginning to fall. Joanna laid the rose in her basket, and then, kicking off her muddy boots, she walked barefoot into the house.

It was the silence that struck her as she closed the door and began to climb up the stairs. An utter absence of sound. No speech, no footsteps, not a whisper of movement. No infant's cry. The basket slipped from her fingers: fungi and nuts bounced down the narrow, winding stairs. Picking up her skirts, she ran to the nursery.

It was empty. An embroidery-frame and a handful of silks lay discarded by the window-seat. No child slept in the carved wooden cradle or played with the scattered toys. She began to run from room to room, throwing open doors, calling, through the terrible silence, her daughter's name.

She went to the solar last. The door was partially open. She could see through it his figure, tall and strong, silhouetted against the light from the oriel window. She cried out, '*Toby!*'

The man turned. She saw her mistake immediately. She could not speak, could not move. Hamon de Bohun, walking forward, took her hands and led her into the room.

In Venice, Toby, for his part in the victory of Marignano, received from Andrea Gritti thanks, money, offers of position and employment. He found himself prowling the city as he had done once before, over a year ago, when he had learned of Eleanor's death. Gritti had offered to him what he had struggled for all his life: a name, a future, the possibility of acceptance into this proud, exquisite city. His sense of achievement was mingled with a sense of loss. It was not enough, it was not complete.

He took gondolas, walked through piazzas and alleyways. Venice was resonant with memory: of Arlotto, of Gilles, of Joanna. Most of all, of Joanna. He dug his hands into his pockets; the breeze from the Adriatic was unusually chill for early autumn. He remembered the first time he had seen Joanna, in the workshops of her uncle. He had looked up from some dull conversation with Taddeo Zulian, and there she had been. Seated in a corner, bent over an easel. Her rich red-brown hair was coiled into her neck, her lovely grey eyes lidded and serious. He smiled with pleasure as he watched her mixing colours on a palette. Then she looked up and their eyes met, just once. Her quick glance noted him, studied him, and then turned haughtily back to her painting. He had been dismissed: she had more important things to do.

Now, looking up, he realized that he was in the square of San Giovanni e San Paolo. The church towered above him, ornate and beautiful. If he turned on his heel, then he would be within a stone's throw of Taddeo Zulian's workshop.

He walked forward, beat on the door. A boy of twelve or thirteen answered it, beckoning him in. The lad had paint on his shirt, and his fingertips were marked crimson, blue and green. Toby followed him up the stairs to the workshop.

As he entered, Toby almost expected to see Joanna there, bundled in her corner, brow creased as she glared at her painting. But she was not there, of course. Joanna Zulian was in Brittany with Guillaume du Chantonnay.

He gave his name. There was no recognition on Taddeo Zulian's face. Taddeo had aged: he was stooped and his hair had thinned so that Toby could see the shining scalp through the grey strands.

Taddeo managed a creaking bow. 'Messer Crow? How can I help you?'

The studio was littered with half-completed wedding-chests, banners and portraits. The apprentices, bored in the late afternoon, glanced curiously at Taddeo's visitor.

'A wedding-chest? You are to be married, perhaps, signor?'

Toby shook his head. 'I'm inquiring about the painter Gaetano Cavazza. I believe that you are related to Messer Cavazza. I would like him to paint a portrait for me. I saw a picture of his – a *Judith and Holofernes* – very fine, I thought.'

'Yes, very fine,' said Taddeo fussily. 'He never did much else, though. Such a disappointment. I was going to leave him this studio. He was my brother-in-law, you know. Now . . .' Taddeo shrugged his shoulders crossly.

Toby's heart began to pound a little faster. 'Gaetano Cavazza is *dead*?'

Taddeo, nodding, clouted an idle apprentice on the side of his head. 'Five years ago. Such a disappointment, as I said. I've had so much interest . . . more than in his lifetime,' he added, his face screwed up with irritation. 'Another gentleman like yourself. He mentioned the *Judith and Holofernes*, too.'

Taddeo began to sort papers on his desk, to clear away brushes and rags. Sun filtered through the dusty windows, a fly whined, trapped in a corner of the high ceiling.

'Another picture like that, and our futures would have been secured. I can do little myself now, of course. My eyesight has grown too poor. But after my niece left him . . . the silly girl . . . Donato's daughter . . .' Taddeo mumbled into his robes, incoherent with past disappointments.

Toby said, 'What gentleman?'

Taddeo looked up, bewildered. Then his brow cleared. 'Oh – a Frenchman, like yourself. You are French, are you not, Messer Crow? He was looking for poor Gaetano. He said that he was going to commission another painting – another biblical subject, I believe, to complement the *Judith and Holofernes*. That's it' – Taddeo seized the bundle of papers and tied them with a ribbon – 'that's it. He said his master *owned* the *Judith and Holofernes*.'

'When?' said Toby, hoarsely.

The fly still whined high above their heads, while the apprentices and the journeyman continued to daub the gaudy canvases. As Taddeo Zulian answered him, Toby suddenly saw in his mind a picture of the three of them, he, Gilles and Penniless, riding side by side back from

Marignano. From behind, to any stray assassin, they would have appeared almost identical. Except for their headgear. Toby's sallet, Penniless's bald pate and stringy pigtail, Gilles's wide-brimmed hat, bright with scarlet feathers . . .

'Why, last winter, Messer Crow,' said Taddeo Zulian. 'Yes, that's it. Last winter.'

'My daughter?' Joanna said when she was able to speak.

'Your daughter is on her way to Marigny,' said Hamon de Bohun smoothly. 'In the company of her nurse.'

She stared at him. She reached into the sleeve of her gown, but she was too clumsy, too fumbling. Hamon de Bohun quickly grabbed her wrist with one hand, while the other drew her knife from the folds of satin.

'Dear Joanna,' he said. 'I would almost welcome such a scratch. Pain and pleasure are such close companions, don't you agree?'

He seized her long braid of hair and dragged her towards him. He held the small dagger-blade upmost, so that the thin shaft of steel caught the sunlight. Joanna closed her eyes.

Hamon de Bohun whispered, 'I wouldn't hurt you, my pet. I wouldn't mark your face. I prize beauty, you see. Houses, gardens, paintings, women. And besides, I wouldn't have to, would I? After all, there is the child.'

She opened her eyes again. She was gasping for breath. His free hand was running over her sleeves, her bodice, her skirts.

'There. No more little surprises,' he said. 'Now we can talk.'

He let her go so suddenly that she fell back against the wall. Her eyes stared wildly back through the doorway: she listened for a sound, any sound.

'Your serving-men have taken to the forest,' said Hamon de Bohun. 'Such loyalty.' He smiled. 'You have to *buy* loyalty, you see, Joanna. You have only your face, your body. Not the right coin for that sort of transaction.'

He added, 'Guillaume du Chantonnay is dead. You know that, of course. You are free of your husband, too. Therefore you will come with me to Marigny. I will make something of you.'

'Never,' Joanna whispered. 'Never. Toby –'

'Ah yes, Toby.'

De Bohun seated himself in a chair. His chin rested on his cupped fingers as he studied her consideringly.

'You were lovers, weren't you? You have been, my dear Joanna, rather indiscriminate with your favours. I shall demand a much greater degree of circumspection when you are my wife.'

She shook her head. She could not speak.

'Yes,' said de Bohun gently. 'Remember the child. Guillaume's bastard.'

She was across the room before she could think, hands outstretched, clawing at his eyes. He seized her wrists, his strong hands pulling her to him. A trickle of blood traced a scratch from his eye to his chin. 'Toby will kill you,' she hissed.

'No, he won't,' said de Bohun. His eyes were dark, amused. 'Toby Crow is dead.'

She struggled to free herself, but he had pinioned her wrists with one hand. 'I don't believe you.'

'A stray crossbow bolt, my dear. After Marignano.'

She stared at him. *'After?'*

'After.' He smiled. 'My messenger arrived this morning.'

She stopped fighting then. The muscles in her arms relaxed, her hands fell shaking to her sides. She had struggled, she thought wearily, all her life, yet quite suddenly, in the space of a few moments, the habit had deserted her.

'Come,' said de Bohun, 'to Marigny.'

He placed his open palms on either side of her face, raising her head to kiss her. She did not resist him. Letting her go at last, he looked down at her.

'Izabel,' she said. Her voice was dry, scratching. She trembled.

He shook his head. 'We shall wed in Marigny's chapel, Joanna. That is your due. You shall stand at my side, and you shall wear cloth-of-gold and pearls. I shall place my ring on your finger, I shall take you to my bed. In the morning, when you rise, you shall look out of your window and see your garden. Marigny will be yours, Joanna, and you shall never, ever leave it.'

He led her out of the house to her horse. She took only the bag that she had packed for herself and Sanchia, clutching it to her as though it were the child he had abducted and taken to Marigny. She remembered nothing of the long ride. In the taverns they rested in she did not sleep, but crouched at the end of the bed, waiting for him to come. He did not come, though: he meant to marry her. To place his ring on her finger, to keep her for ever at Marigny.

Faces flickered through her head as they rode the familiar route. Sanchia, Guillaume, Guy, Eleanor du Chantonnay, and Martin in England. And Toby.

When she thought of Toby her eyes were dry. She had not cried for her father, she would not cry for her lover. Other women wept: women like Eleanor or Izabel Mandeville who were bought and sold in marriage to increase the power of men. She had never been a pawn in that sort of game. She was Joanna Zulian, who made pictures out of flowers, who made stories out of gardens. She was not made for roofs or walls. She was not made for the gold chains that Hamon de Bohun would string around her neck, the rings that he would bind her with.

They reached Marigny. The gate shut behind her; the forest, with its tangle of leaves and branches, enclosed her. Tree branches met over the path, shutting out the sky. They crossed the meadow and the moat. Chains clanked and gears creaked as the drawbridge was raised.

Inside, Hamon showed her her child sleeping safely in her cradle, and the nurse gazing up at her with frightened eyes. She had no word for either of them. She thought, as he led her away from the nursery, that she heard footsteps, a small child's footsteps, but when she turned there was no one. He took her to a bedchamber, where seamstresses fashioned a wedding-gown for her out of lengths of shining cloth, lace and jewels. When they were done, she went to the window.

She looked down at her flower garden below. Hamon de Bohun was standing at her side. 'Look at it,' he whispered. 'You want it, don't you?'

'Yes,' she said. 'Oh, yes.' Her voice was rusty with disuse.

'We are the same, Joanna,' he said, smiling.

She let him take her in his arms and caress her, but her gaze remained always on the four squares of her garden, perfect and ornate, like a tapestry. The Garden of Jealous Love, the Garden of Passionate Love, the Garden of Tender Love, the Garden of Obsessive Love. In the centre of the Garden of Obsessive Love she had planted hemlock and cowbane, thorn apple and nightshade. Destructive plants for a destructive passion. She had led a fractured, hazardous sort of life. But she had learned, long ago, to look after herself. Donato, with his herbal and his remedies, had taught her. She had never forgotten the lessons that he and Sanchia had taught her. Lessons of life, lessons of death. You planned for the worst, you protected what was yours. There was in the end no security. You struggled alone, head bowed against the wind. You took your own sort of justice. Only she remained to see that justice was done; only she had never felt bound by other men's laws.

'I'll walk in the garden,' she said. 'Alone.'

He didn't try to stop her. She walked through the countless perfect passageways of Marigny. They lowered the drawbridge for her, and she circled the château to reach the garden.

It was late evening. The moonlight touched the closed petals and the twilight reduced the colours of her garden to grey. The patterns, their stories, were unreadable now, but in the morning they would be plain to everyone. They were her justice, which she had made herself.

In the Garden of Obsessive Love, she picked her bitter fruits. For Toby, she whispered. For Eleanor. For François. For Izabel. Berries, black and gleaming, spiky and green, rolled into her palms. In the darkness the château de Marigny was shrunken, insubstantial. The moonlight showed only the garden, and the woman in it, surrounded by flowers.

CHAPTER NINETEEN

Yellow is the colour of the Garden of Jealous Love. Yellow is the colour of envy, of distrust. Box trees draw the shape of the horns that the jealous lover always fears. The horns are ugly, unpleasing; the colour that fills them is oppressive.

The Garden of Passionate Love is red. Here the box hedges form a maze: a mad, intricate dance, broken and wild. The colours of the flowers are discordant: scarlet poppies, crimson roses, their thorns sharp, drawing blood.

In the Garden of Obsessive Love, the hedges curve into swords and daggers. That sort of love – whether it is for a house, or for a woman, or for a country – always destroys. It is a love that cares only for itself, that sucks everything into it, crushing the young, the powerless, those who cannot look after themselves. The red flowers represent the blood spilt by war, the white the innocent that are destroyed. The poisonous plants in the centre of the garden are ugly, disrupting the symmetry. The berries of the nightshade are black, glittering, the thorn apple's fruit a misshapen curiosity. The hemlock and cowbane grow tall and gangling; their umbrellas reach out like clutching hands.

In the garden of Marigny, she had painted the story of the de Bohuns and the du Chantonnays, the story of her own life. Not in oil and tempera, but in lily and jasmine and gillyflower and box. The Garden of Jealous Love for Gaetano, the Garden of Passionate Love for Eleanor, the Garden of Obsessive Love for Hamon, the Garden of Tender Love for Toby and the children. They were all there: a red rose for Guy, pink for Sanchia, white for Paolo. The hearts made by the box hedges were coloured with all the flowers of the Italian garden: melilots and carnations and love-lies-bleeding.

Joanna married Hamon de Bohun in the chapel at Marigny. She wore his gold on her back, his pearls in her hair. She kissed him. After the ceremony, she took her daughter in her arms, and hugged Hamon's own small, damaged son. She went with Hamon to the bedchamber, took off the gold, the pearls, the jewels, the wedding-gown. She wore only his ring. She brought him the cup that she had made, and she said, 'Drink, Hamon. Drink.'

When his eyes had closed and his breathing had begun to fade, she dressed herself. Not in cloth-of-gold and silk, but in the black velvet that Isotta had made for her.

It was easy to ride out of Marigny. She was the Seigneur's wife, after all. 'I am taking the children for a ride in the meadow,' she said. Sanchia was perched on the saddlebow, cradled safely in Joanna's arms, and Guy clutched her skirts behind her. Hidden beneath the folds of her cloak were a few clothes and her dowry: a jade necklace, a copy of Dioscorides' herbal, and a few coins in an old silk purse.

She found her father in a small Basque village by the Spanish border. He lay next to Sanchia Zulian, without whom he had been unable to live. The gravestone was overgrown with lichen and ivy. Clearing the ivy away, Joanna learned that Donato Zulian had never reached Valladolid, had lain down and died that first winter he and his daughter had parted.

She sold her horse and bought a mule. She made a tent from a length of sailcloth coaxed from one of the mariners at the docks. It was a precarious living that she scratched for her children. They collected plants and roots by the roads that they travelled along, drying them in the sun, pounding them to powder with a stone. Joanna taught Sanchia and Guy the names of the plants and their properties. She showed them the plants listed in the pages of her herbal, reading from her own neat writing that listed the vernacular names. They sold the powders and dried leaves in the marketplaces and fairs. Once, in Spain, a great lord asked her to visit his wife. You see too little of the sun, Joanna thought, watching the pale young woman as she lay in bed. But she made up a tisane, and the lord rewarded her with a cloak for herself and a pair of sleeves for Sanchia.

In lean times – during winter or famine – she sewed seams for a living and wrote letters for the illiterate. She taught her children how to write, sharpening goose feathers filched from a farmyard, mixing her own pigments in sea-shells. Sometimes, watching Guy, his black head bent as he scrawled careful letters on a fragment of parchment, she feared for him. For his provenance, for his inheritance. For the early years that had marked him, for the future for which she must arm him.

For Sanchia, she never feared. She was her daughter, blithe, happy and fierce. In the summer they danced in the market square, she and Sanchia. Sanchia's pale golden hair fanned out around her, people threw coins into the skirts she held out to them.

The seasons passed, an endless pageant of roads and villages, hills and rivers. France and Savoy, Aragon and Portugal, Navarre and Castile, Lombardy and the Dauphiné. They would walk, Joanna thought, until they were safe again. She could see no end to their journey.

He arrived, of course, too late. By the time Toby Crow reached Marigny, Hamon de Bohun was dead and buried, and Joanna had gone.

She poisoned him, they said when he reached the house. The gates were flung open, the drawbridge lowered, the servants dazed and confused. No one grieved. The funeral had, by all accounts, been a shuffling, mediocre affair. The story of the marriage, told to Toby by Sanchia's nurse, made him shiver.

He saw her garden for the first time. He walked through the hedges and the fading flowers of autumn. A few lily leaves floated on the pond; a late dragonfly, an insubstantial flicker of iridescent blue, darted over the water. The tiny box hedges were shaped into fans, diamonds, hearts, crescents, each shape surrounding a swathe of differently coloured flowers. A few butterflies which had survived the summer floated in the cooling air; the occasional wasp whined as it hovered around overripe windfalls. Petals, heavy with rain, tumbled to the ground. As Toby pushed aside the loose branches of roses that hung from the roof of the pergola, he was sprinkled by drops of scented water. He knew then that she had left him something. A memory, a recollection of something real, something precious. An antidote to despair.

With Penniless beside him, Toby rode first to the house in Finistère. It was silent, empty, cold as he had known it must be. Dead leaves had already swirled through the open doorway, half-blocking the stairs; briars and twisting tendrils of ivy had crawled out of the forest to swallow up the garden. The shutters slammed back and forth in the wind. Penniless scowled and crossed himself.

He spent the winter travelling France and Brittany, looking for her. He found nothing, though, not a trace. Sometimes, when he was half dozing in a tavern, he would hear the rhythms of tabor and fife and the patter of dancing feet. He would look up, expecting to see her, skirts swirling in the darkness, bright hair fanned out like a veil . . .

★

The seasons adopted a different rhythm. There was always work for someone like him, because there was always war. He fed off war, picking at its bones, shaking out his black feathers, looking round him, always watchful. In the summer he fought, hiring out himself and his company to kings and emperors. In the winter, he searched endlessly, Penniless at his side, for a russet-haired woman and two children, a girl and a boy. He had a house in Venice in which he never lived; he had acquired – the thought made him laugh – honours, medals, plate and the prospect of a title.

In the summer of 1517, Toby Crow rode with his most puissant majesty, François I, helping to escort the vast cavalcade of the king's household around the dusty roads of France. Eighteen thousand men and women, twelve thousand of them mounted on horseback, travelled in a slow and stately pilgrimage along the dusty roads of Languedoc. The clothing of the great lords and officers of the realm sparkled; the topazes, agates, emeralds and cornelians in their hair, around their necks, tried to outshine the sun.

Pausing in a forest, they picnicked beneath the trees. Long tables were set under the branches; stewards and servers scuttled about in the leaf-mould, placing silver plates and jewelled goblets on damask tablecloths. The lords and ladies of France chattered and stretched their limbs. The officers of the king's guard, released from their duties for a while, returned to their men, who were sprawled on the forest floor a short distance away.

Penniless, pale-faced, was clutching his jaw. 'Hit me on the head, Toby,' he groaned. 'It worked the last time.'

Toby crouched on the grass beside him. 'There was a dentist's booth in the fair that we passed. That tooth's troubled you for two years, on and off, Penniless.'

The Englishman, fear in his eyes, shook his head, clamping his mouth shut.

Someone called, 'There's a woman sells powders at the fair. She gave Jehan something for his stomach. Stopped him puking within the hour.'

Someone else muttered, 'Get him something, for God's sake, Toby. Else he'll keep us awake again tonight with his moaning.'

Penniless was looking up at him with hopeful, trusting eyes. Toby swore and swung himself into the saddle.

They had ridden past the fair that morning, a ramshackle and tawdry collection of patched tents. Children squabbled in the gutters, a man's hopeful voice implored them to visit the sea-maid with her fish's tail and scaly limbs. Ragged poppies, motionless in the early-morning heat, lined the field's perimeter.

A woman selling powders, though. It was the sort of possibility he always investigated. In the weeks they had spent together in Brittany, Joanna had given him hope, something to replace the blacker philosophies of his childhood. So, always hoping, he visited them all: the old crones with their dubious cures and their mad, exhausted eyes; the witches who offered him love philtres, secret remedies for unspeakable ailments. He visited them, and handed over his sou, and threw their recipes into the first ditch or pool he came across.

The path through the forest was simple to follow. The branches of eucalyptus and olive trees twisted round him, their leaves heavy with dust. The mare trod carefully between the rabbit holes and tree roots. He knew that now he feared nothing except the usual human frailties of sickness, loneliness and death. He hoped for everything. As he reached the edge of the forest, he heard music.

He paused beneath the outermost trees, dismounting from his horse. There was a fiddler and a hurdy-gurdy player. On the baked area of ground beyond the trees, he could see a little girl dancing. A boy was playing the tambourine. The boy was dark-haired, dark-eyed; his hand beat at the parchment drum of the tambourine, his expression was intense, careful. The little girl's long, golden hair whirled around her in the dusty heat; her brightly coloured skirts circled as she skipped and twirled.

A woman was standing beside them. Her clothes were ragged, patched and ornamented with braid. She had unfurled a banner. The banner announced her trade, gave her name. A thousand flowers were painted on the cloth: red and purple and yellow and green and blue. Toby did not have to read the name on the banner; but he looked for a while at the woman, studying the features, the gestures, the smile that he already knew by heart.

He looped his reins around the branch of a tree, and brushed the dust from his clothes. Then he walked forward into the sunlight.